PLUTARCH'S LIVES

VOLUME II

The Dryden translation, edited with preface by Arthur Hugh Clough

Introduction by James Atlas

THE MODERN LIBRARY
NEW YORK

2001 Modern Library Paperback Edition

Library of Congress Cataloging-in-Publication Data
Plutarch.
[Lives. English]
Plutarch's lives / the Dryden translation, edited with notes and preface by Arthur Hugh Clough.
v. ; cm.
Includes index.
ISBN 0-375-75676-0 (v. 1)—ISBN 0-375-75677-9 (v. 2)
1. Greece—Biography. 2. Rome—Biography. I. Dryden, John, 1631–1700. II. Clough, Arthur Hugh, 1819–1861. III. Title.
DE7.P513 2001
920.038—dc21 00-068388

Modern Library website address: www.modernlibrary.com

Printed in the United States of America

21st Printing

PLUTARCH'S LIVES

PLUTARCH

PLUTARCH was born during the reign of Claudius, around A.D. 45, at Chaeronea in Boeotia, a town of historic but somewhat faded importance. His family, originally from Thebes, had long enjoyed local distinction, a tradition he was to maintain in a life full of civic accomplishments. He founded a school of philosophy, served as Archon of Chaeronea, and eventually officiated as a priest of Apollo at Delphi. Only a few details of his life can be gleaned from his writings. At the time of Emperor Nero's visit to Greece in A.D. 66, Plutarch was by his own account a student of philosophy at Athens under the teacher Ammonius. As an exponent of Platonism, he vigorously attacked the positions of the Stoics and Epicureans. He was married and had at least five children.

Plutarch spent some part of his career in Italy, although he describes his experiences there only in passing; for example, in a discussion about his knowledge of Latin writers in his life of Demosthenes, he says that "having had no leisure, while I was in Rome and other parts of Italy, to exercise myself in the Roman language, on account of public business and of those who came to be instructed by me in philosophy, it was very late, and in the decline of my age, before I applied myself to the reading of Latin authors." He traveled in Egypt as well. He was a prolific writer in a variety of genres; his surviving work (representing perhaps half of what he wrote) fills a dozen volumes. In addition to the *Parallel Lives* of celebrated Greeks and Romans, which he produced late in his career, he wrote essays and dialogues on an immense range of subjects, collected in the *Moralia*. The dialogues—involving a cast of philosophers, grammarians, rhetoricians, and physicians—recreate in stylized fashion the table talk, alternately moralizing and frivolous, of Plutarch's milieu. The comings and goings of these participants—from Britain to Tarsus, from

Egypt to Lacedaemonia—emphasize that this was the heyday of Roman imperial unity, and an era of cultural flowering: Plutarch's contemporaries included Epictetus, Dio Chrysostom, Arrian, Quintilian, Tacitus, Suetonius, Pliny the Younger, Martial, and Juvenal.

Plutarch's own life may have been centered on his native town, but his writings move easily through centuries of history and across the length and breadth of the Mediterranean world. His reputation was evidently wide; under Trajan and Hadrian he is said to have received the insignia of a consul and a post as Procurator of Greece. He probably died sometime after A.D. 120. It was during the reign of Trajan that he wrote the *Lives*, which have proven his most enduring work. Intended as moral portraits rather than historical interpretations, the *Lives* are an incomparably rich trove of the facts and legends that Plutarch tirelessly collected, and an epitome of Graeco-Roman concepts of character. In the English translation made by Sir Thomas North in 1579 they contributed enormously, in both incident and language, to Shakespeare's *Julius Caesar, Coriolanus*, and *Antony and Cleopatra*. The present translation, originally published in 1683–86 in conjunction with a life of Plutarch by John Dryden, was revised in 1864 by the poet and scholar Arthur Hugh Clough.

CONTENTS

CONTENTS

INTRODUCTION

by James Atlas

Plutarch, the first modern biographer, chronicler of Mark Antony, Caesar, Pericles, and Brutus, is no less real to us than his mythic subjects. The known facts of his life are few, but enough to provide a vivid glimpse of him. He was born in Chaeronea, a small town in Boeotia "remarkable for nothing," noted one of his translators, "but the tameness and servility of its inhabitants." Even the year of his birth is uncertain: some place it near the middle of the reign of Claudius, others near the end, about 45 or 50 A.D. We know that he was Greek, and had a traditional Greek education; that he was studying philosophy under Ammonius at Athens when Nero made his incursion into Greece, in the twelfth year of the Emperor's reign, the sixty-sixth year of the Christian era; and that he was from a wealthy family. His ancestors were magistrates, and were relatively long-lived. Plutarch knew his great-grandfather Nicarchus, who, we read in his life of Antony, had been whipped by Roman soldiers while forced to carry grain to the coast; and his grandfather Lamprias, fabled for his wine-induced eloquence, also makes a cameo appearance in that narrative, the source of a story about the fantastically lavish banquets Antony and Cleopatra threw for their circle of overindulgent friends, who referred to themselves as the Inimitable Livers.

Plutarch's domestic life was tranquil, by all accounts, though often darkened by the tragedy of early death, a common hazard of that era. He had at least five children—four sons and a daughter—by his wife, Timoxena. Of his daughter, named after his wife, he wrote: "When she was very young she would frequently beg of her nurse to give the breast not only to the other children, but to her babies and dolls, which she considered as her dependents, and under her protection." She died in early childhood, and he also lost two of his sons prematurely. Plutarch's response to the death of his daughter is frequently cited by scholars as a model of calm dignity in mourning. Their evidence is an essay in the form of a letter, entitled *The Consolation to His Wife*, that Plutarch wrote Timoxena, counseling her to grieve "within the reasonable limits": "What our loss really amounts to, I know and estimate for myself. But should I find your distress excessive, my trouble on your account will be greater than on that of our loss. I am not a 'stock or stone,' as you, my partner in the care of our numerous children, every one of whom we have ourselves brought up at home, can testify." Rather than allow themselves to be overwhelmed by loss, they could more profitably recall their good fortune, however brief: "Yet why should we forget the reasonings we have often addressed to others, and regard our present pain as obliterating and effacing our former joys?"

Plutarch was worldly, by the standards of his day and age. In his youth he may have traveled to Egypt—a stage in the classical Grand Tour—and also to Greece and Asia Minor. He certainly visited Italy—"on public business," he tells us in his life of Demosthenes—but he didn't get around to learning Latin until late in life, "having had no leisure, while I was in Rome and other parts of Italy, to exercise myself in the Roman language." He delivered his public lectures on philosophy in Greek. After his Italian sojourn—again, the precise dates elude historians—he retired to Chaeronea to compose his *Lives*. "As to myself, I live in a little town," he famously wrote, "and I choose to live there, lest it should become still less." A loyal and public-spirited member of the community whose population he refused "to make less by the withdrawal of even one inhabitant," he served for a time as the commissioner of sewage and public buildings.

> I make no doubt that the citizens of Chaeronea often smile when they see me employed in such offices as these. On such occasions, I generally call to mind what is said of Antisthenes: when he was bringing home, in his own hands, a dirty fish from the market, some, who observed it, expressed their surprise; "It is for myself," said Antisthenes, "that I carry this fish." On the contrary, for my own part, when I am rallied for measuring tiles, or for calculating a quantity of stones or mortar, I answer, that it is *not* for myself that I do these things, but for my country. For, in all things of this nature, the public utility takes off the disgrace; and the meaner the office you sustain may be, the greater is the compliment that you pay to the public.

Plutarch's job as a magistrate was "to heal private animosities," to conciliate, to be always available to the citizenry, to keep his house open "as a place of refuge for those who sought for justice." He also held a priesthood for life at Delphi, and was an honorary citizen of Athens. In later life, Hadrian made him Procurator of Greece. He "lived to be old," according to Arthur Hugh Clough, the Victorian-age poet who revised Dryden's version of the *Lives.* The exact date of his death, like that of his birth, is unknown, but it was probably early in the reign of Hadrian. He was survived by two sons, Plutarch and Lamprius; the latter was a philosopher who left a catalogue of his father's writings that have since disappeared, and upon which we must look, as Dryden says, with the same emotions that a merchant must feel in perusing a bill of freight after he has lost his vessel.

What we know of Plutarch, then, "forms a picture," as Clough described it, "of a happy domestic life, half academic, half municipal, passed among affectionate relatives and well-known friends"—the life of a cosmopolitan intellectual who lived two thousand years ago. His character, reflected in a handful of anecdotes and in the lively voice that animates his narratives, shines forth from the distance of two millennia like a lamp behind a curtain—faint and diffuse, but still illuminating.

Amidst the endless accounts of wars, the shimmering shields and gilt-edged swords, the massed troops in their elaborate finery, the pageant of blood and sacrifice, Plutarch's observations have a familiar, even intimate tone. That he was a sensitive soul is evident from his attitude toward the elder Cato, whom he reproves for selling off his servants when they got old "like so many beasts of burden." Animals, too, elicited his sympathy. It was important to take care of dogs and horses, he maintained, praising those who gave proper burial to their pets: "The obligations of law and equity reach only to mankind, but kindness and beneficence should be extended to the creatures of every species; and these still flow from the breast of a well-natured man, as streams that issue from the living fountain." Like Dr. Johnson, who once let go a hare that his host had caught in the garden with an eye toward making it their supper, he had kind words for the people of Athens, who spared the lives and put out to pasture animals that had been enlisted in building the temple at Hecatompedon.

Plutarch may have inherited his gentle temperament from his father, who was determined to teach his son the virtue of modesty. Once, he recounts, when a fellow citizen accompanied him on a diplomatic mission and had to stop along the way, Plutarch's father urged his son to share credit for accomplishing the task: "Say not *I went, I spoke, I executed;* but *we went, we spoke, we executed.*" The lesson was to "avoid that envy which necessarily follows all arrogated merit." On another occasion, Arulenus Rusticus, an eminent political figure in Rome, happened to be in the audience at one of Plutarch's lectures when a soldier arrived with a letter from the emperor: "Upon this there was a general silence through the audience, and I stopped to give him time to peruse this letter; but he would not suffer it; nor did he open the letter till I had finished my lecture, and the audience was dispersed—an example of serious and dignified behavior which excited much admiration." This example of self-mastery clearly made an impression on Plutarch; in his discourse on Inquisitiveness, he advised his readers not to open letters in a hurry, biting the strings.

For a contemporary reader, one of the most notable features of the *Lives* is how closely they resemble our own. Plutarch's evocation of the texture of Greek and Roman life has an utterly familiar feel. The architecture of homes; the contrast between city and country; the rituals of meals: all this information is conveyed with a freshness that makes it seem as if we could be reading about the civic culture of twenty-first-century Rome—or of New York City. Writing of Caesar, Plutarch remarks on his "dinner parties and entertainments and a certain splendor about his whole way of life"; Alcibiades is chided for his "drunkenness, debauchery, and insolence," his notorious flamboyance: "He was effeminate in his dress and would walk through the market-place trailing his long purple robes." He also borrowed vessels of gold and silver from the city for his own table—an ancient instance of expense-account abuse. The practice was apparently widespread. Lamachus, a Greek soldier, was said to be so poor that "whenever he sent in his accounts for a campaign, he was in the habit of claiming expenses for his clothes and shoes."

How accurate are these details? Not very. It has to be kept in mind that Plutarch was writing at a time when the world itself had yet to be mapped out. To say that his geography was shaky hardly covers the case. The Cimmerians, he informs us, "lived at the end of the world by the outer ocean in a land of shade and forests so thick that the sun is never visible because of the size and thickness of the trees which extend inland as far as the Hercynii." As for Britain: "The reported size of the island had appeared incredible and it had become a great matter of controversy among writers and scholars, many of whom asserted that the place did not exist at all. . . ." Plutarch's credulity will strike the modern reader as quaint. In his narrative, augurs who study entrails and monitor the flight of birds are in great demand. When a sparrow flies over the Forum with a grasshopper in its bill and throws part of it down on the ground, "this was interpreted by the professionals to mean that there would be quarrels and political disturbances between the great landowners and the common people of the city." Assembling his life of Sulla, he relies on the usual vague sources ("they say") for a story about a satyr that was found on "a holy piece of ground" and brought to the Consul, "but could scarcely speak at all and could certainly say nothing intelligible." And in the life of Marcellus, he passes on rumors that "an ox had uttered human speech, and that a boy had been born with an elephant's head." Plutarch required no evidence: "When a story is so celebrated and is vouched for by so many authorities and, more important still, when it is so much in keeping with Solon's character and bears the stamp of his wisdom and greatness of mind, I cannot agree that it should be rejected because of the so-called rule of chronology."

There was nothing unusual about Plutarch's insouciance toward facts. Scholarship in his day was a highly impressionistic affair. Most of his sources were letters, speeches, and collections of sayings quoted largely from memory, stories heard and written down in a common-book—the *Symposiac*, or Table-Talk, a record of conversations collected from family and friends. Biography itself was only beginning to emerge as a genre. We hear of biographies, and perhaps autobiographies, as early as the fifth century B.C., but biography in a form we would recognize first appears in the Hellenistic Age. "The word is *bios*—not *biographia*," Arnaldo Momigliano explained in *The Development of Greek Biography*—that is to say, it dealt more with the type (generals, philosophers, demagogues) than with the individual. And it built upon another developing genre: "One of the spectacular features of intellectual life in the fifth century is the development of a new branch of research: history." In the work of Herodotus and Thucydides one encounters for the first time a "historiography centred on individuals," according to Momigliano: "The philosophical and rhetorical schools of the fourth century [B.C.] developed the art of talking about individuals, including the most important of individuals—oneself."

What distinguished Plutarch from his predecessors was his awareness of what we would now call the interior life. "My design is not to write Histories, but lives," he declared:

> And the most glorious exploits do not always furnish us with the clearest discoveries of virtue or vice in men; sometimes a matter of less moment, an expression or a jest, informs us better of their character and inclinations, than the most famous sieges, the greatest armaments, or the bloodiest battles whatsoever. Therefore as portrait-painters are more exact in the lines and features of the face, in which the character is seen, than in the other parts of the body, so I must be

> allowed to give my more particular attention to the marks and indications of the souls of men, and while I endeavor by these to portray their lives, may be free to leave more weighty matters and great battles to be treated by others.

It was in a man's private life rather than in his public deeds that character stood revealed. This was Plutarch's credo, as it would become the credo of Aubrey and Boswell, Carlyle and Macaulay, Lytton Strachey and Richard Ellmann. The history of biography begins with Plutarch's discovery that men are defined by their most peculiar traits. Thus, Themistocles put off things until the last minute "in order to deal with an immense quantity of business all at once and have meetings with many different kinds of people and thus make himself out to be a person of great importance and power." And thus the chameleonlike Alcibiades promoted the benefits of physical exercise in Sparta, of indolence in pleasure-loving Ionia, of drink in bibulous Thrace.

Not that Plutarch neglected the astonishing violence of antiquity. Few of his subjects died in their beds; murder, often at the hands of a bloodthirsty mob, was the order of the day. In his life of Gaius Marius, he describes how the Cimbri, routed by the Romans, fell upon their own: "The women, all dressed in black, stood on the wagons and killed the fugitives—their husbands, their brothers, their fathers; then they strangled their little children with their own hands, hurling them down under the wheels of the wagons or the feet of the animals; and finally they cut their own throats." Sulla thought nothing of butchering thousands of captured soldiers in the Circus. Phraates put his own father to death. But Plutarch was less interested in men's acts than in their consequences. He didn't believe in character development; his subjects were static, not evolving. It was "the drama of an individual's success or failure," as the Plutarch scholar D. A. Russell put it, that captured his imagination: "He is a moralist rather than a historian. His interest is less for politics and the changes of empires, and much more for personal character and individual actions and motives to action—duty performed and rewarded; arrogance chastised; hasty anger corrected; humanity, fair dealing, and generosity triumphing in the visible, or relying on the invisible, world."

Plutarch gave the fullest account of his method in the opening pages of his life of Pericles. Why did he write? To "arouse the spirit of emulation," to find in the deeds of heroes an illustration of "moral good" that inspires other men to follow. Of Coriolanus, who lost his father in youth, he noted: "His example shows us that the loss of a father, even though it may impose other disadvantages on a boy, does not prevent him from living a virtuous or a distinguished life, and that it is only worthless men who seek to excuse the deterioration of their character by pleading neglect in their early years." Sertorius, who rose to be one of the great generals of Rome, he praised for his willingness to share power and negotiate fairly with his enemies, as well as for his equable disposition, which "enabled him to resist pleasure and fear alike: he was unmoved in the face of danger, nor did he become overelated with success." So often in Plutarch one reads of men whose successes make them arrogant: "Great powers bring about a change in the previous characters of their holders—a change in the direction of overexcitability, pomposity, and inhumanity." What appealed to him about Sertorius was his gentleness of spirit, his "magnanimity." Here was a man who adopted a fawn as his mascot in battle and grieved so intensely upon learning of his mother's death that he lay in his tent for a week.

Yet despite his efforts to emphasize his subjects' positive attributes, the dark side of humanity is always present in Plutarch's chronicles. The evidence of his subjects' bad qualities is irrepressible. Caesar's lust for distinction; Themistocles' insomniac obsession with the triumphs of his rival Miltiades; Mark Antony's "insane desire to be the first and greatest man in the world"—time and again, the moral good that Plutarch wishes to put before his readers is blotted out by the schemes and machinations, the greed, envy, competitiveness, and lust, that drive the world. Plutarch saw these forces at work even if he failed to grasp their ubiquity. Writing of the civil war led by Pompey and Caesar, he was awed by the spectacle of those two vast armies massed on the plain of Pharsalia, intent on mutual destruction—"a clear enough lesson of how blind and mad a thing human nature is when under the sway of passion."

Plutarch was modest about his chosen form; biography, he cautioned, was a provisional enterprise, dependent on hearsay and fallible memory, the facts obliterated by the remorseless erasures of time and history: "The true history of these events is hidden from us." Perhaps; but it was his insights into their causes, his knowledge of our profoundly divided human nature, that assured his immortality.

PREFACE

by Arthur Hugh Clough

THE collection so well known as *Plutarch's Lives*, is neither in form nor in arrangement what its author left behind him.

To the proper work, the Parallel Lives, narrated in a series of books, each containing the accounts of one Greek and one Roman, followed by a comparison, some single lives have been appended, for no reason but that they are also biographies. Otho and Galba belonged, probably, to a series of Roman Emperors from Augustus to Vitellius. Artaxerxes and Aratus the statesman are detached narratives, like others which once, we are told, existed, Hercules, Aristomenes, Hesiod, Pindar, Daiphantus, Crates the cynic, and Aratus the poet.

In the Parallel Lives themselves there are gaps. There was a book containing those of Epaminondas and Scipio the younger. Many of the comparisons are wanting, have either been lost, or were not completed. And the reader will notice for himself that references made here and there in the extant lives show that their original order was different from the present. In the very first page, for example, of the book, in the life of Theseus, mention occurs of the lives of Lycurgus and Numa, as already written.

The plain facts of Plutarch's own life may be given in a very short compass. He was born, probably, in the reign of Claudius, about A.D. 45 or 50. His native place was Chæronea, in Bœotia, where his family had long been settled and was of good standing and local reputation. He studied at Athens under a philosopher named Ammonius. He visited Egypt. Later in life, some time before A.D. 90, he was at Rome "on public business," a deputation, perhaps, from Chæronea. He continued there long enough to give lectures which attracted attention. Whether he visited Italy once only, or more often, is uncertain.

He was intimate with Sosius Senecio, to all appearances the same who was four times consul. The acquaintance may have sprung up at Rome, where Sosius, a much younger man than himself,[1] may have first seen him as a lecturer; or they may have previously known each other in Greece.

To Greece and to Chæronea he returned, and appears to have spent in the little town, which he was loth "to make less by the withdrawal of even one inhabitant," the remainder of his life. He took part in the public business of the place and the neighbourhood. He was archon in the town, and officiated many years as a priest of Apollo, apparently at Delphi.

He was married, and was the father of at least five children, of whom two sons, at any rate, survived to manhood. His greatest work, his Biographies, and several of his smaller writings, belong to this later period of his life, under the reign of Trajan. Whether he survived to the time of Hadrian is doubtful. If A.D. 45 be taken by way of conjecture for the date of his birth, A.D. 120, Hadrian's fourth year, may be assumed, in like manner, as pretty nearly that of his death. All that is certain is that he lived to be old; that in one of his fictitious dialogues he describes himself as a young man conversing on philosophy with Ammonius in the time of Nero's visit to Greece, A.D. 66–67; and that he was certainly alive and still writing in A.D. 106, the winter which Trajan, after building his bridge over the Danube, passed in Dacia. "We are told," he says, in his Inquiry into the Principle of Cold, "by those who are now wintering with the Emperor on the Danube, that the freezing of water will crush boats to pieces."

To this bare outline of certainties, several names and circumstances may be added from his writings; on which indeed alone we can safely rely for the very outline itself. There are a few allusions and anecdotes in the Lives, and from his miscellaneous compositions, his Essays, Lectures, Dialogues, Table-Talk, etc., the imagination may furnish itself with a great variety of curious and interesting suggestions.

The name of his great-grandfather, Nicarchus, is incidentally recorded in the life of Antony. "My great-grandfather used," he says, "to tell, how in Antony's last war the whole of the citizens of Chæronea were put in requisition to bring down corn to the coast of the gulf of Corinth, each man carrying a certain load, and soldiers standing by to urge them on with the lash." One such journey was made, and they had measured out their burdens for the second, when news arrived of the

[1] Unless the expression "my sons your companions" ought to be taken as a piece of pleasantry.

defeat at Actium.[1] Lamprias, his grandfather, is also mentioned in the same life. Philotas, the physician, had told him an anecdote illustrating the luxuriousness of Antony's life in Egypt. His father is more than once spoken of in the minor works, but never mentioned by his name.

The name of Ammonius, his teacher and preceptor at Athens, occurs repeatedly in the minor works, and is once specially mentioned in the Lives; a descendant of Themistocles had studied with Plutarch under Ammonius. We find it mentioned that he three times held the office, once so momentous in the world's history, of *strategus* at Athens.[2] This, like that of the Bœotarchs in Bœotia, continued under the Empire to be intrusted to native citizens, and judging from what is said in the little treatise of Political Precepts, was one of the more important places under the Roman provincial governor.

"Once," Plutarch tells us, "our teacher, Ammonius, observing at his afternoon lecture that some of his auditors had been indulging too freely at breakfast, gave directions, in our presence, for chastisement to be administered to his own son, *because*, he said, *the young man has declined to take his breakfast unless he has sour wine with it*, fixing his eyes at the same time on the offending members of the class."

The following anecdote appears to belong to some period a little later than that of his studies at Athens. "I remember, when I myself was still a young man, I was sent in company with another on a deputation to the proconsul; my colleague, it so happened, was unable to proceed, and I saw the proconsul and performed the commission alone. Upon my return when I was about to lay down my office, and to give an account of its discharge, my father got up in the assembly and bade me privately to take care not to say *I* went, but *we* went, nor *I* said, but *we* said, and in the whole narration to give my companion his share."

Of his stay in Italy, his visit to or residence in Rome, we know little beyond the statement which he gives us in the life of Demosthenes, that public business and visitors who came to see him on subjects of philosophy, took up so much of his time that he learned, at that time, but little of the Latin language. He must have travelled about, for he saw the bust

[1] There appears, however, to be no sure reason for saying that Plutarch himself remembered seeing his great-grandfather, and hearing him tell the story.

[2] This may throw some doubt on the statement (with which, however, it is perhaps not absolutely incompatible) made by the Byzantine historian Eunapius that "Ammonius, the teacher of the divine Plutarch, was an Egyptian."

Plutarch was certainly skilled in all the wisdom of the Græco-Egyptians; see his treatise addressed to the learned lady Clea, on Isis and Osiris; but he may, for anything we know, have stayed long and studied much at Alexandria.

or statue of Marius at Ravenna, as he informs us in the beginning of Marius's life. He undertook, he tells us in his essay on Brotherly Affection, the office, whilst he was in Rome, of arbitrating between two brothers, one of whom was considered to be a lover of philosophy. "But he had," he says, "in reality, no legitimate title to the name either of brother or of philosopher. When I told him I should expect from him the behaviour of a philosopher towards one, who was, first of all, an ordinary person making no such profession, and, in the second place, a brother, *as for the first point*, replied he, *it may be well enough, but I don't attach any great importance to the fact of two people having come from the same pair of bodies;*" an impious piece of free-thinking which met, of course, with Plutarch's indignant rebuke and reprobation.

A more remarkable anecdote is related in his discourse on Inquisitiveness. Among other precepts for avoiding or curing the fault, "We should habituate ourselves," he says, "when letters are brought to us, not to open them instantly and in a hurry, not to bite the strings in two, as many people will, if they do not succeed at once with their fingers; when a messenger comes, not to run to meet him; not to jump up, when a friend says he has something new to tell us; rather, if he has some good or useful advice to give us. Once when I was lecturing at Rome, Rusticus, whom Domitian afterwards, out of jealousy of his reputation, put to death, was one of my hearers; and while I was going on, a soldier came in and brought him a letter from the Emperor. And when every one was silent, and I stopped in order to let him read the letter, he declined to do so, and put it aside until I had finished and the audience withdrew; an example of serious and dignified behaviour which excited much admiration."

L. Junius Arulenus Rusticus, the friend of Pliny and Tacitus, glorified among the Stoic martyrs whose names are written in the life of Agricola, was in youth the ardent disciple of Thrasea Pætus; and when Pætus was destined by Nero for death, and the Senate was prepared to pass the decree for his condemnation, Rusticus, in the fervour of his feelings, was eager to interpose the veto still attaching in form to the office, which he happened then to hold, of tribune, and was scarcely withheld by his master from a demonstration which would but have added him, before his time, to the catalogue of victims. After performing, in the civil wars ensuing on the death of Nero, the duties of prætor, he published in Domitian's time a life of Thrasea, as did Senecio one of Helvidius, and Tacitus, probably himself, that of Agricola: the bold language of which insured his death. Among the teachers who afterwards gave instruction to the youthful Marcus Aurelius, we read the name of an Arulenus Rusticus, probably his grandson, united with that of Sextus of Chæronea, Plutarch's nephew, "who taught me," says the virtuous Emperor, "by his own example, the just and wise habits he recommended," and to whose door, in late life, he was still seen to go, still desirous, as he said, to be a learner.

It does not, of course, follow from the terms in which the story is related, that the incident occurred in Domitian's time, and that it was to Domitian's letter that Plutarch's discourse was preferred. But that Plutarch was at Rome in or after Domitian's reign, seems to be fairly inferred from the language in which he speaks of the absurd magnificence of Domitian's palaces and other imperial buildings.

His two brothers, Timon and Lamprias, are frequently mentioned in his Essays and Dialogues. They, also, appear to have been pupils of Ammonius. In the treatise on Affection between Brothers, after various examples of the strength of this feeling, occurs the following passage: "And for myself," he says, "that among the many favours for which I have to thank the kindness of fortune, my brother Timon's affection to me is one, past and present, that may be put in the balance against all the rest, is what every one that has so much as met with us must be aware of, and our friends, of course, know well."

His wife was Timoxena, the daughter of Alexion. The circumstances of his domestic life receive their best illustration from his letter addressed to this wife, on the loss of their one daughter, born to them, it would appear, late in life, long after her brothers. "Plutarch to his wife, greeting. The messengers you sent to announce our child's death, apparently missed the road to Athens. I was told about my daughter on reaching Tanagra. Everything relating to the funeral I suppose to have been already performed; my desire is that all these arrangements may have been so made, as will now and in the future be most consoling to yourself. If there is anything which you have wished to do and have omitted, awaiting my opinion, and think would be a relief to you, it shall be attended to, apart from all excess and superstition, which no one would like less than yourself. Only, my wife, let me hope, that you will maintain both me and yourself within the reasonable limits of grief. What our loss really amounts to, I know and estimate for myself. But should I find your distress excessive, my trouble on your account will be greater than on that of our loss. I am not a 'stock or stone,' as you, my partner in the care of our numerous children, every one of whom we have ourselves brought up at home, can testify. And this child, a daughter, born to your wishes after four sons, and affording me the opportunity of recording your name, I am well aware was a special object of recording your name, I am well aware was a special object of affection."

The sweet temper and the pretty ways of the child, he proceeds to say, make the privation peculiarly painful. "Yet why," he says, "should we forget the reasonings we have often addressed to others, and regard our present pain as obliterating and effacing our former joys?" Those who had been present had spoken to him in terms of admiration of the calmness and simplicity of her behaviour. The funeral had been devoid of any useless and idle sumptuosity, and her own house of all display of extravagant lamentation. This was indeed no wonder to him, who knew how much her plain and unluxurious living had surprised his philosophical friends and visitors, and who well remembered her composure under the previous loss of the eldest of her children, and again, "when our beautiful Charon left us." "I recollect," he says, "that some acquaintance from abroad were coming up with me from the sea when the tidings of the child's decease were brought, and they followed with our other friends to the house; but the perfect order and tranquillity they found there made them believe, as I afterwards was informed they had related, that nothing had happened, and that the previous intelligence had been a mistake."

The Consolation (so the letter is named) closes with expressions of belief in the immortality of each human soul; in which the parents are sustained and fortified by the tradition of their ancestors, and the revelations to which they had both been admitted, conveyed in the mystic Dionysian ceremonies.

There is a phrase in the letter which might be taken to imply that, at the time of his domestic misfortune, Plutarch and Timoxena were already grandparents. The marriage of their son Autobulus is the occasion of one of the dinner parties recorded in the Symposiac Questions; and in one of the dialogues there is a distinct allusion to Autobulus's son. Plutarch inscribes the little treatise in explanation of the Timæus to his two sons, Autobulus and Plutarch. They must certainly have been grown-up men, to have anything to do with so difficult a subject. In his Inquiry as to the Way in which the Young should read the Poets, "It is not easy," he says, addressing Marcus Sedatus, "to restrain altogether from such reading young people of the age of my Soclarus and your Cleander." But whether Soclarus was a son, or a grandson, or some more distant relative, or, which is possible, a pupil, does not appear. Eurydice, to whom and to Pollianus, her newly espoused husband, he addresses his Marriage Precepts, seems to be spoken of as a recent inmate of his house; but it cannot be inferred that she was a daughter, nor does it seem likely that the little Timoxena's place was ever filled up.[1]

[1] That he had more than two sons who grew up, at any rate, to youth, appears from a passage where he speaks of his younger sons having stayed too long at the theatre, and being, in consequence, too late at supper.

The office of Archon, which Plutarch held in his native municipality, was probably only an annual one; but very likely he served it more than once. He seems to have busied himself about all the little matters of the town, and to have made it a point to undertake the humblest duties. After relating the story of Epaminondas giving dignity to the office of Chief Scavenger, "And I, too, for that matter," he says, "am often a jest to my neighbours, when they see me, as they frequently do, in public, occupied on very similar duties; but the story told about Antisthenes comes to my assistance. When some one expressed surprise at his carrying home some picked fish from market in his own hands, *It is*, he answered, *for myself.* Conversely, when I am reproached with standing by and watching while tiles are measured out, and stone and mortar brought up, *This service*, I say, *is not for myself*, it is for my country."

In the little essay on the question, Whether an Old Man should continue in Public Life, written in the form of an exhortation of Euphanes, an ancient and distinguished member of the Areopagus at Athens, and of the Amphictyonic council, not to relinquish his duties, "Let there be no severance," he says, "in our long companionship, and let neither the one nor the other of us forsake the life that was our choice." And, alluding to his own functions as priest of Apollo at Delphi, "You know," he adds in another place, "that I have served the Pythian God for many *pythiads*[1] past, yet you would not now tell me, *you have taken part enough in the sacrifices, processions, and dances, and it is high time, Plutarch, now you are an old man, to lay aside your garland, and retire as superannuated from the oracle.*"

Even in these, the comparatively few, more positive and matter-of-fact passages of allusion and anecdote, there is enough to bring up something of a picture of a happy domestic life, half academic, half municipal, passed among affectionate relatives and well-known friends, inclining most to literary and moral studies, yet not cut off from the duties and avocations of the citizen. We cannot, of course, to go yet further, accept the scenery of the fictitious Dialogues as historical; yet there is much of it which may be taken as, so to say, pictorially just; and there is, probably, a good deal here and there that is literally true to the fact. The Symposiac, or After-Dinner Questions, collected in nine books, and dedicated to Sosius Senecio, were discussed, we are told, many of them, in the company of Sosius himself, both at Rome and in Greece, as, for example, when he was with them at the marriage festivities of Autobulus. Lamprias and Timon, the author's brothers, are frequent

[1] Periods of four years elapsing between the celebrations of the Pythian games, like the Olympiads for the Olympic games.

speakers, each with a distinctly traced character, in these conversations; the father, and the elder Lamprias, the grandfather, both take an occasional, and the latter a lively part; there is one whole book in which Ammonius predominates; the scene is now at Delphi, and now at Athens, sometimes perhaps, but rarely, at Rome, sometimes at the celebrations of the Games. Plutarch, in his priestly capacity, gives an entertainment in honour of a poetic victor at the Pythia, there is an Isthmian dinner at Corinth, and an Olympian party at Elis. As an adopted Athenian citizen of the Leontid tribe, he attends the celebration of the success of his friend, the philosophic poet Serapion. The *dramatis personæ* of the various little pieces form a company, when put together, of more than eighty names, philosophers, rhetoricians, and grammarians, several physicians, Euthydemus his colleague in the priesthood, Alexion his father-in-law, and four or five other connections by marriage, Favorinus the philosopher of Arles in Provence, afterwards favoured by Hadrian, to whom he dedicates one of his treatises, and who in return wrote an essay called Plutarchus, on the Academic Philosophy. Serapion entertains them in a garden on the banks of the Cephisus. They dine with a friendly physician on the heights of Hyampolis, and meet in a party at the baths of Ædepsus. The questions are of the most miscellaneous description, grave sometimes, and moral, grammatical and antiquarian, and often festive and humorous. *In what sense does Plato say that God uses geometry? Why do we hear better by night than by day? Why are dreams least true in autumn? Which existed first, the hen or the egg? Which of Venus's hands did Diomed wound?* Lamprias, the grandfather, finds fault with his son, Plutarch's father, for *inviting too many guests* to the parties given "when we came home from Alexandria." Ammonius, in office as general at Athens, gives a dinner to the young men who had distinguished themselves at a trial of skill in grammar, rhetoric, geometry, and poetry; and anecdotes are told on the occasion *of verses aptly or inaptly quoted.*

Of the other minor works, some look a good deal like lectures delivered at Rome, and afterwards published with little dedications prefixed. We have a disquisition on the Advantages we can derive from our Enemies, addressed to Cornelius Pulcher, a discourse On Fate, to Piso, and On Brotherly Affection, to Nigrinus and Quintus. Many, however, are dialogues and conversations, with a good deal of the same varied scenery and exuberant detail which embellish the Table-Talk.

In a conversation which he had been present at, "long ago, when Nero was staying in Greece," between Ammonius and some other friends, the meaning of the strange inscription at Delphi, the two letters EI, is debated. A visitor is conducted by some of Plutarch's friends over the sacred buildings at Delphi, and in the intervals between the somewhat tedious speeches of the professional guides, who showed the sights, a discussion takes place on the Nature of the Oracles. "It happened a little before the Pythian games in the time of Callistratus, there met us at Delphi two travellers, from the extremities of the world, Demetrius, the grammarian, on his way home to Tarsus from Britain, and Cleombrotus the Lacedæmonian, just returned from a journey he had made for his pleasure and instruction in Upper Egypt, and far out into the Erythræan Sea." The question somehow or other occurs, and the dialogue, Of the Cessation of Oracles, ensues; one passage of which is the famous story of the voice that proclaimed the death of the great Pan. Autobulus is talking with Soclarus, the companion of his son, about an encomium which they had heard on hunting; the best praise they can give it is, that it diverts into a less objectionable course the passion which finds one vent in seeing the contests of gladiators. Up come presently a large party of young men, lovers of hunting and fishing, and the question of the Superior Sagacity of Land or of Water Animals is formally pleaded by two selected orators. Stories are told of elephants; and Aristotimus, the advocate of the land animals, relates a sight (of the dog imitating in a play the effects of poison) which he himself, he says, saw in Rome, and which was so perfectly acted as to cause emotion in the spectators, the Emperor included; the aged Vespasian himself being present, in the theatre of Marcellus. It reads very much as if Plutarch, and not Aristotimus, had been the eye-witness.[1]

Autobulus occurs again in the Dialogue on Love. At the request of his friend Flavianus, he repeats a long conversation, attended with curious incidents, in which his father had taken part on Mount Helicon, "once long ago, before we were born, when he brought our mother, after the dispute and variance which had arisen between their parents, that she might offer a sacrifice to Love at the feast held at Thespiæ."

The variance alluded to must clearly have been a fact. And, in general, though these playful fictions or semi-fictions, which form the machinery of the dialogues, are not indeed to be accepted in a literal way, they possess an authenticity which we cannot venture to attribute to the

[1] Something also of a personal remembrance of Vespasian's unrelentingly severe temper may be thought to appear in the story, related in the Dialogue on Love, of the Gaulish rebel Sabinus, and his wife Eponina, mentioned by Tacitus in his Histories, who, after living in an underground concealment several years, were discovered and put to death. Two sons were born to them in their hiding-place, "one of whom," says Plutarch, "was here with us in Delphi only a little while ago," and he is disposed, he adds, "to attribute the subsequent extinction of the race of Vespasian to divine displeasure at this cruel and unfeeling act."

professedly historical statements about their author, given in later writers. Suidas, the lexicographer, repeats a mere romance when he tells us that Trajan gave him the dignity of consul, and issued orders that none of the magistrates in Illyria should do anything without consulting him. Syncellus, the Byzantine historian, under the record of one of the first years of Hadrian's reign, is equally or even more extravagant, relating that Plutarch, the philosopher of Chæronea, was in his old age appointed by the emperor to the office of governor of Greece. Though the period of Trajan and the Antonines was the golden age of philosophers, whose brief persecution under Domitian seems to have won them for a while a sort of spiritual supremacy, similar to that which, after Diocletian, was wrested from them by the ministers of the new religion, still these assertions are on the face of them entirely incredible.

There is a letter, indeed, given among Plutarch's printed works, in which a collection of Sayings of Kings and Commanders is dedicated to Trajan; and though much doubt is entertained, it is not at all improbable that it is Plutarch's own writing. There is nothing remarkable in its contents, and it is most noticeable for the contrast in tone which it presents to another letter, undoubtedly spurious, first published in Latin by John of Salisbury, which is a very preceptorial lecture to Trajan, his pupil, by Plutarch, his supposed former teacher.

A list of Plutarch's works, including many of which nothing remains, is also given by Suidas, as made by Lamprias, Plutarch's son; and a little prefatory letter to a friend, whom he had known in Asia, and who had written to ask for the information, is prefixed to the catalogue. The catalogue itself may be correct enough, but the name of Lamprias occurs nowhere in all Plutarch's extant works as that of one of his sons; and it cannot but be suspected that this family name was adopted, and this letter to the nameless friend in Asia composed, by some grammarian long after, who desired to give interest to an ordinary list of the author's extant writings.

In reading Plutarch, the following points should be remembered. He is a moralist rather than an historian. His interest is less for politics and the changes of empires, and much more for personal character and individual actions and motives to action; duty performed and rewarded; arrogance chastised, hasty anger corrected; humanity, fair dealing, and generosity triumphing in the visible, or relying on the invisible world. His mind in his biographic memoirs is continually running on the Aristotelian Ethics and the high Platonic theories, which formed the religion of the educated population of his time.

The time itself is a second point; that of Nerva, Trajan, and Hadrian;

the commencement of the best and happiest age of the great Roman imperial period. The social system, spreading over all the coasts of the Mediterranean Sea, of which Greece and Italy were the centres, and to which the East and the furthest known West were brought into relation, had then reached its highest mark of advance and consummation. The laws of Rome and the philosophy of Greece were powerful from the Tigris to the British islands. It was the last great era of Greek and Roman literature. Epictetus was teaching in Greek the virtues which Marcus Aurelius was to illustrate as emperor. Dio Chrysostom and Arrian were recalling the memory of the most famous Attic rhetoricians and historians, and while Plutarch wrote in Chæronea, Tacitus, Pliny the Younger, Martial, and Juvenal were writing at Rome. It may be said too, perhaps, not untruly, that the Latin, the metropolitan writers, less faithfully represent the general spirit and character of the time than what came from the pen of a simple Bœotian provincial, writing in a more universal language, and unwarped by the strong local reminiscences of the old home of the Senate and the Republic. Tacitus and Juvenal have more, perhaps, of the "antique Roman" than of the citizen of the great Mediterranean Empire. The evils of the imperial government, as felt in the capital city, are depicted in the Roman prose and verse more vividly and more vehemently than suits a general representation of the state of the imperial world, even under the rule of Domitian himself.

It is, at any rate, the serener aspect and the better era that the life and writings of Plutarch reflect. His language is that of a man happy in himself and in what is around him. His natural cheerfulness is undiminished, his easy and joyous simplicity is unimpaired, his satisfactions are not saddened or imbittered by any overpowering recollections of years passed under the immediate present terrors of imperial wickedness. Though he also could remember Nero, and had been a man when Domitian was an emperor, the utmost we can say is, that he shows, perhaps, the instructed happiness of one who had lived into good times out of evil, and that the very vigour of his content proves that its roots were fixed amongst circumstances not too indulgent or favourable.

Much has been said of Plutarch's inaccuracy; and it cannot be denied that he is careless about numbers, and occasionally contradicts his own statements. A greater fault, perhaps, is his passion for anecdote; he cannot forbear from repeating stories, the improbability of which he is the first to recognise; which, nevertheless, by mere repetition, leave unjust impressions. He is unfair in this way to Demosthenes and to Pericles, against the latter of whom, however, he doubtless inherited the prejudices which Plato handed down to the philosophers.

It is true, also, that his unhistorical treatment of the subjects of his biography makes him often unsatisfactory and imperfect in the portraits he draws. Much, of course, in the public lives of statesmen can find its only explanation in their political position; and of this Plutarch often knows and thinks little. So far as the researches of modern historians have succeeded in really recovering a knowledge of relations of this sort, so far, undoubtedly, these biographies stand in need of their correction. Yet in the uncertainty which must attend all modern restorations, it is agreeable, and surely, also, profitable, to recur to portraits drawn ere new thoughts and views had occupied the civilised world, without reference to such disputable grounds of judgment, simply upon the broad principles of the ancient moral code of right and wrong.

Making some little deductions in cases such as those that have been mentioned, allowing for a little over-love of story, and for some considerable quasi-religious hostility to the democratic leaders who excited the scorn of Plato, if we bear in mind, also, that in narratives like that of Theseus, he himself confesses his inability to disengage fact from fable, it may be said that in Plutarch's Lives the readers of all ages will find instructive and faithful biographies of the great men of Greece and Rome. Or, at any rate, if in Plutarch's time it was too late to think of really faithful biographies, we have here the faithful record of the historical tradition of his age. This is what, in the second century of our era, Greeks and Romans loved to believe about their warriors and statesmen of the past. As a picture, at least, of the best Greek and Roman moral views and moral judgments, as a presentation of the results of Greek and Roman moral thought, delivered not under the pressure of calamity, but as they existed in ordinary times, and actuated plain-living people in country places in their daily life, Plutarch's writings are of indisputable value; and it may be said, also, that Plutarch's character, as depicted in them, possesses a natural charm of pleasantness and amiability which it is not easy to match among all extant classical authors.

The present translation is a revision of that published at the end of the seventeenth century, with a life of Plutarch written by Dryden, whose name, it was presumed, would throw some reflected lustre on the humbler workmen who performed, better or worse, the more serious labour. There is, of course, a great inequality in their work. But the translation by Langhorne, for which, in the middle of the last century, the older volumes were discarded, is so inferior in liveliness, and is in fact so dull and heavy a book that, in default of an entirely new translation, some advantage, it is hoped, may be gained by the revival here attempted. It would not have been needed, had Mr. Long not limited the series which he published, with very useful notes, in Mr. Knight's Shilling Library, to the lives connected with the Civil Wars of Rome.

Dryden's Life of Plutarch is, like many of Dryden's writings, hasty yet well written, inaccurate but agreeable to read; that by Dacier, printed in the last volume of his French translations, is, in many respects, very good. The materials for both were collected, and the references accumulated, by Rualdus, in his laborious Life appended to the old Paris folios of 1624. But everything that is of any value is given in the articles in Fabricius's *Bibliotheca Græca*, and, with the most recent additions, in Pauly's *German Cyclopædia*. Much that is useful is found, as might be expected, in Clinton's *Fasti Romani*, from which the following table is taken:—

Date	Occurrences	Authors
A.D.		
41.	Accession of Claudius.	
54.	Accession of Nero.	
66.	Nero comes into Greece; alluded to in Plutarch's Dialogue, On the EI at Delphi.	Seneca. Lucan. Persius.
67.	Nero celebrates the Isthmian Games; alluded to in Plutarch's Life of Flamininus.	
68.	Galba is Emperor. Civil wars.	
69.	Vitellius, Otho, Vespasian.	
70.	Taking of Jerusalem.	
74.	The Philosophers are expelled from Rome.	Death of Pliny the Elder.
79.	Death of Sabinus, the Gaul. Death of Vespasian, and accession of Titus. Eruption of Vesuvius; alluded to by Plutarch, as a recent occurrence, in his Enquiry why the Pythian Oracles are no longer delivered in verse.	
81.	Accession of Domitian.	Quintilian. Statius. Silius Italicus. Martial.
90.	The Philosophers are again expelled from Rome, after the death of Rusticus.	
96.	Accession of Nerva.	*Dio Chrysostom.* Tacitus, born about A.D. 60. *Plutarch.* *Epictetus.* *Arrian.* Pliny the Younger, born A.D. 61. Juvenal, born A.D. 59. *Favorinus.* Suetonius, born about A.D. 70.
98.	Accession of Trajan.	
100.	Pliny's Panegyric	
103.	Epictetus is teaching at Nicopolis, Arrian attending him.	
104.	Pliny in Bithynia.	
106.	Trajan winters on the Danube; alluded to by Plutarch, On the Principle of Cold	
113.	Erection of Trajan's Column	
114.	Trajan's Parthian Victories. Plutarch had written his life of Antony before these.	
117.	Accession of Hadrian. In Hadrian's third year, Plutarch, according to Eusebius, was still alive.	
138.	Acession of Antoninus.	*Ptolemy.* *Appian.* *Pausanias.* *Galen.* *Lucian.* *Athenœus.* *Dion Cassius.*
161.	Accession of Marcus Aurelius.	
181.	Accession of Commodus.	

NOTE.—*The authors whose names are printed in italics are Greek writers.*

The fault which runs through all the earlier biographies, from that of Rualdus downward, is the assumption, wholly untenable, that Plutarch passed many years, as many, perhaps, as forty, at Rome. The entire character of his life is of course altered by such an impression. It is, therefore, not worth while reprinting here the life originally prefixed by Dryden to the translations which, with more or less of alteration, follow in the present volumes. One or two characteristic extracts may be sufficient. The first may throw some light on a subject which to modern readers is a little obscure. Dryden is wrong in one or two less important points, but his general view of the *dœmonic* belief which pervades Plutarch's writings is tolerably to the purpose.

"We can only trace the rest of his opinions from his philosophy, which we have said in the general to be Platonic, though it cannot also be denied that there was a tincture in it of the Electic[1] sect, which was begun by Potamon under the empire of Augustus, and which selected from all the other sects what seemed most probable in their opinions, not adhering singularly to any of them, nor rejecting everything. I will only touch his belief of spirits. In his two Treatises of Oracles, the one concerning the Reason of their Cessation, the other inquiring Why they were not given in Verse as in former times, he seems to assert the Pythagorean doctrine of Transmigration of Souls. We have formerly shown that he owned the unity of a Godhead; whom, according to his attributes, he calls by several names, as Jupiter from his almighty power, Apollo from his wisdom, and so of the rest; but under him he places those beings whom he styles *Genii* or *Dœmons*, of a middle nature, between divine and human; for he thinks it absurd that there should be no mean between the two extremes of an immortal and a mortal being; that there cannot be in nature so vast a flaw, without some intermedial kind of life, partaking of them both. As, therefore, we find the intercourse between the soul and body to be made by the animal spirits, so between divinity and humanity there is this species of dæmons. Who,[2] having first been men, and followed the strict rules of virtue, have purged off the grossness and feculency of their earthly being, are exalted into these genii; and are from thence either raised higher into an ethereal life, if they still continue virtuous, or tumbled down again into mortal bodies, and sinking into flesh after they have lost that purity which constituted their glorious being. And this sort of Genii are those who, as our author imagines, presided over oracles; spirits which have so much of their ter-

[1] He means the Eclectic as it is more usually called.

[2] He means, I believe, *Those who;* apparently the word *and* should be omitted in line 25, before *sinking into flesh.*

restrial principles remaining in them as to be subject to passions and inclinations; usually beneficent, sometimes malevolent to mankind, according as they refine themselves, or gather dross, and are declining into mortal bodies. The cessation, or rather the decrease of oracles (for some of them were still remaining in Plutarch's time), he attributes either to the death of those dæmons, as appears by the story of the Egyptian Thamus, who was commanded to declare that the great god Pan was dead, or to their forsaking of those places where they formerly gave out their oracles, from whence they were driven by stronger Genii into banishment for a certain revolution of ages. Of this last nature were the war of the giants against the gods, the dispossession of Saturn by Jupiter, the banishment of Apollo from heaven, the fall of Vulcan, and many others; all which, according to our author, were the battles of these Genii or Dæmons amongst themselves. But supposing, as Plutarch evidently does, that these spirits administered, under the Supreme Being, the affairs of men, taking care of the virtuous, punishing the bad, and sometimes communicating with the best, as, particularly, the Genius of Socrates always warned him of approaching dangers, and taught him to avoid them, I cannot but wonder that every one who has hitherto written Plutarch's Life, and particularly Rualdus, the most knowing of them all, should so confidently affirm that these oracles were given by bad spirits, according to Plutarch. As Christians, indeed, we may think them so; but that Plutarch so thought is a most apparent falsehood. 'Tis enough to convince a reasonable man, that our author in his old age (and that then he doted not, we may see by the treatise he has written, That old men ought to have the management of public affairs), I say that then he initiated himself in the sacred rites of Delphos, and died, for ought we know, Apollo's priest. Now it is not to be imagined that he thought the God he served a *Cacodæmon*, or, as we call him, a devil. Nothing could be further from the opinion and practice of this holy philosopher than so gross an impiety. The story of the Pythias, or priestess of Apollo, which he relates immediately before the ending of that treatise, concerning the Cessation of Oracles, confirms my assertion rather than shakes it; for 'tis there delivered, 'That going with great reluctation into the sacred place to be inspired, she came out foaming at the mouth, her eyes goggling, her breast heaving, her voice undistinguishable and shrill, as if she had an earthquake within her, labouring for vent; and, in short, that thus tormented with the god, whom she was not able to support, she died distracted in a few days after. For he had said before that the divineress ought to have no perturbations of mind or impure passions at the time when she was to consult the oracle, and if she had, she was no more fit to be inspired than an instrument untuned to render an harmonious sound.' And he gives us to suspect, by what he says at the close of this relation, 'That this Pythias had not lived chastely for some time before it; so that her death appears more like a punishment inflicted for loose living, by some holy Power, than the mere malignancy of a Spirit delighted naturally in mischief.' There is another observation which indeed comes nearer to their purpose, which I will digress so far as to relate, because it somewhat appertains to our own country. 'There are many islands,' says he, 'which lie scattering about Britain, after the manner of our Sporades; they are unpeopled, and some of them are called the Islands of the Heroes, or the Genii.' One Demetrius was sent by the emperor (who by computation of the time must either be Caligula or Claudius[1]) to discover those parts, and arriving at one of the islands next adjoining to the before mentioned, which was inhabited by some few Britons (but those held sacred and inviolable by all their countrymen), immediately after his arrival, the air grew black and troubled, strange apparitions were seen, the winds raised a tempest, and fiery spouts or whirlwinds appeared dancing towards the earth. When these prodigies were ceased, the islanders informed him that some one of the aerial beings, superior to our nature, then ceased to live. For as a taper, while yet burning, affords a pleasant, harmless light, but is noisome and offensive when extinguished, so those heroes shine benignly on us and do us good, but at their death turn all things topsy-turvy, raise up tempests, and infect the air with pestilential vapours. By those holy and inviolable men, there is no question but he means our Druids, who were nearest to the Pythagoreans of any sect; and this opinion of the Genii might probably be one of theirs. Yet it proves not that all dæmons were thus malicious, only those who were to be condemned hereafter into human bodies, for their misdemeanours in their aerial being. But 'tis time to leave a subject so very fanciful, and so little reasonable as this. I am apt to imagine the natural vapours, arising in the cave where the temple afterwards was built, might work upon the spirits of those who entered the holy place, as they did on the shepherd Coretas, who first found it out by accident, and incline them to enthusiasm and prophetic madness; that as the strength of those vapours diminished (which were generally in caverns, as that of Mopsus, of Trophonius, and this of Delphos), so the inspiration decreased by the same measures; that they happened to be stronger when they killed the Pythias, who being conscious of this, was so unwilling to enter; that the oracles ceased to be given in verse when poets ceased to be the priests, and that the Genius of Socrates (whom he confessed never to

[1] Undoubtedly much later.

have seen, but only to have heard inwardly, and unperceived by others) was no more than the strength of his imagination; or, to speak in the language of a Christian Platonist, his guardian angel."

The concluding passage of the life may serve as a conclusion to this prefatory essay. It is as follows: "And now, with the usual vanity of Dutch prefacers, I could load our author with the praises and commemorations of writers; for both ancient and modern have made honourable mention of him. But to cumber pages with this kind of stuff were to raise a distrust in common readers that Plutarch wants them. Rualdus, indeed, has collected ample testimonies of them; but I will only recite the names of some, and refer you to him for the particular quotations. He reckons Gellius, Eusebius, Himerius the Sophister, Eunapius, Cyrillus of Alexandria, Theodoret, Agathias, Photius and Xiphilin, patriarchs of Constantinople, Johannes Sarisberiensis, the famous Petrarch, Petrus Victorius, and Justus Lipsius.

"But Theodorus Gaza, a man learned in the Latin tongue, and a great restorer of the Greek, who lived above two hundred years ago, deserves to have his suffrage set down in words at length; for the rest have only commended Plutarch more than any single author, but he has extolled him above all together.

" 'Tis said that, having this extravagant question put to him by a friend, that if learning must suffer a general shipwreck, and he had only his choice left him of preserving one author, who should be the man he would preserve, he answered, Plutarch; and probably might give this reason, that in saving him, he should secure the best collection of them all.

"The epigram of Agathias deserves also to be remembered. This author flourished about the year five hundred, in the reign of the Emperor Justinian. The verses are extant in the Anthologia, and with the translation of them I will conclude the praises of our author; having first admonished you, that they are supposed to be written on a statue erected by the Romans to his memory.

" 'Chæronean Plutarch, to thy deathless praise
Does marital Rome this grateful statue raise,
Because both Greece and she thy fame have shared,
(Their heroes written, and their lives compared).
But thou thyself couldst never write thy own;
Their lives have parallels, but thine has none.' "

Plutarch's Lives

SERTORIUS

It is no great wonder if in long process of time, while fortune takes her course hither and thither, numerous coincidences should spontaneously occur. If the number and variety of subjects to be wrought upon be infinite, it is all the more easy for fortune, with such an abundance of material, to effect this similarity of results. Or if, on the other hand, events are limited to the combinations of some finite number, then of necessity the same must often recur, and in the same sequence. There are people who take a pleasure in making collections of all such fortuitous occurrences that they have heard or read of, as look like works of a rational power and design; they observe, for example, that two eminent persons whose names were Attis, the one a Syrian, the other of Arcadia, were both slain by a wild boar; that of two whose names were Actæon, the one was torn in pieces by his dogs, the other by his lovers; that of two famous Scipios, the one overthrew the Carthaginians in war, the other totally ruined and destroyed them; the city of Troy was the first time taken by Hercules for the horses promised him by Laomedon, the second time by Agamemnon, by means of the celebrated great wooden horse, and the third time by Charidemus, by occasion of a horse falling down at the gate, which hindered the Trojans, so that they could not shut them soon enough; and of two cities which take their names from the most agreeable odoriferous plants, Ios and Smyrna, the one from a violet, the other from myrrh, the poet Homer is reported to have been born in the one and to have died in the other. And so to these instances let us further add, that the most warlike commanders, and most remarkable for exploits of skilful stratagem, have had but one eye; as Philip, Antigonus, Hannibal, and Sertorius, whose life and actions we describe at present; of whom, indeed, we might truly say, that he was more continent than Philip, more faithful to his friends than Antigonus, and more merciful to his enemies than Hannibal; and that for prudence and judgment he gave place to none of them, but in fortune was inferior to them all. Yet though he had continually in her a far more difficult adversary to contend against than his open enemies, he nevertheless maintained his ground, with the military skill of Metellus, the boldness of Pompey, the success of Sylla, and the power of the Roman people, all to be encountered by one who was a banished man and a stranger at the head of a body of barbarians. Among Greek commanders, Eumenes of Cardia may be best compared with him; they were both of them men born for command, for warfare, and for stratagem; both banished from their countries, and holding command over strangers; both had fortune for their adversary, in their last days so harshly so, that they were both betrayed and murdered by those who served them, and with whom they had formerly overcome their enemies.

Quintus Sertorius was of a noble family, born in the city of Nursia, in the country of the Sabines; his father died when he was young, and he was carefully and decently educated by his mother, whose name was Rhea, and whom he appears to have extremely loved and honoured. He paid some attention to the study of oratory and pleading in his youth, and acquired some reputation and influence in Rome by his eloquence; but the splendour of his actions in arms, and his successful achievements in the wars, drew off his ambition in that direction.

At his first beginning, he served under Cæpio, when the Cimbri and Teutones invaded Gaul; where the Romans fighting unsuccessfully, and being put to flight, he was wounded in many parts of his body, and lost his horse, yet, nevertheless, swam across the river Rhone in his armour, with his breastplate and shield, bearing himself up against the violence of the current; so strong and so well inured to hardship was his body.

The second time that the Cimbri and Teutones came down with some hundreds of thousands, threatening death and destruction to all, when it was no small piece of service for a Roman soldier to keep his ranks and obey his commander, Sertorius undertook, while Marius led the army, to spy out the enemy's camp. Procuring a Celtic dress, and acquainting himself with the ordinary expressions of their language requisite for common intercourse, he threw himself in amongst the barbarians; where having carefully seen with his own eyes, or having been fully informed by persons upon the place of all their most important concerns, he returned to Marius, from whose hands he received the rewards of valour; and afterwards giving frequent proof both of conduct and courage in all the following war, he was advanced to places of honour and trust under his general. After the wars with the Cimbri and Teutones, he was sent into Spain, having the command of a thousand men under Didius, the Roman general, and wintered in the country of the Celtiberians, in the city of Castulo, where the soldiers enjoying great plenty, and growing insolent and continually drinking, the inhabitants despised them and sent for aid by night to the Gyrisœnians, their near neighbours, who fell upon the Romans in their lodgings and slew a great number of them. Sertorius, with a few of his soldiers, made his way out, and rallying together the rest who escaped, he marched round about the walls, and finding the gate open, by which the Gyrisœnians had made their secret entrance, he gave not them the same opportunity, but placing a guard at the gate, and seizing upon all quarters of the city, he slew all who were of age to bear arms, and then ordering his soldiers to lay aside their weapons and put off their own clothes, and put on the accoutrements of the barbarians, he commanded them to follow him to the city from whence the men came who had made this night attack upon the Romans. And thus deceiving the Gyrisœniana with the sight of their own armour, he found the gates of their city open and took a great number prisoners, who came out thinking to meet their friends and fellow-citizens come home from a successful expedition. Most of them were thus slain by the Romans at their own gates, and the rest within yielded up themselves and were sold for slaves.

This action made Sertorius highly renowned throughout all Spain, and as soon as he returned to Rome he was appointed quæstor of Cisalpine Gaul, at a very seasonable moment for his country, the Marsian war being on the point of breaking out. Sertorius was ordered to raise soldiers and provide arms, which he performed with a diligence and alacrity, so contrasting with the feebleness and slothfulness of other officers of his age, that he got the repute of a man whose life would be one of action. Nor did he relinquish the part of a soldier, now that he had arrived at the dignity of a commander, but performed wonders with his own hands, and never sparing himself, but exposing his body freely in all conflicts, he lost one of his eyes. This he always esteemed an honour to him; observing that others do not continually carry about with them the marks and testimonies of their valour, but must often lay aside their chains of gold, their spears and crowns; whereas his ensigns of honour, and the manifestations of his courage, always remained with him, and those who beheld his misfortune must at the same time recognise his merits. The people also paid him the respect he deserved, and when he came into the theatre, received him with plaudits and joyful acclamations, an honour rarely bestowed even on persons of advanced standing and established reputation. Yet, notwithstanding this popularity, when he stood to be tribune of the people, he was disappointed, and lost the place, being opposed by the party of Sylla, which seems to have been the principal cause of his subsequent enmity to Sylla.

After that Marius was overcome by Sylla and fled into Africa, and Sylla had left Italy to go to the wars against Mithridates, and of the two consuls Octavius and Cinna, Octavius remained steadfast to the policy of Sylla, but Cinna, desirous of a new revolution, attempted to recall the lost interest of Marius, Sertorius joined Cinna's party, more particularly as he saw that Octavius was not very capable, and was also suspicious of any one that was a friend to Marius. When a great battle was fought between the two consuls in the forum, Octavius overcame, and Cinna and Sertorius, having lost not less than ten thousand men, left the city, and gaining over most part of the troops who were dispersed about and remained still in many parts of Italy, they in a short time mustered up a force against Octavius sufficient to give him battle again, and Marius, also, now coming by sea out of Africa, proffered himself to serve under Cinna, as a private soldier under his consul and commander.

Most were for the immediate reception of Marius, but Sertorius openly declared against it, whether he thought that Cinna would not now pay as much attention to himself, when a man of higher military repute was present, or feared that the violence of Marius would bring all things to confusion, by his boundless wrath and vengeance after victory. He insisted upon it with Cinna that they were already victorious, that there remained little to be done, and that if they admitted Marius, he would deprive them of the glory and advantage of the war, as there was no man less easy to deal with, or less to be trusted in, as a partner in power. Cinna answered, that Sertorius rightly judged the affair, but that he himself was at a loss, and ashamed, and knew not how to reject him, after he had sent for him to share in his fortunes. To which Sertorius immediately replied, that he had thought that Marius came into Italy of his own accord, and therefore had deliberated as to what might be most expedient, but that Cinna ought not so much as to have questioned whether he should accept him whom he had already invited, but should have honourably received and employed him, for his word once passed left no room for debate. Thus Marius being sent for by Cinna, and their forces being divided into three parts, under Cinna, Marius, and Sertorius, the war was brought to a successful conclusion; but those about Cinna and Marius committing all manner of insolence and cruelty, made the Romans think the evils of war a golden time in comparison. On the contrary, it is reported of Sertorius that he never slew any man in his anger to satisfy his own private revenge, nor ever insulted over any one whom he had overcome, but was much offended with Marius, and often privately entreated Cinna to use his power more moderately. And in the end, when the slaves whom Marius had freed at his landing to increase his army, being made not only his fellow-soldiers in the war, but also now his guard in his usurpation, enriched and powerful by his favour, either by the command or permission of Marius, or by their own lawless violence, committed all sorts of crimes, killed their masters, ravished their masters' wives and abused their children, their conduct appeared so intolerable to Sertorius that he slew the whole body of them, four thousand in number, commanding his soldiers to shoot them down with their javelins, as they lay encamped together.

Afterwards when Marius died, and Cinna shortly after was slain, when the younger Marius made himself consul against Sertorius's wishes and contrary to law, when Carbo, Norbanus, and Scipio fought unsuccessfully against Sylla, now advancing to Rome, when much was lost by the cowardice and remissness of the commanders, but more by the treachery of their party, when with the want of prudence in the chief leaders, all went so ill that his presence could do no good, in the end when Sylla had placed his camp near to Scipio, and by pretending friendship, and putting him in hopes of a peace, corrupted his army, and Scipio could not be made sensible of this, although often forewarned of it by Sertorius—at last he utterly despaired of Rome, and hasted into Spain, that by taking possession there beforehand, he might secure a refuge to his friends from their misfortunes at home. Having bad weather in his journey, and travelling through mountainous countries, and the inhabitants stopping the way, and demanding a toll and money for passage, those who were with him were out of all patience at the indignity and shame it would be for a proconsul of Rome to pay tribute to a crew of wretched barbarians. But he little regarded their censure, and slighting that which had only the appearance of an indecency, told them he must buy time, the most precious of all things to those who go upon great enterprises; and pacifying the barbarous people with money, he hastened his journey, and took possession of Spain, a country flourishing and populous, abounding with young men fit to bear arms; but on account of the insolence and covetousness of the governors from time to time sent thither from Rome they had generally an aversion to Roman supremacy. He, however, soon gained the affection of their nobles by intercourse with them, and the good opinion of the people by remitting their taxes. But that which won him most popularity was his exempting them from finding lodgings for the soldiers, when he commanded his army to take up their winter quarters outside the cities, and to pitch their camp in the suburbs; and when he himself, first of all, caused his own tent to be raised without the walls. Yet not being willing to rely totally upon the good inclination of the inhabitants he armed all the Romans who lived in those countries that were of military age, and undertook the building of ships and the making of all sorts of warlike engines, by which means he kept the cities in due obedience, showing himself gentle in all peaceful business, and at the same time formidable to his enemies by his great preparations for war.

As soon as he was informed that Sylla had made himself master of Rome, and that the party which sided with Marius and Carbo was going to destruction, he expected that some commander with a considerable army would speedily come against him, and therefore sent away Julius Salinator immediately, with six thousand men fully armed, to fortify and defend the passes of the Pyrenees. And Caius Annius not long after being sent out by Sylla, finding Julius unassailable, sat down short at the foot of the mountains in perplexity. But a certain Calpurnius, surnamed Lanarius, having treacherously slain Julius, and his soldiers then forsaking the heights of the Pyrenees, Caius Annius advanced with large numbers and drove before him all who endeavoured to hinder his march. Sertorius, also, not being strong enough to give him battle, retreated with three thousand men into New Carthage, where he took shipping, and crossed the seas into Africa. And coming near the coast of Mauritania, his men went on shore to water, and straggling about negligently, the natives fell upon them and slew a great number. This new misfortune forced him to sail back again into Spain, whence he was also repulsed, and, some Cilician private ships joining with him, they made for the island of Pityussa, where they landed and overpowered the garrison placed there by Annius, who, however, came not long after with a great fleet of ships and five thousand soldiers. And Sertorius made ready to fight him by sea, although his ships were not built for strength, but for lightness and swift sailing; but a violent west wind raised such a sea that many of them were run aground and shipwrecked, and he himself, with a few vessels, being kept from putting further out to sea by the fury of the weather, and from landing by the power of his enemies, were tossed about painfully for ten days together, amidst the boisterous and adverse waves.

He escaped with difficulty, and after the wind ceased, ran for certain desert islands scattered in those seas, affording no water, and after passing a night there, making out to sea again, he went through the straits of Cadiz, and sailing outward, keeping the Spanish shore on his right hand, landed a little above the mouth of the river Bætis, where it falls into the Atlantic Sea, and gives the name to that part of Spain. Here he met with seamen recently arrived from the Atlantic islands, two in number, divided from one another only by a narrow channel, and distant from the coast of Africa ten thousand furlongs. These are called the Islands of the Blest; rain falls there seldom, and in moderate showers, but for the most part they have gentle breezes, bringing along with them soft dews, which render the soil not only rich for ploughing and planting, but so abundantly fruitful that it produces spontaneously an abundance of delicate fruits, sufficient to feed the inhabitants, who may here enjoy all things without trouble or labour. The seasons of the year are temperate, and the transitions from one to another so moderate that the air is almost always serene and pleasant. The rough northerly and easterly winds which blow from the coasts of Europe and Africa, dissipated in the vast open space, utterly lose their force before they reach the islands. The soft western and southerly winds which breathe upon them sometimes produce gentle sprinkling showers, which they convey along with them from the sea, but more usually bring days of moist, bright weather, cooling and gently fertilising the soil, so that the firm belief prevails, even among the barbarians, that this is the seat of the blessed, and that these are the Elysian Fields celebrated by Homer.

When Sertorius heard this account, he was seized with a wonderful passion for these islands, and had an extreme desire to go and live there in peace and quietness, and safe from oppression and unending wars; but his inclinations being perceived by the Cilician pirates, who desired not peace nor quiet, but riches and spoils, they immediately forsook him and sailed away into Africa to assist Ascalis, the son of Iphtha, and to help to restore him to his kingdom of Mauritania. Their sudden departure noways discouraged Sertorius; he presently resolved to assist the enemies of Ascalis, and by this new adventure trusted to keep his soldiers together, who from this might conceive new hopes, and a prospect of a new scene of action. His arrival in Mauritania being very acceptable to the Moors, he lost no time, but immediately giving battle to Ascalis, beat him out of the field and besieged him; and Paccianus being sent by Sylla, with a powerful supply, to raise the siege, Sertorius slew him in the field, gained over all his forces, and took the city of Tingis, into which Ascalis and his brothers were fled for refuge. The Africans tell that Antæus was buried in this city, and Sertorius had the grave opened, doubting the story because of the prodigious size, and finding there his body, in effect, it is said, full sixty cubits long, he was infinitely astonished, offered sacrifice, and heaped up the tomb again, gave his confirmation to the story, and added new honours to the memory of Antæus. The Africans tell that after the death of Antæus, his wife Tinga lived with Hercules, and had a son by him called Sophax, who was king of these countries, and gave his mother's name to this city, whose son, also, was Diodorus, a great conqueror, who brought the greatest part of the Libyan tribes under his subjection, with an army of Greeks, raised out of the colonies of the Olbians and Myceneans placed here by Hercules. Thus much I may mention for the sake of King Juba, of all monarchs the greatest student of history, whose ancestors are said to have sprung from Diodorus and Sophax.

When Sertorius had made himself absolute master of the whole country, he acted with great fairness to those who had confided in him, and who yielded to his mercy; he restored to them their property, cities, and government, accepting only of such acknowledgments as they themselves freely offered. And whilst he considered which way next to turn his arms, the Lusitanians sent ambassadors to desire him to be their general; for being terrified with the Roman power, and finding the necessity of having a commander of great authority and experience in war, being also sufficiently assured of his worth and valour by those who had formerly known him, they were desirous to commit themselves especially to his care. And in fact Sertorius is said to have been of a temper unassailable either by fear or pleasure, in adversity and dangers undaunted, and noways puffed up with prosperity. In straightforward fighting, no commander in his time was more bold and daring, and in whatever was to be performed in war by stratagem, secrecy, or surprise, if any strong place was to be secured, any pass to be gained speedily, for deceiving and overreaching an enemy, there was no man equal to him in subtlety and skill. In bestowing rewards and conferring honours upon those who had performed good service in the wars, he was bountiful and magnificent, and was no less sparing and moderate in inflicting punishment. It is true that that piece of harshness and cruelty which he executed in the latter part of his days upon the Spanish hostages seems to argue that his clemency was not natural to him, but only worn as a dress, and employed upon calculation, as his occasion or necessity required. As to my own opinion, I am persuaded that pure virtue, established by reason and judgment, can never be totally perverted or changed into its opposite, by any misfortune whatever. Yet I think it at the same time possible that virtuous inclinations and natural good qualities may, when unworthily oppressed by calamities, show, with change of fortune, some change and alteration of their temper; and thus I conceive it happened to Sertorius, who, when prosperity failed him, became exasperated by his disasters against those who had done him wrong.

The Lusitanians having sent for Sertorius, he left Africa, and being made general with absolute authority, he put all in order amongst them, and brought the neighbouring parts of Spain under subjection. Most of the tribes voluntarily submitted themselves, won by the fame of his clemency and of his courage, and, to some extent, also, he availed himself of cunning artifices of his own devising to impose upon them and gain influence over them. Amongst which, certainly, that of the hind was not the least. Spanus, a countryman who lived in those parts, meeting by chance a hind that had recently calved, flying from the hunters, let the dam go, and pursuing the fawn, took it, being wonderfully pleased with the rarity of the colour, which was all milk-white. As at that time Sertorius was living in the neighbourhood, and accepted gladly any presents of fruit, fowl, or venison that the country afforded, and rewarded liberally those who presented them, the countryman brought him his young hind, which he took and was well pleased with at the first sight; but when in time he had made it so tame and gentle that it would come when he called, and follow him wheresoever he went, and could endure the noise and tumult of the camp, knowing well that uncivilised people are naturally prone to superstition, by little and little he raised it into something preternatural, saying that it was given him by the goddess Diana, and that it revealed to him many secrets. He added, also, further contrivances. If he had received at any time private intelligence that the enemies had made an incursion into any part of the districts under his command, or had solicited any city to revolt, he pretended that the hind had informed him of it in his sleep, and charged him to keep his forces in readiness. Or if again he had noticed that any of the commanders under him had got a victory, he would hide the messengers and bring forth the hind crowned with flowers, for joy of the good news that was to come, and would encourage them to rejoice and sacrifice to the gods for the good account they should soon receive of their prosperous success.

By such practices, he brought them to be more tractable and obedient in all things; for now they thought themselves no longer to be led by a stranger, but rather conducted by a god, and the more so, as the facts themselves seemed to bear witness to it, his power, contrary to all expectation or probability, continually increasing. For with two thousand six hundred men, whom for honour's sake he called Romans, combined with seven hundred Africans, who landed with him when he first entered Lusitania, together with four thousand targeteers and seven hundred horse of the Lusitanians themselves, he made war against four Roman generals, who commanded a hundred and twenty thousand foot, six thousand horse, two thousand archers and slingers, and had cities innumerable in their power; whereas at the first he had not above twenty cities in all. From this weak and slender beginning, he raised himself to the command of large nations of men, and the possession of numerous cities; and of the Roman commanders who were sent against him, he overthrew Cotta in a sea-fight, in the channel near the town of Mellaria; he routed Fufidius, the governor of Bætica, with the loss of two thousand Romans, near the banks of the river Bætis; Lucius Domitius, proconsul of the other province of Spain, was overthrown by one of his lieutenants; Thoranius, another commander sent against him by Metellus with a great force, was slain, and Metellus, one of the greatest and most approved Roman generals then living, by a series of defeats, was reduced to such extremities, that Lucius Manlius came to his assistance out of Gallia Narbonensis, and Pompey the Great was sent from Rome itself in all haste with considerable forces. Nor did Metellus know which way to turn himself, in a war with such a bold and ready commander, who was continually molesting him, and yet could not be brought to a set battle, but by the swiftness and dexterity of his Spanish soldiery was enabled to shift and adapt himself to any change of circumstances. Metellus had had experience in battles fought by regular legions of soldiers, fully armed and drawn up in due order into a heavy standing phalanx, admirably trained for encountering and overpowering an enemy who came to close combat, hand to hand, but entirely unfit for climbing among the hills, and competing incessantly with the swift attacks and retreats of a set of fleet mountaineers, or to endure hunger and thirst, and live exposed like them to the wind and weather, without fire or covering.

Besides, being now in years, and having been formerly engaged in many fights and dangerous conflicts, he had grown inclined to a more remiss, easy, and luxurious life, and was the less able to contend with Sertorius, who was in the prime of his strength and vigour, and had a body wonderfully fitted for war, being strong, active, and temperate, continually accustomed to endure hard labour, to take long, tedious journeys, to pass many nights together without sleep, to eat little, and to be satisfied with very coarse fare, and who was never stained with the least excess in wine, even when he was most at leisure. What leisure time he allowed himself he spent in hunting and riding about, and so made himself thoroughly acquainted with every passage for escape when he would fly, and for overtaking and intercepting a pursuit, and gained a perfect knowledge of where he could and where he could not go. Insomuch that Metellus suffered all the inconveniences of defeat, although he earnestly desired to fight, and Sertorius, though he refused the field, reaped all the advantages of a conqueror. For he hindered them from foraging, and cut them off from water; if they advanced, he was nowhere to be found; if they stayed in any place and encamped, he continually molested and alarmed them; if they besieged any town, he presently appeared and besieged them again, and put them to extremities for want of necessaries. Thus he so wearied out the Roman army that when Sertorius challenged Metellus to fight singly with him, they commended it, and cried out it was a fair offer, a Roman to fight against a Roman, and a general against a general; and when Metellus refused the challenge, they reproached him. Metellus derided and contemned this, and rightly so; for, as Theophrastus observes, a general should die like a general, and not like a skirmisher. But perceiving that the town of the Langobritæ, which gave great assistance to Sertorius, might easily be taken for want of water, as there was but one well within the walls, and the besieger would be master of the springs and fountains in the suburbs, he advanced against the place, expecting to carry it in two days' time, there being no more water, and gave command to his soldiers to take five days' provision only. Sertorius, however, resolving to send speedy relief, ordered two thousand skins to be filled with water, naming a considerable sum of money for the carriage of every skin; and many Spaniards and Moors undertaking the work, he chose out those who were the strongest and swiftest of foot, and sent them through the mountains, with order that when they had delivered the water, they should convey away privately all those who would be least serviceable in the siege, that there might be water sufficient for the defendants. As soon as Metellus understood this, he was disturbed, as he had already consumed most part of the necessary provisions for his army, but he sent out Aquinus with six thousand soldiers to fetch in fresh supplies. But Sertorius having notice of it, laid an ambush for him, and having sent out beforehand three thousand men to take post in a thickly wooded water-course, with these he attacked the rear of Aquinus in his return, while he himself, charging him in the front, destroyed part of his army, and took the rest prisoners, Aquinus only escaping, after the loss of both his horse and his armour. And Metellus, being forced shamefully to raise the siege, withdrew amidst the laughter and contempt of the Spaniards; while Sertorius became yet more the object of their esteem and admiration.

He was also highly honoured for his introducing discipline and good order amongst them, for he altered their furious savage manner of fighting, and brought them to make use of the Roman armour, taught them to keep their ranks, and observe signals and watchwords; and out of a confused number of thieves and robbers he constituted a regular, well-disciplined army. He bestowed silver and gold upon them liberally to gild and adorn their helmets, he had their shields worked with various figures and designs, he brought them into the mode of wearing flowered and embroidered cloaks and coats, and by supplying money for these purposes, and joining with them in all improvements, he won the hearts of all. That, however, which delighted them most was the care that he took of their children. He sent for all the boys of noblest parentage out of all their tribes, and placed them in the great city of Osca, where he appointed masters to instruct them in the Grecian and Roman learning, that when they came to be men, they might, as he professed, be fitted to share with him in authority, and in conducting the government, although under this pretext he really made them hostages. However, their fathers were wonderfully pleased to see their children going daily to the schools in good order, handsomely dressed in gowns edged with purple, and that Sertorius paid for their lessons, examined them often, distributed rewards to the most deserving, and gave them the golden bosses to hang about their necks, which the Romans called bullæ.

There being a custom in Spain that when a commander was slain in battle, those who attended his person fought it out till they all died with him, which the inhabitants of those countries called an *offering*, or libation, there were few commanders that had any considerable guard or number of attendants; but Sertorius was followed by many thousands who offered themselves, and vowed to spend their blood with his. And it is told that when his army was defeated near a city in Spain, and the enemy pressed hard upon them, the Spaniards, with no care for themselves, but being totally solicitous to save Sertorius, took him upon their shoulders and passed him from one to another, till they carried him into the city, and only when they had thus placed their general in safety, provided afterwards each man for his own security.

Nor were the Spaniards alone ambitious to serve him, but the Roman soldiers, also, that came out of Italy, were impatient to be under his command; and when Perpenna Vento, who was of the same faction with Sertorius, came into Spain with a quantity of money and a large number of troops, and designed to make war against Metellus on his own account, his own soldiers opposed it, and talked continually of Sertorius, much to the mortification of Perpenna, who was puffed up with the grandeur of his family and his riches. And when they afterwards received tidings that Pompey was passing the Pyrenees, they took up their arms, laid hold on their ensigns, called upon Perpenna to lead them to Sertorius, and threatened him that if he refused they would go without him and place themselves under a commander who was able to defend himself and those that served him. And so Perpenna was obliged to yield to their desires, and joining Sertorius, added to his army three-and-fifty cohorts.

When now all the cities on this side of the river Ebro also united their forces together under his command, his army grew great, for they flocked together and flowed in upon him from all quarters. But when they continually cried out to attack the enemy, and were impatient cf delay, their inexperienced, disorderly rashness caused Sertorius much trouble, who at first strove to restrain them with reason and good counsel; but when he perceived them refractory and unseasonably violent, he gave way to their impetuous desires, and permitted them to engage with the enemy, in such sort that they might, being repulsed, yet not totally routed, become more obedient to his commands for the future. Which happening as he had anticipated, he soon rescued them, and brought them safe into his camp. After a few days, being willing to encourage them again, when he had called all his army together, he caused two horses to be brought into the field, one old, feeble, lean animal, the other a lusty, strong horse, with a remarkably thick and long tail. Near the lean one he placed a tall, strong man, and near the strong young horse a weak, despicable-looking fellow; and at a sign given, the strong man took hold of the weak horse's tail with both his hands, and drew it to him with his whole force, as if he would pull it off;

the other, the weak man, in the meantime, set to work to pluck off hair by hair from the great horse's tail. When the strong man had given trouble enough to himself in vain, and sufficient diversion to the company, and had abandoned his attempt, whilst the weak, pitiful fellow in a short time and with little pains had left not a hair on the great horse's tail, Sertorius rose up and spoke to his army. "You see, fellow-soldiers, that perseverance is more prevailing than violence, and that many things which cannot be overcome when they are together, yield themselves up when taken little by little. Assiduity and persistence are irresistible, and in time overthrow and destroy the greatest powers whatever. Time being the favourable friend and assistant of those who use their judgment to await his occasions, and the destructive enemy of those who are unreasonably urging and pressing forward." With a frequent use of such words and such devices, he soothed the fierceness of the barbarous people, and taught them to attend and watch for their opportunities.

Of all his remarkable exploits, none raised greater admiration than that which he put in practice against the Characitanians. These are a people beyond the river Tagus, who inhabit neither cities nor towns, but live in a vast high hill, within the deep dens and caves of the rocks, the mouths of which open all towards the north. The country below is of a soil resembling a light clay, so loose as easily to break into powder, and is not firm enough to bear any one that treads upon it, and if you touch it in the least it flies about like ashes or unslacked lime. In any danger of war, these people descended into their caves, and carrying in their booty and prey along with them, stayed quietly within, secure from every attack. And when Sertorius, leaving Metellus some distance off, had placed his camp near this hill, they slighted and despised him, imagining that he retired into these parts, being overthrown by the Romans. And whether out of anger or resentment, or out of his unwillingness to be thought to fly from his enemies, early in the morning he rode up to view the situation of the place. But finding there was no way to come at it, as he rode about, threatening them in vain and disconcerted, he took notice that the wind raised the dust and carried it up towards the caves of the Characitanians, the mouths of which, as I said before, opened towards the north; and the northern wind, which some call Cæcias, prevailing most in those parts, coming up out of moist plains or mountains covered with snow, at this particular time, in the heat of summer, being further supplied and increased by the melting of the ice in the northern regions, blew a delightful fresh gale, cooling and refreshing the Characitanians and their cattle all the day long. Sertorius, considering well all circumstances in which either the information of the inhabitants or his own experience had instructed him, commanded his soldiers to shovel up a great quantity of this light, dusty earth, to heap it up together, and make a mount of it over against the hill in which those barbarous people resided, who, imagining that all this preparation was for raising a mound to get at them, only mocked and laughed at it. However, he continued the work till the evening, and brought his soldiers back into their camp.

The next morning a gentle breeze at first arose, and moved the lightest parts of the earth and dispersed it about as the chaff before the wind; but when the sun coming to be higher, the strong northerly wind had covered the hills with the dust, the soldiers came and turned this mound of earth over and over, and broke the hard clods in pieces, whilst others on horseback rode through it backward and forward, and raised a cloud of dust into the air: there with the wind the whole of it was carried away and blown into the dwellings of the Characitanians, all lying open to the north. And there being no other vent or breathing-place than that through which the Cæcias rushed in upon them, it quickly blinded their eyes and filled their lungs, and all but choked them, whilst they strove to draw in the rough air mingled with dust and powdered earth. Nor were they able, with all they could do, to hold out above two days, but yielding up themselves on the third, adding, by their defeat, not so much of the power of Sertorius, as to his renown, in proving that he was able to conquer places by art, which were impregnable by the force of arms.

So long as he had to do with Metellus, he was thought to owe his successes to his opponent's age and slow temper, which were ill suited for coping with the daring and activity of one who commanded a light army more like a band of robbers than regular soldiers. But when Pompey also passed over the Pyrenees, and Sertorius pitched his camp near him, and offered and himself accepted every occasion by which military skill could be put to the proof, and in this contest of dexterity was found to have the better, both in baffling his enemy's designs and in counterscheming himself, the fame of him now spread even to Rome itself, as the most expert commander of his time. For the renown of Pompey was not small, who had already won much honour by his achievements in the wars of Sylla, from whom he received the title of Magnus, and was called Pompey the Great; and who had risen to the honour of a triumph before the beard had grown on his face. And many cities which were under Sertorius were on the very eve of revolting and going over to Pompey, when they were deterred from it by that great action, amongst others, which he performed near the city of Lauron, contrary to the expectation of all.

For Sertorius had laid siege to Lauron, and Pompey came with his whole army to relieve it; and there being a hill near this city very advantageously situated, they both made haste to take it. Sertorius was beforehand,

and took possession of it first, and Pompey, having drawn down his forces, was not sorry that it had thus happened, imagining that he had hereby enclosed his enemy between his own army and the city, and sent in a messenger to the citizens of Lauron, to bid them be of good courage, and to come upon their walls, where they might see their besieger besieged. Sertorius, perceiving their intentions, smiled, and said he would now teach Sylla's scholar, for so he called Pompey in derision, that it was the part of a general to look as well behind him as before him, and at the same time showed them six thousand soldiers, whom he had left in his former camp, from whence he marched out to take the hill, where, if Pompey should assault him, they might fall upon his rear. Pompey discovered this too late, and not daring to give battle, for fear of being encompassed, and yet being ashamed to desert his friends and confederates in their extreme danger, was thus forced to sit still, and see them ruined before his face. For the besieged despaired of relief, and delivered up themselves to Sertorius, who spared their lives and granted them their liberty, but burnt their city, not out of anger or cruelty, for of all commanders that ever were Sertorius seemed least of all to have indulged these passions, but only for the greater shame and confusion of the admirers of Pompey, and that it might be reported amongst the Spaniards, that though he had been so close to the fire which burnt down the city of his confederates as actually to feel the heat of it, he still had not dared to make any opposition.

Sertorius, however, sustained many losses; but he always maintained himself and those immediately with him undefeated, and it was by other commanders under him that he suffered; and he was more admired for being able to repair his losses, and for recovering the victory, than the Roman generals against him for gaining these advantages; as at the battle of Sucro against Pompey, and at the battle near Tuttia, against him and Metellus together. The battle near the Sucro was fought, it is said, through the impatience of Pompey, lest Metellus should share with him in the victory, Sertorius being also willing to engage Pompey before the arrival of Metellus. Sertorius delayed the time till the evening, considering that the darkness of the night would be a disadvantage to his enemies, whether flying or pursuing, being strangers, and having no knowledge of the country.

When the fight began, it happened that Sertorius was not placed directly against Pompey, but against Afranius, who had command of the left wing of the Roman army, as he commanded the right wing of his own; but when he understood that his left wing began to give way, and yield to the assault of Pompey, he committed the care of his right wing to other commanders, and made haste to relieve those in distress; and rallying some that were flying, and encouraging others that still kept their ranks, he renewed the fight, and attacked the enemy in their pursuit so effectively as to cause a considerable rout, and brought Pompey into great danger of his life. For after being wounded and losing his horse, he escaped unexpectedly. For the Africans with Sertorius, who took Pompey's horse, set out with gold, and covered with rich trappings, fell out with one another; and upon the dividing of the spoil, gave over the pursuit. Afranius, in the meantime, as soon as Sertorius had left his right wing, to assist the other part of his army, overthrew all that opposed him; and pursuing them to their camp, fell in together with them, and plundered them till it was dark night; knowing nothing of Pompey's overthrow, nor being able to restrain his soldiers from pillaging; when Sertorius, returning with victory, fell upon him and upon his men, who were all in disorder, and slew many of them. And the next morning he came into the field again well armed, and offered battle, but perceiving that Metellus was near, he drew off, and returned to his camp, saying, "If this old woman had not come up, I would have whipped that boy soundly, and sent him to Rome."

He was much concerned that his white hind could nowhere be found; as he was thus destitute of an admirable contrivance to encourage the barbarous people at a time when he most stood in need of it. Some men, however, wandering in the night, chanced to meet her, and knowing her by her colour, took her; to whom Sertorius promised a good reward, if they would tell no one of it; and immediately shut her up. A few days after, he appeared in public with a very cheerful look, and declared to the chief men of the country that the gods had foretold him in a dream that some great good fortune should shortly attend him; and, taking his seat, proceeded to answer the petitions of those who applied themselves to him. The keepers of the hind, who were not far off, now let her loose, and she no sooner espied Sertorius, but she came leaping with great joy to his feet, laid her head upon his knees, and licked his hands, as she formerly used to do. And Sertorius stroking her, and making much of her again, with that tenderness that the tears stood in his eyes, all that were present were immediately filled with wonder and astonishment, and accompanying him to his house with loud shouts for joy, looked upon him as a person above the rank of mortal men, and highly beloved by the gods; and were in great courage and hope for the future.

When he had reduced his enemies to the last extremity for want of provision, he was forced to give them battle, in the plains near Saguntum, to hinder them from foraging and plundering the country. Both parties fought gloriously. Memmius, the best commander in Pompey's army, was slain in the heat of the battle. Sertorius overthrew all before him, and with great slaughter of his enemies pressed forward towards Metellus. This old commander, making a resistance beyond what could be expected from one of his years, was wounded with a lance; an occurrence which filled all who either saw it or heard of it with shame, to be thought to have left their general in distress, but at the same time to provoke them to revenge and fury against their enemies; they covered Metellus with their shields, and brought him off in safety, and then valiantly repulsed the Spaniards; and so victory changed sides, and Sertorius, that he might afford a more secure retreat to his army, and that fresh forces might more easily be raised, retired into a strong city in the mountains. And though it was the least of his intention to sustain a long siege, yet he began to repair the walls, and to fortify the gates, thus deluding his enemies, who came and sat down before the town, hoping to take it without much resistance; and meantime gave over the pursuit of the Spaniards, and allowed opportunity for raising new forces for Sertorius, to which purpose he had sent commanders to all their cities, with orders, when they had sufficiently increased their numbers, to send him word of it. This news he no sooner received, but he sallied out and forced his way through his enemies, and easily joined them with the rest of his army. Having received this considerable reinforcement, he set upon the Romans again, and by rapidly assaulting them, by alarming them on all sides, by ensnaring, circumventing, and laying ambushes for them, he cut off all provisions by land, while with his piratical vessels he kept all the coast in awe, and hindered their supplies by sea. He thus forced the Roman generals to dislodge and to separate from one another: Metellus departed into Gaul, and Pompey wintered among the Vaccæns, in a wretched condition, where, being in extreme want of money, he wrote a letter to the senate, to let them know that if they did not speedily support him, he must draw off his army; for he had already spent his own money in the defence of Italy. To these extremities, the chiefest and the most powerful commanders of the age were reduced by the skill of Sertorius; and it was the common opinion in Rome that he would be in Italy before Pompey.

How far Metellus was terrified, and at what rate he esteemed him, he plainly declared, when he offered by proclamation an hundred talents and twenty thousand acres of land to any Roman that should kill him, and leave, if he were banished, to return; attempting villainously to buy his life by treachery, when he despaired of ever being able to overcome him in open war. When once he gained the advantage in a battle against Sertorius, he was so pleased and transported with his good fortune, that he caused himself to be publicly proclaimed imperator; and all the cities which he visited received him with altars and sacrifices; he allowed himself, it is said, to have garlands placed on his head, and accepted sumptuous entertainments, at which he sat drinking in triumphal robes, while images and figures of victory were introduced by the motion of machines, bringing in with them crowns and trophies of gold to present to him, and companies of young men and women danced before him, and sang to him songs of joy and triumph. By all which he rendered himself deservedly ridiculous, for being so excessively delighted and puffed up with the thoughts of having followed one who was retiring of his own accord, and for having once had the better of him whom he used to call Sylla's runaway slave, and his forces, the remnant of the defeated troops of Carbo.

Sertorius, meantime, showed the loftiness of his temper in calling together all the Roman senators who had fled from Rome, and had come and resided with him, and giving them the name of a senate; and out of these he chose prætors and quæstors, and adorned his government with all the Roman laws and institutions. And though he made use of the arms, riches, and cities of the Spaniards, yet he would never, even in word, remit to them the imperial authority, but set Roman officers and commanders over them, intimating his purpose to restore liberty to the Romans, not to raise up the Spaniard's power against them. For he was a sincere lover of his country, and had a great desire to return home; but in his adverse fortune he showed undaunted courage, and behaved himself towards his enemies in a manner free from all dejection and mean-spiritedness; and when he was in his prosperity, and in the height of his victories, he sent word to Metellus and Pompey that he was ready to lay down his arms and live a private life if he were allowed to return home, declaring that he had rather live as the meanest citizen in Rome than, exiled from it, be supreme commander of all other cities together. And it is thought that his great desire for his country was in no small measure promoted by the tenderness he had for his mother, under whom he was brought up after the death of his father, and upon whom he had placed his entire affection. After that his friends had sent for him into Spain to be their general, as soon as he heard of his mother's death he had almost cast away himself and died for grief; for he lay seven days together continually in his tent, without giving the word, or being seen by the nearest of his friends; and when the chief commanders of the army and persons of the greatest note came about his tent, with great difficulty they prevailed with him at last to come abroad, and speak to his soldiers, and to take upon him the management of affairs, which were in a prosperous condition. And thus, to many men's judgment, he seemed to have been in himself of a mild and compassionate temper, and naturally given to ease and quietness, and to have accepted of the command of military forces contrary to his own inclination, and not being able to live in safety otherwise, to have been driven by his enemies to have recourse to arms. and to espouse the wars as a necessary guard for the defence of his person.

His negotiations with King Mithridates further argue the greatness of his mind. For when Mithridates recovering himself from his overthrow by Sylla, like a strong wrestler that gets up to try another fall, was again endeavouring to re-establish his power in Asia, at this time the great fame of Sertorius was celebrated in all places; and when the merchants who came out of the western parts of Europe, bringing these, as it were, among their other foreign wares, had filled the kingdom of Pontus with their stories of his exploits in war, Mithridates was extremely desirous to send an embassy to him, being also highly encouraged to it by the boastings of his flattering courtiers, who, comparing Mithridates to Pyrrhus, and Sertorius to Hannibal, professed that the Romans would never be able to make any considerable resistance against such great forces, and such admirable commanders, when they should be set upon on both sides at once, on one by the most warlike general, and on the other by the most powerful prince in existence.

Accordingly, Mithridates sends ambassadors into Spain to Sertorius with letters and instructions, and commission to promise ships and money toward the charge of the war, if Sertorius would confirm his pretensions upon Asia, and authorise him to possess all that he had surrendered to the Romans in his treaty with Sylla. Sertorius summoned a full council which he called a senate, where, when others joyfully approved of the conditions, and were desirous immediately to accept of his offer, seeing that he desired nothing of them but a name, and an empty title to places not in their power to dispose of, in recompense of which they should be supplied with what they then stood most in need of, Sertorius would by no means agree to it; declaring that he was willing that King Mithridates should exercise all royal power and authority over Bithynia and Cappadocia, countries accustomed to a monarchical government, and not belonging to Rome, but he could never consent that he should seize or detain a province, which, by the justest right and title, was possessed by the Romans, which Mithridates had formerly taken away from them, and had afterwards lost in open war to Fimbria, and quitted upon a treaty of peace with Sylla. For he looked upon it as his duty to enlarge the Roman possessions by his conquering arms, and not to increase his own power by the diminution of the Roman territories. Since a noble-minded man, though he willingly accepts of victory when it comes with honour, will never so much as endeavour to save his own life upon any dishonourable terms.

When this was related to Mithridates, he was struck with amazement, and said to his intimate friends, "What will Sertorius enjoin us to do when he comes to be seated in the Palatium in Rome, who at present, when he is driven out to the borders of the Atlantic Sea, sets bounds to our kingdoms in the east, and threatens us with war if we attempt the recovery of Asia?" However, they solemnly, upon oath, concluded a league between them, upon these terms: that Mithridates should enjoy the free possession of Cappadocia and Bithynia, and that Sertorius should send him soldiers and a general for his army, in recompense of which the king was to supply him with three thousand talents and forty ships. Marcus Marius, a Roman senator who had quitted Rome to follow Sertorius, was sent general into Asia, in company with whom, when Mithridates had reduced divers of the Asian cities, Marius made his entrance with rods and axes carried before him, and Mithridates followed in the second place, voluntarily waiting upon him. Some of these cities he set at liberty, and others he freed from taxes, signifying to them that these privileges were granted to them by the favour of Sertorius, and hereby Asia, which had been miserably tormented by the revenue farmers, and oppressed by the insolent pride and covetousness of the soldiers, began to rise again to new hopes and to look forward with joy to the expected change of government.

But in Spain, the senators about Sertorius, and others of the nobility, finding themselves strong enough for their enemies, no sooner laid aside fear, but their minds were possessed by envy and irrational jealousies of Sertorius's power. And chiefly Perpenna, elevated by the thoughts of his noble birth, and carried away with a fond ambition of commanding the army, threw out villainous discourses in private amongst his acquaintance. "What evil genius," he would say, "hurries us perpetually from worse to worse? We who disdained to obey the dictates of Sylla, the ruler of the sea and land, and thus to live at home in peace and quiet, are come hither to our destruction, hoping to enjoy our liberty, and have made ourselves slaves of our own accord; and are become the contemptible guards and attendants of the banished Sertorius, who, that he may expose us the further, gives us a name that renders us ridiculous to all that hear it, and calls us the Senate, when at the same time he makes us undergo as much hard labour, and forces us to be as subject to his haughty commands and insolences, as any Spaniards and Lusitanians." With these mutinous discourses he seduced them; and though the greater number could not be led into open rebellion against Sertorius, fearing his power, they were prevailed with to endeavour to destroy his interest secretly. For by abusing the Lusitanians and Spaniards, by inflicting severe punishments upon them, by raising exorbitant taxes, and by pretending that all this was done by the strict command of Sertorius, they caused great troubles, and made many cities to revolt; and those who were sent to mitigate and heal these differences did rather exasperate them, and increase the number of his enemies, and left them at their return more obstinate and rebellious than they found them. And Sertorius, incensed with all this, now so far forgot his former clemency and goodness as to lay hands on the sons of the Spaniards educated in the city of Osca; and, contrary to all justice, he cruelly put some of them to death, and sold others.

In the meantime, Perpenna, having increased the number of his conspirators, drew in Manlius, a commander in the army, who, at that time being attached to a youth, to gain his affections the more, discovered the confederacy to him, bidding him neglect others, and be constant to him alone; who, in a few days, was to be a person of great power and authority. But the youth having a greater inclination for Aufidius, disclosed all to him, which much surprised and amazed him. For he was also one of the confederacy, but knew not that Manlius was anyways engaged in it; but when the youth began to name Perpenna, Gracinus, and others, whom he knew very well to be sworn conspirators, he was very much terrified and astonished; but made light of it to the youth, and bade him not regard what Manlius said, a vain, boasting fellow. However, he went presently to Perpenna, and giving him notice of the danger they were in, and of the shortness of their time, desired him immediately to put their designs in execution. When all the confederates had consented to it, they provided a messenger who brought feigned letters to Sertorius, in which he had notice of a victory obtained, it said, by one of his lieutenants, and of the great slaughter of his enemies; and as Sertorius, being extremely well pleased, was sacrificing and giving thanks to the gods for his prosperous success, Perpenna invited him, and those with him, who were also of the conspiracy, to an entertainment, and being very importunate, prevailed with him to come. At all suppers and entertainments where Sertorius was present, great order and decency was wont to be observed; for he would not endure to hear or see anything that was rude or unhandsome, but made it the habit of all who kept his company to entertain themselves with quiet and inoffensive amusements. But in the middle of this entertainment, those who sought occasion to quarrel fell into dissolute discourse openly, and making as if they were very drunk, committed many insolences on purpose to provoke him. Sertorius, being offended with their ill-behaviour, or perceiving the state of their minds by their way of speaking and their unusually disrespectful manner, changed the posture of his lying, and leaned backward, as one that neither heard nor regarded them. Perpenna now took a cup full of wine, and, as he was drinking, let it fall out of his hand and made a noise, which was the sign agreed upon amongst them; and Antonius, who was next to Sertorius, immediately wounded him with his sword. And whilst Sertorius, upon receiving the wound, turned himself, and strove to get up, Antonius threw himself upon his breast, and held both his hands, so that he died by a number of blows, without being able even to defend himself.

Upon the first news of his death, most of the Spaniards left the conspirators, and sent ambassadors to Pompey and Metellus, and yielded themselves up to them. Perpenna attempted to do something with those that remained, but he made only so much use of Sertorius's arms and preparations for war as to disgrace himself in them, and to let it be evident to all that he understood no more how to command than he knew how to obey; and when he came against Pompey, he was soon overthrown and taken prisoner. Neither did he bear this last affliction with any bravery, but having Sertorius's papers and writings in his hands, he offered to show Pompey letters from persons of consular dignity, and of the highest quality in Rome, written with their own hands, expressly to call Sertorius into Italy, and to let him know what great numbers there were that earnestly desired to alter the present state of affairs, and to introduce another manner of government. Upon this occasion, Pompey behaved not like a youth, or one of a light inconsiderate mind, but as a man of a confirmed, mature, and solid judgment; and so freed Rome from great fears and dangers of change. For he put all Sertorius's writings and letters together and read not one of them, nor suffered any one else to read them, but burnt them all, and caused Perpenna immediately to be put to death, lest by discovering their names further troubles and revolutions might ensue.

Of the rest of the conspirators with Perpenna, some were taken and slain by the command of Pompey, others fled into Africa, and were set upon by the Moors, and run through with their darts: and in a short time not one of them was left alive, except only Aufidius, the rival of Manlius, who, hiding himself, or not being much inquired after, died an old man, in an obscure village in Spain, in extreme poverty, and hated by all.

EUMENES

DURIS reports that Eumenes, the Cardian, was the son of a poor waggoner in the Thracian Chersonesus, yet liberally educated, both as a scholar and a soldier; and that while he was but young, Philip, passing through Cardia, diverted himself with a sight of the wrestling matches and other exercises of the youth of that place, among whom Eumenes performing with success, and showing signs of intelligence and bravery, Philip was so pleased with him as to take him into his service. But they seem to speak more probably who tell us that Philip advanced Eumenes for the friendship he bore to his father, whose guest he had sometime been. After the death of Philip, he continued in the service of Alexander, with the title of his principal secretary, but in as great favour as the most intimate of his familiars, being esteemed as wise and faithful as any person about him, so that he went with troops under his immediate command as general in the expedition against India, and succeeded to the post of Perdiccas, when Perdiccas was advanced to that of Hephæstion, then newly deceased. And therefore, after the death of Alexander, when Neoptolemus, who had been captain of his life-guard, said that he had followed Alexander with shield and spear, but Eumenes only with pen and paper, the Macedonians laughed at him, as knowing very well that, besides other marks of favour, the king had done him the honour to make him a kind of kinsman to himself by marriage. For Alexander's first mistress in Asia, by whom he had his son Hercules, was Barsine the daughter of Artabazus; and in the distribution of the Persian ladies amongst his captains, Alexander gave Apame, one of his sisters, to Ptolemy and another, also called Barsine, to Eumenes.

Notwithstanding, he frequently incurred Alexander's displeasure, and put himself into some danger, through Hephæstion. The quarters that had been taken up for Eumenes, Hephæstion assigned to Euius, the flute-player. Upon which, in great anger, Eumenes and Mentor came to Alexander and loudly complained, saying that the way to be regarded was to throw away their arms and turn flute-players or tragedians; so much so that Alexander took their part and chid Hephæstion; but soon after changed his mind again, and was angry with Eumenes, and accounted the freedom he had taken to be rather an affront to the king than a reflection upon Hephæstion. Afterwards, when Nearchus, with a fleet, was to be sent to the Southern Sea, Alexander borrowed money of his friends, his own treasury being exhausted, and would have had three hundred talents of Eumenes, but he sent a hundred only, pretending that it was not without great difficulty he had raised so much from his stewards. Alexander neither complained nor took the money, but gave private orders to set Eumenes's tent on fire, designing to take him in a manifest lie, when his money was carried out. But before that could be done the tent was consumed, and Alexander repented of his orders, all his papers being burnt; the gold and silver, however, which was melted down in the fire, being afterwards collected, was found to be more than one thousand talents; yet Alexander took none of it, and only wrote to the several governors and generals to send new copies of the papers that were burnt, and ordered them to be delivered to Eumenes.

Another difference happened between him and Hephæstion concerning a gift, and a great deal of ill language passed between them, yet Eumenes still continued in favour. But Hephæstion dying soon after, the king, in his grief, presuming all those that differed with Hephæstion in his lifetime were now rejoicing at his death, showed much harshness and severity in his behaviour with them, especially towards Eumenes, whom he often upbraided with his quarrels and ill language to Hephæstion. But he, being a wise and dexterous courtier, made advantage of what had done him prejudice, and struck in with the king's passion for glorifying his friend's memory, suggesting various plans to do him honour, and contributing largely and readily towards erecting his monument.

After Alexander's death, when the quarrel broke out between the troops of the phalanx and the officers, his companions, Eumenes, though in his judgment he inclined to the latter, yet in his professions stood neuter, as if he thought it unbecoming him, who was a stranger, to interpose in the private quarrels of the Macedonians. When the rest of Alexander's friends left Babylon, he stayed behind, and did much to pacify the foot-soldiers, and to dispose them towards an accommodation. And when the officers had agreed among themselves, and, recovering from the first disorder, proceeded to share out the several commands and provinces, they made Eumenes governor of Cappadocia and Paphlagonia, and all the coast upon the Pontic Sea as far as Trebizond, which at that time was not subject to the Macedonians, for Ariarathes kept it as king, but Leonnatus and Antigonus, with a large army, were to put him in possession of it.

Antigonus, already filled with hopes of his own, and despising all men, took no notice of Perdiccas's letter; but Leonnatus with his army came down into Phrygia to the service of Eumenes. But being visited by Hecatæus, the tyrant of the Cardians, and requested rather to relieve Antipater and the Macedonians that were besieged in Lamia, he resolved upon that expedition, inviting Eumenes to a share in it, and endeavouring to reconcile him to Hecatæus. For there was an hereditary feud between them, arising out of political differences, and Eumenes had more than once been known to denounce Hecatæus as a tyrant, and to exhort Alexander to restore the Cardians their liberty. Therefore at this time, also, he declined the expedition proposed, pretending that he feared lest Antipater, who already hated him, should for that reason, and to gratify Hecatæus, kill him. Leonnatus so far believed as to impart to Eumenes his whole design, which, as he had pretended and given out, was to aid Antipater, but in truth was to seize the kingdom of Macedon; and he showed him letters from Cleopatra, in which, it appeared, she invited him to Pella, with promises to marry him. But Eumenes, whether fearing Antipater, or looking upon Leonnatus as a rash, headstrong, and unsafe man, stole away from him by night, taking with him all his men, namely, three hundred horse, and two hundred of his own servants armed, and all his gold, to the value of five thousand talents of silver, and fled to Perdiccas, discovered to him Leonnatus's design, and thus gained great interest with him, and was made of the council. Soon after, Perdiccas. with a great army, which he led himself, conducted Eumenes into Cappadocia, and, having taken Ariarathes prisoner, and subdued the whole country, declared him governor of it. He accordingly proceeded to dispose of the chief cities among his own friends, and made captains of garrisons, judges, receivers, and other officers, of such as he thought fit himself, Perdiccas not at all interposing. Eumenes, however, still continued to attend upon Perdiccas, both out of respect to him, and a desire not to be absent from the royal family.

But Perdiccas, believing he was able enough to attain his own further objects without assistance, and that the country he left behind him might stand in need of an active and faithful governor, when he came into Cilicia dismissed Eumenes, under colour of sending him to his command, but in truth to secure Armenia, which was on its frontier, and was unsettled through the practices of Neoptolemus. Him, a proud and vain man, Eumenes exerted himself to gain by personal attentions; but to balance the Macedonian foot, whom he found insolent and self-willed, he contrived to raise an army of horse, excusing from tax and contribution all those of the country that were able to serve on horseback, and buying up a number of horses, which he distributed among such of his own men as he most confided in, stimulating the courage of his new soldiers by gifts and honours, and inuring their bodies to service by frequent marching and exercising; so that the Macedonians were some of them astonished, others overjoyed to see that in so short a time he had got together a body of no less than six thousand three hundred horsemen.

But when Craterus and Antipater, having subdued the Greeks, advanced into Asia, with intentions to quell the power of Perdiccas, and were reported to design an invasion of Cappadocia, Perdiccas, resolving himself to march against Ptolemy, made Eumenes commander-in-chief of all the forces of Armenia and Cappadocia, and to that purpose wrote letters, requiring Alcetas and Neoptolemus to be obedient to Eumenes, and giving full commission to Eumenes to dispose and order all things as he thought fit. Alcetas flatly refused to serve, because his Macedonians, he said, were ashamed to fight against Antipater, and loved Craterus so well, they were ready to receive him for their commander. Neoptolemus designed treachery against Eumenes, but was discovered; and being summoned, refused to obey, and put himself in a posture of defence. Here Eumenes first found the benefit of his own foresight and contrivance, for his foot being beaten, he routed Neoptolemus with his horse, and took all his baggage; and coming up with his whole force upon the phalanx while broken and disordered in its flight, obliged the men to lay down their arms and take an oath to serve under him. Neoptolemus, with some few stragglers whom he rallied, fled to

Craterus and Antipater. From them had come an embassy to Eumenes, inviting him over to their side, offering to secure him in his present government and to give him additional command, both of men and of territory, with the advantage of gaining his enemy Antipater to become his friend, and keeping Craterus his friend from turning to be his enemy. To which Eumenes replied that he could not so suddenly be reconciled to his old enemy Antipater, especially at a time when he saw him use his friends like enemies, but was ready to reconcile Craterus to Perdiccas, upon any just and equitable terms; but in case of any aggression, he would resist the injustice to his last breath, and would rather lose his life than betray his word.

Antipater, receiving this answer, took time to consider upon the whole matter; when Neoptolemus arrived from his defeat and acquainted them with the ill success of his arms, and urged them to give him assistance, to come, both of them, if possible, but Craterus at any rate, for the Macedonians loved him so excessively, that if they saw but his hat, or heard his voice, they would all pass over in a body with their arms. And in truth Craterus had a mighty name among them, and the soldiers after Alexander's death were extremely fond of him, remembering how he had often for their sakes incurred Alexander's displeasure, doing his best to withhold him when he began to follow the Persian fashions, and always maintaining the customs of his country, when, through pride and luxuriousness, they began to be disregarded. Craterus, therefore, sent on Antipater into Cilicia, and himself and Neoptolemus marched with a large division of the army against Eumenes; expecting to come upon him unawares, and to find his army disordered with revelling after the late victory. Now that Eumenes should suspect his coming, and be prepared to receive him, is an argument of his vigilance, but not perhaps a proof of any extraordinary sagacity, but that he should contrive both to conceal from his enemies the disadvantages of his position, and from his own men whom they were to fight with, so that he led them on against Craterus himself, without their knowing that he commanded the enemy, this, indeed, seems to show peculiar address and skill in the general. He gave out that Neoptolemus and Pigres were approaching with some Cappadocian and Paphlagonian horse. And at night, having resolved on marching, he fell asleep, and had an extraordinary dream. For he thought he saw two Alexanders ready to engage, each commanding his several phalanx, the one assisted by Minerva, the other by Ceres; and that after a hot dispute, he on whose side Minerva was, was beaten, and Ceres, gathering ears of corn, wove them into a crown for the victor.

This vision Eumenes interpreted at once as boding success to himself, who was to fight for a fruitful country, and at that very time covered with the young ears, the whole being sown with corn, and the fields so thick with it that they made a beautiful show of a long peace. And he was further emboldened when he understood that the enemy's password was Minerva and Alexander. Accordingly he also gave out as his Ceres and Alexander, and gave his men orders to make garlands for themselves, and to dress their arms with wreaths of corn. He found himself under many temptations to discover to his captains and officers whom they were to engage with, and not to conceal a secret of such moment in his own breast alone, yet he kept to his first resolutions, and ventured to run the hazard of his own judgment.

When he came to give battle, he would not trust any Macedonian to engage Craterus, but appointed two troops of foreign horse, commanded by Pharnabazus, son to Artabazus, and Phœnix of Tenedos, with order to charge as soon as ever they saw the enemy, without giving them leisure to speak or retire, or receiving any herald or trumpet from them. For he was exceedingly afraid about his Macedonians, lest, if they found out Craterus to be there, they should go over to his side. He himself, with three hundred of his best horse, led the right wing against Neoptolemus. When having passed a little hill they came in view, and were seen advancing with more than ordinary briskness, Craterus was amazed, and bitterly reproached Neoptolemus for deceiving him with hopes of the Macedonians' revolt, but he encouraged his men to do bravely, and forthwith charged.

The first engagement was very fierce, and the spears being soon broken to pieces, they came to close fighting with their swords; and here Craterus did by no means dishonour Alexander, but slew many of his enemies and repulsed many assaults, but at last received a wound in his side from a Thracian, and fell off his horse. Being down, many not knowing him went past him, but Gorgias, one of Eumenes's captains, knew him, and alighting from his horse kept guard over him as he lay badly wounded and slowly dying. In the meantime Neoptolemus and Eumenes were engaged; who, being inveterate and mortal enemies, sought for one another, but missed for the two first courses, but in the third discovering one another, they drew their swords, and with loud shouts immediately charged. And their horses striking against one another like two galleys, they quitted their reins, and taking mutual hold pulled at one another's helmets, and at the armour from their shoulders. While they were thus struggling, their horses went from under them, and they fell together to the ground, there again still keeping their hold and wrestling. Neoptolemus was getting up first, but Eumenes wounded him in the ham, and got upon his feet before him. Neoptolemus supporting himself upon one knee, the other leg being disabled, and himself undermost, fought courageously, though his blows were not mortal, but receiving a stroke in the neck he fell and ceased to resist.

Eumenes, transported with passion and his inveterate hatred to him, fell to reviling and stripping him, and perceived not that his sword was still in his hand. And with this he wounded Eumenes under the bottom of his corslet in the groin, but in truth more frightened than hurt him; his blow being faint for want of strength. Having stript the dead body, ill as he was with the wounds he had received in his legs and arms, he took horse again, and hurried towards the left wing of his army, which he supposed to be still engaged. Hearing of the death of Craterus, he rode up to him, and finding there was yet some life in him, alighted from his horse and wept, and laying his right hand upon him, inveighed bitterly against Neoptolemus, and lamented both Craterus's misfortune and his own hard fate, that he should be necessitated to engage against an old friend and acquaintance, and either do or suffer so much mischief.

This victory Eumenes obtained about ten days after the former, and got great reputation alike for his conduct and his valour in achieving it. But, on the other hand, it created him great envy both among his own troops and his enemies that he, a stranger and a foreigner, should employ the forces and arms of Macedon to cut off the bravest and most approved man among them. Had the news of this defeat come timely enough to Perdiccas, he had doubtless been the greatest of all the Macedonians; but now, he being slain in a mutiny in Egypt, two days before the news arrived, the Macedonians in a rage decreed Eumenes's death, giving joint commission to Antigonus and Antipater to prosecute the war against him.

Passing by Mount Ida, where there was a royal establishment of horses, Eumenes took as many as he had occasion for, and sent an account of his doing so to the overseers, at which Antipater is said to have laughed, calling it truly laudable in Eumenes thus to hold himself prepared for giving in to them (or would it be taking from them?) strict account of all matters of administration. Eumenes had designed to engage in the plains of Lydia, near Sardis, both because his chief strength lay in horse, and to let Cleopatra see how powerful he was. But at her particular request, for she was afraid to give any umbrage to Antipater, he marched into the upper Phrygia, and wintered in Celænæ; when Alcetas, Polemon, and Docimus disputing with him who should command in chief, "You know," said he, "the old saying: That destruction regards no punctilios." Having promised his soldiers pay within three days, he sold them all the farms and castles in the country, together with the men and beasts with which they were filled; every captain or officer that bought received from Eumenes the use of his engines to storm the place, and divided the spoils among his company, proportionably to every man's arrears. By this Eumenes came again to be popular, so that when letters were found thrown about the camp by the enemy promising one hundred talents, besides great honours, to any one that should kill Eumenes, the Macedonians were extremely offended, and made an order that from that time forward one thousand of their best men should continually guard his person, and keep strict watch about him by night in their several turns. This order was cheerfully obeyed, and they gladly received of Eumenes the same honours which the kings used to confer upon their favourites. He now had leave to bestow purple hats and cloaks, which among the Macedonians is one of the greatest honours the king can give.

Good fortune will elevate even petty minds, and give them the appearance of a certain greatness and stateliness, as from their high place they look down upon the world; but the truly noble and resolved spirit raises itself, and becomes more conspicuous in times of disaster and ill fortune, as was now the case with Eumenes. For having by the treason of one of his own men lost the field to Antigonus at Orcynii, in Cappadocia, in his flight he gave the traitor no opportunity to escape to the enemy, but immediately seized and hanged him. Then in his flight, taking a contrary course to his pursuers, he stole by them unawares, returned to the place where the battle had been fought, and encamped. There he gathered up the dead bodies and burnt them with the doors and windows of the neighbouring villages, and raised heaps of earth upon their graves; insomuch that Antigonus, who came thither soon after, expressed his astonishment at his courage and firm resolution. Falling afterwards upon the baggage of Antigonus, he might easily have taken many captives, both bond and freemen, and much wealth collected from the spoils of so many wars; but he feared lest his men, overladen with so much booty, might become unfit for rapid retreat, and too fond of their ease to sustain the continual marches and endure the long waiting on which he depended for success, expecting to tire Antigonus into some other course. But then considering it would be extremely difficult to restrain the Macedonians from plunder, when it seemed to offer itself, he gave them order to refresh themselves, and bait their horses, and then attack the enemy. In the meantime he sent privately to Menander, who had care of all this baggage, professing a concern for him upon the score of old friendship and acquaintance; and therefore advising him to quit the plain and secure himself upon the sides of the neighbouring hills, where the horse might not be able to hem him in. When Menander, sensible of his danger, had speedily packed up his goods and decamped, Eumenes openly sent his scouts to discover the enemy's posture, and commanded his men to arm and bridle their horses, as designing immediately to give battle; but the scouts returning with news that Menander had secured so difficult a post it was impossible to take him, Eumenes, pretending to be grieved with the disappointment, drew off his men another way. It is said that when Menander reported this afterwards to Antigonus, and the Macedonians commended Eumenes, imputing it to his singular good-nature, that having it in his power to make slaves of their children and outrage their wives he forbore and spared them all, Antigonus replied, "Alas, good friends, he had no regard to us, but to himself, being loath to wear so many shackles when he designed to fly."

From this time Eumenes, daily flying and wandering about, persuaded many of his men to disband, whether out of kindness to them, or unwillingness to lead about such a body of men as were too few to engage and too many to fly undiscovered. Taking refuge at Nora, a place on the confines of Lycaonia and Cappadocia, with five hundred horse and two hundred heavy-armed foot, he again dismissed as many of his friends as desired it, through fear of the probable hardships to be encountered there, and embracing them with all demonstrations of kindness gave them licence to depart. Antigonus, when he came before this fort, desired to have an interview with Eumenes before the siege; but he returned answer that Antigonus had many friends who might command in his room; but they whom Eumenes defended had nobody to substitute if he should miscarry; therefore, if Antigonus thought it worth while to treat with him, he should first send him hostages. And when Antigonus required that Eumenes should first address himself to him as his superior, he replied, "While I am able to wield a sword, I shall think no man greater than myself." At last, when, according to Eumenes's demand, Antigonus sent his own nephew Ptolemy to the fort, Eumenes went out to him, and they mutually embraced with great tenderness and friendship, as having formerly been very intimate. After long conversation, Eumenes making no mention of his own pardon and security, but requiring that he should be confirmed in his several governments, and restitution be made him of the rewards of his service, all that were present were astonished at his courage and gallantry. And many of the Macedonians flocked to see what sort of person Eumenes was, for since the death of Craterus no man had been so much talked of in the army. But Antigonus, being afraid lest he might suffer some violence, first commanded the soldiers to keep off, calling out and throwing stones at those who pressed forwards. At last, taking Eumenes in his arms, and keeping off the crowd with his guards, not without great difficulty, he returned him safe into the fort.

Then Antigonus, having built a wall round Nora, left a force sufficient to carry on the siege, and drew off the rest of his army; and Eumenes was beleaguered and kept garrison, having plenty of corn and water and salt, but no other thing, either for food or delicacy; yet with such as he had, he kept a cheerful table for his friends, inviting them severally in their turns, and seasoning his entertainment with a gentle and affable behaviour. For he had a pleasant countenance, and looked not like an old and practised soldier, but was smooth and florid, and his shape as delicate as if his limbs had been carved by art in the most accurate proportions. He was not a great orator, but winning and persuasive, as may be seen in his letters.

The greatest distress of the besieged was the narrowness of the place they were in, their quarters being very confined, and the whole place but two furlongs in compass; so that both they and their horses fed without exercise. Accordingly, not only to prevent the listlessness of such inactive living, but to have them in condition to fly if occasion required, he assigned a room one-and-twenty feet long, the largest in all the fort, for the men to walk in, directing them to begin their walk gently, and so gradually mend their pace. And for the horses, he tied them to the roof with great halters, fastening which about their necks, with a pulley he gently raised them, till standing upon the ground with their hinder feet, they just touched it with the very ends of their forefeet. In this posture the grooms plied them with whips and shouts, provoking them to curvet and kick out with their hind legs, struggling and stamping at the same time to find support for their forefeet, and thus their whole body was exercised, till they were all in a foam and sweat; excellent exercise, whether for strength or speed; and then he gave them their corn already coarsely ground, that they might sooner despatch and better digest it.

The siege continuing long, Antigonus received advice that Antipater was dead in Macedon, and that affairs were embroiled by the differences of Cassander and Polysperchon, upon which he conceived no mean hopes, purposing to make himself master of all, and, in order to his design, thought to bring over Eumenes, that he might have his advice and assistance. He, therefore, sent Hieronymus to treat with him, proposing a certain oath, which Eumenes first corrected, and then referred himself to the Macedonians themselves that besieged him, to be judged by them, which of the two forms was the most equitable. Antigonus in the beginning of his had slightly mentioned the kings as by way of ceremony, while all the sequel referred to himself alone; but Eumenes changed the form of it to Olympias and the kings, and proceeded to swear not to be true to Antigonus, only, but to them, and have the same friends and enemies, not with Antigonus, but with Olympias and the kings. This form the Macedonians thinking the more reasonable, swore Eumenes according to it, and raised the siege, sending also to Antigonus that he should swear in the same form to Eumenes. Meantime, all the hostages of the Cappadocians whom Eumenes had in Nora he returned, obtaining from their friends war-horses, beasts of carriage, and tents in exchange. And collecting again all the soldiers who had dispersed at the time of his flight, and were now wandering about the country, he got together a body of near a thousand horse, and with them fled from Antigonus, whom he justly feared. For he had sent orders not only to have him blocked up and besieged again, but had given a very sharp answer to the Macedonians for admitting Eumenes's amendment of the oath.

While Eumenes was flying, he received letters from those in Macedonia, who were jealous of Antigonus's greatness, from Olympias, inviting him thither to take the charge and protection of Alexander's infant son, whose person was in danger, and other letters from Polysperchon and Philip the king, requiring him to make war upon Antigonus, as general of the forces in Cappadocia, and empowering him out of the treasure at Quinda to take five hundred talents' compensation for his own losses, and to levy as much as he thought necessary to carry on the war. They wrote also to the same effect to Antigenes and Teutamus, the chief officers of the Argyraspids; who, on receiving these letters, treated Eumenes with a show of respect and kindness; but it was apparent enough that they were full of envy and emulation, disdaining to give place to him. Their envy Eumenes moderated by refusing to accept the money, as if he had not needed it; and their ambition and emulation, who were neither able to govern nor willing to obey, he conquered by help of superstition. For he told them that Alexander had appeared to him in a dream, and showed him a regal pavilion richly furnished, with a throne in it; and told him if they would sit in council there, he himself would be present, and prosper all the consultations and actions upon which they should enter in his name. Antigenes and Teutamus were easily prevailed upon to believe this, being as little willing to come and consult Eumenes as he himself was to be seen waiting at other men's doors. Accordingly, they erected a tent royal, and a throne, called Alexander's, and there they met to consult upon all affairs of moment.

Afterwards they advanced into the interior of Asia, and in their march met with Peucestes, who was friendly to them and with the other satraps, who joined forces with them, and greatly encouraged the Macedonians with the number and appearance of their men. But they themselves, having since Alexander's decease become imperious and ungoverned in their tempers, and luxurious in their daily habits, imagining themselves great princes, and pampered in their conceit by the flattery of the barbarians, when all these conflicting pretensions now came together, were soon found to be exacting and quarrelsome one with another, while all alike unmeasurably flattered the Macedonians, giving them money for revels and sacrifices, till in a short time they brought the camp to be a dissolute place of entertainment, and the army a mere multitude of voters, canvassed as in a democracy for the election of this or that commander. Eumenes, perceiving they despised one another, and all of them feared him, and sought an opportunity to kill him, pretended to be in want of money, and borrowed many talents, of those especially who most hated him, to make them at once confide in him and forbear all violence to him for fear of losing their own money. Thus his enemies' estates were the guard of his person, and by receiving money he purchased safety, for which it is more common to give it.

The Macedonians, also, while there was no show of danger, allowed themselves to be corrupted, and made all their court to those who gave them presents, who had their body-guards, and affected to appear generals-in-chief. But when Antigonus came upon them with a great army, and their affairs themselves seemed to call out for a true general, then not only the common soldiers cast their eyes upon Eumenes, but these men, who had appeared so great in a peaceful time of ease, submitted all of them to him, and quietly posted themselves severally as he appointed them. And when Antigonus attempted to pass the river Pasitigris, all the rest that were appointed to guard the passes were not so much as aware of his march; only Eumenes met and encountered him, slew many of his men, and filled the river with the dead, and took four thousand prisoners. But it was most particularly when Eumenes was sick that the Macedonians let it be seen how in their judgment, while others could feast them handsomely and make entertainments, he alone knew how to fight and lead an army. For Peucestes, having made a splendid entertainment in Persia, and given each of the soldiers a sheep to sacrifice with, made himself sure of being commander-in-chief. Some few days after the army was to march, and Eumenes having been dangerously ill was carried in a litter apart from the body of the army, that any rest he got might not be disturbed. But when they were a little advanced, unexpectedly they had a view of the enemy, who had passed the hills that lay between them, and was marching down into the plain. At the sight of the golden armour glittering in the Sun as they marched down in their order, the elephants with their castles on their backs, and the men in their purple, as their manner was when they were going to give battle, the front stopped their march, and called out for Eumenes, for they would not advance a step but under his conduct; and fixing their arms in the ground gave the word among themselves to stand, requiring their officers also not to stir or engage or hazard themselves without Eumenes. News of this being brought to Eumenes, he hastened those that carried his litter, and drawing back the curtains on both sides, joyfully put forth his right hand. As soon as the soldiers saw him they saluted him in their Macedonian dialect, and took up their shields, and striking them with their pikes, gave a great shout; inviting the enemy to come on, for now they had a leader.

Antigonus understanding by some prisoners he had taken that Eumenes was out of health, to that degree that he was carried in a litter, presumed it would be no hard matter to crush the rest of them, since he was ill. He therefore made the greater haste to come up with them and engage. But being come so near as to discover how the enemy was drawn up and appointed, he was astonished, and paused for some time; at last he saw the litter carrying from one wing of the army to the other, and, as his manner was, laughing aloud, he said to his friends, "That litter there, it seems, is the thing that offers us battle;" and immediately wheeled about, retired with all his army, and pitched his camp. The men on the other side, finding a little respite, returned to their former habits, and allowing themselves to be flattered, and making the most of the indulgence of their generals, took up for their winter quarters near the whole country of the Gabeni, so that the front was quartered nearly a thousand furlongs from the rear; which Antigonus understanding, marched suddenly towards them, taking the most difficult road through a country that wanted water; but the way was short though uneven; hoping, if he should surprise them thus scattered in their winter quarters, the soldiers would not easily be able to come up in time enough and join with their officers. But having to pass through a country uninhabited, where he met with violent winds and severe frosts, he was much checked in his march, and his men suffered exceedingly. The only possible relief was making numerous fires, by which his enemies got notice of his coming. For the barbarians who dwelt on the mountains overlooking the desert, amazed at the multitude of fires they saw, sent messengers upon dromedaries to acquaint Peucestes. He being astonished and almost out of his senses with the news, and finding the rest in no less disorder, resolved to fly, and collect what men he could by the way. But Eumenes relieved him from his fear and trouble, undertaking so to stop the enemy's advance that he should arrive three days later than he was expected. Having persuaded them, he immediately despatched expresses to all the officers to draw the men out of their winter quarters and muster them with all speed. He himself, with some of the chief officers, rode out, and chose an elevated tract within view, at a distance, of such as travelled the desert; this he occupied and quartered out, and commanded many fires to be made in it, as the custom is in a camp. This done, and the enemies seeing the fire upon the mountains, Antigonus was filled with vexation and despondency, supposing that his enemies had been long since advertised of his march, and were prepared to receive him. Therefore, lest his army, now tired and wearied out with their march, should be immediately forced to encounter with fresh men, who had wintered well and were ready for him, quitting the near way, he marched slowly through the towns and villages to refresh his men. But meeting with no such skirmishes as are usual when two armies lie near one another, and being assured by the people of the country that no army had been seen, but only continual fires at that place, he concluded he had been outwitted by a stratagem of Eumenes, and, much troubled, advanced to give open battle.

By this time, the greater part of the forces were come together to Eumenes, and admiring his sagacity, declared him alone commander-in-chief of the whole army; upon which Antigenes and Teutamus, the commanders of the Argyraspids, being very much offended, and envying Eumenes, formed a conspiracy against him; and assembling the greater part of the satraps and officers, consulted when and how to cut him off. When they had unanimously agreed, first to use his service in the next battle, and then to take an occasion to destroy him, Eudamus, the master of the elephants, and Phædimus gave Eumenes private advice of this design, not out of kindness or good-will to him, but lest they should lose the money they had lent him. Eumenes, having commended them, retired to his tent, and telling his friends he lived among a herd of wild beasts, made his will, and tore up all his letters, lest his correspondents after his death should be questioned or punished on account of anything in his secret papers.

Having thus disposed of his affairs, he thought of letting the enemy win the field, or of flying through Media and Armenia and seizing Cappadocia, but came to no resolution while his friends stayed with him. After turning to many expedients in his mind, which his changeable fortune had made versatile, he at last put his men in array, and encouraged the Greeks and barbarians; as for the phalanx and the Argyraspids, they encouraged him, and bade him be of good heart, for the enemy would never be able to stand them. For indeed they were the oldest of Philip's and Alexander's soldiers, tried men, that had long made war their exercise, that had never been beaten or foiled; most of them seventy, none less than sixty years old. And so when they charged Antigonus's men, they cried out, "You fight against your fathers, you rascals," and furiously falling on, routed the whole phalanx at once, nobody being able to stand them, and the greatest part dying by their hands. So that Antigonus's foot was routed, but his horse got the better, and he became master of the baggage through the cowardice of Peucestes, who behaved himself negligently and basely; while Antigonus used his judgment calmly in the danger, being aided moreover by the ground. For the place where they fought was a large plain, neither deep nor hard under foot, but, like the seashore, covered with a fine soft sand which the treading of so many men and horses in the time of battle reduced to a small white dust, that like a cloud of lime darkened the air, so that one could not see clearly at any distance, and so made it easy for Antigonus to take the baggage unperceived.

After the battle, Teutamus sent a message to Antigonus to demand the baggage. He made answer, he would not only restore it to the Argyraspids, but serve them further in the other things if they would but deliver up Eumenes. Upon which the Argyraspids took a villainous resolution to deliver him up alive into the hands of his enemies. So they came to wait upon him, being unsuspected by him, but watching their opportunity, some lamenting the loss of the baggage, some encouraging him as if he had been victor, some accusing the other commanders, till at last they all fell upon him, and seizing his sword, bound his hands behind him with his own girdle.

When Antigonus had sent Nicanor to receive him he begged he might be led through the body of the Macedonians, and have liberty to speak to them, neither to request nor deprecate anything, but only to advise them what would be for their interest. A silence being made, as he stood upon a rising ground, he stretched out his hands bound, and said, "What trophy, O ye basest of all the Macedonians, could Antigonus have wished for so great as you yourselves have erected for him in delivering up your general captive into his hands? You are not ashamed, when you are conquerors, to own yourselves conquered, for the sake only of your baggage, as if it were wealth, not arms, wherein victory consisted; nay, you deliver up your general to redeem your stuff. As for me I am unvanquished, though a captive, conqueror of my enemies, and betrayed by my fellow-soldiers. For you, I adjure you by Jupiter, the protector of arms, and by all the gods that are the avengers of perjury, to kill me here with your own hands; for it is all one; and if I am murdered yonder it will be esteemed your act, nor will Antigonus complain, for he desires not Eumenes alive, but dead. Or if you withhold your own hands, release but one of mine, it shall suffice to do the work; and if you dare not trust me with a sword, throw me bound as I am under the feet of the wild beasts. This if you do I shall freely acquit you from the guilt of my death, as the most just and kind of men to their general."

While Eumenes was thus speaking, the rest of the soldiers wept for grief, but the Argyraspids shouted out to lead him on, and give no attention to his trifling. For it was no such great matter if this Chersonesian pest should meet his death, who in thousands of battles had annoyed and wasted the Macedonians; it would be a much more grievous thing for the choicest of Philip's and Alexander's soldiers to be defrauded of the fruits of so long service, and in their old age to come to beg their bread, and to leave their wives three nights in the power of their enemies. So they hurried him on with violence. But Antigonus, fearing the multitude, for nobody was left in the camp, sent ten of his strongest elephants with divers of his Mede and Parthian lances to keep off the press. Then he could not endure to have Eumenes brought into his presence, by reason of their former intimacy and friendship; but when they that had taken him inquired how he would have him kept, "As I would," said he, "an elephant, or a lion." A little after, being moved with compassion, he commanded the heaviest of his irons to be knocked off, one of his servants to be admitted to anoint him, and that any of his friends that were willing should have liberty to visit him, and bring him what he wanted. Long time he deliberated what to do with him, sometimes inclining to the advice and promises of Nearchus of Crete and Demetrius his son, who were very earnest to preserve Eumenes, whilst all the rest were unanimously instant and importunate to have him taken off. It is related that Eumenes inquired of Onomarchus, his keeper, why Antigonus, now he had his enemy in his hands, would not forthwith despatch or generously release him? And that Onomarchus contumeliously answered him, that the field had been a more proper place than this to show his contempt of death. To whom Eumenes replied, "And, by heavens, I showed it there; ask the men else that engaged me, but I could never meet a man that was my superior." "Therefore," rejoined Onomarchus, "now you have found such a man, why don't you submit quietly to his pleasure?"

When Antigonus resolved to kill Eumenes, he commanded to keep his food from him, and so with two or three days' fasting he began to draw near his end; but the camp being on a sudden to remove, an executioner was sent to despatch him. Antigonus granted his body to his friends, permitted them to burn it, and having gathered his ashes into a silver urn, to send them to his wife and children.

Eumenes was thus taken off; and Divine Providence assigned to no other man the chastisement of the commanders and soldiers that had betrayed him; but Antigonus himself, abominating the Argyraspids as wicked and inhuman villains, delivered them up to Sibyrtius, the governor of Arachosia, commanding him by all ways and means to destroy and exterminate them, so that not a man of them might ever come to Macedon, or so much as within sight of the Greek Sea.

THE COMPARISON OF SERTORIUS WITH EUMENES

THESE are the most remarkable passages that are come to our knowledge concerning Eumenes and Sertorius. In comparing their lives, we may observe that this was common to them both; that being aliens, strangers, and banished men, they came to be commanders of powerful forces, and had the leading of numerous and warlike armies, made up of divers nations. This was peculiar to Sertorius, that the chief command was, by his whole party, freely yielded to him, as to the person of the greatest merit and renown, whereas Eumenes had many who contested the office with him, and only by his actions obtained the superiority. They followed the one honestly, out of desire to be commanded by him; they submitted themselves to the other for their own security, because they could not command themselves. The one, being a Roman, was the general of the Spaniards and Lusitanians, who for many years had been under the subjection of Rome; and the other, a Chersonesian, who was chief commander of the Macedonians, who were the great conquerors of mankind, and were at that time subduing the world. Sertorius, being already in high esteem for his former services in the wars and his abilities in the senate, was advanced to the dignity of a general; whereas Eumenes obtained this honour from the office of a writer, or secretary, in which he had been despised. Nor did he only at first rise from inferior opportunities, but afterwards, also, met with greater impediments in the progress of his authority, and that not only from those who publicly resisted him, but from many others that privately conspired against him. It was much otherwise with Sertorius, not one of whose party publicly opposed him, only late in life, and secretly, a few of his acquaintance entered into a conspiracy against him. Sertorius put an end to his dangers as often as he was victorious in the field, whereas the victories of Eumenes were the beginning of his perils, through the malice of those that envied him.

Their deeds in war were equal and parallel, but their general inclinations different. Eumenes naturally loved war and contention, but Sertorius esteemed peace and tranquillity; when Eumenes might have lived in safety, with honour, if he would have quietly retired out of their way, he persisted in a dangerous contest with the greatest of the Macedonian leaders; but Sertorius, who was unwilling to trouble himself with any public disturbances, was forced, for the safety of his person, to make war against those who would not suffer him to live in peace. If Eumenes could have contented himself with the second place, Antigonus, freed from his competition for the first, would have used him well, and shown him favour, whereas Pompey's friends would never permit Sertorius so much as to live in quiet. The one made war of his own accord, out of a desire for command; and the other was constrained to accept of command to defend himself from war that was made against him. Eumenes was certainly a true lover of war, for he preferred his covetous ambition before his own security; but Sertorius was truly warlike, who procured his own safety by the success of his arms.

As to the manner of their deaths, it happened to one without the least thought or surmise of it; but to the other when he suspected it daily; which in the first argues an equitable temper, and a noble mind, not to distrust his friends; but in the other it showed some infirmity of spirit, for Eumenes intended to fly and was taken. The death of Sertorius dishonoured not his life; he suffered that from his companions which none of his enemies were ever able to perform. The other, not being able to deliver himself before his imprisonment, being willing also to live in captivity, did neither prevent nor expect his fate with honour or bravery; for by meanly supplicating and petitioning. he made his enemy, that pretended only to have power over his body, to be lord and master of his body and mind.

AGESILAUS

ARCHIDAMUS, the son of Zeuxidamus, having reigned gloriously over the Lacedæmonians, left behind him two sons, Agis the elder, begotten of Lampido, a noble lady, Agesilaus, much the younger, born of Eupolia, the daughter of Melesippidas. Now the succession belonging to Agis by law, Agesilaus, who in all probability was to be but a private man, was educated according to the usual discipline of the country, hard and severe, and meant to teach young men to obey their superiors. Whence it was that, men say, Simonides called Sparta "the tamer of men," because by early strictness of education they, more than any nation, trained the citizens to obedience to the laws, and made them tractable and patient of subjection, as horses that are broken in while colts. The law did not impose this harsh rule on the heirs apparent of the kingdom. But Agesilaus, whose good fortune it was to be born a younger brother, was consequently bred to all the arts of obedience, and so the better fitted for the government, when it fell to his share; hence it was that he proved the most popular-tempered of the Spartan kings, his early life having added to his natural kingly and commanding qualities the gentle and humane feelings of a citizen.

While he was yet a boy, bred up in one of what are called the *flocks*, or classes, he attracted the attachment of Lysander, who was particularly struck with the orderly temper that he manifested. For though he was one of the highest spirits, emulous above any of his companions, ambitious of pre-eminence in everything, and showed an impetuosity and fervour of mind which irresistibly carried him through all opposition or difficulty he could meet with; yet, on the other side, he was so easy and gentle in his nature, and so apt to yield to authority, that though he would do nothing on compulsion, upon ingenuous motives he would obey any commands, and was more hurt by the least rebuke or disgrace than he was distressed by any toil or hardship.

He had one leg shorter than the other, but this deformity was little observed in the general beauty of his person in youth. And the easy way in which he bore it (he being the first always to pass a jest upon himself) went far to make it disregarded. And indeed his high spirit and eagerness to distinguish himself were all the more conspicuous by it, since he never let his lameness withhold him from any toil or any brave action. Neither his statue nor picture are extant, he never allowing them in his life, and utterly forbidding them to be made after his death. He is said to have been a little man, of a contemptible presence; but the goodness of his humour, and his constant cheerfulness and playfulness of temper, always free from anything of moroseness or haughtiness, made him more attractive, even to his old age, than the most beautiful and youthful men of the nation. Theophrastus writes that the Ephors laid a fine upon Archidamus for marrying a little wife, "For," said they, "she will bring us a race of kinglets, instead of kings."

Whilst Agis, the elder brother, reigned, Alcibiades, being then an exile from Athens, came from Sicily to Sparta; nor had he stayed long there before his familiarity with Timæa, the king's wife, grew suspected, insomuch that Agis refused to own a child of hers, which, he said, was Alcibiades's, not his. Nor, if we may believe Duris, the historian, was Timæa much concerned at it, being herself forward enough to whisper among her helot maid-servants that the infant's true name was Alcibiades, not Leotychides. Meanwhile it was believed that the amour he had with her was not the effect of his love but of his ambition, that he might have Spartan kings of his posterity. This affair being grown public, it became needful for Alcibiades to withdraw from Sparta. But the child Leotychides had not the honours due to a legitimate son paid him, nor was he ever owned by Agis, till by his prayers and tears he prevailed with him to declare him his son before several witnesses upon his deathbed. But this did not avail to fix him in the throne of Agis, after whose death Lysander, who had lately achieved his conquest of Athens by sea, and was of the greatest power in Sparta, promoted Agesilaus, urging Leotychides's bastardy as a bar to his pretensions. Many of the other citizens, also, were favourable to Agesilaus, and zealously joined his party, induced by the opinion they had of his merits, of which they themselves had been spectators, in the time that he had been bred up among them. But there was a man, named Diopithes, at Sparta, who had a great knowledge of ancient oracles, and was thought particularly skilful and clever in all points of religion and divination. He alleged, that it was unlawful to make a lame man king of Lacedæmon, citing in the debate the following oracle:—

> "Beware, great Sparta, lest there come of thee,
> Though sound thyself, an halting sovereignty:
> Troubles, both long and unexpected too,
> And storms of deadly warfare shall ensue."

But Lysander was not wanting with an evasion, alleging that if the Spartans were really apprehensive of the oracle, they must have a care of Leotychides; for it was not the limping foot of a king that the gods cared about, but the purity of the Herculean family, into whose rights, if a spurious issue were admitted, it would make the kingdom to halt indeed. Agesilaus likewise alleged that the bastardy of Leotychides was witnessed to by Neptune, who threw Agis out of bed by a violent earthquake, after which time he ceased to visit his wife, yet Leotychides was born above ten months after this.

Agesilaus was upon these allegations declared king, and soon possessed himself of the private estate of Agis, as well as his throne, Leotychides being wholly rejected as a bastard. He now turned his attention to his kindred by the mother's side, persons of worth and virtue, but miserably poor. To them he gave half his brother's estate, and by this popular act gained general good-will and reputation, in the place of the envy and ill-feeling which the inheritance might otherwise have procured him. What Xenophon tells us of him, that by complying with, and, as it were, being ruled by his country, he grew into such great power with them, that he could do what he pleased, is meant to apply to the power he gained in the following manner with the Ephors and Elders. These were at that time of the greatest authority in the state; the former, officers annually chosen; the Elders, holding their places during life; both instituted, as already told in the life of Lycurgus, to restrain the power of the kings. Hence it was that there was always from generation to generation a feud and contention between them and the kings. But Agesilaus took another course. Instead of contending with them, he courted them; in all proceedings he commenced by taking their advice, was always ready to go, nay almost run, when they called him; if he were upon his royal seat, hearing causes, and the Ephors came in, he rose to them; whenever any man was elected into the Council of Elders he presented him with a gown and an ox. Thus, whilst he made a show of deference to them, and of a desire to extend their authority, he secretly advanced his own, and enlarged the prerogatives of the kings by several liberties which their friendship to his person conceded.

To other citizens he so behaved himself as to be less blamable in his enmities than in his friendships; for against his enemy he forbore to take any unjust advantage, but his friends he would assist, even in what was unjust. If an enemy had done anything praiseworthy, he felt it shameful to detract from his due, but his friends he knew not how to reprove when they did ill, nay, he would eagerly join with them, and assist them in their misdeed, and thought all offices of friendship commendable, let the matter in which they were employed be what it would. Again, when any of his adversaries was overtaken in a fault, he would be the first to pity him; and be soon entreated to procure his pardon, by which he won the hearts of all men. Insomuch that his popularity grew at last suspected by the Ephors, who laid a fine on him, professing that he was appropriating the citizens to himself who ought to be the common property of the state. For as it is the opinion of philosophers, that could you take away strife and opposition out of the universe, all the heavenly bodies would stand still, generation and motion would cease in the mutual concord and agreement of all things, so the Spartan legislator seems to have admitted ambition and emulation among the ingredients of his commonwealth, as the incentives of virtue, distinctly wishing that there should be some dispute and competition among his men of worth, and pronouncing the mere idle, uncontested, mutual compliance to unproved deserts to be but a false sort of concord. And some think Homer had an eye to this when he introduces Agamemnon well pleased with the quarrel arising between Ulysses and Achilles, and with the "terrible words" that passed between them, which he would never have done, unless he had thought emulations and dissensions between the noblest men to be of great public benefit. Yet this maxim is not simply to be granted, without restriction, for if animosities go too far they are very dangerous to cities and of most pernicious consequence.

When Agesilaus was newly entered upon the government, there came news from Asia that the Persian king was making great naval preparations, resolving with a high hand to dispossess the Spartans of their maritime supremacy. Lysander was eager for the opportunity of going over and succouring his friends in Asia, whom he had there left governors and masters of the cities, whose maladministration and tyrannical behaviour was causing them to be driven out, and in some cases put to death. He therefore persuaded Agesilaus to claim the command of the expedition, and by carrying the war from Greece into Persia, to anticipate the designs of the barbarian. He also wrote to his friends in Asia, that by embassy they should demand Agesilaus for their captain. Agesilaus, therefore, coming into the public assembly, offered his service, upon condition that he might have thirty Spartans for captains and counsellors; two thousand chosen men of the newly enfranchised helots, and allies to the number of six thousand. Lysander's authority and assistance soon obtained his request, so that he was sent away with the thirty Spartans, of whom Lysander was at once the chief, not only because of his power and reputation, but also on account of his friendship with Agesilaus, who esteemed his procuring him this charge a greater obligation than that of preferring him to the kingdom.

Whilst the army was collecting to the rendezvous at Geræstus, Agesilaus went with some of his friends to Aulis, where in a dream he saw a man approach him, and speak to him after this manner: "O king of the Lacedæmonians, you cannot but know that, before yourself, there hath been but one general captain of the whole of the Greeks, namely, Agamemnon; now, since you succeed him in the same office and command the same men, since you war against the same enemies, and begin your expedition from the same place, you ought also to offer such a sacrifice as he offered before he weighed anchor." Agesilaus at the same moment remembered that the sacrifice which Agamemnon offered was his own daughter, he being so directed by the oracle. Yet was he not at all disturbed by it, but as soon as he arose, he told his dream to his friends, adding that he would propitiate the goddess with the sacrifices a goddess must delight in, and would not follow the ignorant example of his predecessor. He therefore ordered an hind to be crowned with chaplets, and bade his own soothsayer perform the rite, not the usual person whom the Bœotians, in ordinary course, appointed to that office. When the Bœotian magistrates understood it, they were much offended, and sent officers to Agesilaus to forbid his sacrificing contrary to the laws of the country. These, having delivered their message to him, immediately went to the altar and threw down the quarters of the hind that lay upon it. Agesilaus took this very ill, and without further sacrifice immediately sailed away, highly displeased with the Bœotians, and much discouraged in his mind at the omen, boding to himself an unsuccessful voyage and an imperfect issue of the whole expedition.

When he came to Ephesus, he found the power and interest of Lysander, and the honours paid to him, insufferably great; all applications were made to him, crowds of suitors attended at his door, and followed upon his steps, as if nothing but the mere name of commander belonged, to satisfy the usage, to Agesilaus, the whole power of it being devolved upon Lysander. None of all the commanders that had been sent into Asia was either so powerful or so formidable as he; no one had rewarded his friends better, or had been more severe against his enemies; which things having been lately done, made the greater impression on men's minds, especially when they compared the simple and popular behaviour of Agesilaus with the harsh and violent and brief-spoken demeanour which Lysander still retained. Universal preference was yielded to this, and little regard shown to Agesilaus. This first occasioned offence to the other Spartan captains, who resented that they should rather seem the attendants of Lysander, than the councillors of Agesilaus. And at length Agesilaus himself, though not perhaps an envious man in his nature, nor apt to be troubled at the honours redounding upon other men, yet eager for honour and jealous of his glory, began to apprehend that Lysander's greatness would carry away from him the reputation of whatever great action should happen. He therefore went this way to work. He first opposed him in all his counsels; whatever Lysander specially advised was rejected, and other proposals followed. Then whoever made any address to him, if he found him attached to Lysander, certainly lost his suit. So also in judicial cases, any one whom he spoke strongly against was sure to come off with success, and any man whom he was particularly solicitous to procure some benefit for might think it well if he got away without an actual loss.

These things being clearly not done by chance, but constantly and of a set purpose, Lysander was soon sensible of them, and hesitated not to tell his friends, that they suffered for his sake, bidding them apply themselves to the king, and such as were more powerful with him than he was. Such sayings of his seeming to be designed purposely to excite ill-feeling, Agesilaus went on to offer himself a more open affront, appointing him his meat-carver, and would in public companies, scornfully say, "Let them go now and pay their court to my carver." Lysander, no longer able to brook these indignities, complained at last to Agesilaus himself, telling him that he knew very well how to humble his friends. Agesilaus answered, "I know certainly how to humble those who pretend to more power than myself." "That," replied Lysander, "is perhaps rather said by you, than done by me: I desire only that you will assign me some office and place in which I may serve you without incurring your displeasure."

Upon this Agesilaus sent him to the Hellespont, whence he procured Spithridates, a Persian of the province of Pharnabazus, to come to the assistance of the Greeks with two hundred horse and a great supply of money. Yet his anger did not so come down, but he thenceforward pursued the design of wresting the kingdom out of the hands of the two families which then enjoyed it, and making it wholly elective; and it is thought that he would on account of his quarrel have excited a great commotion in Sparta, if he had not died in the Bœotian war. Thus ambitious spirits in a commonwealth, when they transgress their bounds, are apt to do more harm than good. For though Lysander's pride and assumption was most ill-timed and insufferable in its display, yet Agesilaus surely could have found some other way of setting him right, less offensive to a man of his reputation and ambitious temper. Indeed they were both blinded with the same passion, so as one not to recognise the authority of his superior, the other not to bear with the imperfections of his friend.

Tisaphernes, being at first afraid of Agesilaus, treated with him about setting the Grecian cities at liberty, which was agreed on. But soon after finding a sufficient force drawn together, he resolved upon war, for which Agesilaus was not sorry. For the expectation of this expedition was great, and he did not think it for his honour that Xenophon with ten thousand men should march through the heart of Asia to the sea, beating the Persian forces when and how he pleased, and that he at the head of the Spartans, then sovereigns both at sea and land, should not achieve some memorable action for Greece. And so to be even with Tisaphernes, he requites his perjury by a fair stratagem. He pretends to march into Caria, whither, when he has drawn Tisaphernes and his army, he suddenly turns back, and falls upon Phrygia, takes many of their cities, and carries away great booty, showing his allies that to break a solemn league was a downright contempt of the gods, but the circumvention of an enemy in war was not only just but glorious, a gratification at once and an advantage.

Being weak in horse, and discouraged by ill-omens in the sacrifices, he retired to Ephesus, and there raised cavalry. He obliged the rich men, that were not inclined to serve in person, to find each of them a horseman armed and mounted; and there being many who preferred doing this, the army was quickly reinforced by a body, not of unwilling recruits for the infantry, but of brave and numerous horsemen. For those that were not good at fighting themselves hired such as were more military in their inclinations, and such as loved not horse-service substituted in their places such as did. Agamemnon's example had been a good one, when he took the present of an excellent mare to dismiss a rich coward from the army.

When by Agesilaus's order the prisoners he had taken in Phrygia were exposed to sale, they were first stripped of their garments and then sold naked. The clothes found many customers to buy them, but the bodies being, from the want of all exposure and exercise, white and tender-skinned, were derided and scorned as unserviceable, Agesilaus, who stood by at the auction, told his Greeks, "These are the men against whom ye fight, and these the things you will gain by it."

The season of the year being come, he boldly gave out that he would invade Lydia; and this plain dealing of his was now mistaken for a stratagem by Tisaphernes, who by not believing Agesilaus, having been already deceived by him, overreached himself. He expected that he should have made choice of Caria, as a rough country, not fit for horse, in which he deemed Agesilaus to be weak, and directed his own marches accordingly. But when he found him to be as good as his word, and to have entered into the country of Sardis, he made great haste after him, and by great marches of his horse, overtaking the loose stragglers who were pillaging the country, he cut them off. Agesilaus meanwhile, considering that the horse had outridden the foot, but that he himself had the whole body of his own army entire, made haste to engage them. He mingled his light-armed foot, carrying targets, with the horse, commanding them to advance at full speed and begin the battle, whilst he brought up the heavier-armed men in the rear. The success was answerable to the design; the barbarians were put to the rout, the Grecians pursued hard, took their camp, and put many of them to the sword. The consequence of this victory was very great; for they had not only the liberty of foraging the Persian country, and plundering at pleasure, but also saw Tisaphernes pay dearly for all the cruelty he had showed the Greeks, to whom he was a professed enemy. For the King of Persia sent Tithraustes, who took off his head, and presently dealt with Agesilaus about his return into Greece, sending to him ambassadors to that purpose with commission to offer him great sums of money. Agesilaus's answer was that the making of peace belonged to the Lacedæmonians, not to him; as for wealth, he had rather see it in his soldiers' hands than his own; that the Grecians thought it not honourable to enrich themselves with the bribes of their enemies, but with their spoils only. Yet, that he might gratify Tithraustes for the justice he had done upon Tisaphernes, the common enemy of the Greeks, he removed his quarters into Phrygia, accepting thirty talents for his expenses. Whilst he was upon his march, he received a *staff* from the government at Sparta, appointing him admiral as well as general. This was an honour which was never done to any but Agesilaus, who being now undoubtedly the greatest and most illustrious man of his time, still, as Theopompus had said, gave himself more occasion of glory in his own virtue and merit than was given him in this authority and power. Yet he committed a fault in preferring Pisander to the command of the navy, when there were others at hand both older and more experienced; in this not so much consulting the public good as the gratification of his kindred, and especially his wife, whose brother Pisander was.

Having removed his camp into Pharnabazus's province, he not only met with great plenty of provisions, but also raised great sums of money, and marching on to the bounds of Paphlagonia, he soon drew Cotys, the king of it, into a league, to which he of his own accord inclined, out of the opinion he had of Agesilaus's honour and virtue. Spithridates, from the time of his abandoning Pharnabazus, constantly attended Agesilaus in the camp whithersoever he went. This Spithridates had a son, a very handsome boy, called Megabates, of whom Agesilaus was extremely fond, and also a very beautiful daughter that was marriageable. Her Agesilaus matched to Cotys, and taking of him a thousand horse, with two thousand light-armed foot, he returned into Phrygia, and there pillaged the country of Pharnabazus, who durst not meet him in the field, nor yet trust to his garrisons, but getting his valuables together, got out of the way and moved about up and down with a flying army, till Spithridates, joining with Herippidas the Spartan, took his camp and all his property. Herippidas being too severe an inquirer into the plunder with which the barbarian soldiers had enriched themselves, and forcing them to deliver it up with too much strictness, so disobliged Spithridates with his questioning and examining that he changed sides again, and went off with the Paphlagonians to Sardis. This was a very great vexation to Agesilaus, not only that he had lost the friendship of a gallant commander, and with him a considerable part of his army, but still more that it had been done with the disrepute of a sordid and petty covetousness, of which he always had made it a point of honour to keep both himself and his country clear. Besides these public causes, he had a private one, his excessive fondness for the son, which touched him to the quick, though he endeavoured to master it, and, especially in presence of the boy, to suppress all appearance of it; so much so that when Megabates, for that was his name, came once to receive a kiss from him, he declined it. At which, when the young boy blushed and drew back, and afterward saluted him at a more reserved distance, Agesilaus soon repenting his coldness, and changing his mind, pretended to wonder why he did not salute him with the same familiarity as formerly. His friends about him answered, "You are in the fault, who would not accept the kiss of the boy, but turned away in alarm; he would come to you again if you would have the courage to let him do so." Upon this Agesilaus paused a while, and at length answered, "You need not encourage him to it; I think I had rather be master of myself in that refusal, than see all things that are now before my eyes turned into gold." Thus he demeaned himself to Megabates when present, but he had so great a passion for him in his absence, that it may be questioned whether, if the boy had returned again, all the courage he had would have sustained him in such another refusal.

After this Pharnabazus sought an opportunity of conferring with Agesilaus, which Apollophanes of Cyzicus, the common host of them both, procured for him. Agesilaus coming first to the appointed place, threw himself down upon the grass under a tree, lying there in expectation of Pharnabazus, who, bringing with him soft skins and wrought carpets to lie down upon, when he saw Agesilaus's posture, grew ashamed of his luxuries, and made no use of them, but laid himself down upon the grass also, without regard for his delicate and richly dyed clothing. Pharnabazus had matter enough of complaint against Agesilaus, and therefore, after the mutual civilities were over, he put him in mind of the great services he had done the Lacedæmonians in the Attic war, of which he thought it an ill recompense to have his country thus harassed and spoiled by those men who owed so much to him. The Spartans that were present hung down their heads, as conscious of the wrong they had done to their ally. But Agesilaus said, "We, O Pharnabazus, when we were in amity with your master the king, behaved ourselves like friends, and now that we are at war with him, we behave ourselves as enemies. As for you, we must look upon you as a part of his property, and must do these outrages upon you, not intending the harm to you, but to him whom we wound through you. But whenever you will choose rather to be a friend to the Grecians than a slave of the King of Persia, you may then reckon this army and navy to be all at your command, to defend both you, your country, and your liberties, without which there is nothing honourable or indeed desirable among men." Upon this Pharnabazus discovered his mind, and answered, "If the king sends another governor in my room, I will certainly come over to you, but as long as he trusts me with the government I shall be just to him, and not fail to do my utmost endeavours in opposing you." Agesilaus was taken with the answer and shook hands with him; and rising, said, "How much rather had I have so brave a man my friend than my enemy."

Pharnabazus being gone off, his son staying behind, ran up to Agesilaus, and smilingly said, "Agesilaus, I make you my guest;" and thereupon presented him with a javelin which he had in his hand. Agesilaus received it, and being much taken with the good mien and courtesy of the youth, looked about to see if there were anything in his train fit to offer him in return; and observing the horse of Idæus, the secretary, to have very fine trappings on, he took them off, and bestowed them upon the young gentleman. Nor did his kindness rest there, but he continued ever after to be mindful of him, so that when he was driven out of his country by his brothers, and lived in exile in Peloponnesus, he took great care of him and condescended even to assist him in some love matters. He had an attachment for a youth of Athenian birth, who was bred up as an athlete; and when at the Olympic games this boy, on account of his great size and general strong and full-grown appearance, was in some danger of not being admitted into the list, the Persian betook himself to Agesilaus, and made use of his friendship. Agesilaus readily assisted him, and not without a great deal of difficulty effected his desires. He was in all other things a man of great and exact justice, but when the case concerned a friend, to be strait-laced in point of justice, he said, was only a colourable pretence of denying him. There is an epistle written to Idrieus, Prince of Caria, that is ascribed to Agesilaus; it is this: "If Nicias be innocent, absolve him; if he be guilty, absolve him upon my account; however, be sure to absolve him." This was his usual character in his deportment towards his friends. Yet his rule was not without exception; for sometimes he considered the necessity of his affairs more than his friend, of which he once gave an example, when upon a sudden and disorderly removal of his camp, he left a sick friend behind him, and when he called loudly after him, and implored his help, turned his back, and said it was hard to be compassionate and wise too. This story is related by Hieronymus, the philosopher.

Another year of the war being spent, Agesilaus's fame still increased, insomuch that the Persian king received daily information concerning his many virtues, and the great esteem the world had of his temperance, his plain living, and his moderation. When he made any journey, he would usually take up his lodging in a temple, and there make the gods witnesses of his most private actions, which others would scarce permit men to be acquainted with. In so great an army you should scarce find a common soldier lie on a coarser mattress than Agesilaus: he was so indifferent to the varieties of heat and cold that all the seasons, as the gods sent them, seemed natural to him. The Greeks that inhabited Asia were much pleased to see the great lords and governors of Persia, with all the pride, cruelty, and luxury in which they lived, trembling and bowing before a man in a poor threadbare cloak, and, at one laconic word out of his mouth, obsequiously deferring and changing their wishes and purposes. So that it brought to the minds of many the verses of Timotheus—

> "Mars is the tyrant, gold Greece does not fear."

Many parts of Asia now revolting from the Persians, Agesilaus restored order in the cities, and without bloodshed or banishment of any of their members re-established the proper constitution in the governments, and now resolved to carry away the war from the seaside, and to march further up into the country, and to attack the King of Persia himself in his own home in Susa and Ecbatana; not willing to let the monarch sit idle in his chair, playing umpire in the conflicts of the Greeks, and bribing their popular leaders. But these great thoughts were interrupted by unhappy news from Sparta; Epicydidas is from thence sent to remand him home, to assist his own country, which was then involved in a great war:—

> "Greece to herself doth a barbarian grow,
> Others could not, she doth herself o'erthrow."

What better can we say of those jealousies, and that league and conspiracy of the Greeks for their own mischief, which arrested fortune in full career, and turned back arms that were already uplifted against the barbarians, to be used upon themselves, and recalled into Greece the war which had been banished out of her? I by no means assent to Demaratus of Corinth, who said that those Greeks lost a great satisfaction that did not live to see Alexander sit in the throne of Darius. That sight should rather have drawn tears from them, when they considered that they had left that glory to Alexander and the Macedonians, whilst they spent all their own great commanders in playing them against each other in the fields of Leuctra, Coronea, Corinth, and Arcadia.

Nothing was greater or nobler than the behaviour of Agesilaus on this occasion, nor can a nobler instance be found in story of a ready obedience and just deference to orders. Hannibal, though in a bad condition himself and, almost driven out of Italy, could scarcely be induced to obey when he was called home to serve his country. Alexander made a jest of the battle between Agis and Antipater, laughing and saying, "So, whilst we were conquering Darius in Asia, it seems there was a battle of mice in Arcadia." Happy Sparta, meanwhile, in the justice and modesty of Agesilaus, and in the deference he paid to the laws of his country; who, immediately upon receipt of his orders, though in the midst of his high fortune and power, and in full hope of great and glorious success, gave all up and instantly departed, "his object unachieved," leaving many regrets behind him among his allies in Asia, and proving by his example the falseness of that saying of Demostratus, the son of Phæax, "That the Lacedæmonians were better in public, but the Athenians in private." For while approving himself an excellent king and general, he likewise showed himself in private an excellent friend and a most agreeable companion.

The coin of Persia was stamped with the figure of an archer; Agesilaus said, That a thousand Persian archers had driven him out of Asia; meaning the money that had been laid out in bribing the demagogues and the orators in Thebes and Athens, and thus inciting those two states to hostility against Sparta.

Having passed the Hellespont, he marched by land through Thrace, not begging or entreating a passage anywhere, only he sent his messengers to them to demand whether they would have him pass as a friend or as an enemy. All the rest received him as a friend, and assisted him on his journey. But the Trallians, to whom Xerxes is also said to have given money, demanded a price of him, namely, one hundred talents of silver and one hundred women. Agesilaus in scorn asked, Why they were not ready to receive them? He marched on, and finding the Trallians in arms to oppose him, fought them, and slew great numbers of them. He sent the like embassy to the King of Macedonia, who replied, He would take time to deliberate. "Let him deliberate," said Agesilaus, "we will go forward in the meantime." The Macedonian, being surprised and daunted at the resolution of the Spartan, gave orders to let him pass as a friend.

When he came into Thessaly he wasted the country, because they were in league with the enemy. To Larissa, the chief city of Thessaly, he sent Xenocles and Scythes to treat of a peace, whom when the Larissæans had laid hold of, and put into custody, others were enraged, and advised the siege of the town; but he answered, That he valued either of those men at more than the whole country of Thessaly. He therefore made terms with them, and received his men again upon composition. Nor need we wonder at this saying of Agesilaus, since when he had news brought him from Sparta, of several great captains in a battle near Corinth, in which the slaughter fell upon other Greeks, and the Lacedæmonians obtained a great victory with small loss, he did not appear at all satisfied; but with a great sigh cried out, "O Greece, how many brave men hast thou destroyed; who, if they had been preserved to so good an use, had sufficed to have conquered all Persia!" Yet when the Pharsalians grew troublesome to him, by pressing upon his army and incommoding his passage, he led out five hundred horse, and in person fought and routed them, setting up a trophy under the mount Narthacius. He valued himself very much upon that victory, that with so small a number of his own training, he had vanquished a body of men that thought themselves the best horsemen of Greece.

Here Diphridas, the Ephor, met him, and delivered his message from Sparta, which ordered him immediately to make an inroad into Bœotia; and though he thought this fitter to have been done at another time, and with greater force, he yet obeyed the magistrates. He thereupon told his soldiers that the day had come on which they were to enter upon that employment for the performance of which they were brought out of Asia. He sent for two divisions of the army near Corinth to his assistance. The Lacedæmonians at home, in honour to him, made proclamations for volunteers that would serve under the king to come in and be enlisted. Finding all the young men in the city ready to offer themselves, they chose fifty of the strongest, and sent them.

Agesilaus having gained Thermopylæ, and passed quietly through Phocis, as soon as he had entered Bœotia, and pitched his camp near Chæronea, at once met with an eclipse of the sun, and with ill news from the navy, Pisander, the Spartan admiral, being beaten and slain at Cnidos by Pharnabazus and Conon. He was much moved at it, both upon his own and the public account. Yet lest his army, being now near engaging, should meet with any discouragement, he ordered the messengers to give out that the Spartans were the conquerors, and he himself putting on a garland, solemnly sacrificed for the good news, and sent portions of the sacrifices to his friends.

When he came near to Coronea, and was within view of the enemy, he drew up his army, and giving the left wing to the Orchomenians, he himself led the right. The Thebans took the right wing of their army, leaving the left to the Argives. Xenophon, who was present, and fought on Agesilaus's side, reports it to be the hardest-fought battle that he had seen. The beginning of it was not so, for the Thebans soon put the Orchomenians to rout, as also did Agesilaus the Argives. But both parties having news of the misfortune of their left wings, they betook themselves to their relief. Here Agesilaus might have been sure of his victory had he contented himself not to charge them in the front, but in the flank or rear; but being angry and heated in the fight he would not wait the opportunity, but fell on at once, thinking to bear them down before him. The Thebans were not behind him in courage, so that the battle was fiercely carried on on both sides, especially near Agesilaus's person, whose new guard of fifty volunteers stood him in great stead that day, and saved his life. They fought with great valour, and interposed their bodies frequently between him and danger, yet could they not so preserve him, but that he received many wounds through his armour with lances and swords, and was with much difficulty gotten off alive by their making a ring about him, and so guarding him, with the slaughter of many of the enemy, and the loss of many of their own number. At length, finding it too hard a task to break the front of the Theban troops, they opened their own files, and let the enemy march through them (an artifice which in the beginning they scorned), watching in the meantime the posture of the enemy, who, having passed through, grew careless, as esteeming themselves past danger, in which position they were immediately set upon by the Spartans. Yet were they not then put to rout, but marched on to Helicon, proud of what they had done, being able to say that they themselves, as to their part of the army, were not worsted.

Agesilaus, sore wounded as he was, would not be borne to his tent till he had been first carried about the field, and had seen the dead conveyed within his encampment. As many of his enemies as had taken sanctuary in the temple he dismissed. For there stood near the battlefield the temple of Minerva the Itonian, and before it a trophy erected by the Bœotians, for the victory which, under the conduct of Sparton, their general, they obtained over the Athenians under Tolmides, who himself fell in the battle. Next morning early, to make trial of the Theban courage, whether they had any mind to a second encounter, he commanded his soldiers to put on garlands on their heads, and play with their flutes, and raise a trophy before their faces; but when they, instead of fighting, sent for leave to bury their dead, he gave it them; and having so assured himself of the victory, after this he went to Delphi, to the Pythian games, which were then celebrating, at which feast he assisted, and there solemnly offered the tenth part of the spoils he had brought from Asia, which amounted to a hundred talents.

Thence he returned to his own country, where his way and habits of life quickly excited the affection and admiration of the Spartans; for, unlike other generals, he came home from foreign lands the same man that he went out, having not so learned the fashions of other countries, as to forget his own, much less to dislike or despise them. He followed and respected all the Spartan customs, without any change either in the manner of his supping, or bathing, or his wife's apparel, as if he had never travelled over the river Eurotas. So also with his household furniture and his own armour, nay, the very gates of his house were so old that they might well be thought of Aristodemus's setting up. His daughter's *Canathrum*, says Xenophon, was no richer than that of any one else. The Canathrum, as they call it, is a chair or chariot made of wood, in the shape of a griffin, or tragelaphus, on which the children and young virgins are carried in processions. Xenophon has not left us the name of this daughter of Agesilaus; and Dicæarchus expresses some indignation, because we do not know, he says, the name of Agesilaus's daughter, nor of Epaminondas's mother. But in the records of Laconia, we ourselves found his wife's name to have been Cleora, and his two daughters to have been called Eupolia and Prolyta. And you may also to this day see Agesilaus's spear kept in Sparta, nothing differing from that of other men.

There was a vanity he observed among the Spartans, about keeping running horses for the Olympic games, upon which he found they much valued themselves. Agesilaus regarded it as a display not of any real virtue, but of wealth and expense; and to make this evident to the Greeks, induced his sister, Cynisca, to send a chariot into the course. He kept with him Xenophon, the philosopher, and made much of him, and proposed to him to send for his children, and educate them at Sparta, where they would be taught the best of all learning; how to obey, and how to command. Finding on Lysander's death a large faction formed, which he on his return from Asia had established against Agesilaus, he thought it advisable to expose both him and it, by showing what manner of a citizen he had been whilst he lived. To that end, finding among his writings an oration, composed by Cleon the Halicarnassean, but to have been spoken by Lysander in a public assembly, to excite the people to innovations and changes in the government, he resolved to publish it as an evidence of Lysander's practices. But one of the Elders having the perusal of it, and finding it powerfully written, advised him to have a care of digging up Lysander again, and rather bury that oration in the grave with him; and this advice he wisely hearkened to, and hushed the whole thing up; and ever after forbore publicly to affront any of his adversaries, but took occasions of picking out the ringleaders, and sending them away upon foreign services. He thus had means for exposing the avarice and the injustice of many of them in their employments; and again when they were by others brought into question, he made it his business to bring them off, obliging them, by that means, of enemies to become his friends, and so by degrees left none remaining.

Agesipolis, his fellow-king, was under the disadvantage of being born of an exiled father, and himself young, modest, and inactive, meddled not much in affairs. Agesilaus took a course of gaining him over and making him entirely tractable. According to the custom of Sparta, the kings, if they were in town, always dined together. This was Agesilaus's opportunity of dealing with Agesipolis, whom he found quick, as he himself was, in forming attachments for young men, and accordingly talked with him always on such subjects, joining and aiding him, and acting as his confidant, such attachments in Sparta being entirely honourable, and attended always with lively feelings of modesty, love of virtue, and a noble emulation; of which more is said in Lycurgus's life.

Having thus established his power in the city, he easily obtained that his half-brother Teleutias might be chosen admiral, and thereupon making an expedition against the Corinthians, he made himself master of the long walls by land, through the assistance of his brother at sea. Coming thus upon the Argives, who then held Corinth, in the midst of their Isthmian festival, he made them fly from the sacrifice they had just commenced, and leave all their festive provision behind them. The exiled Corinthians that were in the Spartan army desired him to keep the feast, and to preside in the celebration of it. This he refused, but gave them leave to carry on the solemnity if they pleased, and he in the meantime stayed and guarded them.

When Agesilaus marched off, the Argives returned and celebrated the games over again, when some who were victors before became victors a second time; others lost the prizes which before they had gained. Agesilaus thus made it clear to everybody that the Argives must in their own eyes have been guilty of great cowardice since they set such a value on presiding at the games, and yet had not dared to fight for it. He himself was of opinion that to keep a mean in such things was best; he assisted at the sports and dances usual in his own country, and was always ready and eager to be present at the exercises either of the young men or of the girls, but things that many men used to be highly taken with he seemed not at all concerned about. Callippides, the tragic actor, who had a great name in all Greece and was made much of, once met and saluted him; of which when he found no notice taken, he confidently thrust himself into his train, expecting that Agesilaus would pay him some attention. When all that failed, he boldly accosted him, and asked him whether he did not remember him? Agesilaus turned, and looking him in the face, "Are you not," said he, "Callippides the showman?" Being invited once to hear a man who admirably imitated the nightingale, he declined, saying he had heard the nightingale itself. Menecrates, the physician, having had great success in some desperate diseases, was by way of flattery called Jupiter; he was so vain as to take the name, and having occasion to write a letter to Agesilaus, thus addressed it: "Jupiter Menecrates to King Agesilaus, greeting." The king returned answer: "Agesilaus to Menecrates, health and a sound mind."

Whilst Agesilaus was in the Corinthian territories, having just taken the Heræum, he was looking on while his soldiers were carrying away the prisoners and the plunder, when ambassadors from Thebes came to him to treat of peace. Having a great aversion for that city, and thinking it then advantageous to his affairs publicly to slight them, he took the opportunity, and would not seem either to see them or hear them speak. But as if on purpose to punish him in his pride, before they parted from him, messengers came with news of the complete slaughter of one of the Spartan divisions by Iphicrates, a greater disaster than had befallen them for many years, and that the more grievous because it was a choice regiment of full-armed Lacedæmonians overthrown by a parcel of mere mercenary targeteers. Agesilaus leapt from his seat, to go at once to their rescue, but found it too late, the business being over. He therefore returned to the Heræum and sent for the Theban ambassadors to give them audience. They now resolved to be even with him for the affront he gave them, and without speaking one word of the peace, only desired leave to go into Corinth. Agesilaus, irritated with this proposal, told them in scorn, that if they were anxious to go and see how proud their friends were of their success they should do it tomorrow with safety. Next morning, taking the ambassadors with him, he ravaged the Corinthian territories, up to the very gates of the city, where, having made a stand, and let the ambassadors see that the Corinthians durst not come out to defend themselves, he dismissed them. Then gathering up the small remainders of the shattered regiment, he marched homewards, always removing his camp before day, and always pitching his tents after night, that he might prevent their enemies among the Arcadians from taking any opportunity of insulting over their loss.

After this, at the request of the Achæans, he marched with them into Acarnania, and there collected great spoils, and defeated the Acarnanians in battle. The Achæans would have persuaded him to keep his winter quarters there, to hinder the Acarnanians from sowing their corn; but he was of the contrary opinion, alleging that they would be more afraid of a war next summer, when their fields were sown, than they would be if they lay fallow. The event justified his opinion; for next summer, when the Achæans began their expedition again, the Acarnanians immediately made peace with them.

When Conon and Pharnabazus with the Persian navy were grown masters of the sea, and had not only infested the coast of Laconia, but also rebuilt the walls of Athens at the cost of Pharnabazus, the Lacedæmonians thought fit to treat of peace with the King of Persia. To that end, they sent Antalcidas to Tiribazus, basely and wickedly betraying the Asiatic Greeks, on whose behalf Agesilaus had made the war. But no part of this dishonour fell upon Agesilaus, the whole being transacted by Antalcidas, who was his bitter enemy, and was urgent for peace upon any terms, because war was sure to increase his power and reputation. Nevertheless, once being told by way of reproach that the Lacedæmonians had gone over to the Medes, he replied, "No, the Medes had come over to the Lacedæmonians." And when the Greeks were backward to submit to the agreement, he threatened them with war, unless they fulfilled the King of Persia's conditions, his particular end in this being to weaken the Thebans; for it was made one of the articles of peace that the country of Bœotia should be left independent. This feeling of his to Thebes appeared further afterwards, when Phœbidas, in full peace, most unjustifiably seized upon the Cadmea. The thing was much resented by all Greece, and not well liked by the Lacedæmonians themselves; those especially who were enemies to Agesilaus required an account of the action, and by whose authority it was done, laying the suspicion of it at his door. Agesilaus resolutely answered, on the behalf of Phœbidas, that the profitableness of the act was chiefly to be considered; if it were for the advantage of the commonwealth, it was no matter whether it were done with or without authority. This was the more remarkable in him, because in his ordinary language he was always observed to be a great maintainer of justice, and would commend it as the chief of virtues, saying, that valour without justice was useless, and if all the world were just, there would be no need of valour. When any would say to him, the Great King will have it so, he would reply, "How is he greater than I, unless he be juster?" nobly and rightly taking, as a sort of royal measure of greatness, justice and not force. And thus when, on the conclusion of the peace, the King of Persia wrote to Agesilaus, desiring a private friendship and relations of hospitality, he refused it, saying that the public friendship was enough; whilst that lasted there was no need of private. Yet in his acts he was not constant to his doctrine, but sometimes out of ambition, and sometimes out of private pique, he let himself be carried away; and particularly in this case of the Thebans, he not only saved Phœbidas, but persuaded the Lacedæmonians to take the fault upon themselves, and to retain the Cadmea, putting a garrison into it, and to put the government of Thebes into the hands of Archias and Leontidas, who had been betrayers of the castle to them.

This excited strong suspicion that what Phœbidas did was by Agesilaus's order, which was corroborated by after-occurrences. For when the Thebans had expelled the garrison, and asserted their liberty, he, accusing them of the murder of Archias and Leontidas, who indeed were tyrants, though in name holding the office of Polemarchs, made war upon them. He sent Cleombrotus on that errand, who was now his fellow-king, in the place of Agesipolis, who was dead, excusing himself by reason of his age; for it was forty years since he had first borne arms, and he was consequently exempt by the law; meanwhile the true reason was, that he was ashamed, having so lately fought against tyranny in behalf of the Phliasians, to fight now in defence of a tyranny against the Thebans.

One Sphodrias, of Lacedæmonians, of the contrary faction to Agesilaus, was governor in Thespiæ, a bold and enterprising man, though he had perhaps more of confidence than wisdom. This action of Phœbidas fired him, and incited his ambition to attempt some great enterprise, which might render him as famous as he perceived the taking of the Cadmea had made Phœbidas. He thought the sudden capture of the Piræus, and the cutting off thereby the Athenians from the sea, would be a matter of far more glory. It is said, too, that Pelopidas and Melon, the chief captains of Bœotia, put him upon it; that they privately sent men to him, pretending to be of the Spartan faction, who, highly commending Sphodrias, filled him with a great opinion of himself, protesting him to be the only man in the world that was fit for so great an enterprise. Being thus stimulated, he could hold no longer, but hurried into an attempt as dishonourable and treacherous as that of the Cadmea, but executed with less valour and less success; for the day broke whilst he was yet in the Thriasian plain, whereas he designed the whole exploit to have been done in the night. As soon as the soldiers perceived the rays of light reflecting from the temples of Eleusis, upon the first rising of the sun, it is said that their hearts failed them; nay, he himself, when he saw that he could not have the benefit of the night, had not courage enough to go on with his enterprise; but having pillaged the country, he returned with shame to Thespiæ. An embassy was upon this sent from Athens to Sparta, to complain of the breach of peace; but the ambassadors found their journey needless, Sphodrias being then under process by the magistrates of Sparta. Sphodrias durst not stay to expect judgment, which he found would be capital, the city being highly incensed against him, out of the shame they felt at the business, and their desire to appear in the eyes of the Athenians as fellow-sufferers in the wrong, rather than accomplices in its being done.

This Sphodrias had a son of great beauty named Cleonymus, to whom Archidamus, the son of Agesilaus, was extremely attached. Archidamus, as became him, was concerned for the danger of his friend's father, but yet he durst not do anything openly for his assistance, he being one of the professed enemies of Agesilaus. But Cleonymus having solicited him with tears about it, as knowing Agesilaus to be of all his father's enemies the most formidable, the young man for two or three days followed after his father with such fear and confusion that he durst not speak to him. At last, the day of sentence being at hand, he ventured to tell him that Cleonymus had entreated him to intercede for his father. Agesilaus, though well aware of the love between the two young men, yet did not prohibit it, because Cleonymus from his earliest years had been looked upon as a youth of very great promise; yet he gave not his son any kind or hopeful answer in the case, but coldly told him that he would consider what he could honestly and honourably do in it, and so dismissed him. Archidamus being ashamed of his want of success, forbore the company of Cleonymus, whom he usually saw several times every day. This made the friends of Sphodrias to think his case desperate, till Etymocles, one of Agesilaus's friends, discovered to them the king's mind; namely, that he abhorred the fact, but yet he thought Sphodrias a gallant man such as the commonwealth much wanted at that time. For Agesilaus used to talk thus concerning the cause, out of a desire to gratify his son. And now Cleonymus quickly understood that Archidamus had been true to him, in using all his interests with his father; and Sphodrias's friend ventured to be forward in his defence. The truth is, that Agesilaus was excessively fond of his children; and it is to him the story belongs, that when they were little ones, he used to make a horse of a stick, and ride with them; and being caught at this sport by a friend, he desired him not to mention it till he himself were the father of children.

Meanwhile, Sphodrias being acquitted, the Athenians betook themselves to arms, and Agesilaus fell into disgrace with the people; since to gratify the whims of a boy he had been willing to pervert justice, and make the city accessory to the crimes of private men, whose most unjustifiable actions had broken the peace of Greece. He also found his colleague, Cleombrotus, little inclined to the Theban war; so that it became necessary for him to waive the privilege of his age, which he before had claimed, and to lead the army himself into Bœotia; which he did with variety of success, sometimes conquering, and sometimes conquered; insomuch that receiving a wound in a battle, he was reproached by Antalcidas, that the Thebans had paid him well for the lessons he had given them in fighting. And, indeed, they were now grown far better soldiers than ever they had been, being so continually kept in training by the frequency of the Lacedæmonian expeditions against them. Out of the foresight of which it was that anciently Lycurgus, in three several laws, forbade them to make any wars with the same nation, as this would be to instruct their enemies in the art of it. Meanwhile, the allies of Sparra were not a little discontented at Agesilaus, because this war was commenced not upon any fair public ground of quarrel, but merely out of his private hatred to the Thebans; and they complained with indignation that they, being the majority of the army, should from year to year be thus exposed to danger and hardship here and there, at the will of a few persons. It was at this time, we are told, that Agesilaus, to obviate the objection, devised this expedient, to show the allies were not the greater number. He gave orders that all the allies, of whatever country, should sit down promiscuously on one side, and all the Lacedæmonians on the other: which being done, he commanded a herald to proclaim, that all the potters of both divisions should stand out; then all the blacksmiths; then all the masons; next the carpenters; and so he went through all the handicrafts. By this time almost all the allies were risen, but of the Lacedæmonians not a man, they being by law forbidden to learn any mechanical business; and now Agesilaus laughed and said, "You see, my friends, how many more soldiers we send out than you do."

When he brought back his army from Bœotia through Megara, as he was going up to the magistrate's office in the Acropolis, he was suddenly seized with pain and cramp in his sound leg, and great swelling and inflammation ensued. He was treated by a Syracusan physician, who let him blood below the ankle; this soon eased his pain, but then the blood could not be stopped, till the loss of it brought on fainting and swooning; at length, with much trouble, he stopped it. Agesilaus was carried home to Sparta in a very weak condition, and did not recover strength enough to appear in the field for a long time after.

Meanwhile, the Spartan fortune was but ill; they received many losses both by sea and land; but the greatest was that at Tegyræ, when for the first time they were beaten by the Thebans in a set battle.

All the Greeks were, accordingly, disposed to a general peace, and to that end ambassadors came to Sparta. Among these was Epaminondas, the Theban, famous at that time for his philosophy and learning, but he had not yet given proof of his capacity as a general. He, seeing all the others crouch to Agesilaus, and court favour with him, alone maintained the dignity of an ambassador, and with that freedom that became his character made a speech in behalf not of Thebes only, from whence he came, but of all Greece, remonstrating that Sparta alone grew great by war, to the distress and suffering of all her neighbours. He urged that a peace should be made upon just and equal terms, such as alone would be a lasting one, which could not otherwise be done than by reducing all to equality. Agesilaus, perceiving all the other Greeks to give much attention to this discourse, and to be pleased with it, presently asked him whether he thought it a part of this justice and equality that the Bœotian towns should enjoy their independence. Epaminondas instantly and without wavering asked him in return, whether he thought it just and equal that the Laconian towns should enjoy theirs. Agesilaus started from his seat and bade him once for all speak out and say whether or not Bœotia should be independent. And when Epaminondas replied once again with the same inquiry, whether Laconia should be so, Agesilaus was so enraged that, availing himself of the pretext, he immediately struck the name of the Thebans out of the league, and declared war against them. With the rest of the Greeks he made a peace, and dismissed them with this saying, that what could be peaceably adjusted, should; what was otherwise incurable, must be committed to the success of war, it being a thing of too great difficulty to provide for all things by treaty.

The Ephors upon this despatched their orders to Cleombrotus, who was at that time in Phocis, to march directly into Bceotia, and at the same time sent to their allies for aid. The confederates were very tardy in their business and unwilling to engage, but as yet they feared the Spartans too much to dare to refuse. And although many portents and prodigies of ill-presage, which I have mentioned in the life of Epaminondas, had appeared, and though Prothous, the Laconian, did all he could to hinder it, yet Agesilaus would needs go forward, and prevailed so, that the war was decreed. He thought the present juncture of affairs very advantageous for their revenge, the rest of Greece being wholly free, and the Thebans excluded from the peace. But that this war was undertaken more upon passion than judgment the event may prove; for the treaty was finished but the fourteenth of Scirophorion, and the Lacedæmonians received their great overthrow at Leuctra on the fifth of Hecatombæon, within twenty days. There fell at that time a thousand Spartans, and Cleombrotus their king, and around him the bravest men of the nation; particularly the beautiful youth, Cleonymus, the son of Sphodrias, who was thrice struck down at the feet of the king, and as often rose, but was slain at the last.

This unexpected blow, which fell so heavy upon the Lacedæmonians, brought greater glory to Thebes than ever was acquired by any other of the Grecian republics in their civil wars against each other. The behaviour, notwithstanding, of the Spartans, though beaten, was as great, and as highly to be admired, as that of the Thebans. And indeed, if, as Xenophon says, in conversation good men even in their sports and at their wine let fall many sayings that are worth the preserving, how much more worthy to be recorded is an exemplary constancy of mind, as shown both in the words and in the acts of brave men when they are pressed by adverse fortune! It happened that the Spartans were celebrating a solemn feast, at which many strangers were present from other countries, and the town full of them, when this news of the overthrow came. It was the gymnopædiæ, and the boys were dancing in the theatre, when the messengers arrived from Leuctra. The Ephors, though they were sufficiently aware that this blow had ruined the Spartan power, and that their primacy over the rest of Greece was gone for ever, yet gave orders that the dances should not break off, nor any of the celebration of the festival abate; but privately sending the names of the slain to each family, out of which they were lost, they continued the public spectacles. The next morning when they had full intelligence concerning it, and everybody knew who were slain, and who survived, the fathers, relatives, and friends of the slain came out rejoicing in the market-place, saluting each other with a kind of exultation; on the contrary, the fathers of the survivors hid themselves at home among the women. If necessity drove any of them abroad they went very dejectedly, with downcast looks and sorrowful countenances. The women outdid the men in it; those whose sons were slain openly rejoicing, cheerfully making visits to one another, and meeting triumphantly in the temples; they who expected their children home being very silent and much troubled.

But the people in general, when their allies now began to desert them, and Epaminondas, in all the confidence of victory, was expected with an invading army in Peloponnesus, began to think again of Agesilaus's lameness, and to entertain feelings of religious fear and despondency, as if their having rejected the sound-footed, and having chosen the halting king, which the oracle had specially warned them against, was the occasion of all their distresses. Yet the regard they had to the merit and reputation of Agesilaus so far stilled this murmuring of the people that, notwithstanding it, they intrusted themselves to him in this distress, as the only man that was fit to heal the public malady, the arbiter of all their difficulties, whether relating to the affairs of war or peace. One great one was then before them concerning the runaways (as their name is for them) that had fled out of the battle, who being many and powerful, it was feared that they might make some commotion in the republic, to prevent the execution of the law upon them for their cowardice. The law in that case was very severe; for they were not only to be debarred from all honours, but also it was a disgrace to intermarry with them; whoever met any of them in the streets might beat him if he chose, nor was it lawful for him to resist; they, in the meanwhile, were obliged to go about unwashed and meanly dressed, with their clothes patched with divers colours, and to wear their beards half shaved, half unshaven. To execute so rigid a law as this, in a case where the offenders were so many, and many of them of such distinction, and that in a time when the commonwealth wanted soldiers so much as then it did, was of dangerous consequence. Therefore they chose Agesilaus as a sort of new lawgiver for the occasion. But he, without adding to or diminishing from or any way changing the law, came out into the public assembly, and said that the law should sleep for to-day, but from this day forth be vigorously executed. By this means he at once preserved the law from abrogation and the citizens from infamy; and that he might alleviate the despondency and self-distrust of the young men, he made an inroad into Arcadia, where, carefully avoiding all fighting, he contended himself with spoiling the territory, and taking a small town belonging to the Mantineans, thus reviving the hearts of the people, letting them see that they were not everywhere unsuccessful.

Epaminondas now invaded Laconia with an army of forty thousand, besides light-armed men and others that followed the camp only for plunder, so that in all they were at least seventy thousand. It was now six hundred years since the Dorians had possessed Laconia, and in all that time the face of an enemy had not been seen within their territories, no man daring to invade them; but now they made their entrance, and burnt and plundered without resistance the hitherto untouched and sacred territory up to Eurotas and the very suburbs of Sparta; for Agesilaus would not permit them to encounter so impetuous a torrent, as Theopompus calls it, of war. He contented himself with fortifying the chief parts of the city, and with placing guards in convenient places, enduring meanwhile the taunts of the Thebans, who reproached him by name as the kindler of the war, and the author of all that mischief to his country, bidding him defend himself if he could. But this was not all; he was equally disturbed at home with the tumults of the city, the outcries and running about of the old men, who were enraged at their present condition, and the women yet worse, out of their senses with the clamours, and the fires of the enemy in the field. He was also himself afflicted by the sense of his lost glory; who, having come to the throne of Sparta when it was in its most flourishing and powerful condition, now lived to see it laid low in esteem, and all its great vaunts cut down, even that which he himself had been accustomed to use, that the women of Sparta had never seen the smoke of the enemy's fire. As it is said, also, that when Antalcidas, once being in dispute with an Athenian about the valour of the two nations, the Athenian boasted that they had often driven the Spartans from the river Cephisus, "Yes," said Antalcidas, "but we never had occasion to drive you from Eurotas." And a common Spartan of less note, being in company with an Argive, who was bragging how many Spartans lay buried in the fields of Argos, replied, "None of you are buried in the country of Laconia." Yet now the case was so altered that Antalcidas, being one of the Ephors, out of fear sent away his children privately to the island of Cythera.

When the enemy essayed to get over the river, and thence to attack the town, Agesilaus, abandoning the rest, betook himself to the high places and strongholds of it. But it happened Eurotas at that time was swollen to a great height with snow that had fallen and made the passage very difficult to the Thebans, not only by its depth, but much more by its extreme coldness. Whilst this was doing, Epaminondas was seen in the front of the phalanx, and was pointed out to Agesilaus, who looked long at him, and said but these words, "O bold man !" But when he came to the city, and would have fain attempted something within the limits of it that might raise him a trophy there, he could not tempt Agesilaus out of his hold, but was forced to march off again, wasting the country as he went.

Meanwhile, a body of long discontented and bad citizens, about two hundred in number, having got into a strong part of the town called the Issorion, where the temple of Diana stands, seized and garrisoned it. The Spartans would have fallen upon them instantly; but Agesilaus, not knowing how far the sedition might reach, bade them forbear, and going himself in his ordinary dress, with but one servant, when he came near the rebels, called out, and told them that they mistook their orders; this was not the right place; they were to go, one part of them thither, showing them another place in the city, and part to another, which he also showed. The conspirators gladly heard this, thinking themselves unsuspected of treason, and readily went off to the places which he showed them. Whereupon Agesilaus placed in their room a guard of his own; and of the conspirators he apprehended fifteen, and put them to death in the night. But after this a much more dangerous conspiracy was discovered of Spartan citizens, who had privately met in each other's houses, plotting a revolution. These were men whom it was equally dangerous to prosecute publicly according to law and to connive at. Agesilaus took council with the Ephors, and put these also to death privately without process; a thing never before known in the case of any born Spartan.

At this time, also, many of the helots and country people, who were in the army, ran away to the enemy, which was a matter of great consternation to the city. He therefore caused some officers of his, every morning before day, to search the quarters of the soldiers, and where any man was gone, to hide his arms, that so the greatness of the number might not appear.

Historians differ about the cause of the Thebans' departure from Sparta. Some say, the winter forced them; as also that the Arcadian soldiers disbanding, made it necessary for the rest to retire. Others say that they stayed there three months, till they had laid the whole country waste. Theopompus is the only author who says that when the Bœotian generals had already resolved upon the retreat, Phrixus, the Spartan, came to them, and offered them from Agesilaus ten talents to be gone, so hiring them to do what they were already doing of their own accord. How he alone should come to be aware of this I know not; only in this all authors agree, that the saving of Sparta from ruin was wholly due to the wisdom of Agesilaus, who in this extremity of affairs quitted all his ambition and his haughtiness, and resolved to play a saving game. But all his wisdom and courage was not sufficient to recover the glory of it, and to raise it to its ancient greatness. For as we see in human bodies, long used to a very strict and too exquisitely regular diet, any single great disorder is usually fatal; so here one stroke overthrew the whole state's long prosperity. Nor can we be surprised at this. Lycurgus had formed a polity admirably designed for the peace, harmony, and virtuous life of the citizens; and their fall came from their assuming foreign dominion and arbitrary sway, things wholly undesirable, in the judgment of Lycurgus, for a well-conducted and happy state.

Agesilaus being now in years, gave over all military employments; but his son, Archidamus, having received help from Dionysius of Sicily, gave a great defeat to the Arcadians, in the fight known by the name of the Tearless Battle, in which there was a great slaughter of the enemy without the loss of one Spartan. Yet this victory, more than anything else, discovered the present weakness of Sparta; for heretofore victory was esteemed so usual a thing with them that for their greatest successes they merely sacrificed a cock to the gods. The soldiers never vaunted, nor did the citizens display any great joy at the news; even when the great victory, described by Thucydides, was obtained at Mantinea, the messenger that brought the news had no other reward than a piece of meat, sent by the magistrates from the common table. But at the news of this Arcadian victory they were not able to contain themselves; Agesilaus went out in procession with tears of joy in his eyes to meet and embrace his son, and all the magistrates and public officers attended him. The old men and the women marched out as far as the river Eurotas, lifting up their hands, and thanking the gods that Sparta was now cleared again of the disgrace and indignity that had befallen her, and once more saw the light of day. Since before, they tell us, the Spartan men, out of shame at their disasters, did not dare so much as to look their wives in the face.

When Epaminondas restored Messene, and recalled from all quarters the ancient citizens to inhabit it, they were not able to obstruct the design, being not in condition of appearing in the field against them. But it went greatly against Agesilaus in the minds of his countrymen, when they found so large a territory, equal to their own in compass, and for fertility the richest of all Greece, which they had enjoyed so long, taken from them in his reign. Therefore it was that the king broke off treaty with the Thebans when they offered him peace, rather than set his hand to the passing away of that country, though it was already taken from him. Which point of honour had like to have cost him dear; for not long after he was overreached by a stratagem, which had almost amounted to the loss of Sparta. For when the Mantineans again revolted from Thebes to Sparta, and Epaminondas understood that Agesilaus was come to their assistance with a powerful army, he privately in the night quitted his quarters of Tegea, and, unknown to the Mantineans, passing by Agesilaus, marched toward Sparta, insomuch that he failed very little of taking it empty and unarmed.

Agesilaus had intelligence sent him by Euthynus, the Thespian, as Callisthenes says, but Xenophon says by a Cretan; and immediately despatched a horseman to Lacedæmon to apprise them of it, and to let them know that he was hastening to them. Shortly after his arrival the Thebans crossed the Eurotas. They made an assault upon the town, and were received by Agesilaus with great courage, and with exertions beyond what was to be expected at his years. For he did not now fight with that caution and cunning which he formerly made use of, but put all upon a desperate push; which, though not his usual method, succeeded so well, that he rescued the city out of the very hands of Epaminondas, and forced him to retire, and, at the erection of a trophy, was able, in the presence of their wives and children, to declare that the Lacedæmonians had nobly paid their debt to their country, and particularly his son Archidamus, who had that day made himself illustrious, both by his courage and agility of body, rapidly passing about by the short lanes to every endangered point, and everywhere maintaining the town against the enemy with but few to help him.

Isadas, however, the son of Phœbidas, must have been, I think, the admiration of the enemy as well as of his friends. He was a youth of remarkable beauty and stature, in the very flower of the most attractive time of life, when the boy is just rising into the man. He had no arms upon him and scarcely clothes; he had just anointed himself at home, when, upon the alarm, without further awaiting, in that undress, he snatched a spear in one hand and a sword in the other, and broke his way through the combatants to the enemies, striking at all he met. He received no wound, whether it were that a special divine care rewarded his valour with an extraordinary protection, or whether his shape being so large and beautiful, and his dress so unusual, they thought him more than a man. The Ephors gave him a garland; but as soon as they had done so, they fined him a thousand drachmas for going out to battle unarmed.

A few days after this there was another battle fought near Mantinea, in which Epaminondas, having routed the van of the Lacedæmonians, was eager in the pursuit of them, when Anticrates, the Laconian, wounded him with a spear, says Dioscorides; but the Spartans to this day call the posterity of this Anticrates, swordsmen, because he wounded Epaminondas with a sword. They so dreaded Epaminondas when living, that the slayer of him was embraced and admired by all; they decreed honours and gifts to him, and an exemption from taxes to his posterity, a privilege enjoyed at this day by Callicrates, one of his descendants.

Epaminondas being slain, there was a general peace again concluded from which Agesilaus's party excluded the Messenians, as men that had no city, and therefore would not let them swear to the league; to which when the rest of the Greeks admitted them, the Lacedæmonians broke off, and continued the war alone, in hopes of subduing the Messenians. In this Agesilaus was esteemed a stubborn and headstrong man, and insatiable of war, who took such pains to undermine the general peace, and to protract the war at a time when he had not money to carry it on with, but was forced to borrow of his friends and raise subscriptions, with much difficulty, while the city, above all things, needed repose. And all this to recover the one poor town of Messene, after he had lost so great an empire both by sea and land, as the Spartans were possessed of, when he began to reign.

But it added still more to his ill-repute when he put himself into the service of Tachos, the Egyptian. They thought it too unworthy of a man of his high station, who was then looked upon as the first commander in all Greece, who had filled all countries with his renown, to let himself out to hire to a barbarian, an Egyptian rebel (for Tachos was no better), and to fight for pay, as captain only of a band of mercenaries. If, they said, at those years of eighty and odd, after his body had been worn out with age, and enfeebled with wounds, he had resumed that noble undertaking the liberation of the Greeks from Persia, it had been worthy of some reproof. To make an action honourable, it ought to be agreeable to the age and other circumstances of the person; since it is circumstance and proper measure that give an action its character, and make it either good or bad. But Agesilaus valued not other men's discourses; he thought no public employment dishonourable; the ignoblest thing in his esteem was for a man to sit idle and useless at home, waiting for his death to come and take him. The money, therefore, that he received from Tachos, he laid out in raising men, with whom, having filled his ships, he took also thirty Spartan counsellors with him, as formerly he had done in his Asiatic expedition, and set sail for Egypt.

As soon as he arrived in Egypt, all the great officers of the kingdom came to pay their compliments to him at his landing. His reputation, being so great, had raised the expectation of the whole country, and crowds flocked in to see him; but when they found, instead of the splendid prince whom they looked for, a little old man of contemptible appearance, without ceremony lying down upon the grass, in coarse and threadbare clothes, they fell into laughter and scorn of him, crying out that the old proverb was now made good, "The mountain had brought forth a mouse." They were yet more astonished at his stupidity, as they thought it, who, when presents were made him of all sorts of provisions, took only the meal, the calves, and the geese, but rejected the sweetmeats, the confections, and perfumes: and when they urged him to the acceptance of them, took them and gave them to the helots in his army. Yet he was taken, Theophrastus tells us, with the garlands they made of the papyrus, because of their simplicity, and when he returned home, he demanded one of the king which he carried with him.

When he joined with Tachos, he found his expectation of being general-in-chief disappointed. Tachos reserved that place for himself, making Agesilaus only captain of the mercenaries, and Chabrias, the Athenian, commander of the fleet. This was the first occasion of his discontent, but there followed others; he was compelled daily to submit to the insolence and vanity of this Egyptian, and was at length forced to attend him into Phœnicia, in a condition much below his character and dignity, which he bore and put up with for a time, till he had opportunity of showing his feelings. It was afforded him by Nectanabis, the cousin of Tachos, who commanded a large force under him, and shortly after deserted him, and was proclaimed king by the Egyptians. This man invited Agesilaus to join his party, and the like he did to Chabrias, offering great rewards to both. Tachos, suspecting it, immediately applied himself both to Agesilaus and Chabrias, with great humility beseeching their continuance in his friendship. Chabrias consented to it, and did what he could by persuasion and good words to keep Agesilaus with them. But he gave this short reply, "You, O Chabrias, came hither a volunteer, and may go and stay as you see cause; but I am the servant of Sparta, appointed to head the Egyptians, and therefore I cannot fight against those to whom I was sent as a friend, unless I am commanded to do so by my country." This being said, he despatched messengers to Sparta, who were sufficiently supplied with matter both for dispraise of Tachos and commendation of Nectanabis. The two Egyptians also sent their ambassadors to Lacedæmon, the one to claim continuance of the league already made, the other to make great offers for the breaking of it, and making a new one. The Spartans having heard both sides, gave in their public answer, that they referred the whole matter to Agesilaus; but privately wrote to him to act as he should find it best for the profit of the commonwealth. Upon receipt of his orders he at once changed sides, carrying all the mercenaries with him to Nectanabis, covering, with the plausible pretence of acting for the benefit of his country, a most questionable piece of conduct, which, stripped of that disguise, in real truth was no better than downright treachery. But the Lacedæmonians, who make it their first principle of action to serve their country's interest, know not anything to be just or unjust by any measure but that.

Tachos, being thus deserted by the mercenaries, fled for it; upon which a new king of the Mendesian province was proclaimed his successor, and came against Nectanabis with an army of one hundred thousand men. Nectanabis, in his talk with Agesilaus, professed to despise them as newly raised men, who, though many in number, were of no skill in war, being most of them mechanics and tradesmen, never bred to war. To whom Agesilaus answered, that he did not fear their numbers, but did fear their ignorance, which gave no room for employing stratagem against them. Stratagem only avails with men who are alive to suspicion, and, expecting to be assailed, expose themselves by their attempts at defence; but one who has no thought or expectation of anything, gives as little opportunity to the enemy as he who stands stock-still does to a wrestler. The Mendesian was not wanting in solicitations of Agesilaus, insomuch that Nectanabis grew jealous. But when Agesilaus advised to fight the enemy at once, saying it was folly to protract the war and rely on time, in a contest with men who had no experience in fighting battles, but with their great numbers might be able to surround them, and cut off their communications by entrenchments, and anticipate them in many matters of advantage, this altogether confirmed him in his fears and suspicions. He took quite the contrary course, and retreated into a large and strongly fortified town. Agesilaus, finding himself mistrusted, took it very ill, and was full of indignation, yet was ashamed to change sides back again, or to go away without effecting anything, so that he was forced to follow Nectanabis into the town.

When the enemy came up, and began to draw lines about the town, and to entrench, the Egyptian now resolved upon a battle out of fear of a siege. And the Greeks were eager for it, provisions growing already scarce in the town. When Agesilaus opposed it, the Egyptians then suspected him much more, publicly calling him the betrayer of the king. But Agesilaus, being now satisfied within himself, bore these reproaches patiently, and followed the design which he had laid, of over-reaching the enemy, which was this.

The enemy were forming a deep ditch and high wall, resolving to shut up the garrison and starve it. When the ditch was brought almost quite round and the two ends had all but met, he took the advantage of the night and armed all his Greeks. Then going to the Egyptian, "This, young man, is your opportunity," said he, "of saving yourself, which I all this while durst not announce, lest discovery should prevent it; but now the enemy has, at his own cost, and the pains and labour of his own men, provided for our security. As much of this wall as is built will prevent them from surrounding us with their multitude, the gap yet left will be sufficient for us to sally out by; now play the man, and follow the example the Greeks will give you, and by fighting valiantly save yourself and your army; their front will not be able to stand against us, and their rear we are sufficiently secured from by a wall of their own making."

Nectanabis, admiring the sagacity of Agesilaus, immediately placed himself in the middle of the Greek troops, and fought with them; and upon the first charge soon routed the enemy. Agesilaus having now gained credit with the king, proceeded to use, like a trick in wrestling, the same stratagem over again. He sometimes pretended a retreat, at other times advanced to attack their flanks, and by this means at last drew them into a place enclosed between two ditches that were very deep and full of water. When he had them at this advantage, he soon charged them, drawing up the front of his battle equal to the space between the two ditches, so that they had no way of surrounding him, being enclosed themselves on both sides. They made but little resistance; many fell, others fled and were dispersed.

Nectanabis, being thus settled and fixed in his kingdom, with much kindness and affection invited Agesilaus to spend his winter in Egypt, but he made haste home to assist in wars of his own country, which was, he knew, in want of money, and forced to hire mercenaries, whilst their own men were fighting abroad. The king, therefore, dismissed him very honourably, and among other gifts presented him with two hundred and thirty talents of silver toward the charge of the war. But the weather being tempestuous, his ships kept inshore, and passing along the coast of Africa he reached an uninhabited spot called the Port of Menelaus, and here, when his ships were just upon landing, he expired, being eighty-four years old, and having reigned in Lacedæmon forty-one. Thirty of which years he passed with the reputation of being the greatest and most powerful man of all Greece, and was looked upon as, in a manner, general and king of it, until the battle of Leuctra. It was the custom of the Spartans to bury their common dead in the place where they died, whatsoever country it was, but their kings they carried home. The followers of Agesilaus, for want of honey, enclosed his body in wax, and so conveyed him to Lacedæmon.

His son, Archidamus, succeeded him on his throne; so did his posterity successively to Agis, the fifth from Agesilaus; who was slain by Leonidas, while attempting to restore the ancient discipline of Sparta.

POMPEY

THE people of Rome seem to have entertained for Pompey from his childhood the same affection that Prometheus, in the tragedy of Æschylus, expresses for Hercules, speaking of him as the author of his deliverance, in these words:—

> "Ah cruel Sire! how dear thy son to me!
> The generous offspring of my enemy!"

For on the one hand, never did the Romans give such demonstrations of a vehement and fierce hatred against any of their generals as they did against Strabo, the father of Pompey; during whose lifetime, it is true, they stood in awe of his military power, as indeed he was a formidable warrior, but immediately upon his death, which happened by a stroke of thunder, they treated him with the utmost contumely, dragging his corpse from the bier, as it was carried to his funeral. On the other side, never had any Roman the people's good-will and devotion more zealous throughout all the changes of fortune, more early in its first springing up, or more steadily rising with his prosperity, or more constant in his adversity than Pompey had. In Strabo, there was one great cause of their hatred, his insatiable covetousness; in Pompey, there were many that helped to make him the object of their love; his temperance, his skill and exercise in war, his eloquence of speech, integrity of mind, and affability in conversation and address; insomuch that no man ever asked a favour with less offence, or conferred one with a better grace. When he gave, it was without assumption; when he received, it was with dignity and honour.

In his youth, his countenance pleaded for him, seeming to anticipate his eloquence, and win upon the affections of the people before he spoke. His beauty even in his bloom of youth had something in it at once of gentleness and dignity; and when his prime of manhood came, the majesty and kingliness of his character at once became visible in it. His hair sat somewhat hollow or rising a little; and this, with the languishing motion of his eyes, seemed to form a resemblance in his face, though perhaps more talked of than really apparent, to the statues of the King Alexander. And because many applied that name to him in his youth, Pompey himself did not decline it, insomuch that some called him so in derision. And Lucius

Philippus, a man of consular dignity, when he was pleading in favour of him, thought it not unfit to say, that people could not be surprised if Philip was a lover of Alexander.

It is related of Flora, the courtesan, that when she was now pretty old, she took great delight in speaking of her early familiarity with Pompey, and was wont to say that she could never part after being with him without a bite. She would further tell, that Geminius, a companion of Pompey's, fell in love with her, and made his court with great importunity; and on her refusing, and telling him, however her inclinations were, yet she could not gratify his desires for Pompey's sake, he therefore made his request to Pompey, and Pompey frankly gave his consent, but never afterwards would have any converse with her, notwithstanding that he seemed to have a great passion for her; and Flora, on this occasion, showed none of the levity that might have been expected of her, but languished for some time after under a sickness brought on by grief and desire. This Flora, we are told, was such a celebrated beauty, that Cæcilius Metellus, when he adorned the temple of Castor and Pollux with paintings and statues, among the rest dedicated hers for her singular beauty. In his conduct also to the wife of Demetrius, his freed servant (who had great influence with him in his lifetime, and left an estate of four thousand talents), Pompey acted contrary to his usual habits, not quite fairly or generously, fearing lest he should fall under the common censure of being enamoured and charmed with her beauty, which was irresistible, and became famous everywhere. Nevertheless, though he seemed to be so extremely circumspect and cautious, yet even in matters of this nature he could not avoid the calumnies of his enemies, but upon the score of married women, they accused him, as if he had connived at many things, and embezzled the public revenue to gratify their luxury.

Of his easiness of temper and plainness, in what related to eating and drinking, the story is told that, once in a sickness, when his stomach nauseated common meats, his physician prescribed him a thrush to eat, but upon search, there was none to be bought, for they were not then in season, and one telling him they were to be had at Lucullus's, who kept them all the year round, "So then," said he, "if it were not for Lucullus's luxury, Pompey should not live;" and thereupon, not minding the prescription of the physician, he contented himself with such meat as could easily be procured. But this was at a later time.

Being as yet a very young man, and upon an expedition in which his father was commanding against Cinna, he had in his tent with him one Lucius Terentius, as his companion and comrade, who, being corrupted by Cinna, entered into an engagement to kill Pompey, as others had done to set the general's tent on fire. This conspiracy being discovered to Pompey at supper, he showed no discomposure at it, but on the contrary drank more liberally than usual, and expressed great kindness to Terentius; but about bedtime, pretending to go to his repose, he stole away secretly out of the tent, and setting a guard about his father, quietly expected the event. Terentius, when he thought the proper time come, rose with his naked sword, and coming to Pompey's bedside stabbed several strokes through the bedclothes, as if he were Iying there. Immediately after this there was a great uproar throughout all the camp, arising from the hatred they bore to the general, and an universal movement of the soldiers to revolt, all tearing down their tents and betaking themselves to their arms. The general himself all this while durst not venture out because of the tumult; but Pompey, going about in the midst of them, besought them with tears; and at last threw himself prostrate upon his face before the gate of the camp, and lay there in the passage at their feet shedding tears, and bidding those that were marching off, if they would go, trample upon him. Upon which, none could help going back again, and all, except eight hundred, either through shame or compassion, repented, and were reconciled to the general.

Immediately upon the death of Strabo, there was an action commenced against Pompey, as his heir, for that his father had embezzled the public treasure. But Pompey, having traced the principal thefts, charged them upon one Alexander, a freed slave of his father's, and proved before the judges that he had been the appropriator. But he himself was accused of having in his possession some hunting tackle, and books, that were taken at Asculum. To this he confessed thus far, that he received them from his father when he took Asculum, but pleaded further, that he had lost them since, upon Cinna's return to Rome, when his house was broken open and plundered by Cinna's guards. In this cause he had a great many preparatory pleadings against his accuser, in which he showed in activity and steadfastness beyond his years, and gained great reputation and favour, insomuch that Antistius, the prætor and judge of the cause, took a great liking to him, and offered him his daughter in marriage, having had some communications with his friends about it. Pompey accepted the proposal, and they were privately contracted; however, the secret was not so closely kept as to escape the multitude, but it was discernible enough, from the favour shown him by Antistius in his cause. And at last, when Antistius pronounced the absolutory sentence of the judges, the people, as if it had been upon a signal given, made the acclamation used according to ancient custom at marriages, *Talasio.* The origin of which custom is related to be this. At the time when the daughters of the Sabines came to Rome, to see the shows and sports there, and were violently seized upon by the most distinguished and bravest of the Romans for wives, it happened that some goatswains and herdsmen of the meaner rank were carrying off a beautiful and tall maiden; and lest any of their betters should meet them, and take her away, as they ran, they cried out with one voice, *Talasio*, Talasius being a well-known and popular person among them, insomuch that all that heard the name clapped their hands for joy, and joined with them in the shout, as applauding and congratulating the chance. Now, say they, because this proved a fortunate match to Talasius, hence it is that this acclamation is sportively used as a nuptial cry at all weddings. This is the most credible of the accounts that are given of the Talasio. And some few days after this judgment, Pompey married Antistia.

After this he went to Cinna's camp, where, finding some false suggestions and calumnies prevailing against him, he began to be afraid, and presently withdrew himself secretly; which sudden disappearance occasioned great suspicion. And there went a rumour and speech through all the camp that Cinna had murdered the young man; upon which all that had been anyways disobliged, and bore any malice to him, resolved to make an assault upon him. He, endeavouring to make his escape, was seized by a centurion, who pursued him with his naked sword. Cinna, in this distress, fell upon his knees, and offered him his seal-ring, of great value, for his ransom; but the centurion repulsed him insolently, saying, "I did not come to seal a covenant, but to be revenged upon a lawless and wicked tyrant;" and so despatched him immediately.

Thus Cinna being slain, Carbo, a tyrant yet more senseless than he, took the command and exercised it, while Sylla meantime was approaching, much to the joy and satisfaction of most people, who in their present evils were ready to find some comfort if it were but in the exchange of a master. For the city was brought to that pass by oppression and calamities that, being utterly in despair of liberty, men were only anxious for the mildest and most tolerable bondage. At that time Pompey was in Picenum in Italy, where he spent some time amusing himself, as he had estates in the country there, though the chief motive of his stay was the liking he felt for the towns of that district, which all regarded him with hereditary feelings of kindness and attachment. But when he now saw that the noblest and best of the city began to forsake their homes and property, and fly from all quarters to Sylla's camp, as to their haven, he likewise was desirous to go; not, however, as a fugitive, alone and with nothing to offer, but as a friend rather than a suppliant, in a way that would gain him honour, bringing help along with him, and at the head of a body of troops. Accordingly he solicited the Picentines for their assistance, who as cordially embraced his motion, and rejected the messengers sent from Carbo; insomuch that a certain Vindius taking upon him to say that Pompey was come from the school-room to put himself at the head of the people, they were so incensed that they fell forthwith upon this Vindius and killed him.

From henceforward Pompey, finding a spirit of government upon him, though not above twenty-three years of age, nor deriving an authority by commission from any man, took the privilege to grant himself full power, and, causing a tribunal to be erected in the market-place of Auximum, a populous city, expelled two of their principal men, brothers, of the name of Ventidius, who were acting against him in Carbo's interest, commanding them by a public edict to depart the city; and then proceeding to levy soldiers, issuing out commissions to centurions and other officers, according to the form of military discipline. And in this manner he went round all the rest of the cities in the district. So that those of Carbo's faction flying, and all others cheerfully submitting to his command, in a little time he mustered three entire legions, having supplied himself besides with all manner of provisions, beasts of burden, carriages, and other necessaries of war. And with this equipage he set forward on his march toward Sylla, not as if he were in haste, or desirous of escaping observation, but by small journeys, making several halts upon the road, to distress and annoy the enemy, and exerting himself to detach from Carbo's interest every part of Italy that he passed through.

Three commanders of the enemy encountered him at once, Carinna, Clœlius, and Brutus, and drew up their forces, not all in the front, nor yet together on any one part, but encamping three several armies in a circle about him, they resolved to encompass and overpower him. Pompey was noway alarmed at this, but collecting all his troops into one body, and placing his horse in the front of the battle, where he himself was in person, he singled out and bent all his forces against Brutus, and when the Celtic horsemen from the enemy's side rode out to meet him, Pompey himself encountering hand to hand with the foremost and stoutest among them, killed him with his spear. The rest seeing this turned their backs and fled, and breaking the ranks of their own foot, presently caused a general rout; whereupon the commanders fell out among themselves, and marched off, some one way, some another, as their fortunes led them, and the towns round about came in and surrendered themselves to Pompey, concluding that the enemy was dispersed for fear. Next after these, Scipio, the consul, came to attack him, and with as little success; for before the armies could join, or be within the throw of their javelins, Scipio's soldiers saluted Pompey's, and came over to them, while Scipio made his escape by flight. Last of all, Carbo himself sent down several troops of horse against him by the river Arsis, which Pompey assailed with the same courage and success as before; and having routed and put them to flight, he forced them in the pursuit into difficult ground, unpassable for horse, where, seeing no hopes of escape, they yielded themselves with their horses and armour, all to his mercy.

Sylla was hitherto unacquainted with all these actions; and on the first intelligence he received of his movements was in great anxiety about him, fearing lest he should be cut off among so many and such experienced commanders of the enemy, and marched therefore with all speed to his aid. Now Pompey, having advice of his approach, sent out orders to his officers to marshal and draw up all his forces in full array, that they might make the finest and noblest appearance before the commander-in-chief; for he expected indeed great honours from him, but met with even greater. For as soon as Sylla saw him thus advancing, his army so well appointed, his men so young and strong, and their spirits so high and hopeful with their successes, he alighted from his horse, and being first, as was his due, saluted by them with the title of Imperator, he returned the salutation upon Pompey, in the same term and style of Imperator, which might well cause surprise, as none could have ever anticipated that he would have imparted, to one so young in years and not yet a senator, a title which was the object of contention between him and the Scipios and Marii. And indeed all the rest of his deportment was agreeable to this first compliment; whenever Pompey came into his presence, he paid some sort of respect to him, either in rising and being uncovered, or the like, which he was rarely seen to do with any one else, notwithstanding that there were many about him of great rank and honour. Yet Pompey was not puffed up at all, or exalted with these favours. And when Sylla would have sent him with all expedition into Gaul, a province in which it was thought Metellus, who commanded in it, had done nothing worthy of the large forces at his disposal, Pompey urged that it could not be fair or honourable for him to take a province out of the hands of his senior in command and his superior in reputation; however, if Metellus were willing, and should request his service, he should be very ready to accompany and assist him in the war, which when Metellus came to understand, he approved of the proposal, and invited him over by letter. On this Pompey fell immediately into Gaul, where he not only achieved wonderful exploits of himself, but also fired up and kindled again that bold and warlike spirit, which old age had in a manner extinguished in Metellus, into a new heat; just as molten copper, they say, when poured upon that which is cold and solid, will dissolve and melt it faster than fire itself. But as when a famous wrestler has gained the first place among men, and borne away the prizes at all the games, it is not usual to take account of his victories as a boy, or to enter them upon record among the rest; so with the exploits of Pompey in his youth, though they were extraordinary in themselves, yet because they were obscured and buried in the multitude and greatness of his later wars and conquests, I dare not be particular in them, lest, by trifling away time in the lesser moments of his youth, we should be driven to omit those greater actions and fortunes which best illustrate his character.

Now, when Sylla had brought all Italy under his dominion, and was proclaimed dictator, he began to reward the rest of his followers, by giving them wealth, appointing them to offices in the state, and granting them freely and without restriction any favours they asked for. But as for Pompey, admiring his valour and conduct, and thinking that he might prove a great stay and support to him hereafter in his affairs, he sought means to attach him to himself by some personal alliance, and his wife Metella joining in his wishes, they two persuaded Pompey to put away Antistia, and marry Æmilia, the step-daughter of Sylla, born by Metella to Scaurus, her former husband, she being at that very time the wife of another man, living with him, and with child by him. These were the very tyrannies of marriage, and much more agreeable to the times under Sylla than to the nature and habits of Pompey; that Æmilia great with child should be, as it were, ravished from the embraces of another for him, and that Antistia should be divorced with dishonour and misery by him, for whose sake she had been but just before bereft of her father. For Antistius was murdered in the senate, because he was suspected to be a favourer of Sylla for Pompey's sake; and her mother, likewise, after she had seen all these indignities, made away with herself, a new calamity to be added to the tragic accompaniments of this marriage, and that there might be nothing wanting to complete them, Æmilia herself died, almost immediately after entering Pompey's house, in childbed.

About this time news came to Sylla that Perpenna was fortifying himself in Sicily, that the island was now become a refuge and receptacle for the relics of the adverse party, that Carbo was hovering about those seas with a navy, that Domitius had fallen in upon Africa, and that many of the exiled men of note who had escaped from the proscriptions were daily flocking into those parts. Against these, therefore, Pompey was sent with a large force; and no sooner was he arrived in Sicily, but Perpenna immediately departed, leaving the whole island to him. Pompey received the distressed cities into favour, and treated all with great humanity, except the Mamertines in Messena; for when they protested against his court and jurisdiction, alleging their privilege and exemption founded upon an ancient charter or grant of the Romans, he replied sharply, "What! will you never cease prating of laws to us that have swords by our sides?" It was thought, likewise, that he showed some inhumanity to Carbo, seeming rather to insult over his misfortunes than to chastise his crimes. For if there had been a necessity, as perhaps there was, that he should be taken off, that might have been done at first, as soon as he was taken prisoner, for then it would have been the act of him that commanded it. But here Pompey commanded a man that had been thrice consul of Rome to be brought in fetters to stand at the bar, he himself sitting upon the bench in judgment, examining the cause with the formalities of law, to the offence and indignation of all that were present, and afterwards ordered him to be taken away and put to death. It is related, by the way, of Carbo, that as soon as he was brought to the place, and saw the sword drawn for execution, he was suddenly seized with a looseness or pain in his bowels, and desired a little respite of the executioner, and a convenient place to relieve himself. And yet further, Caius Oppius, the friend of Cæsar, tells us, that Pompey dealt cruelly with Quintus Valerius, a man of singular learning and science. For when he was brought to him, he walked aside, and drew him into conversation, and after putting a variety of questions to him, and receiving answers from him, he ordered his officers to take him away and put him to death. But we must not be too credulous in the case of narratives told by Oppius, especially when he undertakes to relate anything touching the friends or foes of Cæsar. This is certain, that there lay a necessity upon Pompey to be severe upon many of Sylla's enemies, those at least that were eminent persons in themselves, and notoriously known to be taken; but for the rest, he acted with all the clemency possible for him, conniving at the concealment of some, and himself being the instrument in the escape of others. So in the case of the Himeræans; for when Pompey had determined on severely punishing their city, as they had been abettors of the enemy, Sthenis, the leader of the people there, craving liberty of speech, told him that what he was about to do was not at all consistent with justice, for that he would pass by the guilty and destroy the innocent; and on Pompey demanding who that guilty person was that would assume the offences of them all, Sthenis replied it was himself, who had engaged his friends by persuasion to what they had done, and his enemies by force; whereupon Pompey, being much taken with the frank speech and noble spirit of the man, first forgave his crime, and then pardoned all the rest of the Himeræans. Hearing, likewise, that his soldiers were very disorderly in their march, doing violence upon the roads, he ordered their swords to be sealed up in their scabbards, and whosoever kept them not so were severely punished.

Whilst Pompey was thus busy in the affairs and government of Sicily, he received a decree of the senate, and a commission from Sylla, commanding him forthwith to sail into Africa, and make war upon Domitius with all his forces: for Domitius had rallied up a far greater army than Marius had had not long since, when he sailed out of Africa into Italy, and caused a revolution in Rome, and himself, of a fugitive outlaw, became a tyrant. Pompey, therefore, having prepared everything with the utmost speed, left Memmius, his sister's husband, governor of Sicily, and set sail with one hundred and twenty galleys, and eight hundred other vessels laden with provisions, money, ammunition, and engines of battery. He arrived with his fleet, part at the port of Utica, part at Carthage; and no sooner was he landed, but seven thousand of the enemy revolted and came over to him, while his own forces that he brought with him consisted of six entire legions. Here they tell us of a pleasant incident that happened to him at his first arrival.

Some of his soldiers having by accident stumbled upon a treasure, by which they got a good sum of money, the rest of the army hearing this, began to fancy that the field was full of gold and silver, which had been hid there of old by the Carthaginians in the time of their calamities, and thereupon fell to work, so that the army was useless to Pompey for many days, being totally engaged in digging for the fancied treasure, he himself all the while walking up and down only, and laughing to see so many thousands together, digging and turning up the earth. Until at last, growing weary and hopeless, they came to themselves and returned to their general, begging him to lead them where he pleased, for that they had already received the punishment of their folly.

By this time Domitius had prepared himself and drawn out his army in array against Pompey; but there was a watercourse betwixt them craggy, and difficult to pass over; and this, together with a great storm of wind and rain pouring down even from break of day, seemed to leave but little possibility of their coming together; so that Domitius, not expecting any engagement that day, commanded his forces to draw off and retire to the camp. Now Pompey, who was watchful upon every occasion, making use of the opportunity, ordered a march forthwith, and having passed over the torrent, fell in immediately upon their quarters. The enemy was in great disorder and tumult, and in that confusion attempted a resistance; but they neither were all there, nor supported one another; besides, the wind having veered about beat the rain full in their faces. Neither indeed was the storm less troublesome to the Romans, for that they could not clearly discern one another, insomuch that even Pompey himself, being unknown, escaped narrowly; for when one of his soldiers demanded of him the word of battle, it happened that he was somewhat slow in his answer, which might have cost him his life.

The enemy being routed with a great slaughter (for it is said that of twenty thousand there escaped but three thousand), the army saluted Pompey by the name of Imperator; but he declined it, telling them that he could not by any means accept of that title as long as he saw the camp of the enemy standing; but if they designed to make him worthy of the honour, they must first demolish that. The soldiers on hearing this went at once and made an assault upon the works and trenches, and there Pompey fought without his helmet, in memory of his former danger, and to avoid the like. The camp was thus taken by storm, and among the rest Domitius was slain. After that overthrow, the cities of the country thereabouts were all either secured by surrender, or taken by storm. King Iarbas, likewise, a confederate and auxiliary of Domitius, was taken prisoner, and his kingdom was given to Hiempsal.

Pompey could not rest here, but being ambitious to follow the good fortune and use the valour of his army, entered Numidia; and marching forward many days' journey up into the country, he conquered all where-ever he came. And having revived the terror of the Roman power, which was now almost obliterated among the barbarous nations, he said likewise, that the wild beasts of Africa ought not to be left without some experience of the courage and success of the Romans, and therefore he bestowed some few days in hunting lions and elephants. And it is said that it was not above the space of forty days at the utmost in which he gave a total overthrow to the enemy, reduced Africa, and established the affairs of the kings and kingdoms of all that country, being then in the twenty-fourth year of his age.

When Pompey returned back to the city of Utica, there were presented to him letters and orders from Sylla, commanding him to disband the rest of his army, and himself with one legion only to wait there the coming of another general, to succeed him in the government. This, inwardly, was extremely grievous to Pompey, though he made no show of it. But the army resented it openly, and when Pompey besought them to depart and go home before him, they began to revile Sylla, and declared broadly that they were resolved not to forsake him, neither did they think it safe for him to trust the tyrant. Pompey at first endeavoured to appease and pacify them by fair speeches; but when he saw that his persuasions were vain, he left the bench, and retired to his tent with tears in his eyes. But the soldiers followed him, and seizing upon him, by force brought him again, and placed him in his tribunal; where great part of that day was spent in dispute, they on their part persuading him to stay and command them, he, on the other side, pressing upon them obedience and the danger of mutiny. At last, when they grew yet more importunate and clamourous, he swore that he would kill himself if they attempted to force him; and scarcely even thus appeased them. Nevertheless, the first tidings brought to Sylla were that Pompey was up in rebellion; on which he remarked to some of his friends,

"I see, then, it is my destiny to contend with children in my old age;" alluding at the same time to Marius, who, being but a mere youth, had given him great trouble, and brought him into extreme danger. But being undeceived afterwards by better intelligence, and finding the whole city prepared to meet Pompey, and receive him with every display of kindness and honour, he resolved to exceed them all. And, therefore, going out foremost to meet him and embracing him with great cordiality, he gave him his welcome aloud in the title of Magnus, or the Great, and bade all that were present call him by that name. Others say that he had this title first given him by a general acclamation of all the army in Africa, but that it was fixed upon him by this ratification of Sylla. It is certain that he himself was the last that owned the title; for it was a long time after, when he was sent proconsul into Spain against Sertorius, that he began to write himself in his letters and commissions by the name of Pompeius Magnus; common and familiar use having then worn off the invidiousness of the title. And one cannot but accord respect and admiration to the ancient Romans, who did not reward the successes of action and conduct in war alone with such honourable titles, but adorned likewise the virtue and services of eminent men in civil government with the same distinctions and marks of honour. Two persons received from the people the name of Maximus, or the Greatest, Valerius for reconciling the senate and people, and Fabius Rullus, because he put out of the senate certain sons of freed slaves who had been admitted into it because of their wealth.

Pompey now desired the honour of a triumph, which Sylla opposed, alleging that the law allowed that honour to none but consuls and prætors, and therefore Scipio the elder, who subdued the Carthaginians in Spain in far greater and nobler conflicts, never petitioned for a triumph, because he had never been consul or prætor; and if Pompey, who had scarcely yet fully grown a beard, and was not of age to be a senator, should enter the city in triumph, what a weight of envy would it bring, he said, at once upon his government and Pompey's honour. This was his language to Pompey, intimating that he could not by any means yield to his request, but if he would persist in his ambition, that he was resolved to interpose his power to humble him. Pompey, however, was not daunted; but bade Sylla recollect that more worshipped the rising than the setting sun; as if to tell him that his power was increasing and Sylla's in the wane. Sylla did not perfectly hear the words, but observing a sort of amazement and wonder in the looks and gestures of those that did hear them, he asked what it was that he said. When it was told him, he seemed astounded at Pompey's boldness, and cried out twice together, "Let him triumph," and when others began to show their disapprobation and offence at it, Pompey, it is said, to gall and vex them the more, designed to have his triumphant chariot drawn with four elephants (having brought over several which belonged to the African kings), but the gates of the city being too narrow, he was forced to desist from that project, and be content with horses. And when his soldiers, who had not received as large rewards as they had expected, began to clamour, and interrupt the triumph, Pompey regarded these as little as the rest, and plainly told them that he had rather lose the honour of his triumph than flatter them. Upon which Servilius, a man of great distinction, and at first one of the chief opposers of Pompey's triumph, said, he now perceived that Pompey was truly great and worthy of a triumph. It is clear that he might easily have been a senator, also, if he had wished, but he did not sue for that, being ambitious, it seems, only of unusual honours. For what wonder had it been for Pompey to sit in the senate before his time? But to triumph before he was in the senate was really an excess of glory.

And, moreover, it did not a little ingratiate him with the people, who were much pleased to see him after his triumph take his place again among the Roman knights. On the other side, it was no less distasteful to Sylla to see how fast he came on, and to what a height of glory and power he was advancing; yet being ashamed to hinder him, he kept quiet. But when, against his direct wishes, Pompey got Lepidus made consul, having openly joined in the canvass and, by the good-will the people felt for himself, conciliated their favour for Lepidus, Sylla could forbear no longer; but when he saw him coming away from the election through the forum with a great train after him, cried out to him, "Well, young man, I see you rejoice in your victory. And, indeed, is it not a most generous and worthy act, that the consulship should be given to Lepidus, the vilest of men, in preference to Catulus, the best and most deserving in the city, and all by your influence with the people? It will be well, however, for you to be wakeful and look to your interests; as you have been making your enemy stronger than yourself." But that which gave the clearest demonstration of Sylla's ill-will to Pompey was his last will and testament; for whereas he had bequeathed several legacies to all the rest of his friends, and appointed some of them guardians to his son, he passed by Pompey without the least remembrance. However, Pompey bore this with great moderation and temper; and when Lepidus and others were disposed to obstruct his interment in the Campus Martius, and to prevent any public funeral taking place, came forward in support of it, and saw his obsequies performed with all honour and security.

Shortly after the death of Sylla, his prophetic words were fulfilled; and Lepidus proposing to be the successor to all his power and authority, without any ambiguities or pretences, immediately appeared in arms, rousing once more and gathering about him all the long dangerous remains of the old factions, which had escaped the hand of Sylla. Catulus, his colleague who was followed by the sounder part of the senate and people, was a man of the greatest esteem among the Romans for wisdom and justice; but his talent lay in the government of the city rather than the camp, whereas the exigency required the skill of Pompey. Pompey, therefore, was not long in suspense which way to dispose of himself, but joining with the nobility, was presently appointed general of the army against Lepidus, who had already raised up war in great part of Italy, and held Cisalpine Gaul in subjection with an army under Brutus. As for the rest of his garrisons, Pompey subdued them with ease in his march, but Mutina in Gaul resisted in a formal siege, and he lay here a long time encamped against Brutus. In the meantime Lepidus marched in all haste against Rome, and sitting down before it with a crowd of followers, to the terror of those within, demanded a second consulship. But that fear quickly vanished upon letters sent from Pompey, announcing that he had ended the war without a battle; for Brutus, either betraying his army, or being betrayed by their revolt, surrendered himself to Pompey, and receiving a guard of horse, was conducted to a little town upon the river Po, where he was slain the next day by Geminius, in execution of Pompey's commands. And for this Pompey was much censured; for, having at the beginning of the revolt written to the senate that Brutus had voluntarily surrendered himself, immediately afterward he sent other letters, with matter of accusation against the man after he was taken off. Brutus, who, with Cassius, slew Cæsar, was son to this Brutus; neither in war nor in his death like his father, as appears at large in his life. Lepidus, upon this being driven out of Italy, fled to Sardinia, where he fell sick and died of sorrow, not for his public misfortunes, as they say, but upon the discovery of a letter proving his wife to have been unfaithful to him.

There yet remained Sertorius, a very different general from Lepidus, in possession of Spain, and making himself formidable to Rome; the final disease, as it were, in which the scattered evils of the civil wars had now collected. He had already cut off various inferior commanders, and was at this time coping with Metellus Pius, a man of repute and a good soldier, though perhaps he might now seem too slow, by reason of his age, to second and improve the happier moments of war, and might be sometimes wanting to those advantages which Sertorius, by his quickness and dexterity, would wrest out of his hands. For Sertorius was always hovering about, and coming upon him unawares, like a captain of thieves rather than soldiers, disturbing him perpetually with ambuscades and light skirmishes: whereas Metellus was accustomed to regular conduct, and fighting in battle array with full-armed soldiers. Pompey, therefore, keeping his army in readiness, made it his object to be sent in aid to Metellus; neither would he be induced to disband his forces, notwithstanding that Catulus called upon him to do so, but by some colourable device or other he still kept them in arms about the city, until the senate at last thought fit, upon the report of Lucius Philippus, to decree him that government. At that time, they say, one of the senators there expressing his wonder and demanding of Philippus whether his meaning was that Pompey should be sent into Spain as proconsul, "No," replied Philippus, "but as pro*consuls*," as if both consuls for that year were in his opinion wholly useless.

When Pompey was arrived in Spain, as is usual upon the fame of a new leader, men began to be inspired with new hopes, and those nations that had not entered into a very strict alliance with Sertorius began to waver and revolt; whereupon Sertorius uttered various arrogant and scornful speeches against Pompey, saying, in derision, that he should want no other weapon but a ferula and rod to chastise this boy with, if he were not afraid of that old woman, meaning Metellus. Yet in deed and reality he stood in awe of Pompey, and kept on his guard against him, as appeared by his whole management of the war, which he was observed to conduct much more warily than before: for Metellus, which one would not have imagined, was grown excessively luxurious in his habits, having given himself over to self-indulgence and pleasure, and from a moderate and temperate became suddenly a sumptuous and ostentatious liver, so that this very thing gained Pompey great reputation and good-will, as he made himself somewhat specially an example of frugality, although that virtue was habitual in him, and required no great industry to exercise it, as he was naturally inclined to temperance, and no ways inordinate in his desires. The fortune of the war was very various; nothing, however, annoyed Pompey so much as the taking of the town of Lauron by Sertorius. For when Pompey thought he had him safe enclosed, and had boasted somewhat largely of raising the siege, he found himself all of a sudden encompassed; insomuch that he durst not move out of his camp; but was forced to sit still whilst the city was taken and burnt before his face. However, afterwards, in a battle near Valentia, he gave a great defeat to Herennius and Perpenna, two commanders among the refugees who had fled to Sertorius, and now lieutenants under him, in which he slew above ten thousand men.

Pompey, being elated and filled with confidence by this victory, made all haste to engage Sertorius himself, and the rather lest Metellus should come in for a share in the honour of the victory. Late in the day towards sunset they joined battle near the river Sucro, both being in fear lest Metellus should come: Pompey, that he might engage alone, Sertorius, that he might have one alone to engage with. The issue of the battle proved doubtful, for a wing of each side had the better, but of the generals Sertorius had the greater honour, for that he maintained his post, having put to flight the entire division that was opposed to him, whereas Pompey was himself almost made a prisoner; for being set upon by a strong man at-arms that fought on foot (he being on horseback), as they were closely engaged hand to hand the strokes of their swords chanced to light upon their hands, but with a different success; for Pompey's was a slight wound only, whereas he cut off the other's hand. However, it happened so, that many now falling upon Pompey together, and his own forces there being put to the rout, he made his escape beyond expectation, by quitting his horse, and turning him out among the enemy. For the horse being richly adorned with golden trappings, and having a caparison of great value, the soldiers quarrelled among themselves for the booty, so that while they were fighting with one another, and dividing the spoil, Pompey made his escape. By break of day the next morning each drew out his forces into the field to claim the victory; but Metellus coming up, Sertorius vanished, having broken up and dispersed his army. For this was the way in which he used to raise and disband his armies, so that sometimes he would be wandering up and down all alone, and at other times again he would come pouring into the field at the head of no less than one hundred and fifty thousand fighting men, swelling of a sudden like a winter torrent.

When Pompey was going, after the battle, to meet and welcome Metellus, and when they were near one another, he commanded his attendants to lower their rods in honour of Metellus, as his senior and superior. But Metellus on the other side forbade it, and behaved himself in general very obligingly to him, not claiming any prerogative either in respect of his consular rank or seniority; excepting only that when they encamped together, the watchword was given to the whole camp by Metellus. But generally they had their camps asunder, being divided and distracted by the enemy, who took all shapes, and being always in motion, would by some skilful artifice appear in a variety of places almost in the same instant, drawing them from one attack to another, and at last keeping them from foraging, wasting the country, and holding the dominion of the sea, Sertorius drove them both out of that part of Spain which was under his control, and forced them, for want of necessaries, to retreat into provinces that did not belong to them.

Pompey, having made use of and expended the greatest part of his own private revenues upon the war, sent and demanded moneys of the senate, adding that, in case they did not furnish him speedily, he should be forced to return into Italy with his army. Lucullus being consul at that time, though at variance with Pompey, yet in consideration that he himself was a candidate for the command against Mithridates, procured and hastened these supplies, fearing lest there should be any pretence or occasion given to Pompey of returning home, who of himself was no less desirous of leaving Sertorius and of undertaking the war against Mithridates, as an enterprise which by all appearance would prove much more honourable and not so dangerous. In the meantime Sertorius died, being treacherously murdered by some of his own party; and Perpenna, the chief among them, took the command and attempted to carry on the same enterprises with Sertorius, having indeed the same forces and the same means, only wanting the same skill and conduct in the use of them. Pompey therefore marched directly against Perpenna, and finding him acting merely at random in his affairs, had a decoy ready for him, and sent out a detachment of ten cohorts into the level country with orders to range up and down and disperse themselves abroad. The bait took accordingly, and no sooner had Perpenna turned upon the prey and had them in chase, but Pompey appeared suddenly with all his army, and joining battle, gave him a total overthrow. Most of his officers were slain in the field, and he himself being brought prisoner to Pompey, was by his order put to death. Neither was Pompey guilty in this of ingratitude or unmindfulness of what had occurred in Sicily, which some have laid to his charge, but was guided by a high-minded policy and a deliberate counsel for the security of his country. For Perpenna, having in his custody all Sertorius's papers, offered to produce several letters from the greatest men in Rome, who, desirous of a change and subversion of the government, had invited Sertorius into Italy. And Pompey, fearing that these might be the occasion of worse wars than those which were now ended, thought it advisable to put Perpenna to death, and burnt the letters without reading them.

Pompey continued in Spain after this so long a time as was necessary for the suppression of all the greatest disorders in the province; and after moderating and allaying the more violent heats of affairs there, returned with his army into Italy, where he arrived, as chance would have it, in the height of the servile war. Accordingly, upon his arrival, Crassus, the commander in that war, at some hazard, precipitated a battle, in which he had great success, and slew upon the place twelve thousand three hundred of the insurgents. Nor yet was he so quick, but that fortune reserved to Pompey some share of honour in the success of this war, for five thousand of those that had escaped out of the battle fell into his hands; and when he had totally cut them off, he wrote to the senate, that Crassus had overthrown the slaves in battle, but that he had plucked up the whole war by the roots. And it was agreeable in Rome both thus to say, and thus to hear said, because of the general favour of Pompey. But of the Spanish war and the conquest of Sertorius, no one, even in jest, could have ascribed the honour to any one else. Nevertheless, all this high respect for him, and this desire to see him come home, were not unmixed with apprehensions and suspicions that he might perhaps not disband his army, but take his way by force of arms and a supreme command to the seat of Sylla. And so in the number of all those that ran out to meet him and congratulate his return, as many went out of fear as affection. But after Pompey had removed this alarm, by declaring beforehand that he would discharge the army after his triumph, those that envied him could now only complain that he affected popularity, courting the common people more than the nobility, and that whereas Sylla had abolished the tribuneship of the people, he designed to gratify the people by restoring that office, which was indeed the fact. For there was not any one thing that the people of Rome were more wildly eager for, or more passionately desired, than the restoration of that office, insomuch that Pompey thought himself extremely fortunate in this opportunity, despairing (if he were anticipated by some one else in this) of ever meeting with any other sufficient means of expressing his gratitude for the favours which he had received from the people.

Though a second triumph was decreed him, and he was declared consul, yet all these honours did not seem so great an evidence of his power and glory as the ascendant which he had over Crassus; for he, the wealthiest among all the statesmen of his time, and the most eloquent and greatest too, who had looked down on Pompey himself and on all others beneath him, durst not appear a candidate for the consulship before he had applied to Pompey. The request was made accordingly, and was eagerly embraced by Pompey, who had long sought an occasion to oblige him in some friendly office; so that he solicited for Crassus, and entreated the people heartily, declaring that their favour would be no less to him in choosing Crassus his colleague, than in making himself consul. Yet for all this, when they were created consuls, they were always at variance, and opposing one another. Crassus prevailed most in the senate, and Pompey's power was no less with the people, he having restored to them the office of tribune, and having allowed the courts of judicature to be transferred back to the knights by a new law. He himself in person, too, afforded them a most grateful spectacle, when he appeared and craved his discharge from the military service. For it is an ancient custom among the Romans that the knights, when they had served out their legal time in the wars, should lead their horses into the market-place before the two officers, called censors, and having given an account of the commanders and generals under whom they served, as also of the places and actions of their service, should be discharged, every man with honour or disgrace, according to his deserts. There were then sitting in state upon the bench two censors, Gellius and Lentulus, inspecting the knights, who were passing by in muster before them, when Pompey was seen coming down into the forum, with all the ensigns of a consul, but leading his horse in his hand. When he came up, he bade his lictors make way for him, and so he led his horse to the bench; the people being all this while in a sort of a maze, and all in silence, and the censors themselves regarding the sight with a mixture of respect and gratification. Then the senior censor examined him: "Pompeius Magnus, I demand of you whether you have served the full time in the wars that is prescribed by the law?" "Yes," replied Pompey, with a loud voice, "I have served all, and all under myself as general." The people hearing this gave a great shout, and made such an outcry for delight, that there was no appeasing it; and the censors rising from their judgment-seat accompanied him home to gratify the multitude who followed after, clapping their hands and shouting.

Pompey's consulship was now expiring, and yet his difference with Crassus increasing, when one Caius Aurelius, a knight, a man who had declined public business all his lifetime, mounted the hustings, and addressed himself in an oration to the assembly, declaring that Jupiter had appeared to him in a dream, commanding him to tell the consuls that they should not give up office until they were friends. After this was said, Pompey stood silent, but Crassus took him by the hand, and spoke in this manner: "I do not think, fellow-citizens, that I shall do anything mean or dishonourable in yielding first to Pompey, whom you were pleased to ennoble with the title of Great, when as yet he scarce had a hair on his face; and granted the honour of two triumphs before he had a place in the senate." Hereupon they were reconciled and laid down their office. Crassus resumed the manner of life which he had always pursued before; but Pompey in the great generality of causes for judgment declined appearing on either side, and by degrees withdrew himself totally from the forum, showing himself but seldom in public; and, whenever he did, it was with a great train after him. Neither was it easy to meet or visit him without a crowd of people about him; he was most pleased to make his appearance before large numbers at once, as though he wished to maintain in this way his state and majesty, and as if he held himself bound to preserve his dignity from contact with the addresses and conversation of common people. And life in the robe of peace is only too apt to lower the reputation of men that have grown great by arms, who naturally find difficulty in adapting themselves to the habits of civil equality. They expect to be treated as the first in the city, even as they were in the camp; and on the other hand, men who in war were nobody think it intolerable if in the city at any rate they are not to take the lead. And so when a warrior renowned for victories and triumphs shall turn advocate and appear among them in the forum, they endeavour their utmost to obscure and depress him; whereas, if he gives up any pretensions here and retires, they will maintain his military honour and authority beyond the reach of envy. Events themselves not long after showed the truth of this.

The power of the pirates first commenced in Cilicia, having in truth but a precarious and obscure beginning, but gained life and boldness afterwards in the wars of Mithridates, where they hired themselves out and took employment in the king's service. Afterwards, whilst the Romans were embroiled in their civil wars, being engaged against one another even before the very gates of Rome, the seas lay waste and unguarded, and by degrees enticed and drew them on not only to seize upon and spoil the merchants and ships upon the seas, but also to lay waste the islands and seaport towns. So that now there embarked with these pirates men of wealth and noble birth and superior abilities, as if it had been a natural occupation to gain distinction in. They had divers arsenals, or piratic harbours, as likewise watch-towers and beacons, all along the sea-coast; and fleets were here received that were well manned with the finest mariners, and well served with the expertest pilots, and composed of swift-sailing and light-built vessels adapted for their special purpose. Nor was it merely their being thus formidable that excited indignation; they were even more odious for their ostentation than they were feared for their force. Their ships had gilded masts at their stems; the sails woven of purple, and the oars plated with silver, as if their delight were to glory in their iniquity. There was nothing but music and dancing, banqueting and revels, all along the shore. Officers in command were taken prisoners, and cities put under contribution, to the reproach and dishonour of the Roman supremacy.

There were of these corsairs above one thousand sail, and they had taken no less than four hundred cities, committing sacrilege upon the temples of the gods, and enriching themselves with the spoils of many never violated before, such as were those of Claros, Didyma, and Samothrace; and the temple of the Earth in Hermione, and that of Æsculapius in Epidaurus, those of Neptune at the Isthmus, at Tænarus, and at Calauria; those of Apollo at Actium and Leucas, and those of Juno in Samos, at Argos, and at Lacinium. They themselves offered strange sacrifices upon Mount Olympus, and performed certain secret rites or religious mysteries, among which those of Mithras have been preserved to our own time, having received their previous institution from them. But besides these insolencies by sea, they were also injurious to the Romans by land; for they would often go inland up the roads, plundering and destroying their villages and country-houses. Once they seized upon two Roman prætors, Sextilius and Bellinus, in their purple-edged robes, and carried them off together with their officers and lictors. The daughter also of Antonius, a man that had had the honour of a triumph, taking a journey into the country, was seized, and redeemed upon payment of a large ransom. But it was most abusive of all that, when any of the captives declared himself to be a Roman, and told his name, they affected to be surprised, and feigning fear, smote their thighs and fell down at his feet, humbly beseeching him to be gracious and forgive them.

The captives, seeing them so humble and suppliant, believed them to be in earnest; and some of them now would proceed to put Roman shoes on his feet, and to dress him in a Roman gown, to prevent, they said, his being mistaken another time. After all this pageantry, when they had thus deluded and mocked him long enough, at last putting out a ship's ladder, when they were in the midst of the sea, they told him he was free to go, and wished him a pleasant journey; and if he resisted they themselves threw him overboard and drowned him.

This piratic power having got the dominion and control of all the Mediterranean, there was left no place for navigation or commerce. And this it was which most of all made the Romans, finding themselves to be extremely straitened in their markets, and considering that if it should continue, there would be a dearth and famine in the land, determined at last to send out Pompey to recover the seas from the pirates. Gabinius, one of Pompey's friends, preferred a law, whereby there was granted to him, not only the government of the seas as admiral, but, in direct words, sole and irresponsible sovereignty over all men. For the decree gave him absolute power and authority in all the seas within the pillars of Hercules, and in the adjacent mainland for the space of four hundred furlongs from the sea. Now there were but few regions in the Roman empire out of that compass; and the greatest of the nations and most powerful of the kings were included in the limit. Moreover, by this decree he had a power of selecting fifteen lieutenants out of the senate, and of assigning to each his province in charge; then he might take likewise out of the treasury and out of the hands of the revenue-farmers what moneys he pleased; as also two hundred sail of ships, with a power to press and levy what soldiers and seamen he thought fit.

When this law was read, the common people approved of it exceedingly, but the chief men and most important among the senators looked upon it as an exorbitant power, even beyond the reach of envy, but well deserving their fears. Therefore concluding with themselves that such unlimited authority was dangerous, they agreed unanimously to oppose the bill, and all went against it, except Cæsar, who gave his vote for the law, not to gratify Pompey, but the people, whose favour he had courted underhand from the beginning, and hoped to compass for himself. The rest inveighed bitterly against Pompey, insomuch that one of the consuls told him that, if he was ambitious of the place of Romulus, he would scarce avoid his end, but he was in danger of being torn to pieces by the multitude for his speech. Yet when Catulus stood up to speak against the law, the people in reverence to him were silent and attentive. And when, after saying much in the most honourable terms in favour of Pompey, he proceeded to advise the people in kindness to spare him, and not to expose a man of his value to such a succession of dangers and wars, "For," said he, "where could you find another Pompey, or whom would you have in case you should chance to lose him?" they all cried out with one voice, "Yourself." And so Catulus, finding all his rhetoric ineffectual, desisted. Then Roscius attempted to speak, but could obtain no hearing, and made signs with his fingers, intimating, "Not him alone," but that there might be a second Pompey or colleague in authority with him. Upon this, it is said, the multitude, being extremely incensed, made such a loud outcry, that a crow flying over the market-place at that instant was struck, and dropped down among the crowd; whence it would appear that the cause of birds falling down to the ground is not any rupture or division of the air causing a vacuum, but purely the actual stroke of the voice, which, when carried up in a great mass and with violence, raises a sort of tempest and billow, as it were, in the air.

The assembly broke up for that day; and when the day was come on which the bill was to pass by suffrage into a decree, Pompey went privately into the country; but hearing that it was passed and confirmed, he returned again into the city by night, to avoid the envy that might be occasioned by the concourse of people that would meet and congratulate him. The next morning he came abroad and sacrificed to the gods, and having audience at an open assembly, so handled the matter that they enlarged his power, giving him many things besides what was already granted, and almost doubling the preparation appointed in the former decree. Five hundred ships were manned for him, and an army raised of one hundred and twenty thousand foot and five thousand horse. Twenty-four senators that had been generals of armies were appointed to serve as lieutenants under him, and to these were added two quæstors. Now it happened within this time that the prices of provisions were much reduced which gave an occasion to the joyful people of saying that the very name of Pompey had ended the war. However, Pompey, in pursuance of his charge, divided all the seas and the whole Mediterranean into thirteen parts, allotting a squadron to each, under the command of his officers; and having thus dispersed his power into all quarters, and encompassed the pirates everywhere, they began to fall into his hands by whole shoals, which he seized and brought into his harbours. As for those that withdrew themselves betimes, or otherwise escaped his general chase, they all made to Cilicia, where they hid themselves as in their hives; against whom Pompey now proceeded in person with sixty of his best ships, not, however, until he had first scoured and cleared all the seas near Rome, the Tyrrhenian, and the African, and all the waters of Sardinia, Corsica, and Sicily; all which he performed in the space of forty days by his own indefatigable industry and the zeal of his lieutenants.

Pompey met with some interruption in Rome, through the malice and envy of Piso, the consul, who had given some check to his proceedings by withholding his stores and discharging his seamen; whereupon he sent his fleet round to Brundusium, himself going the nearest way by land through Tuscany to Rome; which was no sooner known by the people than they all flocked out to meet him upon the way as if they had not sent him out but a few days before. What chiefly excited their joy was the unexpectedly rapid change in the markets, which abounded now with the greatest plenty, so that Piso was in great danger to have been deprived of his consulship, Gabinius having a law ready prepared for that purpose; but Pompey forbade it, behaving himself as in that, so in all things else, with great moderation, and when he had made sure of all that he wanted or desired, he departed for Brundusium, whence he set sail in pursuit of the pirates. And though he was straitened in time, and his hasty voyage forced him to sail by several cities without touching, yet he would not pass by the city of Athens unsaluted; but landing there, after he had sacrificed to the gods, and made an address to the people, as he was returning out of the city, he read at the gates two epigrams, each in a single line, written in his own praise; one within the gate:—

> "Thy humbler thoughts make thee a god the more;"

the other without:—

> "Adieu we bid, who welcome bade before."

Now because Pompey had shown himself merciful to some of these pirates that were yet roving in bodies about the seas, having upon their supplication ordered a seizure of their ships and persons only, without any further process or severity, therefore the rest of their comrades, in hopes of mercy too, made their escape from his other commanders, and surrendered themselves with their wives and children into his protection. He continued to pardon all that came in, and the rather because by them he might make discovery of those who fled from his justice, as conscious that their crimes were beyond an act of indemnity. The most numerous and important part of these conveyed their families and treasures, with all their people that were unfit for war, into castles and strong forts about Mount Taurus; but they themselves, having well manned their galleys, embarked for Coracesium in Cilicia, where they received Pompey and gave him battle. Here they had a final overthrow, and retired to the land, where they were besieged. At last, having despatched their heralds to him with a submission, they delivered up to his mercy themselves, their towns, islands, and strongholds, all which they had so fortified that they were almost impregnable, and scarcely even accessible.

Thus was this war ended, and the whole power of the pirates at sea dissolved everywhere in the space of three months, wherein, besides a great number of other vessels, he took ninety men-of-war with brazen beaks; and likewise prisoners of war to the number of no less than twenty thousand.

As regarded the disposal of these prisoners, he never so much as entertained the thought of putting them to death; and yet it might be no less dangerous on the other hand to disperse them, as they might reunite and make head again, being numerous, poor, and warlike. Therefore wisely weighing with himself that man by nature is not a wild or unsocial creature, neither was he born so, but makes himself what he naturally is not by vicious habit; and that again, on the other side, he is civilised and grows gentle by a change of place, occupation, and manner of life, as beasts themselves that are wild by nature become tame and tractable by housing and gentler usage, upon this consideration he determined to translate these pirates from sea to land, and give them a taste of an honest and innocent course of life by living in towns and tilling the ground. Some therefore were admitted into the small and half-peopled towns of the Cilicians, who, for an enlargement of their territories, were willing to receive them. Others he planted in the city of the Solians, which had been lately laid waste by Tigranes, King of Armenia, and which he now restored. But the largest number were settled in Dyme, the town of Achæa, at that time extremely depopulated, and possessing an abundance of good land.

However, these proceedings could not escape the envy and censure of his enemies; and the course he took against Metellus in Crete was disapproved of even by the chiefest of his friends. For Metellus, a relation of Pompey's former colleague in Spain, had been sent prætor into Crete, before this province of the seas was assigned to Pompey. Now Crete was the second source of pirates next to Cilicia, and Metellus having shut up a number of them in their strongholds there was engaged in reducing and extirpating them. Those that were yet remaining and besieged sent their supplications to Pompey, and invited him into the island as a part of his province, alleging it to fall, every part of it, within the distance from the sea specified in his commission, and so within the precincts of his charge. Pompey receiving the submission, sent letters to Metellus, commanding him to leave off the war; and others in like manner to the cities, in which he charged them not to yield any obedience to the commands of Metellus. And after these he sent Lucius Octavius, one of his lieutenants, to act as general, who entering the besieged fortifications, and fighting in defence of the pirates, rendered Pompey not odious only, but even ridiculous too; that he should lend his name as a guard to a nest of thieves, that knew neither god nor law, and made his reputation serve as a sanctuary to them, only out of pure envy and emulation to Metellus. For neither was Achilles thought to act the part of a man, but rather of a mere boy, mad after glory, when by signs he forbade the rest of the Greeks to strike at Hector—

> "For fear
> Some other hand should give the blow, and he
> Lose the first honour of the victory."

Whereas Pompey even sought to preserve the common enemies of the world only that he might deprive a Roman prætor, after all his labours, of the honour of a triumph. Metellus, however, was not daunted, but prosecuted the war against the pirates, expelled them from their strongholds and punished them; and dismissed Octavius with the insults and reproaches of the whole camp.

When the news came to Rome that the war with the pirates was at an end, and that Pompey was unoccupied, diverting himself in visits to the cities for want of employment, one Manlius, a tribune of the people, preferred a law that Pompey should have all the forces of Lucullus, and the provinces under his government, together with Bithynia, which was under the command of Glabrio; and that he should forthwith conduct the war against the two kings, Mithridates and Tigranes, retaining still the same naval forces and the sovereignty of the seas as before. But this was nothing less than to constitute one absolute monarch of all the Roman empire. For the provinces which seemed to be exempt from his commission by the former decree, such as were Phrygia, Lycaonia, Galatia, Cappadocia, Cilicia, the upper Colchis, and Armenia, were all added in by this latter law, together with all the troops and forces with which Lucullus had defeated Mithridates and Tigranes. And though Lucullus was thus simply robbed of the glory of his achievements in having a successor assigned him, rather to the honour of his triumph than the danger of the war; yet this was of less moment in the eyes of the aristocratical party, though they could not but admit the injustice and ingratitude to Lucullus. But their great grievance was that the power of Pompey should be converted into a manifest tyranny;

and they therefore exhorted and encouraged one another privately to bend all their forces in opposition to this law, and not tamely to cast away their liberty; yet when the day came on which it was to pass into a decree, their hearts failed them for fear of the people, and all were silent except Catulus, who boldly inveighed against the law and its proposer, and when he found that he could do nothing with the people, turned to the senate, crying out and bidding them seek out some mountain as their forefathers had done, and fly to the rocks where they might preserve their liberty. The law passed into a decree, as it is said, by the suffrages of all the tribes. And Pompey, in his absence, was made lord of almost all that power which Sylla only obtained by force of arms, after a conquest of the very city itself.

When Pompey had advice by letters of the decree, it is said that in the presence of his friends, who came to give him joy of his honour, he seemed displeased, frowning and smiting his thigh, and exclaimed as one overburdened and weary of government, "Alas, what a series of labours upon labours! If I am never to end my service as a soldier, nor to escape from this invidious greatness and live at home in the country with my wife, I had better have been an unknown man." But all this was looked upon as mere trifling, neither indeed could the best of his friends call it anything else, well knowing that his enmity with Lucullus, setting a flame just now to his natural passion for glory and empire, made him feel more than usually gratified.

As indeed appeared not long afterwards by his actions, which clearly unmasked him; for, in the first place, he sent out his proclamations into all quarters, commanding the soldiers to join him, and summoned all the tributary kings and princes within his charge; and in short, as soon as he had entered upon his province, he left nothing unaltered that had been done and established by Lucullus. To some he remitted their penalties, and deprived others of their rewards, and acted in all respects as if with the express design that the admirers of Lucullus might know that all his authority was at an end.

Lucullus expostulated by friends, and it was thought fitting that there should be a meeting betwixt them; and accordingly they met in the country of Galatia. As they were both great and successful generals, their officers bore their rods before them all wreathed with branches of laurel; Lucullus came through a country full of green trees and shady woods, but Pompey's march was through a cold and barren district. Therefore the lictors of Lucullus, perceiving that Pompey's laurels were withered and dry, helped him to some of their own, and adorned and crowned his rods with fresh laurels. This was thought ominous, and looked as if Pompey came to take away the reward and honour of Lucullus's victories. Lucullus had the priority in the order of consulships, and also in age; but Pompey's two triumphs made him the greater man. Their first addresses in this interview were dignified and friendly, each magnifying the other's actions, and offering congratulations upon his success. But when they came to the matter of their conference or treaty, they could agree on no fair or equitable terms of any kind, but even came to harsh words against each other, Pompey upbraiding Lucullus with avarice, and Lucullus retorting ambition upon Pompey, so that their friends could hardly part them. Lucullus remaining in Galatia, made a distribution of the lands within his conquests, and gave presents to whom he pleased; and Pompey encamping not far distant from him, sent out his prohibitions, forbidding the execution of any of the orders of Lucullus, and commanded away all his soldiers, except sixteen hundred, whom he thought likely to be unserviceable to himself, being disorderly and mutinous, and whom he knew to be hostile to Lucullus; and to these acts he added satirical speeches, detracting openly from the glory of his actions, and giving out that the battles of Lucullus had been but with the mere stage-shows and idle pictures of royal pomp, whereas the real war against a genuine army, disciplined by defeat, was reserved to him, Mithridates having now begun to be in earnest, and having betaken himself to his shields, swords, and horses. Lucullus, on the other side, to be even with him, replied, that Pompey came to fight with the mere image and shadow of war, it being his usual practice, like a lazy bird of prey, to come upon the carcass when others had slain the dead, and to tear in pieces the relics of a war.

Thus he had appropriated to himself the victories over Sertorius, over Lepidus, and over the insurgents under Spartacus; whereas this last had been achieved by Crassus, that obtained by Catulus, and the first won by Metellus. And therefore it was no great wonder that the glory of the Pontic and Armenian war should be usurped by a man who had condescended to any artifices to work himself into the honour of a triumph over a few run-away slaves.

After this Lucullus went away, and Pompey having placed his whole navy in guard upon the seas betwixt Phœnicia and Bosphorus, himself marched against Mithridates, who had a phalanx of thirty thousand foot, with two thousand horse, yet durst not bid him battle. He had encamped upon a strong mountain where it would have been hard to attack him, but abandoned it in no long time as destitute of water. No sooner was he gone but Pompey occupied it, and observing the plants that were thriving there, together with the hollows which he found in several places, conjectured that such a plot could not be without springs, and therefore ordered his men to sink wells in every corner. After which there was, in a little time, great plenty of water throughout all the camp, insomuch that he wondered how it was possible for Mithridates to be ignorant of this, during all that time of his encampment there. After this Pompey followed him to his next camp, and there drawing lines round about him, shut him in. But he, after having endured a siege of forty-five days, made his escape secretly, and fled away with all the best part of his army, having first put to death all the sick and unserviceable. Not long after Pompey overtook him again near the banks of the river Euphrates, and encamped close by him; but fearing lest he should pass over the river and give him the slip there too, he drew up his army to attack him at midnight. And at that very time Mithridates, it is said, saw a vision in his dream foreshowing what should come to pass. For he seemed to be under sail in the Euxine Sea with a prosperous gale, and just in view of Bosphorus, discoursing pleasantly with the ship's company, as one overjoyed for his past danger and present security, when on a sudden he found himself deserted of all, and floating upon a broken plank of the ship at the mercy of the sea. Whilst he was thus labouring under these passions and phantasms, his friends came and awaked him with the news of Pompey's approach; who was now indeed so near at hand that the fight must be for the camp itself, and the commanders accordingly drew up the forces in battle array.

Pompey perceiving how ready they were and well prepared for defence began to doubt with himself whether he should put it to the hazard of a fight in the dark, judging it more prudent to encompass them only at present, lest they should fly, and to give them battle with the advantage of numbers the next day. But his oldest officers were of another opinion, and by entreaties and encouragements obtained permission that they might charge them immediately. Neither was the night so very dark, but that, though the moon was going down, it yet gave light enough to discern a body, and indeed this was one especial disadvantage to the king's army. For the Romans coming upon them with the moon on their backs, the moon, being very low, and just upon setting, cast the shadows a long way before their bodies, reaching almost to the enemy, whose eyes were thus so much deceived that not exactly discerning the distance, but imagining them to be near at hand, they threw their darts at the shadows without the least execution. The Romans therefore, perceiving this, ran in upon them with a great shout; but the barbarians, all in a panic, unable to endure the charge, turned and fled, and were put to great slaughter, above ten thousand being slain; the camp also was taken. As for Mithridates himself, he at the beginning of the onset, with a body of eight hundred horse, charged through the Roman army, and made his escape. But before long all the rest dispersed, some one way, some another, and he was left only with three persons, among whom was his concubine, Hypsicratia, a girl always of a manly and daring spirit, and the king called her on that account Hypsicrates. She being attired and mounted like a Persian horseman, accompanied the king in all his flight, never weary even in the longest journey, nor ever failing to attend the king in person, and look after his horse too, until they came to Inora, a castle of the king's well stored with gold and treasure. From thence Mithridates took his richest apparel, and gave it among those that had resorted to him in their flight; and so to every one of his friends he gave a deadly poison, that they might not fall into the power of the enemy against their wills. From thence he designed to have gone to Tigranes in Armenia, but being prohibited by Tigranes, who put out a proclamation with a reward of one hundred talents to any one that should apprehend him, he passed by the headwaters of the river Euphrates and fled through the country of Colchis.

Pompey in the meantime made an invasion into Armenia upon the invitation of young Tigranes, who was now in rebellion against his father, and gave Pompey a meeting about the river Araxes, which rises near the head of Euphrates, but turning its course and bending towards the east, falls into the Caspian Sea. They two, therefore, marched together through the country, taking in all the cities by the way, and receiving their submission. But King Tigranes, having lately suffered much in the war with Lucullus, and understanding that Pompey was of a kind and gentle disposition, admitted Roman troops into his royal palaces, and taking along with him his friends and relations, went in person to surrender himself into the hands of Pompey. He came as far as the trenches on horseback, but there he was met by two of Pompey's lictors, who commanded him to alight and walk on foot, for no man ever was seen on horseback within a Roman camp. Tigranes submitted to this immediately, and not only so, but loosing his sword, delivered up that too; and last of all, as soon as he appeared before Pompey, he pulled off his royal turban, and attempted to have laid it at his feet. Nay, worst of all, even he himself had fallen prostrate as an humble suppliant at his knees had not Pompey prevented it, taking him by the hand and placing him near him, Tigranes himself on one side of him and his son upon the other. Pompey now told him that the rest of his losses were chargeable upon Lucullus, by whom he had been dispossessed of Syria, Phœnicia, Cilicia, Galatia, and Sophene; but all that he had preserved to himself entire till that time he should peaceably enjoy, paying the sum of six thousand talents as a fine or penalty for injuries done to the Romans, and that his son should have the kingdom of Sophene. Tigranes himself was well pleased with these conditions of peace, and when the Romans saluted him king, seemed to be overjoyed, and promised to every common soldier half a mina of silver, to every centurion ten minas, and to every tribune a talent; but the son was displeased, insomuch that when he was invited to supper he replied, that he did not stand in need of Pompey for that sort of honour, for he would find out some other Roman to sup with. Upon this he was put into close arrest, and reserved for the triumph.

Not long after this Phraates, King of Parthia, sent to Pompey, and demanded to have young Tigranes, as his son-in-law, given up to him, and that the river Euphrates should be the boundary of the empires. Pompey replied, that for Tigranes, he belonged more to his own natural father than his father-in-law, and for the boundaries, he would take care that they should be according to right and justice.

So Pompey, leaving Armenia in the custody of Afranius, went himself in chase of Mithridates; to do which he was forced of necessity to march through several nations inhabiting about Mount Caucasus. Of these the Albanians and Iberians were the two chiefest. The Iberians stretch out as far as the Moschian mountains and the Pontus; the Albanians lie more eastwardly, and towards the Caspian Sea. These Albanians at first permitted Pompey, upon his request, to pass through the country; but when winter had stolen upon the Romans whilst they were still in the country, and they were busy celebrating the festival of Saturn, they mustered a body of no less than forty thousand fighting men, and set upon them, having passed over the river Cyrnus, which rising from the mountains of Iberia, and receiving the river Araxes in its course from Armenia, discharges itself by twelve mouths into the Caspian. Or, according to others, the Araxes does not fall into it, but they flow near one another, and so discharge themselves as neighbours into the same sea. It was in the power of Pompey to have obstructed the enemy's passage over the river, but he suffered them to pass over quietly; and then leading on his forces and giving battle he routed them and slew great numbers of them in the field. The king sent ambassadors with his submission, and Pompey upon his supplication pardoned the offence, and making a treaty with him, he marched directly against the Iberians, a nation no less in number than the other, but much more warlike, and extremely desirous of gratifying Mithridates and driving out Pompey.

These Iberians were never subject to the Medes or Persians, and they happened likewise to escape the dominion of the Macedonians, because Alexander was so quick in his march through Hyrcania. But these also Pompey subdued in a great battle, where there were slain nine thousand upon the spot, and more than ten thousand taken prisoners. From thence he entered into the country of Colchis, where Servilius met him by the river Phasis, bringing the fleet with which he was guarding the Pontus.

The pursuit of Mithridates, who had thrown himself among the tribes inhabiting Bosphorus and the shores of the Mæotian Sea, presented great difficulties. News was also brought to Pompey that the Albanians had again revolted. This made him turn back, out of anger and determination not to be beaten by them, and with difficulty and great danger passed back over the Cyrnus, which the barbarous people had fortified a great way down the banks with palisadoes. And after this, having a tedious march to make through a waterless and difficult country, he ordered ten thousand skins to be filled with water, and so advanced towards the enemy, whom he found drawn up in order of battle near the river Abas, to the number of sixty thousand horse and twelve thousand foot, ill-armed generally, and most of them covered only with the skins of wild beasts. Their general was Cosis, the king's brother, who, as soon as the battle was begun, singled out Pompey, and rushing in upon him darted his javelin into the joints of his breastplate; while Pompey, in return, struck him through the body with his lance and slew him. It is related that in this battle there were Amazons fighting as auxiliaries with the barbarians, and that they came down from the mountains by the river Thermodon. For that after the battle, when the Romans were taking the spoils and plunder of the field, they met with several targets and buskins of the Amazons; but no woman's body was found among the dead. They inhabit the parts of Mount Caucasus that reach down to the Hyrcanian Sea, not immediately bordering upon the Albanians, for the Gelæ and the Leges lie betwixt; and they keep company with these people yearly, for two months only, near the river Thermodon; after which they retire to their own habitations, and live alone all the rest of the year.

After this engagement, Pompey was eager to advance with his forces upon the Hyrcanian and Caspian Sea, but was forced to retreat at a distance of three days' march from it by the number of venomous serpents, and so he retreated into Armenia the Less. Whilst he was there, the kings of the Elymæans and Medes sent ambassadors to him, to whom he gave friendly answer by letter; and sent against the King of Parthia, who had made incursions upon Gordyene, and despoiled the subjects of Tigranes an army under the command of Afranius, who put him to the rout, and followed him in chase as far as the district of Arbela.

Of the concubines of King Mithridates that were brought before Pompey, he took none to himself, but sent them all away to their parents and relations; most of them being either the daughters or wives of princes and great commanders. Stratonice, however, who had the greatest power and influence with him and to whom he had committed the custody of his best and richest fortress, had been, it seems, the daughter of a musician, an old man, and of no great fortune, and happening to sing one night before Mithridates at a banquet, she struck his fancy so that immediately he took her with him, and sent away the old man much dissatisfied, the king having not so much as said one kind word to himself. But when he rose in the morning, and saw tables in his house richly covered with gold and silver plate, a great retinue of servants, eunuchs, and pages bringing him rich garments, and a horse standing before the door richly caparisoned, in all respects as was usual with the king's favourites, he looked upon it all as a piece of mockery, and thinking himself trifled with, attempted to make off and run away. But the servants laying hold upon him, and informing him really that the king had bestowed on him the house and furniture of a rich man lately deceased, and that these were but the first fruits or earnests of greater riches and possession that were to come, he was persuaded at last with much difficulty to believe them. And so putting on his purple robes, and mounting his horse, he rode through the city, crying out, "All this is mine;" and to those that laughed at him, he said, there was no such wonder in this, but it was a wonder rather that he did not throw stones at all he met, he was so transported with joy. Such was the parentage and blood of Stratonice. She now delivered up this castle into the hands of Pompey, and offered him many presents of great value, of which he accepted only such as he thought might serve to adorn the temples of the gods and add to the splendour of his triumph: the rest he left to Stratonice's disposal, bidding her please herself in the enjoyment of them.

And in the same manner he dealt with the presents offered him by the King of Iberia, who sent him a bedstead, table, and a chair of state, all of gold, desiring him to accept of them; but he delivered them all into the custody of the public treasurers, for the use of the commonwealth.

In another castle called Cænum, Pompey found and read with pleasure several secret writings of Mithridates, containing much that threw light on his character. For there were memoirs by which it appeared that, besides others, he had made away with his son Ariarathes by poison, as also with Alcæus the Sardian, for having robbed him of the first honours in a horse-race. There. were several judgments upon the interpretation of dreams, which either he himself or some of his mistresses had had; and besides these, there was a series of wanton letters to and from his concubine Monime. Theophanes tells us that there was found also an address by Rutilius, in which he attempted to exasperate him to the slaughter of all the Romans in Asia; though most men justly conjecture this to be a malicious invention of Theophanes, who probably hated Rutilius because he was a man in nothing like himself; or perhaps it might be to gratify Pompey, whose father is described by Rutilius in his history as the vilest man alive.

From thence Pompey came to the city of Amisus, where his passion for glory put him into a position which might be called a punishment on himself. For whereas he had often sharply reproached Lucullus, in that while the enemy was still living he had taken upon him to issue decrees, and distribute rewards and honours, as conquerors usually do only when the war is brought to an end, yet now was he himself, while Mithridates was paramount in the kingdom of Bosphorus, and at the head of a powerful army, as if all were ended, just doing the same thing, regulating the provinces, and distributing rewards, many great commanders and princes having flocked to him, together with no less than twelve barbarian kings; insomuch that to gratify these other kings, when he wrote to the King of Parthia, he would not condescend, as others used to do, in the superscription of his letter, to give him his title of king of kings.

Moreover, he had a great desire and emulation to occupy Syria, and to march through Arabia to the Red Sea, that he might thus extend his conquests every way to the great ocean that encompasses the habitable earth; as in Africa he was the first Roman that advanced his victories to the ocean; and again in Spain he made the Atlantic Sea the limit of the empire: and then thirdly, in his late pursuit of the Albanians, he had wanted but little of reaching the Hyrcanian Sea. Accordingly he raised his camp, designing to bring the Red Sea within the circuit of his expedition; especially as he saw how difficult it was to hunt after Mithridates with an army, and that he would prove a worse enemy flying than fighting. But yet he declared that he would leave a sharper enemy behind him than himself, namely, famine; and therefore he appointed a guard of ships to lie in wait for the merchants that sailed to Bosphorus, death being the penalty for any who should attempt to carry provisions thither.

Then he set forward with the greatest part of his army, and in his march casually fell in with several dead bodies, still uninterred, of those soldiers who were slain with Triarius in his unfortunate engagement with Mithridates: these he buried splendidly and honourably. The neglect of whom, it is thought, caused, as much as anything, the hatred that was felt against Lucullus, and alienated the affections of the soldiers from him. Pompey having now by his forces under the command of Afranius subdued the Arabians about the mountain Amanus, himself entered Syria, and finding it destitute of any natural and lawful prince, reduced it into the form of a province, as a possession of the people of Rome. He conquered also Judæa, and took its king, Aristobulus, captive. Some cities he built anew, and to others he gave their liberty, chastising their tyrants. Most part of the time that he spent there was employed in the administration of justice, in deciding controversies of kings and states; and where he himself could not be present in person, he gave commissions to his friends, and sent them. Thus when there arose a difference betwixt the Armenians and Parthians about some territory, and the judgment was referred to him, he gave a power by commission to three judges and arbiters to hear and determine the controversy. For the reputation of his power was great; nor was the fame of his justice and clemency inferior to that of his power, and served indeed as a veil for a multitude of faults committed by his friends and familiars. For although it was not in his nature to check or chastise wrongdoers, yet he himself always treated those that had to do with him in such a manner that they submitted to endure with patience the acts of covetousness and oppression done by others.

Among these friends of his there was one Demetrius, who had the greatest influence with him of all; he was a freed slave, a youth of good understanding, but somewhat too insolent in his good fortune, of whom there goes this story. Cato, the philosopher, being as yet a very young man, but of great repute and a noble mind, took a journey of pleasure to Antioch, at a time when Pompey was not there, having a great desire to see the city. He, as his custom was, walked on foot, and his friends accompanied him on horseback; and seeing before the gates of the city a multitude dressed in white, the young men on one side of the road and the boys on the other, he was somewhat offended at it, imagining that it was officiously done in honour of him, which was more than he had any wish for. However, he desired his companions to alight and walk with him; but when they drew near, the master of the ceremonies in this procession came out with a garland and a rod in his hand and met them, inquiring where they had left Demetrius, and when he would come? Upon which Cato's companions burst out into laughter, but Cato said only, "Alas, poor city!" and passed by without any other answer. However, Pompey rendered Demetrius less odious to others by enduring his presumption and impertinence to himself. For it is reported how that Pompey, when he had invited his friends to an entertainment, would be very ceremonious in waiting till they all came and were placed, while Demetrius would be already stretched upon the couch as if he cared for no one, with his dress over his ears, hanging down from his head. Before his return into Italy, he had purchased the pleasantest country-seat about Rome, with the finest walks and places for exercise, and there were sumptuous gardens, called by the name of Demetrius, while Pompey his master, up to his third triumph, was contented with an ordinary and simple habitation. Afterwards, it is true, when he had erected his famous and stately theatre for the people of Rome, he built as a sort of appendix to it a house for himself, much more splendid than his former, and yet no object even this to excite men's envy, since he who came to be master of it after Pompey could not but express wonder and inquire where Pompey the Great used to sup. Such is the story told us.

The king of the Arabs near Petra, who had hitherto despised the power of the Romans, now began to be in great alarm at it, and sent letters to him promising to be at his commands, and to do whatever he should see fit to order. However, Pompey having a desire to confirm and keep him in the same mind, marched forwards for Petra, an expedition not altogether irreprehensible in the opinion of many; who thought it a mere running away from their proper duty, the pursuit of Mithridates, Rome's ancient and inveterate enemy, who was now rekindling the war once more, and taking preparations, it was reported, to lead his army through Scythia and Pæonia into Italy. Pompey, on the other side, judging it easier to destroy his forces in battle than to seize his person in flight, resolved not to tire himself out in a vain pursuit, but rather to spend his leisure upon another enemy, as a sort of digression in the meanwhile. But fortune resolved the doubt, for when he was now not far from Petra, and had pitched his tents and encamped for that day, as he was taking exercise with his horse outside the camp, couriers came riding up from Pontus, bringing good news, as was known at once by the heads of their javelins, which it is the custom to carry crowned with branches of laurel. The soldiers, as soon as they saw them, flocked immediately to Pompey, who, notwithstanding, was minded to finish his exercise; but when they began to be clamorous and importunate, he alighted from his horse, and taking the letters went before them into the camp.

Now there being no tribunal erected there, not even that military substitute for one which they make by cutting up thick turfs of earth, and piling them one upon another, they, through eagerness and impatience, heaped up a pile of pack-saddles, and Pompey standing upon that, told them the news of Mithridates's death, how that he had himself put an end to his life upon the revolt of his son Pharnaces, and that Pharnaces had taken all things there into his hands and possession, which he did, his letters said, in right of himself and the Romans. Upon this news the whole army, expressing their joy, as was to be expected, fell to sacrificing to the gods, and feasting as if in the person of Mithridates alone there had died many thousands of their enemies.

Pompey by this event having brought this war to its completion, with much more ease than was expected, departed forthwith out of Arabia, and passing rapidly through the intermediate provinces, he came at length to the city Amisus. There he received many presents brought from Pharnaces, with several dead bodies of the royal blood, and the corpse of Mithridates himself, which was not easy to be known by the face, for the physicians that embalmed him had not dried up his brain, but those who were curious to see him knew him by the scars there. Pompey himself would not endure to see him, but to deprecate the divine jealousy sent it away to the city of Sinope. He admired the richness of his robes no less than the size and splendour of his armour. His sword-belt, however, which had cost four hundred talents, was stolen by Publius, and sold to Ariarathes; his tiara also, a piece of admirable workmanship, Gaius, the foster-brother of Mithridates, gave secretly to Faustus, the son of Sylla, at his request. All which Pompey was ignorant of, but afterwards, when Pharnaces came to understand it, he severely punished those that embezzled them.

Pompey now having ordered all things, and established that province, took his journey homewards in greater pomp and with more festivity. For when he came to Mitylene, he gave the city their freedom upon the intercession of Theophanes, and was present at the contest, there periodically held, of the poets, who took at that time no other theme or subject than the actions of Pompey. He was extremely pleased with the theatre itself, and had a model of it taken, intending to erect one in Rome on the same design, but larger and more magnificent. When he came to Rhodes, he attended the lectures of all the philosophers there, and gave to every one of them a talent. Posidonius has published the disputation which he held before him against Hermagoras the rhetorician, upon the subject of Invention in general. At Athens, also, he showed similiar munificence to the philosophers, and gave fifty talents towards the repairing and beautifying the city. So that now by all these acts he well hoped to return into Italy in the greatest splendour and glory possible to man, and find his family as desirous to see him as he felt himself to come home to them. But that supernatural agency, whose province and charge it is always to mix some ingredient of evil with the greatest and most glorious goods of fortune, had for some time back been busy in his household, preparing him a sad welcome. For Mucia during his absence had dishonoured his bed. Whilst he was abroad at a distance he had refused all credence to the report; but when he drew nearer to Italy, where his thoughts were more at leisure to give consideration to the charge, he sent her a bill of divorce; but neither then in writing, nor afterwards by word of mouth, did he ever give a reason why he discharged her; the cause of it is mentioned in Cicero's epistles.

Rumours of every kind were scattered abroad about Pompey, and were carried to Rome before him, so that there was a great tumult and stir, as if he designed forthwith to march with his army into the city and establish himself securely as sole ruler. Crassus withdrew himself, together with his children and property, out of the city, either that he was really afraid, or that he counterfeited rather, as is most probable, to give credit to the calumny and exasperate the jealousy of the people. Pompey, therefore, as soon as he entered Italy, called a general muster of the army; and having made a suitable address and exchanged a kind farewell with his soldiers he commanded them to depart every man to his country and place of habitation, only taking care that they should not fail to meet again at his triumph. Thus the army being disbanded, and the news commonly reported, a wonderful result ensued. For when the cities saw Pompey the Great passing through the country unarmed, and with a small train of familiar friends only, as if he was returning from a journey of pleasure, not from his conquests, they came pouring out to display their affection for him, attending and conducting him to Rome with far greater forces than he disbanded; insomuch that if he had designed any movement or innovation in the state, he might have done it without his army.

Now, because the law permitted no commander to enter into the city before his triumph, he sent to the senate, entreating them as a favour to him to prorogue the election of consuls, that thus he might be able to attend and give countenance to Piso, one of the candidates. The request was resisted by Cato, and met with a refusal. However, Pompey could not but admire the liberty and boldness of speech which Cato alone had dared to use in the maintenance of law and justice. He therefore had a great desire to win him over, and purchase his friendship at any rate; and to that end, Cato having two nieces, Pompey asked for one in marriage for himself, the other for his son. But Cato looked unfavourably on the proposal, regarding it as a design for undermining his honesty, and in a manner bribing him by a family alliance; much to the displeasure of his wife and sister, who were indignant that he should reject a connection with Pompey the Great. About that time Pompey having a design of setting up Afranius for the consulship, gave a sum of money among the tribes for their votes, and people came and received it in his own gardens, a proceeding which, when it came to be generally known, excited great disapprobation, that he should thus, for the sake of men who could not obtain the honour by their own merits, make merchandise of an office which had been given to himself as the highest reward of his services. "Now," said Cato, to his wife and sister, "had we contracted an alliance with Pompey, we had been allied to this dishonour too;" and this they could not but acknowledge, and allow his judgment of what was right and fitting to have been wiser and better than theirs.

The splendour and magnificence of Pompey's triumph was such that though it took up the space of two days, yet they were extremely straitened in time, so that of what was prepared for that pageantry, there was as much withdrawn as would have set out and adorned another triumph. In the first place, there were tables carried, inscribed with the names and titles of the nations over whom he triumphed, Pontus, Armenia, Cappadocia, Paphlagonia, Media, Colchis, the Iberians, the Albanians, Syria, Cilicia, and Mesopotamia, together with Phœnicia and Palestine, Judæa, Arabia, and all the power of the pirates subdued by sea and land. And in these different countries there appeared the capture of no less than one thousand fortified places, nor much less than nine hundred cities, together with eight hundred ships of the pirates, and the foundation of thirty-nine towns. Besides, there was set forth in these tables an account of all the tributes throughout the empire, and how that before these conquests the revenue amounted but to fifty millions, whereas from his acquisitions they had a revenue of eighty-five millions; and that in present payment he was bringing into the common treasury ready money, and gold and silver plate, and ornaments, to the value of twenty thousand talents, over and above what had been distributed among the soldiers, of whom he that had least had fifteen hundred drachmas for his share. The prisoners of war that were led in triumph, besides the chief pirates, were the son of Tigranes, King of Armenia with his wife and daughter; as also Zosime, wife of King Tigranes himself, and Aristobulus, King of Judæa, the sister of King Mithridates, and her five sons, and some Scythian women. There were likewise the hostages of the Albanians and Iberians, and of the King of Commagene, besides a vast number of trophies, one for every battle in which he was conqueror, either himself in person or by his lieutenants. But that which seemed to be his greatest glory, being one which no other Roman ever attained to, was this, that he made his third triumph over the third division of the world. For others among the Romans had the honour of triumphing thrice, but his first triumph was over Africa, his second over Europe, and this last over Asia; so that he seemed in these three triumphs to have led the whole world captive.

As for his age, those who affect to make the parallel exact in all things betwixt him and Alexander the Great, do not allow him to have been quite thirty-four, whereas in truth at that time he was near forty. And well had it been for him had he terminated his life at this date, while he still enjoyed Alexander's fortune, since all his after-time served only either to bring him prosperity that made him odious, or calamities too great to be retrieved. For that great authority which he had gained in the city by his merits he made use of only in patronising the iniquities of others, so that by advancing their fortunes he detracted from his own glory, till at last he was overthrown even by the force and greatness of his own power. And as the strongest citadel or fort in a town, when it is taken by an enemy, does then afford the same strength to the foe as it had done to friends before, so Cæsar, after Pompey's aid had made him strong enough to defy his country, ruined and overthrew at last the power which had availed him against the rest. The course of things was as follows. Lucullus, when he returned out of Asia, where he had been treated with insult by Pompey, was received by the senate with great honour, which was yet increased when Pompey came home; to check whose ambition they encouraged him to assume the administration of the government, whereas he was now grown cold and disinclined to business, having given himself over to the pleasures of ease and the enjoyment of a splendid fortune. However, he began for the time to exert himself against Pompey, attacked him sharply, and succeeded in having his own acts and decrees, which were repealed by Pompey, re-established, and, with the assistance of Cato, gained the superiority in the senate.

Pompey having fallen from his hopes in such an unworthy repulse, was forced to fly to the tribunes of the people for refuge, and to attach himself to the young men, among whom was Clodius, the vilest and most impudent wretch alive, who took him about, and exposed him as a tool to the people, carrying him up and down among the throngs in the marketplace, to countenance those laws and speeches which he made to cajole the people and ingratiate himself. And at last, for his reward, he demanded Pompey, as if he had not disgraced, but done him a great kindness, that he should forsake (as in the end he did forsake) Cicero, his friend, who on many public occasions had done him the greatest service. And so when Cicero was in danger, and implored his aid, he would not admit him into his presence, but shutting up his gates against those that came to mediate for him, slipt out at a back door, whereupon Cicero, fearing the result of his trial, departed privately from Rome.

About that time Cæsar, returning from military service, started a course of policy which brought him great present favour, and much increased his power for the future, and proved extremely destructive both to Pompey and the commonwealth. For now he stood candidate for his first consulship, and well observing the enmity betwixt Pompey and Crassus, and finding that by joining with one he should make the other his enemy, he endeavoured by all means to reconcile them, an object in itself honourable and tending to the public good, but, as he undertook it, a mischievous and subtle intrigue. For he well knew that opposite parties or factions in a commonwealth, like passengers in a boat, serve to trim and balance the unsteady motions of power there; whereas if they combine and come all over to one side, they cause a shock which will be sure to overset the vessel and carry down everything. And therefore Cato wisely told those who charged all the calamities of Rome upon the disagreement betwixt Pompey and Cæsar that they were in error in charging all the crime upon the last cause; for it was not their discord and enmity, but their unanimity and friendship, that gave the first and greatest blow to the commonwealth.

Cæsar being thus elected consul, began at once to make an interest with the poor and meaner sort, by preferring and establishing laws for planting colonies and dividing lands, lowering the dignity of his office, and turning his consulship into a sort of tribuneship rather. And when Bibulus, his colleague, opposed him, and Cato was prepared to second Bibulus, and assist him vigorously, Cæsar brought Pompey upon the hustings, and addressing him in the sight of the people, demanded his opinion upon the laws that were proposed. Pompey gave his approbation. "Then," said Cæsar, "in case any man should offer violence to these laws, will you be ready to give assistance to the people?" "Yes," replied Pompey, "I shall be ready, and against those that threaten the sword, I will appear with sword and buckler." Nothing ever was said or done by Pompey up to that day that seemed more insolent or overbearing; so that his friends endeavoured to apologise for it as a word spoken inadvertently; but by his actions afterwards it appeared plainly that he was totally devoted to Cæsar's service. For on a sudden, contrary to all expectation, he married Julia, the daughter of Cæsar, who had been affianced before and was to be married within a few days to Cæpio. And to appease Cæpio's wrath, he gave him his own daughter in marriage, who had been espoused before to Faustus, the son of Sylla. Cæsar himself married Calpurnia, the daughter of Piso.

Upon this Pompey, filling the city with soldiers, carried all things by force as he pleased. As Bibulus, the consul, was going to the forum, accompanied by Lucullus and Cato, they fell upon him on a sudden and broke his rods; and somebody threw a vessel of ordure upon the head of Bibulus himself; and two tribunes of the people, who escorted him, were desperately wounded in the fray. And thus having cleared the forum of all their adversaries, they got their bill for the division of lands established and passed into an act; and not only so, but the whole populace, being taken with this bait, became totally at their devotion, inquiring into nothing and without a word giving their suffrages to whatever they propounded. Thus they confirmed all those acts and decrees of Pompey which were questioned and contested by Lucullus; and to Cæsar they granted the provinces of Gaul, both within and without the Alps, together with Illyricum, for five years, and likewise an army of four entire legions; then they created consuls for the year ensuing, Piso, the father-in-law of Cæsar, and Gabinius, the most extravagant of Pompey's flatterers.

During all these transactions, Bibulus kept close within doors, nor did he appear publicly in person for the space of eight months together, notwithstanding he was consul, but sent out proclamations full of bitter invectives and accusations against them both. Cato turned prophet, and as if he had been possessed with a spirit of divination, did nothing else in the senate but foretell what evils should befall the commonwealth and Pompey. Lucullus pleaded old age, and retired to take his ease, as superannuated for affairs of state; which gave occasion to the saying of Pompey, that the fatigues of luxury were not more seasonable for an old man than those of government. Which in truth proved a reflection upon himself; for he not long after let his fondness for his young wife seduce him also into effeminate habits. He gave all his time to her, and passed his days in her company in country-houses and gardens, paying no heed to what was going on in the forum. Insomuch that Clodius, who was then tribune of the people, began to despise him, and engage in the most audacious attempts. For when he had banished Cicero, and sent away Cato into Cyprus under pretence of military duty, and when Cæsar was gone upon his expedition to Gaul, finding the populace now looking to him as the leader who did everything according to their pleasure, he attempted forthwith to repeal some of Pompey's decrees; he took Tigranes, the captive, out of prison, and kept him about him as his companion; and commenced actions against several of Pompey's friends, thus designing to try the extent of his power. At last, upon a time when Pompey was present at the hearing of a certain cause, Clodius, accompanied with a crowd of profligate and impudent ruffians, standing up in a place above the rest, put questions to the populace as follows: "Who is the dissolute general? who is the man that seeks another man? who scratches his head with one finger?" and the rabble, upon the signal of his shaking his gown, with a great shout to every question, like singers making responses in a chorus, made answer, "Pompey."

This indeed was no small annoyance to Pompey, who was quite unaccustomed to hear anything ill of himself, and unexperienced altogether in such encounters; and he was yet more vexed when he saw that the senate rejoiced at this foul usage, and regarded it as a just punishment upon him for his treachery to Cicero. But when it came even to blows and wounds in the forum, and that one of Clodius's bond-slaves was apprehended creeping through the crowd towards Pompey with a sword in his hand, Pompey laid hold of this pretence, though perhaps otherwise apprehensive of Clodius's insolence and bad language, and never appeared again in the forum during all the time he was tribune, but kept close at home, and passed his time in consulting with his friends by what means he might best allay the displeasure of the senate and nobles against him. Among other expedients, Culleo advised the divorce of Julia, and to abandon Cæsar's friendship to gain that of the senate; this he would not hearken to. Others again advised him to call home Cicero from banishment, a man who was always the great adversary of Clodius, and as great a favourite of the senate; to this he was easily persuaded. And therefore he brought Cicero's brother into the forum, attended with a strong party, to petition for his return; where, after a warm dispute, in which several were wounded and some slain, he got the victory over Clodius.

No sooner was Cicero returned home upon this decree, but immediately he used his efforts to reconcile the senate to Pompey; and by speaking in favour of the law upon the importations of corn, did again, in effect, make Pompey sovereign lord of all the Roman possessions by sea and land. For by that law there were placed under his control all ports, markets, and storehouses, and, in short, all the concerns both of the merchants and the husbandmen; which gave occasion to the charge brought against it by Clodius, that the law was not made because of the scarcity of corn, but the scarcity of corn was made that they might pass a law, whereby that power of his, which was now grown feeble and consumptive, might be revived again, and Pompey reinstated in a new empire. Others look upon it as a politic device of Spinther, the consul, whose design it was to secure Pompey in a greater authority, that he himself might be sent in assistance to King Ptolemy. However, it is certain that Canidius, the tribune, preferred a law to despatch Pompey in the character of an ambassador, without an army, attended only with two lictors, as a mediator betwixt the king and his subjects of Alexandria.

Neither did this proposal seem unacceptable to Pompey, though the senate cast it out upon the specious pretence that they were unwilling to hazard his person. However, there were found several writings scattered about the forum and near the senate-house intimating how grateful it would be to Ptolemy to have Pompey appointed for his general instead of Spinther. And Timagenes even asserts that Ptolemy went away and left Egypt, not out of necessity, but purely upon the persuasion of Theophanes, who was anxious to give Pompey the opportunity for holding a new command and gaining further wealth. But Theophanes's want of honesty does not go so far to make this story credible as does Pompey's own nature, which was averse, with all its ambition, to such base and disingenuous acts, to render it improbable.

Thus Pompey, being appointed chief purveyor, and having within his administration and management all the corn trade, sent abroad his factors and agents into all quarters, and he himself sailing into Sicily, Sardinia and Africa, collected vast stores of corn. He was just ready to set sail upon his voyage home, when a great storm arose upon the sea, and the ships' commanders doubted whether it were safe. Upon which Pompey himself went first aboard, and bid the mariners weigh anchor, declaring with a loud voice that there was a necessity to sail, but no necessity to live. So that with this spirit and courage, and having met with favourable fortune, he made a prosperous return, and filled the markets with corn, and the sea with ships. So much so that this great plenty and abundance of provisions yielded a sufficient supply, not only to the city of Rome but even to other places too, dispersing itself, like waters from a spring, into all quarters.

Meantime Cæsar grew great and famous with his wars in Gaul, and while in appearance he seemed far distant from Rome, entangled in the affairs of the Belgians, Suevians, and Britons, in truth he was working craftily by secret practices in the midst of the people, and countermining Pompey in all political matters of most importance. He himself, with his army close about him, as if it had been his own body, not with mere views of conquest over the barbarians, but as though his contests with them were but mere sports and exercises of the chase, did his utmost with this training and discipline to make it invincible and alarming. In the meantime his gold and silver and other spoils and treasure which he took from the enemy in his conquests, he sent to Rome in presents, tempting people with his gifts, and aiding ædiles, prætors, and consuls, as also their wives, in their expenses, and thus purchasing himself numerous friends. Insomuch, that when he passed back again over the Alps, and took up his winter quarters in the city of Luca, there flocked to him an infinite number of men and women, striving who should get first to him, two hundred senators included, among whom were Pompey and Crassus; so that there were to be seen at once before Cæsar's door no less than six score rods of proconsuls and prætors. The rest of his addressers he sent all away full fraught with hopes and money; but with Crassus and Pompey he entered into special articles of agreement, that they should stand candidates for the consulship next year; that Cæsar on his part should send a number of his soldiers to give their votes at the election; that as soon as they were elected, they should use their interest to have the command of some provinces and legions assigned to themselves, and that Cæsar should have his present charge confirmed to him for five years more. When these arrangements came to be generally known, great indignation was excited among the chief men in Rome; and Marcellinus, in an open assembly of the people, demanded of them both, whether they designed to sue for the consulship or no. And being urged by the people for their answer, Pompey spoke first, and told them, perhaps he would sue for it, perhaps he would not. Crassus was more temperate, and said, that he would do what should be judged most agreeable with the interest of the commonwealth; and when Marcellinus persisted in his attack on Pompey, and spoke, as it was thought, with some vehemence, Pompey remarked that Marcellinus was certainly the unfairest of men, to show him no gratitude for having thus made him an orator out of a mute, and converted him from a hungry starveling into a man so full-fed that he could not contain himself.

Most of the candidates nevertheless abandoned their canvass for the consulship; Cato alone persuaded and encouraged Lucius Domitius not to desist, "since," said he, "the contest now is not for office, but for liberty against tyrants and usurpers." Therefore those of Pompey's party, fearing this inflexible constancy in Cato, by which he kept with him the whole senate, lest by this he should likewise pervert and draw after him all the whole senate part of the commonalty, resolved to withstand Domitius at once, and to prevent his entrance into the forum. To this end, therefore, they sent in a band of armed men, who slew the torchbearer of Domitius, as he was leading the way before him, and put all the rest to flight; last of all, Cato himself retired, having received a wound in his right arm while defending Domitius. Thus by these means and practices they obtained the consulship; neither did they behave themselves with more decency in their further proceedings; but in the first place, when the people were choosing Cato prætor, and just ready with their votes for the poll, Pompey broke up the assembly, upon a pretext of some inauspicious appearance, and having gained the tribes by money, they publicly proclaimed Vatinius prætor. Then, in pursuance of their covenants with Cæsar, they introduced several laws by Trebonius, the tribune, continuing Cæsar's commission to another five years' charge of his province; to Crassus there were appointed Syria and the Parthian war; and to Pompey himself, all Africa, together with both Spains, and four legions of soldiers, two of which he lent to Cæsar upon his request for the wars in Gaul.

Crassus, upon the expiration of his consulship, departed forthwith into his province; but Pompey spent some time in Rome, upon the opening or dedication of his theatre, where he treated the people with all sorts of games, shows, and exercises, in gymnastics alike and in music. There was likewise the hunting or baiting of wild beasts, and combats with them, in which five hundred lions were slain; but above all, the battle of elephants was a spectacle full of horror and amazement.

These entertainments brought him great honour and popularity; but on the other side he created no less envy to himself, in that he committed the government of his provinces and legions into the hands of friends as his lieutenants, whilst he himself was going about and spending his time with his wife in all the places of amusement in Italy; whether it were he was so fond of her himself, or she so fond of him, and he unable to distress her by going away, for this also is stated. And the love displayed by this young wife for her elderly husband was a matter of general note, to be attributed, it would seem, to his constancy in married life, and to his dignity of manner, which in familiar intercourse was tempered with grace and gentleness, and was particularly attractive to women, as even Flora, the courtesan, may be thought good enough evidence to prove.

It once happened in a public assembly, as they were at an election of the ædiles, that the people came to blows, and several about Pompey were slain, so that he, finding himself all bloody, ordered a change of apparel; but the servants who brought home his clothes, making a great bustle and hurry about the house, it chanced that the young lady, who was then with child, saw his gown all stained with blood; upon which she dropped immediately into a swoon, and was hardly brought to life again; however, what with her fright and suffering, she fell into labour and miscarried; even those who chiefly censured Pompey for his friendship to Cæsar could not reprove him for his affection to so attached a wife. Afterwards she was great again, and brought to bed of a daughter, but died in childbed; neither did the infant outlive her mother many days. Pompey had prepared all things for the interment of her corpse at his house near Alba, but the people seized upon it by force, and performed the solemnities in the field of Mars, rather in compassion for the young lady, than in favour either for Pompey or Cæsar; and yet of these two, the people seemed at that time to pay Caesar a greater share of honour in his absence, than to Pompey, though he was present.

For the city now at once began to roll and swell, so to say, with the stir of the coming storm. Things everywhere were in a state of agitation, and everybody's discourse tended to division, now that death had put an end to that relation which hitherto had been a disguise rather than restraint to the ambition of these men. Besides, not long after came messengers from Parthia with intelligence of the death of Crassus there, by which another safeguard against civil war was removed, since both Cæsar and Pompey kept their eyes on Crassus, and awe of him held them together more or less within the bounds of fair-dealing all his lifetime. But when fortune had taken away this second, whose province it might have been to revenge the quarrel of the conquered, you might then say with the comic poet—

> "The combatants are waiting to begin,
> Smearing their hands with dust and oiling each his skin."

So inconsiderable a thing is fortune in respect of human nature, and so insufficient to give content to a covetous mind, that an empire of that mighty extent and sway could not satisfy the ambition of two men; and though they knew and had read, that—

> "The gods, when they divided out 'twixt three,
> This massive universe, heaven, hell, and sea,
> Each one sat down contented on his throne,
> And undisturbed each god enjoys his own,"

yet they thought the whole Roman empire not sufficient to contain them, though they were but two.

Pompey once in an oration to the people told them that he had always come into office before he expected he should, and that he had always left it sooner than they expected he would; and, indeed, the disbanding of all his armies witnessed as much. Yet when he perceived that Cæsar would not so willingly discharge his forces, he endeavoured to strengthen himself against him by offices and commands in the city; but beyond this he showed no desire for any change, and would not seem to distrust, but rather to disregard and contemn him. And when he saw how they bestowed the places of government quite contrary to his wishes because the citizens were bribed in their elections, he let things take their course, and allowed the city to be left without any government at all. Hereupon there was mention straightway made of appointing a dictator. Lucullus, a tribune of the people, was the man who first adventured to propose it, urging the people to make Pompey dictator. But the tribune was in danger of being turned out of his office by the opposition that Cato made against it. And for Pompey, many of his friends appeared and excused him, alleging that he never was desirous of that government, neither would he accept of it. When Cato therefore made a speech in commendation of Pompey and exhorted him to support the cause of good order in the commonwealth, he could not for shame but yield to it, and so for the present Domitius and Messala were elected consuls. But shortly afterwards, when there was another anarchy, or vacancy in the government, and the talk of a dictator was much louder and more general than before, those of Cato's party, fearing lest they should be forced to appoint Pompey, thought it policy to keep him from that arbitrary and tyrannical power by giving him an office of more legal authority. Bibulus himself, who was Pompey's enemy, first gave his vote in the senate, that Pompey should be created consul alone; alleging, that by these means either the commonwealth would be freed from its present confusion, or that its bondage should be lessened by serving the worthiest. This was looked upon as a very strange opinion, considering the man that spoke it; and therefore on Cato's standing up, everybody expected that he would have opposed it; but after silence made, he said that he would never have been the author of that advice himself, but since it was propounded by another, his advice was to follow it, adding, that any form of government was better than none at all; and that in a time so full of distraction, he thought no man fitter to govern than Pompey. This counsel was unanimously approved of, and a decree passed that Pompey should be made sole consul, with this clause, that if he thought it necessary to have a colleague, he might choose whom he pleased, provided it were not till after two months expired.

Thus was Pompey created and declared sole consul by Sulpicius, regent in this vacancy; upon which he made very cordial acknowledgments to Cato, professing himself much his debtor, and requesting his good advice in conducting the government; to this Cato replied, that Pompey had no reason to thank him, for all that he had said was for the service of the commonwealth, not of Pompey; but that he would be always ready to give his advice privately, if he were asked for it; and if not, he should not fail to say what he thought in public. Such was Cato's conduct on all occasions.

On his return into the city Pompey married Cornelia, the daughter of Metellus Scipio, not a maiden, but lately left a widow by Publius, the son of Crassus, her first husband, who had been killed in Parthia. The young lady had other attractions besides those of youth and beauty; for she was highly educated, played well upon the lute, and understood geometry, and had been accustomed to listen with profit to lectures on philosophy; all this, too, without in any degree becoming unamiable or pretentious, as sometimes young women do when they pursue such studies. Nor could any fault be found either with her father's family or reputation. The disparity of their ages was, however, not liked by everybody; Cornelia being in this respect a fitter match for Pompey's son. And wiser judges thought it rather a slight upon the commonwealth when he, to whom alone they had committed their broken fortunes, and from whom alone, as from their physician, they expected a cure to these distractions, went about crowned with garlands and celebrating his nuptial feasts, never considering that his very consulship was a public calamity, which would never have been given him, contrary to the rules of law, had his country been in a flourishing state. Afterwards, however, he took cognisance of the cases of those that had obtained offices by gifts and bribery, and enacted laws and ordinances, setting forth the rules of judgment by which they should be arraigned; and regulating all things with gravity and justice, he restored security, order, and silence to their courts of judicature, himself giving his presence there with a band of soldiers. But when his father-in-law, Scipio, was accused, he sent for the three hundred and sixty judges to his house, and entreated them to be favourable to him whereupon his accuser, seeing Scipio come into the court, accompanied by the judges themselves, withdrew the prosecution. Upon this Pompey was very ill spoken of, and much worse in the case of Plancus; for whereas he himself had made a law putting a stop to the practice of making speeches in praise of persons under trial, yet notwithstanding this prohibition, he came into court and spoke openly in commendation of Plancus, insomuch that Cato, who happened to be one of the judges at that time, stopping his ears with his hands, told him he could not in conscience listen to commendations contrary to law. Cato upon this was refused, and set aside from being a judge, before sentence was given, but Plancus was condemned by the rest of the judges, to Pompey's dishonour. Shortly after, Hypsæus, a man of consular dignity, who was under accusation, waited for Pompey's return from his bath to his supper, and falling down at his feet, implored his favour; but he disdainfully passed him by, saying, that he did nothing else but spoil his supper. Such partiality was looked upon as a great fault in Pompey and highly condemned; however, he managed all things else discreetly, and having put the government in very good order, he chose his father-in-law to be his colleague in the consulship for the last five months. His provinces were continued to him for the term of four years longer, with a commission to take one thousand talents yearly out of the treasury for the payment of his army.

This gave occasion to some of Cæsar's friends to think it reasonable, that some consideration should be had of him too, who had done such signal services in war and fought so many battles for the empire, alleging, that he deserved at least a second consulship, or to have the government of his province continued, that so he might command and enjoy in peace what he had obtained in war, and no successor come in to reap the fruits of his labour and carry off the glory of his actions. There arising some debate about this matter, Pompey took upon him, as it were out of kindness to Cæsar, to plead his cause, and allay any jealousy that was conceived against him, telling them that he had letters from Cæsar, expressing his desire for a successor, and his own discharge from the command; but it would be only right that they should give him leave to stand for the consulship though in his absence. But those of Cato's party withstood this, saying, that if he expected any favour from the citizens, he ought to leave his army and come in a private capacity to canvass for it. And Pompey's making no rejoinder, but letting it pass as a matter in which he was overruled, increased the suspicion of his real feelings towards Cæsar. Presently, also, under pretence of a war with Parthia, he sent for his two legions which he had lent him. However, Cæsar, though he well knew why they were asked for, sent them home very liberally rewarded.

About that time Pompey recovered of a dangerous fit of sickness which seized him at Naples, where the whole city, upon the suggestion of Praxagoras, made sacrifices of thanksgiving to the gods for his recovery. The neighbouring towns likewise happening to follow their example, the thing then went its course throughout all Italy, so that there was not a city, either great or small, that did not feast and rejoice for many days together. And the company of those that came from all parts to meet him was so numerous that no place was able to contain them, but the villages, seaport towns, and the very highways were all full of people, feasting and sacrificing to the gods. Nay, many went to meet him with garlands on their heads, and flambeaux in their hands, casting flowers and nosegays upon him as he went along; so that this progress of his, and reception, was one of the noblest and most glorious sights imaginable. And yet it is thought that this very thing was not one of the least causes and occasions of the civil war. For Pompey, yielding to a feeling of exultation, which in the greatness of the present display of joy lost sight of more solid grounds of consideration, and abandoning that prudent temper which had guided him hitherto to a safe use of all his good fortune and his successes, gave himself up to an extravagant confidence in his own contempt of Cæsar's power; insomuch that he thought neither force of arms nor care necessary against him, but that he could pull him down much easier than he had set him up. Besides this, Appius, under whose command those legions which Pompey lent to Cæsar were returned, coming lately out of Gaul, spoke slightingly of Cæsar's actions there, and spread scandalous reports about him, at the same time telling Pompey that he was unacquainted with his own strength and reputation if he made use of any other forces against Cæsar than Cæsar's own; for such was the soldiers' hatred to Cæsar, and their love to Pompey so great, that they would all come over to him upon his first appearance. By these flatteries Pompey was so puffed up, and led on into such a careless security, that he could not choose but laugh at those who seemed to fear a war; and when some were saying, that if Cæsar should march against the city, they could not see what forces there were to resist him, he replied with a smile, bidding them be in no concern, "for," said he, "whenever I stamp with my foot in any part of Italy there will rise up forces enough in an instant, both horse and foot."

Cæsar, on the other side, was more and more vigorous in his proceedings, himself always at hand about the frontiers of Italy, and sending his soldiers continually into the city to attend all elections with their votes. Besides, he corrupted several of the magistrates, and kept them in his pay; among others, Paulus, the consul, who was brought over by a bribe of one thousand and five hundred talents; and Curio, tribune of the people, by a discharge of the debts with which he was overwhelmed; together with Mark Antony, who, out of friendship to Curio, had become bound with him in the same obligations for them all. And it was stated as a fact, that a centurion of Cæsar's, waiting at the senate-house, and hearing that the senate refused to give him a longer term of his government, clapped his hand upon his sword, and said, "But this shall give it." And indeed all his practices and preparations seemed to bear this appearance. Curio's demands, however, and requests in favour of Cæsar, were more popular in appearance; for he desired one of these two things, either that Pompey also should be called upon to resign his army, or that Cæsar's should not be taken away from him; for if both of them became private persons, both would be satisfied with simple justice; or if both retained their present power, each being a match for the other, they would be contented with what they already had; but he that weakens one, does at the same time strengthen the other, and so doubles that very strength and power which he stood in fear of before.

Marcellus, the consul, replied nothing to all this, but that Cæsar was a robber, and should be proclaimed an enemy to the state if he did not disband his army. However, Curio, with the assistance of Antony and Piso, prevailed, that the matter in debate should be put to the question, and decided by vote in the senate. So that it being ordered upon the question for those to withdraw who were of opinion that Cæsar only should lay down his army, and Pompey command, the majority withdrew. But when it was ordered again for those to withdraw whose vote was that both should lay down their arms, and neither command, there were but twenty-two for Pompey, all the rest remained on Curio's side. Whereupon he, as one proud of his conquest, leaped out in triumph among the people, who received him with as great tokens of joy, clapping their hands and crowning him with garlands and flowers. Pompey was not then present in the senate, because it is not lawful for generals in command of an army to come into the city. But Marcellus rising up, said, that he would not sit there hearing speeches, when he saw ten legions already passing the Alps on their march toward the city, but on his own authority would send some one to oppose them in defence of the country.

Upon this the city went into mourning, as in a public calamity, and Marcellus, accompanied by the senate, went solemnly through the forum to meet Pompey, and made him this address: "I hereby give you orders, O Pompey, to defend your country, to employ the troops you now command, and to levy more." Lentulus, consul elect for the year following, spoke to the same purpose. Antony, however, contrary to the will of the senate, having in a public assembly read a letter of Cæsar's, containing various plausible overtures such as were likely to gain the common people, proposing, namely, that both Pompey and he, quitting their governments and dismissing their armies, should submit to the judgment of the people, and give an account of their actions before them, the consequence was that when Pompey began to make his levies, he found himself disappointed in his expectations. Some few, indeed, came in, but those very unwillingly; others would not answer to their names, and the generality cried out for peace. Lentulus, notwithstanding he was now entered upon his consulship, would not assemble the senate; but Cicero, who was lately returned from Cilicia, laboured for a reconciliation, proposing that Cæsar should leave his province of Gaul and army, reserving two legions only, together with the government of Illyricum and should thus be put in nomination for a second consulship. Pompey disliking this motion, Cæsar's friends were contented that he should surrender one of the two; but Lentulus still opposing, and Cato crying out that Pompey did ill to be deceived again, the reconciliation did not take effect.

In the meantime, news was brought that Cæsar had occupied Ariminum, a great city in Italy, and was marching directly towards Rome with all his forces. But this latter was altogether false, for he had no more with him at that time than three hundred horse and five thousand foot; and he did not mean to tarry for the body of his army, which lay beyond the Alps, choosing rather to fall in on a sudden upon his enemies, while they were in confusion, and did not expect him, than to give them time, and fight them after they had made preparations. For when he came to the banks of the Rubicon, a river that made the bounds of his province there he made a halt, pausing a little, and considering, we may suppose, with himself the greatness of the enterprise which he had undertaken; then, at last, like men that are throwing themselves headlong from some precipice into a vast abyss, having shut, as it were, his mind's eyes and put away from his sight the idea of danger, he merely uttered to those near him in Greek the words, "Anerriphtho kubos" (let the die be cast), and led his army through it. No sooner was the news arrived, but there was an uproar throughout all the city, and a consternation in the people even to astonishment, such as never was known in Rome before; all the senate ran immediately to Pompey, and the magistrates followed. And when Tullus made inquiry about his legions and forces, Pompey seemed to pause a little, and answered with some hesitation that he had those two legions ready that Cæsar sent back, and that out of the men who had been previously enrolled he believed he could shortly make up a body of thirty thousand men. On which Tullus crying out aloud, "O Pompey, you have deceived us," gave his advice to send off a deputation to Cæsar. Favonius, a man of fair character, except that he used to suppose his own petulance and abusive talking a copy of Cato's straightforwardness, bade Pompey stamp upon the ground, and call forth the forces he had promised. But Pompey bore patiently with this unseasonable raillery; and on Cato putting him in mind of what he had foretold from the very beginning about Cæsar, made this answer only, that Cato indeed had spoken more like a prophet, but he had acted more like a friend. Cato then advised them to choose Pompey general with absolute power and authority, saying that the same men who do great evils know best how to cure them. He himself went his way forthwith into Sicily, the province that was allotted him, and all the rest of the senators likewise departed every one to his respective government.

Thus all Italy in a manner being up in arms, no one could say what was best to be done. For those that were without came from all parts flocking into the city; and they who were within, seeing the confusion and disorder so great there, all good things impotent, and disobedience and insubordination grown too strong to be controlled by the magistrates, were quitting it as fast as the others came in. Nay, it was so far from being possible to allay their fears, that they would not suffer Pompey to follow out his own judgment, but every man pressed and urged him according to his particular fancy, whether it proceeded from doubt, fear, grief, or any meaner passion; so that even in the same day quite contrary counsels were acted upon. Then, again, it was as impossible to have any good intelligence of the enemy; for what each man heard by chance upon a flying rumour he would report for truth, and exclaim against Pompey if he did not believe it. Pompey, at length, seeing such a confusion in Rome, determined with himself to put an end to their clamours by his departure, and therefore commanding all the senate to follow him, and declaring that whosoever tarried behind should be judged a confederate of Cæsar's, about the dusk of the evening he went out and left the city. The consuls also followed after in a hurry, without offering the sacrifices to the gods usual before a war. But in all this, Pompey himself had the glory that, in the midst of such calamities, he had so much of men's love and good-will. For though many found fault with the conduct of the war, yet no man hated the general; and there were more to be found of those that went out of Rome, because that they could not forsake Pompey, than of those that fled for love of liberty.

Some few days after Pompey was gone out, Cæsar came into the city, and made himself master of it, treating every one with a great deal of courtesy, and appeasing their fears, except only Metellus, one of the tribunes; on whose refusing to let him take any money out of the treasury, Cæsar threatened him with death, adding words yet harsher than the threat, that it was far easier for him to do it than say it. By this means removing Metellus, and taking what moneys were of use for his occasions, he set forward in pursuit of Pompey, endeavouring with all speed to drive him out of Italy before his army, that was in Spain, could join him.

But Pompey arriving at Brundusium, and having plenty of ships there, bade the two consuls embark immediately, and with them shipped thirty cohorts of foot, bound before him for Dyrrhachium. He sent likewise his father-in-law, Scipio, and Cnæus, his son, into Syria, to provide and fit out a fleet there; himself in the meantime having blocked up the gates, placed his lightest soldiers as guards upon the walls; and giving express orders that the citizens should keep within doors, he dug up all the ground inside the city, cutting trenches, and fixing stakes and palisades throughout all the streets of the city, except only two that led down to the seaside. Thus in three days' space having with ease put all the rest of his army on shipboard, he suddenly gave the signal to those that guarded the walls, who nimbly repairing to the ships were received on board and carried off. Cæsar meantime perceiving their departure by seeing the walls unguarded, hastened after, and in the heat of pursuit was all but entangled himself among the stakes and trenches. But the Brundusians discovering the danger to him, and showing him the way, he wheeled about, and taking a circuit round the city, made towards the haven, where he found all the ships on their way excepting only two vessels that had but a few soldiers aboard.

Most are of opinion that this departure of Pompey's is to be counted among the best of his military performances, but Cæsar himself could not but wonder that he, who was thus engarrisoned in a city well fortified, who was in expectation of his forces from Spain, and was master of the sea besides, should leave and abandon Italy. Cicero accuses him of imitating the conduct of Themistocles, rather than of Pericles, when the circumstances were more like those of Pericles than they were like those of Themistocles. However, it appeared plainly, and Cæsar showed it by his actions, that he was in great fear of delay, for when he had taken Numerius, a friend of Pompey's, prisoner, he sent him as an ambassador to Brundusium, with offers of peace and reconciliation upon equal terms; but Numerius sailed away with Pompey. And now Cæsar having become master of all Italy in sixty days, without a drop of bloodshed, had a great desire forthwith to follow Pompey; but being destitute of shipping, he was forced to divert his course and march into Spain, designing to bring over Pompey's forces there to his own.

In the meantime Pompey raised a mighty army both by sea and land. As for his navy, it was irresistible. For there were five hundred men-of-war, besides an infinite company of light vessels, Liburnians, and others; and for his land forces, the cavalry made up a body of seven thousand horse, the very flower of Rome and Italy, men of family, wealth, and high spirit; but the infantry was a mixture of inexperienced soldiers drawn from different quarters, and these he exercised and trained near Berœa, where he quartered his army; himself noways slothful, but performing all his exercises as if he had been in the flower of his youth, conduct which raised the spirits of his soldiers extremely. For it was no small encouragement for them to see Pompey the Great, sixty years of age wanting two, at one time handling his arms among the foot, then again mounted among the horse, drawing out his sword with ease in full career, and sheathing it up as easily; and in darting the javelin, showing not only skill and dexterity in hitting the mark, but also strength and activity in throwing it so far that few of the young men went beyond him.

Several kings and princes of nations came thither to him, and there was a concourse of Roman citizens who had held the magistracies, so numerous that they made up a complete senate. Labienus forsook his old friend Cæsar, whom he had served throughout all his wars in Gaul, and came over to Pompey; and Brutus, son to that Brutus that was put to death in Gaul, a man of a high spirit, and one that to that day had never so much as saluted or spoke to Pompey, looking upon him as the murderer of his father, came then and submitted himself to him as the defender of their liberty. Cicero likewise, though he had written and advised otherwise, yet was ashamed not to be accounted in the number of those that would hazard their lives and fortunes for the safeguard of their country. There came to him also into Macedonia, Tidius Sextius, a man extremely old, and lame af one leg; so that others indeed mocked and laughed at the spectacle, but Pompey, as soon as he saw him, rose and ran to meet him, esteeming it no small testimony in his favour, when men of such age and infirmities should rather choose to be with him in danger than in safety at home. Afterwards in a meeting of their senate they passed a decree, on the motion of Cato, that no Roman citizen should be put to death but in battle, and that they should not sack or plunder any city that was subject to the Roman empire, a resolution which gained Pompey's party still greater reputation, insomuch that those who were noways at all concerned in the war, either because they dwelt afar off, or were thought incapable of giving help, were yet, in their good wishes, upon his side, and in all their words, so far as that went, supported the good or just cause, as they called it; esteeming those as enemies to the gods and men that wished not victory to Pompey.

Neither was Pompey's clemency such but that Cæsar likewise showed himself as merciful a conqueror; for when he had taken and overthrown all Pompey's forces in Spain, he gave them easy terms, leaving the commanders at their liberty, and taking the common soldiers into his own pay. Then repassing the Alps, and making a running march through Italy, he came to Brundusium about the winter solstice, and crossing the sea there, landed at the port of Oricum. And having Jubius, an intimate friend of Pompey's, with him as his prisoner, he despatched him to Pompey with an invitation that they, meeting together in a conference, should disband their armies within three days, and renewing their former friendship with solemn oaths, should return together into Italy. Pompey looked upon this again as some new stratagem, and therefore marching down in all haste to the seacoast, possessed himself of all forts and places of strength suitable to encamp in, and to secure his land-forces, as likewise of all ports and harbours commodious to receive any that came by sea, so that what wind soever blew, it must needs, in some way or other, be favourable to him, bringing in either provision, men, or money; while Cæsar, on the contrary, was so hemmed in both by sea and land that he was forced to desire battle, daily provoking the enemy, and assailing them in their very forts, and in these light skirmishes for the most part had the better. Once only he was dangerously overthrown, and was within a little of losing his whole army, Pompey having fought nobly, routing the whole force and killing two thousand on the spot. But either he was not able, or was afraid, to go on and force his way into their camp with them; so that Cæsar made the remark, that "To-day the victory had been the enemy's had there been any one among them to gain it." Pompey's soldiers were so encouraged by this victory that they were eager now to have all put to the decision of a battle; but Pompey himself, though he wrote to distant kings, generals, and states in confederacy with him as a conqueror, yet was afraid to hazard the success of a battle, choosing rather by delays and distress of provisions to tire out a body of men who had never yet been conquered by force of arms, and had long been used to fight and conquer together; while their time of life, now an advanced one, which made them quickly weary of those other hardships of war, such as were long marches and frequent decampings, making trenches, and building fortifications, made them eager to come to close combat and venture a battle with all speed.

Pompey had all along hitherto by his persuasions pretty well quieted his soldiers; but after this last engagement, when Cæsar, for want of provisions, was forced to raise his camp, and passed through Athamania into Thessaly, it was impossible to curb or allay the heat of their spirits any longer. For all crying out with a general voice that Cæsar was fled, some were for pursuing and pressing upon him, others for returning into Italy; some there were that sent their friends and servants beforehand to Rome to hire houses near the forum, that they might be in readiness to sue for offices; several of their own motion sailed off at once to Lesbos to carry to Cornelia (whom Pompey had conveyed thither to be in safety) the joyful news that the war was ended. And a senate being called and the matter being under debate, Afranius was of opinion that Italy should first be regained, for that it was the grand prize and crown of all the war; and they who were masters of that would quickly have at their devotion all the provinces of Sicily, Sardinia, Corsica, Spain, and Gaul; but what was of greatest weight and moment to Pompey, it was his own native country that lay near, reaching out her hand for his help; and certainly it could not be consistent with his honour to leave her thus exposed to all indignities, and in bondage under slaves and the flatterers of a tyrant. But Pompey himself, on the contrary, thought it neither honourable to fly a second time before Cæsar, and be pursued, when fortune had given him the advantage of a pursuit; nor indeed lawful before the gods to forsake Scipio and divers other men of consular dignity dispersed throughout Greece and Thessaly, who must necessarily fall into Cæsar's hands, together with large sums of money and numerous forces; and as to his care for the city of Rome, that would most eminently appear by removing the scene of war to a greater distance, and leaving her, without feeling the distress or even hearing the sound of these evils, to await in peace the return of whichever should be the victor.

With this determination, Pompey marched forwards in pursuit of Cæsar, firmly resolved with himself not to give him battle, but rather to besiege and distress him, by keeping close at his heels, and cutting him short. There were other reasons that made him continue this resolution, but especially because a saying that was current among the Romans serving in the cavalry came to his ear, to the effect that they ought to beat Cæsar as soon as possible, and then humble Pompey too. And some report it was for this reason that Pompey never employed Cato in any matter of consequence during the whole war, but now, when he pursued Cæsar, left him to guard his baggage by sea, fearing lest, if Cæsar should be taken off, he himself also by Cato's means not long after should be forced to give up his power.

Whilst he was thus slowly attending the motions of the enemy, he was exposed on all sides to outcries and imputations of using his generalship to defeat, not Cæsar, but his country and the senate, that he might always continue in authority, and never cease to keep those for his guards and servants who themselves claimed to govern the world. Domitius Ænobarbus, continually calling him Agamemnon, the king of kings, excited jealousy against him; and Favonius, by his unseasonable raillery, did him no less injury than those who openly attacked him, as when he cried out, "Good friends, you must not expect to gather any figs in Tusculum this year." But Lucius Afranius, who had lain under an imputation of treachery for the loss of the army in Spain, when he saw Pompey purposely declining an engagement, declared openly that he could not but admire why those who were so ready to accuse him did not go themselves and fight this buyer and seller of their provinces.

With these and many such speeches they wrought upon Pompey, who never could bear reproach, or resist the expectations of his friends; and thus they forced him to break his measures, so that he forsook his own prudent resolution to follow their vain hopes and desires: weakness that would have been blamable in the pilot of a ship, how much more in the sovereign commander of such an army, and so many nations. But he, though he had often commended those physicians who did not comply with the capricious appetites of their patients, yet himself could not but yield to the malady and disease of his companions and advisers in the war, rather than use some severity in their cure. Truly who could have said that health was not disordered and a cure not required in the case of men who went up and down the camp, suing already for the consulship and office of prætor, while Spinther, Domitius, and Scipio made friends, raised factions, and quarrelled among themselves who should succeed Cæsar in the dignity of his high-priesthood, esteeming all as lightly as if they were to engage only with Tigranes, King of Armenia, or some petty Nabathæan king, not with that Cæsar and his army that had stormed a thousand towns, and subdued more than three hundred several nations; that had fought innumerable battles with the Germans and Gauls, and always carried the victory; that had taken a million of men prisoners, and slain as many upon the spot in pitched battles?

But they went on soliciting and clamouring, and on reaching the plain of Pharsalia, they forced Pompey by their pressure and importunities to call a council of war, where Labienus, general of the horse, stood up first and swore that he would not return out of the battle if he did not rout the enemies; and all the rest took the same oath. That night Pompey dreamed that, as he went into the theatre, the people received him with great applause, and that he himself adorned the temple of Venus the Victorious with many spoils. This vision partly encouraged, but partly also disheartened him, fearing lest that splendour and ornament to Venus should be made with spoils furnished by himself to Cæsar, who derived his family from that goddess. Besides there were some panic fears and alarms that ran through the camp, with such a noise that it awakened him out of his sleep. And about the time of renewing the watch towards morning, there appeared a great light over Cæsar's camp whilst they were all at rest, and from thence a ball of flaming fire was carried into Pompey's camp, which Cæsar himself says he saw as he was walking his rounds.

Now Cæsar having designed to raise his camp with the morning and move to Scotussa, whilst the soldiers were busy in pulling down their tents, and sending on their cattle and servants before them with their baggage, there came in scouts who brought word that they saw arms carried to and fro in the enemy's camp, and heard a noise and running up and down as of men preparing for battle; not long after there came in other scouts with further intelligence, that the first ranks were already set in battle array. Thereupon Cæsar, when he had told them that the wished for day was come at last, when they should fight with men, not with hunger and famine, instantly gave orders for the red colours to be set up before his tent, that being the ordinary signal of battle among the Romans. As soon as the soldiers saw that, they left their tents, and with great shouts of joy ran to their arms; the officers likewise, on their part, drawing up their companies in order of battle, every man fell into his proper rank without any trouble or noise, as quietly and orderly as if they had been in a dance.

Pompey himself led the right wing of his army against Antony, and placed his father-in-law, Scipio, in the middle against Lucius Calvinus. The left wing was commanded by Lucius Domitius, and supported by the great mass of the horse. For almost the whole cavalry was posted there in the hope of crushing Cæsar, and cutting off the tenth legion, which was spoken of as the stoutest in all the army, and in which Cæsar himself usually fought in person. Cæsar observing the left wing of the enemy to be lined and fortified with such a mighty guard of horse, and alarmed at the gallantry of their appearance, sent for a detachment of six cohorts out of the reserves, and placed them in the rear of the tenth legion, commanding them not to stir, lest they should be discovered by the enemy; but when the enemy's horse should begin to charge, and press upon them, that they should make up with all speed to the front through the foremost ranks, and not throw their javelins at a distance, as is usual with brave soldiers, that they come to a close fight with their swords the sooner, but that they should strike them upwards into the eyes and faces of the enemy; telling them that those fine young dancers would never endure the steel shining in their eyes, but would fly to save their handsome faces. This was Cæsar's employment at that time. But while he was thus instructing his soldiers, Pompey on horseback was viewing the order of both armies, and when he saw how well the enemy kept their ranks, expecting quietly the signal of battle, and, on the contrary, how impatient and unsteady his own men were, waving up and down in disorder for want of experience, he was very much afraid that their ranks would be broken upon the first onset; and therefore he gave out orders that the van should make a stand, and keeping close in their ranks should receive the enemy's charge. Cæsar much condemns this command; which, he says, not only took off from the strength of the blows, which would otherwise have been made with a spring, but also lost the men the impetus, which, more than anything, in the moment of their coming upon the enemy, fills soldiers with impulse and inspiration, the very shouts and rapid pace adding to their fury; of which Pompey deprived his men, arresting them in their course and cooling down their heat.

Cæsar's army consisted of twenty-two thousand, and Pompey's of somewhat above twice as many. When the signal of battle was given on both sides, and the trumpets began to sound a charge, most men of course were fully occupied with their own matters; only some few of the noblest Romans, together with certain Greeks there present, standing as spectators without the battle, seeing the armies now ready to join, could not but consider in themselves to what a pass private ambition and emulation had brought the empire. Common arms, and kindred ranks drawn up under the selfsame standards, the whole flower and strength of the same single city here meeting in collision with itself, offered plain proof how blind and how mad a thing human nature is when once possessed with any passion; for if they had been desirous only to rule, and enjoy in peace what they had conquered in war, the greatest and best part of the world was subject to them both by sea and land. But if there was yet a thirst in their ambition, that must still be fed with new trophies and triumphs, the Parthian and German wars would yield matter enough to satisfy the most covetous of honour. Scythia, moreover, was yet unconquered, and the Indians too, where their ambition might be coloured over with the specious pretext of civilising barbarous nations. And what Scythian horse, Parthian arrows, or Indian riches could be able to resist seventy thousand Roman soldiers, well appointed in arms, under the command of two such generals as Pompey and Cæsar,whose names they had heard of before that of the Romans, and whose prowess, by their conquests of such wild, remote, savage, and brutish nations, was spread further than the fame of the Romans themselves? Today they met in conflict, and could no longer be induced to spare their country, even out of regard for their own glory or the fear of losing the name which till this day both had held, of having never yet been defeated. As for their former private ties, and the charms of Julia, and the marriage that had made them near connections, these could now only be looked upon as tricks of state, the mere securities of a treaty made to serve the needs of an occasion, not the pledges of any real friendship.

Now, therefore, as soon as the plains of Pharsalia were covered with men, horse, and armour, and that the signal of battle was raised on either side, Caius Crassianus, a centurion, who commanded a company of one hundred and twenty men, was the first that advanced out of Cæsar's army to give the charge and acquit himself of a solemn engagement that he had made to Cæsar. He had been the first man that Cæsar had seen going out of the camp in the morning, and Cæsar, after saluting him, had asked him what he thought of the coming battle. To which he, stretching out his right hand, replied aloud, "Thine is the victory, O Cæsar, thou shalt conquer gloriously, and I myself this day will be the subject of thy praise either alive or dead." In pursuance of this promise he hastened forward, and being followed by many more, charged into the midst of the enemy. There they came at once to a close fight with their swords, and made a great slaughter; but as he was still pressing forward, and breaking the ranks of the vanguard, one of Pompey's soldiers ran him in at the mouth, so that the point of the sword came out behind at his neck; and Crassianus being thus slain, the fight became doubtful, and continued equal on that part of the battle.

Pompey had not yet brought on the right wing, but stayed and looked about, waiting to see what execution his cavalry would do on the left. They had already drawn out their squadrons in form, designing to turn Cæsar's flank, and force those few horse, which he had placed in the front, to give back upon the battalion of foot. But Cæsar, on the other side, having given the signal, his horse retreated back a little, and gave way to those six subsidiary cohorts, which had been posted in the rear, as a reserve to cover the flank, and which now came out, three thousand men in number, and met the enemy; and when they came up, standing by the horses, struck their javelins upwards, according to their instructions, and hit the horsemen full in their faces. They, unskillful in any manner of fight, and least of all expecting or understanding such a kind as this, had not courage enough to endure the blows upon their faces, but turning their backs, and covering their eyes with their hands, shamefully took to flight. Cæsar's men, however, did not follow them, but marched upon the foot, and attacked the wing, which the flight of the cavalry had left unprotected, and liable to be turned and taken in the rear, so that this wing now being attacked in the flank by these, and charged in the front by the tenth legion, was not able to abide the charge, or make any longer resistance, especially when they saw themselves surrounded and circumvented in the very way in which they had designed to invest the enemy. Thus these being likewise routed and put to flight, when Pompey, by the dust flying in the air, conjectured the fate of his horse, it were very hard to say what his thoughts or intentions were, but looking like one distracted and beside himself and without any recollection or reflection that he was Pompey the Great, he retired slowly towards his camp, without speaking a word to any man, exactly according to the description in the verses—

> "But Jove from heaven struck Ajax with a fear;
> Ajax the bold then stood astonished there,
> Flung o'er his back the mighty sevenfold shield,
> And trembling gazed and spied about the field."

In this state and condition he went into his own tent and sat down, speechless still, until some of the enemy fell in together with his men that were flying into the camp, and then he let fall only this one word, "What! into the very camp?" and said no more, but rose up, and putting on a dress suitable to his present fortune, made his way secretly out.

By this time the rest of the army was put to flight, and there was a great slaughter in the camp among the servants and those that guarded the tents, but of the soldiers themselves there were not above six thousand slain, as is stated by Asinius Pollio, who himself fought in this battle on Cæsar's side. When Cæsar's soldiers had taken the camp, they saw clearly the folly and vanity of the enemy; for all their tents and pavilions were richly set out with garlands of myrtle, embroidered carpets and hangings, and tables laid and covered with goblets. There were large bowls of wine ready, and everything prepared and put in array, in the manner rather of people who had offered sacrifice and were going to celebrate a holiday, than of soldiers who had armed themselves to go out to battle, so possessed with the expectation of success and so full of empty confidence had they gone out that morning.

When Pompey had got a little way from the camp, he dismounted and forsook his horse, having but a small retinue with him; and finding that no man pursued him, walked on softly afoot, taken up altogether with thoughts, such as probably might possess a man that for the space of thirty-four years together had been accustomed to conquest and victory, and was then at last, in his old age, learning for the first time what defeat and flight were. And it was no small affliction to consider that he had lost in one hour all that glory and power which he had been getting in so many wars and bloody battles; and that he who but a little before was guarded with such an army of foot, so many squadrons of horse, and such a mighty fleet, was now flying in so mean a condition, and with such a slender retinue, that his very enemies who fought him could not know him. Thus, when he had passed by the city of Larissa, and came into the pass of Tempe, being very thirsty, he kneeled down and drank out of the river; then rising up again, he passed through Tempe, until he came to the seaside, and there he betook himself to a poor fisherman's cottage, where he rested the remainder of the night. The next morning about break of day he went into one of the river boats, and taking none of those that followed him except such as were free, dismissed his servants, advising them to go boldly to Caesar and not be afraid. As he was rowing up and down near the shore, he chanced to spy a large merchant ship, lying off, just ready to set sail; the master of which was a Roman citizen, named Peticius, who, though he was not familiarly acquainted with Pompey, yet knew him well by sight. Now it happened that this Peticius dreamed, the night before, that he saw Pompey, not like the man he had often seen him, but in a humble and dejected condition, and in that posture discoursing with him. He was then telling his dream to the people on board, as men do when at leisure, and especially dreams of that consequence, when of a sudden one of the mariners told him he saw a river boat with oars putting off from shore, and that some of the men there shook their garments, and held out their hands, with signs to take them in; thereupon Peticius, looking attentively, at once recognised Pompey, just as he appeared in his dream, and smiting his hand on his head, ordered the mariners to let down the ship's boat, he himself waving his hand, and calling to him by his name, already assured of his change and the change of his fortune by that of his garb. So that without waiting for any further entreaty or discourse he took him into his ship, together with as many of his company as he thought fit, and hoisted sail. There were with him the two Lentuli and Favonius; and a little after they spied King Deiotarus, making up towards them from the shore; so they stayed and took him in along with them. At supper time, the master of the ship having made ready such provisions as he had aboard, Pompey, for want of his servants, began to undo his shoes himself, which Favonius noticing, ran to him and undid them, and helped him to anoint himself, and always after continued to wait upon, and attended him in all things, as servants do their masters, even to the washing of his feet and preparing his supper. Insomuch that any one there present, observing the free and unaffected courtesy of these services, might have well exclaimed—

> "O heavens, in those that noble are,
> Whate'er they do is fit and fair."

Pompey, sailing by the city of Amphipolis, crossed over from thence to Mitylene, with a design to take in Cornelia and his son; and as soon as he arrived at the port in that island, he despatched a messenger into the city with news very different from Cornelia's expectation. For she, by all the former messages and letters sent to please her, had been put in hopes that the war was ended at Dyrrhachium, and that there was nothing more remaining for Pompey but the pursuit of Cæsar. The messenger, finding her in the same hopes still, was not able to salute or speak to her, but declaring the greatness of her misfortune by his tears rather than his words, desired her to make haste if she would see Pompey, with one ship only, and that not of his own. The young lady hearing this, fell down in a swoon, and continued a long time senseless and speechless. And when with some trouble she was brought to her senses again, being conscious to herself that this was no time for lamentation and tears, she started up and ran through the city towards the seaside, where Pompey meeting and embracing her, as she sank down, supported by his arms, "This, sir," she exclaimed, "is the effect of my fortune, not of yours, that I see you thus reduced to one poor vessel, who before your marriage with Cornelia were wont to sail in these seas with a fleet of five hundred ships. Why therefore should you come to see me, or why not rather have left to her evil genius one who has brought upon you her own ill fortune? How happy a woman had I been if I had breathed out my last before the news came from Parthia of the death of Publius, the husband of my youth, and how prudent if I had followed his destiny, as I designed! But I was reserved for a greater mischief, even the ruin of Pompey the Great."

Thus, they say, Cornelia spoke to him, and this was Pompey's reply: "You have had, Cornelia, but one season of a better fortune, which, it may be, gave you unfounded hopes, by attending me a longer time than is usual. It behooves us, who are mortals born, to endure these events, and to try fortune yet again; neither is it any less possible to recover our former state than it was to fall from that into this." Thereupon Cornelia sent for her servants and baggage out of the city. The citizens also of Mitylene came out to salute and invite Pompey into the city, but he refused, advising them to be obedient to the conqueror and fear not, for that Cæsar was a man of great goodness and clemency. Then turning to Cratippus, the philosopher, who came among the rest out of the city to visit him, he began to find some fault, and briefly argued with him upon Providence, but Cratippus modestly declined the dispute, putting him in better hopes only, lest by opposing he might seem too austere or unseasonable. For he might have put Pompey a question in his turn in defence of Providence; and might have demonstrated the necessity there was that the commonwealth should be turned into a monarchy, because of their ill government in the state; and could have asked, "How, O Pompey, and by what token or assurance can we ascertain, that if the victory had been yours, you would have used your fortune better than Cæsar? We must leave the divine power to act as we find it do."

Pompey having taken his wife and friends aboard, set sail, making no port, or touching anywhere, but when he was necessitated to take in provisions or fresh water. The first city he entered was Attalia, in Pamphylia, and whilst he was there, there came some galleys thither to him out of Cilicia, together with a small body of soldiers, and he had almost sixty senators with him again; then hearing that his navy was safe too, and that Cato had rallied a considerable body of soldiers after their overthrow, and was crossing with them over into Africa, he began to complain and blame himself to his friends that he had allowed himself to be driven into engaging by land, without making use of his other forces, in which he was irresistibly the stronger, and had not kept near enough to his fleet, that failing by land, he might have reinforced himself from the sea, and would have been again at the head of a power quite sufficient to encounter the enemy on equal terms. And, in truth, neither did Pompey during all the war commit a greater oversight, nor Cæsar use a more subtle stratagem, than in drawing the fight so far off from the naval forces.

As it now was, however, since he must come to some decision and try some plan within his present ability, he despatched his agents to the neighbouring cities, and himself sailed about in person to others, requiring their aid in money and men for his ships. But, fearing lest the rapid approach cf the enemy might cut off all his preparations, he began to consider what place would yield him the safest refuge and retreat at present. A consultation was held, and it was generally agreed that no province of the Romans was secure enough. As for foreign kingdoms, he himself was of opinion that Parthia would be the fittest to receive and defend them in their present weakness, and best able to furnish them with new means, and send them out again with large forces. Others of the council were for going into Africa, and to King Juba. But Theophanes the Lesbian thought it madness to leave Egypt, that was but at a distance of three days' sailing, and make no use of Ptolemy, who was still a boy, and was highly indebted to Pompey for the friendship and favour he had shown to his father, only to put himself under the Parthian, and trust the most treacherous nation in the world; and rather than make any trial of the clemency of a Roman, and his own near connection, to whom if he would but yield to be second he might be the first and chief over all the rest, to go and place himself at the mercy of Arsaces, which even Crassus had not submitted to while alive; and, moreover, to expose his young wife, of the family of the Scipios, among a barbarous people, who govern by their lusts, and measure their greatness by their power to commit affronts and insolences; from whom, though she suffered no dishonour, yet it might be thought she did, being in the hands of those who had the power to do it. This argument alone, they say, was persuasive enough to divert his course, that was designed towards Euphrates, if it were so indeed that any counsel of Pompey's, and not some superior power, made him take this other way.

As soon, therefore, as it was resolved upon that he should fly into Egypt, setting sail from Cyprus in a galley of Seleucia, together with Cornelia, while the rest of his company sailed along near him, some in ships of war, and others in merchant vessels, he passed over sea without danger. But on hearing that King Ptolemy was posted with his army at the city of Pelusium, making war against his sister, he steered his course that way, and sent a messenger before to acquaint the king with his arrival, and to crave his protection. Ptolemy himself was quite young, and therefore Pothinus, who had the principal administration of affairs, called a council of the chief men, those being the greatest whom he pleased to make so, and commanded them every man to deliver his opinion touching the reception of Pompey. It was, indeed, a miserable thing that the fate of the great Pompey should be left to the determinations of Pothinus the eunuch, Theodotus of Chois, the paid rhetoric master, and Achillas the Egyptian. For these, among the chamberlains and menial domestics that made up the rest of the council, were the chief and leading men. Pompey, who thought it dishonourable for him to owe his safety to Cæsar, riding at anchor at a distance from shore, was forced to wait the sentence of this tribunal. It seems they were so far different in their opinions that some were for sending the man away, and others, again, for inviting and receiving him; but Theodotus, to show his cleverness and the cogency of his rhetoric, undertook to demonstrate that neither the one nor the other was safe in that juncture of affairs. For if they entertained him, they would be sure to make Cæsar their enemy and Pompey their master; or if they dismissed him, they might render themselves hereafter obnoxious to Pompey, for that inhospitable expulsion, and to Cæsar, for the escape; so that the most expedient course would be to send for him and take away his life, for by that means they would ingratiate themselves with the one, and have no reason to fear the other; adding, it is related, with a smile, that "a dead man cannot bite."

This advice being approved of, they committed the execution of it to Achillas. He, therefore, taking with him as his accomplices one Septimius, a man that had formerly held a command under Pompey, and Salvius, another centurion, with three or four attendants, made up towards Pompey's galley. In the meantime, all the chiefest of those who accompanied Pompey in this voyage were come into his ship to learn the event of their embassy. But when they saw the manner of their reception, that in appearance it was neither princely nor honourable, nor indeed in any way answerable to the hopes of Theophanes, or their expectation (for there came but a few men in a fisherman's boat to meet them), they began to suspect the meanness of their entertainment, and gave warning to Pompey that he should row back his galley, whilst he was out of their reach, and make for the sea. By this time the Egyptian boat drew near, and Septimius standing up first, saluted Pompey, in the Latin tongue, by the title of imperator. Then Achillas, saluting him in the Greek language, desired him to come aboard his vessel, telling him that the sea was very shallow towards the shore, and that a galley of that burden could not avoid striking upon the sands. At the same time they saw several of the king's galleys getting their men on board, and all the shore covered with soldiers; so that even if they changed their minds, it seemed impossible for them to escape, and besides, their distrust would have given the assassins a pretence for their cruelty. Pompey, therefore, taking his leave of Cornelia, who was already lamenting his death before it came, bade two centurions, with Philip, one of his freedmen, and a slave called Scythes, go on board the boat before him. And as some of the crew with Achillas were reaching out their hands to help him, he turned about towards his wife and son, and repeated those iambics of Sophocles—

> "He that once enters at a tyrant's door
> Becomes a slave, though he were free before."

These were the last words he spoke to his friends, and so he went aboard. Observing presently that notwithstanding there was a considerable distance betwixt his galley and the shore, yet none of the company addressed any words of friendliness or welcome to him all the way, he looked earnestly upon Septimius, and said, "I am not mistaken, surely, in believing you to have been formerly my fellow-soldier." But he only nodded with his head, making no reply at all, nor showing any other courtesy. Since, therefore, they continued silent, Pompey took a little book in his hand, in which was written out an address in Greek, which he intended to make to King Ptolemy and began to read it. When they drew near to the shore, Cornelia, together with the rest of his friends in the galley, was very impatient to see the event, and began to take courage at last when she saw several of the royal escort coming to meet him, apparently to give him a more honourable reception; but in the meantime, as Pompey took Philip by the hand to rise up more easily, Septimius first stabbed him from behind with his sword, and after him likewise Salvius and Achillas drew out their swords. He, therefore, taking up his gown with both hands, drew it over his face, and neither saying nor doing anything unworthy of himself, only groaning a little, endured the wounds they gave him, and so ended his life, in the fifty-ninth year of his age, the very next day after the day of his birth.

Cornelia, with her company from the galley, seeing him murdered, gave such a cry that it was heard on the shore, and weighing anchor with all speed, they hoisted sail, and fled. A strong breeze from the shore assisted their flight into the open sea, so that the Egyptians, though desirous to overtake them, desisted from the pursuit. But they cut off Pompey's head, and threw the rest of his body overboard, leaving it naked upon the shore, to be viewed by any that had the curiosity to see so sad a spectacle. Philip stayed by and watched till they had glutted their eyes in viewing it; and then washing it with sea-water, having nothing else, he wrapped it up in a shirt of his own for a winding-sheet. Then seeking up and down about the sands, at last he found some rotten planks of a little fisher-boat, not much, but yet enough to make up a funeral pile for a naked body, and that not quite entire. As Philip was busy in gathering and putting these old planks together, an old Roman citizen, who in his youth had served in the wars under Pompey, came up to him and demanded who he was that was preparing the funeral of Pompey the Great. And Philip making answer that he was his freedman, "Nay, then," said he, "you shall not have this honour alone; let even me, too, I pray you, have my share in such a pious office, that I may not altogether repent me of this pilgrimage in a strange land, but in compensation of many misfortunes may obtain this happiness at last, even with mine own hands to touch the body of Pompey, and do the last duties to the greatest general among the Romans." And in this manner were the obsequies of Pompey performed. The next day Lucius Lentulus, not knowing what had passed, came sailing from Cyprus along the shore of that coast, and seeing a funeral pile, and Philip standing by, exclaimed, before he was yet seen by any one, "Who is this that has found his end here?" adding after a short pause, with a sigh, "Possibly even thou, Pompeius Magnus" and so going ashore, he was presently apprehended and slain. This was the end of Pompey.

Not long after, Cæsar arrived in the country that was polluted with this foul act, and when one of the Egyptians was sent to present him with Pompey's head, he turned away from him with abhorrence as from a murderer; and on receiving his seal, on which was engraved a lion holding a sword in his paw, he burst into tears. Achillas and Pothinus he put to death; and King Ptolemy himself, being overthrown in battle upon the banks of the Nile, fled away and was never heard of afterwards. Theodotus, the rhetorician, flying out of Egypt, escaped the hands of Cæsar's justice, but lived a vagabond in banishment, wandering up and down, despised and hated of all men, till at last Marcus Brutus, after he had killed Cæsar, finding him in his province of Asia, put him to death with every kind of ignominy. The ashes of Pompey were carried to his wife Cornelia, who deposited them at his country-house near Alba.

THE COMPARISON OF POMPEY WITH AGESILAUS

THUS having drawn out the history of the lives of Agesilaus and Pompey the next thing is to compare them; and in order to this, to take a cursory view, and bring together the points in which they chiefly disagree; which are these. In the first place, Pompey attained to all his greatness and glory by the fairest and justest means, owing his advancement to his own efforts, and to the frequent and important aid which he rendered Sylla, in delivering Italy from its tyrants. But Agesilaus appears to have obtained his kingdom, not without offence both towards gods and towards men, towards these, by procuring judgment of bastardy against Leotychides, whom his brother had declared his lawful son, and towards those, by putting a false gloss upon the oracle, and eluding its sentence against his lameness. Secondly,

Pompey never ceased to display his respect for Sylla during his lifetime, and expressed it also after his death, by enforcing the honourable interment of his corpse, in despite of Lepidus, and by giving his daughter in marriage to his son Faustus. But Agesilaus, upon a slight pretence, cast off Lysander with reproach and dishonour. Yet Sylla in fact had owed to Pompey services as much as Pompey ever received from him, whereas Lysander made Agesilaus King of Sparta and general of all Greece. Thirdly, Pompey's transgressions of right and justice in his political life were occasioned chiefly by his relations with other people, and most of his errors had some affinity, as well as himself, to Cæsar and Scipio, his fathers-in-law. But Agesilaus, to gratify the fondness of his son, saved the life of Sphodrias by a sort of violence, when he deserved death for the wrong he had done to the Athenians; and when Phœbidas treacherously broke the peace with Thebes, zealously abetted him for the sake, it was clear, of the unjust act itself. In short, what mischief soever Pompey might be said to have brought on Rome through compliance with the wishes of his friends or through inadvertency, Agesilaus may be said to have brought on Sparta out of obstinacy and malice, by kindling the Bœotian war. And if, moreover, we are to attribute any part of these disasters to some personal ill-fortune, attaching to the men themselves, in the case of Pompey, certainly the Romans had no reason to anticipate it. Whereas Agesilaus would not suffer the Lacedæmonians to avoid what they foresaw and were forewarned must attend the "lame sovereignty." For had Leotychides been chargeable ten thousand times as foreign and spurious, yet the race of the Eurypontids was still in being, and could easily have furnished Sparta with a lawful king that was sound in his limbs, had not Lysander darkened and disguised the true sense of the oracle in favour of Agesilaus.

Such a politic piece of sophistry as was devised by Agesilaus, in that great perplexity of the people as to the treatment to be given to those who had played the coward at the battle of Leuctra, when after that unhappy defeat he decreed that the laws should sleep for that day, it would be hard to find any parallel to; neither have we the fellow of it in all Pompey's story. But on the contrary, Pompey for a friend thought it no sin to break those very laws which he himself had made, as if to show at once the force of his friendship, and the greatness of his power; whereas Agesilaus, under the necessity, as it seemed, of either rescinding the laws, or not saving the citizens, contrived an expedient by the help of which the laws should not touch these citizens, and yet should not, to avoid it, be overthrown. Then I must commend it as an incomparable act of civil virtue and obedience in Agesilaus, that immediately upon the receipt of the scytala, he left the wars in Asia and returned into his country. For he did not, like Pompey, merely advance his country's interest by acts that contributed at the same time to promote his own greatness, but looking to his country's good, for its sake laid aside as great authority and honour as ever any man had before or since, except Alexander the Great.

But now to take another point of view, if we sum up Pompey's military expeditions and exploits of war, the number of his trophies, and the greatness of the powers which he subdued, and the multitude of battles in which he triumphed, I am persuaded even Xenophon himself would not put the victories of Agesilaus in balance with his, though Xenophon has this privilege allowed him, as a sort of special reward for his other excellences, that he may write and speak, in favour of his hero, whatever he pleases. Methinks, too, there is a great deal of difference betwixt these men in their clemency and moderation towards their enemies. For Agesilaus, while attempting to enslave Thebes and exterminate Messene, the latter, his country's ancient associate, and Thebes, the mother-city of his own royal house, almost lost Sparta itself, and did really lose the government of Greece; whereas Pompey gave cities to those of the pirates who were willing to change their manner of life; and when it was in his power to lead Tigranes, King of Armenia, in triumph, he chose rather to make him a confederate of the Romans, saying, that a single day was worth less than all future time. But if the pre-eminence in that which relates to the office and virtues of a general should be determined by the greatest and most important acts and counsels of war, the Lacedæmonian would not a little exceed the Roman. For Agesilaus never deserted his city, though it was besieged by an army of seventy thousand men, when there were very few soldiers within to defend it, and those had been defeated too, but a little before, at the battle of Leuctra. But Pompey, when Cæsar, with a body only of fifty-three hundred men, had taken but one town in Italy, departed in a panic out of Rome, either through cowardice, when there were so few, or at least through a false and mistaken belief that there were more; and having conveyed away his wife and children, he left all the rest of the citizens defenceless, and fled; whereas he ought either to have conquered in fight for the defence of his country, or yielded upon terms to the conqueror, who was, moreover, his fellow-citizen and allied to him; but now to the same man to whom he refused a prolongation of the terms of his government, and thought it intolerable to grant another consulship, to him he gave the power, by letting him take the city, to tell Metellus, together with all the rest, that they were his prisoners.

That which is chiefly the office of a general, to force the enemy into fighting when he finds himself the stronger, and to avoid being driven into it himself when he is the weaker, this excellence Agesilaus always displayed and by it kept himself invincible; whereas in contending with Pompey, Cæsar, who was the weaker, successfully declined the danger, and his own strength being in his land-forces, drove him into putting the conflict to issue with these, and thus made himself master of the treasure, stores, and the sea too, which were all in his enemy's hands, and by the help of which the victory could have been secured without fighting. And what is alleged as an apology in vindication of Pompey, is to a general of his age and standing the greatest of disgraces. For, granting that a young commander might by clamour and outcry be deprived of his fortitude and strength of mind, and weakly forsake his better judgment, and the thing be neither strange nor altogether unpardonable, yet for Pompey the Great, whose camp the Romans called their country, and his tent the senate, styling the consuls, prætors, and all other magistrates who were conducting the government at Rome by no better title than that of rebels and traitors, for him, whom they well knew never to have been under the command of any but himself, having served all his campaigns under himself as sole general, for him upon so small a provocation as the scoffs of Favonius and Domitius, and lest he should bear the nickname of Agamemnon, to be wrought upon, and even forced to hazard the whole empire and liberty of Rome upon the cast of a die, was surely indeed intolerable. Who, if he had so much regarded a present infamy, should have guarded the city at first with his arms, and fought the battle in defence of Rome, not have left it as he did: nor while declaring his flight from Italy an artifice in the manner of Themistocles, nevertheless be ashamed in Thessaly of a prudent delay before engaging. Heaven had not appointed the Pharsalian fields to be the stage and theatre upon which they should contend for the empire of Rome, neither was he summoned thither by any herald upon challenge, with intimation that he must either undergo the combat or surrender the prize to another. There were many other fields, thousands of cities, and even the whole earth placed at his command, by the advantage of his fleet and his superiority at sea, if he would but have followed the examples of Maximus, Marius, Lucullus, and even Agesilaus himself, who endured no less tumults within the city of Sparta, when the Thebans provoked him to come out and fight in defence of the land, and sustained in Egypt also numerous calumnies, slanders, and suspicions on the part of the king, whom he counselled to abstain from a battle. And thus following always what he had determined in his own judgment upon mature advice, by that means he not only preserved the Egyptians against their wills, not only kept Sparta, in those desperate convulsions, by his sole act, safe from overthrow, but even was able to set up trophies likewise in the city over the Thebans, having given his countrymen an occasion of being victorious afterwards by not at first leading them out, as they tried to force him to do, to their own destruction. The consequence was that in the end Agesilaus was commended by the very men, when they found themselves saved, upon whom he had put this compulsion, whereas Pompey, whose error had been occasioned by others, found those his accusers whose advice had misled him. Some indeed profess that he was deceived by his father-in-law Scipio, who, designing to conceal and keep to himself the greatest part of that treasure which he had brought out of Asia, pressed Pompey to battle, upon the pretence that there would be a want of money. Yet admitting he was deceived, one in his place ought not to have been so, nor should have allowed so slight an artifice to cause the hazard of such mighty interests. And thus we have taken a view of each, by comparing together their conduct and actions in war.

As to their voyages into Egypt, one steered his course thither out of necessity in flight; the other neither honourably, nor of necessity, but as a mercenary soldier, having enlisted himself into the service of a barbarous nation for pay, that he might be able afterwards to wage war upon the Greeks. And secondly, what we charge upon the Egyptians in the name of Pompey, the Egyptians lay to the charge of Agesilaus. Pompey trusted them and was betrayed and murdered by them; Agesilaus accepted their confidence and deserted them, transferring his aid to the very enemies who were now attacking those whom he had been brought over to assist.

ALEXANDER

It being my purpose to write the lives of Alexander the king, and of Cæsar, by whom Pompey was destroyed, the multitude of their great actions affords so large a field that I were to blame if I should not by way of apology forewarn my reader that I have chosen rather to epitomise the most celebrated parts of their story, than to insist at large on every particular circumstance of it. It must be borne in mind that my design is not to write histories, but lives. And the most glorious exploits do not always furnish us with the clearest discoveries of virtue or vice in men; sometimes a matter of less moment, an expression or a jest, informs us better of their characters and inclinations, than the most famous sieges, the greatest armaments, or the bloodiest battles whatsoever. Therefore as portrait-painters are more exact in the lines and features of the face, in which the character is seen, than in the other parts of the body, so I must be allowed to give my more particular attention to the marks and indications of the souls of men, and while I endeavour by these to portray their lives, may be free to leave more weighty matters and great battles to be treated of by others.

It is agreed on by all hands, that on the father's side, Alexander descended from Hercules by Caranus, and from Æacus by Neoptolemus on the mother's side. His father Philip, being in Samothrace, when he was quite young, fell in love there with Olympias, in company with whom he was initiated in the religious ceremonies of the country, and her father and mother being both dead, soon after, with the consent of her brother, Arymbas, he married her. The night before the consummation of their marriage, she dreamed that a thunderbolt fell upon her body, which kindled a great fire, whose divided flames dispersed themselves all about, and then were extinguished. And Philip, some time after he was married, dreamt that he sealed up his wife's body with a seal, whose impression, as he fancied, was the figure of a lion. Some of the diviners interpreted this as a warning to Philip to look narrowly to his wife; but Aristander of Telmessus, considering how unusual it was to seal up anything that was empty, assured him the meaning of his dream was that the queen was with child of a boy, who would one day prove as stout and courageous as a lion. Once, moreover, a serpent was found lying by Olympias as she slept, which more than anything else, it is said, abated Philip's passion for her; and whether he feared her as an enchantress, or thought she had commerce with some god, and so looked on himself as excluded, he was ever after less fond of her conversation. Others say, that the women of this country having always been extremely addicted to the enthusiastic Orphic rites, and the wild worship of Bacchus (upon which account they were called Clodones, and Mimallones), imitated in many things the practices of the Edonian and Thracian women about Mount Hæmus, from whom the word *threskeuein* seems to have been derived, as a special term for superfluous and over-curious forms of adoration; and that Olympias, zealously affecting these fanatical and enthusiastic inspirations, to perform them with more barbaric dread, was wont in the dances proper to these ceremonies to have great tame serpents about her, which sometimes creeping out of the ivy in the mystic fans, sometimes winding themselves about the sacred spears, and the women's chaplets, made a spectacle which men could not look upon without terror.

Philip, after this vision, sent Chæron of Megalopolis to consult the oracle of Apollo at Delphi, by which he was commanded to perform sacrifice, and henceforth pay particular honour, above all other gods, to Ammon; and was told he should one day lose that eye with which he presumed to peep through that chink of the door, when he saw the god, under the form of a serpent, in the company of his wife. Eratosthenes says that Olympias, when she attended Alexander on his way to the army in his first expedition, told him the secret of his birth, and bade him behave himself with courage suitable to his divine extraction. Others again affirm that she wholly disclaimed any pretensions of the kind, and was wont to say, "When will Alexander leave off slandering me to Juno?" Alexander was born the sixth of Hecatombæon, which month the Macedonians call Lous, the same day that the temple of Diana at Ephesus was burnt; which Hegesias of Magnesia makes the occasion of a conceit, frigid enough to have stopped the conflagration. The temple, he says, took fire and was burnt while its mistress was absent, assisting at the birth of Alexander. And all the Eastern soothsayers who happened to be then at Ephesus, looking upon the ruin of this temple to be the forerunner of some other calamity, ran about the town, beating their faces, and crying that this day had brought forth something that would prove fatal and destructive to all Asia.

Just after Philip had taken Potidæa, he received these three messages at one time, that Parmenio had overthrown the Illyrians in a great battle, that his race-horse had won the course at the Olympic games, and that his wife had given birth to Alexander; with which being naturally well pleased, as an addition to his satisfaction, he was assured by the diviners that a son, whose birth was accompanied with three such successes, could not fail of being invincible.

The statues that gave the best representation of Alexander's person were those of Lysippus (by whom alone he would suffer his image to be made), those peculiarities which many of his successors afterwards and his friends used to affect to imitate, the inclination of his head a little on one side towards his left shoulder, and his melting eye, having been expressed by this artist with great exactness. But Apelles, who drew him with thunderbolts in his hand, made his complexion browner and darker than it was naturally; for he was fair and of a light colour, passing into ruddiness in his face and upon his breast. Aristoxenus in his Memoirs tells us that a most agreeable odour exhaled from his skin, and that his breath and body all over was so fragrant as to perfume the clothes which he wore next him; the cause of which might probably be the hot and adust temperament of his body. For sweet smells, Theophrastus conceives, are produced by the concoction of moist humours by heat, which is the reason that those parts of the world which are driest and most burnt up afford spices of the best kind and in the greatest quantity; for the heat of the sun exhausts all the superfluous moisture which lies in the surface of bodies, ready to generate putrefaction. And this hot constitution, it may be, rendered Alexander so addicted to drinking, and so choleric. His temperance, as to the pleasures of the body, was apparent in him in his very childhood, as he was with much difficulty incited to them, and always used them with great moderation; though in other things he was extremely eager and vehement, and in his love of glory, and the pursuit of it, he showed a solidity of high spirit and magnanimity far above his age. For he neither sought nor valued it upon every occasion, as his father Philip did (who affected to show his eloquence almost to a degree of pedantry, and took care to have the victories of his racing chariots at the Olympic games engraven on his coin), but when he was asked by some about him, whether he would run a race in the Olympic games, as he was very swift-footed, he answered, he would, if he might have kings to run with him. Indeed, he seems in general to have looked with indifference, if not with dislike, upon the professed athletes. He often appointed prizes, for which not only tragedians and musicians, pipers and harpers, but rhapsodists also, strove to outvie one another; and delighted in all manner of hunting and cudgel-playing, but never gave any encouragement to contests either of boxing or of the pancratium.

While he was yet very young, he entertained the ambassadors from the King of Persia, in the absence of his father, and entering much into conversation with them, gained so much upon them by his affability, and the questions he asked them, which were far from being childish or trifling (for he inquired of them the length of the ways, the nature of the road into inner Asia, the character of their king, how he carried himself to his enemies, and what forces he was able to bring into the field), that they were struck with admiration of him, and looked upon the ability so much famed of Philip to be nothing in comparison with the forwardness and high purpose that appeared thus early in his son. Whenever he heard Philip had taken any town of importance, or won any signal victory, instead of rejoicing at it altogether, he would tell his companions that his father would anticipate everything, and leave him and them no opportunities of performing great and illustrious actions. For being more bent upon action and glory than either upon pleasure or riches, he esteemed all that he should receive from his father as a diminution and prevention of his own future achievements; and would have chosen rather to succeed to a kingdom involved in troubles and wars, which would have afforded him frequent exercise of his courage, and a large field of honour, than to one already flourishing and settled where his inheritance would be an inactive life, and the mere enjoyment of wealth and luxury.

The care of his education, as it might be presumed, was committed to a great many attendants, preceptors, and teachers, over the whole of whom Leonidas, a near kinsman of Olympias, a man of an austere temper, presided, who did not indeed himself decline the name of what in reality is a noble and honourable office, but in general his dignity, and his near relationship, obtained him from other people the title of Alexander's foster-father and governor. But he who took upon him the actual place and style of his pedagogue was Lysimachus the Acarnanian, who, though he had nothing specially to recommend him, but his lucky fancy of calling himself Phœnix, Alexander Achilles, and Philip Peleus, was therefore well enough esteemed, and ranked in the next degree after Leonidas.

Philonicus the Thessalian brought the horse Bucephalus to Philip, offering to sell him for thirteen talents; but when they went into the field to try him, they found him so very vicious and unmanageable, that he reared up when they endeavoured to mount him, and would not so much as endure the voice of any of Philip's attendants. Upon which, as they were leading him away as wholly useless and untractable, Alexander, who stood by, said, "What an excellent horse do they lose for want of address and boldness to manage him!" Philip at first took no notice of what he said; but when he heard him repeat the same thing several times, and saw he was much vexed to see the horse sent away, "Do you reproach," said he to him, "those who are older than yourself, as if you knew more, and were better able to manage him than they?" "I could manage this horse," replied he, "better than others do." "And if you do not," said Philip, "what will you forfeit for your rashness?" "I will pay," answered Alexander, "the whole price of the horse." At this the whole company fell a-laughing; and as soon as the wager was settled amongst them, he immediately ran to the horse, and taking hold of the bridle, turned him directly towards the sun, having, it seems, observed that he was disturbed at and afraid of the motion of his own shadow; then letting him go forward a little still keeping the reins in his hands, and stroking him gently when he found him begin to grow eager and fiery, he let fall his upper garment softly, and with one nimble leap securely mounted him, and when he was seated, by little and little drew in the bridle, and curbed him without either striking or spurring him. Presently, when he found him free from all rebelliousness, and only impatient for the course, he let him go at full speed, inciting him now with a commanding voice, and urging him also with his heel. Philip and his friends looked on at first in silence and anxiety for the result, till seeing him turn at the end of his career, and come back rejoicing and triumphing for what he had performed, they all burst out into acclamations of applause; and his father shedding tears, it is said, for joy, kissed him as he came down from his horse, and in his transport said, "O my son, look thee out a kingdom equal to and worthy of thyself, for Macedonia is too little for thee."

After this, considering him to be of a temper easy to be led to his duty by reason, but by no means to be compelled, he always endeavoured to persuade rather than to command or force him to anything; and now looking upon the instruction and tuition of his youth to be of greater difficulty and importance than to be wholly trusted to the ordinary masters in music and poetry, and the common school subjects, and to require, as Sophocles says—

"The bridle and the rudder too,"

he sent for Aristotle, the most learned and most celebrated philosopher of his time, and rewarded him with a munificence proportionable to and becoming the care he took to instruct his son. For he repeopled his native city Stagira, which he had caused to be demolished a little before, and restored all the citizens, who were in exile or slavery, to their habitations. As a place for the pursuit of their studies and exercise, he assigned the temple of the Nymphs, near Mieza, where, to this very day, they show you Aristotle's stone seats, and the shady walks which he was wont to frequent. It would appear that Alexander received from him not only his doctrines of Morals and of Politics, but also something of those more abstruse and profound theories which these philosophers, by the very names they gave them, professed to reserve for oral communication to the initiated, and did not allow many to become acquainted with. For when he was in Asia, and heard Aristotle had published some treatises of that kind, he wrote to him, using very plain language to him in behalf of philosophy, the following letter. "Alexander to Aristotle, greeting. You have not done well to publish your books of oral doctrine; for what is there now that we excel others in, if those things which we have been particularly instructed in be laid open to all? For my part, I assure you, I had rather excel others in the knowledge of what is excellent, than in the extent of my power and dominion. Farewell." And Aristotle, soothing this passion for pre-eminence, speaks, in his excuse for himself, of these doctrines as in fact both published and not published: as indeed, to say the truth, his books on metaphysics are written in a style which makes them useless for ordinary teaching, and instructive only, in the way of memoranda, for those who have been already conversant in that sort of learning.

Doubtless also it was to Aristotle that he owed the inclination he had, not to the theory only, but likewise to the practice of the art of medicine. For when any of his friends were sick, he would often prescribe them their course of diet, and medicines proper to their disease, as we may find in his epistles. He was naturally a great lover of all kinds of learning and reading; and Onesicritus informs us that he constantly laid Homer's Iliads, according to the copy corrected by Aristotle, called the casket copy, with his dagger under his pillow, declaring that he esteemed it a perfect portable treasure of all military virtue and knowledge. When he was in the upper Asia, being destitute of other books, he ordered Harpalus to send him some; who furnished him with Philistus's History, a great many of the plays of Euripides, Sophocles, and Æschylus, and some dithyrambic odes, composed by Telestes and Philoxenus. For a while he loved and cherished Aristotle no less, as he was wont to say himself, than if he had been his father, giving this reason for it, that as he had received life from the one, so the other had taught him to live well. But afterwards, upon some mistrust of him, yet not so great as to make him do him any hurt, his familiarity and friendly kindness to him abated so much of its former force and affectionateness, as to make it evident he was alienated from him. However, his violent thirst after and passion for learning, which were once implanted, still grew up with him, and never decayed; as appears by his veneration of Anaxarchus, by the present of fifty talents which he sent to Xenocrates, and his particular care and esteem of Dandamis and Calanus.

While Philip went on his expedition against the Byzantines, he left Alexander, then sixteen years old, his lieutenant in Macedonia, committing the charge of his seal to him; who, not to sit idle, reduced the rebellious Mædi, and having taken their chief town by storm, drove out the barbarous inhabitants, and planting a colony of several nations in their room, called the place after his own name, Alexandropolis. At the battle of Chæronea, which his father fought against the Grecians, he is said to have been the first man that charged the Thebans' sacred band. And even in my remembrance, there stood an old oak near the river Cephisus, which people called Alexander's oak, because his tent was pitched under it. And not far off are to be seen the graves of the Macedonians who fell in that battle. This early bravery made Philip so fond of him, that nothing pleased him more than to hear his subjects call himself their general and Alexander their king.

But the disorders of his family, chiefly caused by his new marriages and attachments (the troubles that began in the women's chambers spreading, so to say, to the whole kingdom), raised various complaints and differences between them, which the violence of Olympias, a woman of a jealous and implacable temper, made wider, by exasperating Alexander against his father. Among the rest, this accident contributed most to their falling out. At the wedding of Cleopatra, whom Philip fell in love with and married, she being much too young for him, her uncle Attalus in his drink desired the Macedonians would implore the gods to give them a lawful successor to the kingdom by his niece. This so irritated Alexander, that throwing one of the cups at his head, "You villain," said he, "what, am I then a bastard?" Then Philip, taking Attalus's part, rose up and would have run his son through; but by good fortune for them both, either his over-hasty rage, or the wine he had drunk, made his foot slip, so that he fell down on the floor. At which Alexander reproachfully insulted over him: "See there," said he, "the man who makes preparations to pass out of Europe into Asia, overturned in passing from one seat to another." After this debauch, he and his mother Olympias withdrew from Philip's company, and when he had placed her in Epirus, he himself retired into Illyria.

About this time, Demaratus the Corinthian, an old friend of the family, who had the freedom to say anything among them without offence, coming to visit Philip, after the first compliments and embraces were over, Philip asked him whether the Grecians were at amity with one another. "It ill becomes you," replied Demaratus, "to be so solicitous about Greece, when you have involved your own house in so many dissensions and calamities." He was so convinced by this seasonable reproach, that he immediately sent for his son home, and by Demaratus's mediation prevailed with him to return. But this reconciliation lasted not long; for when Pixodorus, viceroy of Caria, sent Aristocritus to treat for a match between his eldest daughter and Philip's son, Arrhidæus, hoping by this alliance to secure his assistance upon occasion, Alexander's mother, and some who pretended to be his friends, presently filled his head with tales and calumnies, as if Philip, by a splendid marriage and important alliance, were preparing the way for settling the kingdom upon Arrhidæus. In alarm at this, he despatched Thessalus, the tragic actor, into Caria, to dispose Pixodorus to slight Arrhidæus, both illegitimate and a fool, and rather to accept of himself for his son-in-law. This proposition was much more agreeable to Pixodorus than the former. But Philip, as soon as he was made acquainted with this transaction, went to his son's apartment, taking with him Philotas, the son of Parmenio, one of Alexander's intimate friends and companions, and there reproved him severely, and reproached him bitterly, that he should be so degenerate, and unworthy of the power he was to leave him, as to desire the alliance of a mean Carian, who was at best but the slave of a barbarous prince. Nor did this satisfy his resentment, for he wrote to the Corinthians to send Thessalus to him in chains, and banished Harpalus, Nearchus, Erigyius, and Ptolemy, his son's friends and favourites, whom Alexander afterwards recalled and raised to great honour and preferment.

Not long after this, Pausanias, having had an outrage done to him at the instance of Attalus and Cleopatra, when he found he could get no reparation for his disgrace at Philip's hands, watched his opportunity and murdered him. The guilt of which fact was laid for the most part upon Olympias, who was said to have encouraged and exasperated the enraged youth to revenge; and some sort of suspicion attached even to Alexander himself, who, it was said, when Pausanias came and complained to him of the injury he had received, repeated the verse out of Euripides's Medea—

"On husband, and on father, and on bride."

However, he took care to find out and punish the accomplices of the conspiracy severely, and was very angry with Olympias for treating Cleopatra inhumanly in his absence.

Alexander was but twenty years old when his father was murdered, and succeeded to a kingdom, beset on all sides with great dangers and rancorous enemies. For not only the barbarous nations that bordered on Macedonia were impatient of being governed by any but their own native princes, but Philip likewise, though he had been victorious over the Grecians, yet, as the time had not been sufficient for him to complete his conquest and accustom them to his sway, had simply left all things in a general disorder and confusion. It seemed to the Macedonians a very critical time; and some would have persuaded Alexander to give up all thought of retaining the Grecians in subjection by force of arms, and rather to apply himself to win back by gentle means the allegiance of the tribes who were designing revolt, and try the effect of indulgence in arresting the first motions towards revolution. But he rejected this counsel as weak and timorous, and looked upon it to be more prudence to secure himself by resolution and magnanimity, than, by seeming to truckle to any, to encourage all to trample on him. In pursuit of this opinion, he reduced the barbarians to tranquillity, and put an end to all fear of war from them, by a rapid expedition into their country as far as the river Danube, where he gave Syrmus, King of the Triballians, an entire overthrow. And hearing the Thebans were in revolt, and the Athenians in correspondence with them, he immediately marched through the pass of Thermopylæ, saying that to Demosthenes, who had called him a child while he was in Illyria and in the country of the Triballians, and a youth when he was in Thessaly, he would appear a man before the walls of Athens.

When he came to Thebes, to show how willing he was to accept of their repentance for what was past, he only demanded of them Phœnix and Prothytes, the authors of the rebellion, and proclaimed a general pardon to those who would come over to him. But when the Thebans merely retorted by demanding Philotas and Antipater to be delivered into their hands, and by a proclamation on their part invited all who would assert the liberty of Greece to come over to them, he presently applied himself to make them feel the last extremities of war. The Thebans indeed defended themselves with a zeal and courage beyond their strength, being much outnumbered by their enemies. But when the Macedonian garrison sallied out upon them from the citadel, they were so hemmed in on all sides that the greater part of them fell in the battle; the city itself being taken by storm was sacked and razed. Alexander's hope being that so severe an example might terrify the rest of Greece into obedience, and also in order to gratify the hostility of his confederates, the Phocians and Platæans. So that, except the priests, and some few who had heretofore been the friends and connections of the Macedonians, the family of the poet Pindar, and those who were known to have opposed the public vote for the war, all the rest, to the number of thirty thousand, were publicly sold for slaves; and it is computed that upwards of six thousand were put to the sword.

Among the other calamities that befell the city, it happened that some Thracian soldiers, having broken into the house of a matron of high character and repute, named Timoclea, their captain, after he had used violence with her, to satisfy his avarice as well as lust, asked her, if she knew of any money concealed; to which she readily answered she did, and bade him follow her into a garden, where she showed him a well, into which, she told him, upon the taking of the city, she had thrown what she had of most value. The greedy Thracian presently stooping down to view the place where he thought the treasure lay, she came behind him and pushed him into the well, and then flung great stones in upon him, till she had killed him. After which, when the soldiers led her away bound to Alexander, her very mien and gait showed her to be a woman of dignity, and of a mind no less elevated, not betraying the least sign of fear or astonishment. And when the king asked her who she was, "I am," said she, "the sister of Theagenes, who fought the battle of Chæronea with your father Philip, and fell there in command for the liberty of Greece." Alexander was so surprised, both at what she had done and what she said, that he could not choose but give her and her children their freedom to go whither they pleased. After this he received the Athenians into favour, although they had shown themselves so much concerned at the calamity of Thebes that out of sorrow they omitted the celebration of the Mysteries, and entertained those who escaped with all possible humanity. Whether it were, like the lion, that his passion was now satisfied, or that, after an example of extreme cruelty, he had a mind to appear merciful, it happened well for the Athenians; for he not only forgave them all past offences, but bade them look to their affairs with vigilance, remembering that if he should miscarry, they were likely to be the arbiters of Greece. Certain it is, too, that in aftertime he often repented of his severity to the Thebans, and his remorse had such influence on his temper as to make him ever after less rigorous to all others. He imputed also the murder of Clitus, which he committed in his wine, and the unwillingness of the Macedonians to follow him against the Indians, by which his enterprise and glory was left imperfect, to the wrath and vengeance of Bacchus, the protector of Thebes. And it was observed that whatsoever any Theban, who had the good fortune to survive this victory, asked of him, he was sure to grant without the least difficulty.

Soon after, the Grecians, being assembled at the Isthmus, declared their resolution of joining with Alexander in the war against the Persians, and proclaimed him their general. While he stayed here, many public ministers and philosophers came from all parts to visit him and congratulated him on his election, but contrary to his expectation, Diogenes of Sinope, who then was living at Corinth, thought so little of him, that instead of coming to compliment him, he never so much as stirred out of the suburb called the Cranium, where Alexander found him lying along in the sun. When he saw so much company near him, he raised himself a little, and vouchsafed to look upon Alexander; and when he kindly asked him whether he wanted anything, "Yes," said he, "I would have you stand from between me and the sun." Alexander was so struck at this answer, and surprised at the greatness of the man, who had taken so little notice of him, that as he went away he told his followers, who were laughing at the moroseness of the philosopher, that if he were not Alexander, he would choose to be Diogenes.

Then he went to Delphi, to consult Apollo concerning the success of the war he had undertaken, and happening to come on one of the forbidden days, when it was esteemed improper to give any answer from the oracle, he sent messengers to desire the priestess to do her office; and when she refused, on the plea of a law to the contrary, he went up himself, and began to draw her by force into the temple, until tired and overcome with his importunity, "My son," said she, "thou art invincible." Alexander taking hold of what she spoke, declared he had received such an answer as he wished for, and that it was needless to consult the god any further. Among other prodigies that attended the departure of his army, the image of Orpheus at Libethra, made of cypress-wood, was seen to sweat in great abundance, to the discouragement of many. But Aristander told him that, far from presaging any ill to him, it signified he should perform acts so important and glorious as would make the poets and musicians of future ages labour and sweat to describe and celebrate them.

His army, by their computation who make the smallest amount, consisted of thirty thousand foot and four thousand horse; and those who make the most of it, speak but of forty-three thousand foot and three thousand horse. Aristobulus says, he had not a fund of above seventy talents for their pay, nor had he more than thirty days' provision, if we may believe Duris; Onesicritus tells us he was two hundred talents in debt. However narrow and disproportionable the beginnings of so vast an undertaking might seem to be, yet he would not embark his army until he had informed himself particularly what means his friends had to enable them to follow him, and supplied what they wanted, by giving good farms to some, a village to one, and the revenue of some hamlet or harbour-town to another. So that at last he had portioned out or engaged almost all the royal property; which giving Perdiccas an occasion to ask him what he would leave himself, he replied, his hopes. "Your soldiers," replied Perdiccas, "will be your partners in those," and refused to accept of the estate he had assigned him. Some others of his friends did the like, but to those who willingly received or desired assistance of him, he liberally granted it, as far as his patrimony in Macedonia would reach, the most part of which was spent in these donations.

With such vigorous resolutions, and his mind thus dispersed, he passed the Hellespont, and at Troy sacrificed to Minerva, and honoured the memory of the heroes who were buried there, with solemn libations; especially Achilles, whose gravestone he anointed, and with his friends, as the ancient custom is, ran naked about his sepulchre, and crowned it with garlands, declaring how happy he esteemed him, in having while he lived so faithful a friend, and when he was dead, so famous a poet to proclaim his actions. While he was viewing the rest of the antiquities and curiosities of the place, being told he might see Paris's harp, if he pleased, he said he thought it not worth looking on, but he should be glad to see that of Achilles, to which he used to sing the glories and great actions of brave men.

In the meantime, Darius's captains, having collected large forces, were encamped on the further bank of the river Granicus, and it was necessary to fight, as it were, in the gate of Asia for an entrance into it. The depth of the river, with the unevenness and difficult ascent of the opposite bank, which was to be gained by main force, was apprehended by most, and some pronounced it an improper time to engage, because it was unusual for the kings of Macedonia to march with their forces in the month called Dæsius. But Alexander broke through these scruples, telling them they should call it a second Artemisius. And when Parmenio advised him not to attempt anything that day, because it was late, he told him that he should disgrace the Hellespont should he fear the Granicus. And so, without more saying, he immediately took the river with thirteen troops of horse, and advanced against whole showers of darts thrown from the steep opposite side,which was covered with armed multitudes of the enemy's horse and foot, notwithstanding the disadvantage of the ground and the rapidity of the stream; so that the action seemed to have more frenzy and desperation in it, than of prudent conduct. However, he persisted obstinately to gain the passage, and at last with much ado making his way up the banks, which were extremely muddy and slippery, he had instantly to join in a mere confused hand-to-hand combat with the enemy, before he could draw up his men, who were still passing over, into any order. For the enemy pressed upon him with loud and warlike outcries; and charging horse against horse, with their lances, after they had broken and spent these, they fell to it with their swords. And Alexander, being easily known by his buckler, and a large plume of white feathers on each side of his helmet, was attacked on all sides, yet escaped wounding, though his cuirass was pierced by a javelin in one of the joinings. And Rhœsaces and Spithridates, two Persian commanders, falling upon him at once, he avoided one of them, and struck at Rhœsaces, who had a good cuirass on, with such force that, his spear breaking in his hand, he was glad to betake himself to his dagger. While they were thus engaged, Spithridates came up on one side of him, and raising himself upon his horse, gave him such a blow with his battle-axe on the helmet that he cut off the crest of it with one of his plumes, and the helmet was only just so far strong enough to save him, that the edge of the weapon touched the hair of his head. But as he was about to repeat his stroke, Clitus, called the black Clitus, prevented him, by running him through the body with his spear. At the same time Alexander despatched Rhœsaces with his sword. While the horse were thus dangerously engaged, the Macedonian phalanx passed the river, and the foot on each side advanced to fight. But the enemy hardly sustaining the first onset, soon gave ground and fled, all but the mercenary Greeks, who, making a stand upon a rising ground, desired quarter, which Alexander, guided rather by passion than judgment refused to grant, and charging them himself first, had his horse (not Bucephalus, but another) killed under him. And this obstinacy of his to cut off these experienced desperate men cost him the lives of more of his own soldiers than all the battle before, besides those who were wounded. The Persians lost in this battle twenty thousand foot and two thousand five hundred horse. On Alexander's side, Aristobulus says there were not wanting above four-and-thirty, of whom nine were foot-soldiers; and in memory of them he caused so many statues of brass, of Lysippus's making, to be erected. And that the Grecians might participate in the honour of his victory he sent a portion of the spoils home to them, particularly to the Athenians three hundred bucklers, and upon all the rest he ordered this inscription to be set: "Alexander the son of Philip, and the Grecians, except the Lacedæmonians, won these from the barbarians who inhabit Asia." All the plate and purple garments, and other things of the same kind that he took from the Persians, except a very small quantity which he reserved for himself, he sent as a present to his mother.

This battle presently made a great change of affairs to Alexander s advantage. For Sardis itself, the chief seat of the barbarian's power in the maritime provinces, and many other considerable places, were surrendered to him; only Halicarnassus and Miletus stood out, which he took by force together with the territory about them. After which he was a little unsettled in his opinion how to proceed. Sometimes he thought it best to find out Darius as soon as he could, and put all to the hazard of a battle; another while he looked upon it as a more prudent course to make an entire reduction of the sea-coast, and not to seek the enemy till he had first exercised his power here and made himself secure of the resources of these provinces. While he was thus deliberating what to do, it happened that a spring of water near the city of Xanthus in Lycia, of its own accord swelled over its banks, and threw up a copper plate, upon the margin of which was engraven in ancient characters, that the time would come when the Persian empire should be destroyed by the Grecians. Encouraged by this accident, he proceeded to reduce the maritime parts of Cilicia and Phœnicia, and passed his army along the sea-coasts of Pamphylia with such expedition that many historians have described and extolled it with that height of admiration, as if it were no less than a miracle, and an extraordinary effect of divine favour, that the waves which usually come rolling in violently from the main, and hardly ever leave so much as a narrow beach under the steep, broken cliffs at any time uncovered, should on a sudden retire to afford him passage. Menander, in one of his comedies, alludes to this marvel when he says—

"Was Alexander ever favoured more?
Each man I wish for meets me at my door,
And should I ask for passage through the sea,
The sea I doubt not would retire for me."

But Alexander himself in his epistles mentions nothing unusual in this at all, but says he went from Phaselis, and passed through what they call the Ladders. At Phaselis he stayed some time, and finding the statue of Theodectes, who was a native of this town and was now dead, erected in the market-place, after he had supped, having drunk pretty plentifully, he went and danced about it, and crowned it with garlands, honouring not ungracefully, in his sport, the memory of a philosopher whose conversation he had formerly enjoyed when he was Aristotle's scholar.

Then he subdued the Pisidians who made head against him, and conquered the Phrygians, at whose chief city, Gordium, which is said to be the seat of the ancient Midas, he saw the famous chariot fastened with cords made of the rind of the cornel-tree, which whosoever should untie, the inhabitants had a tradition, that for him was reserved the empire of the world. Most authors tell the story that Alexander finding himself unable to untie the knot, the ends of which were secretly twisted round and folded up within it, cut it asunder with his sword. But Aristobulus tells us it was easy for him to undo it, by only pulling the pin out of the pole, to which the yoke was tied, and afterwards drawing off the yoke itself from below. From hence he advanced into Paphlagonia and Cappadocia, both which countries he soon reduced to obedience, and then hearing of the death of Memnon, the best commander Darius had upon the sea-coasts, who, if he had lived, might, it was supposed, have put many impediments and difficulties in the way of the progress of his arms, he was the rather encouraged to carry the war into the upper provinces of Asia.

Darius was by this time upon his march from Susa, very confident, not only in the number of his men, which amounted to six hundred thousand, but likewise in a dream, which the Persian soothsayers interpreted rather in flattery to him than according to the natural probability. He dreamed that he saw the Macedonian phalanx all on fire, and Alexander waiting on him, clad in the same dress which he himself had been used to wear when he was courier to the late king; after which, going into the temple of Belus, he vanished out of his sight. The dream would appear to have supernaturally signified to him the illustrious actions the Macedonians were to perform, and that as he, from a courier's place, had risen to the throne, so Alexander should come to be master of Asia, and not long surviving his conquests, conclude his life with glory. Darius's confidence increased the more, because Alexander spent so much time in Cilicia, which he imputed to his cowardice. But it was sickness that detained him there, which some say he contracted from his fatigues, others from bathing in the river Cydnus, whose waters were exceedingly cold. However it happened, none of his physicians would venture to give him any remedies, they thought his case so desperate, and were so afraid of the suspicions and ill-will of the Macedonians if they should fail in the cure; till Philip, the Acarnanian, seeing how critical his case was, but relying on his own well-known friendship for him, resolved to try the last efforts of his art, and rather hazard his own credit and life than suffer him to perish for want of physic, which he confidently administered to him, encouraging him to take it boldly, if he desired a speedy recovery, in order to prosecute the war. At this very time, Parmenio wrote to Alexander from the camp, bidding him have a care of Philip, as one who was bribed by Darius to kill him, with great sums of money, and a promise of his daughter in marriage. When he had perused the letter, he put it under his pillow, without showing it so much as to any of his most intimate friends, and when Philip came in with the potion, he took it with great cheerfulness and assurance, giving him meantime the letter to read. This was a spectacle well worth being present at, to see Alexander take the draught and Philip read the letter at the same time, and then turn and look upon one another, but with different sentiments; for Alexander's looks were cheerful and open, to show his kindness to and confidence in his physician, while the other was full of surprise and alarm at the accusation, appealing to the gods to witness his innocence, sometimes lifting up his hands to heaven, and then throwing himself down by the bedside, and beseeching Alexander to lay aside all fear, and follow his directions without apprehension. For the medicine at first worked so strongly as to drive, so to say, the vital forces into the interior; he lost his speech, and falling into a swoon, had scarce any sense or pulse left. However, in no long time, by Philip's means, his health and strength returned, and he showed himself in public to the Macedonians, who were in continual fear and dejection until they saw him abroad again.

There was at this time in Darius's army a Macedonian refugee, named Amyntas, one who was pretty well acquainted with Alexander's character. This man, when he saw Darius intended to fall upon the enemy in the passes and defiles, advised him earnestly to keep where he was, in the open and extensive plains, it being the advantage of a numerous army to have field-room enough when it engaged with a lesser force. Darius, instead of taking his counsel, told him he was afraid the enemy would endeavour to run away, and so Alexander would escape out of his hands. "That fear," replied Amyntas, "is needless, for assure yourself that far from avoiding you, he will make all the speed he can to meet you, and is now most likely on his march toward you." But Amyntas's counsel was to no purpose, for Darius immediately decamping, marched into Cilicia at the same time that Alexander advanced into Syria to meet him; and missing one another in the night, they both turned back again. Alexander, greatly pleased with the event, made all the haste he could to fight in the defiles, and Darius to recover his former ground, and draw his army out of so disadvantageous a place. For now he began to perceive his error in engaging himself too far in a country in which the sea, the mountains, and the river Pinarus running through the midst of it, would necessitate him to divide his forces, render his horse almost unserviceable, and only cover and support the weakness of the enemy. Fortune was not kinder to Alexander in the choice of the ground, than he was careful to improve it to his advantage. For being much inferior in numbers, so far from allowing himself to be outflanked, he stretched his right wing much further out than the left wing of his enemies, and fighting there himself in the very foremost ranks, put the barbarians to flight. In this battle he was wounded in the thigh, Chares says, by Darius, with whom he fought hand to hand. But in the account which he gave Antipater of the battle, though indeed he owns he was wounded in the thigh with a sword, though not dangerously, yet he takes no notice who it was that wounded him.

Nothing was wanting to complete this victory, in which he overthrew above an hundred and ten thousand of his enemies, but the taking the person of Darius, who escaped very narrowly by flight. However, having taken his chariot and his bow, he returned from pursuing him, and found his own men busy in pillaging the barbarians' camp, which (though to disburden themselves they had left most of their baggage at Damascus) was exceedingly rich. But Darius's tent, which was full of splendid furniture and quantities of gold and silver, they reserved for Alexander himself, who, after he had put off his arms, went to bathe himself saying, "Let us now cleanse ourselves from the toils of war in the bath of Darius." "Not so," replied one of his followers, "but in Alexander's rather; for the property of the conquered is and should be called the conqueror's." Here, when he beheld the bathing vessels, the water-pots, the pans, and the ointment boxes, all of gold curiously wrought, and smelt the fragrant odours with which the whole place was exquisitely perfumed, and from thence passed into a pavilion of great size and height, where the couches and tables and preparations for an entertainment were perfectly magnificent, he turned to those about him and said, "This, it seems, is royalty."

But as he was going to supper, word was brought him that Darius's mother and wife and two unmarried daughters, being taken among the rest of the prisoners, upon the sight of his chariot and bow, were all in mourning and sorrow, imagining him to be dead. After a little pause, more lively affected with their affliction than with his own success, he sent Leonnatus to them, to let them know Darius was not dead, and that they need not fear any harm from Alexander, who made war upon him only for dominion; they should themselves be provided with everything they had been used to receive from Darius. This kind message could not but be very welcome to the captive ladies, especially being made good by actions no less humane and generous. For he gave them leave to bury whom they pleased of the Persians, and to make use for this purpose of what garments and furniture they thought fit out of the booty. He diminished nothing of their equipage, or of the attentions and respect formerly paid them, and allowed larger pensions for their maintenance than they had before. But the noblest and most royal part of their usage was, that he treated these illustrious prisoners according to their virtue and character, not suffering them to hear, or receive, or so much as to apprehend anything that was unbecoming. So that they seemed rather lodged in some temple, or some holy virgin chambers, where they enjoyed their privacy sacred and uninterrupted, than in the camp of an enemy. Nevertheless Darius's wife was accounted the most beautiful princess then living, as her husband the tallest and handsomest man of his time, and the daughters were not unworthy of their parents. But Alexander, esteeming it more kingly to govern himself than to conquer his enemies, sought no intimacy with any one of them, nor indeed with any other women before marriage, except Barsine, Memnon's widow, who was taken prisoner at Damascus. She had been instructed in the Grecian learning, was of a gentle temper, and by her father, Artabazus, royally descended, with good qualities, added to the solicitations and encouragement of Parmenio, as Aristobulus tells us, made him the more willing to attach himself to so agreeable and illustrious a woman. Of the rest of the female captives, though remarkably handsome and well proportioned, he took no further notice than to say jestingly that Persian women were terrible eyesores. And he himself, retaliating, as it were, by the display of the beauty of his own temperance and self-control, bade them be removed, as he would have done so many lifeless images. When Philoxenus, his lieutenant on the sea-coast, wrote to him to know if he would buy two young boys of great beauty, whom one Theodorus, a Tarentine, had to sell, he was so offended that he often expostulated with his friends what baseness Philoxenus had ever observed in him that he should presume to make him such a reproachful offer. And he immediately wrote him a very sharp letter, telling him Theodorus and his merchandise might go with his good-will to destruction. Nor was he less severe to Hagnon, who sent him word he would buy a Corinthian youth named Crobylus, as a present for him. And hearing that Damon and Timotheus, two of Parmenio's Macedonian soldiers, had abused the wives of some strangers who were in his pay, he wrote to Parmenio, charging him strictly, if he found them guilty, to put them to death, as wild beasts that were only made for the mischief of mankind. In the same letter he added, that he had not so much as seen or desired to see the wife of Darius, no, nor suffered anybody to speak of her beauty before him. He was wont to say that sleep and the act of generation chiefly made him sensible that he was mortal; as much as to say, that weariness and pleasure proceed both from the same frailty and imbecility of human nature.

In his diet, also, he was most temperate, as appears, omitting many other circumstances, by what he said to Ada, whom he adopted, with the title of mother, and afterwards created Queen of Caria. For when she, out of kindness, sent him every day many curious dishes and sweetmeats, and would have furnished him with some cooks and pastry-men, who were thought to have great skill, he told her he wanted none of them, his preceptor, Leonidas, having already given him the best, which were a night march to prepare for breakfast, and a moderate breakfast to create an appetite for supper. Leonidas also, he added, used to open and search the furniture of his chamber and his wardrobe, to see if his mother had left him anything that was delicate or superfluous. He was much less addicted to wine than was generally believed; that which gave people occasion to think so of him was, that when he had nothing else to do, he loved to sit long and talk, rather than drink, and over every cup hold a long conversation. For when his affairs called upon him, he would not be detained, as other generals often were, either by wine, or sleep, nuptial solemnities, spectacles, or any other diversion whatsoever; a convincing argument of which is, that in the short time he lived, he accomplished so many and so great actions. When he was free from employment, after he was up, and had sacrificed to the gods, he used to sit down to breakfast, and then spend the rest of the day in hunting, or writing memoirs, giving decisions on some military questions, or reading. In marches that required no great haste, he would practise shooting as he went along, or to mount a chariot and alight from it in full speed. Sometimes, for sport's sake, as his journals tell us, he would hunt foxes and go fowling. When he came in for the evening, after he had bathed and was anointed, he would call for his bakers and chief cooks, to know if they had his dinner ready. He never cared to dine till it was pretty late and beginning to be dark, and was wonderfully circumspect at meals that every one who sat with him should be served alike and with proper attention; and his love of talking, as was said before, made him delight to sit long at his wine. And then, though otherwise no prince's conversation was ever so agreeable, he would fall into a temper of ostentation and soldierly boasting, which gave his flatterers a great advantage to ride him, and made his better friends very uneasy. For though they thought it too base to strive who should flatter him most, yet they found it hazardous not to do it; so that between the shame and the danger, they were in a great strait how to behave themselves. After such an entertainment, he was wont to bathe, and then perhaps he would sleep till noon, and sometimes all day long. He was so very temperate in his eating, that when any rare fish or fruits were sent him, he would distribute them among his friends, and often reserve nothing for himself. His table, however, was always magnificent, the expense of it still increasing with his good fortune, till it amounted to ten thousand drachmas a day, to which sum he limited it, and beyond this he would suffer none to lay out in any entertainment where he himself was the guest.

After the battle of Issus, he sent to Damascus to seize upon the money and baggage, the wives and children, of the Persians, of which spoil the Thessalian horsemen had the greatest share; for he had taken particular notice of their gallantry in the fight, and sent them thither on purpose to make their reward suitable to their courage. Not but that the rest of the army had so considerable a part of the booty as was sufficient to enrich them all. This first gave the Macedonians such a taste of the Persian wealth and women and barbaric splendour of living, that they were ready to pursue and follow upon it with all the eagerness of hounds upon a scent. But Alexander, before he proceeded any further, thought it necessary to assure himself of the sea-coast. Those who governed in Cyprus put that island into his possession, and Phœnicia, Tyre only excepted, was surrendered to him. During the siege of this city, which, with mounds of earth cast up, and battering engines, and two hundred galleys by sea, was carried on for seven months together, he dreamt that he saw Hercules upon the walls, reaching out his hands, and calling to him. And many of the Tyrians in their sleep fancied that Apollo told them he was displeased with their actions, and was about to leave them and go over to Alexander. Upon which, as if the god had been a deserting soldier, they seized him, so to say, in the act, tied down the statue with ropes, and nailed it to the pedestal, reproaching him that he was a favourer of Alexander. Another time Alexander dreamed he saw a satyr mocking him at a distance, and when he endeavoured to catch him, he still escaped from him, till at last with much perseverance, and running about after him, he got him into his power. The soothsayers, making two words of *Satyrus*, assured him that Tyre should be his own. The inhabitants at this time show a spring of water, near which they say Alexander slept when he fancied the satyr appeared to him.

While the body of the army lay before Tyre, he made an excursion against the Arabians who inhabit the Mount Antilibanus, in which he hazarded his life extremely to bring off his master Lysimachus, who would needs go along with him, declaring he was neither older nor inferior in courage to Phœnix, Achilles's guardian. For when, quitting their horses, they began to march up the hills on foot, the rest of the soldiers outwent them a great deal, so that night drawing on, and the enemy near, Alexander was fain to stay behind so long, to encourage and help up the lagging and tired old man, that before he was aware he was left behind, a great way from his soldiers, with a slender attendance, and forced to pass an extremely cold night in the dark, and in a very inconvenient place; till seeing a great many scattered fires of the enemy at some distance, and trusting to his agility of body, and as he was always wont by undergoing toils and labours himself to cheer and support the Macedonians in any distress, he ran straight to one of the nearest fires, and with his dagger despatching two of the barbarians that sat by it, snatched up a lighted brand, and returned with it to his own men. They immediately made a great fire, which so alarmed the enemy that most of them fled, and those that assaulted them were soon routed, and thus they rested securely the remainder of the night. Thus Chares writes.

But to return to the siege, it had this issue. Alexander, that he might refresh his army, harassed with many former encounters, had led only a small party towards the walls, rather to keep the enemy busy than with any prospect of much advantage. It happened at this time that Aristander, the soothsayer, after he had sacrificed, upon view of the entrails, affirmed confidently to those who stood by that the city should be certainly taken that very month, upon which there was a laugh and some mockery among the soldiers, as this was the last day of it. The king, seeing him in perplexity, and always anxious to support the credit of the predictions, gave order that they should not count it as the thirtieth, but as the twenty third of the month, and ordering the trumpets to sound, attacked the walls more seriously than he at first intended. The sharpness of the assault so inflamed the rest of his forces who were left in the camp, that they could not hold from advancing to second it, which they performed with so much vigour that the Tyrians retired, and the town was carried that very day. The next place he sat down before was Gaza, one of the largest cities of Syria, when this accident befell him. A large bird flying over him let a clod of earth fall upon his shoulder, and then settling upon one of the battering engines, was suddenly entangled and caught in the nets, composed of sinews, which protected the ropes with which the machine was managed. This fell out exactly according to Aristander's prediction, which was, that Alexander should be wounded and the city reduced.

From hence he sent great part of the spoils to Olympias, Cleopatra, and the rest of his friends, not omitting his preceptor Leonidas, on whom he bestowed five hundred talents' weight of frankincense and an hundred of myrrh, in remembrance of the hopes he had once expressed of him when he was but a child. For Leonidas, it seems, standing by him one day while he was sacrificing, and seeing him take both his hands full of incense to throw into the fire, told him it became him to be more sparing in his offerings, and not to be so profuse till he was master of the countries which those sweet gums and spices come from. So Alexander now wrote to him, saying, "We have sent you abundance of myrrh and frankincense, that for the future you may not be stingy to the gods." Among the treasures and other booty that was taken from Darius, there was a very precious casket, which being brought to Alexander for a great rarity, he asked those about him what they thought fittest to be laid up in it; and when they had delivered their various opinions, he told them he should keep Homer's Iliad in it. This is attested by many credible authors, and if what those of Alexandria tell us, relying upon the authority of Heraclides, be true, Homer was neither an idle nor an unprofitable companion to him in his expedition. For when he was master of Egypt, designing to settle a colony of Grecians there, he resolved to build a large and populous city, and give it his own name. In order to which, after he had measured and staked out the ground with the advice of the best architects, he chanced one night in his sleep to see a wonderful vision; a grey-headed old man, of a venerable aspect, appeared to stand by him, and pronounce these verses:—

"An island lies, where loud the billows roar,
Pharos they call it, on the Egyptian shore."

Alexander upon this immediately rose up and went to Pharos, which, at that time, was an island lying a little above the Canobic mouth of the river Nile, though it has now been joined to the mainland by a mole. As soon as he saw the commodious situation of the place, it being a long neck of land, stretching like an isthmus between large lagoons and shallow waters on one side and the sea on the other, the latter at the end of it making a spacious harbour, he said, Homer, besides his other excellences, was a very good architect, and ordered the plan of a city to be drawn out answerable to the place. To do which, for want of chalk, the soil being black, they laid out their lines with flour, taking in a pretty large compass of ground in a semi-circular figure, and drawing into the inside of the circumference equal straight lines from each end, thus giving it something of the form of a cloak or cape; while he was pleasing himself with his design, on a sudden an infinite number of great birds of several kinds, rising like a black cloud out of the river and the lake, devoured every morsel of the flour that had been used in setting out the lines; at which omen even Alexander himself was troubled, till the augurs restored his confidence again by telling him it was a sign the city he was about to build would not only abound in all things within itself, but also be the nurse and feeder of many nations. He commanded the workmen to proceed, while he went to visit the temple of Ammon.

This was a long and painful, and, in two respects, a dangerous journey; first, if they should lose their provision of water, as for several days none could be obtained; and, secondly, if a violent south wind should rise upon them, while they were travelling through the wide extent of deep sands, as it is said to have done when Cambyses led his army that way, blowing the sand together in heaps, and raising, as it were, the whole desert like a sea upon them, till fifty thousand were swallowed up and destroyed by it. All these difficulties were weighed and represented to him; but Alexander was not easily to be diverted from anything he was bent upon. For fortune having hitherto seconded him in his designs, made him resolute and firm in his opinions, and the boldness of his temper raised a sort of passion in him for surmounting difficulties; as if it were not enough to be always victorious in the field, unless places and seasons and nature herself submitted to him. In this journey, the relief and assistance the gods afforded him in his distresses were more remarkable, and obtained greater belief than the oracles he received afterwards, which, however, were valued and credited the more on account of those occurrences. For first, plentiful rains that fell preserved them from any fear of perishing by drought, and, allaying the extreme dryness of the sand, which now became moist and firm to travel on, cleared and purified the air. Besides this, when they were out of their way, and were wandering up and down, because the marks which were wont to direct the guides were disordered and lost, they were set right again by some ravens, which flew before them when on their march, and waited for them when they lingered and fell behind; and the greatest miracle, as Callisthenes tells us, was that if any of the company went astray in the night, they never ceased croaking and making a noise till by that means they had brought them into the right way again. Having passed through the wilderness, they came to the place where the high priest, at the first salutation, bade Alexander welcome from his father Ammon. And being asked by him whether any of his father's murderers had escaped punishment, he charged him to speak with more respect, since his was not a mortal father. Then Alexander, changing his expression, desired to know of him if any of those who murdered Philip were yet unpunished, and further concerning dominion, whether the empire of the world was reserved for him? This, the god answered, he should obtain, and that Philip's death was fully revenged, which gave him so much satisfaction that he made splendid offerings to Jupiter, and gave the priests very rich presents. This is what most authors write concerning the oracles. But Alexander, in a letter to his mother, tells her there were some secret answers, which at his return he would communicate to her only. Others say that the priest, desirous as a piece of courtesy to address him in Greek, "O Paidion," by a slip in pronunciation ended with the *s* instead of the *n*, and said "O Paidios," which mistake Alexander was well enough pleased with, and it went for current that the oracle had called him so.

Among the sayings of one Psammon, a philosopher, whom he heard in Egypt, he most approved of this, that all men are governed by God, because in everything, that which is chief and commands is divine. But what he pronounced himself upon this subject was even more like a philosopher, for he said, God was the common father of us all, but more particularly of the best of us. To the barbarians he carried himself very haughtily, as if he were fully persuaded of his divine birth and parentage; but to the Grecians more moderately, and with less affectation of divinity, except it were once in writing to the Athenians about Samos, when he tells them that he should not himself have bestowed upon them that free and glorious city; "You received it," he says, "from the bounty of him who at that time was called my lord and father," meaning Philip. However, afterwards being wounded with an arrow, and feeling much pain, he turned to those about him, and told them, "This, my friends, is real flowing blood, not Ichor—

"Such as immortal gods are wont to shed."

And another time, when it thundered so much that everybody was afraid, and Anaxarchus, the sophist, asked him if he who was Jupiter's son could do anything like this, "Nay," said Alexander, laughing, "I have no desire to be formidable to my friends, as you would have me, who despised my table for being furnished with fish, and not with the heads of governors of provinces." For in fact it is related as true, that Anaxarchus, seeing a present of small fishes, which the king sent to Hephæstion, had used this expression, in a sort of irony, and disparagement of those who undergo vast labours and encounter great hazards in pursuit of magnificent objects which after all bring them little more pleasure or enjoyment than what others have. From what I have said upon this subject, it is apparent that Alexander in himself was not foolishly affected, or had the vanity to think himself really a god, but merely used his claims to divinity as a means of maintaining among other people the sense of his superiority.

At his return out of Egypt into Phœnicia, he sacrificed and made solemn processions, to which were added shows of lyric dances and tragedies, remarkable not merely for the splendour of the equipage and decorations, but for the competition among those who exhibited them. For the kings of Cyprus were here the exhibitors, just in the same manner as at Athens those who are chosen by lot out of the tribes. And, indeed, they showed the greatest emulation to outvie each other; especially Nicocreon, King of Salamis, and Pasicrates of Soli, who furnished the chorus, and defrayed the expenses of the two most celebrated actors, Athenodorus and Thessalus, the former performing for Pasicrates, and the latter for Nicocrean. Thessalus was most favoured by Alexander, though it did not appear till Athenodorus was declared victor by the plurality of votes. For then at his going away, he said the judges deserved to be commended for what they had done, but that he would willingly have lost part of his kingdom rather than to have seen Thessalus overcome. However, when he understood Athenodorus was fined by the Athenians for being absent at the festivals of Bacchus, though he refused his request that he would write a letter in his behalf, he gave him a sufficient sum to satisfy the penalty. Another time, when Lycon of Scarphia happened to act with great applause in the theatre, and in a verse which he introduced into the comic part which he was acting, begged for a present of ten talents, he laughed and gave him the money.

Darius wrote him a letter, and sent friends to intercede with him, requesting him to accept as a ransom of his captives the sum of a thousand talents, and offering him in exchange for his amity and alliance all the countries on this side the river Euphrates, together with one of his daughters in marriage. These propositions he communicated to his friends, and when

Parmenio told him that, for his part, if he were Alexander, he should readily embrace them, "So would I," said Alexander, "if I were Parmenio." Accordingly, his answer to Darius was, that if he would come and yield himself up into his power he would treat him with all possible kindness; if not, he was resolved immediately to go himself and seek him. But the death of Darius's wife in childbirth made him soon after regret one part of this answer, and he showed evident marks of grief at being thus deprived of a further opportunity of exercising his clemency and good nature, which he manifested, however, as far as he could, by giving her a most sumptuous funeral.

Among the eunuchs who waited in the queen's chamber, and were taken prisoners with the women, there was one Tireus, who, getting out of the camp, fled away on horseback to Darius, to inform him of his wife's death. He, when he heard it, beating his head, and bursting into tears and lamentations, said, "Alas! how great is the calamity of the Persians! Was it not enough that their king's consort and sister was a prisoner in her lifetime, but she must, now she is dead, also be but meanly and obscurely buried?" "O king," replied the eunuch, "as to her funeral rites, or any respect or honour that should have been shown in them, you have not the least reason to accuse the ill fortune of your country; for to my knowledge neither your queen Statira when alive, nor your mother, nor children, wanted anything of their former happy condition, unless it were the light of your countenance, which I doubt not but the lord Oromasdes will yet restore to its former glory. And after her decease, I assure you, she had not only all due funeral ornaments, but was honoured also with the tears of your very enemies; for Alexander is as gentle after victory as he is terrible in the field." At the hearing of these words, such was the grief and emotion on Darius's mind, that they carried him into extravagant suspicions; and taking Tireus aside into a more private part of his tent, "Unless thou likewise," said he to him, "hast deserted me, together with the good fortune of Persia, and art become a Macedonian in thy heart; if thou yet ownest me for thy master Darius, tell me, I charge thee, by the veneration thou payest the light of Mithras, and this right hand of thy king, do I not lament the least of Statira's misfortunes in her captivity and death? Have I not suffered something more injurious and deplorable in her lifetime? And had I not been miserable with less dishonour if I had met with a more severe and inhuman enemy? For how is it possible a young man as he is should treat the wife of his opponent with so much distinction, were it not from some motive that does me disgrace?" Whilst he was yet speaking, Tireus threw himself at his feet, and besought him neither to wrong Alexander so much, nor his dead wife and sister, as to give utterance to any such thoughts, which deprived him of the greatest consolation left him in his adversity, the belief that he was overcome by a man whose virtues raised him above human nature; that he ought to look upon Alexander with love and admiration, who had given no less proofs of his continence towards the Persian women, than of his valour among the men. The eunuch confirmed all he said with solemn and dreadful oaths, and was further enlarging upon Alexander's moderation and magnanimity on other occasions, when Darius, breaking away from him into the other division of the tent, where his friends and courtiers were, lifted up his hands to heaven and uttered this prayer, "Ye gods," said he, " of my family, and of my kingdom, if it be possible, I beseech you to restore the declining affairs of Persia, that I may leave them in as flourishing a condition as I found them, and have it in my power to make a grateful return to Alexander for the kindness which in my adversity he has shown to those who are dearest to me. But if, indeed, the fatal time be come, which is to give a period to the Persian monarchy, if our ruin be a debt that must be paid to the divine jealousy and the vicissitude of things, then I beseech you grant that no other man but Alexander may sit upon the throne of Cyrus." Such is the narrative given by the greater number of the historians.

But to return to Alexander. After he had reduced all Asia on this side the Euphrates, he advanced towards Darius, who was coming down against him with a million of men. In his march a very ridiculous passage happened. The servants who followed the camp for sport's sake divided themselves into two parties, and named the commander of one of them Alexander, and the other Darius. At first they only pelted one another with clods of earth, but presently took to their fists, and at last, heated with contention, they fought in good earnest with stones and clubs, so that they had much ado to part them; till Alexander, upon hearing of it, ordered the two captains to decide the quarrel by single combat, and armed him who bore his name himself, while Philotas did the same to him who represented Darius. The whole army were spectators of this encounter, willing from the event of it to derive an omen of their own future success. After they had fought stoutly a pretty long while, at last he who was called Alexander had the better, and for a reward of his prowess had twelve villages given him, with leave to wear the Persian dress. So we are told by Eratosthenes.

But the great battle of all that was fought with Darius was not, as most writers tell us, at Arbela, but at Gaugamela, which, in their language, signifies the camel's house, forasmuch as one of their ancient kings having escaped the pursuit of his enemies on a swift camel, in gratitude to his beast, settled him at this place, with an allowance of certain villages and rents for his maintenance. It came to pass that in the month Boëdromion, about the beginning of the feast of Mysteries at Athens, there was an eclipse of the moon, the eleventh night after which, the two armies being now in view of one another, Darius kept his men in arms, and by torchlight took a general review of them. But Alexander, while his soldiers slept, spent the night before his tent with his diviner, Aristander, performing certain mysterious ceremonies, and sacrificing to the god Fear. In the meanwhile the oldest of his commanders, and chiefly Parmenio, when they beheld all the plain between Niphates and the Gordyæan mountains shining with the lights and fires which were made by the barbarians, and heard the uncertain and confused sounds of voices out of their camp, like the distant roaring of a vast ocean, were so amazed at the thoughts of such a multitude, that after some conference among themselves, they concluded it an enterprise too difficult and hazardous for them to engage so numerous an enemy in the day, and therefore meeting the king as he came from sacrificing, besought him to attack Darius by night, that the darkness might conceal the danger of the ensuing battle. To this he gave them the celebrated answer, "I will not steal a victory," which though some at the time thought a boyish and inconsiderate speech, as if he played with danger, others, however, regarded as an evidence that he confided in his present condition, and acted on a true judgment of the future, not wishing to leave Darius, in case he were worsted, the pretext of trying his fortune again, which he might suppose himself to have, if he could impute his overthrow to the disadvantage of the night, as he did before to the mountains, the narrow passages, and the sea. For while he had such numerous forces and large dominions still remaining, it was not any want of men or arms that could induce him to give up the war, but only the loss of all courage and hope upon the conviction of an undeniable and manifest defeat.

After they were gone from him with this answer, he laid himself down in his tent and slept the rest of the night more soundly than was usual with him, to the astonishment of the commanders, who came to him early in the morning, and were fain themselves to give order that the soldiers should breakfast. But at last, time not giving them leave to wait any longer, Parmenio went to his bedside, and called him twice or thrice by his name, till he waked him, and then asked him how it was possible, when he was to fight the most important battle of all, he could sleep as soundly as if he were already victorious. "And are we not so, indeed," replied Alexander, smiling, "since we are at last relieved from the trouble of wandering in pursuit of Darius through a wide and wasted country, hoping in vain that he would fight us?" And not only before the battle, but in the height of the danger, he showed himself great, and manifested the self-possession of a just foresight and confidence. For the battle for some time fluctuated and was dubious.

The left wing, where Parmenio commanded, was so impetuously charged by the Bactrian horse that it was disordered and forced to give ground, at the same time that Mazæus had sent a detachment round about to fall upon those who guarded the baggage, which so disturbed Parmenio that he sent messengers to acquaint Alexander that the camp and baggage would be all lost unless he immediately relieved the rear by a considerable reinforcement drawn out of the front. This message being brought him just as he was giving the signal to those about him for the onset, he bade them tell Parmenio that he must have surely lost the use of his reason, and had forgotten, in his alarm, that soldiers, if victorious, became masters of their enemies' baggage; and if defeated, instead of taking care of their wealth or their slaves, have nothing more to do but to fight gallantly and die with honour. When he had said this, he put on his helmet, having the rest of his arms on before he came out of his tent, which were a coat of the Sicilian make, girt close about him, and over that a breast-piece of thickly quilted linen, which was taken among other booty at the battle of Issus. The helmet, which was made by Theophilus, though of iron, was so well wrought and polished that it was as bright as the most refined silver. To this was fitted a gorget of the same metal, set with precious stones. His sword, which was the weapon he most used in fight, was given him by the King of the Citieans, and was of an admirable temper and lightness. The belt which he also wore in all engagements was of much richer workmanship than the rest of his armour. It was a work of the ancient Helicon, and had been presented to him by the Rhodians, as a mark of their respect to him. So long as he was engaged in drawing up his men, or riding about to give orders or directions, or to view them, he spared Bucephalus, who was now growing old, and made use of another horse; but when he was actually to fight, he sent for him again, and as soon as he was mounted, commenced the attack.

He made the longest address that day to the Thessalians and other Greeks, who answered him with loud shouts, desiring him to lead them on against the barbarians, upon which he shifted his javelin into his left hand, and with his right lifted up towards heaven, besought the gods, as Callisthenes tells us, that if he was of a truth the son of Jupiter, they would be pleased to assist and strengthen the Grecians. At the same time the augur Aristander, who had a white mantle about him, and a crown of gold on his head, rode by and showed them an eagle that soared just over Alexander, and directed his flight towards the enemy; which so animated the beholders, that after mutual encouragements and exhortations, the horse charged at full speed, and were followed in a mass by the whole phalanx of the foot. But before they could well come to blows with the first ranks, the barbarians shrunk back, and were hotly pursued by Alexander, who drove those that fled before him into the middle of the battle, where Darius himself was in person, whom he saw from a distance over the foremost ranks, conspicuous in the midst of his life-guard, a tall and fine-looking man, drawn in a lofty chariot, defended by an abundance of the best horse, who stood close in order about it ready to receive the enemy. But Alexander's approach was so terrible, forcing those who gave back upon those who yet maintained their ground, that he beat down and dispersed them almost all. Only a few of the bravest and valiantest opposed the pursuit, who were slain in their king's presence, falling in heaps upon one another, and in the very pangs of death striving to catch hold of the horses. Darius now seeing all was lost, that those who were placed in front to defend him were broken and beat back upon him, that he could not turn or disengage his chariot without great difficulty, the wheels being clogged and entangled among the dead bodies, which lay in such heaps as not only stopped, but almost covered the horses, and made them rear and grow so unruly that the frightened charioteer could govern them no longer, in this extremity was glad to quit his chariot and his arms, and mounting, it is said, upon a mare that had been taken from her foal, betook himself to flight. But he had not escaped so either, if Parmenio had not sent fresh messengers to Alexander, to desire him to return and assist him against a considerable body of the enemy which yet stood together, and would not give ground. For, indeed, Parmenio is on all hands accused of having been sluggish and unserviceable in this battle, whether age had impaired his courage, or that, as Callisthenes says, he secretly disliked and envied Alexander's growing greatness. Alexander, though he was not a little vexed to be so recalled and hindered from pursuing his victory, yet concealed the true reason from his men, and causing a retreat to be sounded, as if it were too late to continue the execution any longer, marched back towards the place of danger, and by the way met the news of the enemy's total overthrow and flight.

This battle being thus over, seemed to put a period to the Persian empire; and Alexander, who was now proclaimed King of Asia, returned thanks to the gods in magnificent sacrifices, and rewarded his friends and followers with great sums of money, and places, and governments of provinces. Eager to gain honour with the Grecians, he wrote to them that he would have all tyrannies abolished, that they might live free according to their own laws, and specially to the Platæans, that their city should be rebuilt, because their ancestors had permitted their countrymen of old to make their territory the seat of the war when they fought with the barbarians for their common liberty. He sent also part of the spoils into Italy, to the Crotoniats, to honour the zeal and courage of their citizen Phayllus, the wrestler, who, in the Median war, when the other Grecian colonies in Italy disowned

Greece, that he might have a share in the danger, joined the fleet at Salamis, with a vessel set forth at his own charge. So affectionate was Alexander to all kind of virtue, and so desirous to preserve the memory of laudable actions.

From hence he marched through the province of Babylon, which immediately submitted to him, and in Ecbatana was much surprised at the sight of the place where fire issues in a continuous stream, like a spring of water, out of a cleft in the earth, and the stream of naphtha, which, not far from this spot, flows out so abundantly as to form a sort of lake. This naphtha, in other respects resembling bitumen, is so subject to take fire, that before it touches the flame it will kindle at the very light that surrounds it, and often inflame the intermediate air also. The barbarians, to show the power and nature of it, sprinkled the street that led to the king's lodgings with little drops of it, and when it was almost night, stood at the further end with torches, which being applied to the moistened places, the first at once taking fire, instantly, as quick as a man could think of it, it caught from one end to another, in such a manner that the whole street was one continued flame. Among those who used to wait on the king and find occasion to amuse him when he anointed and washed himself, there was one Athenophanes, an Athenian, who desired him to make an experiment of the naphtha upon Stephanus, who stood by in the bathing place, a youth with a ridiculously ugly face, whose talent was singing well, "For," said he, "if it take hold of him and is not put out, it must undeniably be allowed to be of the most invincible strength." The youth, as it happened, readily consented to undergo the trial, and as soon as he was anointed and rubbed with it, his whole body broke out into such a flame, and was so seized by the fire, that Alexander was in the greatest perplexity and alarm for him, and not without reason; for nothing could have prevented his being consumed by it, if by good chance there had not been people at hand with a great many vessels of water for the service of the bath, with all which they had much ado to extinguish the fire; and his body was so burned all over that he was not cured of it for a good while after. Thus it is not without some plausibility that they endeavour to reconcile the fable to truth, who say this was the drug in the tragedies with which Medea anointed the crown and veil which she gave to Creon's daughter. For neither the things themselves, nor the fire, could kindle of its own accord, but being prepared for it by the naphtha, they imperceptibly attracted and caught a flame which happened to be brought near them. For the rays and emanations of fire at a distance have no other effect upon some bodies than bare light and heat, but in others, wherethey meet with airy dryness, and also sufficient rich moisture, they collect themselves and soon kindle and create a transformation. The manner, however, of the production of naphtha admits of a diversity of opinion. . .or whether this liquid substance that feeds the flame does not rather proceed from a soil that is unctuous and productive of fire, as that of the province of Babylon is, where the ground is so very hot that oftentimes the grains of barley leap up and are thrown out, as if the violent inflammation had made the earth throb; and in the extreme heats the inhabitants are wont to sleep upon skins filled with water. Harpalus, who was left governor of this country, and was desirous to adorn the palace gardens and walks with Grecian plants, succeeding in raising all but ivy, which the earth would not bear, but constantly killed. For being a plant that loves a cold soil, the temper of this hot and fiery earth was improper for it. But such digressions as these the impatient reader will be more willing to pardon if they are kept within a moderate compass.

At the taking of Susa, Alexander found in the palace forty thousand talents in money ready coined, besides an unspeakable quantity of other furniture and treasure; amongst which was five thousand talents' worth of Hermionian purple, that had been laid up there an hundred and ninety years, and yet kept its colour as fresh and lively as at first. The reason of which, they say, is that in dyeing the purple they made use of honey, and of white oil in the white tincture, both which after the like space of time preserve the clearness and brightness of their lustre. Dinon also relates that the Persian kings had water fetched from the Nile and the Danube, which they laid up in their treasuries as a sort of testimony of the greatness of their power and universal empire.

The entrance into Persia was through a most difficult country, and was guarded by the noblest of the Persians, Darius himself having escaped further. Alexander, however, chanced to find a guide in exact correspondence with what the Pythia had foretold when he was a child, that a lycus should conduct him into Persia. For by such an one, whose father was a Lycian, and his mother a Persian, and who spoke both languages, he was now led into the country, by a way something about, yet without fetching any considerable compass. Here a great many of the prisoners were put to the sword, of which himself gives this account, that he commanded them to be killed in the belief that it would be for his advantage. Nor was the money found here less, he says, than at Susa, besides other movables and treasure, as much as ten thousand pair of mules and five thousand camels could well carry away. Amongst other things he happened to observe a large statue of Xerxes thrown carelessly down to the ground in the confusion made by the multitude of soldiers pressing into the palace. He stood still, and accosting it as if it had been alive, "Shall we," said he, "neglectfully pass thee by, now thou art prostrate on the ground because thou once invadedst Greece, or shall we erect thee again in consideration of the greatness of thy mind and thy other virtues?" But at last, after he had paused some time, and silently considered with himself, he went on without taking any further notice of it. In this place he took up his winter quarters, and stayed four months to refresh his soldiers. It is related that the first time he sat on the royal throne of Persia under the canopy of gold, Demaratus the Corinthian, who was much attached to him and had been one of his father's friends, wept, in an old man's manner, and deplored the misfortune of those Greeks whom death had deprived of the satisfaction of seeing Alexander seated on the throne of Darius.

From hence designing to march against Darius, before he set out he diverted himself with his officers at an entertainment of drinking and other pastimes, and indulged so far as to let every one's mistress sit by and drink with them. The most celebrated of them was Thais, an Athenian, mistress of Ptolemy, who was afterwards King of Egypt. She, partly as a sort of well-turned compliment to Alexander, partly out of sport, as the drinking went on, at last was carried so far as to utter a saying, not misbecoming her native country's character, though somewhat too lofty for her own condition. She said it was indeed some recompense for the toils she had undergone in following the camp all over Asia, that she was that day treated in, and could insult over, the stately palace of the Persian monarchs. But, she added, it would please her much better if, while the king looked on, she might in sport, with her own hands, set fire to the court of that Xerxes who reduced the city of Athens to ashes, that it might be recorded to posterity that the women who followed Alexander had taken a severer revenge on the Persians for the sufferings and affronts of Greece, than all the famed commanders had been able to do by sea or land. What she said was received with such universal liking and murmurs of applause, and so seconded by the encouragement and eagerness of the company, that the king himself, persuaded to be of the party, started from his seat, and with a chaplet of flowers on his head and a lighted torch in his hand, led them the way, while they went after him in a riotous manner, dancing and making loud cries about the place; which when the rest of the Macedonians perceived, they also in great delight ran thither with torches; for they hoped the burning and destruction of the royal palace was an argument that he looked homeward, and had no design to reside among the barbarians. Thus some writers give their account of this action, while others say it was done deliberately; however, all agree that he soon repented of it, and gave order to put out the fire.

Alexander was naturally most munificent, and grew more so as his fortune increased, accompanying what he gave with that courtesy and freedom which, to speak truth, is necessary to make a benefit really obliging. I will give a few instances of this kind. Ariston, the captain of the Pæonians, having killed an enemy, brought his head to show him, and told him that in his country such a present was recompensed with a cup of gold. "With an empty one," said Alexander, smiling, "but I drink to you in this, which I give you full of wine." Another time, as one of the common soldiers was driving a mule laden with some of the king's treasure, the beast grew tired, and the soldier took it upon his own back, and began to march with it, till Alexander seeing the man so overcharged asked what was the matter; and when he was informed, just as he was ready to lay down his burden for weariness, "Do not faint now," said he to him, "but finish the journey, and carry what you have there to your own tent for yourself." He was always more displeased with those who would not accept of what he gave than with those who begged of him. And therefore he wrote to Phocion, that he would not own him for his friend any longer if he refused his presents. He had never given anything to Serapion, one of the youths that played at ball with him, because he did not ask of him, till one day, it coming to Serapion's turn to play, he still threw the ball to others, and when the king asked him why he did not direct it to him, "Because you do not ask for it," said he; which answer pleased him so that he was very liberal to him afterwards. One Proteas, a pleasant, jesting, drinking fellow, having incurred his displeasure, got his friends to intercede for him, and begged his pardon himself with tears, which at last prevailed, and Alexander declared he was friends with him. "I cannot believe it," said Proteas, "unless you first give me some pledge of it." The king understood his meaning, and presently ordered five talents to be given him. How magnificent he was in enriching his friends, and those who attended on his person, appears by a letter which Olympias wrote to him, where she tells him he should reward and honour those about him in a more moderate way. "For now," said she, "you make them all equal to kings, you give them power and opportunity of making many friends of their own, and in the meantime you leave yourself destitute." She often wrote to him to this purpose, and he never communicated her letters to anybody, unless it were one which he opened when Hephæstion was by, whom he permitted, as his custom was, to read it along with him; but then as soon as he had done, he took off his ring, and set the seal upon Hephæstion's lips. Mazæus, who was the most considerable man in Darius's court, had a son who was already governor of a province. Alexander bestowed another upon him that was better; he, however, modestly refused, and told him, instead of one Darius, he went the way to make many Alexanders. To Parmenio he gave Bagoas's house, in which he found a wardrobe of apparel worth more than a thousand talents. He wrote to Antipater, commanding him to keep a life-guard about him for the security of his person against conspiracies. To his mother he sent many presents, but would never suffer her to meddle with matters of state or war, not indulging her busy temper, and when she fell out with him on this account, he bore her ill-humour very patiently. Nay more, when he read a long letter from Antipater full of accusations against her, "Antipater," he said, "does not know that one tear of a mother effaces a thousand such letters as these."

But when he perceived his favourites grow so luxurious and extravagant in their way of living and expenses that Hagnon, the Teian, wore silver nails in his shoes, that Leonnatus employed several camels only to bring him powder out of Egypt to use when he wrestled, and that Philotas had hunting nets a hundred furlongs in length, that more used precious ointment than plain oil when they went to bathe, and that they carried about servants everywhere with them to rub them and wait upon them in their chambers, he reproved them in gentle and reasonable terms, telling them he wondered that they who had been engaged in so many single battles did not know by experience, that those who labour sleep more sweetly and soundly than those who are laboured for, and could fail to see by comparing the Persians' manner of living with their own that it was the most abject and slavish condition to be voluptuous, but the most noble and royal to undergo pain and labour. He argued with them further, how it was possible for any one who pretended to be a soldier, either to look well after his horse, or to keep his armour bright and in good order, who thought it much to let his hands be serviceable to what was nearest to him, his own body. "Are you still to learn," said he, "that the end and perfection of our victories is to avoid the vices and infirmities of those whom we subdue?" And to strengthen his precepts by example, he applied himself now more vigorously than ever to hunting and warlike expeditions, embracing all opportunities of hardship and danger, insomuch that a Lacedæmonian, who was there on an embassy to him, and chanced to be by when he encountered with and mastered a huge lion, told him he had fought gallantly with the beast, which of the two should be king. Craterus caused a representation to be made of this adventure, consisting of the lion and the dogs, of the king engaged with the lion, and himself coming in to his assistance, all expressed in figures of brass, some of which were by Lysippus, and the rest by Leochares; and had it dedicated in the temple of Apollo at Delphi. Alexander exposed his person to danger in this manner, with the object both of inuring himself and inciting others to the performance of brave and virtuous actions.

But his followers, who were grown rich, and consequently proud, longed to indulge themselves in pleasure and idleness, and were weary of marches and expeditions, and at last went on so far as to censure and speak ill of him. All which at first he bore very patiently, saying it became a king well to do good to others, and be evil spoken of. Meantime, on the smallest occasions that called for a show of kindness to his friends, there was every indication on his part of tenderness and respect. Hearing Peucestes was bitten by a bear, he wrote to him that he took it unkindly he should send others notice of it and not make him acquainted with it; "But now," said he, "since it is so, let me know how you do, and whether any of your companions forsook you when you were in danger, that I may punish them." He sent Hephæstion, who was absent about some business, word how, while they were fighting for their diversion with an ichneumon, Craterus was by chance run through both thighs with Perdiccas's javelin. And upon Peucestes's recovery from a fit of sickness, he sent a letter of thanks to his physician Alexippus. When Craterus was ill, he saw a vision in his sleep, after which he offered sacrifices for his health, and bade him do so likewise. He wrote also to Pausanias, the physician, who was about to purge Craterus with hellebore, partly out of an anxious concern for him, and partly to give him a caution how he used that medicine. He was so tender of his friends' reputation that he imprisoned Ephialtes and Cissus, who brought him the first news of Harpalus's flight and withdrawal from his service, as if they had falsely accused him. When he sent the old and infirm soldiers home, Eurylochus, a citizen of Ægæ, got his name enrolled among the sick, though he ailed nothing, which being discovered, he confessed he was in love with a young woman named Telesippa, and wanted to go along with her to the sea-side. Alexander inquired to whom the woman belonged, and being told she was a free courtesan, "I will assist you," said he to Eurylochus, "in your amour if your mistress be to be gained either by presents or persuasions; but we must use no other means, because she is free-born."

It is surprising to consider upon what slight occasions he would write letters to serve his friends. As when he wrote one in which he gave order to search for a youth that belonged to Seleucus, who was run away into Cilicia; and in another thanked and commanded Peucestes for apprehending Nicon, a servant of Craterus; and in one to Megabyzus, concerning a slave that had taken sanctuary in a temple, gave direction that he should not meddle with him while he was there, but if he could entice him out by fair means, then he gave him leave to seize him. It is reported of him that when he first sat in judgment upon capital causes he would lay his hand upon one of his ears while the accuser spoke, to keep it free and unprejudiced in behalf of the party accused. But afterwards such a multitude of accusations were brought before him, and so many proved true, that he lost his tenderness of heart, and gave credit to those also that were false; and especially when anybody spoke ill of him, he would be transported out of his reason, and show himself cruel and inexorable, valuing his glory and reputation beyond his life or kingdom.

He now, as we said, set forth to seek Darius, expecting he should be put to the hazard of another battle, but heard he was taken and secured by Bessus, upon which news he sent home the Thessalians, and gave them a largess of two thousand talents over and above the pay that was due to them. This long and painful pursuit of Darius—for in eleven days he marched thirty-three hundred furlongs—harassed his soldiers so that most of them were ready to give it up, chiefly for want of water. While they were in this distress, it happened that some Macedonians who had fetched water in skins upon their mules from a river they had found out came about noon to the place where Alexander was, and seeing him almost choked with thirst, presently filled an helmet and offered it him. He asked them to whom they were carrying the water; they told him to their children, adding, that if his life were but saved, it was no matter for them, they should be able well enough to repair that loss, though they all perished. Then he took the helmet into his hands, and looking round about, when he saw all those who were near him stretching their heads out and looking earnestly after the drink, he returned it again with thanks without tasting a drop of it. "For," said he, "if I alone drink, the rest will be out of heart." The soldiers no sooner took notice of his temperance and magnanimity upon this occasion, but they one and all cried out to him to lead them forward boldly, and began whipping on their horses. For whilst they had such a king they said they defied both weariness and thirst, and looked upon themselves to be little less than immortal. But though they were all equally cheerful and willing, yet not above threescore horse were able, it is said, to keep up, and to fall in with Alexander upon the enemy's camp, where they rode over abundance of gold and silver that lay scattered about, and passing by a great many chariots full of women that wandered here and there for want of drivers, they endeavoured to overtake the first of those that fled, in hopes to meet with Darius among them. And at last, after much trouble, they found him lying in a chariot, wounded all over with darts, just at the point of death. However, he desired they would give him some drink, and when he had drunk a little cold water, he told Polystratus, who gave it him, that it had become the last extremity of his ill fortune to receive benefits and not be able to return them. "But Alexander," said he, "whose kindness to my mother, my wife, and my children I hope the gods will recompense, will doubtless thank you for your humanity to me. Tell him, therefore, in token of my acknowledgment, I give him this right hand," with which words he took hold of Polystratus's hand and died. When Alexander came up to them, he showed manifest tokens of sorrow, and taking off his own cloak, threw it upon the body to cover it. And some time afterwards, when Bessus was taken, he ordered him to be torn in pieces in this manner. They fastened him to a couple of trees which were bound down so as to meet, and then being let loose, with a great force returned to their places, each of them carrying that part of the body along with it that was tied to it. Darius's body was laid in state, and sent to his mother with pomp suitable to his quality. His brother Exathres, Alexander received into the number of his intimate friends.

And now with the flower of his army he marched into Hyrcania, where he saw a large bay of an open sea, apparently not much less than the Euxine, with water, however, sweeter than that of other seas, but could learn nothing of certainty concerning it, further than that in all probability it seemed to him to be an arm issuing from the lake of Mæotis. However, the naturalists were better informed of the truth, and had given an account of it many years before Alexander's expedition; that of four gulfs which out of the main sea enter into the continent, this, known indifferently as the Caspian and as the Hyrcanian Sea, is the most northern. Here the barbarians, unexpectedly meeting with those who led Bucephalus, took them prisoners, and carried the horse away with them, at which Alexander was so much vexed that he sent an herald to let them know he would put them all to the sword, men, women, and children, without mercy, if they did not restore him. But on their doing so, and at the same time surrendering their cities into his hands, he not only treated them kindly, but also paid a ransom for his horse to those who took him.

From hence he marched into Parthia, where not having much to do, he first put on the barbaric dress, perhaps with the view of making the work of civilising them the easier, as nothing gains more upon men than a conformity to their fashions and customs. Or it may have been as a first trial, whether the Macedonians might be brought to *adore* as the Persians did their kings, by accustoming them by little and little to bear with the alteration of his rule and course of life in other things. However, he followed not the Median fashion, which was altogether foreign and uncouth, and adopted neither the trousers nor the sleeved vest, nor the tiara for the head, but taking a middle way between the Persian mode and the Macedonian, so contrived his habit that it was not so flaunting as the one, and yet more pompous and magnificent than the other. At first he wore this habit only when he conversed with the barbarians, or within doors, among his intimate friends and companions, but afterwards he appeared in it abroad, when he rode out, and at public audiences, a sight which the Macedonians beheld with grief; but they so respected his other virtues and good qualities that they felt it reasonable in some things to gratify his fancies and his passion of glory, in pursuit of which he hazarded himself so far, that, besides his other adventures, he had but lately been wounded in the leg by an arrow, which had so shattered the shank-bone that splinters were taken out. And on another occasion he received a violent blow with a stone upon the nape of the neck, which dimmed his sight for a good while afterwards. And yet all this could not hinder him from exposing himself freely to any dangers, insomuch that he passed the river Orexartes, which he took to be the Tanais, and putting the Scythians to flight, followed them above a hundred furlongs, though suffering all the time from a diarrhœa.

Here many affirm that the Amazon came to give him a visit. So Clitarchus, Polyclitus, Onesicritus, Antigenes, and Ister tell us. But Aristobulus and Chares, who held the office of reporter of requests, Ptolemy and Anticlides, Philon the Theban, Philip of Theangela, Hecatæus the Eretrian, Philip the Chalcidian, and Duris the Samian, say it is wholly a fiction. And truly Alexander himself seems to confirm the latter statement, for in a letter in which he gives Antipater an account of all that happened, he tells him that the King of Scythia offered him his daughter in marriage, but makes no mention at all of the Amazon. And many years after, when Onesicritus read this story in his fourth book to Lysimachus, who then reigned, the king laughed quietly and asked, "Where could I have been at that time?"

But it signifies little to Alexander whether this be credited or no. Certain it is, that apprehending the Macedonians would be weary of pursuing the war, he left the greater part of them in their quarters; and having with him in Hyrcania the choice of his men only, amounting to twenty thousand foot and three thousand horse, he spoke to them to this effect: That hitherto the barbarians had seen them no otherwise than as it were in a dream, and if they should think of returning when they had only alarmed Asia, and not conquered it, their enemies would set upon them as upon so many women. However he told them he would keep none of them with him against their will, they might go if they pleased; he should merely enter his protest, that when on his way to make the Macedonians the masters of the world, he was left alone with a few friends and volunteers. This is almost word for word, as he wrote in a letter to Antipater, where he adds, that when he had thus spoken to them, they all cried out, they would go along with him whithersoever it was his pleasure to lead them. After succeeding with these, it was no hard matter for him to bring over the multitude, which easily followed the example of their betters. Now, also, he more and more accommodated himself in his way of living to that of the natives, and tried to bring them also as near as he could to the Macedonian customs, wisely considering that whilst he was engaged in an expedition which would carry him far from thence, it would be wiser to depend upon the good-will which might arise from intermixture and association as a means of maintaining tranquillity, than upon force and compulsion. In order to this, he chose out thirty thousand boys, whom he put under masters to teach them the Greek tongue, and to train them up to arms in the Macedonian discipline. As for his marriage with Roxana, whose youthfulness and beauty had charmed him at a drinking entertainment, where he first happened to see her taking part in a dance, it was, indeed a love affair, yet it seemed at the same time to be conducive to the object he had in hand. For it gratified the conquered people to see him choose a wife from among themselves, and it made them feel the most lively affection for him, to find that in the only passion which he, the most temperate of men, was overcome by, he yet forbore till he could obtain her in a lawful and honourable way.

Noticing also that among his chief friends and favourites, Hephæstion most approved all that he did, and complied with and imitated him in his change of habits, while Craterus continued strict in the observation of the customs and fashions of his own country, he made it his practice to employ the first in all transactions with the Persians, and the latter when he had to do with the Greeks or Macedonians. And in general he showed more affection for Hephæstion, and more respect for Craterus; Hephæstion, as he used to say, being Alexander's, and Craterus the king's friend. And so these two friends always bore in secret a grudge to each other, and at times quarrelled openly, so much so that once in India they drew upon one another, and were proceeding in good earnest, with their friends on each side to second them, when Alexander rode up and publicly reproved Hephæstion, calling him fool and madman, not to be sensible that without his favour he was nothing. He rebuked Craterus also in private, severely, and then causing them both to come into his presence, he reconciled them, at the same time swearing by Ammon and the rest of the gods, that he loved them two above all other men, but if ever he perceived them fall out again he would be sure to put both of them to death, or at least the aggressor. After which they neither ever did or said anything, so much as in jest, to offend one another.

There was scarcely any one who had greater repute among the Macedonians than Philotas, the son of Parmenio. For besides that he was valiant and able to endure any fatigue of war, he was also next to Alexander himself the most munificent, and the greatest lover of his friends, one of whom asking him for some money, he commanded his steward to give it him; and when he told him he had not wherewith, "Have you not any plate, then," said he, "or any clothes of mine to sell?" But he carried his arrogance and his pride of wealth and his habits of display and luxury to a degree of assumption unbecoming a private man; and affecting all the loftiness without succeeding in showing any of the grace or gentleness of true greatness, by this mistaken and spurious majesty he gained so much envy and ill-will, that Parmenio would sometimes tell him, "My son, to be not quite so great would be better." For he had long before been complained of, and accused to Alexander. Particularly when Darius was defeated in Cilicia, and an immense booty was taken at Damascus, among the rest of the prisoners who were brought into the camp, there was one Antigone of Pydna, a very handsome woman, who fell to Philotas's share. The young man one day in his cups, in the vaunting, outspoken, soldier's manner, declared to his mistress, that all the great actions were performed by him and his father, the glory and benefit of which, he said, together with the title of king, the boy Alexander reaped and enjoyed by their means. She could not hold, but discovered what he had said to one of her acquaintance, and he, as is usual in such cases, to another, till at last the story came to the ears of Craterus, who brought the woman secretly to the king. When Alexander had heard what she had to say, he commanded her to continue her intrigue with Philotas, and give him an account from time to time of all that should fall from him to this purpose. He, thus unwittingly caught in a snare, to gratify sometimes a fit of anger, sometimes a love of vainglory, let himself utter numerous foolish, indiscreet speeches against the king in Antigone's hearing, of which, though Alexander was informed and convinced by strong evidence, yet he would take no notice of it at present, whether it was that he confided in Parmenio's affection and loyalty, or that he apprehended their authority and interest in the army. But about this time, one Limnus, a Macedonian of Chalastra, conspired against Alexander's life, and communicated his design to a youth whom he was fond of, named Nicomachus, inviting him to be of the party. But he not relishing the thing, revealed it to his brother Balinus, who immediately addressed himself to Philotas, requiring him to introduce them both to Alexander, to whom they had something of great moment to impart which very nearly concerned him. But he, for what reason is uncertain, went not with them, professing that the king was engaged with affairs of more importance. And when they had urged him a second time, and were still slighted by him, they applied themselves to another, by whose means being admitted into Alexander's presence, they first told about Limnus's conspiracy, and by the way let Philotas's negligence appear who had twice disregarded their application to him. Alexander was greatly incensed, and on finding that Limnus had defended himself, and had been killed by the soldier who was sent to seize him, he was still more discomposed, thinking he had thus lost the means of detecting the plot. As soon as his displeasure against Philotas began to appear, presently all his old enemies showed themselves, and said openly, the king was too easily imposed on, to imagine that one so inconsiderable as Limnus, a Chalastrian, should of his own head undertake such an enterprise; that in all likelihood he was but subservient to the design, an instrument that was moved by some greater spring; that those ought to be more strictly examined about the matter whose interest it was so much to conceal it. When they had once gained the king's ear for insinuations of this sort, they went on to show a thousand grounds of suspicion against Philotas, till at last they prevailed to have him seized and put to the torture, which was done in the presence of the principal officers, Alexander himself being placed behind some tapestry to understand what passed. Where, when he heard in what a miserable tone, and with what abject submissions Philotas applied himself to Hephæstion, he broke out, it is said, in this manner: "Are you so mean-spirited and effeminate, Philotas, and yet can engage in so desperate a design?" After his death, he presently sent into Media, and put also Parmenio, his father, to death, who had done brave service under Philip, and was the only man of his older friends and counsellors who had encouraged Alexander to invade Asia. Of three sons whom he had had in the army, he had already lost two, and now was himself put to death with the third. These actions rendered Alexander an object of terror to many of his friends, and chiefly to Antipater, who, to strengthen himself, sent messengers privately to treat for an alliance with the Ætolians, who stood in fear of Alexander, because they had destroyed the town of the Œniadæ; on being informed of which, Alexander had said the children of the Œniadæ need not revenge their father's quarrel, for he would himself take care to punish the Ætolians.

Not long after this happened, the deplorable end of Clitus, which, to those who barely hear the matter, may seem more inhuman than that of Philotas; but if we consider the story with its circumstance of time, and weigh the cause, we shall find it to have occurred rather through a sort of mischance of the king's, whose anger and over-drinking offered an occasion to the evil genius of Clitus. The king had a present of Grecian fruit brought him from the sea-coast, which was so fresh and beautiful that he was surprised at it, and called Clitus to him to see it, and to give him a share of it. Clitus was then sacrificing, but he immediately left off and came, followed by three sheep, on whom the drink-offering had been already poured preparatory to sacrificing them. Alexander, being informed of this, told his diviners, Aristander and Cleomantis the Lacedæmonian, and asked them what it meant; on whose assuring him it was an ill omen, he commanded them in all haste to offer sacrifices for Clitus's safety, forasmuch as three days before he himself had seen a strange vision in his sleep, of Clitus all in mourning, sitting by Parmenio's sons who were dead. Clitus, however, stayed not to finish his devotions, but came straight to supper with the king, who had sacrificed to Castor and Pollux. And when they had drunk pretty hard, some of the company fell a-singing the verses of one Pranichus, or as others say of Pierion, which were made upon those captains who had been lately worsted by the barbarians, on purpose to disgrace and turn them to ridicule. This gave offence to the older men who were there, and they upbraided both the author and the singer of the verses, though Alexander and the younger men about him were much amused to hear them, and encouraged them to go on, till at last Clitus, who had drunk too much, and was besides of a forward and wilful temper, was so nettled that he could hold no longer, saying it was not well done to expose the Macedonians before the barbarians and their enemies, since though it was their unhappiness to be overcome, yet they were much better men than those who laughed at them. And when Alexander remarked, that Clitus was pleading his own cause, giving cowardice the name of misfortune, Clitus started up: "This cowardice, as you are pleased to term it," said he to him, "saved the life of a son of the gods, when in flight from Spithridates's sword; it is by the expense of Macedonian blood, and by these wounds, that you are now raised to such a height as to be able to disown your father Philip, and call yourself the son of Ammon." "Thou base fellow," said Alexander, who was now thoroughly exasperated, "dost thou think to utter these things everywhere of me, and stir up the Macedonians to sedition, and not be punished for it?" "We are sufficiently punished already," answered Clitus, "if this be the recompense of our toils, and we must esteem theirs a happy lot who have not lived to see their countrymen scourged with Median rods and forced to sue to the Persians to have access to their king." While he talked thus at random, and those near Alexander got up from their seats and began to revile him in turn, the elder men did what they could to compose the disorder. Alexander, in the meantime turning about to Xenodochus, the Pardian, and Artemius, the Colophonian, asked him if they were not of opinion that the Greeks, in comparison with the Macedonians, behaved themselves like so many demigods among wild beasts. But Clitus for all this would not give over, desiring Alexander to speak out if he had anything more to say, or else why did he invite men who were freeborn and accustomed to speak their minds openly without restraint to sup with him. He had better live and converse with barbarians and slaves who would not scruple to bow the knee to his Persian girdle and his white tunic. Which words so provoked Alexander that, not able to suppress his anger any longer, he threw one of the apples that lay upon the table at him, and hit him, and then looked about for his sword. But Aristophanes, one of his life-guard, had hid that out of the way, and others came about him and besought him, but in vain; for, breaking from them, he called out aloud to his guards in the Macedonian language, which was a certain sign of some great disturbance in him, and commanded a trumpeter to sound, giving him a blow with his clenched fist for not instantly obeying him; though afterwards the same man was commended for disobeying an order which would have put the whole army into tumult and confusion. Clitus still refusing to yield, was with much trouble forced by his friends out of the room. But he came in again immediately at another door, very irreverently and confidently singing the verses out of Euripides's Andromache—

"In Greece, alas! how ill things ordered are!"

Upon this, at last, Alexander, snatching a spear from one of the soldiers, met Clitus as he was coming forward and was putting by the curtain that hung before the door, and ran him through the body. He fell at once with a cry and a groan. Upon which the king's anger immediately vanishing, he came perfectly to himself, and when he saw his friends about him all in a profound silence, he pulled the spear out of the dead body, and would have thrust it into his own throat, if the guards had not held his hands, and by main force carried him away into his chamber, where all that night and the next day he wept bitterly, till being quite spent with lamenting and exclaiming, he lay as it were speechless, only fetching deep sighs. His friends apprehending some harm from his silence, broke into the room, but he took no notice of what any of them said, till Aristander putting him in mind of the vision he had seen concerning Clitus, and the prodigy that followed, as if all had come to pass by an unavoidable fatality, he then seemed to moderate his grief. They now brought Callisthenes, the philosopher, who was the near friend of Aristotle, and Anaxarchus of Abdera, to him. Callisthenes used moral language, and gentle and soothing means, hoping to find access for words of reason, and get a hold upon the passion. But Anaxarchus, who had always taken a course of his own in philosophy, and had a name for despising and slighting his contemporaries, as soon as he came in, cried aloud, "Is this the Alexander whom the whole world looks to, lying here weeping like a slave, for fear of the censure and reproach of men, to whom he himself ought to be a law and measure of equity, if he would use the right his conquests have given him as supreme lord and governor of all, and not be the victim of a vain and idle opinion? Do not you know," said he, "that Jupiter is represented to have Justice and Law on each hand of him, to signify that all the actions of a conqueror are lawful and just?" With these and the like speeches, Anaxarchus indeed allayed the king's grief, but withal corrupted his character, rendering him more audacious and lawless than he had been. Nor did he fail these means to insinuate himself into his favour, and to make Callisthenes's company, which at all times, because of his austerity, was not very acceptable, more uneasy and disagreeable to him.

It happened that these two philosophers met at an entertainment where conversation turned on the subject of climate and the temperature of the air. Callisthenes joined with their opinion, who held that those countries were colder, and the winter sharper there than in Greece. Anaxarchus would by no means allow this, but argued against it with some heat. "Surely," said Callisthenes, "you cannot but admit this country to be colder than Greece, for there you used to have but one threadbare cloak to keep out the coldest winter, and here you have three good warm mantles one over another." This piece of raillery irritated Anaxarchus and the other pretenders to learning, and the crowd of flatterers in general could not endure to see Callisthenes so much admired and followed by the youth, and no less esteemed by the older men for his orderly life and his gravity and for being contented with his condition; and confirming what he had professed about the object he had in his journey to Alexander, that it was only to get his countrymen recalled from banishment, and to rebuild and repeople his native town. Besides the envy which his great reputation raised, he also, by his own deportment, gave those who wished him ill opportunity to do him mischief. For when he was invited to public entertainments, he would most times refuse to come, or if he were present at any, he put a constraint upon the company by his austerity and silence, which seemed to intimate his disapproval of what he saw. So that Alexander himself said in application to him,—

> "That vain pretence to wisdom I detest,
> Where a man's blind to his own interest."

Being with many more invited to sup with the king, he was called upon when the cup came to him, to make an oration extempore in praise of the Macedonians; and he did it with such a flow of eloquence, that all who heard it rose from their seats to clap and applaud him, and threw their garland upon him; only Alexander told him out of Euripides—

> "I wonder not that you have spoke so well,
> 'Tis easy on good subjects to excel."

"Therefore," said he, "if you will show the force of your eloquence, tell my Macedonians their faults, and dispraise them, that by hearing their errors they may learn to be better for the future." Callisthenes presently obeyed him, retracting all he had said before, and, inveighing against the

Macedonians with great freedom, added, that Philip thrived and grew powerful, chiefly by the discord of the Grecians, applying this verse to him—

"In civil strife e'en villains rise to fame;"

which so offended the Macedonians, that he was odious to them ever after. And Alexander said, that instead of his eloquence, he had only made his ill-will appear in what he had spoken. Hermippus assures us that one Strœbus, a servant whom Callisthenes kept to read to him, gave this account of these passages afterwards to Aristotle; and that when he perceived the king grow more and more averse to him, two or three times, as he was going away, he repeated the verses—

"Death seiz'd at last on great Patroclus too,
Though he in virtue far exceeded you."

Not without reason, therefore, did Aristotle give this character of Callisthenes, that he was, indeed, a powerful speaker, but had no judgment. He acted certainly a true philosopher's part in positively refusing, as he did, to pay adoration; and by speaking out openly against that which the best and gravest of the Macedonians only repined at in secret, he delivered the Grecians and Alexander himself from a great disgrace, when the practice was given up. But he ruined himself by it, because he went too roughly to work, as if he would have forced the king to that which he should have effected by reason and persuasion. Chares of Mitylene writes, that at a banquet Alexander, after he had drunk, reached the cup to one of his friends, who, on receiving it, rose up towards the domestic altar, and when he had drunk, first adored and then kissed Alexander, and afterwards laid himself down at the table with the rest. Which they all did one after another, till it came to Callisthenes's turn, who took the cup and drank, while the king, who was engaged in conversation with Hephæstion, was not observing, and then came and offered to kiss him. But Demetrius, surnamed Phidon, interposed, saying, "Sir, by no means let him kiss you, for he only of us all has refused to adore you;" upon which the king declined it, and all the concern Callisthenes showed was, that he said aloud, "Then I go away with a kiss less than the rest." The displeasure he incurred by this action procured credit for Hephæstion's declaration that he had broken his word to him in not paying the king the same veneration that others did, as he had faithfully promised to do. And to finish his disgrace, a number of such men as Lysimachus and Hagnon now came in with their asseverations that the sophist went about everywhere boasting of his resistance to arbitrary power, and that the young men all ran after him, and honoured him as the only man among so many thousands who had the courage to preserve his liberty.

Therefore when Hermolaus's conspiracy came to be discovered, the charges which his enemies brought against him were the more easily believed, particularly that when the young man asked him what he should do to be the most illustrious person on earth, he told him the readiest way was to kill him who was already so, and that to incite him to commit the deed, he bade him not be awed by the golden couch, but remember Alexander was a man equally infirm and vulnerable as another. However, none of Hermolaus's accomplices, in the utmost extremity, made any mention of Callisthenes's being engaged in the design. Nay, Alexander himself, in the letters which he wrote soon after to Craterus, Attalus, and Alcetas, tells them that the young men who were put to the torture declared they had entered into the conspiracy of themselves, without any others being privy to or guilty of it. But yet afterwards, in a letter to Antipater, he accuses Callisthenes. "The young men," he says, "were stoned to death by the Macedonians, but for the sophist" (meaning Callisthenes), "I will take care to punish him with them too who sent him to me, and who harbour those in their cities who conspire against my life," an unequivocal declaration against Aristotle, in whose house Callisthenes, for his relationship's sake, being his niece Hero's son, had been educated. His death is variously related. Some say he was hanged by Alexander's orders; others, that he died of sickness in prison; but Chares writes he was kept in chains seven months after he was apprehended, on purpose that he might be proceeded against in full council, when Aristotle should be present; and that growing very fat, and contracting a disease of vermin, he there died, about the time that Alexander was wounded in India, in the country of the Malli Oxydracæ, all which came to pass afterwards.

For to go on in order, Demaratus of Corinth, now quite an old man, had made a great effort, about this time, to pay Alexander a visit; and when he had seen him, said he pitied the misfortune of those Grecians, who were so unhappy as to die before they had beheld Alexander seated on the throne of Darius. But he did not long enjoy the benefit of the king's kindness for him, any otherwise than that soon after falling sick and dying, he had a magnificent funeral, and the army raised him a monument of earth fourscore cubits high, and of a vast circumference. His ashes were conveyed in a very rich chariot, drawn by four horses, to the seaside.

Alexander, now intent upon his expedition into India, took notice that his soldiers were so charged with booty that it hindered their marching. Therefore, at break of day, as soon as the baggage waggons were laden, first he set fire to his own, and to those of his friends, and then commanded those to be burnt which belonged to the rest of the army. An act which in the deliberation of it had seemed more dangerous and difficult than it proved in the execution, with which few were dissatisfied; for most of the soldiers, as if they had been inspired, uttering loud outcries and warlike shoutings, supplied one another with what was absolutely necessary, and burnt and destroyed all that was superfluous, the sight of which redoubled Alexander's zeal and eagerness for his design. And, indeed, he was now grown very severe and inexorable in punishing those who committed any fault. For he put Menander, one of his friends, to death for deserting a fortress where he had placed him in garrison, and shot Orsodates, one of the barbarians who revolted from him, with his own hand.

At this time a sheep happened to yean a lamb, with the perfect shape and colour of a tiara upon the head, and testicles on each side; which portent Alexander regarded with such dislike, that he immediately caused his Babylonian priests, whom he usually carried about with him for such purposes, to purify him, and told his friends he was not so much concerned for his own sake as for theirs, out of an apprehension that after his death the divine power might suffer his empire to fall into the hands of some degenerate, impotent person. But this fear was soon removed by a wonderful thing that happened not long after, and was thought to presage better. For Proxenus, a Macedonian, who was the chief of those who looked to the king's furniture, as he was breaking up the ground near the river Oxus, to set up the royal pavilion, discovered a spring of a fat oily liquor, which, after the top was taken off, ran pure, clear oil, without any difference either of taste or smell, having exactly the same smoothness and brightness, and that, too, in a country where no olives grew. The water, indeed, of the river Oxus, is said to be the smoothest to the feeling of all waters, and to leave a gloss on the skins of those who bathe themselves in it. Whatever might be the cause, certain it is that Alexander was wonderfully pleased with it, as appears by his letters to Antipater, where he speaks of it as one of the most remarkable presages that God had ever favoured him with. The diviners told him it signified his expedition would be glorious in the event, but very painful and attended with many difficulties; for oil, they said, was bestowed on mankind by God as a refreshment of their labours.

Nor did they judge amiss, for he exposed himself to many hazards in the battles which he fought, and received very severe wounds, but the greatest loss in his army was occasioned through the unwholesomeness of the air and the want of necessary provisions. But he still applied himself to overcome fortune and whatever opposed him, by resolution and virtue, and thought nothing impossible to true intrepidity, and on the other hand nothing secure or strong for cowardice. It is told of him that when he besieged Sisimithres, who held an inaccessible, impregnable rock against him, and his soldiers began to despair of taking it, he asked Oxyartes whether

Sisimithres was a man of courage, who assuring him he was the greatest coward alive, "Then you tell me," said he, "that the place may easily be taken, since what is in command of it is weak." And in a little time he so terrified Sisimithres that he took it without any difficulty. At an attack which he made upon such another precipitous place with some of his Macedonian soldiers, he called to one whose name was Alexander, and told him he at any rate must fight bravely if it were but for his name's sake. The youth fought gallantly and was killed in the action, at which he was sensibly afflicted. Another time, seeing his men march slowly and unwillingly to the siege of the place called Nysa, because of a deep river between them and the town, he advanced before them, and standing upon the bank, "What a miserable man," said he, "am I, that I have not learned to swim!" and then was hardly dissuaded from endeavouring to pass it upon his shield. Here, after the assault was over, the ambassadors who from several towns which he had blocked up came to submit to him and make their peace, were surprised to find him still in his armour, without any one in waiting or attendance upon him, and when at last some one brought him a cushion, he made the eldest of them, named Acuphis, take it and sit down upon it. The old man, marvelling at his magnanimity and courtesy, asked him what his countrymen should do to merit his friendship. "I would have them," said Alexander, "choose you to govern them, and send one hundred of the most worthy men among them to remain with me as hostages." Acuphis laughed and answered, "I shall govern them with more ease, sir, if I send you so many of the worst, rather than the best of my subjects."

The extent of King Taxiles's dominions in India was thought to be as large as Egypt, abounding in good pastures, and producing beautiful fruits. The king himself had the reputation of a wise man, and at his first interview with Alexander he spoke to him in these terms: "To what purpose," said he, "should we make war upon one another, if the design of your coming into these parts be not to rob us of our water or our necessary food, which are the only things that wise men are indispensably obliged to fight for? As for other riches and possessions, as they are accounted in the eye of the world, if I am better provided of them than you, I am ready to let you share with me; but if fortune has been more liberal to you than me, I have no objection to be obliged to you." This discourse pleased Alexander so much that, embracing him, "Do you think," said he to him, "your kind words and courteous behaviour will bring you off in this interview without a contest? No, you shall not escape so. I shall contend and do battle with you so far, that how obliging soever you are, you shall not have the better of me." Then receiving some presents from him, he returned him others of greater value, and to complete his bounty gave him in money ready coined one thousand talents; at which his old friends were much displeased, but it gained him the hearts of many of the barbarians. But the best soldiers of the Indians now entering into the pay of several of the cities, undertook to defend them, and did it so bravely, that they put Alexander to a great deal of trouble, till at last, after a capitulation, upon the surrender of the place, he fell upon them as they were marching away, and put them all to the sword. This one breach of his word remains as a blemish upon his achievements in war, which he otherwise had performed throughout with that justice and honour that became a king. Nor was he less incommoded by the Indian philosophers, who inveighed against those princes who joined his party, and solicited the free nations to oppose him. He took several of these also and caused them to be hanged.

Alexander, in his own letters, has given us an account of his war with Porus. He says the two armies were separated by the river Hydaspes, on whose opposite bank Porus continually kept his elephants in order of battle, with their heads towards their enemies, to guard the passage; that he, on the other hand, made every day a great noise and clamour in his camp, to dissipate the apprehensions of the barbarians; that one stormy dark night he passed the river, at a distance from the place where the enemy lay, into a little island, with part of his foot and the best of his horse. Here there fell a most violent storm of rain, accompanied with lightning and whirlwinds, and seeing some of his men burnt and dying with the lightning, he nevertheless quitted the island and made over to the other side. The Hydaspes, he says, now after the storm, was so swollen and grown so rapid as to have made a breach in the bank, and a part of the river was now pouring in here, so that when he came across it was with difficulty he got a footing on the land, which was slippery and unsteady, and exposed to the force of the currents on both sides. This is the occasion when he is related to have said, "O ye Athenians, will ye believe what dangers I incur to merit your praise?" This, however, is Onesicritus's story. Alexander says, here the men left their boats, and passed the breach in their armour, up to the breast in water, and that then he advanced with his horse about twenty furlongs before his foot, concluding that if the enemy charged him with their cavalry he should be too strong for them; if with their foot, his own would come up time enough to his assistance. Nor did he judge amiss; for being charged by a thousand horse and sixty armed chariots, which advanced before their main body, he took all the chariots, and killed four hundred horse upon the place. Porus, by this time, guessing that Alexander himself had crossed over, came on with his whole army, except a party which he left behind, to hold the rest of the Macedonians in play, if they should attempt to pass the river. But he, apprehending the multitude of the enemy, and to avoid the shock of their elephants, dividing his forces, attacked their left wing himself, and commanded Cœnus to fall upon the right, which was performed with good success. For by this means both wings being broken, the enemies fell back in their retreat upon the centre, and crowded in upon their elephants. There rallying, they fought a hand-to-hand battle, and it was the eighth hour of the day before they were entirely defeated. This description the conqueror himself has left us in his own epistles.

Almost all the historians agree in relating that Porus was four cubits and a span high, and that when he was upon his elephant, which was of the largest size, his stature and bulk were so answerable, that he appeared to be proportionately mounted, as a horseman on his horse. This elephant, during the whole battle, gave many singular proofs of sagacity and of particular care of the king, whom as long as he was strong and in a condition to fight, he defended with great courage, repelling those who set upon him; and as soon as he perceived him overpowered with his numerous wounds and the multitude of darts that were thrown at him, to prevent his falling off, he softly knelt down and began to draw out the darts with his proboscis. When Porus was taken prisoner, and Alexander asked him how he expected to be used, he answered, "As a king." For that expression, he said, when the same question was put to him a second time, comprehended everything. And Alexander, accordingly, not only suffered him to govern his own kingdom as satrap under himself, but gave him also the additional territory of various independent tribes whom he subdued, a district which, it is said, contained fifteen several nations, and five thousand considerable towns, besides abundance of villages. To another government, three times as large as this, he appointed Philip, one of his friends.

Some little time after the battle with Porus, Bucephalus died, as most of the authorities state, under cure of his wounds, or, as Onesicritus says, of fatigue and age, being thirty years old. Alexander was no less concerned at his death than if he had lost an old companion or an intimate friend, and built a city, which he named Bucephalia, in memory of him, on the bank of the river Hydaspes. He also, we are told, built another city, and called it after the name of a favourite dog, Peritas, which he had brought up himself. So Sotion assures us he was informed by Potamon of Lesbos.

But this last combat with Porus took off the edge of the Macedonians' courage, and stayed their further progress into India. For having found it hard enough to defeat an enemy who brought but twenty thousand foot and two thousand horse into the field, they thought they had reason to oppose Alexander's design of leading them on to pass the Ganges, too, which they were told was thirty-two furlongs broad and a hundred fathoms deep, and the banks on the further side covered with multitudes of enemies. For they were told the kings of the Gandaritans and Præsians expected them there with eighty thousand horse, two hundred thousand foot, eight thousand armed chariots, and six thousand fighting elephants. Nor was this a mere vain report, spread to discourage them. For Androcottus, who not long after reigned in those parts, made a present of five hundred elephants at once to Seleucus, and with an army of six hundred thousand men subdued all India. Alexander at first was so grieved and enraged at his men's reluctancy that he shut himself up in his tent and threw himself upon the ground, declaring, if they would not pass the Ganges, he owed them no thanks for anything they had hitherto done, and that to retreat now was plainly to confess himself vanquished. But at last the reasonable persuasions of his friends and the cries and lamentations of his soldiers, who in a suppliant manner crowded about the entrance of his tent, prevailed with him to think of returning. Yet he could not refrain from leaving behind him various deceptive memorials of his expedition, to impose upon aftertimes, and to exaggerate his glory with posterity, such as arms larger than were really worn, and mangers for horses, with bits and bridles above the usual size, which he set up, and distributed in several places. He erected altars, also, to the gods, which the kings of the Præsians even in our time do honour to when they pass the river, and offer sacrifice upon them after the Grecian manner. Androcottus, then a boy, saw Alexander there, and is said often afterwards to have been heard to say, that he missed but little of making himself master of those countries; their king, who then reigned, was so hated and despised for the viciousness of his life and the meanness of his extraction.

Alexander was now eager to see the ocean. To which purpose he caused a great many tow-boats and rafts to be built, in which he fell gently down the rivers at his leisure, yet so that his navigation was neither unprofitable nor inactive. For by several descents upon the bank, he made himself master of the fortified towns, and consequently of the country on both sides. But at a siege of a town of the Mallians, who have the repute of being the bravest people of India, he ran in great danger of his life. For having beaten off the defendants with showers of arrows, he was the first man that mounted the wall by a scaling-ladder, which, as soon as he was up, broke and left him almost alone, exposed to the darts which the barbarians threw at him in great numbers from below. In this distress, turning himself as well as he could, he leaped down in the midst of his enemies, and had the good fortune to light upon his feet. The brightness and clattering of his armour when he came to the ground made the barbarians think they saw rays of light, or some bright phantom playing before his body, which frightened them so at first that they ran away and dispersed. Till seeing him seconded but by two of his guards, they fell upon him hand to hand, and some, while he bravely defended himself, tried to wound him through his armour with their swords and spears. And one who stood further off drew a bow with such strength that the arrow, finding its way through his cuirass, stuck in his ribs under the breast. This stroke was so violent that it made him give back, and set one knee to the ground, upon which the man ran up with his drawn scimitar, thinking to despatch him, and had done it, if Peucestes and Limnæus had not interposed, who were both wounded, Limnæus mortally, but Peucestes stood his ground, while Alexander killed the barbarians. But this did not free him from danger; for, besides many other wounds, at last he received so weighty a stroke of a club upon his neck that he was forced to lean his body against the wall, still, however, facing the enemy. At this extremity, the Macedonians made their way in and gathered round him. They took him up, just as he was fainting away, having lost all sense of what was done near him, and conveyed him to his tent, upon which it was presently reported all over the camp that he was dead. But when they had with great difficulty and pains sawed off the shaft of the arrow, which was of wood, and so with much trouble got off his cuirass, they came to cut the head of it, which was three fingers broad and four long, and stuck fast in the bone. During the operation he was taken with almost mortal swoonings, but when it was out he came to himself again. Yet though all danger was past, he continued very weak, and confined himself a great while to a regular diet and the method of his cure, till one day hearing the Macedonians clamouring outside in their eagerness to see him, he took his cloak and went out. And having sacrificed to the gods, without more delay he went on board again, and as he coasted along subdued a great deal of the country on both sides, and several considerable cities.

In this voyage he took ten of the Indian philosophers prisoners who had been most active in persuading Sabbas to revolt, and had caused the Macedonians a great deal of trouble. These men, called Gymnosophists, were reputed to be extremely ready and succinct in their answers, which he made trial of, by putting difficult questions to them, letting them know that those whose answers were not pertinent should be put to death, of which he made the eldest of them judge. The first being asked which he thought the most numerous, the dead or the living, answered, "The living because those who are dead are not at all." Of the second, he desired to know whether the earth or the sea produced the largest beasts; who told him, "The earth, for the sea is but a part of it." His question to the third was, Which is the cunningest of beasts? "That," said he, "which men have not yet found out." He bade the fourth tell him what argument he used to Sabbas to persuade him to revolt. "No other," said he, "than that he should either live or die nobly." Of the fifth he asked, Which was the eldest, night or day? The philosopher replied, "Day was eldest, by one day at least." But perceiving Alexander not well satisfied with that account, he added, that he ought not to wonder if strange questions had as strange answers made to them. Then he went on and inquired of the next, what a man should do to be exceedingly beloved. "He must be very powerful," said he, "without making himself too much feared." The answer of the seventh to his question, how a man might become a god, was, "By doing that which was impossible for men to do." The eighth told him, "Life is stronger than death, because it supports so many miseries." And the last being asked, how long he thought it decent for a man to live, said, "Till death appeared more desirable than life." Then Alexander turned to him whom he had made judge, and commanded him to give sentence. "All that I can determine," said he, "is, that they have every one answered worse than another." "Nay," said the king, "then you shall die first, for giving such a sentence." "Not so, O king," replied the gymnosophist, "unless you said falsely that he should die first who made the worst answer." In conclusion he gave them presents and dismissed them.

But to those who were in greatest reputation among them, and lived a private quiet life, he sent Onesicritus, one of Diogenes the Cynic's disciples, desiring them to come to him. Calanus, it is said, very arrogantly and roughly commanded him to strip himself and hear what he said naked, otherwise he would not speak a word to him, though he came from Jupiter himself. But Dandamis received him with more civility, and hearing him discourse of Socrates, Pythagoras, and Diogenes, told him he thought them men of great parts and to have erred in nothing so much as in having too great respect for the laws and customs of their country. Others say Dandamis only asked him the reason why Alexander undertook so long a journey to come into those parts. Taxiles, however, persuaded Calanus to wait upon Alexander. His proper name was Sphines, but because he was wont to say *Cale*, which in the Indian tongue is a form of salutation to those he met with anywhere, the Greeks called him Calanus. He is said to have shown Alexander an instructive emblem of government, which was. this. He threw a dry shrivelled hide upon the ground, and trod upon the edges of it. The skin when it was pressed in one place still rose up in another, wheresoever he trod round about it, till he set his foot in the middle, which made all the parts lie even and quiet. The meaning of this similitude being that he ought to reside most in the middle of his empire, and not spend too much time on the borders of it.

His voyage down the rivers took up seven months' time, and when he came to the sea, he sailed to an island which he himself called Scillustis, others Psiltucis, where going ashore, he sacrificed, and made what observations he could as to the nature of the sea and the sea-coast. Then having besought the gods that no other man might ever go beyond the bounds of this expedition, he ordered his fleet, of which he made Nearchus admiral and Onesicritus pilot, to sail round about, keeping the Indian shore on the right hand, and returned himself by land through the country of the Orites, where he was reduced to great straits for want of provisions, and lost a vast number of his men, so that of an army of one hundred and twenty thousand foot and fifteen thousand horse, he scarcely brought back above a fourth part out of India, they were so diminished by disease, ill diet, and the scorching heats, but most by famine. For their march was through an uncultivated country whose inhabitants fared hardly, possessing only a few sheep, and those of a wretched kind, whose flesh was rank and unsavoury, by their continual feeding upon sea-fish.

After sixty days' march he came into Gedrosia, where he found great plenty of all things, which the neighbouring kings and governors of provinces, hearing of his approach, had taken care to provide. When he had here refreshed his army, he continued his march through Carmania, feasting all the way for seven days together. He with his most intimate friends banqueted and revelled night and day upon a platform erected on a lofty, conspicuous scaffold, which was slowly drawn by eight horses. This was followed by a great many chariots, some covered with purple and embroidered canopies, and some with green boughs, which were continually supplied afresh, and in them the rest of his friends and commanders drinking, and crowned with garlands of flowers. Here was now no target or helmet or spear to be seen; instead of armour, the soldiers handled nothing but cups and goblets and Thericlean drinking vessels, which, along the whole way, they dipped into large bowls and jars, and drank healths to one another, some seating themselves to it, others as they went along. All places resounded with music of pipes and flutes, with harping and singing, and women dancing as in the rites of Bacchus. For this disorderly, wandering march, besides the drinking part of it, was accompanied with all the sportiveness and insolence of bacchanals, as much as if the god himself had been there to countenance and lead the procession. As soon as he came to the royal palace of Gedrosia, he again refreshed and feasted his army; and one day after he had drunk pretty hard, it is said, he went to see a prize of dancing contended for, in which his favourite Bagoas, having gained the victory, crossed the theatre in his dancing habit, and sat down close by him, which so pleased the Macedonians that they made loud acclamations for him to kiss Bagoas, and never stopped clapping their hands and shouting till Alexander put his arms round him and kissed him.

Here his admiral, Nearchus, came to him, and delighted him so with the narrative of his voyage, that he resolved himself to sail out of the mouth of the Euphrates with a great fleet, with which he designed to go round by Arabia and Africa, and so by Hercules's Pillars into the Mediterranean; in order for which, he directed all sorts of vessels to be built at Thapsacus, and made great provisions everywhere of seamen and pilots. But the tidings of the difficulties he had gone through in his Indian expedition, the danger of his person among the Mallians, the reported loss of a considerable part of his forces, and a general doubt as to his own safety, had begun to give occasion for revolt among many of the conquered nations, and for acts of great injustice, avarice, and insolence on the part of the satraps and commanders in the provinces, so that there seemed to be an universal fluctuation and disposition to change. Even at home, Olympias and Cleopatra had raised a faction against Antipater, and divided his government between them, Olympias seizing upon Epirus, and Cleopatra upon Macedonia. When Alexander was told of it, he said his mother had made the best choice, for the Macedonians would never endure to be ruled by a woman. Upon this he despatched Nearchus again to his fleet, to carry the war into the maritime provinces, and as he marched that way himself he punished those commanders who had behaved ill, particularly Oxyartes, one of the sons of Abuletes, whom he killed with his own hand, thrusting him through the body with his spear. And when Abuletes, instead of the necessary provisions which he ought to have furnished, brought him three thousand talents in coined money, he ordered it to be thrown to his horses, and when they would not touch it, "What good," he said, "will this provision do us?" and sent him away to prison.

When he came into Persia, he distributed money among the women, as their own kings had been wont to do, who as often as they came thither gave every one of them a piece of gold; on account of which custom, some of them, it is said, had come but seldom, and Ochus was so sordidly covetous that, to avoid this expense, he never visited his native country once in all his reign. Then finding Cyrus's sepulchre opened and rifled, he put Polymachus, who did it, to death, though he was a man of some distinction, a born Macedonian of Pella. And after he had read the inscription, he caused it to be cut again below the old one in Greek characters; the words being these: "O man, whosoever thou art, and from whencesoever thou comest (for I know thou wilt come), I am Cyrus, the founder of the Persian empire; do not grudge me this little earth which covers my body." The reading of this sensibly touched Alexander, filling him with the thought of the uncertainty and mutability of human affairs. At the same time Calanus, having been a little while troubled with a disease in the bowels, requested that he might have a funeral pile erected, to which he came on horseback, and, after he had said some prayers and sprinkled himself and cut off some of his hair to throw into the fire, before he ascended it, he embraced and took leave of the Macedonians who stood by, desiring them to pass that day in mirth and good-fellowship with their king, whom in a little time, he said, he doubted not to see again at Babylon. Having this said, he lay down, and covering up his face, he stirred not when the fire came near him, but continued still in the same posture as at first, and so sacrificed himself, as it was the ancient custom of the philosophers in those countries to do. The same thing was done long after by another Indian who came with Cæsar to Athens, where they still show you, "the Indian's monument." At his return from the funeral pile, Alexander invited a great many of his friends and principal officers to supper, and proposed a drinking match, in which the victor should receive a crown. Promachus drank twelve quarts of wine, and won the prize, which was a talent from them all; but he survived his victory but three days, and was followed, as Chares says, by forty-one more, who died of the same debauch, some extremely cold weather having set in shortly after.

At Susa, he married Darius's daughter Statira, and celebrated also the nuptials of his friends, bestowing the noblest of the Persian ladies upon the worthiest of them, at the same time making it an entertainment in honour of the other Macedonians whose marriages had already taken place. At this magnificent festival, it is reported, there were no less than nine thousand guests, to each of whom he gave a golden cup for the libations. Not to mention other instances of his wonderful magnificence, he paid the debts of his army, which amounted to nine thousand eight hundred and seventy talents. But Antigenes, who had lost one of his eyes, though he owed nothing, got his name set down in the list of those who were in debt, and bringing one who pretended to be his creditor, and to have supplied him from the bank, received the money. But when the cheat was found out, the king was so incensed at it, that he banished him from court, and took away his command, though he was an excellent soldier and a man of great courage. For when he was but a youth, and served under Philip at the siege of Perinthus, where he was wounded in the eye by an arrow shot out of an engine, he would neither let the arrow be taken out nor be persuaded to quit the field till he had bravely repulsed the enemy and forced them to retire into the town. Accordingly he was not able to support such a disgrace with any patience, and it was plain that grief and despair would have made him kill himself, but the king fearing it, not only pardoned him, but let him also enjoy the benefit of his deceit.

The thirty thousand boys whom he left behind him to be taught and disciplined were so improved at his return, both in strength and beauty, and performed their exercises with such dexterity and wonderful agility, that he was extremely pleased with them, which grieved the Macedonians, and made them fear he would have the less value for them. And when he proceeded to send down the infirm and maimed soldiers to the sea, they said they were unjustly and infamously dealt with, after they were worn out in his service upon all occasions, now to be turned away with disgrace and sent home into their country among their friends and relations in a worse condition than when they came out; therefore they desired him to dismiss them one and all, and to account his Macedonians useless, now he was so well furnished with a set of dancing boys, with whom, if he pleased, he might go on and conquer the world. These speeches so incensed Alexander that, after he had given them a great deal of reproachful language in his passion, he drove them away, and committed the watch to Persians, out of whom he chose his guards and attendants. When the Macedonians saw him escorted by these men, and themselves excluded and shamefully disgraced, their high spirits fell, and conferring with one another, they found that jealousy and rage had almost distracted them. But at last coming to themselves again, they went without their arms, with only their under garments on, crying and weeping to offer themselves at his tent, and desired him to deal with them as their baseness and ingratitude deserved. However, this would not prevail; for though his anger was already something mollified, yet he would not admit them into his presence, nor would they stir from thence, but continued two days and nights before his tent, bewailing themselves, and imploring him as their lord to have compassion on them. But the third day he came out to them, and seeing them very humble and penitent, he wept himself a great while, after a gentle reproof spoke kindly to them, and dismissed those who were unserviceable with magnificent rewards, and with his recommendation to Antipater, that when they came home, at all public shows and in the theatres, they should sit on the best and foremost seats, crowned with chaplets of flowers. He ordered, also, that the children of those who had lost their lives in his service should have their father's pay continued to them.

When he came to Ecbatana in Media, and had despatched his most urgent affairs, he began to divert himself again with spectacles and public entertainments, to carry on which he had a supply of three thousand actors and artists, newly arrived out of Greece. But they were soon interrupted by Hephæstion falling sick of a fever, in which, being a young man and a soldier, too, he could not confine himself to so exact a diet as was necessary; for whilst his physician, Glaucus, was gone to the theatre, he ate a fowl for his dinner, and drank a large draught of wine, upon which he became very ill, and shortly after died. At this misfortune, Alexander was so beyond all reason transported that, to express his sorrow, he immediately ordered the manes and tails of all his horses and mules to be cut, and threw down the battlements of the neighbouring cities. The poor physician he crucified, and forbade playing on the flute or any other musical instrument in the camp a great while, till directions came from the oracle of Ammon, and enjoined him to honour Hephæstion, and sacrifice to him as a hero. Then seeking to alleviate his grief in war, he set out, as it were, to a hunt and chase of men, for he fell upon the Cossæans, and put the whole nation to the sword. This was called a sacrifice to Hephæstion's ghost. In his sepulchre and monument and the adorning of them he intended to bestow ten thousand talents; and designing that the excellence of the workmanship and the singularity of the design might outdo the expense, his wishes turned, above all other artists, to Stasicrates, because he always promised something very bold, unusual, and magnificent in his projects. Once when they had met before, he had told him that, of all the mountains he knew, that of Athos in Thrace was the most capable of being adapted to represent the shape and lineaments of a man; that if he pleased to command him, he would make it the noblest and most durable statue in the world, which in its left hand should hold a city of ten thousand inhabitants, and out of its right should pour a copious river into the sea. Though Alexander declined this proposal, yet now he spent a great deal of time with workmen to invent and contrive others even more extravagant and sumptuous.

As he was upon his way to Babylon, Nearchus, who had sailed back out of the ocean up the mouth of the river Euphrates, came to tell him he had met with some Chaldæan diviners, who had warned him against Alexander's going thither. Alexander, however, took no thought of it, and went on, and when he came near the walls of the place, he saw a great many crows fighting with one another, some of whom fell down just by him. After this, being privately informed that Apollodorus, the governor of Babylon, had sacrificed, to know what would become of him, he sent for Pythagoras, the soothsayer, and on his admitting the thing, asked him in what condition he found the victim; and when he told him the liver was defective in its lobe, "A great presage indeed!" said Alexander. However, he offered Pythagoras no injury, but was sorry that he had neglected Nearchus's advice, and stayed for the most part outside the town, removing his tent from place to place, and sailing up and down the Euphrates. Besides this, he was disturbed by many other prodigies. A tame ass fell upon the biggest and handsomest lion that he kept, and killed him by a kick. And one day after he had undressed himself to be anointed, and was playing at ball, just as they were going to bring his clothes again, the young men who played with him perceived a man clad in the king's robes with a diadem upon his head, sitting silently upon his throne. They asked him who he was, to which he gave no answer a good while, till at last, coming to himself, he told them his name was Dionysius, that he was of Messenia, that for some crime of which he was accused he was brought thither from the seaside, and had been kept long in prison, that Serapis appeared to him, had freed him from his chains, conducted him to that place, and commanded him to put on the king's robe and diadem, and to sit where they found him, and to say nothing. Alexander, when he heard this, by the direction of his soothsayers, put the fellow to death, but he lost his spirits, and grew diffident of the protection and assistance of the gods, and suspicious of his friends. His greatest apprehension was of Antipater and his sons, one of whom, Iolaus, was his chief cupbearer; and Cassander, who had lately arrived, and had been bred up in Greek manners, the first time he saw some of the barbarians adore the king could not forbear laughing at it aloud, which so incensed Alexander that he took him by the hair with both hands and dashed his head against the wall. Another time, Cassander would have said something in defence of Antipater to those who accused him, but Alexander interrupting him, said, "What is it you say? Do you think people, if they had received no injury, would come such a journey only to calumniate your father?" To which when Cassander replied, that their coming so far from the evidence was a great proof of the falseness of their charges, Alexander smiled, and said those were some of Aristotle's sophisms, which would serve equally on both sides; and added, that both he and his father should be severely punished, if they were found guilty of the least injustice towards those who complained. All which made such a deep impression of terror in Cassander's mind that, long after, when he was King of Macedonia and master of Greece, as he was walking up and down at Delphi, and looking at the statues, at the sight of that of Alexander he was suddenly struck with alarm, and shook all over, his eyes rolled, his head grew dizzy, and it was long before he recovered himself.

When once Alexander had given way to fears of supernatural influence, his mind grew so disturbed and so easily alarmed that, if the least unusual or extraordinary thing happened, he thought it a prodigy or a presage, and his court was thronged with diviners and priests whose business was to sacrifice and purify and foretell the future. So miserable a thing is incredulity and contempt of divine power on the one hand, and so miserable, also, superstition on the other, which like water, where the level has been lowered, flowing in and never stopping, fills the mind with slavish fears and follies, as now in Alexander's case. But upon some answers which were brought him from the oracle concerning Hephæstion, he laid aside his sorrow, and fell again to sacrificing and drinking; and having given

Nearchus a splendid entertainment, after he had bathed, as was his custom, just as he was going to bed, at Medius's request he went to supper with him. Here he drank all the next day, and was attacked with a fever, which seized him, not as some write, after he had drunk of the bowl of Hercules, nor was he taken with any sudden pain in his back, as if he had been struck with a lance, for these are the inventions of some authors who thought it their duty to make the last scene of so great an action as tragical and moving as they could. Aristobulus tells us, that in the rage of his fever and a violent thirst, he took a draught of wine, upon which he fell into delirium, and died on the thirtieth day of the month Dæsius.

But the journals give the following record. On the eighteenth day of the month he slept in the bathing-room on account of his fever. The next day he bathed and removed into his chamber, and spent his time in playing at dice with Medius. In the evening he bathed and sacrificed, and ate freely and had the fever on him through the night. On the twentieth, after the usual sacrifices and bathing, he lay in the bathing-room and heard Nearchus's narrative of his voyage, and the observations he had made in the great sea. The twenty-first he passed in the same manner, his fever still increasing, and suffered much during the night. The next day the fever was very violent. and he had himself removed and his bed set by the great bath, and discoursed with his principal officers about finding fit men to fill up the vacant places in the army. On the twenty-fourth he was much worse, and was carried out of his bed to assist at the sacrifices, and gave order that the general officers should wait within the court, whilst the inferior officers kept watch without doors. On the twenty-fifth he was removed to his palace on the other side the river, where he slept a little, but his fever did not abate, and when the generals came into his chamber, he was speechless and continued so the following day. The Macedonians, therefore, supposing he was dead, came with great clamours to the gates, and menaced his friends so that they were forced to admit them, and let them all pass through unarmed by his bedside. The same day Python and Seleucus were despatched to the temple of Serapis to inquire if they should bring Alexander thither, and were answered by the god that they should not remove him. On the twenty-eighth, in the evening, he died. This account is most of it word for word as it is written in the diary.

At the time, nobody had any suspicion of his being poisoned, but upon some information given six years after, they say Olympias put many to death, and scattered the ashes of Iolaus, then dead, as if he had given it him. But those who affirm that Aristotle counselled Antipater to do it, and that by his means the poison was brought, adduced one Hagnothemis as their authority, who, they say, heard King Antigonus speak of it, and tell us that the poison was water, deadly cold as ice, distilled from a rock in the district of Nonacris, which they gathered like a thin dew, and kept in an ass's hoof; for it was so very cold and penetrating that no other vessel would hold it. However, most are of opinion that all this is a mere made-up story, no slight evidence of which is, that during the dissensions among the commanders, which lasted several days, the body continued clear and fresh, without any sign of such taint or corruption, though it lay neglected in a close sultry place.

Roxana, who was now with child, and upon that account much honoured by the Macedonians, being jealous of Statira, sent for her by a counterfeit letter, as if Alexander had been still alive; and when she had her in her power, killed her and her sister, and threw their bodies into a well, which they filled up with earth, not without the privity and assistance of Perdiccas, who in the time immediately following the king's death, under cover of the name of Arrhidæus, whom he carried about him as a sort of guard to his person, exercised the chief authority. Arrhidæus, who was Philip's son by an obscure woman of the name of Philinna, was himself of weak intellect, not that he had been originally deficient either in body or mind, on the contrary, in his childhood, he had showed a happy and promising character enough. But a diseased habit of body, caused by drugs which Olympias gave him, had ruined, not only his health, but his understanding.

CÆSAR

AFTER Sylla became master of Rome, he wished to make Cæsar put away his wife Cornelia, daughter of Cinna, the late sole ruler of the commonwealth, but was unable to effect it either by promises or intimidation, and so contented himself with confiscating her dowry. The ground of Sylla's hostility to Cæsar was the relationship between him and Marius; for Marius, the elder, married Julia, the sister of Cæsar's father, and had by her the younger Marius, who consequently was Cæsar's first cousin. And though at the beginning, while so many were to be put to death, and there was so much to do, Cæsar was overlooked by Sylla, yet he would not keep quiet, but presented himself to the people as a candidate for the priesthood, though he was yet a mere boy. Sylla, without any open opposition, took measures to have him rejected, and in consultation whether he should be put to death, when it was urged by some that it was not worth his while to contrive the death of a boy, he answered, that they knew little who did not see more than one Marius in that boy. Cæsar, on being informed of this saying, concealed himself, and for a considerable time kept out of the way in the country of the Sabines, often changing his quarters, till one night, as he was removing from one house to another on account of his health, he fell into the hands of Sylla's soldiers, who were searching those parts in order to apprehend any who had absconded. Cæsar, by a bribe of two talents, prevailed with Cornelius, their captain, to let him go, and was no sooner dismissed but he put to sea and made for Bithynia. After a short stay there with Nicomedes, the king, in his passage back he was taken near the island of Pharmacusa by some of the pirates, who, at that time, with large fleets of ships and innumerable smaller vessels, infested the seas everywhere.

When these men at first demanded of him twenty talents for his ransom, he laughed at them for not understanding the value of their prisoner, and voluntarily engaged to give them fifty. He presently despatched those about him to several places to raise the money, till at last he was left among a set of the most bloodthirsty people in the world, the Cilicians, only with one friend and two attendants. Yet he made so little of them, that when he had a mind to sleep, he would send to them, and order them to make no noise. For thirty-eight days, with all the freedom in the world, he amused himself with joining in their exercises and games, as if they had not been his keepers, but his guards. He wrote verses and speeches, and made them his auditors, and those who did not admire them, he called to their faces illiterate and barbarous, and would often, in raillery, threaten to hang them. They were greatly taken with this, and attributed his free talking to a kind of simplicity and boyish playfulness. As soon as his ransom was come from Miletus, he paid it, and was discharged, and proceeded at once to man some ships at the port of Miletus, and went in pursuit of the pirates, whom he surprised with their ships still stationed at the island, and took most of them. Their money he made his prize, and the men he secured in prison at Pergamus, and he made application to Junius, who was then governor of Asia, to whose office it belonged, as prætor, to determine their punishment. Junius, having his eye upon the money, for the sum was considerable, said he would think at his leisure what to do with the prisoners, upon which Cæsar took his leave of him, and went off to Pergamus, where he ordered the pirates to be brought forth and crucified; the punishment he had often threatened them with whilst he was in their hands, and they little dreamt he was in earnest.

In the meantime Sylla's power being now on the decline, Cæsar's friends advised him to return to Rome, but he went to Rhodes, and entered himself in the school of Apollonius, Molon's son, a famous rhetorician, one who had the reputation of a worthy man, and had Cicero for one of his scholars. Cæsar is said to have been admirably fitted by nature to make a great statesman and orator, and to have taken such pains to improve his genius this way that without dispute he might challenge the second place. More he did not aim at, as choosing to be first rather amongst men of arms and power, and, therefore, never rose to that height of eloquence to which nature would have carried him, his attention being diverted to those expeditions and designs which at length gained him the empire. And he himself, in his answer to Cicero's panegyric on Cato, desires his reader not to compare the plain discourse of a soldier with the harangues of an orator who had not only fine parts, but had employed his life in this study.

When he was returned to Rome, he accused Dolabella of mal-administration, and many cities of Greece came in to attest it. Dolabella was acquitted, and Cæsar, in return for the support he had received from the Greeks, assisted them in their prosecution of Publius Antonius for corrupt practices, before Marcus Lucullus, prætor of Macedonia. In this course he so far succeeded, that Antonius was forced to appeal to the tribunes at Rome, alleging that in Greece he could not have fair play against Grecians. In his pleadings at Rome, his eloquence soon obtained him great credit and favour, and he won no less upon the affections of the people by the affability of his manners and address, in which he showed a tact and consideration beyond what could have been expected at his age; and the open house he kept, the entertainments he gave, and the general splendour of his manner of life contributed little by little to create and increase his political influence. His enemies slighted the growth of it at first, presuming it would soon fail when his money was gone; whilst in the meantime it was growing up and flourishing among the common people. When his power at last was established and not to be overthrown, and now openly tended to the altering of the whole constitution, they were aware too late that there is no beginning so mean, which continued application will not make considerable, and that despising a danger at first will make it at last irresistible. Cicero was the first who had any suspicions of his designs upon the government, and as a good pilot is apprehensive of a storm when the sea is most smiling, saw the designing temper of the man through this disguise of good humour and affability, and said that, in general, in all he did and undertook, he detected the ambition for absolute power, "but when I see his hair so carefully arranged, and observe him adjusting it with one finger, I cannot imagine it should enter into such a man's thoughts to subvert the Roman state." But of this more hereafter.

The first proof he had of the people's good-will to him was when he received by their suffrages a tribuneship in the army, and came out on the list with a higher place than Caius Popilius. A second and clearer instance of their favour appeared upon his making a magnificent oration in praise of his aunt Julia, wife to Marius, publicly in the forum, at whose funeral he was so bold as to bring forth the images of Marius, which nobody had dared to produce since the government came into Sylla's hands, Marius's party having from that time been declared enemies of the state. When some who were present had begun to raise a cry against Cæsar, the people answered with loud shouts and clapping in his favour, expressing their joyful surprise and satisfaction at his having, as it were, brought up again from the grave those honours of Marius, which for so long a time had been lost to the city. It had always been the custom at Rome to make funeral orations in praise of elderly matrons, but there was no precedent of any upon young women till Cæsar first made one upon the death of his own wife. This also procured him favour, and by this show of affection he won upon the feelings of the people, who looked upon him as a man of great tenderness and kindness of heart. After he had buried his wife, he went as quæstor into Spain under one of the prætors, named Vetus, whom he honoured ever after, and made his son his own quæstor, when he himself came to be prætor. After this employment was ended, he married Pompeia, his third wife, having then a daughter by Cornelia, his first wife, whom he afterwards married to Pompey the Great. He was so profuse in his expenses that, before he had any public employment, he was in debt thirteen hundred talents, and many thought that by incurring such expense to be popular he changed a solid good for what would prove but a short and uncertain return; but in truth he was purchasing what was of the greatest value at an inconsiderable rate. When he was made surveyor of the Appian Way, he disbursed, besides the public money, a great sum out of his private purse; and when he was ædile, he provided such a number of gladiators, that he entertained the people with three hundred and twenty single combats, and by his great liberality and magnificence in theatrical shows, in processions, and public feastings, he threw into the shade all the attempts that had been made before him, and gained so much upon the people, that every one was eager to find out new offices and new honours for him in return for his munificence.

There being two factions in the city, one that of Sylla, which was very powerful, the other that of Marius, which was then broken and in a low condition, he undertook to revive this and to make it his own. And to this end, whilst he was in the height of his repute with the people for the magnificent shows he gave as ædile, he ordered images of Marius and figures of Victory, with trophies in their hands, to be carried privately in the night and placed in the capitol. Next morning when some saw them bright with gold and beautifully made, with inscriptions upon them, referring them to Marius's exploits over the Cimbrians, they were surprised at the boldness of him who had set them up, nor was it difficult to guess who it was. The fame of this soon spread and brought together a great concourse of people. Some cried out that it was an open attempt against the established government thus to revive those honours which had been buried by the laws and decrees of the senate; that Cæsar had done it to sound the temper of the people whom he had prepared before, and to try whether they were tame enough to bear his humour, and would quietly give way to his innovations. On the other hand, Marius's party took courage, and it was incredible how numerous they were suddenly seen to be, and what a multitude of them appeared and came shouting into the capitol. Many, when they saw Marius's likeness, cried for joy, and Cæsar was highly extolled as the one man, in the place of all others, who was a relation worthy of Marius. Upon this the senate met, and Catulus Lutatius, one of the most eminent Romans of that time, stood up and inveighed against Cæsar, closing his speech with the remarkable saying that Cæsar was now not working mines, but planting batteries to overthrow the state. But when Cæsar had made an apology for himself, and satisfied the senate, his admirers were very much animated, and advised him not to depart from his own thoughts for any one, since with the people's good favour he would ere long get the better of them all, and be the first man in the commonwealth.

At this time, Metellus, the high priest, died, and Catulus and Isauricus, persons of the highest reputation, and who had great influence in the senate, were competitors for the office, yet Cæsar would not give way to them, but presented himself to the people as a candidate against them. The several parties seeming very equal, Catulus, who, because he had the most honour to lose, was the most apprehensive of the event, sent to Cæsar to buy him off, with offers of a great sum of money. But his answer was, that he was ready to borrow a larger sum than that to carry on the contest. Upon the day of election, as his mother conducted him out of doors with tears, after embracing her, "My mother," he said, "to-day you will see me either high priest or an exile." When the votes were taken, after a great struggle, he carried it, and excited among the senate and nobility great alarm lest he might now urge on the people to every kind of insolence. And Piso and Catulus found fault with Cicero for having let Cæsar escape, when in the conspiracy of Catiline he had given the government such advantage against him. For Catiline, who had designed not only to change the present state of affairs, but to subvert the whole empire and confound all, had himself taken to flight, while the evidence was yet incomplete against him, before his ultimate purposes had been properly discovered. But he had left Lentulus and Cethegus in the city to supply his place in the conspiracy, and whether they received any secret encouragement and assistance from Cæsar is uncertain; all that is certain is, that they were fully convicted in the senate, and when Cicero, the consul, asked the several opinions of the senators, how they would have them punished, all who spoke before Cæsar sentenced them to death; but Cæsar stood up and made a set speech, in which he told them that he thought it without precedent and not just to take away the lives of persons of their birth and distinction before they were fairly tried, unless there was an absolute necessity for it; but that if they were kept confined in any towns of Italy Cicero himself should choose till Catiline was defeated, then the senate might in peace and at their leisure determine what was best to be done.

This sentence of his carried so much appearance of humanity, and he gave it such advantage by the eloquence with which he urged it, that not only those who spoke after him closed with it, but even they who had before given a contrary opinion now came over to his, till it came about to Catulus's and Cato's turn to speak. They warmly opposed it, and Cato intimated in his speech the suspicion of Cæsar himself, and pressed the matter so strongly that the criminals were given up to suffer execution. As Cæsar was going out of the senate, many of the young men who at that time acted as guards to Cicero ran in with their naked swords to assault him. But Curio, it is said, threw his gown over him, and conveyed him away, and Cicero himself, when the young men looked up to see his wishes, gave a sign not to kill him, either for fear of the people or because he thought the murder unjust and illegal. If this be true, I wonder how Cicero came to omit all mention of it in his book about his consulship. He was blamed, however, afterwards, for not having made use of so fortunate an opportunity against Cæsar, as if he had let it escape him out of fear of the populace, who, indeed, showed remarkable solicitude about Cæsar, and some time after, when he went into the senate to clear himself of the suspicions he lay under, and found great clamours raised against him, upon the senate in consequence sitting longer than ordinary, they went up to the house in a tumult, and beset it, demanding Cæsar, and requiring them to dismiss him. Upon this, Cato, much fearing some movement among the poor citizens, who were always the first to kindle the flame among the people, and placed all their hopes in Cæsar, persuaded the senate to give them a monthly allowance of corn, an expedient which put the commonwealth to the extraordinary charge of seven million five hundred thousand drachmas in the year, but quite succeeded in removing the great cause of terror for the present, and very much weakened Cæsar's power, who at that time was just going to be made prætor, and consequently would have been more formidable by his office.

But there was no disturbance during his prætorship, only what misfortune he met with in his own domestic affairs. Publius Clodius was a patrician by descent, eminent both for his riches and eloquence, but in licentiousness of life and audacity exceeded the most noted profligates of the day. He was in love with Pompeia, Cæsar's wife, and she had no aversion to him. But there was strict watch kept on her apartment, and Cæsar's mother, Aurelia, who was a discreet woman, being continually about her, made any interview very dangerous and difficult. The Romans have a goddess whom they call Bona, the same whom the Greeks call Gyncæcea. The Phrygians, who claim a peculiar title to her, say she was mother to Midas. The Romans profess she was one of the Dryads, and married to Faunus. The Grecians affirm that she is that mother of Bacchus whose name is not to be uttered, and, for this reason, the women who celebrate her festival cover the tents with vine-branches, and, in accordance with the fable, a consecrated serpent is placed by the goddess. It is not lawful for a man to be by, nor so much as in the house, whilst the rites are celebrated, but the women by themselves perform the sacred offices, which are said to be much the same with those used in the solemnities of Orpheus. When the festival comes, the husband, who is either consul or prætor, and with him every male creature, quits the house. The wife then taking it under her care sets it in order, and the principal ceremonies are performed during the night, the women playing together amongst themselves as they keep watch, and music of various kinds going on.

As Pompeia was at that time celebrating this feast, Clodius, who as yet had no beard, and so thought to pass undiscovered, took upon him the dress and ornaments of a singing woman, and so came thither, having the air of a young girl. Finding the doors open, he was without any stop introduced by the maid, who was in the intrigue. She presently ran to tell Pompeia, but as she was away a long time, he grew uneasy in waiting for her, and left his post and traversed the house from one room to another, still taking care to avoid the lights, till at last Aurelia's woman met him, and invited him to play with her, as the women did among themselves. He refused to comply, and she presently pulled him forward, and asked him who he was and whence he came. Clodius told her he was waiting for Pompeia's own maid, Abra, being in fact her own name also, and as he said so, betrayed himself by his voice. Upon which the woman shrieking, ran into the company where there were lights, and cried out she had discovered a man. The women were all in a fright. Aurelia covered up the sacred things and stopped the proceedings, and having ordered the doors to be shut, went about with lights to find Clodius, who was got into the maid's room that he had come in with, and was seized there. The women knew him, and drove him out of doors, and at once, that same night, went home and told their husbands the story. In the morning, it was all about the town, what an impious attempt Clodius had made, and how he ought to be punished as an offender, not only against those whom he had offended, but also against the public and the gods. Upon which one of the tribunes impeached him for profaning the holy rites, and some of the principal senators combined together and gave evidence against him, that besides many other horrible crimes, he had been guilty of incest with his own sister, who was married to Lucullus. But the people set themselves against this combination of the nobility, and defended Clodius, which was of great service to him with the judges, who took alarm and were afraid to provoke the multitude. Cæsar at once dismissed Pompeia, but being summoned as a witness against Clodius, said he had nothing to charge him with. This looking like a paradox, the accuser asked him why he parted with his wife. Cæsar replied, "I wished my wife to be not so much as suspected." Some say that Cæsar spoke this as his real thought, others, that he did it to gratify the people, who were very earnest to save Clodius. Clodius, at any rate, escaped; most of the judges giving their opinions so written as to be illegible that they might not be in danger from the people by condemning him, nor in disgrace with the nobility by acquitting him.

Cæsar, in the meantime, being out of his prætorship, had got the province of Spain, but was in great embarrassment with his creditors, who, as he was going off, came upon him, and were very pressing and importunate. This led him to apply himself to Crassus, who was the richest man in Rome, but wanted Cæsar's youthful vigour and heat to sustain the opposition against Pompey. Crassus took upon him to satisfy those creditors who were most uneasy to him, and would not be put off any longer, and engaged himself to the amount of eight hundred and thirty talents, upon which Cæsar was now at liberty to go to his province. In his journey, as he was crossing the Alps, and passing by a small village of the barbarians with but few inhabitants, and those wretchedly poor, his companions asked the question among themselves by way of mockery, if there were any canvassing for offices there; any contention which should be uppermost, or feuds of great men one against another. To which Cæsar made answer seriously, "For my part, I had rather be the first man among these fellows, than the second man in Rome." It is said that another time, when free from business in Spain, after reading some part of the history of Alexander, he sat a great while very thoughtful, and at last burst out into tears. His friends were surprised, and asked him the reason of it. "Do you think," said he, "I have not just cause to weep, when I consider that Alexander at my age had conquered so many nations, and I have all this time done nothing that is memorable." As soon as he came into Spain he was very active, and in a few days had got together ten new cohorts of foot in addition to the twenty which were there before. With these he marched against the Calaici and Lusitani and conquered them, and advancing as far as the ocean, subdued the tribes which never before had been subject to the Romans. Having managed his military affairs with good success, he was equally happy in the course of his civil government. He took pains to establish a good understanding amongst the several states, and no less care to heal the differences between debtors and creditors. He ordered that the creditor should receive two parts of the debtor's yearly income, and that the other part should be managed by the debtor himself, till by this method the whole debt was at last discharged. This conduct made him leave his province with a fair reputation; being rich himself, and having enriched his soldiers, and having received from them the honourable name of Imperator.

There is a law among the Romans, that whoever desires the honour of a triumph must stay without the city and expect his answer. And another, that those who stand for the consulship shall appear personally upon the place. Cæsar was come home at the very time of choosing consuls, and being in a difficulty between these two opposite laws, sent to the senate to desire that, since he was obliged to be absent, he might sue for the consulship by his friends. Cato, being backed by the law, at first opposed his request; afterwards perceiving that Cæsar had prevailed with a great part of the senate to comply with it, he made it his business to gain time, and went on wasting the whole day in speaking. Upon which Cæsar thought fit to let the triumph fall, and pursued the consulship. Entering the town and coming forward immediately, he had recourse to a piece of state policy by which everybody was deceived but Cato. This was the reconciling of Crassus and Pompey, the two men who then were most powerful in Rome. There had been a quarrel between them, which he now succeeded in making up, and by this means strengthened himself by the united power of both, and so under the cover of an action which carried all the appearance of a piece of kindness and good-nature, caused what was in effect a revolution in the government. For it was not the quarrel between Pompey and Cæsar, as most men imagine, which was the origin of the civil wars, but their union, their conspiring together at first to subvert the aristocracy, and so quarrelling afterwards between themselves. Cato, who often foretold what the consequence of this alliance would be, had then the character of a sullen, interfering man, but in the end the reputation of a wise but unsuccessful counsellor.

Thus Cæsar, being doubly supported by the interests of Crassus and Pompey, was promoted to the consulship, and triumphantly proclaimed with Calpurnius Bibulus. When he entered on his office he brought in bills which would have been preferred with better grace by the most audacious of the tribunes than by a consul, in which he proposed the plantation of colonies and the division of lands, simply to please the commonality. The best and most honourable of the senators opposed it, upon which, as he had long wished for nothing more than for such a colourable pretext, he loudly protested how much it was against his will to be driven to seek support from the people, and how the senate's insulting and harsh conduct left no other course possible for him than to devote himself henceforth to the popular cause and interest. And so he hurried out of the senate, and presenting himself to the people, and there placing Crassus and Pompey, one on each side of him, he asked them whether they consented to the bills he had proposed. They owned their assent, upon which he desired them to assist him against those who had threatened to oppose him with their swords. They engaged they would, and Pompey added further, that he would meet their swords with a sword and buckler too. These words the nobles much resented, as neither suitable to his own dignity, nor becoming the reverence due to the senate, but resembling rather the vehemence of a boy or the fury of a madman. But the people were pleased with it. In order to get a yet firmer hold upon Pompey, Cæsar having a daughter, Julia, who had been before contracted to Servilius Cæpio, now betrothed her to Pompey, and told Servilius he should have Pompey's daughter, who was not unengaged either, but promised to Sylla's son, Faustus. A little time after, Cæsar married Calpurnia, the daughter of Piso, and got Piso made consul for the year following. Cato exclaimed loudly against this, and protested, with a great deal of warmth, that it was intolerable the government should be prostituted by marriages, and that they should advance one another to the commands of armies, provinces, and other great posts, by means of women. Bibulus, Cæsar's colleague, finding it was to no purpose to oppose his bills, but that he was in danger of being murdered in the forum, as also was Cato, confined himself to his house, and there let the remaining part of his consulship expire. Pompey, when he was married, at once filled the forum with soldiers, and gave the people his help in passing the new laws, and secured Cæsar the government of all Gaul, both on this and the other side of the Alps, together with Illyricum, and the command of four legions for five years. Cato made some attempts against these proceedings, but was seized and led off on the way to prison by Cæsar, who expected that he would appeal to the tribunes. But when he saw that Cato went along without speaking a word, and not only the nobility were indignant, but the people also, out of respect for Cato's virtue, were following in silence, and with dejected looks, he himself privately desired one of the tribunes to rescue Cato. As for the other senators, some few of them attended the house, the rest, being disgusted, absented themselves. Hence Considius, a very old man, took occasion one day to tell Cæsar that the senators did not meet because they were afraid of his soldiers. Cæsar asked, "Why don't you, then, out of the same fear, keep at home?" To which Considius replied, that age was his guard against fear, and that the small remains of his life were not worth much caution. But the most disgraceful thing that was done in Cæsar's consulship was his assisting to gain the tribuneship for the same Clodius who had made the attempt on his wife's chastity and intruded upon the secret vigils. He was elected on purpose to effect Cicero's downfall; nor did Cæsar leave the city to join his army till they two had overpowered Cicero and driven him out of Italy.

Thus far have we followed Cæsar's actions before the wars of Gaul. After this, he seems to begin his course afresh, and to enter upon a new life and scene of action. And the period of those wars which he now fought, and those many expeditions in which he subdued Gaul, showed him to be a soldier and general not in the least inferior to any of the greatest and most admired commanders who had ever appeared at the head of armies. For if we compare him with the Fabii, the Metelli, the Scipios, and with those who were his contemporaries, or not long before him, Sylla, Marius, the Luculli, or even Pompey himself, whose glory, it may be said, went up at that time to heaven for every excellence in war, we shall find Cæsar's actions to have surpassed them all. One he may be held to have outdone in consideration of the difficulty of the country in which he fought, another in the extent of territory which he conquered; some, in the number and strength of the enemy whom he defeated; one man, because of the wildness and perfidiousness of the tribes whose good-will he conciliated, another in his humanity and clemency to those he overpowered; others, again, in his gifts and kindnesses to his soldiers; all alike in the number of the battles which he fought and the enemies whom he killed. For he had not pursued the wars in Gaul full ten years when he had taken by storm above eight hundred towns, subdued three hundred states, and of the three millions of men, who made up the gross sum of those with whom at several times he engaged, he had killed one million and taken captive a second.

He was so much master of the good-will and hearty service of his soldiers that those who in other expeditions were but ordinary men displayed a courage past defeating or withstanding when they went upon any danger where Cæsar's glory was concerned. Such a one was Acilius, who, in the sea-fight before Marseilles, had his right hand struck off with a sword, yet did not quit his buckler out of his left, but struck the enemies in the face with it, till he drove them off and made himself master of the vessel. Such another was Cassius Scæva, who, in a battle near Dyrrhachium, had one of his eyes shot out with an arrow, his shoulder pierced with one javelin, and his thigh with another: and having received one hundred and thirty darts upon his target, called to the enemy, as though he would surrender himself. But when two of them came up to him, he cut off the shoulder of one with a sword, and by a blow over the face forced the other to retire, and so with the assistance of his friends, who now came up, made his escape. Again, in Britain, when some of the foremost officers had accidentally got into a morass full of water, and there were assaulted by the enemy, a common soldier, whilst Cæsar stood and looked on, threw himself in the midst of them, and after many signal demonstrations of his valour, rescued the officers and beat off the barbarians. He himself, in the end, took to the water, and with much difficulty, partly by swimming, partly by wading, passed it, but in the passage lost his shield. Cæsar and his officers saw it and admired, and went to meet him with joy and acclamation. But the soldier, much dejected and in tears, threw himself down at Cæsar's feet and begged his pardon for having let go his buckler. Another time in Africa, Scipio having taken a ship of Cæsar's in which Granius Petro, lately appointed quæstor, was sailing, gave the other passengers as free prize to his soldiers, but thought fit to offer the quæstor his life. But he said it was not usual for Cæsar's soldiers to take but give mercy, and having said so, fell upon his sword and killed himself.

This love of honour and passion for distinction were inspired into them and cherished in them by Cæsar himself, who, by his unsparing distribution of money and honours, showed them that he did not heap up wealth from the wars for his own luxury, or the gratifying his private pleasures, but that all he received was but a public fund laid by the reward and encouragement of valour, and that he looked upon all he gave to deserving soldiers as so much increase to his own riches. Added to this also, there was no danger to which he did not willingly expose himself, no labour from which he pleaded an exemption. His contempt of danger was not so much wondered at by his soldiers because they knew how much he coveted honour. But his enduring so much hardship, which he did to all appearance beyond his natural strength, very much astonished them. For he was a spare man, had a soft and white skin, was distempered in the head and subject to an epilepsy, which, it is said, first seized him at Corduba. But he did not make the weakness of his constitution a pretext for his ease, but rather used war as the best physic against his indispositions; whilst, by indefatigable journeys, coarse diet, frequent lodging in the field, and continual laborious exercise, he struggled with his diseases and fortified his body against all attacks. He slept generally in his chariots or litters, employing even his rest in pursuit of action. In the day he was thus carried to the forts, garrisons, and camps, one servant sitting with him, who used to write down what he dictated as he went, and a soldier attending behind him with his sword drawn. He drove so rapidly that when he first left Rome he arrived at the river Rhone within eight days. He had been an expert rider from his childhood; for it was usual with him to sit with his hands joined together behind his back, and so to put his horse to its full speed. And in this war he disciplined himself so far as to be able to dictate letters from on horseback, and to give directions to two who took notes at the same time or, as Oppius says, to more. And it is thought that he was the first who contrived means for communicating with friends by cipher, when either press of business, or the large extent of the city, left him no time for a personal conference about matters that required despatch. How little nice he was in his diet may be seen in the following instance. When at the table of Valerius Leo, who entertained him at supper at Milan, a dish of asparagus was put before him on which his host instead of oil had poured sweet ointment, Cæsar partook of it without any disgust, and reprimanded his friends for finding fault with it. "For it was enough," said he, "not to eat what you did not like; but he who reflects on another man's want of breeding, shows he wants it as much himself." Another time upon the road he was driven by a storm into a poor man's cottage, where he found but one room, and that such as would afford but a mean reception to a single person, and therefore told his companions places of honour should be given up to the greater men, and necessary accommodations to the weaker, and accordingly ordered that Oppius, who was in bad health, should lodge within, whilst he and the rest slept under a shed at the door.

His first war in Gaul was against the Helvetians and Tigurini, who having burnt their own towns, twelve in number, and four hundred villages, would have marched forward through that part of Gaul which was included in the Roman province, as the Cimbrians and Teutons formerly had done. Nor were they inferior to these in courage; and in numbers they were equal, being in all three hundred thousand, of which one hundred and ninety thousand were fighting men. Cæsar did not engage the Tigurini in person, but Labienus, under his directions, routed them near the river Arar. The Helvetians surprised Cæsar, and unexpectedly set upon him as he was conducting his army to a confederate town. He succeeded, however, in making his retreat into a strong position, where, when he had mustered and marshalled his men, his horse was brought to him; upon which he said, "When I have won the battle, I will use my horse for the chase, but at present let us go against the enemy," and accordingly charged them on foot. After a long and severe combat, he drove the main army out of the field, but found the hardest work at their carriages and ramparts, where not only the men stood and fought, but the women also and children defended themselves till they were cut to pieces; insomuch that the fight was scarcely ended till midnight. This action, glorious in itself, Cæsar crowned with another yet more noble, by gathering in a body all the barbarians that had escaped out of the battle, above one hundred thousand in number, and obliging them to re-occupy the country which they had deserted and the cities which they had burnt. This he did for fear the Germans should pass it and possess themselves of the land whilst it lay uninhabited.

His second war was in defence of the Gauls against the Germans, though some time before he had made Ariovistus, their king, recognised at Rome as an ally. But they were very insufferable neighbours to those under his government; and it was probable, when occasion offered, they would renounce the present arrangements, and march on to occupy Gaul. But finding his officers timorous, and especially those of the young nobility who came along with him in hopes of turning their campaigns with him into a means for their own pleasure or profit, he called them together, and advised them to march off, and not run the hazard of a battle against their inclinations, since they had such weak unmanly feelings; telling them that he would take only the tenth legion and march against the barbarians, whom he did not expect to find an enemy more formidable than the Cimbri nor, he added, should they find him a general inferior to Marius. Upon this, the tenth legion deputed some of their body to pay him their acknowledgments and thanks, and the other legions blamed their officers, and all, with great vigour and zeal, followed him many days' journey, till they encamped within two hundred furlongs of the enemy. Ariovistus's courage to some extent was cooled upon their very approach; for never expecting the Romans would attack the Germans whom he had thought it more likely they would not venture to withstand even in defence of their own subjects, he was the more surprised at Cæsar's conduct, and saw his army to be in consternation. They were still more discouraged by the prophecies of their holy women, who foretell the future by observing the eddies of rivers, and taking signs from the windings and noise of streams, and who now warned them not to engage before the next new moon appeared. Cæsar having had intimation of this, and seeing the Germans lie still, thought it expedient to attack them whilst they were under these apprehensions, rather than sit still and wait their time. Accordingly he made his approaches to the strongholds and hills on which they lay encamped, and so galled and fretted them that at last they came down with great fury to engage. But he gained a signal victory, and pursued them for four hundred furlongs, as far as the Rhine; all which space was covered with spoils and bodies of the slain. Ariovistus made shift to pass the Rhine with the small remains of an army, for it is said the number of the slain amounted to eighty thousand.

After this action, Cæsar left his army at their winter quarters in the country of the Sequani, and, in order to attend to affairs at Rome, went into that part of Gaul which lies on the Po, and was part of his province; for the river Rubicon divides Gaul, which is on this side the Alps, from the rest of Italy. There he sat down and employed himself in courting people's favour; great numbers coming to him continually, and always finding their requests answered; for he never failed to dismiss all with present pledges of his kindness in hand, and further hopes for the future. And during all this time of the war in Gaul, Pompey never observed how Cæsar was on the one hand using the arms of Rome to effect his conquests, and on the other was gaining over and securing to himself the favour of the Romans with the wealth which those conquests obtained him. But when he heard that the Belgæ, who were the most powerful of all the Gauls, and inhabited a third part of the country, were revolted, and had got together a great many thousand men in arms, he immediately set out and took his way hither with great expedition, and falling upon the enemy as they were ravaging the Gauls, his allies, he soon defeated and put to flight the largest and least scattered division of them. For though their numbers were great, yet they made but a slender defence, and the marshes and deep rivers were made passable to the Roman foot by the vast quantity of dead bodies. Of those who revolted, all the tribes that lived near the ocean came over without fighting, and he, therefore, led his army against the Nervii, the fiercest and most warlike people of all in those parts. These live in a country covered with continuous woods, and having lodged their children and property out of the way in the depth of the forest, fell upon Cæsar with a body of sixty thousand men, before he was prepared for them, while he was making his encampment. They soon routed his cavalry, and having surrounded the twelfth and seventh legions, killed all the officers, and had not Cæsar himself snatched up a buckler and forced his way through his own men to come up to the barbarians, or had not the tenth legion, when they saw him in danger, run in from the tops of the hills, where they lay, and broken through the enemy's ranks to rescue him, in all probability not a Roman would have been saved. But now, under the influence of Cæsar's bold example, they fought a battle, as the phrase is, of more than human courage, and yet with their utmost efforts they were not able to drive the enemy out of the field, but cut them down fighting in their defence. For out of sixty thousand men, it is stated that not above five hundred survived the battle, and of four hundred of their senators not above three.

When the Roman senate had received news of this, they voted sacrifices and festivals to the gods, to be strictly observed for the space of fifteen days, a longer space than ever was observed for any victory before. The danger to which they had been exposed by the joint outbreak of such a number of nations was felt to have been great; and the people's fondness for Cæsar gave additional lustre to successes achieved by him. He now, after settling everything in Gaul, came back again, and spent the winter by the Po, in order to carry on the designs he had in hand at Rome. All who were candidates for offices used his assistance, and were supplied with money from him to corrupt the people and buy their votes, in return of which, when they were chosen, they did all things to advance his power. But what was more considerable, the most eminent and powerful men in Rome in great numbers came to visit him at Lucca, Pompey, and Crassus and Appius, the governor of Sardinia, and Nepos, the pro-consul of Spain, so that there were in the place at one time one hundred and twenty lictors and more than two hundred senators. In deliberation here held, it was determined that Pompey and Crassus should be consuls again for the following year; that Cæsar should have a fresh supply of money, and that his command should be renewed to him for five years more. It seemed very extravagant to all thinking men that those very persons who had received so much money from Cæsar should persuade the senate to grant him more, as if he were in want. Though in truth it was not so much upon persuasion as compulsion that, with sorrow and groans for their own acts, they passed the measure. Cato was not present, for they had sent him seasonably out of the way into Cyprus; but Favonius, who was a zealous imitator of Cato, when he found he could do no good by opposing it, broke out of the house, and loudly declaimed against these proceedings to the people, but none gave him any hearing; some slighting him out of respect to Crassus and Pompey, and the greater part to gratify Cæsar, on whom depended their hopes.

After this, Cæsar returned again to his forces in Gaul, when he found that country involved in a dangerous war, two strong nations of the Germans having lately passed the Rhine to conquer it; one of them called the Usipes, the other the Tenteritæ. Of the war with the people, Cæsar himself has given this account in his commentaries, that the barbarians, having sent ambassadors to treat with him, did, during the treaty, set upon him in his march, by which means with eight hundred men they routed five thousand of his horse, who did not suspect their coming; that afterwards they sent other ambassadors to renew the same fraudulent practices, whom he kept in custody, and led on his army against the barbarians, as judging it mere simplicity to keep faith with those who had so faithlessly broken the terms they had agreed to. But Tanusius states that when the senate decreed festivals and sacrifices for this victory, Cato declared it to be his opinion that Cæsar ought to be given into the hands of the barbarians, that so the guilt which this breach of faith might otherwise bring upon the state might be expiated by transferring the curse on him, who was the occasion of it. Of those who passed the Rhine, there were four hundred thousand cut off; those few who escaped were sheltered by the Sugambri, a people of Germany. Cæsar took hold of this pretence to invade the Germans, being at the same time ambitious of the honour of being the first man that should pass the Rhine with an army. He carried a bridge across it, though it was very wide, and the current at that particular point very full, strong, and violent, bringing down with its waters trunks of trees, and other lumber, which much shook and weakened the foundations of his bridge. But he drove great piles of wood into the bottom of the river above the passage, to catch and stop these as they floated down, and thus fixing his bridle upon the stream, successfully finished his bridge, which no one who saw could believe to be the work but of ten days.

In the passage of his army over it he met with no opposition: the Suevi themselves, who are the most warlike people of all Germany, flying with their effects into the deepest and most densely wooded valleys. When he had burnt all the enemy's country, and encouraged those who embraced the Roman interest, he went back into Gaul, after eighteen days' stay in Germany. But his expedition into Britain was the most famous testimony of his courage. For he was the first who brought a navy into the western ocean, or who sailed into the Atlantic with an army to make war; and by invading an island, the reported extent of which had made its existence a matter of controversy among historians, many of whom questioned whether it were not a mere name and fiction, not a real place, he might be said to have carried the Roman empire beyond the limits of the known world. He passed thither twice from that part of Gaul which lies over against it, and in several battles which he fought did more hurt to the enemy than service to himself, for the islanders were so miserably poor that they had nothing worth being plundered of. When he found himself unable to put such an end to the war as he wished, he was content to take hostages from the king, and to impose a tribute, and then quitted the island. At his arrival in Gaul, he found letters which lay ready to be conveyed over the water to him from his friends at Rome, announcing his daughter's death, who died in labour of a child by Pompey. Cæsar and Pompey both were much afflicted with her death, nor were their friends less disturbed, believing that the alliance was now broken which had hitherto kept the sickly commonwealth in peace, for the child also died within a few days after the mother. The people took the body of Julia, in spite of the opposition of the tribunes, and carried it into the field of Mars, and there her funeral rites were performed, and her remains are laid.

Cæsar's army was now grown very numerous, so that he was forced to disperse them into various camps for their winter quarters, and he having gone himself to Italy as he used to do, in his absence a general outbreak throughout the whole of Gaul commenced, and large armies marched about the country, and attacked the Roman quarters, and attempted to make themselves masters of the forts where they lay. The greatest and strongest party of the rebels, under the command of Abriorix, cut off Cotta and Titurius with all their men, while a force sixty thousand strong besieged the legion under the command of Cicero, and had almost taken it by storm, the Roman soldiers being all wounded, and having quite spent themselves by a defence beyond their natural strength. But Cæsar, who was at a great distance, having received the news, quickly got together seven thousand men, and hastened to relieve Cicero. The besiegers were aware of it, and went to meet him, with great confidence that they should easily overpower such a handful of men. Cæsar, to increase their presumption, seemed to avoid fighting, and still marched off till he found a place conveniently situated for a few to engage against many, where he encamped. He kept his soldiers from making any attack upon the enemy, and commanded them to raise the ramparts higher and barricade the gates, that by show of fear they might heighten the enemy's contempt of them. Till at last they came without any order in great security to make an assault, when he issued forth and put them in flight with the loss of many men.

This quieted the greater part of the commotions in these parts of Gaul, and Cæsar, in the course of the winter, visited every part of the country, and with great vigilance took precautions against all innovations. For there were three legions now come to him to supply the place of the men he had lost, of which Pompey furnished him with two out of those under his command; the other was newly raised in the part of Gaul by the Po. But in a while the seeds of war, which had long since been secretly sown and scattered by the most powerful men in those warlike nations, broke forth into the greatest and most dangerous war that was in those parts, both as regards the number of men in the vigour of their youth who were gathered and armed from all quarters, the vast funds of money collected to maintain it, the strength of the towns, and the difficulty of the country where it was carried on. It being winter, the rivers were frozen, the woods covered with snow, and the level country flooded, so that in some places the ways were lost through the depth of the snow; in others, the overflowing of marshes and streams made every kind of passage uncertain. All which difficulties made it seem impracticable for Cæsar to make any attempt upon the insurgents. Many tribes had revolted together, the chief of them being the Arverni and Carnutini; the general who had the supreme command in war was Vergentorix, whose father the Gauls had put to death on suspicion of his aiming at absolute government.

He having disposed his army in several bodies, and set officers over them, drew over to him all the country round about as far as those that lie upon the Arar, and having intelligence of the opposition which Cæsar now experienced at Rome, thought to engage all Gaul in the war. Which if he had done a little later, when Cæsar was taken up with the civil wars, Italy had been put into as great a terror as before it was by the Cimbri. But Cæsar, who above all men was gifted with the faculty of making the right use of everything in war, and most especially of seizing the right moment, as soon as he heard of the revolt, returned immediately the same way he went, and showed the barbarians, by the quickness of his march in such a severe season, that an army was advancing against them which was invincible. For in the time that one would have thought it scarce credible that a courier or express should have come with a message from him, he himself appeared with all his army, ravaging the country, reducing their posts, subduing their towns, receiving into his protection those who declared for him. Till at last the Edui, who hitherto had styled themselves brethren to the Romans, and had been much honoured by them, declared against him, and joined the rebels, to the great discouragement of his Army. Accordingly he removed thence, and passed the country of the Ligones, desiring to reach the territories of the Sequani, who were his friends, and who lay like a bulwark in front of Italy against the other tribes of Gaul. There the enemy came upon him, and surrounded him with many myriads, whom he also was eager to engage; and at last, after some time and with much slaughter, gained on the whole a complete victory; though at first he appears to have met with some reverse, and the Aruveni show you a small sword hanging up in a temple, which they say was taken from Cæsar. Cæsar saw this afterwards himself, and smiled, and when his friends advised it should be taken down, would not permit it, because he looked upon it as consecrated.

After the defeat, a great part of those who had escaped fled with their king into a town called Alesia, which Cæsar besieged, though the height of the walls, and number of those who defended them, made it appear impregnable; and meantime, from without the walls, he was assailed by a greater danger than can be expressed. For the choice men of Gaul, picked out of each nation, and well armed, came to relieve Alesia, to the number of three hundred thousand; nor were there in the town less than one hundred and seventy thousand. So that Cæsar being shut up betwixt two such forces, was compelled to protect himself by two walls, one towards the town, the other against the relieving army, as knowing if these forces should join, his affairs would be entirely ruined. The danger that he underwent before Alesia justly gained him great honour on many accounts, and gave him an opportunity of showing greater instances of his valour and conduct than any other contest had done. One wonders much how he should be able to engage and defeat so many thousands of men without the town, and not be perceived by those within, but yet more, that the Romans themselves, who guarded their wall which was next to the town, should be strangers to it. For even they knew nothing of the victory, till they heard the cries of the men and lamentations of the women who were in the town, and had from thence seen the Romans at a distance carrying into their camp a great quantity of bucklers, adorned with gold and silver, many breastplates stained with blood, besides cups and tents made in the Gallic fashion. So soon did so vast an army dissolve and vanish like a ghost or dream, the greatest part of them being killed upon the spot. Those who were in Alesia, having given themselves and Cæsar much trouble, surrendered at last; and Vergentorix, who was the chief spring of all the war, putting his best armour on, and adorning his horse, rode out of the gates, and made a turn about Cæsar as he was sitting, then quitting his horse, threw off his armour, and remained quietly sitting at Cæsar's feet until he was led away to be reserved for the triumph.

Cæsar had long ago resolved upon the overthrow of Pompey, as had Pompey, for that matter, upon his. For Crassus, the fear of whom had hitherto kept them in peace, having now been killed in Parthia, if the one of them wished to make himself the greatest man in Rome, he had only to overthrow the other; and if he again wished to prevent his own fall, he had nothing for it but to be beforehand with him whom he feared. Pompey had not been long under any such apprehensions, having till lately despised Cæsar, as thinking it no difficult matter to put down him whom he himself had advanced. But Cæsar had entertained this design from the beginning against his rivals, and had retired, like an expert wrestler, to prepare himself apart for the combat. Making the Gallic wars his exercise ground, he had at once improved the strength of his soldiery, and had heightened his own glory by his great actions, so that he was looked on as one who might challenge comparison with Pompey. Nor did he let go any of those advantages which were now given him both by Pompey himself and the times, and the ill-government of Rome, where all who were candidates for offices publicly gave money, and without any shame bribed the people, who, having received their pay, did not contend for their benefactors with their bare suffrages, but with bows, swords, and slings. So that after having many times stained the place of election with blood of men killed upon the spot, they left the city at last without a government at all, to be carried about like a ship without a pilot to steer her; while all who had any wisdom could only be thankful if a course of such wild and stormy disorder and madness might end no worse than in a monarchy. Some were so bold as to declare openly that the government was incurable but by a monarchy, and that they ought to take that remedy from the hands of the gentlest physician, meaning Pompey, who, though in words he pretended to decline it, yet in reality made his utmost efforts to be declared dictator. Cato, perceiving his design, prevailed with the senate to make him sole consul, that with the offer of a more legal sort of monarchy he might be withheld from demanding the dictatorship. They over and above voted him the continuance of his provinces, for he had two, Spain and all Africa, which he governed by his lieutenants, and maintained armies under him, at the yearly charge of a thousand talents out of the public treasury.

Upon this Cæsar also sent and petitioned for the consulship and the continuance of his provinces. Pompey at first did not stir in it, but Marcellus and Lentulus opposed it, who had always hated Cæsar, and now did everything, whether fit or unfit, which might disgrace and affront him. For they took away the privilege of Roman citizens from the people of New Comum, who were a colony that Cæsar had lately planted in Gaul, and Marcellus, who was then consul, ordered one of the senators of that town, then at Rome, to be whipped, and told him he laid that mark upon him to signify he was no citizen of Rome, bidding him, when he went back again, to show it to Cæsar. After Marcellus's consulship, Cæsar began to lavish gifts upon all the public men out of the riches he had taken from the Gauls; discharged Curio, the tribune, from his great debts; gave Paulus, then consul, fifteen hundred talents, with which he built the noble court of justice adjoining the forum, to supply the place of that called the Fulvian. Pompey, alarmed at these preparations, now openly took steps, both by himself and his friends, to have a successor appointed in Cæsar's room, and sent to demand back the soldiers whom he had lent him to carry on the wars in Gaul. Cæsar returned them, and made each soldier a present of two hundred and fifty drachmas. The officer who brought them home to Pompey spread amongst the people no very fair or favourable report of Cæsar, and flattered Pompey himself with false suggestions that he was wished for by Cæsar's army; and though his affairs here were in some embarrassment through the envy of some, and the ill state of the government, yet there the army was at his command, and if they once crossed into Italy would presently declare for him; so weary were they of Cæsar's endless expeditions, and so suspicious of his designs for a monarchy. Upon this Pompey grew presumptuous, and neglected all warlike preparations as fearing no danger, and used no other means against him than mere speeches and votes, for which Cæsar cared nothing. And one of his captains, it is said, who was sent by him to Rome, standing before the senate house one day, and being told that the senate would not give Cæsar longer time in his government, clapped his hand on the hilt of his sword and said, "But this shall."

Yet the demands which Cæsar made had the fairest colours of equity imaginable. For he proposed to lay down his arms, and that Pompey should do the same, and both together should become private men, and each expect a reward of his services from the public. For that those who proposed to disarm him, and at the same time to confirm Pompey in all the power he held, were simply establishing the one in the tyranny which they accused the other of aiming at. When Curio made these proposals to the people in Cæsar's name, he was loudly applauded, and some threw garlands towards him, and dismissed him as they do successful wrestlers, crowned with flowers. Antony, being tribune, produced a letter sent from Cæsar on this occasion, and read it though the consuls did what they could to oppose it. But Scipio, Pompey's father-in-law, proposed in the senate, that if Cæsar did not lay down his arms within such a time he should be voted an enemy; and the consuls putting it to the question, whether Pompey should dismiss his soldiers, and again, whether Cæsar should disband his, very few assented to the first, but almost all to the latter. But Antony proposing again, that both should lay down their commissions, all but a very few agreed to it. Scipio was upon this very violent, and Lentulus, the consul, cried aloud, that they had need of arms, and not of suffrages, against a robber; so that the senators for the present adjourned, and appeared in mourning as a mark of their grief for the dissension.

Afterwards there came other letters from Cæsar, which seemed yet more moderate, for he proposed to quit everything else, and only to retain Gaul within the Alps, Illyricum, and two legions, till he should stand a second time for consul. Cicero, the orator, who was lately returned from Cilicia, endeavoured to reconcile differences, and softened Pompey, who was willing to comply in other things, but not to allow him the soldiers. At last Cicero used his persuasions with Cæsar's friends to accept of the provinces and six thousand soldiers only, and so to make up the quarrel. And Pompey was inclined to give way to this, but Lentulus, the consul would not hearken to it, but drove Antony and Curio out of the senate-house with insults, by which he afforded Cæsar the most plausible pretence that could be, and one which he could readily use to inflame the soldiers, by showing them two persons of such repute and authority who were forced to escape in a hired carriage in the dress of slaves. For so they were glad to disguise themselves when they fled out of Rome.

There were not about him at that time above three hundred horse and five thousand foot; for the rest of his army, which was left behind the Alps, was to be brought after him by officers who had received orders for that purpose. But he thought the first motion towards the design which he had on foot did not require large forces at present, and that what was wanted was to make this first step suddenly, and so to astound his enemies with the boldness of it; as it would be easier, he thought, to throw them into consternation by doing what they never anticipated than fairly to conquer them, if he had alarmed them by his preparations. And therefore he commanded his captains and other officers to go only with their swords in their hands, without any other arms, and make themselves masters of Ariminum, a large city of Gaul, with as little disturbance and bloodshed as possible. He committed the care of these forces to Hortensius, and himself spent the day in public as a stander-by and spectator of the gladiators, who exercised before him. A little before night he attended to his person, and then went into the hall, and conversed for some time with those he had invited to supper, till it began to grow dusk, when he rose from table and made his excuses to the company, begging them to stay till he came back, having already given private directions to a few immediate friends that they should follow him, not all the same way, but some one way, some another. He himself got into one of the hired carriages, and drove at first another way, but presently turned towards Ariminum. When he came to the river Rubicon, which parts Gaul within the Alps from the rest of Italy, his thoughts began to work, now he was just entering upon the danger, and he wavered much in his mind when he considered the greatness of the enterprise into which he was throwing himself. He checked his course and ordered a halt, while he revolved with himself, and often changed his opinion one way and the other, without speaking a word. This was when his purposes fluctuated most; presently he also discussed the matter with his friends who were about him (of which number Asinius Pollio was one), computing how many calamities his passing that river would bring upon mankind, and what a relation of it would be transmitted to posterity. At last, in a sort of passion, casting aside calculation, and abandoning himself to what might come, and using the proverb frequently in their mouths who enter upon dangerous and bold attempts, "The die is cast," with these words he took the river. Once over, he used all expedition possible, and before it was day reached Ariminum and took it. It is said that the night before he passed the river he had an impious dream, that he was unnaturally familiar with his own mother.

As soon as Ariminum was taken, wide gates, so to say, were thrown open, to let in war upon every land alike and sea, and with the limits of the province, the boundaries of the laws were transgressed. Nor would one have thought that, as at other times, the mere men and women fled from one town of Italy to another in their consternation, but that the very towns themselves left their sites and fled for succour to each other. The city of Rome was overrun, as it were, with a deluge, by the conflux of people flying in from all the neighbouring places. Magistrates could not longer govern, nor the eloquence of any orator quiet it; it was all but suffering shipwreck by the violence of its own tempestuous agitation. The most vehement contrary passions and impulses were at work everywhere. Nor did those who rejoiced at the prospect of the change altogether conceal their feelings, but when they met, as in so great a city they frequently must, with the alarmed and dejected of the other party, they provoked quarrels by their bold expressions of confidence in the event. Pompey, sufficiently disturbed of himself, was yet more perplexed by the clamours of others; some telling him that he justly suffered for having armed Cæsar against himself and the government; others blaming him for permitting Cæsar to be insolently used by Lentulus, when he made such ample concessions, and offered such reasonable proposals towards an accommodation. Favonius bade him now stamp upon the ground; for once talking big in the senate, he desired them not to trouble themselves about making any preparations for the war, for that he himself, with one stamp of his foot, would fill all Italy with soldiers. Yet still Pompey at that time had more forces than Cæsar; but he was not permitted to pursue his own thoughts, but, being continually disturbed with false reports and alarms, as if the enemy was close upon him and carrying all before him, he gave way and let himself be borne down by the general cry. He put forth an edict declaring the city to be in a state of anarchy, and left it with orders that the senate should follow him, and that no one should stay behind who did not prefer tyranny to their country and liberty.

The consuls at once fled, without making even the usual sacrifices; so did most of the senators, carrying off their own goods in as much haste as if they had been robbing their neighbours. Some, who had formerly much favoured Cæsar's cause, in the prevailing alarm quitted their own sentiments, and without any prospect of good to themselves, were carried along by the common stream. It was a melancholy thing to see the city tossed in these tumults, like a ship given up by her pilots, and left to run, as chance guides her, upon any rock in her way. Yet, in spite of their sad condition people still esteemed the place of their exile to be their country for Pompey's sake, and fled from Rome, as if it had been Cæsar's camp. Labienus even, who had been one of Cæsar's nearest friends, and his lieutenant, and who had fought by him zealously in the Gallic wars, now deserted him, and went over to Pompey. Caesar sent all his money and equipage after him and then sat down before Corfinium, which was garrisoned with thirty cohorts under the command of Domitius. He, in despair of maintaining the defence, requested a physician, whom he had among his attendants, to give him poison; and taking the dose, drank it, in hopes of being despatched by it. But soon after, when he was told that Cæsar showed the utmost clemency towards those he took prisoners, he lamented his misfortune, and blamed the hastiness of his resolution. His physician consoled him by informing him that he had taken a sleeping draught, not a poison; upon which, much rejoiced, and rising from his bed, he went presently to Cæsar and gave him the pledge of his hand, yet afterwards again went over to Pompey. The report of these actions at Rome quieted those who were there, and some who had fled thence returned.

Cæsar took into his army Domitius's soldiers, as he did all those whom he found in any town enlisted for Pompey's service. Being now strong and formidable enough, he advanced against Pompey himself, who did not stay to receive him, but fled to Brundusium, having sent the consuls before with a body of troops to Dyrrhachium. Soon after, upon Cæsar's approach, he set to sea, as shall be more particularly related in his Life. Cæsar would have immediately pursued him, but wanted shipping, and therefore went back to Rome, having made himself master of all Italy without bloodshed in the space of sixty days. When he came thither, he found the city more quiet than he expected, and many senators present, to whom he addressed himself with courtesy and deference, desiring them to send to Pompey about any reasonable accommodation towards a peace. But nobody complied with this proposal; whether out of fear of Pompey, whom they had deserted, or that they thought Cæsar did not mean what he said, but thought it his interest to talk plausibly. Afterwards, when Mettellus, the tribune, would have hindered him from taking money out of the public treasure, and adduced some laws against it, Cæsar replied that arms and laws had each their own time; "If what I do displeases you, leave the place; war allows no free talking. When I have laid down my arms, and made peace, come back and make what speeches you please. And this," he added, "I tell you in diminution of my own just right, as indeed you and all others who have appeared against me and are now in my power may be treated as I please." Having said this to Metellus, he went to the doors of the treasury, and the keys being not to be found, sent for smiths to force them open. Metellus again making resistance and some encouraging him in it, Cæsar, in a louder tone, told him he would put him to death if he gave him any further disturbance. "And this," said he, "you know, young man, is more disagreeable for me to say than to do." These words made Metellus withdraw for fear, and obtained speedy execution henceforth for all orders that Cæsar gave for procuring necessaries for the war.

He was now proceeding to Spain, with the determination of first crushing Afranius and Varro, Pompey's lieutenants, and making himself master of the armies and provinces under them, that he might then more securely advance against Pompey, when he had no enemy left behind him. In this expedition his person was often in danger from ambuscades, and his army by want of provisions, yet he did not desist from pursuing the enemy, provoking them to fight, and hemming them with his fortifications, till by main force he made himself master of their camps and their forces. Only the generals got off, and fled to Pompey.

When Cæsar came back to Rome, Piso, his father-in-law advised him to send men to Pompey to treat of a peace; but Isauricus, to ingratiate himself with Cæsar, spoke against it. After this, being created dictator by the senate, he called home the exiles, and gave back their rights as citizens to the children of those who had suffered under Sylla; he relieved the debtors by an act remitting some part of the interest on their debts, and passed some other measures of the same sort, but not many. For within eleven days he resigned his dictatorship, and having declared himself consul, with Servilius Isauricus, hastened again to the war. He marched so fast that he left all his army behind him, except six hundred chosen horse and five legions, with which he put to sea in the very middle of winter, about the beginning of the month of January (which corresponds pretty nearly with the Athenian month Posideon), and having passed the Ionian Sea, took Oricum and Apollonia, and then sent back the ships to Brundusium, to bring over the soldiers who were left behind in the march. They, while yet on the march, their bodies now no longer in the full vigour, and they themselves weary with such a multitude of wars, could not but exclaim against Cæsar, "When at last, and where, will this Cæsar let us be quiet? He carries us from place to place, and uses us as if we were not to be worn out, and had no sense of labour. Even our iron itself is spent by blows, and we ought to have some pity on our bucklers, and breastplates, which have been used so long. Our wounds, if nothing else, should make him see that we are mortal men whom he commands, subject to the same pains and sufferings as other human beings. The very gods themselves cannot force the winter season, or hinder the storms in their time; yet he pushes forward, as if he were not pursuing, but flying from an enemy." So they talked as they marched leisurely towards Brundusium. But when they came thither, and found Cæsar gone off before them, their feelings changed, and they blamed themselves as traitors to their general. They now railed at their officers for marching so slowly, and placing themselves on the heights overlooking the sea towards Epirus, they kept watch to see if they could espy the vessels which were to transport them to Cæsar.

He in the meantime was posted in Apollonia, but had not an army with him able to fight the enemy, the forces from Brundusium being so long in coming, which put him to great suspense and embarrassment what to do. At last he resolved upon a most hazardous experiment, and embarked, without any one's knowledge, in a boat of twelve oars, to cross over to Brundusium, though the sea was at that time covered with a vast fleet of the enemies. He got on board in the night-time, in the dress of a slave, and throwing himself down like a person of no consequence lay along at the bottom of the vessel. The river Anius was to carry them down to sea, and there used to blow a gentle gale every morning from the land, which made it calm at the mouth of the river, by driving the waves forward; but this night there had blown a strong wind from the sea, which overpowered that from the land, so that where the river met the influx of the seawater and the opposition of the waves it was extremely rough and angry; and the current was beaten back with such a violent swell that the master of the boat could not make good his passage, but ordered his sailors to tack about and return. Cæsar, upon this, discovers himself, and taking the man by the hand who was surprised to see him there, said, "Go on, my friend, and fear nothing; you carry Cæsar and his fortune in your boat." The mariners, when they heard that, forgot the storm, and laying all their strength to their oars, did what they could to force their way down the river. But when it was to no purpose, and the vessel now took in much water, Cæsar finding himself in such danger in the very mouth of the river, much against his will permitted the master to turn back. When he was come to land, his soldiers ran to him in a multitude, reproaching him for what he had done, and indignant that he should think himself not strong enough to get a victory by their sole assistance, but must disturb himself, and expose his life for those who were absent, as if he could not trust those who were with him.

After this, Antony came over with the forces from Brundusium, which encouraged Cæsar to give Pompey battle, though he was encamped very advantageously, and furnished with plenty of provisions both by sea and land, whilst he himself was at the beginning but ill supplied, and before the end was extremely pinched for want of necessaries, so that his soldiers were forced to dig up a kind of root which grew there, and tempering it with milk, to feed on it. Sometimes they made a kind of bread of it, and advancing up to the enemy's outposts, would throw in these loaves, telling them, that as long as the earth produced such roots they would not give up blockading Pompey. But Pompey took what care he could that neither the loaves nor the words should reach his men, who were out of heart and despondent through terror at the fierceness and hardihood of their enemies, whom they looked upon as a sort of wild beasts. There were continual skirmishes about Pompey's outworks, in all which Cæsar had the better, except one, when his men were forced to fly in such a manner that he had like to have lost his camp. For Pompey made such a vigorous sally on them that not a man stood his ground; the trenches were filled with the slaughter, many fell upon their own ramparts and bulwarks, whither they were driven in flight by the enemy. Cæsar met them and would have turned them back, but could not. When he went to lay hold of the ensigns, those who carried them threw them down, so that the enemy took thirty-two of them. He himself narrowly escaped; for taking hold of one of his soldiers, a big and strong man, that was flying by him, he bade him stand and face about; but the fellow, full of apprehensions from the danger he was in, laid hold of his sword, as if he would strike Cæsar, but Cæsar's armour-bearer cut off his arm. Cæsar's affairs were so desperate at that time that when Pompey, either through over-cautiousness or his ill fortune, did not give the finishing stroke to that great success, but retreated after he had driven the routed enemy within their camp, Cæsar, upon seeing his withdrawal, said to his friends, "The victory to-day had been on the enemies' side if they had had a general who knew how to gain it." When he was retired into his tent, he laid himself down to sleep, but spent that night as miserable as ever he did any, in perplexity and consideration with himself, coming to the conclusion that he had conducted the war amiss. For when he had a fertile country before him, and all the wealthy cities of Macedonia and Thessaly, he had neglected to carry the war thither and had sat down by the seaside, where his enemies had such a powerful fleet. so that he was in fact rather besieged by the want of necessaries than besieging others with his arms. Being thus distracted in his thoughts with the view of the difficulty and distress he was in, he raised his camp with the intention of advancing towards Scipio, who lay in Macedonia; hoping either to entice Pompey into a country where he should fight without the advantage he now had of supplies from the sea, or to overpower Scipio if not assisted.

This set all Pompey's army and officers on fire to hasten and pursue Cæsar, whom they concluded to be beaten and flying. But Pompey was afraid to hazard a battle on which so much depended, and being himself provided with all necessaries for any length of time, thought to tire out and waste the vigour of Cæsar's army, which could not last long. For the best part of his men, though they had great experience, and showed irresistible courage in all engagements, yet by their frequent marches, changing their camps, attacking fortifications, and keeping long night-watches, were getting worn out and broken; they being now old, their bodies less fit for labour, and their courage, also, beginning to give way with the failure of their strength. Besides, it was said that an infectious disease, occasioned by their irregular diet, was prevailing in Cæsar's army, and what was of greatest moment, he was neither furnished with money nor provisions, so that in a little time he must needs fall of himself.

For these reasons Pompey had no mind to fight him, but was thanked for it by none but Cato, who rejoiced at the prospect of sparing his fellow-citizens. For he, when he saw the dead bodies of those who had fallen in the last battle on Cæsar's side, to the number of a thousand, turned away, covered his face, and shed tears. But every one else upbraided Pompey for being reluctant to fight, and tried to goad him on by such nicknames as Agamemnon, and king of kings, as if he were in no hurry to lay down his sovereign authority, but was pleased to see so many commanders attending on him, and paying their attendance at his tent. Favonius, who affected Cato's free way of speaking his mind, complained bitterly that they should eat no figs even this year at Tusculum, because of Pompey's love of command. Afranius, who was lately returned out of Spain, and, on account of his ill success there, laboured under the suspicion of having been bribed to betray the army, asked why they did not fight this purchaser of provinces. Pompey was driven, against his own will, by this kind of language, into offering battle, and proceeded to follow Cæsar. Cæsar had found great difficulties in his march, for no country would supply him with provisions, his reputation being very much fallen since his late defeat. But after he took Gomphi, a town of Thessaly, he not only found provisions for his army, but physic too. For there they met with plenty of wine, which they took very freely, and heated with this, sporting and revelling on their march in bacchanalian fashion, they shook off the disease, and their whole constitution was relieved and changed into another habit.

When the two armies were come into Pharsalia, and both encamped there, Pompey's thoughts ran the same way as they had done before, against fighting, and the more because of some unlucky presages, and a vision he had in a dream. But those who were about him were so confident of success, that Domitius, and Spinther, and Scipio, as if they had already conquered, quarrelled which should succeed Cæsar in the pontificate. And many sent to Rome to take houses fit to accommodate consuls and prætors, as being sure of entering upon those offices as soon as the battle was over. The cavalry especially were obstinate for fighting, being splendidly armed and bravely mounted, and valuing themselves upon the fine horses they kept, and upon their own handsome persons, as also upon the advantage of their numbers, for they were five thousand against one thousand of Cæsar's. Nor were the numbers of the infantry less disproportionate, there being forty-five thousand of Pompey's against twenty-two thousand of the enemy.

Cæsar, collecting his soldiers together, told them that Corfinius was coming up to them with two legions, and that fifteen cohorts more under Calenus were posted at Megara and Athens; he then asked him whether they would stay till these joined them, or would hazard the battle by themselves. They all cried out to him not to wait, but on the contrary to do whatever he could to bring about an engagement as soon as possible. When he sacrificed to the gods for the lustration of his army, upon the death of the first victim, the augur told him, within three days he should come to a decisive action. Cæsar asked him whether he saw anything in the entrails which promised a happy event. "That," said the priest, "you can best answer yourself; for the gods signify a great alteration from the present posture of affairs. If, therefore, you think yourself well off now, expect worse fortune; if unhappy, hope for better." The night before the battle, as he walked the rounds about midnight, there was a light seen in the heavens, very bright and flaming, which seemed to pass over Cæsar's camp and fall into Pompey's. And when Cæsar's soldiers came to relieve the watch in the morning, they perceived a panic disorder among the enemies. However, he did not expect to fight that day, but set about raising his camp with the intention of marching towards Scotussa.

But when the tents were now taken down, his scouts rode up to him, and told him the enemy would give him battle. With this news he was extremely pleased, and having performed his devotions to the gods, set his army in battle array, dividing them into three bodies. Over the middlemost he placed Domitius Calvinus; Antony commanded the left wing, and he himself the right, being resolved to fight at the head of the tenth legion. But when he saw the enemy's cavalry taking position against him, being struck with their fine appearance and their number, he gave private orders that six cohorts from the rear of the army should come and join him, whom he posted behind the right wing, and instructed them what they should do when the enemy's horse came to charge. On the other side, Pompey commanded the right wing, Domitius the left, and Scipio, Pompey's father-in-law, the centre. The whole weight of the cavalry was collected on the left wing, with the intent that they should outflank the right wing of the enemy, and rout that part where the general himself commanded. For they thought no phalanx of infantry could be solid enough to sustain such a shock, but that they must necessarily be broken and shattered all to pieces upon the onset of so immense a force of cavalry. When they were ready on both sides to give the signal for battle, Pompey commanded his foot, who were in the front, to stand their ground, and without breaking their order, receive, quietly, the enemy's first attack, till they came within javelin's cast. Cæsar, in this respect, also, blames Pompey's generalship, as if he had not been aware how the first encounter, when made with an impetus and upon the run, gives weight and force to the strokes, and fires the men's spirits into a flame, which the general concurrence fans to full heat. He himself was just putting the troops into motion and advancing to the action, when he found one of his captains, a trusty and experienced soldier, encouraging his men to exert their utmost. Cæsar called him by his name, and said, "What hopes, Caius Crassinius, and what grounds for encouragement?" Crassinius stretched out his hand, and cried in a loud voice, "We shall conquer nobly, Cæsar; and I this day will deserve your praises, either alive or dead." So he said, and was the first man to run in upon the enemy, followed by the hundred and twenty soldiers about him, and breaking through the first rank, still pressed on forwards with much slaughter of the enemy, till at last he was struck back by the wound of a sword, which went in at his mouth with such force that it came out at his neck behind.

Whilst the foot was thus sharply engaged in the main battle, on the flank Pompey's horse rode up confidently, and opened their ranks very wide, that they might surround the right wing of Cæsar. But before they engaged, Cæsar's cohorts rushed out and attacked them, and did not dart their javelins at a distance, nor strike at the thighs and legs, as they usually did in close battle, but aimed at their faces. For thus Cæsar had instructed them, in hopes that young gentlemen, who had not known much of battles and wounds, but came wearing their hair long, in the flower of their age and height of their beauty, would be more apprehensive of such blows, and not care for hazarding both a danger at present and a blemish for the future. And so it proved, for they were so far from bearing the stroke of the javelins, that they could not stand the sight of them, but turned about, and covered their faces to secure them. Once in disorder, presently they turned about to fly; and so most shamefully ruined all. For those who had beat them back at once outflanked the infantry, and falling on their rear, cut them to pieces. Pompey, who commanded the other wing of the army, when he saw his cavalry thus broken and flying, was no longer himself, nor did he now remember that he was Pompey the Great, but, like one whom some god had deprived of his senses, retired to his tent without speaking a word, and there sat to expect the event, till the whole army was routed and the enemy appeared upon the works which were thrown up before the camp, where they closely engaged with his men who were posted there to defend it. Then first he seemed to have recovered his senses, and uttering, it is said, only these words, "What, into the camp too?" he laid aside his general's habit, and putting on such clothes as might best favour his flight, stole off. What fortune he met with afterwards, how he took shelter in Egypt, and was murdered there, we tell you in his Life.

Cæsar, when he came to view Pompey's camp, and saw some of his opponents dead upon the ground, others dying, said, with a groan, "This they would have; they brought me to this necessity. I, Caius Cæsar, after succeeding in so many wars, had been condemned had I dismissed my army." These words, Pollio says, Cæsar spoke in Latin at that time, and that he himself wrote them in Greek; adding, that those who were killed at the taking of the camp were most of them servants; and that not above six thousand soldiers fell. Cæsar incorporated most of the foot whom he took prisoners with his own legions, and gave a free pardon to many of the distinguished persons, and amongst the rest to Brutus, who afterwards killed him. He did not immediately appear after the battle was over, which put Cæsar, it is said, into great anxiety for him; nor was his pleasure less when he saw him present himself alive.

There were many prodigies that foreshadowed this victory, but the most remarkable that we are told of was that at Tralles. In the temple of Victory stood Cæsar's statue. The ground on which it stood was naturally hard and solid, and the stone with which it was paved still harder; yet it is said that a palm-tree shot itself up near the pedestal of this statue. In the city of Padua, one Caius Cornelius, who had the character of a good augur, the fellow-citizen and acquaintance of Livy, the historian, happened to be making some augural observations that very day when the battle was fought. And first, as Livy tells us, he pointed out the time of the fight, and said to those who were by him that just then the battle was begun and the men engaged. When he looked a second time, and observed the omens, he leaped up as if he had been inspired, and cried out, "Cæsar, you are victorious." This much surprised the standers-by, but he took the garland which he had on from his head, and swore he would never wear it again till the event should give authority to his art. This Livy positively states for a truth.

Cæsar, as a memorial of his victory, gave the Thessalians their freedom, and then went in pursuit of Pompey. When he was come into Asia, to gratify Theopompus, the author of the collection of fables, he enfranchised the Cnidians, and remitted one-third of their tribute to all the people of the province of Asia. When he came to Alexandria, where Pompey was already murdered, he would not look upon Theodotus, who presented him with his head, but taking only his signet, shed tears. Those of Pompey's friends who had been arrested by the King of Egypt, as they were wandering in those parts, he relieved, and offered them his own friendship. In his letter to his friends at Rome, he told them that the greatest and most signal pleasure his victory had given him was to be able continually to save the lives of fellow-citizens who had fought against him. As to the war in Egypt, some say it was at once dangerous and dishonourable, and noways necessary, but occasioned only by his passion for Cleopatra. Others blame the ministers of the king, and especially the eunuch Pothinus, who was the chief favourite and had lately killed Pompey, who had banished Cleopatra, and was now secretly plotting Cæsar's destruction (to prevent which, Cæsar from that time began to sit up whole nights, under pretence of drinking, for the security of his person), while openly he was intolerable in his affronts to Cæsar, both by his words and actions. For when Cæsar's soldiers had musty and unwholesome corn measured out to them, Pothinus told them they must be content with it, since they were fed at another's cost. He ordered that his table should be served with wooden and earthen dishes, and said Cæsar had carried off all the gold and silver plate, under pretence of arrears of debt. For the present king's father owed Cæsar one thousand seven hundred and fifty myriads of money. Cæsar had formerly remitted to his children the rest, but thought fit to demand the thousand myriads at that time to maintain his army. Pothinus told him that he had better go now and attend to his other affairs of greater consequence, and that he should receive his money at another time with thanks. Cæsar replied that he did not want Egyptians to be his counsellors, and soon after privately sent for Cleopatra from her retirement.

She took a small boat, and one only of her confidants, Apollodorus, the Sicilian, along with her, and in the dusk of the evening landed near the palace. She was at a loss how to get in undiscovered, till she thought of putting herself into the coverlet of a bed and lying at length, whilst Apollodorus tied up the bedding and carried it on his back through the gates to Cæsar's apartment. Cæsar was first captivated by this proof of Cleopatra's bold wit, and was afterwards so overcome by the charm of her society that he made a reconciliation between her and her brother, on the condition that she should rule as his colleague in the kingdom. A festival was kept to celebrate this reconciliation, where Cæsar's barber, a busy listening fellow, whose excessive timidity made him inquisitive into everything, discovered that there was a plot carrying on against Cæsar by Achillas, general of the king's forces, and Pothinus, the eunuch. Cæsar, upon the first intelligence of it, set a guard upon the hall where the feast was kept and killed Pothinus. Achillas escaped to the army, and raised a troublesome and embarrassing war against Cæsar, which it was not easy for him to manage with his few soldiers against so powerful a city and so large an army. The first difficulty he met with was want of water, for the enemies had turned the canals. Another was, when the enemy endeavoured to cut off his communication by sea, he was forced to divert that danger by setting fire to his own ships, which, after burning the docks, thence spread on and destroyed the great library. A third was, when in an engagement near Pharos, he leaped from the mole into a small boat to assist his soldiers who were in danger, and when the Egyptians pressed him on every side, he threw himself into the sea, and with much difficulty swam off. This was the time when, according to the story, he had a number of manuscripts in his hand, which, though he was continually darted at, and forced to keep his head often under water, yet he did not let go, but held them up safe from wetting in one hand, whilst he swam with the other. His boat in the meantime, was quickly sunk. At last, the king having gone off to Achillas and his party, Cæsar engaged and conquered them. Many fell in that battle, and the king himself was never seen after. Upon this, he left Cleopatra queen of Egypt, who soon after had a son by him, whom the Alexandrians called Cæsarion, and then departed for Syria.

Thence he passed to Asia, where he heard that Domitius was beaten by Pharnaces, son of Mithridates, and had fled out of Pontus with a handful of men; and that Pharnaces pursued the victory so eagerly, that though he was already master of Bithynia and Cappadocia, he had a further design of attempting the Lesser Armenia, and was inviting all the kings and tetrarchs there to rise. Cæsar immediately marched against him with three legions, fought him near Zela, drove him out of Pontus, and totally defeated his army. When he gave Amantius, a friend of his at Rome, an account of this action, to express the promptness and rapidity of it he used three words, I came, saw, and conquered, which in Latin, having all the same cadence, carry with them a very suitable air of brevity.

Hence he crossed into Italy, and came to Rome at the end of that year, for which he had been a second time chosen dictator, though that office had never before lasted a whole year, and was elected consul for the next. He was ill spoken of, because upon a mutiny of some soldiers, who killed Cosconius and Galba, who had been prætors, he gave them only the slight reprimand of calling them *Citizens* instead of *Fellow-Soldiers*, and afterwards assigned to each man a thousand drachmas, besides a share of lands in Italy. He was also reflected on for Dolabella's extravagance, Amantius's covetousness, Antony's debauchery, and Corfinius's profuseness, who pulled down Pompey's house, and rebuilt it, as not magnificent enough; for the Romans were much displeased with all these. But Cæsar, for the prosecution of his own scheme of government, though he knew their characters and disapproved them, was forced to make use of those who would serve him.

After the battle of Pharsalia, Cato and Scipio fled into Africa, and there, with the assistance of King Juba, got together a considerable force, which Cæsar resolved to engage. He accordingly passed into Sicily about the winter solstice, and to remove from his officers' minds all hopes of delay there, encamped by the seashore, and as soon as ever he had a fair wind, put to sea with three thousand foot and a few horse. When he had landed them, he went back secretly, under some apprehensions for the larger part of his army, but met them upon the sea, and brought them all to the same camp. There he was informed that the enemies relied much upon an ancient oracle, that the family of the Scipios should be always victorious in Africa. There was in his army a man, otherwise mean and contemptible, but of the house of the Africani, and his name Scipio Sallutio. This man Cæsar (whether in raillery to ridicule Scipio, who commanded the enemy, or seriously to bring over the omen to his side, it were hard to say), put at the head of his troops, as if he were general, in all the frequent battles which he was compelled to fight. For he was in such want both of victualling for his men and forage for his horses, that he was forced to feed the horses with seaweed, which he washed thoroughly to take off its saltness, and mixed with a little grass to give it a more agreeable taste. The Numidians, in great numbers, and well horsed, whenever he went, came up and commanded the country. Cæsar's cavalry, being one day unemployed, diverted themselves with seeing an African, who entertained them with dancing and at the same time played upon the pipe to admiration. They were so taken with this, that they alighted, and gave their horses to some boys, when on a sudden the enemy surrounded them, killed some, pursued the rest and fell in with them into their camp; and had not Cæsar himself and Asinius Pollio come to their assistance, and put a stop to their flight, the war had been then at an end. In another engagement, also, the enemy had again the better, when Cæsar, it is said, seized a standard-bearer, who was running away, by the neck, and forcing him to face about, said, "Look, that is the way to the enemy."

Scipio, flushed with this success at first, had a mind to come to one decisive action. He therefore left Afranius and Juba in two distinct bodies not far distant and marched himself towards Thapsus, where he proceeded to build a fortified camp above a lake, to serve as a centre-point for their operations, and also as a place of refuge. Whilst Scipio was thus employed, Cæsar with incredible despatch made his way through thick woods, and a country supposed to be impassable, cut off one part of the enemy and attacked another in the front. Having routed these, he followed up his opportunity and the current of his good fortune, and on the first onset carried Afranius's camp, and ravaged that of the Numidians, Juba, their king, being glad to save himself by flight; so that in a small part of a single day he made himself master of three camps, and killed fifty thousand of the enemy, with the loss only of fifty of his own men. This is the account some give of that fight. Others say he was not in the action, but that he was taken with his usual distemper just as he was setting his army in order. He perceived the approaches of it, and before it had too far disordered his senses, when he was already beginning to shake under its influence, withdrew into a neighbouring fort where he reposed himself. Of the men of consular and prætorian dignity that were taken after the fight, several Cæsar put to death, others anticipated him by killing themselves.

Cato had undertaken to defend Utica, and for that reason was not in the battle. The desire which Cæsar had to take him alive made him hasten thither; and upon the intelligence that he had despatched himself, he was much discomposed, for what reason is not so well agreed. He certainly said, "Cato, I must grudge you your death, as you grudged me the honour of saving your life." Yet the discourse he wrote against Cato after his death is no great sign of his kindness, or that he was inclined to be reconciled to him. For how is it probable that he would have been tender of his life when he was so bitter against his memory? But from his clemency to Cicero, Brutus, and many others who fought against him, it may be divined that Cæsar's book was not written so much out of animosity to Cato, as in his own vindication. Cicero had written an encomium upon Cato, and called it by his name. A composition by so great a master upon so excellent a subject was sure to be in every one's hands. This touched Cæsar, who looked upon a panegyric on his enemies as no better than an invective against himself; and therefore he made in his Anti-Cato a collection of whatever could be said in his derogation. The two compositions, like Cato and Cæsar themselves, have each of them their several admirers.

Cæsar, upon his return to Rome, did not omit to pronounce before the people a magnificent account of his victory, telling them that he had subdued a country which would supply the public every year with two hundred thousand attic bushels of corn and three million pounds' weight of oil. He then led three triumphs for Egypt, Pontus, and Africa, the last for the victory over, not Scipio, but King Juba, as it was professed, whose little son was then carried in the triumph, the happiest captive that ever was,who, of a barbarian Numidian, came by this means to obtain a place among the most learned historians of Greece. After the triumphs, he distributed rewards to his soldiers, and treated the people with feasting and shows. He entertained the whole people together at one feast, where twenty-two thousand dining couches were laid out; and he made a display of gladiators, and of battles by sea, in honour, as he said, of his daughter Julia, though she had been long since dead. When these shows were over, an account was taken of the people who, from three hundred and twenty thousand, were now reduced to one hundred and fifty thousand. So great a waste had the civil war made in Rome alone, not to mention what the other parts of Italy and the provinces suffered.

He was now chosen a fourth time consul, and went into Spain against Pompey's sons. They were but young, yet had gathered together a very numerous army, and showed they had courage and conduct to command it, so that Cæsar was in extreme danger. The great battle was near the town of Munda, in which Cæsar, seeing his men hard pressed, and making but a weak resistance, ran through the ranks among the soldiers, and crying out, asked them whether they were not ashamed to deliver him into the hands of boys? At last, with great difficulty, and the best efforts he could make, he forced back the enemy, killing thirty thousand of them, though with the loss of one thousand of his best men. When he came back from the fight, he told his friends that he had often fought for victory, but this was the first time he had ever fought for life. This battle was won on the feast of Bacchus, the very day in which Pompey, four years before, had set out for the war. The younger of Pompey's sons escaped; but Didius, some days after the fight, brought the head of the elder to Cæsar. This was the last war he was engaged in. The triumph which he celebrated for this victory displeased the Romans beyond anything, for he had not defeated foreign generals or barbarian kings, but had destroyed the children and family of one of the greatest men of Rome, though unfortunate; and it did not look well to lead a procession in celebration of the calamities of his country, and to rejoice in those things for which no other apology could be made either to gods or men than their being absolutely necessary. Besides that, hitherto he had never sent letters or messengers to announce any victory over his fellow-citizens, but had seemed rather to be ashamed of the action than to expect honour from it.

Nevertheless his countrymen, conceding all to his fortune, and accepting the bit, in the hope that the government of a single person would give them time to breathe after so many civil wars and calamities, made him dictator for life. This was indeed a tyranny avowed, since his power now was not only absolute, but perpetual too. Cicero made the first proposals to the senate for conferring honours upon him, which might in some sort be said not to exceed the limits of ordinary human moderation. But others, striving which should deserve most, carried them so excessively high, that they made Cæsar odious to the most indifferent and moderate sort of men, by the pretentions and extravagance of the titles which they decreed him. His enemies, too, are thought to have had some share in this, as well as his flatterers. It gave them advantage against him, and would be their justification for any attempt they should make upon him; for since the civil wars were ended, he had nothing else that he could be charged with. And they had good reason to decree a temple to Clemency, in token of their thanks for the mild use he made of his victory. For he not only pardoned many of those who fought against him, but, further, to some gave honours and offices; as particularly to Brutus and Cassius, who both of them were prætors.

Pompey's images that were thrown down he set up again, upon which Cicero also said that by raising Pompey's statues he had fixed his own. When his friends advised him to have a guard, and several offered their services, he would not hear of it; but said it was better to suffer death once than always to live in fear of it. He looked upon the affections of the people to be the best and surest guard, and entertained them again with public feasting and general distributions of corn; and to gratify his army, he sent out colonies to several places, of which the most remarkable were Carthage and Corinth; which as before they had been ruined at the same time, so now were restored and repeopled together.

As for the men of high rank, he promised to some of them future consulships and prætorship, some he consoled with other offices and honours, and to all held out hopes of favour by the solicitude he showed to rule with the general good-will, insomuch that upon the death of Maximus one day before his consulship was ended, he made Caninius Revilius consul for that day. And when many went to pay the usual compliments and attentions to the new consul, "Let us make haste," said Cicero, "lest the man be gone out of his office before we come."

Cæsar was born to do great things, and had a passion after honour, and the many noble exploits he had done did not now serve as an inducement to him to sit still and reap the fruit of his past labours, but were incentives and encouragements to go on, and raised in him ideas of still greater actions, and a desire of new glory, as if the present were all spent. It was in fact a sort of emulous struggle with himself, as it had been with another, how he might outdo his past actions by his future. In pursuit of these thoughts, he resolved to make war upon the Parthians, and when he had subdued them, to pass through Hyrcania; thence to march along by the Caspian Sea to Mount Caucasus, and so on about Pontus till he came into Scythia; then to overrun all the countries bordering upon Germany, and Germany itself; and so to return through Gaul into Italy, after completing the whole circle of his intended empire, and bounding it on every side by the ocean. While preparations were making for this expedition, he proposed to dig through the isthmus on which Corinth stands; and appointed Anienus to superintend the work. He had also a design of diverting the Tiber, and carrying it by a deep channel directly from Rome to Circeii, and so into the sea near Tarracina, that there might be a safe and easy passage for all merchants who traded to Rome. Besides this, he intended to drain all the marshes by Pomentium and Setia, and gain ground enough from the water to employ many thousands of men in tillage. He proposed further to make great mounds on the shore nearest Rome, to hinder the sea from breaking in upon the land, to clear the coast at Ostia of all the hidden rocks and shoals that made it unsafe for shipping and to form ports and harbours fit to receive the large number of vessels that would frequent them.

These things were designed without being carried into effect; but his reformation of the calendar in order to rectify the irregularity of time was not only projected with great scientific ingenuity, but was brought to its completion, and proved of very great use. For it was not only in ancient time that the Romans had wanted a certain rule to make the revolutions of their months fall in with the course of the year, so that their festivals and solemn days for sacrifice were removed by little and little, till at last they came to be kept at seasons quite the contrary to what was at first intended, but even at this time the people had no way of computing the solar year; only the priests could say the time, and they, at their pleasure, without giving any notice, slipped in the intercalary month, which they called Mercedonius. Numa was the first who put in this month, but his expedient was but a poor one and quite inadequate to correct all the errors that arose in the returns of the annual cycles, as we have shown in his life. Cæsar called in the best philosophers and mathematicians of his time to settle the point, and out of the systems he had before him formed a new and more exact method of correcting the calendar, which the Romans use to this day, and seem to succeed better than any nation in avoiding the errors occasioned by the inequality of the cycles. Yet even this gave offence to those who looked with an evil eye on his position, and felt oppressed by his power. Cicero the orator, when some one in his company chanced to say the next morning Lyra would rise, replied, "Yes, in accordance with the edict," as if even this were a matter of compulsion.

But that which brought upon him the most apparent and mortal hatred was his desire of being king; which gave the common people the first occasion to quarrel with him, and proved the most specious pretence to those who had been his secret enemies all along. Those who would have procured him that title gave it out that it was foretold in the Sibyls' books that the Romans should conquer the Parthians when they fought against them under the conduct of a king, but not before. And one day, as Cæsar was coming down from Alba to Rome, some were so bold as to salute him by the name of king; but he, finding the people disrelish it, seemed to resent it himself, and said his name was Cæsar, not king. Upon this there was a general silence, and he passed on looking not very well pleased or contented. Another time, when the senate had conferred on him some extravagant honours, he chanced to receive the message as he was sitting on the rostra, where, though the consuls and praetors themselves waited on him, attended by the whole body of the senate, he did not rise, but behaved himself to them as if they had been private men, and told them his honours wanted rather to be retrenched than increased. This treatment offended not only the senate, but the commonalty too, as if they thought the affront upon the senate equally reflected upon the whole republic; so that all who could decently leave him went off, looking much discomposed. Cæsar, perceiving the false step he had made, immediately retired home; and laying his throat bare, told his friends that he was ready to offer this to any one who would give the stroke. But afterwards he made the malady from which he suffered the excuse for his sitting, saying that those who are attacked by it lose their presence of mind if they talk much standing; that they presently grow giddy, fall into convulsions, and quite lose their reason. But this was not the reality, for he would willingly have stood up to the senate, had not Cornelius Balbus, one of his friends, or rather flatterers, hindered him. "Will you not remember," said he, "you are Cæsar, and claim the honour which is due to your merit?"

He gave a fresh occasion of resentment by his affront to the tribunes. The Lupercalia were then celebrated, a feast at the first institution belonging, as some writers say, to the shepherds, and having some connection with the Arcadian Lycæ. Many young noblemen and magistrates run up and down the city with their upper garments off, striking all they meet with thongs of hide, by way of sport; and many women, even of the highest rank, place themselves in the way, and hold out their hands to the lash, as boys in a school do to the master, out of a belief that it procures an easy labour to those who are with child, and makes those conceive who are barren. Cæsar, dressed in a triumphal robe, seated himself in a golden chair at the rostra to view this ceremony. Antony, as consul, was one of those who ran this course, and when he came into the forum, and the people made way for him, he went up and reached to Cæsar a diadem wreathed with laurel. Upon this there was a shout, but only a slight one, made by the few who were planted there for that purpose; but when Cæsar refused it, there was universal applause. Upon the second offer, very few, and upon the second refusal, all again applauded. Cæsar finding it would not take, rose up, and ordered the crown to be carried into the capitol. Cæsar's statues were afterwards found with royal diadems on their heads. Flavius and Marullus, two tribunes of the people, went presently and pulled them off, and having apprehended those who first saluted Cæsar as king committed them to prison. The people followed them with acclamations, and called them by the name of Brutus, because Brutus was the first who ended the succession of kings, and transferred the power which before was lodged in one man into the hands of the senate and people. Cæsar so far resented this, that he displaced Marullus and Flavius; and in urging his charges against them, at the same time ridiculed the people, by himself giving the men more than once the names of Bruti and Cumæi.

This made the multitude turn their thoughts to Marcus Brutus, who, by his father's side, was thought to be descended from that first Brutus, and by his mother's side from the Servilii, another noble family, being besides nephew and son-in-law to Cato. But the honours and favours he had received from Cæsar took off the edge from the desires he might himself have felt for overthrowing the new monarchy. For he had not only been pardoned himself after Pompey's defeat at Pharsalia, and had procured the same grace for many of his friends, but was one in whom Cæsar had a particular confidence. He had at that time the most honourable prætorship for the year, and was named for the consulship four years after, being preferred before Cassius, his competitor. Upon the question as to the choice, Cæsar, it is related, said that Cassius had the fairer pretensions, but that he could not pass by Brutus. Nor would he afterwards listen to some who spoke against Brutus, when the conspiracy against him was already afoot, but laying his hand on his body, said to the informers, "Brutus will wait for this skin of mine," intimating that he was worthy to bear rule on account of his virtue, but would not be base and ungrateful to gain it. Those who desired a change, and looked on him as the only, or at least the most proper, person to effect it, did not venture to speak with him; but in the night-time laid papers about his chair of state, where he used to sit and determine causes, with such sentences in them as, "You are asleep, Brutus," "You are no longer Brutus." Cassius, when he perceived his ambition a little raised upon this, was more instant than before to work him yet further, having himself a private grudge against Cæsar for some reasons that we have mentioned in the Life of Brutus. Nor was Cæsar without suspicions of him, and said once to his friends, "What do you think Cassius is aiming at? I don't like him, he looks so pale." And when it was told him that Antony and Dolabella were in a plot against him, he said he did not fear such fat, luxurious men, but rather the pale, lean fellows, meaning Cassius and Brutus.

Fate, however, is to all appearance more unavoidable than unexpected. For many strange prodigies and apparitions are said to have been observed shortly before this event. As to the lights in the heavens, the noises heard in the night, and the wild birds which perched in the forum, these are not perhaps worth taking notice of in so great a case as this. Strabo, the philosopher, tells us that a number of men were seen, looking as if they were heated through with fire, contending with each other; that a quantity of flame issued from the hand of a soldier's servant, so that they who saw it thought he must be burnt, but that after all he had no hurt. As Cæsar was sacrificing, the victim's heart was missing, a very bad omen, because no living creature can subsist without a heart. One finds it also related by many that a soothsayer bade him prepare for some great danger on the Ides of March. When this day was come, Cæsar, as he went to the senate, met this soothsayer, and said to him by way of raillery, "The Ides of March are come," who answered him calmly, "Yes, they are come, but they are not past." The day before his assassination he supped with Marcus Lepidus; and as he was signing some letters according to his custom, as he reclined at table, there arose a question what sort of death was the best. At which he immediately, before any one could speak, said, "A sudden one."

After this, as he was in bed with his wife, all the doors and windows of the house flew open together; he was startled at the noise, and the light which broke into the room, and sat up in his bed, where by the moonshine he perceived Calpurnia fast asleep, but heard her utter in her dream some indistinct words and inarticulate groans. She fancied at that time she was weeping over Cæsar, and holding him butchered in her arms. Others say this was not her dream, but that she dreamed that a pinnacle, which the senate, as Livy relates, had ordered to be raised on Cæsar's house by way of ornament and grandeur, was tumbling down, which was the occasion of her tears and ejaculations. When it was day, she begged of Cæsar, if it were possible, not to stir out, but to adjourn the senate to another time; and if he slighted her dreams, that she would be pleased to consult his fate by sacrifices and other kinds of divination. Nor was he himself without some suspicion and fears; for he never before discovered any womanish superstition in Calpurnia, whom he now saw in such great alarm. Upon the report which the priests made to him, that they had killed several sacrifices, and still found them inauspicious, he resolved to send Antony to dismiss the senate.

In this juncture, Decimus Brutus, surnamed Albinus, one whom Caesar had such confidence in that he made him his second heir, who nevertheless was engaged in the conspiracy with the other Brutus and Cassius, fearing lest if Cæsar should put off the senate to another day, the business might get wind, spoke scoffingly and in mockery of the diviners, and blamed Cæsar for giving the senate so fair an occasion of saying he had put a slight upon them, for that they were met upon his summons, and were ready to vote unanimously that he should be declared king of all the provinces out of Italy, and might wear a diadem in any other place but Italy, by sea or land. If any one should be sent to tell them they might break up for the present, and meet again when Calpurnia should chance to have better dreams, what would his enemies say? Or who would with any patience hear his friends, if they should presume to defend his government as not arbitrary and tyrannical? But if he was possessed so far as to think this day unfortunate, yet it were more decent to go himself to the senate, and to adjourn it in his own person. Brutus, as he spoke these words, took Cæsar by the hand, and conducted him forth. He was not gone far from the door, when a servant of some other person's made towards him, but not being able to come up to him, on account of the crowd of those who pressed about him, he made his way into the house, and committed himself to Calpurnia, begging of her to secure him till Cæsar returned, because he had matters of great importance to communicate to him.

Artemidorus, a Cnidian, a teacher of Greek logic, and by that means so far acquainted with Brutus and his friends as to have got into the secret, brought Cæsar in a small written memorial the heads of what he had to depose. He had observed that Cæsar, as he received any papers, presently gave them to the servants who attended on him; and therefore came as near to him as he could, and said, "Read this, Cæsar, alone, and quickly, for it contains matter of great importance which nearly concerns you." Cæsar received it, and tried several times to read it, but was still hindered by the crowd of those who came to speak to him. However, he kept it in his hand by itself till he came into the senate. Some say it was another who gave Cæsar this note, and that Artemidorus could not get to him, being all along kept off by the crowd.

All these things might happen by chance. But the place which was destined for the scene of this murder, in which the senate met that day, was the same in which Pompey's statue stood, and was one of the edifices which Pompey had raised and dedicated with his theatre to the use of the public, plainly showing that there was something of a supernatural influence which guided the action and ordered it to that particular place. Cassius, just before the act, is said to have looked towards Pompey's statue, and silently implored his assistance, though he had been inclined to the doctrines of Epicurus. But this occasion, and the instant danger, carried him away out of all his reasonings, and filled him for the time with a sort of inspiration. As for Antony, who was firm to Cæsar, and a strong man, Brutus Albinus kept him outside the house, and delayed him with a long conversation contrived on purpose. When Cæsar entered, the senate stood up to show their respect to him, and of Brutus's confederates, some came about his chair and stood behind it, others met him, pretending to add their petitions to those of Tillius Cimber, in behalf of his brother, who was in exile; and they followed him with their joint applications till he came to his seat. When he was sat down, he refused to comply with their requests,and upon their urging him further began to reproach them severely for their importunities, when Tillius, laying hold of his robe with both his hands, pulled it down from his neck, which was the signal for the assault. Casca gave him the first cut in the neck, which was not mortal nor dangerous, as coming from one who at the beginning of such a bold action was probably very much disturbed;

Cæsar immediately turned about, and laid his hand upon the dagger and kept hold of it. And both of them at the same time cried out, he that received the blow, in Latin, "Vile Casca, what does this mean?" and he that gave it, in Greek to his brother, "Brother, help! " Upon this first onset, those who were not privy to the design were astonished, and their horror and amazement at what they saw were so great that they durst not fly nor assist Cæsar, nor so much as speak a word. But those who came prepared for the business enclosed him on every side, with their naked daggers in their hands. Which way soever he turned he met with blows, and saw their swords levelled at his face and eyes, and was encompassed like a wild beast in the toils on every side. For it had been agreed they should each of them make a thrust at him, and flesh themselves with his blood; for which reason Brutus also gave him one stab in the groin. Some say that he fought and resisted all the rest, shifting his body to avoid the blows, and calling out for help, but that when he saw Brutus's sword drawn, he covered his face with his robe and submitted, letting himself fall, whether it were by chance or that he was pushed in that direction by his murderers, at the foot of the pedestal on which Pompey's statue stood, and which was thus wetted with his blood. So that Pompey himself seemed to have presided, as it were, over the revenge done upon his adversary, who lay here at his feet, and breathed out his soul through his multitude of wounds, for they say he received three-and-twenty. And the conspirators themselves were many of them wounded by each other, whilst they all levelled their blows at the same person.

When Cæsar was despatched, Brutus stood forth to give a reason for what they had done, but the senate would not hear him, but flew out of doors in all haste, and filled the people with so much alarm and distraction, that some shut up their houses, others left their counters and shops. All ran one way or the other, some to the place to see the sad spectacle, others back again after they had seen it. Antony and Lepidus, Cæsar's most faithful friends, got off privately, and hid themselves in some friends' houses. Brutus and his followers, being yet hot from the deed, marched in a body from the senate-house to the capitol with their drawn swords, not like persons who thought of escaping, but with an air of confidence and assurance, and as they went along, called to the people to resume their liberty, and invited the company of any more distinguished people whom they met. And some of these joined the procession and went up along with them, as if they also had been of the conspiracy, and could claim a share in the honour of what had been done. As, for example, Caius Octavius and Lentulus Spinther, who suffered afterwards for their vanity, being taken off by Antony and the young Cæsar, and lost the honour they desired, as well as their lives, which it cost them, since no one believed they had any share in the action. For neither did those who punished them profess to revenge the fact, but the ill-will. The day after, Brutus with the rest came down from the capitol and made a speech to the people, who listened without expressing either any pleasure or resentment, but showed by their silence that they pitied Cæsar and respected Brutus. The senate passed acts of oblivion for what was past, and took measures to reconcile all parties. They ordered that Cæsar should be worshipped as a divinity, and nothing, even of the slightest consequence, should be revoked which he had enacted during his government. At the same time they gave Brutus and his followers the command of provinces, and other considerable posts. So that all the people now thought things were well settled, and brought to the happiest adjustment.

But when Cæsar's will was opened, and it was found that he had left a considerable legacy to each one of the Roman citizens, and when his body was seen carried through the market-place all mangled with wounds, the multitude could no longer contain themselves within the bounds of tranquility and order, but heaped together a pile of benches, bars, and tables, which they placed the corpse on, and setting fire to it, burnt it on them. Then they took brands from the pile and ran some to fire the houses of the conspirators, others up and down the city, to find out the men and tear them to pieces, but met, however, with none of them, they having taken effectual care to secure themselves.

One Cinna, a friend of Cæsar's, chanced the night before to have an odd dream. He fancied that Cæsar invited him to supper, and that upon his refusal to go with him, Cæsar took him by the hand and forced him, though he hung back. Upon hearing the report that Cæsar's body was burning in the market-place, he got up and went thither, out of respect to his memory, though his dream gave him some ill apprehensions, and though he was suffering from a fever. One of the crowd who saw him there asked another who that was, and having learned his name, told it to his neighbour. It presently passed for a certainty that he was one of Cæsar's murderers, as, indeed, there was another Cinna, a conspirator, and they, taking this to be the man, immediately seized him and tore him limb from limb upon the spot.

Brutus and Cassius, frightened at this, within a few days retired out of the city. What they afterwards did and suffered, and how they died, is written in the Life of Brutus. Cæsar died in his fifty-sixth year, not having survived Pompey above four years. That empire and power which he had pursued through the whole course of his life with so much hazard, he did at last with much difficulty compass, but reaped no other fruits from it than the empty name and invidious glory. But the great genius which attended him through his lifetime even after his death remained as the avenger of his murder, pursuing through every sea and land all those who were concerned in it, and suffering none to escape, but reaching all who in any sort or kind were either actually engaged in the fact, or by their counsels any way promoted it.

The most remarkable of mere human coincidences was that which befell Cassius, who, when he was defeated at Philippi, killed himself with the same dagger which he had made use of against Cæsar. The most signal preternatural appearances were the great comet, which shone very bright for seven nights after Cæsar's death, and then disappeared, and the dimness of the sun, whose orb continued pale and dull for the whole of that year, never showing its ordinary radiance at its rising, and giving but a weak and feeble heat. The air consequently was damp and gross for want of stronger rays to open and rarefy it. The fruits, for that reason, never properly ripened, and began to wither and fall off for want of heat before they were fully formed. But above all, the phantom which appeared to Brutus showed the murder was not pleasing to the gods. The story of it is this.

Brutus, being to pass his army from Abydos to the continent on the other side, laid himself down one night, as he used to do, in his tent, and was not asleep, but thinking of his affairs, and what events he might expect. For he is related to have been the least inclined to sleep of all men who have commanded armies, and to have had the greatest natural capacity for continuing awake, and employing himself without need of rest. He thought he heard a noise at the door of his tent, and looking that way, by the light of his lamp, which was almost out, saw a terrible figure, like that of a man, but of unusual stature and severe countenance. He was somewhat frightened at first, but seeing it neither did nor spoke anything to him, only stood silently by his bedside, he asked who it was. The spectre answered him, "Thy evil genius, Brutus, thou shalt see me at Philippi." Brutus answered courageously, "Well, I shall see you," and immediately the appearance vanished. When the time was come, he drew up his army near Philippi against Antony and Cæsar, and in the first battle won the day, routed the enemy, and plundered Cæsar's camp. The night before the second battle, the same phantom appeared to him again, but spoke not a word. He presently understood his destiny was at hand, and exposed himself to all the danger of the battle. Yet he did not die in the fight, but seeing his men defeated, got up to the top of a rock, and there presenting his sword to his naked breast, and assisted, as they say, by a friend, who helped him to give the thrust, met his death.

PHOCION

DEMADES, the orator, when in the height of the power which he obtained at Athens, by advising the state in the interest of Antipater and the Macedonians, being necessitated to write and speak many things below the dignity, and contrary to the character, of the city, was wont to excuse himself by saying he steered only the shipwrecks of the commonwealth. This hardy saying of his might have some appearance of truth, if applied to Phocion's government. For Demades, indeed, was himself the mere wreck of his country, living and ruling so dissolutely, that Antipater took occasion to say of him, when he was now grown old, that he was like a sacrificed beast, all consumed except the tongue and the belly. But Phocion's was a real virtue, only overmatched in the unequal contest with an adverse time, and rendered, by the ill fortunes of Greece, inglorious and obscure. We must not, indeed, allow ourselves to concur with Sophocles in so far diminishing the force of virtue as to say that—

> "When fortune fails, the sense we had before
> Deserts us also, and is ours no more."

Yet thus much, indeed, must be allowed to happen in the conflicts between good men and ill fortune, that instead of due returns of honour and gratitude, obloquy and unjust surmises may often prevail, to weaken, in a considerable degree, the credit of their virtue.

It is commonly said that public bodies are most insulting and contumelious to a good man, when they are puffed up with prosperity and success. But the contrary often happens; afflictions and public calamities naturally embittering and souring the minds and tempers of men, and disposing them to such peevishness and irritability that hardly any word or sentiment of common vigour can be addressed to them, but they will be apt to take offence. He that remonstrates with them on their errors is presumed to be insulting over their misfortunes, and any free-spoken expostulation is construed into contempt. Honey itself is searching in sore and ulcerated parts; and the wisest and most judicious counsels prove provoking to distempered minds, unless offered with those soothing and compliant approaches which made the poet, for instance, characterise agreeable things in general by a word expressive of a grateful and easy touch, exciting nothing of offence or resistance. Inflamed eyes require a retreat into dusky places, amongst colours of the deepest shades, and are unable to endure the brilliancy of light. So fares it in the body politic, in times of distress and humiliation; a certain sensitiveness and soreness of humour prevail, with a weak incapacity of enduring any free and open advice, even when the necessity of affairs most requires such plain dealing, and when the consequences of any single error may be beyond retrieving. At such times the conduct of public affairs is on all hands most hazardous. Those who humour the people are swallowed up in the common ruin; those who endeavour to lead them aright perish the first in their attempt.

Astronomers tell us, the sun's motion is neither exactly parallel with that of the heavens in general, nor yet directly and diametrically opposite, but describing an oblique line, with insensible declination he steers his course in such a gentle, easy curve, as to dispense his light and influence, in his annual revolution, at several seasons in just proportions to the whole creation. So it happens in political affairs; if the motions of rulers be constantly opposite and cross to the tempers and inclinations of the people, they will be resented as arbitrary and harsh; as, on the other side, too much deference, or encouragement, as too often it has been, to popular faults and errors, is full of danger and ruinous consequences. But where concession is the response to willing obedience, and a statesman gratifies his people, that he may the more imperatively recall them to a sense of the common interest, then, indeed, human beings, who are ready enough to serve well and submit to much, if they are not always ordered about and roughly handled, like slaves, may be said to be guided and governed upon the method that leads to safety. Though it must be confessed it is a nice point, and extremely difficult, so to temper this lenity as to preserve the authority of the government. But if such a blessed mixture and temperament may be obtained, it seems to be of all concords and harmonies the most concordant and most harmonious. For thus we are taught even God governs the world, not by irresistible force, but persuasive argument and reason, controlling it into compliance with his eternal purposes.

Cato the younger is a similar instance. His manners were little agreeable or acceptable to the people, and he received very slender marks of their favour; witness his repulse when he sued for the consulship, which he lost, as Cicero says, for acting rather like a citizen in Plato's commonwealth, than among the dregs of Romulus's posterity, the same thing happening to him, in my opinion, as we observe in fruits ripe before their season, which we rather take pleasure in looking at and admiring than actually use; so much was his old-fashioned virtue out of the present mode, among the depraved customs which time and luxury had introduced, that it appeared, indeed, remarkable and wonderful, but was too great and too good to suit the present exigencies, being so out of all proportion to the times. Yet his circumstances were not altogether like Phocion's, who came to the helm when the ship of the state was just upon sinking. Cato's time was, indeed, stormy and tempestuous, yet so, as he was able to assist in managing the sails, and lend his helping hand to those who, which he was not allowed to do, commanded at the helm, others were to blame for the result; yet his courage and virtue made it in spite of all a hard task for fortune to ruin the commonwealth, and it was only with long time and effort and by slow degrees, when he himself had all but succeeded in averting it, that the catastrophe was at last effected.

Phocion and he may be well compared together, not for any mere general resemblances, as though we should say both were good men and great statesmen. For, assuredly, there is difference enough among virtues of the same denomination, as between the bravery of Alcibiades and that of Epaminondas, the prudence of Themistocles and that of Aristides, the justice of Numa and that of Agesilaus. But these men's virtue, even looking to the most minute points of difference, bear the same colour, stamp, and character impressed upon them, so as not to be distinguishable. The mixture is still made in the same exact proportions whether we look at the combination to be found in them, both of lenity on the one hand, with austerity on the other; their boldness upon some occasions, and caution on others; their extreme solicitude for the public, and perfect neglect of themselves; their fixed and immovable bent to all virtuous and honest actions, accompanied with an extreme tenderness and scrupulosity as to doing anything which might appear mean or unworthy; so that we should need a very nice and subtle logic of discrimination to detect and establish the distinctions between them.

As to Cato's extraction, it is confessed by all to have been illustrious, as will be said hereafter, nor was Phocion's, I feel assured, obscure or ignoble. For had he been the son of a turner, as Idomeneus reports, it had certainly not been forgotten to his disparagement by Glaucippus, the son of Hyperides, when heaping up a thousand spiteful things to say against him. Nor, indeed, had it been possible for him, in such circumstances, to have had such a liberal breeding and education in his youth, as to be first Plato's and afterwards Xenocrates's scholar in the Academy, and to have devoted himself from the first to the pursuit of the noblest studies and practices. His countenance was so composed that scarcely was he ever seen by any Athenian either laughing or in tears. He was rarely known, so Duris has recorded, to appear in the public baths, or was observed with his hand exposed outside his cloak, when he wore one. Abroad, and in the camp, he was so hardy in going always thin clad and barefoot, except in a time of excessive and intolerable cold, that the soldiers used to say in merriment, that it was like to be a hard winter when Phocion wore his coat.

Although he was most gentle and humane in his disposition, his aspect was stern and forbidding, so that he was seldom accosted alone by any who were not intimate with him. When Chares once made some remark on his frowning looks, and the Athenians laughed at the jest, "My sullenness," said Phocion, "never yet made any of you sad, but these men's jollities have given you sorrow enough." In like manner Phocion's language, also, was full of instruction, abounding in happy maxims and wise thoughts, but admitted no embellishment to its austere and commanding brevity. Zeno said a philosopher should never speak till his words had been steeped in meaning; and such, it may be said, were Phocion's, crowding the greatest amount of significance into the smallest allowance of space. And to this, probably, Polyeuctus, the Sphettian, referred, when he said that Demosthenes was, indeed, the best orator of his time, but Phocion the most powerful speaker. His oratory, like small coin of great value, was to be estimated, not by its bulk, but its intrinsic worth. He was once observed, it is said, when the theatre was filling with the audience, to walk musing alone behind the scenes, which one of his friends taking notice of said, "Phocion, you seem to be thoughtful." "Yes," replied he, "I am considering how I may shorten what I am going to say to the Athenians." Even Demosthenes himself, who used to despise the rest of the haranguers, when Phocion stood up, was wont to say quietly to those about him, "Here is the pruning-knife of my periods." This, however, might refer, perhaps, not so much to his eloquence as to the influence of his character, since not only a word, but even a nod from a person who is esteemed, is of more force than a thousand arguments or studied sentences from others.

In his youth he followed Chabrias, the general, from whom he gained many lessons in military knowledge, and in return did something to correct his unequal and capricious humour. For whereas at other times Chabrias was heavy and phlegmatic, in the heat of battle he used to be so fired and transported that he threw himself headlong into danger beyond the forwardest, which indeed, in the end, cost him his life in the island of Chios, he having pressed his own ship foremost to force a landing. But Phocion, being a man of temper as well as courage, had the dexterity at some times to rouse the general, when in his procrastinating mood, to action, and at others to moderate and cool the impetuousness of his unseasonable fury. Upon which account Chabrias, who was a good-natured, kindly-tempered man, loved him much, and procured him commands and opportunities for action, giving him means to make himself known in Greece, and using his assistance in all his affairs of moment. Particularly the sea-fight of Naxos added not a little to Phocion's reputation, when he had the left squadron committed to him by Chabrias, as in this quarter the battle was sharply contested, and was decided by a speedy victory. And this being the first prosperous sea-battle the city had engaged in with its own force since its captivity, Chabrias won great popularity by it, and Phocion, also, got the reputation of a good commander. The victory was gained at the time of the Great Mysteries, and Chabrias used to keep the commemoration of it by distributing wine among the Athenians, yearly, on the sixteenth day of Boëdromion.

After this, Chabrias sent Phocion to demand their quota of the charges of the war from the islanders, and offered him a guard of twenty ships. Phocion told him, if he intended him to go against them as enemies, that force was insignificant; if as to friends and allies, one vessel was sufficient. So he took his own single galley, and having visited the cities, and treated with the magistrates in an equitable and open manner, he brought back a number of ships, sent by the confederates to Athens, to convey the supplies. Neither did his friendship and attention close with Chabrias's life, but after his decease he carefully maintained it to all that were related to him, and chiefly to his son, Ctesippus, whom he laboured to bring to some good, and although he was a stupid and intractable young fellow, always endeavoured, so far as in him lay, to correct and cover his faults and follies. Once, however, when the youngster was very impertinent and troublesome to him in the camp, interrupting him with idle questions, and putting forward his opinions and suggestions of how the war should be conducted, he could not forbear exclaiming, "O Chabrias, Chabrias, how grateful I show myself for your friendship, in submitting to endure your son!"

Upon looking into public matters, and the way in which they were now conducted, he observed that the administration of affairs was cut and parcelled out, like so much land by allotment, between the military men and the public speakers, so that neither these nor those should interfere with the claims of the others. As the one were to address the assemblies, to draw up votes and prepare motions, men, for example, like Eubulus, Aristophon, Demosthenes, Lycurgus, and Hyperides, and were to push their interests here; so, in the meantime, Liopithes, Menestheus, Leosthenes, and Chares were to make their profit by war and in military commands. Phocion, on the other hand, was desirous to restore and carry out the old system, more complete in itself, and more harmonious and uniform, which prevailed in the times of Pericles, Aristides, and Solon; when statesmen showed themselves, to use Archilochus's words—

"Mars' and the Muses' friends alike designed,
To arts and arms indifferently inclined."

and the presiding goddess of his country was, he did not fail to see, the patroness and protectress of both civil and military wisdom. With these views, while his advice at home was always for peace and quietness, he nevertheless held the office of general more frequently than any of the statesmen, not only of his own times, but of those preceding, never, indeed, promoting or encouraging military expeditions, yet never, on the other hand, shunning or declining, when he was called upon by the public voice. Thus much is well known, that he was no less than forty-five several times chosen general, he being never on any one of those occasions present at the election, but having the command, in his absence, by common suffrage, conferred on him, and he sent for on purpose to undertake it. Insomuch that it amazed those who did not well consider to see the people always prefer Phocion, who was so far from humouring them or courting their favour, that he always thwarted and opposed them. But so it was, as great men and princes are said to call in their flatterers when dinner has been served, so the Athenians, upon slight occasions, entertained and diverted themselves with their spruce speakers and trim orators, but when it came to action, they were sober and considerate enough to single out the austerest and wisest for public employment, however much he might be opposed to their wishes and sentiments. This, indeed, he made no scruple to admit, when the oracle from Delphi was read, which informed them that the Athenians were all of one mind, a single dissentient only excepted, frankly coming forward and declaring that they need look no further; he was the man; there was no one but he who was dissatisfied with everything they did. And when once he gave his opinion to the people, and was met with the general approbation and applause of the assembly, turning to some of his friends, he asked them, "Have I inadvertently said something foolish?"

Upon occasion of a public festivity, being solicited for his contribution by the example of others, and the people pressing him much, he bade them apply themselves to the wealthy; for his part he should blush to make a present here, rather than a repayment there, turning and pointing to Callicles, the money-lender. Being still clamoured upon and importuned, he told them this tale. A certain cowardly fellow setting out for the wars, hearing the ravens croak in his passage, threw down his arms, resolving to wait. Presently he took them and ventured out again, but hearing the same music, once more made a stop. "For," said he, "you may croak till you are tired, but you shall make no dinner upon me."

The Athenians urging him at an unseasonable time to lead them out against the enemy, he peremptorily refused, and being upbraided by them with cowardice and pusillanimity, he told them, "Just now, do what you will, I shall not be brave; and do what I will, you will not be cowards. Nevertheless, we know well enough what we are." And when again, in a time of great danger, the people were very harsh upon him, demanding a strict account how the public money had been employed, and the like, he bade them, "First, good friends, make sure you are safe." After a war, during which they had been very tractable and timorous, when, upon peace being made, they began again to be confident and overbearing, and to cry out upon Phocion, as having lost them the honour of victory, to all their clamour he made only this answer, "My friends, you are fortunate in having a leader who knows you; otherwise, you had long since been undone."

Having a controversy with the Bœotians about boundaries, which he counselled them to decide by negotiation, they inclined to blows. "You had better," said he, "carry on the contest with the weapons in which you excel (your tongues), and not by war, in which you are inferior." Once when he was addressing them, and they would not hear him or let him go on, said he, "You may compel me to act against my wishes, but you shall never force me to speak against my judgment." Among the many public speakers who opposed him, Demosthenes, for example, once told him, "The Athenians, Phocion, will kill you some day when they once are in a rage." "And you," said he, "if they once are in their senses." Polyeuctus, the Sphettian, once on a hot day was urging war with Philip, and being a corpulent man, and out of breath and in a great heat with speaking, took numerous draughts of water as he went on. "Here, indeed," said Phocion, "is a fit man to lead us into a war! What think you he will do when he is carrying his corselet and his shield to meet the enemy, if even here, delivering a prepared speech to you, has almost killed him with exhaustion?" When Lycurgus in the assembly made many reflections on his past conduct, upbraiding him above all for having advised them to deliver up the ten citizens whom Alexander had demanded, he replied that he had been the author of much safe and wholesome counsel, which had not been followed.

There was a man called Archibiades, nicknamed the Lacedæmonian, who used to go about with a huge, over-grown beard, wearing an old threadbare cloak, and affecting a very stern countenance. Phocion once, when attacked in council by the rest, appealed to this man for his support and testimony. And when he got up and began to speak on the popular side, putting his hand to his beard, "O Archibiades," said he, "it is time you should shave." Aristogiton, a common accuser, was a terrible man of war within the assembly, always inflaming the people to battle, but when the muster-roll came to be produced, he appeared limping on a crutch, with a bandage on his leg; Phocion descried him afar off, coming in, and cried out to the clerk, "Put down Aristogiton, too, as lame and worthless."

So that it is a little wonderful, how a man so severe and harsh upon all occasions should, notwithstanding, obtain the name of the Good. Yet, though difficult, it is not, I suppose, impossible for men's tempers, any more than for wines, to be at the same time harsh and agreeable to the taste; just as on the other hand many that are sweet at the first taste are found, on further use, extremely disagreeable and unwholesome. Hyperides, we are told, once said to the people, "Do not ask yourselves, men of Athens, whether or not I am bitter, but whether or not I am paid for being so," as though a covetous purpose were the only thing that should make a harsh temper insupportable, and as if men might not even more justly render themselves obnoxious to popular dislike and censure, by using their power and influence in the indulgence of their own private passions of pride and jealousy, anger and animosity. Phocion never allowed himself from any feeling of personal hostility to do hurt to any fellow-citizen, nor, indeed, reputed any man his enemy, except so far as he could not but contend sharply with such as opposed the measures he urged for the public good; in which argument he was, indeed, a rude, obstinate, and uncompromising adversary. For his general conversation, it was easy, courteous, and obliging to all, to that point that he would befriend his very opponents in their distress, and espouse the cause of those who differed most from him, when they needed his patronage. His friends reproaching him for pleading in behalf of a man of indifferent character, he told them the innocent had no need of an advocate. Aristogiton, the sycophant, whom we mentioned before, having, after sentence passed upon him, sent earnestly to Phocion to speak with him in the prison, his friends dissuaded him from going; "Nay, by your favour," said he, "where should I rather choose to pay Aristogiton a visit ? "

As for the allies of the Athenians, and the islanders, whenever any admiral besides Phocion was sent, they treated him as an enemy suspect, barricaded their gates, blocked up their havens, brought in from the country their cattle, slaves, wives, and children, and put them in garrison; but upon Phocion's arrival, they went out to welcome him in their private boats and barges, with streamers and garlands, and received him at landing with every demonstration of joy and pleasure.

When King Philip was effecting his entry into Eubœa, and was bringing over troops from Macedonia, and making himself master of the cities, by means of the tyrants who ruled in them, Plutarch of Eretria sent to request aid of the Athenians for the relief of the island, which was in imminent danger of falling wholly into the hands of the Macedonians. Phocion was sent thither with a handful of men in comparison, in expectation that the Eubœans themselves would flock in and join him. But when he came, he found all things in confusion, the country all betrayed, the whole ground, as it were, undermined under his feet, by the secret pensioners of

King Philip, so that he was in the greatest risk imaginable. To secure himself as far as he could, he seized a small rising ground, which was divided from the level plains about Tamynæ by a deep watercourse, and here he enclosed and fortified the choicest of his army. As for the idle talkers and disorderly bad citizens who ran off from his camp and made their way back, he bade his officers not regard them, since here they would have been not only useless and ungovernable themselves, but an actual hindrance to the rest: and further, being conscious to themselves of the neglect of their duty, they would be less ready to misrepresent the action, or raise a cry against them at their return home. When the enemy drew nigh, he bade his men stand to their arms, until he had finished the sacrifice, in which he spent a considerable time, either by some difficulty of the thing itself, or on purpose to invite the enemy nearer. Plutarch, interpreting this tardiness as a failure in his courage, fell on alone with the mercenaries, which the cavalry perceiving, could not be contained, but issuing also out of the camp, confusedly and in disorder, spurred up to the enemy. The first who came up were defeated, the rest were put to the rout. Plutarch himself took to flight, and a body of the enemy advanced in the hope of carrying the camp, supposing themselves to have secured the victory. But by this time, the sacrifice being over, the Athenians within the camp came forward, and falling upon them put them to flight, and killed the greater number as they fled among the intrenchments, while Phocion, ordering his infantry to keep on the watch and rally those who came in from the previous flight, himself, with a body of his best men, engaged the enemy in a sharp and bloody fight, in which all of them behaved with signal courage and gallantry. Thallus, the son of Cineas, and Glaucus of Polymedes, who fought near the general, gained the honours of the day. Cleophanes, also, did good service in the battle. Recovering the cavalry from its defeat, and with his shouts and encouragement bringing them up to succour the general, who was in danger, he confirmed the victory obtained by the infantry. Phocion now expelled Plutarch from Eretria, and possessed himself of the very important fort of Zaretra, situated where the island is pinched in, as it were, by the seas on each side, and its breadth most reduced to a narrow girth. He released all the Greeks whom he took, out of fear of the public speakers at Athens, thinking they might very likely persuade the people in their anger into committing some act of cruelty.

This affair thus despatched and settled, Phocion set sail homewards, and the allies had soon as good reason to regret the loss of his just and humane dealing as the Athenians that of his experience and courage. Molossus, the commander who took his place, had no better success than to fall alive into the enemy's hands.

Philip, full of great thoughts and designs, now advanced with all his forces into the Hellespont, to seize the Chersonesus and Perinthus, and after them Byzantium. The Athenians raised a force to relieve them, but the popular leaders made it their business to prefer Chares to be general, who, sailing thither, effected nothing worthy of the means placed in his hands. The cities were afraid, and would not receive his ships into their harbours, so that he did nothing but wander about, raising money from their friends, and despised by their enemies. When the people, chafed by the orators, were extremely indignant, and repented having ever sent any help to the Byzantines, Phocion rose and told them they ought not to be angry with the allies for distrusting, but with their generals for being distrusted. "They make you suspected," he said, "even by those who cannot possibly subsist without your succour." The assembly being moved with this speech of his, changed their minds on the sudden, and commanded him immediately to raise another force, and go himself to assist their confederates in the Hellespont; an appointment which, in effect, contributed more than anything to the relief of Byzantium.

For Phocion's name was already honourably known; and an old acquaintance of his, who had been his fellow-student in the Academy, Leon, a man of high renown for virtue among the Byzantines, having vouched for Phocion to the city, they opened their gates to receive him, not permitting him, though he desired it, to encamp without the walls, but entertained him and all the Athenians with perfect reliance, while they, to requite their confidence, behaved among their new hosts soberly and inoffensively, and exerted themselves on all occasions with the greatest zeal and resolution for their defence. Thus King Philip was driven out of the Hellespont, and was despised to boot, whom, till now, it had been thought impossible to match, or even to oppose. Phocion also took some of his ships, and recaptured some of the places he had garrisoned, making besides several inroads into the country, which he plundered and overran, until he received a wound from some of the enemy who came to the defence, and, thereupon, sailed away home.

The Megarians at this time privately praying aid of the Athenians, Phocion, fearing lest the Bœotians should hear of it, and anticipate them, called an assembly at sunrise, and brought forward the petition of the Megarians, and immediately after the vote had been put, and carried in their favour, he sounded the trumpet, and led the Athenians straight from the assembly, to arm and put themselves in posture. The Megarians received them joyfully, and he proceeded to fortify Nisæa, and built two new long walls from the city to the arsenal, and so joined it to the sea, so that having now little reason to regard the enemies on the land side, it placed its dependence entirely on the Athenians.

When final hostilities with Philip were now certain, and in Phocion's absence other generals had been nominated, he, on his arrival from the islands, dealt earnestly with the Athenians, that since Philip showed peaceable inclinations towards them, and greatly apprehended the danger, they would consent to a treaty. Being contradicted in this by one of the ordinary frequenters of the courts of justice, a common accuser, who asked him if he durst presume to persuade the Athenians to peace, now their arms were in their hands, "Yes," said he, "though I know that if there be war, I shall be in office over you, and if peace, you over me." But when he could not prevail, and Demosthenes's opinion carried it, advising them to make war as far off from home as possible, and fight the battle out of Attica, "Good friends," said Phocion, "let us not ask where we shall fight, but how we may conquer in the war. That will be the way to keep it at a distance. If we are beaten, it will be quickly at our doors." After the defeat, when the clamourers and incendiaries in the town would have brought up Charidemus to the hustings, to be nominated to the command, the best of the citizens were in a panic, and supporting themselves with the aid of the council of the Areopagus, with entreaties and tears, hardly prevailed upon the people to have Phocion entrusted with the care of the city. He was of opinion, in general, that the fair terms to be expected from Philip should be accepted, yet after Demades had made a motion that the city should receive the common conditions of peace in concurrence with the rest of the states of Greece, he opposed it, till it were known what the particulars were which Philip demanded. He was overborne in this advice, under the pressure of the time, but almost immediately after the Athenians repented it, when they understood that by these articles they were obliged to furnish Philip both with horse and shipping. "It was the fear of this," said Phocion, "that occasioned my opposition. But since the thing is done, let us make the best of it, and not be discouraged. Our forefathers were sometimes in command, and sometimes under it; and by doing their duty, whether as rulers or as subjects, saved their own country and the rest of Greece."

Upon the news of Philip's death, he opposed himself to any public demonstrations of joy and jubilee, saying it would be ignoble to show malice upon such an occasion, and that the army that had fought them at Chæronea was only diminished by a single man.

When Demosthenes made his invectives against Alexander, now on his way to attack Thebes, he repeated those verses of Homer:—

> "Unwise one, wherefore to a second stroke
> His anger be foolhardy to provoke?"

and asked, "Why stimulate his already eager passion for glory? Why take pains to expose the city to the terrible conflagration now so near? We, who accepted office to save our fellow-citizens, will not, however they desire it, be consenting to their destruction."

After Thebes was lost, and Alexander had demanded Demosthenes, Lycurgus, Hyperides, and Charidemus to be delivered up, the whole assembly turning their eyes to him, and calling on him by name to deliver his opinion, at last he rose up, and showing them one of his most intimate friends, whom he loved and confided in above all others, told them, "You have brought things amongst you to that pass, that for my part, should he demand this my friend Nicocles, I would not refuse to give him up. For as for myself, to have it in my power to sacrifice my own life and fortune for the common safety, I should think the greatest of good fortune. Truly," he added, "it pierces my heart to see those who are fled hither for succour from the desolation of Thebes. Yet it is enough for Greece to have Thebes to deplore. It will be more for the interest of all that we should deprecate the conqueror's anger, and intercede for both, than run the hazard of another battle."

When this was decreed by the people, Alexander is said to have rejected their first address when it was presented, throwing it from him scornfully, and turning his back upon the deputation, who left him in affright. But the second, which was presented by Phocion, he received, understanding from the older Macedonians how much Philip had admired and esteemed him. And he not only gave him audience and listened to his memorial and petition, but also permitted him to advise him, which he did to this effect, that if his designs were for quietness, he should make peace at once; if glory were his aim, he should make war, not upon Greece, but on the barbarians. With various counsels and suggestions, happily designed to meet the genius and feelings of Alexander, he so won upon him, and softened his temper, that he bade the Athenians not forget their position, as if anything went wrong with him, the supremacy belonged to them. And to Phocion himself, whom he adopted as his friend and guest, he showed a respect, and admitted him to distinctions, which few of those who were continually near his person ever received. Duris, at any rate, tells us, that when he became great, and had conquered Darius, in the heading of all his letters he left off the word *Greeting*, except in those he wrote to Phocion. To him, and to Antipater alone, he condescended to use it. This also is stated by Chares.

As for his munificence to him, it is well known he sent him a present at one time of one hundred talents; and this being brought to Athens, Phocion asked of the bearers how it came to pass that among all the Athenians he alone should be the object of this bounty. Being told that Alexander esteemed him alone a person of honour and worth, "Let him, then," said he, "permit me to continue so and be still so reputed." Following him to his house, and observing his simple and plain way of living, his wife employed in kneading bread with her own hands, himself drawing water to wash his feet, they pressed him to accept it, with some indignation, being ashamed, as they said, that Alexander's friend should live so poorly and pitifully. So Phocion, pointing out to them a poor old fellow, in a dirty worn-out coat, passing by, asked them if they thought him in worse condition than this man. They bade him not mention such a comparison. "Yet," said Phocion, "he, with less to live upon than I, finds it sufficient, and in brief," he continued, "if I do not use this money, what good is there in my having it; and if I do use it, I shall procure an ill name, both for myself and for Alexander, among my countrymen." So the treasure went back again from Athens, to prove to Greece, by a signal example, that he who could afford to give so magnificent a present, was yet not so rich as he who could afford to refuse it. And when Alexander was displeased, and wrote back to him to say that he could not esteem those his friends who would not be obliged by him, not even would this induce Phocion to accept the money, but he begged leave to intercede with him in behalf of Echecratides, the sophist, and Athenodorus, the Imbrian, as also for Demaratus and Sparton, two Rhodians, who had been arrested upon some charges, and were in custody at Sardis. This was instantly granted by Alexander, and they were set at liberty. Afterwards, when sending Craterus into Macedonia, he commanded him to make him an offer of four cities in Asia, Cius, Gergithus, Mylasa, and Elæa, any one of which, at his choice, should be delivered to him; insisting yet more positively with him, and declaring he should resent it, should he continue obstinate in his refusal. But Phocion was not to be prevailed with at all, and shortly after, Alexander died.

Phocion's house is shown to this day in Melita, ornamented with small plates of copper, but otherwise plain and homely. Concerning his wives, of the first of them there is little said, except that she was sister of Cephisodotus, the statuary. The other was a matron of no less reputation for her virtues and simple living among the Athenians than Phocion was for his probity. It happened once when the people were entertained with a new tragedy, that the actor, just as he was to enter the stage to perform the part of a queen, demanded to have a number of attendants sumptuously dressed, to follow in his train, and on their not being provided, was sullen and refused to act, keeping the audience waiting, till at last Melanthius, who had to furnish the chorus, pushed him on the stage, crying out, "What, don't you know that Phocion's wife is never attended by more than a single waiting-woman, but you must needs be grand, and fill our women's heads with vanity?" This speech of his, spoken loud enough to be heard, was received with great applause, and clapped all round the theatre. She herself, when once entertaining a visitor out of Ionia, who showed her all her rich ornaments, made of gold and set with jewels, her wreaths, necklaces, and the like, "For my part," said she, "all my ornament is my husband, Phocion, now for the twentieth year in office as general at Athens."

He had a son named Phocus, who wished to take part in the games at the great feast of Minerva. He permitted him so to do, in the contest of leaping, not with any view to the victory, but in the hope that the training and discipline for it would make him a better man, the youth being in a general way a lover of drinking, and ill-regulated in his habits. On his having succeeded in the sports, many were eager for the honour of his company at banquets in celebration of the victory. Phocion declined all these invitations but one, and when he came to this entertainment and saw the costly preparations, even the water brought to wash the guests' feet being mingled with wine and spices, he reprimanded his son, asking him why he would so far permit his friend to sully the honour of his victory. And in the hope of wholly weaning the young man from such habits and company, he sent him to Lacedæmon, and placed him among the youths then under the course of the Spartan discipline. This the Athenians took offence at, as though he slighted and contemned the education at home; and Demades twitted him with it publicly. "Suppose, Phocion, you and I advise the Athenians to adopt the Spartan constitution. If you like, I am ready to introduce a bill to that effect, and to speak in its favour." "Indeed," said Phocion, "you, with that strong scent of perfumes about you, and with that mantle on your shoulders, are just the very man to speak in honour of Lycurgus, and recommend the Spartan table."

When Alexander wrote to demand a supply of galleys, and the public speakers objected to sending them, Phocion, on the council requesting his opinion, told them freely, "Sirs, I would either have you victorious yourselves, or friends of those who are so." He took up Pytheas, who about this time first began to address the assembly, and already showed himself a confident, talking fellow, by saying that a young slave whom the people had but bought yesterday ought to have the manners to hold his tongue. And when Harpalus, who had fled from Alexander out of Asia, carrying off a large sum of money, came to Attica, and there was a perfect race among the ordinary public men of the assembly who should be the first to take his pay, he distributed amongst these some trifling sums by way of a bait and provocative, but to Phocion he made an offer of no less than seven hundred talents and all manner of other advantages he pleased to demand; with the compliment that he would entirely commit himself and all his affairs to his disposal. Phocion answered sharply, Harpalus should repent of it, if he did not quickly leave off corrupting and debauching the city, which for the time silenced him, and checked his proceedings. But afterwards, when the Athenians were deliberating in council about him, he found those that had received money from him to be his greatest enemies, urging and aggravating matters against him, to prevent themselves being discovered, whereas Phocion, who had never touched his pay, now, so far as the public interest would admit of it, showed some regard to his particular security. This encouraged him once more to try his inclinations, and upon further survey finding that he himself was a fortress, inaccessible on every quarter to the approaches of corruption, he professed a particular friendship to Phocion's son-in-law, Charicles. And admitting him into his confidence in all his affairs, and continually requesting his assistance, he brought him under some suspicion. Upon the occasion, for example, of the death of Pythonice, who was Harpalus's mistress, for whom he had a great fondness, and had a child by her, he resolved to build her a sumptuous monument, and committed the care of it to his friend Charicles. This commission, disreputable enough in itself, was yet further disparaged by the figure the piece of workmanship made after it was finished. It is yet to be seen in the Hermenum, as you go from Athens to Eleusis, with nothing in its appearance answerable to the sum of thirty talents, with which Charicles is said to have charged Harpalus for its erection. After Harpalus's own decease, his daughter was educated by Phocion and Charicles with great care. But when Charicles was called to account for his dealings with Harpalus, and entreated his-father-in-law's protection, begging that he would appear for him in the court, Phocion refused, telling him, "I did not choose you for my son-in-law for any but honourable purposes."

Asclepiades, the son of Hipparchus, brought the first tidings of Alexander's death to Athens, which Demades told them was not to be credited; for were it true, the whole world would ere this have stunk with the dead body. But Phocion, seeing the people eager for an instant revolution, did his best to quiet and repress them. And when numbers of them rushed up to the hustings to speak, and cried out that the news was true, and Alexander was dead, "If he is dead to-day," said, "he will be so to-morrow and the day after to-morrow equally. So that there is no need to take counsel hastily or before it is safe."

When Leosthenes now had embarked the city in the Lamian war, greatly against Phocion's wishes, to raise a laugh against Phocion, he asked him scoffingly, what the state had been benefited by his having now so many years been general. "It is not a little," said Phocion, "that the citizens have been buried in their own sepulchres." And when Leosthenes continued to speak boldly and boastfully in the assembly, "Young man," he said, "your speeches are like cypress-trees, stately and tall, and no fruit to come of them." When he was then attacked by Hyperides, who asked him when the time would come that he would advise the Athenians to make war, "As soon," said he, "as I find the young men keep their ranks, the rich men contribute their money, and the orators leave off robbing the treasury." Afterwards, when many admired the forces raised, and the preparations for war that were made by Leosthenes, they asked Phocion how he approved of the new levies. "Very well," said he, "for the short course; but what I fear is the long race. Since, however late the war may last, the city has neither money, ships, nor soldiers, but these." The event justified his prognostics. At first all things appeared fair and promising. Leosthenes gained great reputation by worsting the Bœotians in battle, and driving Antipater within the walls of Lamia, and the citizens were so transported with the first successes, that they kept solemn festivities for them, and offered public sacrifices to the gods. So that some, thinking Phocion must now be convinced of his error, asked him whether he would not willingly have been author of these successful actions. "Yes," said he, "most gladly, but also of the former counsel." And when one express after another came from the camp, confirming and magnifying the victories, "When," said he, "will the end of them come?"

Leosthenes, soon after, was killed, and now those who feared lest if Phocion obtained the command he would put an end to the war, arranged with an obscure person in the assembly, who should stand up and profess himself to be a friend and old confidant of Phocion's, and persuade the people to spare him at this time, and reserve him (with whom none could compare) for a more pressing occasion, and now to give Antiphilus the command of the army. This pleased the generality, but Phocion made it appear he was so far from having any friendship with him of old standing, that he had not so much as the least familiarity with him; "Yet now, sir," says he, "give me leave to put you down among the number of my friends and well-wishers, as you have given a piece of advice so much to my advantage."

When the people were eager to make an expedition against the Bœotians, he at first opposed it; and on his friends telling him the people would kill him for always running counter to them, "That will be unjust of them," he said, "if I give them honest advice, if not, it will be just of them." But when he found them persisting and shouting to him to lead them out, he commanded the crier to make proclamation, that all the Athenians under sixty should instantly provide themselves with five days' provision, and follow him from the assembly. This caused a great tumult. Those in years were startled, and clamoured against the order; he demanded wherein he injured them, "For I," says he, "am now fourscore, and am ready to lead you." This succeeded in pacifying them for the present.

But when Micion, with a large force of Macedonians and mercenaries, began to pillage the sea-coast, having made a descent upon Rhamnus, and overrun the neighbouring country, Phocion led out the Athenians to attack him. And when sundry private persons came, intermeddling with his dispositions, and telling him that he ought to occupy such or such a hill. detach the cavalry in this or that direction, engage the enemy on this point or that, "Oh Hercules," said he, "how many generals have we here, and how few soldiers!" Afterwards, having formed the battle, one who wished to show his bravery advanced out of his post before the rest, but on the enemy's approaching, lost heart, and retired back into his rank. "Young man," said Phocion, "are you not ashamed twice in one day to desert your station, first that on which I had placed you, and secondly that on which you had placed yourself?" However, he entirely routed the enemy, killing Micion and many more on the spot. The Grecian army, also, in Thessaly. after Leonnatus and the Macedonians who came with him out of Asia had arrived and joined Antipater, fought and beat them in a battle. Leonnatus was killed in the fight, Antiphilus commanding the foot, and Menon, the Thessalian, the horse.

But not long after, Craterus crossed from Asia with numerous forces; a pitched battle was fought at Cranon; the Greeks were beaten; though not, indeed, in a signal defeat, nor with any great loss of men. But what with their want of obedience to their commanders, who were young and over-indulgent with them, and what with Antipater's tampering and treating with their separate cities, one by one, the end of it was that the army was dissolved, and the Greeks shamefully surrendered the liberty of their country.

Upon the news of Antipater's now advancing at once against Athens, with all his force, Demosthenes and Hyperides deserted the city, and Demades, who was altogether insolvent for any part of the fines that had been laid upon him by the city, for he had been condemned no less than seven times for introducing bills contrary to the laws, and who had been disfranchised, and was no longer competent to vote in the assembly, laid hold of this season of impunity to bring in a bill for sending ambassadors with plenipotentiary power to Antipater, to treat about a peace. But the people distrusted him, and called upon Phocion to give his opinion, as the person they only and entirely confided in. He told them, "If my former counsels had been prevalent with you, we had not been reduced to deliberate on the question at all." However, the vote passed; and a decree was made, and he with others deputed to go to Antipater, who lay now encamped in the Theban territories, but intended to dislodge immediately, and pass into

Attica. Phocion's first request was, that he would make the treaty without moving his camp. And when Craterus declared that it was not fair to ask them to be burdensome to the country of their friends and allies by their stay, when they might rather use that of their enemies for provisions and the support of their army, Antipater, taking him by the hand, said, "We must grant this favour to Phocion." For the rest he bade them return to their principals, and acquaint them that he could only offer them the same terms, namely, to surrender at discretion, which Leosthenes had offered to him when he was shut up in Lamia.

When Phocion had returned to the city and acquainted them with this answer, they made a virtue of necessity and complied, since it would be no better. So Phocion returned to Thebes with the other ambassadors, and among the rest Xenocrates, the philosopher, the reputation of whose virtue and wisdom was so great and famous everywhere, that they conceived there could not be any pride, cruelty, or anger arising in the heart of man, which would not at the mere sight of him be subdued into something of reverence and admiration. But the result, as it happened, was the very opposite, Antipater showed such a want of feeling, and such a dislike of goodness. He saluted every one else, but would not so much as notice Xenocrates. Xenocrates, they tell us, observed upon it, that Antipater, when meditating such cruelty to Athens, did well to be ashamed of seeing him. When he began to speak, he would not hear him, but broke in and rudely interrupted him, until at last he was obliged to be silent. But when Phocion had declared the purport of their embassy, he replied shortly, that he would make peace with the Athenians on these conditions, and no others; that Demosthenes and Hyperides should be delivered up to him; that they should retain their ancient form of government, the franchise being determined by a property qualification; that they should receive a garrison into Munychia, and pay a certain sum of the cost of the war. As things stood, these terms were judged tolerable by the rest of the ambassadors; Xenocrates only said, that if Antipater considered the Athenians slaves, he was treating them fairly; but if free, severely. Phocion pressed him only to spare them the garrison, and used many arguments and entreaties. Antipater replied, "Phocion, we are ready to do you any favour, which will not bring ruin both on ourselves and on you." Others report it differently; that Antipater asked Phocion, supposing he remitted the garrison to the Athenians, would he, Phocion, stand surety for the city's observing the terms and attempting no revolution? And when he hesitated, and did not at once reply, Callimedon, the Carabus, a hot partisan and professed enemy of free states, cried out, "And if he should talk so idly, Antipater, will you be so much abused as to believe him and not carry out your own purpose?" So the Athenians received the garrison, and Menyllus for the governor, a fair-dealing man, and one of Phocion's acquaintance.

But the proceeding seemed sufficiently imperious and arbitrary, indeed rather a spiteful and insulting ostentation of power, than that the possession of the fortress would be of any great importance. The resentment felt upon it was heightened by the time it happened in, for the garrison was brought in on the twentieth of the month of Boëdromion, just at the time of the great festival, when they carry forth Iacchus with solemn pomp from the city to Eleusis; so that the solemnity being disturbed, many began to call to mind instances, both ancient and modern, of divine interventions and intimations. For in old time, upon the occasions of their happiest successes, the presence of the shapes and voices of the mystic ceremonies had been vouchsafed to them, striking terror and amazement into their enemies; but now, at the very season of their celebration, the gods themselves stood witnesses of the saddest oppressions of Greece, the most holy time being profaned, and their greatest jubilee made the unlucky date of their most extreme calamity. Not many years before, they had a warning from the oracle at Dodona, that they should carefully guard the summits of Diana, lest haply strangers should seize them. And about this very time, when they dyed the ribbons and garlands with which they adorn the couches and cars of the procession, instead of a purple, they received only a faint yellow colour; and to make the omen yet greater, all the things that were dyed for common use, took the natural colour. While a candidate for initiation was washing a young pig in the haven of Cantharus, a shark seized him, bit off his lower parts up to the belly, and devoured them, by which the god gave them manifestly to understand, that having lost the lower town and sea-coast, they should keep only the upper city.

Menyllus was sufficient security that the garrison should behave itself inoffensively. But those who were now excluded from the franchise by property amounted to more than twelve thousand; so that both those that remained in the city thought themselves oppressed and shamefully used, and those who on this account left their homes and went away into Thrace, where Antipater offered them a town and some territory to inhabit, regarded themselves only as a colony of slaves and exiles. And when to this was added the deaths of Demosthenes at Calauria, and of Hyperides at Clonæ, as we have elsewhere related, the citizens began to think with regret of Philip and Alexander, and almost to wish the return of those times. And as, after Antigonus was slain, when those that had taken him off were afflicting and oppressing the people, a countryman in Phrygia, digging in the fields, was asked what he was doing, "I am," said he, fetching a deep sigh, "searching for Antigonus;" so said many that remembered those days, and the contests they had with those kings, whose anger, however great, was yet generous and placable; whereas Antipater, with the counterfeit humility of appearing like a private man, in the meanness of his dress and his homely fare, merely belied his real love of that arbitrary power, which he exercised, as a cruel master and despot, to distress those under his command. Yet Phocion had interest with him to recall many from banishment by his intercession, and prevailed also for those who were driven out, that they might not, like others, be hurried beyond Tænarus, and the mountains of Ceraunia, but remain in Greece, and plant themselves in Peloponnesus, of which number was Agnonides, the sycophant. He was no less studious to manage the affairs within the city with equity and moderation, preferring constantly those that were men of worth and good education to the magistracies, and recommending the busy and turbulent talkers, to whom it was a mortal blow to be excluded from office and public debating, to learn to stay at home, and be content to till their land. And observing that Xenocrates paid his alien-tax as a foreigner, he offered him the freedom of the city, which he refused, saying he could not accept a franchise which he had been sent as an ambassador to deprecate.

Menyllus wished to give Phocion a considerable present of money, who, thanking him, said, neither was Menyllus greater than Alexander, nor his own occasions more urgent to receive it now, than when he refused it from him. And on his pressing him to permit his son Phocus to receive it, he replied, "If my son returns to a right mind, his patrimony is sufficient; if not, all supplies will be insufficient." But to Antipater he answered more sharply, who would have him engaged in something dishonourable. "Antipater," said he, "cannot have me both as his friend and his flatterer." And, indeed, Antipater was wont to say he had two friends at Athens, Phocion and Demades; the one would never suffer him to gratify him at all, the other would never be satisfied. Phocion might well think that poverty a virtue, in which, after having so often been general of the Athenians, and admitted to the friendship of potentates and princes, he had now grown old. Demades, meantime, delighted in lavishing his wealth even in positive transgressions of the law. For there having been an order that no foreigner should be hired to dance in any chorus on the penalty of a fine of one thousand drachmas on the exhibitor, he had the vanity to exhibit an entire chorus of a hundred foreigners, and paid down the penalty of a thousand drachmas a head upon the stage itself. Marrying his son Demeas, he told him with the like vanity, "My son, when I married your mother, it was done so privately it was not known to the next neighbours, but kings and princes give presents at your nuptials."

The garrison in Munychia continued to be felt as a great grievance, and the Athenians did not cease to be importunate upon Phocion, to prevail with Antipater for its removal; but whether he despaired of effecting it, or perhaps observed the people to be more orderly, and public matters more reasonably conducted by the awe that was thus created, he constantly declined the office, and contented himself with obtaining from Antipater the postponement for the present of the payment of the sum of money in which the city was fined. So the people, leaving him off, applied themselves to Demades, who readily undertook the employment, and took along with him his son also into Macedonia; and some superior power, as it seems, so ordering it, he came just at that nick of time when Antipater was already seized with his sickness, and Cassander, taking upon himself the command, had found a letter of Demades's, formerly written by him to Antigonus in Asia, recommending him to come and possess himself of the empire of Greece and Macedon, now hanging, he said (a scoff at Antipater), "by an old and rotten thread." So when Cassander saw him come, he seized him; and first brought out the son, and killed him so close before his face, that the blood ran all over his clothes and person, and then, after bitterly taunting and upbraiding him with his ingratitude and treachery, despatched him himself.

Antipater being dead, after nominating Polysperchon general-in-chief and Cassander commander of the cavalry, Cassander at once set up for himself, and immediately despatched Nicanor to Menyllus, to succeed him in the command of the garrison, commanding him to possess himself of Munychia before the news of Antipater's death should be heard; which being done, and some days after the Athenians hearing the report of it, Phocion was taxed as privy to it before, and censured heavily for dissembling it, out of friendship for Nicanor. But he slighted their talk, and making it his duty to visit and confer continually with Nicanor, he succeeded in procuring his good-will and kindness for the Athenians, and induced him even to put himself to trouble and expense to seek popularity with them, by undertaking the office of presiding at the games.

In the meantime Polysperchon, who was entrusted with the charge of the king, to countermine Cassander, sent a letter to the city, declaring, in the name of the king, that he restored them their democracy, and that the whole Athenian people were at liberty to conduct their commonwealth according to their ancient customs and constitutions. The object of these pretences was merely the overthrow of Phocion's influence, as the event manifested. For Polysperchon's design being to possess himself of the city, he despaired altogether of bringing it to pass whilst Phocion retained his credit; and the most certain way to ruin him would be again to fill the city with a crowd of disfranchised citizens, and let loose the tongues of the demagogues and common accusers.

With this prospect the Athenians were all in excitement, and Nicanor, wishing to confer with them on the subject, at a meeting of the Council in Piræus, came himself, trusting for the safety of his person to Phocion. And when Dercyllus, who commanded the guard there, made an attempt to seize him, upon notice of it beforehand, he made his escape, and there was little doubt he would now lose no time in righting himself upon the city for the affront; and when Phocion was found fault with for letting him get off and not securing him, he defended himself by saying that he had no mistrust of Nicanor, nor the least reason to expect any mischief from him, but should it prove otherwise, for his part he would have them all know, he would rather receive than do the wrong. And so far as he spoke for himself alone, the answer was honourable and high-minded enough, but he who hazards his country's safety, and that, too, when he is her magistrate and chief commander, can scarcely be acquitted, I fear, of transgressing a higher and more sacred obligation of justice, which he owed to his fellow-citizens. For it will not even do to say that he dreaded the involving the city in war, by seizing Nicanor, and hoped by professions of confidence and just-dealing to retain him in the observance of the like; but it was, indeed, his credulity and confidence in him, and an overweening opinion of his sincerity, that imposed upon him. So that notwithstanding the sundry intimations he had of his making preparations to attack Piræus, sending soldiers over into Salamis, and tampering with and endeavouring to corrupt various residents in Piræus, he would, notwithstanding all this evidence, never be persuaded to believe it. And even when Philomedes of Lampra had got a decree passed, that all the Athenians should stand to their arms, and be ready to follow Phocion their general, he yet sat still and did nothing, until Nicanor actually led his troops out from Munychia, and drew trenches about Piræus; upon which, when Phocion at last would have let out the Athenians, they cried out against him, and slighted his orders.

Alexander, the son of Polysperchon, was at hand with a considerable force, and professed to come to give them succour against Nicanor, but intended nothing less, if possible, than to surprise the city, whilst they were in tumult and divided among themselves. For all that had previously been expelled from the city, now coming back with him, made their way into it, and were joined by a mixed multitude of foreigners and disfranchised persons, and of these a motley and irregular public assembly came together, in which they presently divested Phocion of all power, and chose other generals; and if by chance Alexander had not been spied from the walls, alone in close conference with Nicanor, and had not this, which was often repeated, given the Athenians cause of suspicion, the city had not escaped the snare. The orator Agnonides, however, at once fell foul upon

Phocion, and impeached him of treason; Callimedon and Charicles, fearing the worst, consulted their own security by flying from the city. Phocion, with a few of his friends that stayed with him went over to Polysperchon, and out of respect for him, Solon of Platæa, and Dinarchus of Corinth, who were reputed friends and confidants of Polysperchon, accompanied him. But on account of Dinarchus falling ill, they remained several days in Elatea, during which time, upon the persuasion of Agnonides and on the motion of Archestratus, a decree passed that the people should send delegates thither to accuse Phocion. So both parties reached Polysperchon at the same time, who was going through the country with the king, and was then at a small village of Phocis, Pharygæ, under the mountain now called Galate, but then Acrurium.

There Polysperchon, having set up the golden canopy, and seated the king and his company under it, ordered Dinarchus at once to be taken, and tortured, and put to death; and that done, gave audience to the Athenians, who filled the place with noise and tumult, accusing and recriminating on one another, till at last Agnonides came forward, and requested they might all be shut up together in one cage, and conveyed to Athens, there to decide the controversy. At that the king could not forbear smiling, but the company that attended, for their own amusement, Macedonians and strangers, were eager to hear the altercation, and made signs to the delegates to go on with their case at once. But it was no sort of fair hearing. Polysperchon frequently interrupted Phocion, till at last Phocion struck his staff on the ground and declined to speak further. And when Hegemon said, Polysperchon himself could bear witness to his affection for the people, Polysperchon called out fiercely, "Give over slandering me to the king," and the king starting up was about to have run him through with his javelin, but Polysperchon interposed and hindered him: so that the assembly dissolved.

Phocion, then, and those about him, were seized; those of his friends that were not immediately by him, on seeing this, hid their faces, and saved themselves by flight. The rest Clitus took and brought to Athens, to be submitted to trial; but, in truth, as men already sentenced to die. The manner of conveying them was indeed extremely moving; they were carried in chariots through the Ceramicus, straight to the place of judicature, where Clitus secured them till they had convoked an assembly of the people, which was open to all comers, neither foreigners, nor slaves, nor those who had been punished with disfranchisement being refused admittance. but all alike, both men and women, being allowed to come into the court, and even upon the place of speaking. So having read the king's letters, in which he declared he was satisfied himself that these men were traitors, however, they

being a free city, he willingly accorded them the grace of trying and judging them according to their own laws, Clitus brought in his prisoners. Every respectable citizen, at the sight of Phocion, covered up his face, and stooped down to conceal his tears. And one of them had the courage to say, that since the king had committed so important a cause to the judgment of the people, it would be well that the strangers, and those of servile condition, should withdraw. But the populace would not endure it, crying out they were oligarchs, and enemies to the liberty of the people, and deserved to be stoned; after which no man durst offer anything further in Phocion's behalf. He was himself with difficulty heard at all, when he put the question, "Do you wish to put us to death lawfully or unlawfully?" Some answered, "According to law." He replied, "How can you, except we have a fair hearing?" But when they were deaf to all he said, approaching nearer, "As to myself," said he, "I admit my guilt, and pronounce my public conduct to have deserved sentence of death. But why O men of Athens, kill others who have offended in nothing?" The rabble cried out they were his friends, that was enough. Phocion therefore drew back, and said no more.

Then Agnonides read the bill, in accordance with which the people should decide by show of hands whether they judged them guilty, and if so it should be found, the penalty should be death. When this had been read out, some desired it might be added to the sentence, that Phocion should be tortured also, and the rack should be produced with the executioners. But Agnonides perceiving even Clitus to dislike this, and himself thinking it horrid and barbarous, said, "When we catch that slave, Callimedon, men of Athens, we will put him to the rack, but I shall make no motion of the kind in Phocion's case." Upon which one of the better citizens remarked, he was quite right; "If he should torture Phocion, what could we do to you?" So the form of the bill was approved of, and the show of hands called for; upon which, not one man retaining his seat, but all rising up, and some with garlands on their heads, they condemned them all to death.

There were present with Phocion, Nicocles, Thudippus, Hegemon, and Pythocles. Demetrius the Phalerian, Callimedon, Charicles, and some others, were included in the condemnation, being absent.

After the assembly was dismissed, they were carried to the prison; the rest with cries and lamentations, their friends and relatives following and clinging about them, but Phocion looking (as men observed with astonishment at his calmness and magnanimity), just the same as when he had been used to return to his home attended, as general, from the assembly. His enemies ran along by his side, reviling and abusing him. And one of them coming up to him, spat in his face; at which Phocion, turning to the officers, only said, "You should stop this indecency." Thudippus, on their reaching

the prison, when he observed the executioner tempering the poison and preparing it for them, gave away to his passion, and began to bemoan his condition and the hard measure he received, thus unjustly to suffer with Phocion. "You cannot be contented," said he, "to die with Phocion?" One of his friends that stood by, asked him if he wished to have anything said to his son. "Yes, by all means," said he, "bid him bear no grudge against the Athenians." Then Nicocles, the dearest and most faithful of his friends, begged to be allowed to drink the poison first. "My friend," said he, "you ask what I am loath and sorrowful to give, but as I never yet in all my life was so thankless as to refuse you, I must gratify you in this also." After they had all drunk of it, the poison ran short; and the executioner refused to prepare more, except they would pay him twelve drachmas, to defray the cost of the quantity required. Some delay was made, and time spent, when Phocion called one of his friends, and observing that a man could not even die at Athens without paying for it, requested him to give the sum.

It was the nineteenth day of the month Munychion, on which it was the usage to have a solemn procession in the city, in honour of Jupiter. The horsemen, as they passed by, some of them threw away their garlands, others stopped, weeping, and casting sorrowful looks towards the prison doors, and all the citizens whose minds were not absolutely debauched by spite and passion, or who had any humanity left, acknowledged it to have been most impiously done, not, at least, to let that day pass, and the city so be kept pure from death and a public execution at the solemn festival. But as if this triumph had been insufficient, the malice of Phocion's enemies went yet further; his dead body was excluded from burial within the boundaries of the country, and none of the Athenians could light a funeral pile to burn the corpse; neither durst any of his friends venture to concern themselves about it. A certain Conopion, a man who used to do these offices for hire, took the body and carried it beyond Eleusis, and procuring fire from over the frontier of Megara, burned it. Phocion's wife, with her servant-maids, being present and assisting at the solemnity, raised there an empty tomb, and performed the customary libations, and gathering up the bones in her lap, and bringing them home by night, dug a place for them by the fireside in her house, saying, "Blessed hearth, to your custody I commit the remains of a good and brave man, and, I beseech you, protect and restore them to the sepulchre of his fathers, when the Athenians return to their right minds."

And, indeed, a very little time and their own sad experience soon informed them what an excellent governor, and how great an example and guardian of justice and of temperance they had bereft themselves of. And now they decreed him a statue of brass, and his bones to be buried honourably at the public charge; and for his accusers, Agnonides they took themselves, and caused him to be put to death. Epicurus and Demophilus, who fled from the city for fear, his son met with, and took his revenge upon them. This son of his, we are told, was in general of an indifferent character, and once when enamoured of a slave girl kept by a common harlot merchant, happened to hear Theodorus, the atheist, arguing in the Lyceum, that if it were a good and honourable thing to buy the freedom of a friend in the masculine, why not also of a friend in the feminine, if, for example, a master, why not also a mistress? So putting the good argument and his passion together, he went off and purchased the girl's freedom. The death which was thus suffered by Phocion revived among the Greeks the memory of that of Socrates, the two cases being so similar, and both equally the sad fault and misfortune of the city.

CATO THE YOUNGER

THE family of Cato derived its first lustre from his great-grandfather Cato, whose virtue gained him such great reputation and authority among the Romans, as we have written in his life.

This Cato was, by the loss of both his parents, left an orphan, together with his brother Cæpio, and his sister Porcia. He had also a half-sister, Servilia, by the mother's side. All these lived together, and were bred up in the house of Livius Drusus, their uncle by the mother, who, at that time, had a great share in the government, being a very eloquent speaker, a man of the greatest temperance, and yielding in dignity to none of the Romans.

It is said of Cato that even from his infancy, in his speech, his countenance, and all his childish pastimes, he discovered an inflexible temper, unmoved by any passion, and firm in everything. He was resolute in his purposes, much beyond the strength of his age, to go through with whatever he undertook. He was rough and ungentle toward those that flattered him, and still more unyielding to those who threatened him. It was difficult to excite him to laughter, his countenance seldom relaxed even into a smile; he was not quickly or easily provoked to anger, but if once incensed, he was no less difficult to pacify.

When he began to learn, he proved dull, and slow to apprehend, but of what he once received, his memory was remarkably tenacious. And such in fact, we find generally to be the course of nature; men of fine genius are readily reminded of things, but those who receive with most pains and difficulty, remember best; every new thing they learn, being, as it were, burnt and branded in on their minds. Cato's natural stubbornness and slowness to be persuaded may also have made it more difficult for him to be taught. For to learn is to submit to have something done to one and persuasion comes soonest to those who have least strength to resist it. Hence young men are sooner persuaded than those that are more in years, and sick men, than those that are well in health. In fine, where there is least previous doubt and difficulty, the new impression is most easily accepted. Yet Cato, they say, was very obedient to his preceptor, and would do whatever he was commanded; but he would also ask the reason, and inquire the cause of everything. And, indeed, his teacher was a very well-bred man, more ready to instruct than to beat his scholars. His name was Sarpedon.

When Cato was a child, the allies of the Romans sued to be made free citizens of Rome. Pompædius Silo, one of their deputies, a brave soldier and a man of great repute, who had contracted a friendship with Drusus, lodged at his house for several days, in which time being grown familiar with the children, "Well," said he to them, "will you entreat your uncle to befriend us in our business?" Cæpio, smiling, assented, but Cato made no answer, only he looked steadfastly and fiercely on the strangers. Then said Pompædius, "And you, young sir, what say you to us? will not you, as well as your brother, intercede with your uncle in our behalf?" And when Cato continued to give no answer, by his silence and his countenance seeming to deny their petition, Pompædius snatched him up to the window as if he would throw him out, and told him to consent, or he would fling him down, and, speaking in a harsher tone, held his body out of the window, and shook him several times. When Cato had suffered this a good while, unmoved and unalarmed, Pompædius, setting him down, said in an undervoice to his friend, "What a blessing for Italy that he is but a child! If he were a man, I believe we should not gain one voice among the people." Another time, one of his relations, on his birthday, invited Cato and some other children to supper, and some of the company diverted themselves in a separate part of the house, and were at play, the elder and the younger together, their sport being to act the pleadings before the judges, accusing one another, and carrying away the condemned to prison. Among these a very beautiful young child, being bound and carried by a bigger into prison, cried out to Cato, who seeing what was going on, presently ran to the door, and thrusting away those who stood there as a guard, took out the child, and went home in anger, followed by some of his companions.

Cato at length grew so famous among them, that when Sylla designed to exhibit the sacred game of young men riding courses on horseback, which they called Troy, having gotten together the youth of good birth, he appointed two for their leaders. One of them they accepted for his mother's sake, being the son of Metella, the wife of Sylla; but as for the other, Sextus, the nephew of Pompey, they would not be led by him, nor exercise under him. Then Sylla asking whom they would have, they all cried out, Cato; and Sextus willingly yielded the honour to him, as the more worthy.

Sylla, who was a friend of their family, sent at times for Cato and his brother to see them and talk with them; a favour which he showed to very few, after gaining his great power and authority. Sarpedon, full of the advantage it would be, as well for the honour as the safety of his scholars, would often bring Cato to wait upon Sylla at his house, which, for the multitude of those that were being carried off in custody, and tormented there, looked like a place of execution. Cato was then in his fourteenth year, and seeing the heads of men said to be of great distinction brought thither, and observing the secret sighs of those that were present, he asked his preceptor, "Why does nobody kill this man?" "Because," said he, "they fear him, child, more than they hate him." "Why, then," replied Cato, "did you not give me a sword, that I might stab him, and free my country from this slavery?" Sarpedon hearing this, and at the same time seeing his countenance swelling with anger and determination, took care thenceforward to watch him strictly, lest he should hazard any desperate attempt.

While he was yet very young, to some that asked him whom he loved best, he answered, his brother. And being asked, whom next, he replied, his brother, again. So likewise the third time, and still the same, till they left off to ask any further. As he grew in age, this love to his brother grew yet the stronger. When he was about twenty years old, he never supped, never went out of town, nor into the forum, without Cæpio. But when his brother made use of precious ointments and perfumes, Cato declined them; and he was, in all his habits, very strict and austere, so that when Cæpio was admired for his moderation and temperance, he would acknowledge that indeed he might be accounted such, in comparison with some other men, "but," said he, "when I compare myself with Cato, I find myself scarcely different from Sippius," one at that time notorius for his luxurious and effeminate living.

Cato being made priest of Apollo, went to another house, took his portion of their paternal inheritance, amounting to a hundred and twenty talents, and began to live yet more strictly than before. Having gained the intimate acquaintance of Antipater the Tyrian, the Stoic philosopher, he devoted himself to the study, above everything, of moral and political doctrine. And though possessed, as it were, by a kind of inspiration for the pursuit of every virtue, yet what most of all virtue and excellence fixed his affection was that steady and inflexible justice which is not to be wrought upon by favour or compassion. He learned also the art of speaking and debating in public, thinking that political philosophy, like a great city, should maintain for its security the military and warlike element. But he would never recite his exercises before company, nor was he ever heard to declaim. And to one that told him men blamed his silence, "But I hope not my life," he replied, "I will begin to speak, when I have that to say which had not better be unsaid."

The great Porcian Hall, as it was called, had been built and dedicated to the public use by the old Cato, when ædile. Here the tribunes of the people used to transact their business, and because one of the pillars was thought to interfere with the convenience of their seats, they deliberated whether it were best to remove it to another place, or to take it away. This occasion first drew Cato, much against his will, into the forum; for he opposed the demand of the tribunes, and in so doing gave a specimen both of his courage and his powers of speaking, which gained him great admiration. His speech had nothing youthful or refined in it, but was straightforward, full of matter, and rough, at the same time that there was a certain grace about his rough statements which won the attention; and the speaker's character, showing itself in all he said, added to his severe language something that excited feelings of natural pleasure and interest. His voice was full and sounding, and sufficient to be heard by so great a multitude, and its vigour and capacity of endurance quite indefatigable, for he often would speak a whole day and never stop.

When he had carried this cause, he betook himself again to study and retirement. He employed himself in inuring his body to labour and violent exercise; and habituated himself to go bareheaded in the hottest and the coldest weather, and to walk on foot at all seasons. When he went on a journey with any of his friends, though they were on horseback and he on foot, yet he would often join now one, then another, and converse with them on the way. In sickness the patience he showed in supporting, and the abstinence he used for curing, his distempers were admirable. When he had an ague, he would remain alone, and suffer nobody to see him, till he began to recover, and found the fit was over. At supper, when he threw dice for the choice of dishes, and lost, and the company offered him nevertheless his choice, he declined to dispute, as he said, the decision of Venus. At first, he was wont to drink only once after supper, and then go away; but in process of time he grew to drink more, insomuch that oftentimes he would continue till morning. This his friends explained by saying that state affairs and public business took him up all day, and being desirous of knowledge, he liked to pass the night at wine in the conversation of philosophers. Hence, upon one Memmius saying in public, that Cato spent whole nights in drinking, "You should add," replied Cicero, "that he spends whole days in gambling." And in general Cato esteemed the customs and manners of men at that time so corrupt, and a reformation in them so necessary, that he thought it requisite, in many things, to go contrary to the ordinary way of the world. Seeing the lightest and gayest purple was then most in fashion, he would always wear that which was the nearest black; and he would often go out of doors, after his morning meal, without either shoes or tunic; not that he sought vain-glory from such novelties, but he would accustom himself to be ashamed only of what deserves shame, and to despise all other sorts of disgrace.

The estate of one Cato, his cousin, which was worth one hundred talents, falling to him, he turned it all into ready money, which he kept by him for any of his friends that should happen to want, to whom he would lend it without interest. And for some of them, he suffered his own land and his slaves to be mortgaged to the public treasury.

When he thought himself of an age fit to marry, having never before known any woman, he was contracted to Lepida, who had before been contracted to Metellus Scipio, but on Scipio's own withdrawal from it, the contract had been dissolved, and she left at liberty. Yet Scipio afterwards repenting himself, did all he could to regain her, before the marriage with Cato was completed, and succeeded in so doing. At which Cato was violently incensed, and resolved at first to go to law about it; but his friends persuaded him to the contrary. However, he was so moved by the heat of youth and passion that he wrote a quantity of iambic verses against Scipio, in the bitter, sarcastic style of Archilochus, without, however, his licence and scurrility. After this, he married Atilia, the daughter of Soranus, the first but not the only woman he ever knew, less happy thus far than Lælius, the friend of Scipio, who in the whole course of so long a life never knew but the one woman, to whom he was united in his first and only marriage.

In the war of the slaves, which took its name from Spartacus, their ringleader, Gellius was general, and Cato went a volunteer, for the sake of his brother Cæpio, who was a tribune in the army. Cato could find here no opportunity to show his zeal or exercise his valour, on account of the ill conduct of the general. However, amidst the corruption and disorders of that army, he showed such a love of discipline, so much bravery upon occasion, and so much courage and wisdom in everything, that it appeared he was in no way inferior to the old Cato. Gellius offered him great rewards, and would have decreed him the first honours; which, however, he refused, saying he had done nothing that deserved them. This made him be thought a man of strange and eccentric temper.

There was a law passed, moreover, that the candidates who stood for any office should not have prompters in their canvass, to tell them the names of the citizens; and Cato, when he sued to be elected tribune, was the only man that obeyed this law. He took great pains to learn by his own knowledge to salute those he had to speak with, and to call them by their names; yet even those who praised him for this, did not do so without some envy and jealousy, for the more they considered the excellence of what he did, the more they were grieved at the difficulty they found to do the like.

Being chosen tribune, he was sent into Macedon to join Rubrius, who was general there. It is said that his wife showing much concern, and weeping at his departure, Munatius, one of Cato's friends, said to her, "Do not trouble yourself, Atilia, I will engage to watch over him for you." "By all means," replied Cato; and when they had gone one day's journey together, "Now," said he to Munatius, after they had supped, "that you may be sure to keep your promise to Atilia, you must not leave me day nor night," and from that time, he ordered two beds to be made in his own chamber, that Munatius might lie there. And so he continued to do, Cato making it his jest to see that he was always there. There went with him fifteen slaves, two freedmen, and four of his friends; these rode on horseback, but Cato always went on foot, yet would he keep by them, and talk with each of them in turn as they went.

When he came to the army, which consisted of several legions, the general gave him the command of one; and as he looked upon it as a small matter, and not worthy a commander, to give evidence of his own signal valour, he resolved to make his soldiers, as far as he could, like himself, not, however, in this relaxing the terrors of his office, but associating reason with his authority. He persuaded and instructed every one in particular, and bestowed rewards or punishments according to desert; and at length his men were so well disciplined, that it was hard to say whether they were more peaceable or more warlike, more valiant or more just; they were alike formidable to their enemies and courteous to their allies, fearful to do wrong, and forward to gain honour. And Cato himself acquired in the fullest measure, what it had been his least desire to seek, glory and good repute; he was highly esteemed by all men, and entirely beloved by the soldiers. Whatever he commanded to be done, he himself took part in the performing; in his apparel, his diet, and mode of travelling, he was more like a common soldier than an officer; but in character, high purpose, and wisdom, he far exceeded all that had the names and titles of commanders, and he made himself, without knowing it, the object of general affection. For the true love of virtue is in all men produced by the love and respect they bear to him that teaches it; and those who praise good men, yet do not love them, may respect their reputation, but do not really admire, and will never imitate their virtue.

There dwelt at that time in Pergamus, Athenodorus, surnamed Cordylio, a man of high repute for his knowledge of the Stoic philosophy, who was now grown old, and had always steadily refused the friendship and acquaintance of princes and great men. Cato understood this; so that imagining he should not be able to prevail with him by sending or writing, and being by the laws allowed two months' absence from the army, he resolved to go into Asia to see him in person, trusting to his own good qualities not to lose his labour. And when he had conversed with him, and succeeded in persuading him out of his former resolutions, he returned and brought him to the camp as joyful and as proud of this victory as if he had done some heroic exploit, greater than any of those of Pompey or Lucullus, who with their armies at that time were subduing so many nations and kingdoms.

While Cato was yet in the service, his brother, on a journey towards Asia, fell sick at Ænus in Thrace, letters with intelligence of which were immediately despatched to him. The sea was very rough, and no convenient ship of any size to be had; so Cato getting into a small trading-vessel, with only two of his friends, and three servants, set sail from Thessalonica, and having very narrowly escaped drowning, he arrived at Ænus just as Cæpio expired. Upon this occasion, he was thought to have showed himself more a fond brother than a philosopher, not only in the excess of his grief, bewailing and embracing the dead body, but also in the extravagant expenses of the funeral, the vast quantity of rich perfumes and costly garments which were burnt with the corpse, and the monument of Thasian marble, which he erected, at the cost of eight talents, in the public place of the town of Ænus. For there were some who took upon them to cavil at all this, as not consistent with his usual calmness and moderation, not discerning that though he were steadfast, firm, and inflexible to pleasure, fear or foolish entreaties, yet he was full of natural tenderness and brotherly affection. Divers of the cities and princes of the country sent him many presents, to honour the funeral of his brother; but he took none of their money, only the perfumes and ornaments he received, and paid for them also. And afterwards, when the inheritance was divided between him and Cæpio's daughter, he did not require any portion of the funeral expenses to be discharged out of it. Notwithstanding this, it has been affirmed that he made his brother's ashes be passed through a sieve, to find the gold that was melted down when burnt with the body. But he who made this statement appears to have anticipated an exemption for his pen, as much as for his sword, from all question and criticism.

The time of Cato's service in the army being expired, he received, at his departure, not only the prayers and praises, but the tears and embraces of the soldiers, who spread their clothes at his feet and kissed his hand as he passed, an honour which the Romans at that time scarcely paid even to a very few of their generals and commanders-in-chief. Having left the army, he resolved, before he would return home and apply himself to state affairs, to travel in Asia, and observe the manners, the customs, and the strength of every province. He was also unwilling to refuse the kindness of Deiotarus, King of Galatia, who having had great familiarity and friendship with his father, was very desirous to receive a visit from him. Cato's arrangements in his journey were as follows. Early in the morning he sent out his baker and his cook towards the place where he designed to stay the next night; these went soberly and quietly into the town, in which, if there happened to be no friend or acquaintance of Cato or his family, they provided for him in an inn, and gave no disturbance to anybody; but if there were no inn, then and in this case only, they went to the magistrates, and desiring them to help them to lodgings, took without complaint whatever was allotted to them. His servants thus behaving themselves towards the magistrates, without noise and threatening, were often discredited, or neglected by them, so that Cato many times arrived and found nothing provided for him. And it was all the worse when he appeared himself; still less account was taken of him. When they saw him sitting, without saying anything, on his baggage, they set him down at once as a person of no consequence, who did not venture to make any demand. Sometimes, on such occasions, he would call them to him and tell them, "Foolish People, lay aside this inhospitality. All your visitors will not be Catos. Use your courtesy, to take off the sharp edge of power. There are men enough who desire but a pretence, to take from you by force, what you give with such reluctance."

While he travelled in this manner, a diverting accident befell him in Syria. As he was going into Antioch, he saw a great multitude of people outside the gates, ranged in order on either side the way; here the young men with long cloaks, there the children decently dressed; others wore garlands and white garments who were the priests and magistrates. Cato imagining all this could mean nothing but a display in honour of his reception, began to be angry with his servants, who had been sent before, for suffering it to be done; then making his friends alight, he walked along with them on foot. As soon as he came near the gate, an elderly man, who seemed to be master of these ceremonies, with a wand and a garland in his hand, came up to Cato, and without saluting him, asked him where he had left Demetrius, and how soon he thought he would be there. This Demetrius was Pompey's servant, and as at this time the whole world, so to say, had its eyes fixed upon Pompey, this man also was highly honoured, on account of his influence with his master. Upon this Cato's friends fell into such violent laughter, that they could not restrain themselves while they passed through the crowd; and he himself, ashamed and distressed, uttered the words, "Unfortunate city!" and said no more. Afterwards, however, it always made him laugh, when he either told the story or was otherwise reminded of it.

Pompey himself shortly after made the people ashamed of their ignorance and folly in thus neglecting him, for Cato, coming in his journey to Ephesus, went to pay his respects to him, who was the elder man, had gained much honour, and was then general of a great army. Yet Pompey would not receive him sitting, but as soon as he saw him, rose up, and going to meet him, as the more honourable person, gave him his hand and embraced him with great show of kindness. He said much in commendation of his virtue both at that time when receiving him, and also yet more after he had withdrawn. So that now all men began at once to display their respect for Cato, and discovered in him the very same things for which they despised him before, an admirable mildness of temper and greatness of spirit. And indeed the civility that Pompey himself showed him appeared to come from one that rather respected than loved him; and the general opinion was, that while Cato was there he paid him admiration but was not sorry when he was gone. For when other young men came to see him he usually urged and entreated them to continue with him. Now he did not at all invite Cato to stay, but as if his own power were lessened by the other's presence, he very willingly allowed him to take his leave. Yet to Cato alone, of all those who went for Rome, he recommended his children and his wife, who was indeed connected by relationship with Cato.

After this, all the cities through which he passed strove and emulated each other in showing him respect and honour. Feasts and entertainments were made for his reception, so that he bade his friends keep strict watch and take care of him, lest he should end by making good what was said by Curio, who though he were his familiar friend, yet disliking the austerity of his temper, asked him one day if, when he left the army, he designed to see Asia, and Cato answering, "Yes, by all means." "You do well," replied Curio, "you will bring back with you a better temper and pleasanter manners; " pretty nearly the very words he used.

Deiotarus, being now an old man, had sent for Cato, to recommend his children and family to his protection; and as soon as he came, brought him presents of all sorts of things, which he begged and entreated him to accept. And his importunities displeased Cato so much, that though he came but in the evening, he stayed only that night, and went away early the next morning. After he was gone one day's journey, he found at Pessinus a yet greater quantity of presents provided for him there, and also letters from Deiotarus entreating him to receive them, or at least to permit his friends to take them, who for his sake deserved some gratification, and could not have much done for them out of Cato's own means. Yet he would not suffer it, though he saw some of them very willing to receive such gifts, and ready to complain of his severity; but he answered, that corruption would never want pretence, and his friends should share with him in whatever he should justly and honestly obtain, and so returned the presents to Deiotarus.

When he took ship for Brundusium, his friends would have persuaded him to put his brother's ashes into another vessel; but he said he would sooner part with his life than leave them, and so set sail. And as it chanced, he, we are told, had a very dangerous passage, though others at the same time went over safely enough.

After he was returned to Rome, he spent his time for the most part either at home, in conversation with Athenodorus, or at the forum, in the service of his friends. Though it was now the time that he should become quæstor, he would not stand for the place till he had studied the laws relating to it, and by inquiry from persons of experience, had attained a distinct understanding of the duty and authority belonging to it. With this knowledge, as soon as he came into the office, he made a great reformation among the clerks and under-officers of the treasury, people who had long practice and familiarity in all the public records and the laws, and, when new magistrates came in year by year so ignorant and unskilful as to be in absolute need of others to teach them what to do, did not submit and give way, but kept the power in their own hands, and were in effect the treasurers themselves. Till Cato, applying himself roundly to the work, showed that he possessed not only the title and honour of a quæstor, but the knowledge and understanding and full authority of his office. So that he used the clerks and under-officers like servants as they were, exposing their corrupt practices, and instructing their ignorance. Being bold, impudent fellows, they flattered the other quæstors his colleagues, and by their means endeavoured to maintain an opposition against him. But he convicted the chiefest of them of a breach of trust in the charge of an inheritance, and turned him out of his place. A second he brought to trial for dishonesty, who was defended by Lutatius Catulus, at that time censor, a man very considerable for his office, but yet more for his character, as he was eminent above all the Romans of that age for his reputed wisdom and integrity. He was also intimate with Cato, and much commended his way of living. So perceiving he could not bring off his client, if he stood a fair trial, he openly began to beg him off. Cato objected to his doing this. And when he continued still to be importunate, "It would be shameful, Catulus," he said, "that the censor, the judge of all our lives, should incur the dishonour of removal by our officers." At this expression, Catulus looked as if he would have made some answer; but he said nothing and either through anger or shame went away silent, and out of countenance. Nevertheless, the man was not found guilty, for the voices that acquitted him were but one in number less than those that condemned him, and Marcus Lollius, one of Cato's colleagues, who was absent by reason of sickness, was sent for by Catulus, and entreated to come and save the man. So Lollius was brought into court in a chair, and gave his voice also for acquitting him. Yet Cato never after made use of that clerk, and never paid him his salary, nor would he make any account of the vote given by Lollius. Having thus humbled the clerks, and brought them to be at command, he made use of the books and registers as he thought fit, and in a little while gained the treasury a higher name than the senate house itself; and all men said, Cato had made the office of a quæstor equal to the dignity of a consul. When he found many indebted to the state upon old accounts, and the state also in debt to many private persons, he took care that the public might no longer either do or suffer wrong; he strictly and punctually exacted what was due to the treasury, and as freely and speedily paid all those to whom it was indebted. So that the people were filled with sentiments of awe and respect, on seeing those made to pay, who thought to have escaped with their plunder, and others receiving all their due, who despaired of getting anything. And whereas usually those who brought false bills and pretended orders of the senate, could through favour get them accepted, Cato would never be so imposed upon; and in the case of one particular order, on the question arising whether it had passed the senate, he would not believe a great many witnesses that attested it, nor would admit of it, till the consuls came and affirmed it upon oath.

There were at that time a great many whom Sylla had made use of as his agents in the proscription, and to whom he had for their service in putting men to death, given twelve thousand drachmas apiece. These men everybody hated as wicked and polluted wretches, but nobody durst be revenged upon them. Cato called every one to account, as wrongfully possessed of the public money, and exacted it of them, and at the same time sharply reproved them for their unlawful and impious actions. After these proceedings they were presently accused of murder, and being already in a manner prejudged as guilty, they were easily found so, and accordingly suffered; at which the whole people rejoiced and thought themselves now to see the old tyranny finally abolished, and Sylla himself, so to say, brought to punishment.

Cato's assiduity also, and indefatigable diligence, won very much upon the people. He always came first of any of his colleagues to the treasury, and went away the last. He never missed any assembly of the people, or sitting of the senate; being always anxious and on the watch for those who lightly, or as a matter of interest, passed votes in favour of this or that person, for remitting debts or granting away customs that were owing to the state. And at length, having kept the exchequer pure and clear from base informers, and yet having filled it with treasure, he made it appear that the state might be rich without oppressing the people. At first he excited feelings of dislike and irritation in some of his colleagues, but after a while they were well contented with him, since he was perfectly willing that they should cast all the odium on him, when they declined to gratify their friends with the public money, or to give dishonest judgments in passing their accounts; and when hard-pressed by suitors, they could readily answer it was impossible to do anything unless Cato would consent. On the last day of his office, he was honourably attended to his house by almost all the people; but on the way he was informed that several powerful friends were in the treasury with Marcellus, using all their interest with him to pass a certain debt to the public revenue, as if it had been a gift. Marcellus had been one of Cato's friends from his childhood, and so long as Cato was with him, was one of the best of his colleagues in this office, but when alone, was unable to resist the importunity of suitors, and prone to do anybody a kindness. So Cato immediately turned back, and finding that Marcellus had yielded to pass the thing, he took the book, and while Marcellus silently stood by and looked on, struck it out. This done, he brought Marcellus out of the treasury, and took him home with him; who for all this, neither then, nor ever after, complained of him, but always continued his friendship and familiarity with him.

Cato, after he had laid down his office, yet did not cease to keep a watch upon the treasury. He had his servants who continually wrote out the details of the expenditure, and he himself kept always by him certain books, which contained the accounts of the revenue from Sylla's time to his own quæstorship, which he had bought for five talents.

He was always first at the senate, and went out last; and often, while the others were slowly collecting, he would sit and read by himself, holding his gown before his book. He was never once out of town when the senate was to meet. And when afterwards Pompey and his party, finding that he could never be either persuaded or compelled to favour their unjust designs, endeavoured to keep him from the senate, by engaging him in business for his friends, to plead their causes, or arbitrate in their differences, or the like, he quickly discovered the trick, and to defeat it, fairly told all his acquaintance that he would never meddle in any private business when the senate was assembled. Since it was not in the hope of gaining honour or riches, nor out of mere impulse, or by chance that he engaged himself in politics, but he undertook the service of the state as the proper business of an honest man, and therefore he thought himself obliged to be as constant to his public duty as the bee to the honeycomb. To this end, he took care to have his friends and correspondents everywhere, to send him reports of the edicts, decrees, judgments, and all the important proceedings that passed in any of the provinces. Once when Clodius, the seditious orator, to promote his violent and revolutionary projects, traduced to the people some of the priests and priestesses (among whom Fabia, sister to Cicero's wife, Terentia, ran great danger), Cato having boldly interfered, and having made Clodius appear so infamous that he was forced to leave the town, was addressed, when it was over, by Cicero, who came to thank him for what he had done. "You must thank the commonwealth," said he, for whose sake alone he professed to do everything. Thus he gained a great and wonderful reputation; so that an advocate in a cause, where there was only one witness against him, told the judges they ought not to rely upon a single witness, though it were Cato himself. And it was a sort of proverb with many people, if any very unlikely and incredible thing were asserted, to say, they would not believe it, though Cato himself should affirm it. One day a debauched and sumptuous liver talking in the senate about frugality and temperance, Anæus standing up, cried, "Who can endure this, sir, to have you feast like Crassus, build like Lucullus, and talk like Cato." So likewise those who were vicious and dissolute in their manners, yet affected to be grave and severe in their language, were in derision called Catos.

At first, when his friends would have persuaded him to stand to be tribune of the people. he thought it undesirable; for that the power of so great an office ought to be reserved, as the strongest medicines, for occasions of the last necessity. But afterwards in a vacation time, as he was going, accompanied with his books and philosophers, to Lucania, where he had lands with a pleasant residence, they met by the way a great many horses, carriages, and attendants, of whom they understood, that Metellus Nepos was going to Rome, to stand to be tribune of the people. Hereupon Cato stopped, and after a little pause, gave orders to return back immediately; at which the company seeming to wonder, "Don't you know," said he, "how dangerous of itself the madness of Metellus is? and now that he comes armed with the support of Pompey, he will fall like lightning on the state, and bring it to utter disorder; therefore this is no time for idleness and diversion, but we must go and prevent this man in his designs, or bravely die in defence of our liberty." Nevertheless, by the persuasion of his friends, he went first to his country-house, where he stayed but a very little time, and then returned to town.

He arrived in the evening, and went straight the next morning to the forum, where he began to solicit for the tribuneship, in opposition to Metellus. The power of this office consists rather in controlling than performing any business; for though all the rest except any one tribune should be agreed, yet his denial or intercession could put a stop to the whole matter. Cato, at first, had not many that appeared for him; but as soon as his design was known, all the good and distinguished persons of the city quickly came forward to encourage and support him, looking upon him, not as one that desired a favour of them, but one that proposed to do a great favour to his country and all honest men; who had many times refused the same office, when he might have had it without trouble, but now sought it with danger, that he might defend their liberty and their government. It is reported that so great a number flocked about him that he was like to be stifled amidst the press, and could scarce get through the crowd. He was declared tribune, with several others, among whom was Metellus.

When Cato was chosen into this office, observing that the election of consuls was become a matter of purchase, he sharply rebuked the people for this corruption, and in the conclusion of his speech protested he would bring to trial whomever he should find giving money, making an exception only in the case of Silanus, on account of their near connection, he having married Servilia, Cato's sister. He therefore did not prosecute him, but accused Lucius Murena, who had been chosen consul by corrupt means with Silanus. There was a law that the party accused might appoint a person to keep watch upon his accuser, that he might know fairly what means he took in preparing the accusation. He that was set upon Cato by Murena, at first followed and observed him strictly, yet never found him dealing any way unfairly or insidiously, but always generously and candidly going on in the just and open methods of proceeding. And he so admired Cato's great spirit, and so entirely trusted to his integrity, that meeting him in the forum, or going to his house, he would ask him if he designed to do anything that day in order to the accusation, and if Cato said no, he went away, relying on his word. When the cause was pleaded Cicero, who was then consul and defended Murena, took occasion to be extremely witty and jocose, in reference to Cato, upon the Stoic philosophers, and their paradoxes, as they call them, and so excited great laughter among the judges; upon which Cato, smiling, said to the standers-by, "What a pleasant consul we have, my friends." Murena was acquitted, and afterwards showed himself a man of no ill-feeling or want of sense; for when he was consul, he always took Cato's advice in the most weighty affairs and, during all the time of his office, paid him much honour and respect. Of which not only Murena's prudence, but also Cato's own behaviour, was the cause; for though he were terrible and severe as to matters of justice, in the senate, and at the bar, yet after the thing was over his manner to all men was perfectly friendly and humane.

Before he entered on the office of tribune, he assisted Cicero, at that time consul, in many contests that concerned his office, but most especially in his great and noble acts at the time of Catiline's conspiracy; which owed their last successful issue to Cato. Catiline had plotted a dreadful and entire subversion of the Roman state by sedition and open war, but being convicted by Cicero, was forced to fly the city. Yet Lentulus and Cethegus remained, with several others, to carry on the same plot; and blaming Catiline, as one that wanted courage, and had been timid and petty in his designs, they themselves resolved to set the whole town on fire, and utterly to overthrow the empire, rousing whole nations to revolt and exciting foreign wars. But the design was discovered by Cicero (as we have written in his life), and the matter brought before the senate. Silanus, who spoke first, delivered his opinion, that the conspirators ought to suffer the last of punishments, and was therein followed by all who spoke after him; till it came to Cæsar, who being an excellent speaker, and looking upon all changes and commotions in the state as materials useful for his own purposes, desired rather to increase than extinguish them; and standing up, he made a very merciful and persuasive speech, that they ought not to suffer death without fair trial according to law, and moved that they might be kept in prison. Thus was the house almost wholly turned by Cæsar, apprehending also the anger of the people; insomuch that even Silanus retracted, and said he did not mean to propose death, but imprisonment, for that was the utmost a Roman could suffer.

Upon this they were all inclined to the milder and more merciful opinion, when Cato, standing up, began at once with great passion and vehemence to reproach Silanus for his change of opinion, and to attack Cæsar, who would, he said, ruin the commonwealth by soft words and popular speeches, and was endeavouring to frighten the senate, when he himself ought to fear, and be thankful, if he escaped unpunished or unsuspected, who thus openly and boldly dared to protect the enemies of the state, and while finding no compassion for his own native country, brought, with all its glories, so near to utter ruin, could yet be full of pity for those men who had better never have been born, and whose death must deliver the commonwealth from bloodshed and destruction. This only of all Cato's speeches, it is said, was preserved; for Cicero, the consul, had disposed in various parts of the senate-house, several of the most expert and rapid writers, whom he had taught to make figures comprising numerous words in a few short strokes; as up to that time they had not used those we call shorthand writers, who then, as it is said, established the first example of the art. Thus Cato carried it, and so turned the house again, that it was decreed the conspirators should be put to death.

Not to omit any small matters that may serve to show Cato's temper, and add something to the portraiture of his mind, it is reported, that while Cæsar and he were in the very heat, and the whole senate regarding them two, a little note was brought in to Cæsar which Cato declared to be suspicious, and urging that some seditious act was going on, bade the letter be read. Upon which Cæsar handed the paper to Cato; who, discovering it to be a love-letter from his sister Servilia to Cæsar, by whom she had been corrupted, threw it to him again, saying, "Take it, drunkard," and so went on with his discourse. And, indeed, it seems Cato had but ill-fortune in women; for this lady was ill-spoken of for her familiarity with Cæsar, and the other Servilia, Cato's sister also, was yet more ill-conducted; for being married to Lucullus, one of the greatest men in Rome, and having brought him a son, she was afterwards divorced for incontinency. But what was worst of all, Cato's own wife Atilia was not free from the same fault; and after she had borne him two children, he was forced to put her away for her misconduct. After that, he married Marcia, the daughter of Philippus, a woman of good reputation, who yet has occasioned much discourse; and the life of Cato, like a dramatic piece, has this one scene or passage full of perplexity and doubtful meaning.

It is thus related by Thrasea, who refers to the authority of Munatius, Cato's friend and constant companion. Among many that loved and admired Cato, some were more remarkable and conspicuous than others. Of these was Quintus Hortensius, a man of high repute and approved virtue, who desired not only to live in friendship and familiarity with Cato, but also to unite his whole house and family with him by some sort or other of alliance in marriage. Therefore he set himself to persuade Cato that his daughter Porcia, who was already married to Bibulus, and had borne him two children, might nevertheless be given to him, as a fair plot of land, to bear fruit also for him. "For," said he, "though this in the opinion of men may seem strange, yet in nature it is honest, and profitable for the public that a woman in the prime of her youth should not lie useless, and lose the fruit of her womb, nor, on the other side, should burden and impoverish one man, by bringing him too many children. Also by this communication of families among worthy men, virtue would increase, and be diffused through their posterity; and the commonwealth would be united and cemented by their alliances." Yet if Bibulus would not part with his wife altogether, he would restore her as soon as she had brought him a child, whereby he might be united to both their families. Cato answered, that he loved Hortensius very well, and much approved of uniting their houses, but he thought it strange to speak of marrying his daughter, when she was already given to another. Then Hortensius, turning the discourse. did not hesitate to speak openly and ask for Cato's own wife, for she was young and fruitful, and he had already children enough. Neither can it be thought that Hortensius did this, as imagining Cato did not care for Marcia; for, it is said, she was then with child. Cato, perceiving his earnest desire, did not deny his request, but said that Philippus, the father of Marcia, ought also to be consulted. Philippus, therefore, being sent for, came; and finding they were well agreed, gave his daughter Marcia to Hortensius in the presence of Cato, who himself also assisted at the marriage. This was done at a later time, but since I was speaking of women, I thought it well to mention it now.

Lentulus and the rest of the conspirators were put to death; but Cæsar, finding so much insinuated and charged against him in the senate, betook himself to the people, and proceeded to stir up the most corrupt and dissolute elements of the state to form a party in his support. Cato, apprehensive of what might ensue, persuaded the senate to win over the poor and unprovided-for multitude by a distribution of corn, the annual charge of which amounted to twelve hundred and fifty talents. This act of humanity and kindness unquestionably dissipated the present danger. But Metellus, coming into his office of tribune, began to hold tumultuous assemblies, and had prepared a decree, that Pompey the Great should presently be called into Italy, with all his forces, to preserve the city from the danger of Catiline's conspiracy. This was the fair pretence; but the true design was to deliver all into the hands of Pompey, and to give him an absolute power. Upon this the senate was assembled, and Cato did not fall sharply upon Metellus, as he often did, but urged his advice in the most reasonable and moderate tone. At last he descended even to entreaty, and extolled the house of Metellus as having always taken part with the nobility. At this Metellus grew the more insolent, and despising Cato, as if he yielded and were afraid, let himself proceed to the most audacious menaces, openly threatening to do whatever he pleased in spite of the senate. Upon this Cato changed his countenance, his voice, and his language; and after many sharp expressions, boldly concluded that, while he lived, Pompey should never come armed into the city. The senate thought them both extravagant, and not well in their safe senses; for the design of Metellus seemed to be mere rage and frenzy, out of excess of mischief bringing all things to ruin and confusion, and Cato's virtue looked like a kind of ecstasy of contention in the cause of what was good and just.

But when the day came for the people to give their voices for the passing this decree, and Metellus beforehand occupied the forum with armed men, strangers, gladiators, and slaves, those that in hopes of change followed Pompey were known to be no small part of the people, and besides, they had great assistance from Cæsar, who was then prætor; and though the best and chiefest men of the city were no less offended at these proceedings than Cato, they seemed rather likely to suffer with him than able to assist him. In the meantime Cato's whole family were in extreme fear and apprehension for him; some of his friends neither ate nor slept all the night, passing the whole time in debating and perplexity; his wife and sisters also bewailed and lamented him. But he himself, void of all fear, and full of assurance, comforted and encouraged them by his own words and conversation with them. After supper he went to rest at his usual hour, and was the next day waked out of a profound sleep by Minucius Thermus, one of his colleagues. So soon as he was up, they two went together into the forum, accompanied by very few, but met by a great many, who bade them have a care of themselves. Cato, therefore, when he saw the temple of Castor and Pollux encompassed with armed men, and the steps guarded by gladiators, and at the top Metellus and Cæsar seated together, turning to his friends, "Behold," said he, "this audacious coward, who has levied a regiment of soldiers against one unarmed naked man;" and so he went on with Thermus. Those who kept the passages gave way to these two only, and would not let anybody else pass. Yet Cato taking Munatius by the hand, with much difficulty pulled him through along with him. Then going directly to Metellus and Cæsar, he sat himself down between them, to prevent their talking to one another, at which they were both amazed and confounded. And those of the honest party, observing the countenance, and admiring the high spirit and boldness of Cato, went nearer, and cried out to him to have courage, exhorting also one another to stand together, and not betray their liberty nor the defender of it.

Then the clerk took out the bill, but Cato forbade him to read it, whereupon Metellus took it, and would have read it himself, but Cato snatched the book away. Yet Metellus, having the decree by heart, began to recite it without book; but Thermus put his hand to his mouth, and stopped his speech. Metellus seeing them fully bent to withstand him, and the people cowed, and inclining to the better side, sent to his house for armed men. And on their rushing in with great noise and terror, all the rest dispersed and ran away, except Cato, who alone stood still, while the other party threw sticks and stones at him from above, until Murena, whom he had formerly accused, came up to protect him, and holding his gown before him, cried out to them to leave off throwing; and, in fine, persuading and pulling him along, he forced him into the temple of Castor and Pollux. Metellus, now seeing the place clear, and all the adverse party fled out of the forum, thought he might easily carry his point; so he commanded the soldiers to retire, and recommencing in an orderly manner, began to proceed to passing the decree. But the other side having recovered themselves, returned very boldly, and with loud shouting, insomuch that Metellus's adherents were seized with a panic, supposing them to be coming with a reinforcement of armed men, fled every one out of the place. They being thus dispersed, Cato came in again, and confirmed the courage, and commended the resolution of the people; so that now the majority were, by all means, for deposing Metellus from his office. The senate also being assembled, gave orders once more for supporting Cato, and resisting the motion, as of a nature to excite sedition and perhaps civil war in the city.

But Metellus continued still very bold and resolute; and seeing his party stood greatly in fear of Cato, whom they looked upon as invincible, he hurried out of the senate into the forum, and assembled the people, to whom he made a bitter and invidious speech against Cato, crying out, he was forced to fly from his tyranny, and this conspiracy against Pompey; that the city would soon repent their having dishonoured so great a man. And from hence he started to go to Asia, with the intention, as would be supposed, of laying before Pompey all the injuries that were done him. Cato was highly extolled for having delivered the state from this dangerous tribuneship, and having in some measure defeated, in the person of Metellus, the power of Pompey; but he was yet more commended when, upon the senate proceeding to disgrace Metellus and depose him from his office, he altogether opposed and at length diverted the design. The common people admired his moderation and humanity, in not trampling wantonly on an enemy whom he had overthrown, and wiser men acknowledged his prudence and policy in not exasperating Pompey.

Lucullus soon after returned from the war in Asia, the finishing of which, and thereby the glory of the whole, was thus, in all appearance, taken out of his hands by Pompey. And he was also not far from losing his triumph, for Caius Memmius traduced him to the people, and threatened to accuse him; rather, however, out of love to Pompey, than for any particular enmity to him. But Cato, being allied to Lucullus, who had married his sister Servilia, and also thinking it a great injustice, opposed Memmius, thereby exposing himself to much slander and misrepresentation, insomuch that they would have turned him out of his office, pretending that he used his power tyrannically. Yet at length Cato so far prevailed against Memmius that he was forced to let fall the accusations, and abandon the contest. And Lucullus having thus obtained his triumph, yet more sedulously cultivated Cato's friendship, which he looked upon as a great guard and defence for him against Pompey's power.

And now Pompey also returning with glory from the war, and confiding in the good-will of the people, shown in their splendid reception of him, thought he should be denied nothing, and sent therefore to the senate to put off the assembly for the election of consuls, till he could be present to assist Piso, who stood for that office. To this most of the senators were disposed to yield; Cato only not so much thinking that this delay would be of great importance, but, desiring to cut down at once Pompey's high expectations and designs, withstood his request, and so overruled the senate that it was carried against him. And this not a little disturbed Pompey, who found he should very often fail in his projects unless he could bring over Cato to his interest. He sent, therefore, for Munatius, his friend; and Cato having two nieces that were marriageable, he offered to marry the eldest himself, and take the youngest for his son. Some say they were not his nieces, but his daughters. Munatius proposed the matter to Cato, in presence of his wife and sisters; the women were full of joy at the prospect of an alliance with so great and important a person. But Cato, without delay or balancing, forming his decision at once, answered, "Go, Munatius, go and tell Pompey that Cato is not assailable on the side of the women's chamber; I am grateful indeed for the intended kindness, and so long as his actions are upright, I promise him a friendship more sure than any marriage alliance, but I will not give hostages to Pompey's glory against my country's safety." This answer was very much against the wishes of the women, and to all his friends it seemed somewhat harsh and haughty. But afterwards, when Pompey, endeavouring to get the consulship for one of his friends, gave pay to the people for their votes, and the bribery was notorious, the money being counted out in Pompey's own gardens, Cato then said to the women, they must necessarily have been concerned in the contamination of these misdeeds of Pompey, if they had been allied to his family; and they acknowledged that he did best in refusing it. Yet if we may judge by the event, Cato was much to blame in rejecting that alliance, which thereby fell to Cæsar. And then that match was made, which, uniting his and Pompey's power, had well-nigh ruined the Roman empire, and did destroy the commonwealth. Nothing of which, perhaps, had come to pass, but that Cato was too apprehensive of Pompey's least faults, and did not consider how he forced him into conferring on another man the opportunity of committing the greatest.

These things, however, were yet to come. Lucullus and Pompey, meantime, had a great dispute concerning their orders and arrangements in Pontus, each endeavouring that his own ordinances might stand. Cato took part with Lucullus, who was manifestly suffering wrong; and Pompey, finding himself the weaker in the senate, had recourse to the people, and to gain votes he proposed a law for dividing the lands among the soldiers. Cato opposing him in this also made the bill be rejected. Upon this he joined himself with Clodius, at that time the most violent of all the demagogues, and entered also into friendship with Cæsar, upon an occasion of which also Cato was the cause. For Cæsar, returning from his government in Spain, at the same time sued to be chosen consul, and yet desired not to lose his triumph. Now the law requiring that those who stood for any office should be present, and yet that whoever expected a triumph should continue without the walls, Cæsar requested the senate that his friends might be permitted to canvass for him in his absence. Many of the senators were willing to consent to it, but Cato opposed it, and perceiving them inclined to favour Cæsar, spent the whole day in speaking, and so prevented the senate from coming to any conclusion. Cæsar, therefore, resolving to let fall his pretensions to the triumph, came into the town, and immediately made a friendship with Pompey, and stood for the consulship. As soon as he was declared consul elect, he married his daughter Julia to Pompey. And having thus combined themselves together against the commonwealth, the one proposed laws for dividing the lands among the poor people, and the other was present to support the proposals. Lucullus, Cicero, and their friends, joined with Bibulus, the other consul, to hinder their passing, and, foremost of them all, Cato, who already looked upon the friendship and alliance of Pompey and Cæsar as very dangerous, declared he did not so much dislike the advantage the people should get by this division of the lands, as he feared the reward these men would gain, by thus courting and cozening the people. And in this he gained over the senate to his opinion, as likewise many who were not senators, who were offended at Cæsar's ill conduct, that he, in the office of consul, should thus basely and dishonourably flatter the people; practising, to win their favour, the same means that were wont to be used only by the most rash and rebellious tribunes. Cæsar, therefore, and his party, fearing they should not carry it by fair dealing, fell to open force. First a basket of dung was thrown upon Bibulus as he was going to the forum; then they set upon his lictors and broke their rods; at length several darts were thrown, and many men wounded; so that all that were against those laws fled out of the forum, the rest with what haste they could, and Cato, last of all, walking out slowly, often turning back and calling down vengeance upon them.

Thus the other party not only carried their point of dividing the lands, but also ordained that all the senate should swear to confirm this law, and to defend it against whoever should attempt to alter it, inflicting great penalties on those that should refuse the oath. All these senators, seeing the necessity they were in, took the oath, remembering the example of Metellus in old time, who, refusing to swear upon the like occasion, was forced to leave Italy. As for Cato, his wife and children with tears besought him, his friends and familiars persuaded and entreated him, to yield and take the oath; but he that principally prevailed with him was Cicero, the orator, who urged upon him that it was perhaps not even right in itself, that a private man should oppose what the public had decreed; that the thing being already past altering, it were folly and madness to throw himself into danger without the chance of doing his country any good; it would be the greatest of all evils to embrace, as it were, the opportunity to abandon the commonwealth, for whose sake he did everything, and to let it fall into the hands of those who designed nothing but its ruin, as if he were glad to be saved from the trouble of defending it. "For," said he, "though Cato have no need of Rome, yet Rome has need of Cato, and so likewise have all his friends." Of whom Cicero professed he himself was the chief, being at that time aimed at by Clodius, who openly threatened to fall upon him, as soon as ever he should get to be tribune. Thus Cato, they say, moved by the entreaties and the arguments of his friends, went unwillingly to take the oath, which he did the last of all, except only Favonius, one of his intimate acquaintance.

Cæsar, exalted with this success, proposed another law, for dividing almost all the country of Campania among the poor and needy citizens. Nobody durst speak against it but Cato, whom Cæsar therefore pulled from the rostra and dragged to prison: yet Cato did not even thus remit his freedom of speech, but as he went along continued to speak against the law, and advised the people to put down all legislators who proposed the like. The senate and the best of the citizens followed him with sad and dejected looks, showing their grief and indignation by their silence, so that Cæsar could not be ignorant how much they were offended; but for contention's sake he still persisted, expecting Cato should either supplicate him, or make an appeal. But when he saw that he did not so much as think of doing either, ashamed of what he was doing and of what people thought of it, he himself privately bade one of the tribunes interpose and procure his release. However, having won the multitude by these laws and gratifications, they decreed that Cæsar should have the government of Illyricum, and all Gaul, with an army of four legions, for the space of five years, though Cato still cried out they were, by their own vote, placing a tyrant in their citadel. Publius Clodius, a patrician, who illegally became a plebeian, was declared tribune of the people, as he had promised to do all things according to their pleasure, on condition he might banish Cicero. And for consuls, they set up Calpurnius Piso, the father of Cæsar's wife, and Aulus Gabinius, one of Pompey's creatures, as they tell us, who best knew his life and manners.

Yet when they had thus firmly established all things, having mastered one part of the city by favour, and the other by fear, they themselves were still afraid of Cato, and remembered with vexation what pains and trouble their success over him had cost them, and indeed what shame and disgrace, when at last they were driven to use violence to him. This made Clodius despair of driving Cicero out of Italy while Cato stayed at home. Therefore, having first laid his design, as soon as he came into his office, he sent for Cato, and told him that he looked upon him as the most incorrupt of all the Romans, and was ready to show he did so. "For whereas," said he, "many have applied to be sent to Cyprus on the commission in the case of Ptolemy and have solicited to have the appointment, I think you alone are deserving of it, and I desire to give you the favour of the appointment." Cato at once cried out it was a mere design upon him, and no favour, but an injury. Then Clodius proudly and fiercely answered, "If you will not take it as a kindness, you shall go, though never so unwillingly;" and immediately going into the assembly of the people he made them pass a decree, that Cato should be sent to Cyprus. But they ordered him neither ship, nor soldier, nor any attendant, except two secretaries, one of whom was a thief and a rascal, and the other a retainer to Clodius. Besides, as if Cyprus and Ptolemy were not work sufficient, he was ordered also to restore the refugees of Byzantium. For Clodius was resolved to keep him far enough off whilst himself continued tribune.

Cato, being in this necessity of going away, advised Cicero, who was next to be set upon, to make no resistance, lest he should throw the state into civil war and confusion, but to give way to the times, and thus become once more the preserver of his country. He himself sent forward Canidius, one of his friends, to Cyprus, to persuade Ptolemy to yield, without being forced; which if he did, he should want neither riches nor honour, for the Romans would give him the priesthood of the goddess at Paphos. He himself stayed at Rhodes, making some preparations, and expecting an answer from Cyprus. In the meantime, Ptolemy, King of Egypt, who had left Alexandria, upon some quarrel between him and his subjects, and was sailing for Rome, in hopes that Pompey and Cæsar would send troops to restore him, in his way thither desired to see Cato, to whom he sent, supposing he would come to him. Cato had taken purging medicine at the time when the messenger came, and made answer, that Ptolemy had better come to him, if he thought fit. And when he came, he neither went forward to meet him, nor so much as rose up to him, but saluting him as an ordinary person, bade him sit down. This at once threw Ptolemy into some confusion, who was surprised to see such stern and haughty manners in one who made so plain and unpretending an appearance; but afterwards, when he began to talk about his affairs, he was no less astonished at the wisdom and freedom of his discourse. For Cato blamed his conduct, and pointed out to him what honour and happiness he was abandoning, and what humiliations and troubles he would run himself into; what bribery he must resort to, and what cupidity he would have to satisfy when he came to the leading men at Rome, whom all Egypt turned into silver would scarcely content. He therefore advised him to return home and be reconciled to his subjects, offering to go along with him, and assist him in composing the differences. And by this language Ptolemy being brought to himself, as it might be out of a fit of madness or delirium, and discerning the truth and wisdom of what Cato said, resolved to follow his advice; but he was again over-persuaded by his friends to the contrary, and so, according to his first design, went to Rome. When he came there, and was forced to wait at the gate of one of the magistrates, he began to lament his folly in having rejected, rather, as it seemed to him, the oracle of a god than the advice merely of a good and wise man.

In the meantime, the other Ptolemy, in Cyprus, very luckily for Cato, poisoned himself. It was reported he had left great riches; therefore, Cato designing to go first to Byzantium, sent his nephew Brutus to Cyprus, as he would not wholly trust Canidius. Then, having reconciled the refugees and the people of Byzantium, he left the city in peace and quietness; and so sailed to Cyprus, where he found a royal treasure of plate, tables, precious stones and purple, all which was to be turned into ready money. And being determined to do everything with the greatest exactness, and to raise the price of everything to the utmost, to this end he was always present at selling the things, and went carefully into all the accounts. Nor would he trust to the usual customs of the market, but looked doubtfully upon all alike, the officers, criers, purchasers, and even his own friends; and so in fine he himself talked with the buyers, and urged them to bid high, and conducted in this manner the greatest part of the sales.

This mistrustfulness offended most of his friends, and in particular, Munatius, the most intimate of them all, became almost irreconcilable. And this afforded Cæsar the subject of his severest censures in the book he wrote against Cato. Yet Munatius himself relates, that the quarrel was not so much occasioned by Cato's mistrust, as by his neglect of him, and by his own jealousy of Canidius. For Munatius also wrote a book concerning Cato, which is the chief authority followed by Thrasea. Munatius says, that coming to Cyprus after the other, and having a very poor lodging provided for him, he went to Cato's house, but was not admitted, because he was engaged in private with Canidius; of which he afterwards complained in very gentle terms to Cato, but received a very harsh answer, that too much love, according to Theophrastus, often causes hatred; "and you," he said, "because you bear me much love, think you receive too little honour, and presently grow angry. I employ Canidius on account of his industry and his fidelity; he has been with me from the first, and I have found him to be trusted." These things were said in private between them two, but Cato afterwards told Canidius what had passed, on being informed of which, Munatius would no more go to sup with him, and when he was invited to give his counsel, refused to come. Then Cato threatened to seize his goods, as was the custom in the case of those who were disobedient; but Munatius not regarding his threats, returned to Rome, and continued a long time thus discontented. But afterwards, when Cato was come back also, Marcia, who as yet lived with him, contrived to have them both invited to sup together at the house of one Barca; Cato came in last of all, when the rest were laid down, and asked, where he should be. Barca answered him, where he pleased; then looking about, he said he would be near Munatius, and went and placed himself next to him; yet he showed him no other mark of kindness all the time they were at table together. But another time, at the entreaty of Marcia, Cato wrote to Munatius that he desired to speak with him. Munatius went to his house in the morning, and was kept by Marcia till all the company was gone; then Cato came, threw both his arms about him, and embraced him very kindly, and they were reconciled. I have the more fully related this passage, for that I think the manners and tempers of men are more clearly discovered by things of this nature, than by great and conspicuous actions.

Cato got together little less than seven thousand talents of silver; but apprehensive of what might happen in so long a voyage by sea, he provided a great many coffers that held two talents and five hundred drachmas apiece, to each of these he fastened a long rope, and to the other end of the rope a piece of cork, so that if the ship should miscarry, it might be discovered whereabout the chests lay under water. Thus all the money, except a very little, was safely transported. But he had made two books, in which all the accounts of his commission were carefully written out, and neither of these was preserved. For his freedman Philargyrus, who had the charge of one of them, setting sail from Cenchreæ, was lost, together with the ship and all her freight. And the other Cato himself kept safe till he came to Corcyra, but there he set up his tent in the marketplace, and the sailors, being very cold in the night, made a great many fires, some of which caught the tents, so that they were burnt, and the book lost. And though he had brought with him several of Ptolemy's, stewards, who could testify to his integrity, and stop the mouths of enemies and false accusers, yet the loss annoyed him, and he was vexed with himself about the matter, as he had designed them not so much for a proof of his own fidelity, as for a pattern of exactness to others.

The news did not fail to reach Rome that he was coming up the river. All the magistrates, the priests, and the whole senate, with great part of the people, went out to meet him; both the banks of the Tiber were covered with people; so that his entrance was in solemnity and honour not inferior to a triumph. But it was thought somewhat strange, and looked like wilfulness and pride, that when the consuls and prætors appeared, he did not disembark, nor stay to salute them, but rowed up the stream in a royal galley of six banks of oars, and stopped not till he brought his vessels to the dock. However, when the money was carried through the streets, the people much wondered at the vast quantity of it, and the senate being assembled, decreed him in honourable terms an extraordinary prætorship, and also the privilege of appearing at the public spectacles in a robe faced with purple. Cato declined all these honours, but declaring what diligence and fidelity he had found in Nicias, the steward of Ptolemy, he requested the senate to give him his freedom.

Philippus, the father of Marcia, was that year consul, and the authority and power of the office rested in a manner in Cato; for the other consul paid him no less regard for his virtue's sake than Philippus did on account of the connection between them. And Cicero, now being returned from his banishment, into which he was driven by Clodius, and having again obtained great credit among the people, went, in the absence of Clodius, and by force took away the records of his tribuneship, which had been laid up in the capitol. Hereupon the senate was assembled and Clodius complained of Cicero, who answered, that Clodius was never legally tribune, and therefore whatever he had done was void, and of no authority. But Cato interupted him while he spoke, and at last standing up said, that indeed he in no way justified or approved of Clodius's proceedings: but if they questioned the validity of what had been done in his tribuneship, they might also question what himself had done at Cyprus, for the expedition was unlawful, if he that sent him had no lawful authority: for himself, he thought Clodius was legally made tribune, who, by permission of the law, was from a patrician adopted into a plebeian family; if he had done ill in his office, he ought to be called to account for it; but the authority of the magistracy ought not to suffer for the faults of the magistrate. Cicero took this ill, and for a long time discontinued his friendship with Cato; but they were afterwards reconciled.

Pompey and Crassus, by agreement with Cæsar, who crossed the Alps to see them, had formed a design, that they two should stand to be chosen consuls a second time, and when they should be in their office, they would continue to Cæsar his government for five years more, and take to themselves the greatest provinces, with armies and money to maintain them. This seemed a plain conspiracy to subvert the constitution and parcel out the empire. Several men of high character had intended to stand to be consuls that year, but upon the appearance of these great competitors. they all desisted, except only Lucius Domitius, who had married Porcia, the sister of Cato, and was by him persuaded to stand it out, and not abandon such an undertaking, which, he said, was not merely to gain the consulship, but to save the liberty of Rome. In the meantime, it was the common topic among the more prudent part of the citizens, that they ought not to suffer the power of Pompey and Crassus to be united, which would then be carried beyond all bounds, and become dangerous to the state; that therefore one of them must be denied. For these reasons they took part with Domitius, whom they exhorted and encouraged to go on, assuring him that many who feared openly to appear for him, would privately assist him. Pompey's party fearing this, laid wait for Domitius, and set upon him as he was going before daylight, with torches, into the Field. First, he that bore the light next before Domitius was knocked down and killed; then several others being wounded, all the rest fled, except Cato and Domitius, whom Cato held, though himself were wounded in the arm, and crying out, conjured the others to stay, and not, while they had any breath, forsake the defence of their liberty against those tyrants, who plainly showed with what moderation they were likely to use the power which they endeavoured to gain by such violence. But at length Domitius, also, no longer willing to face the danger, fled to his own house, and so Pompey and Crassus were declared elected.

Nevertheless, Cato would not give over, but resolved to stand himself to be prætor that year, which he thought would be some help to him in his design of opposing them; that he might not act as a private man, when he was to contend with public magistrates. Pompey and Crassus apprehended this; and fearing that the office of prætor in the person of Cato might be equal in authority to that of consul, they assembled the senate unexpectedly, without giving notice to a great many of the senators, and made an order, that those who were chosen prætors should immediately enter upon their office, without attending the usual time, in which, according to law, they might be accused, if they had corrupted the people with gifts. When by this order they had got leave to bribe freely, without being called to account, they set up their own friends and dependents to stand for the prætorship, giving money, and watching the people as they voted. Yet the virtue and reputation of Cato was like to triumph over all these stratagems; for the people generally felt it to be shameful that a price should be paid for the rejection of Cato, who ought rather to be paid himself to take upon him the office. So he carried it by the voices of the first tribe. Hereupon Pompey immediately framed a lie, crying out, it thundered; and straight broke up the assembly, for the Romans religiously observed this as a bad omen, and never concluded any matter after it had thundered. Before the next time, they had distributed larger bribes, and driving also the best men out of the Field, by these foul means they procured Vatinius to be chosen prætor, instead of Cato. It is said, that those who had thus corruptly and dishonestly given their voices hurried, as if it were in flight, out of the Field. The others staying together, and exclaiming at the event, one of the tribunes continued the assembly, and Cato standing up, as it were by inspiration, foretold all the miseries that afterwards befell the state, exhorted them to beware of Pompey and Crassus, who were guilty of such things, and had laid such designs, that they might well fear to have Cato prætor. When he had ended this speech, he was followed to his house by a greater number of people than all the new prætors elect put together.

Caius Trebonius now proposed the law for allotting provinces to the consuls, one of whom was to have Spain and Africa, the other Egypt and Syria, with full power of making war, and carrying it on both by sea and land, as they should think fit. When this was proposed, all others despaired of putting any stop to it, and neither did nor said anything against it. But Cato, before the voting began, went up into the place of speaking, and desiring to be heard, was with much difficulty allowed two hours to speak. Having spent that time in informing them and reasoning with them, and in foretelling to them much that was to come, he was not suffered to speak any longer; but as he was going on, a serjeant came and pulled him down; yet when he was down, he still continued speaking in a loud voice, and finding many to listen to him, and join in his indignation. Then the serjeant took him, and forced him out of the forum; but as soon as he got loose, he returned again to the place of speaking, crying out to the people to stand by him. When he had done thus several times, Trebonius grew very angry, and commanded him to be carried to prison; but the multitude followed him, and listened to the speech which he made to them as he went along; so that Trebonius began to be afraid again, and ordered him to be released. Thus that day was expended, and the business staved off by Cato. But in the days succeeding, many of the citizens being overawed by fears and threats, and others won by gifts and favours, Aquillius, one of the tribunes, they kept by an armed force within the senate-house; Cato, who cried it thundered, they drove out of the forum; many were wounded, and some slain; and at length by open force they passed the law. At this many were so incensed that they got together and were going to throw down the statues of Pompey; but Cato went and diverted them from that design.

Again, another law was proposed, concerning the provinces and legions of Cæsar. Upon this occasion Cato did not apply himself to the people, but appealed to Pompey himself; and told him, he did not consider now that he was setting Cæsar upon his own shoulders, who would shortly grow too weighty for him; and at length, not able to lay down the burden, nor yet to bear it any longer, he would precipitate both it and himself with it upon the commonwealth; and then he would remember Cato's advice, which was no less advantageous to him than just and honest in itself. Thus was Pompey often warned, but still disregarded and slighted it, never mistrusting Cæsar's change, and always confiding in his own power and good fortune.

Cato was made prætor the following year; but, it seems, he did not do more honour and credit to the office by his signal integrity than he disgraced and diminished it by his strange behaviour. For he would often come to the court without his shoes, and sit upon the bench without any undergarment, and in this attire would give judgment in capital causes, and upon persons of the highest rank. It is said, also, he used to drink wine after his morning meal, and then transact the business of his office; but this was wrongfully reported of him. The people were at that time extremely corrupted by the gifts of those who sought offices, and most made a constant trade of selling their voices. Cato was eager utterly to root this corruption out of the commonwealth; he therefore persuaded the senate to make an order, that those who were chosen into any office, though nobody should accuse them, should be obliged to come into the court, and give account upon oath of their proceedings in their election. This was extremely obnoxious to those who stood for the offices, and yet more to those vast numbers who took the bribes. Insomuch that one morning, as Cato was going to the tribunal, a great multitude of people flocked together, and with loud cries and maledictions reviled him, and threw stones at him. Those that were about the tribunal presently fled, and Cato himself being forced thence, and jostled about in the throng, very narrowly escaped the stones that were thrown at him, and with much difficulty got hold of the rostra; where, standing up with a bold and undaunted countenance, he at once mastered the tumult, and silenced the clamour; and addressing them in fit terms for the occasion, was heard with great attention, and perfectly quelled the sedition. Afterwards, on the senate commending him for this, "But I," said he, "do not commend you for abandoning your prætor in danger, and bringing him no assistance."

In the meantime, the candidates were in great perplexity; for every one dreaded to give money himself, and yet feared lest his competitors should. At length they agreed to lay down one hundred and twenty-five thousand drachmas apiece, and then all of them to canvass fairly and honestly, on condition, that if any one was found to make use of bribery he should forfeit the money. Being thus agreed, they chose Cato to keep the stakes, and arbitrate the matter; to him they brought the sum concluded on, and before him subscribed the agreement. The money he did not choose to have paid for them, but took their securities who stood bound for them. Upon the day of election, he placed himself by the tribune who took the votes, and very watchfully observing all that passed, he discovered one who had broken the agreement, and immediately ordered him to pay his money to the rest. They, however, commending his justice highly, remitted the penalty, as thinking the discovery a sufficient punishment. It raised, however, as much envy against Cato as it gained him reputation, and many were offended at his thus taking upon himself the whole authority of the senate, the courts of judicature, and the magistracies. For there is no virtue, the honour and credit for which procures a man more odium than that of justice; and this, because more than any other, it acquires a man power and authority among the common people. For they only honour the valiant and admire the wise, while in addition they also love just men, and put entire trust and confidence in them. They fear the bold man, and mistrust the clever man, and moreover think them rather beholding to their natural complexion, than to any goodness of their will, for these excellences; they look upon valour as a certain natural strength of the mind, and wisdom as a constitutional acuteness; whereas a man has it in his power to be just, if he have but the will to be so, and therefore injustice is thought the most dishonourable, because it is least excusable.

Cato upon this account was opposed by all the great men, who thought themselves reproved by his virtue. Pompey especially looked upon the increase of Cato's credit as the ruin of his own power, and therefore continually set up men to rail against him. Among these was the seditious Clodius, now again united to Pompey, who declared openly, that Cato had conveyed away a great deal of the treasure that was found in Cyprus; and that he hated Pompey only because he refused to marry his daughter. Cato answered, that although they had allowed him neither horse nor man, he had brought more treasure from Cyprus alone, than Pompey had, after so many wars and triumphs, from the ransacked world; that he never sought the alliance of Pompey; not that he thought him unworthy of being related to him, but because he differed so much from him in things that concerned the commonwealth. "For," said he, "I laid down the province that was given me, when I went out of my prætorship; Pompey, on the contrary, retains many provinces for himself, and he bestows many on others; and but now he sent Cæsar a force of six thousand men into Gaul, which Cæsar never asked the people for, nor had Pompey obtained their consent to give. Men, and horse and arms, in any number, are become the mutual gifts of private men to one another; and Pompey, keeping the titles of commander and general, hands over the armies and provinces to others to govern, while he himself stays at home to preside at the contests of the canvass, and to stir up tumults at elections; out of the anarchy he thus creates among us, seeking, we see well enough, a monarchy for himself." Thus he retorted on Pompey.

He had an intimate friend and admirer of the name of Marcus Favonius, much the same to Cato as we are told Apollodorus, the Phalerian, was in old time to Socrates, whose words used to throw him into perfect transports and ecstasies, getting into his head, like strong wine, and intoxicating him to a sort of frenzy. This Favonius stood to be chosen ædile, and was like to lose it; but Cato, who was there to assist him, observed that all the votes were written in one hand, and discovering the cheat, appealed to the tribunes, who stopped the election. Favonius was afterwards chosen ædile, and Cato, who assisted him in all things that belonged to his office, also undertook the care of the spectacles that were exhibited in the theatre; giving the actors crowns, not of gold, but of wild olive, such as used to be given at the Olympic games; and instead of the magnificent presents that were usually made, he offered to the Greeks beet root, lettuces, radishes, and pears; and to the Romans earthen pots of wine, pork, figs, cucumbers, and little faggots of wood. Some ridiculed Cato for his economy, others looked with respect on this gentle relaxation of his usual rigour and austerity. In fine, Favonius himself mingled with the crowd, and sitting among the spectators, clapped and applauded Cato, bade him bestow rewards on those who did well, and called on the people to pay their honours to him, as for himself he had placed his whole authority in Cato's hands. At the same time, Curio, the colleague of Favonius, gave very magnificent entertainments in another theatre; but the people left his, and went to those of Favonius, which they much applauded, and joined heartily in the diversion, seeing him act the private man, and Cato the master of the shows, who, in fact, did all this in derision of the great expenses that others incurred, and to teach them, that in amusements men ought to seek amusement only, and the display of a decent cheerfulness, not great preparations and costly magnificence, demanding the expenditure of endless care and trouble about things of little concern.

After this, Scipio, Hypsæus, and Milo, stood to be consuls, and that not only with the usual and now recognised disorders of bribery and corruption, but with arms and slaughter, and every appearance of carrying their audacity and desperation to the length of actual civil war. Whereupon it was proposed that Pompey might be empowered to preside over that election. This Cato at first opposed, saying that the laws ought not to seek protection from Pompey, but Pompey from the laws. Yet the confusion lasting a long time, the forum continually, as it were, besieged with three armies, and no possibility appearing of a stop being put to these disorders, Cato at length agreed that, rather than fall into the last extremity, the senate should freely confer all on Pompey; since it was necessary to make use of a lesser illegality as a remedy against the greatest of all, and better to set up a monarchy themselves than to suffer a sedition to continue that must certainly end in one. Bibulus, therefore, a friend of Cato's, moved the senate to create Pompey sole consul; for that either he would reestablish the lawful government, or they should serve under the master. Cato stood up, and, contrary to all expectation, seconded this motion, concluding that any government was better than mere confusion, and that he did not question but Pompey would deal honourably, and take care of the commonwealth thus committed to his charge. Pompey being hereupon declared consul, invited Cato to see him in the suburbs. When he came, he saluted and embraced him very kindly, acknowledged the favour he had done him, and desired his counsel and assistance, in the management of this office. Cato made answer, that what he had spoken on any former occasion was not out of hate to Pompey, nor what he had now done out of love to him, but all for the good of the commonwealth; that in private, if he asked him, he would freely give his advice; and in public, though he asked him not, he would always speak his opinion. And he did accordingly. For first, when Pompey made severe laws, for punishing and laying great fines on those who had corrupted the people with gifts, Cato advised him to let alone what was already passed, and to provide for the future; for if he should look up past misdemeanours, it would be difficult to know where to stop; and if he would ordain new penalties, it would be unreasonable to punish men by a law, which at that time they had not the opportunity of breaking. Afterwards, when many considerable men, and some of Pompey's own relations, were accused, and he grew remiss, and disinclined to the prosecution, Cato sharply reproved him, and urged him to proceed. Pompey had made a law, also, to forbid the custom of making commendatory orations in behalf of those that were accused; yet he himself wrote one for Munatius Plancus, and sent it while the cause was pleading; upon which Cato, who was sitting as one of the judges, stopped his ears with his hands, and would not hear it read. Whereupon Plancus, before sentence was given, excepted against him, but was condemned notwithstanding. And indeed Cato was a great trouble and perplexity to almost all that were accused of anything, as they feared to have him one of their judges, yet did not dare to demand his exclusion. And many had been condemned because, by refusing him, they seemed to show that they could not trust to their own innocence; and it was a reproach thrown in the teeth of some by their enemies, that they had not accepted Cato for their judge.

In the meanwhile, Cæsar kept close with his forces in Gaul, and continued in arms; and at the same time employed his gifts, his riches, and his friends above all things, to increase his power in the city. And now Cato's old admonitions began to rouse Pompey out of the negligent security in which he lay, into a sort of imagination of danger at hand; but seeing him slow and unwilling, and timorous to undertake any measures of prevention against Cæsar, Cato resolved himself to stand for the consulship, and presently force Cæsar either to lay down his arms or discover his intentions. Both Cato's competitors were persons of good position; Sulpicius, who was one, owed much to Cato's credit and authority in the city, and it was thought unhandsome and ungratefully done, to stand against him; not that Cato himself took it ill, "For it is no wonder," said he, "if a man will not yield to another, in that which he esteems the greatest good." He had persuaded the senate to make an order, that those who stood for offices should themselves ask the people for their votes, and not solicit by others, nor take others about with them to speak for them, in their canvass. And this made the common people very hostile to him, if they were to lose not only the means of receiving money, but also the opportunity of obliging several persons, and so to become by his means both poor and less regarded. Besides this, Cato himself was by nature altogether unfit for the business of canvassing, as he was more anxious to sustain the dignity of his life and character than to obtain the office. Thus by following his own way of soliciting, and not suffering his friends to do those things which take away the multitude, he was rejected and lost the consulship.

But whereas, upon such occasions, not only those who missed the office, but even their friends and relations, used to feel themselves disgraced and humiliated, and observed a sort of mourning for several days after, Cato took it so unconcernedly that he anointed himself, and played at ball in the field, and after breakfasting, went into the forum, as he used to do, without his shoes or his tunic, and there walked about with his acquaintance. Cicero blames him, for that when affairs required such a consul, he would not take more pains, nor condescend to pay some court to the people, as also because that he afterwards neglected to try again; whereas he had stood a second time to be chosen prætor. Cato answered that he lost the prætorship the first time, not by the voice of the people, but by the violence and corrupt dealing of his adversaries; whereas in the election of consuls there had been no foul play. So that he plainly saw the people did not like his manners, which an honest man ought not to alter for their sake;

nor yet would a wise man attempt the same thing again, while liable to the same prejudices.

Cæsar was at this time engaged with many warlike nations, and was subduing them at great hazards. Among the rest, it was believed he had set upon the Germans, in a time of truce, and had thus slain three hundred thousand of them. Upon which, some of his friends moved the senate for a public thanksgiving; but Cato declared they ought to deliver Cæsar into the hands of those who had been thus unjustly treated, and so expiate the offence and not bring a curse upon the city; "Yet we have reason," said he, "to thank the gods, for that they spared the commonwealth, and did not take vengeance upon the army, for the madness and folly of the general." Hereupon Cæsar wrote a letter to the senate which was read openly, and was full of reproachful language and accusations against Cato; who, standing up, seemed not at all concerned, and without any heat or passion, but in a calm and, as it were, premeditated discourse, made all Cæsar's charges against him show like mere common scolding and abuse, and in fact a sort of pleasantry and play on Cæsar's part; and proceeding then to go into all Cæsar's political courses, and to explain and reveal (as though he had been not his constant opponent, but his fellow-conspirator) his whole conduct and purpose from its commencement, he concluded by telling the senate, it was not the sons of the Britons or the Gauls they need fear, but Cæsar himself, if they were wise. And this discourse so moved and awakened the senate, that Cæsar's friends repented they had had a letter read, which had given Cato an opportunity of saying so many reasonable things, and such severe truths against him. However, nothing was then decided upon; it was merely said, that it would be well to send him a successor. Upon that, Cæsar's friends required that Pompey also should lay down his arms, and resign his provinces, or else that Cæsar might not be obliged to either. Then Cato cried out, what he had foretold was come to pass; now it was manifest he was using his forces to compel their judgment, and was turning against the state those armies he had got from it by imposture and trickery. But out of the senate-house Cato could do but little, as the people were ever ready to magnify Cæsar; and the senate, though convinced by Cato, were afraid of the people.

But when the news was brought that Cæsar had seized Ariminum, and was marching with his army toward Rome, then all men, even Pompey, and the common people too, cast their eyes on Cato, who had alone foreseen and first clearly declared Cæsar's intentions. He therefore told them, "If you had believed me, or regarded my advice, you would not now have been reduced to stand in fear of one man, or to put all your hopes in one alone." Pompey acknowledged that Cato indeed had spoken most like a prophet, while he himself had acted too much like a friend. And Cato advised the senate to put all into the hands of Pompey; "For those who can raise up great evils," said he, "can best allay them."

Pompey, finding he had not sufficient forces, and that those he could raise were not very resolute, forsook the city. Cato, resolving to follow Pompey into exile, sent his younger son to Munatius, who was then in the country of Bruttium, and took his eldest son with him; but wanting somebody to keep his house and take care of his daughters, he took Marcia again, who was now a rich widow, Hortensius being dead, and having left her all his estate. Cæsar afterward made use of this action also, to reproach him with covetousness, and a mercenary design in his marriage. "For," said he, "if he had need of a wife why did he part with her? And if he had not, why did he take her again? Unless he gave her only as a bait to Hortensius; and lent her when she was young, to have her again when she was rich." But in answer to this, we might fairly apply the saying of Euripides—

> "To speak of mysteries—the chief of these
> Surely were cowardice in Hercules."

For it is much the same thing to reproach Hercules for cowardice, and to accuse Cato of covetousness; though otherwise, whether he did altogether right in this marriage, might be disputed. As soon, however, as he had again taken Marcia, he committed his house and his daughters to her, and himself followed Pompey. And it is said, that from that day he never cut his hair, nor shaved his beard, nor wore a garland, but was always full of sadness, grief, and dejectedness for the calamities of his country, and continually showed the same feeling to the last, whatever party had misfortune or success.

The government of Sicily being allotted to him, he passed over to Syracuse; where, understanding that Asinius Pollio was arrived at Messena, with forces from the enemy, Cato sent to him, to know the reason of his coming thither: Pollio, on the other side, called upon him to show reason for the present convulsions. And being at the same time informed how Pompey had quite abandoned Italy, and lay encamped at Dyrrhachium, he spoke of the strangeness and incomprehensibility of the divine government of things; "Pompey, when he did nothing wisely nor honestly, was always successful; and now that he would preserve his country, and defend her liberty, he is altogether unfortunate." As for Asinius, he said, he could drive him out of Sicily, but as there were larger forces coming to his assistance, he would not engage the island in a war. He therefore advised the Syracusans to join the conquering party and provide for their own safety; and so set sail from thence.

When he came to Pompey, he uniformly gave advice to protract the war; as he always hoped to compose matters, and was by no means desirous that they should come to action; for the commonwealth would suffer extremely, and be the certain cause of its own ruin, whoever were conqueror by the sword. In like manner, he persuaded Pompey and the council to ordain that no city should be sacked that was subject to the people of Rome; and that no Roman should be killed but in the heat of battle; and hereby he got himself great honour, and brought over many to Pompey's party, whom his moderation and humanity attracted. Afterwards being sent into Asia, to assist those who were raising men and preparing ships in those parts, he took with him his sister Servilia, and a little boy whom she had by Lucullus. For since her widowhood, she had lived with her brother, and much recovered her reputation, having put herself under his care, followed him in his voyages, and complied with his severe way of living. Yet Cæsar did not fail to asperse him upon her account also.

Pompey's officers in Asia, it seems, had no great need of Cato; but he brought over the people of Rhodes by his persuasions, and leaving his sister Servilia and her child there, he returned to Pompey, who had now collected very great forces both by sea and land. And here Pompey, more than in any other act, betrayed his intentions. For at first he designed to give Cato the command of the navy, which consisted of no less than five hundred ships of war, besides a vast number of light galleys, scouts, and open boats. But presently bethinking himself, or put in mind by his friends, that Cato's principal and only aim being to free his country from all usurpation, if he were master of such great forces, as soon as ever Cæsar should be conquered, he would certainly call upon Pompey, also, to lay down his arms, and be subject to the laws, he changed his mind, and though he had already mentioned it to Cato, nevertheless made Bibulus admiral. Notwithstanding this, he had no reason to suppose that Cato's zeal in the cause was in any way diminished. For before one of the battles at Dyrrhachium, when Pompey himself, we are told, made an address to the soldiers and bade the officers do the like, the men listened to them but coldly and with silence, until Cato, last of all, came forward, and in the language of philosophy, spoke to them, as the occasion required, concerning liberty, manly virtue, death, and a good name; upon all which he delivered himself with strong natural passion, and concluded with calling in the aid of the gods, to whom he directed his speech, as if they were present to behold them fight for their country. And at this the army gave such a shout and showed such excitement that their officers led them on full of hope and confidence to the danger. Cæsar's party were routed and put to flight; but his presiding fortune used the advantage of Pompey's cautiousness and diffidence to render the victory incomplete. But of this we have spoken in the life of Pompey.

While, however, all the rest rejoiced, and magnified their success, Cato alone bewailed his country, and cursed that fatal ambition which made so many brave Romans murder one another.

After this Pompey, following Cæsar into Thessaly, left at Dyrrhachium a quantity of munitions, money, and stores, and many of his domestics and relations; the charge of all which he gave to Cato, with the command only of fifteen cohorts. For though he trusted him much, yet he was afraid of him too, knowing full well, that if he had bad success, Cato would be the last to forsake him, but if he conquered, would never let him use his victory at his pleasure. There were, likewise, many persons of high rank that stayed with Cato at Dyrrhachium. When they heard of the overthrow at Pharsalia, Cato resolved with himself, that if Pompey were slain, he would conduct those that were with him into Italy, and then retire as far from the tyranny of Cæsar as he could, and live in exile; but if Pompey were safe, he would keep the army together for him. With this resolution he passed over to Corcyra, where the navy lay; there he would have resigned his command to Cicero, because he had been consul, and himself only a prætor: but Cicero refused it, and was going for Italy. At which Pompey's son being incensed, would rashly and in heat have punished all those who were going away, and in the first place have laid hands on Cicero; but Cato spoke with him in private, and diverted him from that design. And thus he clearly saved the life of Cicero, and rescued several others also from ill-treatment.

Conjecturing that Pompey the Great was fled toward Egypt or Africa, Cato resolved to hasten after him; and having taken all his men aboard, he set sail; but first to those who were not zealous to continue the contest, he gave free liberty to depart. When they came to the coast of Africa they met with Sextus, Pompey's youngest son, who told them of the death of his father in Egypt; at which they were all exceedingly grieved, and declared that after Pompey they would follow no other leader but Cato. Out of compassion, therefore, to so many worthy persons, who had given such testimonies of their fidelity, and whom he could not for shame leave in a desert country, amidst so many difficulties, he took upon him the command, and marched toward the city of Cyrene, which presently received him, though not long before they had shut their gates against Labienus. Here he was informed that Scipio, Pompey's father-in-law, was received by King Juba, and that Attius Varus, whom Pompey had made governor of Africa, had joined them with his forces. Cato therefore resolved to march toward them by land, it being now winter; and got together a number of asses to carry water, and furnished himself likewise with plenty of all other provision, and a number of carriages. He took also with him some of those they call Psylli, who cure the biting of serpents, by sucking out the poison with their mouths, and have likewise certain charms, by which they stupefy and lay asleep the serpents.

Thus they marched seven days together, Cato all the time going on foot at the head of his men, and never making use of any horse or chariot. Ever since the battle of Pharsalia, he used to sit at table, and added this to his other ways of mourning, that he never lay down but to sleep.

Having passed the winter in Africa, Cato drew out his army, which amounted to little less than ten thousand. The affairs of Scipio and Varus went very ill, by reason of their dissensions and quarrels among themselves, and their submissions and flatteries to King Juba, who was insupportable for his vanity, and the pride he took in his strength and riches. The first time he came to a conference with Cato, he had ordered his own seat to be placed in the middle, between Scipio and Cato; which Cato observing, took up his chair and set himself on the other side of Scipio, to whom he thus gave the honour of sitting in the middle, though he were his enemy, and had formerly published some scandalous writing against him. There are people who speak as if this were quite an insignificant matter, and who, nevertheless, find fault with Cato, because in Sicily, walking one day with Philostratus, he gave him the middle place, to show his respect for philosophy. However, he now succeeded both in humbling the pride of Juba, who was treating Scipio and Varus much like a pair of satraps under his orders, and also in reconciling them to each other. All the troops desired him to be their leader; Scipio, likewise, and Varus gave way to it, and offered him the command; but he said he would not break those laws which he sought to defend, and he, being but proprætor, ought not to command in the presence of a proconsul (for Scipio had been created proconsul), besides that people took it as a good omen to see a Scipio command in Africa, and the very name inspired the soldiers with hopes of success.

Scipio, having taken upon him the command, presently resolved, at the instigation of Juba, to put all the inhabitants of Utica to the sword, and to raze the city, for having, as they professed, taken part with Cæsar. Cato would by no means suffer this; but invoking the gods, exclaiming and protesting against it in the council of war, he with much difficulty delivered the poor people from this cruelty. And afterwards, upon the entreaty of the inhabitants, and at the instance of Scipio, Cato took upon himself the government of Utica, lest, one way or the other, it should fall into Cæsar's hands; for it was a strong place, and very advantageous for either party. And it was yet better provided and more strongly fortified by Cato, who brought in great store of corn, repaired the walls, erected towers, and made deep trenches and palisades around the town. The young men of Utica he lodged among these works, having first taken their arms from them; the rest of the inhabitants he kept within the town, and took the greatest care that no injury should be done nor affront offered them by the Romans. From hence he sent great quantity of arms, money, and provision to the camp, and made this city their chief magazine.

He advised Scipio, as he had before done Pompey, by no means to hazard a battle against a man experienced in war, and formidable in the field, but to use delay; for time would gradually abate the violence of the crisis, which is the strength of usurpation. But Scipio out of pride rejected this counsel, and wrote a letter to Cato, in which he reproached him with cowardice; and that he could not be content to lie secure himself within walls and trenches, but he must hinder others from boldly using their own good sense to seize the right opportunity. In answer to this, Cato wrote word again, that he would take the horse and foot which he had brought into Africa, and go over into Italy, to make a diversion there, and draw Cæsar off from them. But Scipio derided this proposition also. Then Cato openly let it be seen that he was sorry he had yielded the command to Scipio. who he saw would not carry on the war with any wisdom, and if, contrary to all appearance, he should succeed, he would use his success as unjustly at home. For Cato had then made up his mind, and so he told his friends, that he could have but slender hopes in those generals that had so much boldness and so little conduct; yet if anything should happen beyond expectation, and Cæsar should be overthrown, for his part he would not stay at Rome, but would retire from the cruelty and inhumanity of Scipio, who had already uttered fierce and proud threats against many.

But what Cato had looked for, fell out sooner than he expected. Late in the evening came one from the army, whence he had been three days coming, who brought word there had been a great battle near Thapsus that all was utterly lost; Cæsar had taken the camps, Scipio and Juba were fled with a few only, and all the rest of the army were lost. This news arriving in time of war, and in the night, so alarmed the people, that they were almost out of their wits, and could scarce keep themselves within the walls of the city. But Cato came forward, and meeting the people in this hurry and clamour, did all he could to comfort and encourage them, and somewhat appeased the fear and amazement they were in, telling them that very likely things were not so bad in truth, but much exaggerated in the report. And so he pacified the tumult for the present. The next morning he sent for three hundred, whom he used as his council; these were Romans, who were in Africa upon business, in commerce and money-lending; there were also several senators and their sons. They were summoned to meet in the temple of Jupiter. While they were coming together, Cato walked about very quietly and unconcerned, as if nothing new had happened. He had a book in his hand, which he was reading; in this book was an account of what provision he had for war, armour, corn, ammunition, and soldiers.

When they were assembled, he began his discourse; first, as regarded the three hundred themselves, and very much commended the courage and fidelity they had shown, and their having very well served their country with their persons, money, and counsel. Then he entreated them by no means to separate, as if each single man could hope for any safety in forsaking his companions; on the contrary, while they kept together, Cæsar would have less reason to despise them, if they fought against him, and be more forward to pardon them, if they submitted to him. Therefore he advised them to consult among themselves, nor should he find fault whichever course they adopted. If they thought fit to submit to fortune, he would impute their change to necessity; but if they resolved to stand firm, and undertake the danger for the sake of liberty, he should not only commend, but admire their courage, and would himself be their leader and companion too, till they had put to the proof the utmost fortune of their country; which was not Utica or Adrumetum but Rome, and she had often, by her own greatness, raised herself after worse disasters. Besides, as there were many things that would conduce to their safety, so chiefly this, that they were to fight against one whose affairs urgently claimed his presence in various quarters. Spain was already revolted to the younger Pompey; Rome was unaccustomed to the bridle, and impatient of it, and would therefore be ready to rise in insurrection upon any turn of affairs. As for themselves, they ought not to shrink from the danger; and in this might take example from their enemy, who so freely exposes his life to effect the most unrighteous designs, yet never can hope for so happy a conclusion as they may promise themselves; for notwithstanding the uncertainty of war, they will be sure of a most happy life if they succeed, or a most glorious death if they miscarry. However, he said, they ought to deliberate among themselves; and he joined with them in praying the gods that in recompense of their former courage and good-will, they would prosper their present determinations. When Cato had thus spoken, many were moved and encouraged by his arguments, but the greatest part were so animated by the sense of his intrepidity, generosity, and goodness, that they forgot the present danger, and as if he were the only invincible leader, and above all fortune, they entreated him to employ their persons, arms, and estates, as he thought fit; for they esteemed it far better to meet death in following his counsel, than to find their safety in betraying one of so great virtue. One of the assembly proposed the making a decree to set the slaves at liberty; and most of the rest approved the motion. Cato said that it ought not to be done, for it was neither just nor lawful; but if any of their masters would willingly set them free, those that were fit for service should be received. Many promised so to do, whose names he ordered to be enrolled, and then withdrew.

Presently after this he received letters from Juba and Scipio. Juba, with some few of his men, was retired to a mountain, where he waited to hear what Cato would resolve upon; and intended to stay there for him, if he thought fit to leave Utica, or to come to his aid with his troops, if he were besieged. Scipio was on shipboard, near a certain promontory, not far from Utica, expecting an answer upon the same account. But Cato thought fit to retain the messengers till the three hundred should come to some resolution.

As for the senators that were there, they showed great forwardness, and at once set free their slaves, and furnished them with arms. But the three hundred being men occupied in merchandise and money-lending, much of their substance also consisting in slaves, the enthusiasm that Cato's speech had raised in them did not long continue. As there are substances that easily admit heat, and as suddenly lose it, when the fire is removed, so these men were heated and inflamed while Cato was present; but when they began to reason among themselves, the fear they had of Cæsar soon overcame their reverence for Cato and for virtue. "For who are we," said they, "and who is it we refuse to obey? Is it not that Cæsar who is now invested with all the power of Rome? and which of us is a Scipio, a Pompey, or a Cato? But now that all men make their honour give way to their fear, shall we alone engage for the liberty of Rome, and in Utica declare war against him, before whom Cato and Pompey the Great fled out of Italy? Shall we set free our slaves against Cæsar, who have ourselves no more liberty than he is pleased to allow? No, let us, poor creatures, know ourselves, submit to the victor, and send deputies to implore his mercy." Thus said the most moderate of them; but the greatest part were for seizing the senators, that by securing them they might appease Cæsar's anger. Cato, though he perceived the change, took no notice of it; but wrote to Juba and Scipio to keep away from Utica, because he mistrusted the three hundred.

A considerable body of horse, which had escaped from the late fight, riding up towards Utica, sent three men before to Cato, who yet did not all bring the same message; for one party was for going to Juba, another for joining with Cato, and some again were afraid to go into Utica. When Cato heard this, he ordered Marcus Rubrius to attend upon the three hundred, and quietly take the names of those who, of their own accord, set their slaves at liberty, but by no means to force anybody. Then taking with him the senators, he went out of the town, and met the principal officers of these horsemen, whom he entreated not to abandon so many Roman senators, not to prefer Juba for their commander before Cato, but consult the common safety, and to come into the city, which was impregnable, and well furnished with corn and other provision, sufficient for many years. The senators likewise with tears besought them to stay. Hereupon the officers went to consult their soldiers, and Cato with the senators sat down upon an embankment, expecting their resolution. In the meantime comes Rubrius in great disorder, crying out, the three hundred were all in commotion, and exciting revolt and tumult in the city. At this all the rest fell into despair, lamenting and bewailing their condition. Cato endeavoured to comfort them, and sent to the three hundred, desiring them to have patience. Then the officers of the horse returned with no very reasonable demands. They said, they did not desire to serve Juba for his pay, nor should they fear Cæsar, while they followed Cato, but they dreaded to be shut up with the Uticans, men of traitorous temper, and Carthaginian blood; for though they were quiet at present, yet as soon as Cæsar should appear, without doubt they would conspire together, and betray the Romans. Therefore, if he expected they should join with him, he must drive out of the town or destroy all the Uticans, that he might receive them into a place clear both of enemies and barbarians. This Cato thought utterly cruel and barbarous; but he mildly answered, he would consult the three hundred.

Then he returned to the city, where he found the men, not framing excuses, or dissembling out of reverence to him, but openly declaring that no one should compel them to make war against Cæsar; which, they said, they were neither able nor willing to do. And some there were who muttered words about retaining the senators till Cæsar's coming; but Cato seemed not to hear this, as indeed he had the excuse of being a little deaf. At the same time came one to him and told him the horse were going away. And now, fearing lest the three hundred should take some desperate resolution concerning the senators, he presently went out with some of his friends, and seeing they were gone some way, he took horse, and rode after them. They, when they saw him coming, were very glad, and received him very kindly, entreating him to save himself with them. At this time, it is said, Cato shed tears, while entreating them on behalf of the senators, and stretching out his hands in supplication. He turned some of their horses' heads, and laid hold of the men by their armour, till in fine he prevailed with them out of compassion, to stay only that one day, to procure a safe retreat for the senators. Having thus persuaded them to go along with him, some he placed at the gates of the town, and to others gave the charge of the citadel. The three hundred began to fear they should suffer for their inconstancy, and sent to Cato, entreating him by all means to come to them; but the senators flocking about him, would not suffer him to go, and said they would not trust their guardian and saviour to the hands of perfidious traitors.

For there had never, perhaps, been a time when Cato's virtue appeared more manifestly; and every class of men in Utica could clearly see, with sorrow and admiration, how entirely free was everything that he was doing from any secret motives or any mixture of self-regard; he, namely, who had long before resolved on his own death, was taking such extreme pains, toil, and care, only for the sake of others, that when he had secured their lives, he might put an end to his own. For it was easily perceived that he had determined to die, though he did not let it appear.

Therefore, having pacified the senators, he complied with the request of the three hundred, and went to them alone without any attendance. They gave him many thanks, and entreated him to employ and trust them for the future; and if they were not Catos, and could not aspire to his greatness of mind, they begged he would pity their weakness; and told him they had determined to send to Cæsar and entreat him, chiefly and in the first place, for Cato, and if they could not prevail for him, they would not accept of pardon for themselves, but as long as they had breath, would fight in his defence. Cato commended their good intentions, and advised them to send speedily, for their own safety, but by no means to ask anything in his behalf; for those who are conquered, entreat, and those who have done wrong, beg pardon; for himself, he did not confess to any defeat in all his life, but rather, so far as he had thought fit, he had got the victory, and had conquered Cæsar in all points of justice and honesty. It was Cæsar that ought to be looked upon as one surprised and vanquished; for he was now convicted and found guilty of those designs against his country, which he had so long practised and so constantly denied. When he had thus spoken, he went out of the assembly, and being informed that Cæsar was coming with his whole army, "Ah," said he, "he expects to find us brave men." Then he went to the senators, and urged them to make no delay, but hasten to be gone, while the horsemen were yet in the city. So ordering all the gates to be shut, except one towards the sea, he assigned their several ships to those that were to depart, and gave money and provision to those that wanted; all which he did with great order and exactness, taking care to suppress all tumults, and that no wrong should be done to the people.

Marcus Octavius, coming with two legions, now encamped near Utica, sent to Cato to arrange about the chief command. Cato returned him no answer; but said to his friends, "Can we wonder all has gone ill with us, when our love of office survives even in our very ruin?" In the meantime, word was brought him, that the horse were going away, and were beginning to spoil and plunder the citizens. Cato ran to them, and from the first he met, snatched what they had taken; the rest threw down all they had gotten, and went away silent and ashamed of what they had done. Then he called all the people of Utica, and requested them, upon the behalf of the three hundred, not to exasperate Cæsar against them, but all to seek their common safety together with them. After that, he went again to the port to see those who were about to embark; and there he embraced and dismissed those of his friends and acquaintance whom he had persuaded to go. As for his son, he did not counsel him to be gone, nor did he think fit to persuade him to forsake his father. But there was one Statyllius, a young man, in the flower of his age, of a brave spirit, and very desirous to imitate the constancy of Cato. Cato entreated him to go away, as he was a noted enemy to Cæsar, but without success. Then Cato looked at Apollonides, the stoic philosopher, and Demetrius, the peripatetic; "It belongs to you to cool the fever of this young man's spirit, and to make him know what is good for him." And thus, in setting his friends upon their way, and in despatching the business of any that applied to him, he spent that night and the greatest part of the next day.

Lucius Cæsar, a kinsman of Cæsar's, being appointed to go deputy for the three hundred, came to Cato, and desired he would assist him to prepare a persuasive speech for them; "And as to you yourself," said he, "it will be an honour for me to kiss the hands and fall at the knees of Cæsar, in your behalf." But Cato would by no means permit him to do any such thing; "For as to myself," said he, "if I would be preserved by Cæsar's favour, I should myself go to him; but I would not be beholden to a tyrant for his acts of tyranny. For it is but usurpation in him to save, as their rightful lord, the lives of men over whom he has no title to reign. But if you please, let us consider what you had best say for the three hundred." And when they had continued some time together, as Lucius was going away, Cato recommended to him his son and the rest of his friends; and taking him by the hand bade him farewell.

Then he retired to his house again, and called together his son and his friends, to whom he conversed on various subjects; among the rest he forbade his son to engage himself in the affairs of state. For to act therein as became him was now impossible; and to do otherwise, would be dishonourable. Toward evening he went into his bath. As he was bathing, he remembered Statyllius and called out loud, "Apollonides, have you tamed the high spirit of Statyllius, and is he gone without bidding us farewell?" "No," said Apollonides, "I have said much to him, but to little purpose; he is still resolute and unalterable, and declares he is determined to follow your example." At this, it is said, Cato smiled, and answered, "That will soon be tried."

After he had bathed, he went to supper, with a great deal of company; at which he sat up, as he had always used to do ever since the battle of Pharsalia; for since that time he never lay down but when he went to sleep. There supped with him all his own friends and the magistrates of Utica.

After supper, the wine produced a great deal of lively and agreeable discourse, and a whole series of philosophical questions was discussed. At length they came to the strange dogmas of the stoics, called their Paradoxes; and to this in particular. That the good man only is free, and that all wicked men are slaves. The peripatetic, as was to be expected, opposing this, Cato fell upon him very warmly; and somewhat raising his voice, he argued the matter at great length, and urged the point with such vehemence, that it was apparent to everybody he was resolved to put an end to his life, and set himself at liberty. And so, when he had done speaking, there was a great silence and evident dejection. Cato, therefore, to divert them from any suspicion of his design, turned the conversation, and began again to talk of matters of present interest and expectation, showing great concern for those that were at sea, as also for the others, who, travelling by land, were to pass through a dry and barbarous desert.

When the company was broke up, he walked with his friends, as he used to do after supper, gave the necessary orders to the officers of the watch, and going into his chamber, he embraced his son and every one of his friends with more than usual warmth, which again renewed their suspicion of his design. Then laying himself down, he took into his hand Plato's dialogue concerning the soul. Having read more than half the book, he looked up, and missing his sword, which his son had taken away while he was at supper, he called his servant, and asked who had taken away his sword. The servant making no answer, he fell to reading again; and a little after, not seeming importunate, or hasty for it, but as if he would only know what had become of it, he bade it be brought. But having waited some time, when he had read through the book, and still nobody brought the sword, he called up all his servants, and in a louder tone demanded his sword. To one of them he gave such a blow in the mouth, that he hurt his own hand; and now grew more angry, exclaiming that he was betrayed and delivered naked to the enemy by his son and his servants. Then his son, with the rest of his friends, came running into the room, and falling at his feet, began to lament and beseech him. But Cato raising himself, and looking fiercely, "When," said he, "and how did I become deranged, and out of my senses, that thus no one tries to persuade me by reason, or show me what is better, if I am supposed to be ill-advised? Must I be disarmed, and hindered from using my own reason? And you, young man, why do you not bind your father's hands behind him that, when Cæsar comes, he may find me unable to defend myself? To despatch myself I want no sword; I need but hold my breath awhile, or strike my head against the wall."

When he had thus spoken, his son went weeping out of the chamber, and with him all the rest, except Demetrius and Apollonides, to whom, being left alone with him, he began to speak more calmly. "And you," said he, "do you also think to keep a man of my age alive by force, and to sit here and silently watch me? Or do you bring me some reasons to prove, that it will not be base and unworthy for Cato, when he can find his safety no other way, to seek it from his enemy? If so, adduce your arguments, and show cause why we should now unlearn what we formerly were taught, in order that rejecting all the convictions in which we lived, we may now by Cæsar's help grow wiser, and be yet more obliged to him for life only. Not that I have determined aught concerning myself, but I would have it in my power to perform what I shall think fit to resolve; and I shall not fail to take you as my advisers, in holding counsel, as I shall do, with the doctrines which your philosophy teaches; in the meantime do not trouble yourselves, but go tell my son that he should not compel his father to what he cannot persuade him to." They made him no answer, but went weeping out of the chamber. Then the sword being brought in by a little boy, Cato took it, drew it out, and looked at it; and when he saw the point was good, "Now," said he, "I am master of myself;" and laying down the sword, he took his book again, which, it is related, he read twice over. After this he slept so soundly that he was heard to snore by those that were without.

About midnight, he called up two of his freedmen, Cleanthes, his physician, and Butas, whom he chiefly employed in public business. Him he sent to the port, to see if all his friends had sailed; to the physician he gave his hand to be dressed, as it was swollen with the blow he had struck one of his servants. At this they all rejoiced, hoping that now he designed to live.

Butas, after a while, returned, and brought word they were all gone except Crassus, who had stayed about some business, but was just ready to depart; he said, also, that the wind was high, and the sea very rough. Cato, on hearing this, sighed, out of compassion to those who were at sea, and sent Butas again to see if any of them should happen to return for anything they wanted, and to acquaint him therewith.

Now the birds began to sing, and he again fell into a little slumber. At length Butas came back, and told him all was quiet in the port. Then Cato, laying himself down, as if he would sleep out the rest of the night, bade him shut the door after him. But as soon as Butas was gone out, he took his sword, and stabbed it into his breast; yet not being able to use his hand so well, on account of the swelling, he did not immediately die of the wound; but struggling, fell off the bed, and throwing down a little mathematical table that stood by, made such a noise that the servants, hearing it, cried out. And immediately his son and all his friends came into the chamber, where, seeing him lie weltering in his blood, great part of his bowels out of his body, but himself still alive and able to look at them, they all stood in horror. The physician went to him, and would have put in his bowels, which were not pierced, and sewed up the wound; but Cato, recovering himself, and understanding the intention, thrust away the physician, plucked out his own bowels, and tearing open the wound, immediately expired.

In less time than one would think his own family could have known this accident, all the three hundred were at the door. And a little after, the people of Utica flocked thither, crying out with one voice, he was their benefactor and their saviour, the only free and only undefeated man. At the very same time, they had news that Cæsar was coming; yet neither fear of the present danger, nor desire to flatter the conqueror, nor the commotions and discord among themselves, could divert them from doing honour to Cato. For they sumptuously set out his body, made him a magnificent funeral, and buried him by the seaside, where now stands his statue, holding a sword. And only when this had been done, they returned to consider of preserving themselves and their city.

Cæsar had been informed that Cato stayed at Utica, and did not seek to fly; that he had sent away the rest of the Romans, but himself, with his son and a few of his friends, continued there very unconcernedly, so that he could not imagine what might be his design. But having a great consideration for the man, he hastened thither with his army. When he heard of his death, it is related he said these words, "Cato, I grudge you your death, as you have grudged me the preservation of your life." And, indeed, if Cato would have suffered himself to owe his life to Cæsar, he would not so much have impaired his own honour, as augmented the other's glory. What would have been done, of course, we cannot know, but from Cæsar's usual clemency, we may guess what was most likely.

Cato was forty-eight years old when he died. His son suffered no injury from Cæsar; but, it is said, he grew idle, and was thought to be dissipated among women. In Cappadocia, he stayed at the house of Marphadates, one of the royal family there, who had a very handsome wife; and continuing his visit longer than was suitable, he made himself the subject of various epigrams; such as, for example—

"To-morrow (being the thirtieth day)
Cato, 'tis thought, will go away;"

"Porcius and Marphadates, friends so true,
One *Soul*, they say, suffices for the two,"

that being the name of the woman, and so again,—

"To Cato's greatness every one confesses,
A royal Soul he certainly possesses."

But all these stains were entirely wiped off by the bravery of his death. For in the battle of Philippi, where he fought for his country's liberty against Cæsar and Antony, when the ranks were breaking, he, scorning to fly, or to escape unknown, called out to the enemy, showed himself to them in front, and encouraged those of his party who stayed; and at length fell, and left his enemies full of admiration of his valour.

Nor was the daughter of Cato inferior to the rest of her family for sober-living and greatness of spirit. She was married to Brutus, who killed Cæsar; was acquainted with the conspiracy, and ended her life as became one of her birth and virtue. All which is related in the life of Brutus.

Statyllius, who said he would imitate Cato, was at that time hindered by the philosophers, when he would have put an end to his life. He afterwards followed Brutus, to whom he was very faithful and very serviceable, and died in the field of Philippi.

AGIS

THE fable of Ixion, who, embracing a cloud instead of Juno, begot the Centaurs, has been ingeniously enough supposed to have been invented to represent to us ambitious men, whose minds, doting on glory, which is a mere image of virtue, produce nothing that is genuine or uniform, but only, as might be expected of such a conjunction, misshapen and unnatural actions. Running after their emulations and passions, and carried away by the impulses of the moment, they may say with the herdsmen in the tragedy of Sophocles—

"We follow these, though born their rightful lords,
And they command us, though they speak no words."

For this is indeed the true condition of men in public life, who, to gain the vain title of being the people's leaders and governors, are content to make themselves the slaves and followers of all the people's humours and caprices. For as the lookout men at the ship's prow, though they see what is ahead before the men at the helm, yet constantly look back to the pilots there, and obey the orders they give; so these men, steered, as I may say, by popular applause, though they bear the name of governors, are in reality the mere underlings of the multitude. The man who is completely wise and virtuous has no need at all of glory, except so far as it disposes and eases his way to action by the greater trust that it procures him. A young man, I grant, may be permitted, while yet eager for distinction, to pride himself a little in his good deeds; for (as Theophrastus says) his virtues, which are yet tender and, as it were, in the blade, cherished and supported by praises, grow stronger, and take the deeper root. But when this passion is exorbitant, it is dangerous in all men, and in those who govern a commonwealth, utterly destructive. For in the possession of large power and authority, it transports men to a degree of madness; so that now they no more think what is good, glorious, but will have those actions only esteemed good that are glorious. As Phocion, therefore, answered King Antipater, who sought his approbation of some unworthy action, "I cannot be your flatterer, and your friend," so these men should answer the people, "I cannot govern and obey you." For it may happen to the commonwealth, as to the serpent in the fable, whose tail, rising in rebellion against the head, complained, as of a great grievance, that it was always forced to follow, and required that it should be permitted by turns to lead the way. And taking the command accordingly, it soon inflicted, by its senseless courses, mischiefs in abundance upon itself, while the head was torn and lacerated with following, contrary to nature, a guide that was deaf and blind. And such we see to have been the lot of many, who, submitting to be guided by the inclinations of an uninformed and unreasoning multitude, could neither stop, nor recover themselves out of the confusion.

This is what has occurred to us to say of that glory which depends on the voice of large numbers, considering the sad effects of it in the misfortunes of Caius and Tiberius Gracchus, men of noble nature, and whose generous natural dispositions were improved by the best of educations, and who came to the administration of affairs with the most laudable intentions; yet they were ruined, I cannot say by an immoderate desire of glory, but by a more excusable fear of disgrace. For being excessively beloved and favoured by the people, they thought it a discredit to them not to make full repayment, endeavouring by new public acts to outdo the honours they had received, and again, because of these new kindnesses, incurring yet further distinctions; till the people and they, mutually inflamed, and vying thus with each other in honours and benefits, brought things at last to such a pass that they might say that to engage so far was indeed a folly, but to retreat would now be a shame.

This the reader will easily gather from the story. I will now compare with them two Lacedæmonian popular leaders, the kings Agis and Cleomenes. For they, being desirous also to raise the people, and to restore the noble and just form of government, now long fallen into disuse, incurred the hatred of the rich and powerful, who could not endure to be deprived of the selfish enjoyment to which they were accustomed. These were not indeed brothers by nature, as the two Romans, but they had a kind of brotherly resemblance in their actions and designs, which took a rise from such beginnings and occasions as I am now about to relate.

When the love of gold and silver had once gained admittance into the Lacedæmonian commonwealth, it was quickly followed by avarice and baseness of spirit in the pursuit of it, and by luxury, effeminacy, and prodigality in the use. Then Sparta fell from almost all her former virtue and repute, and so continued till the days of Agis and Leonidas, who both together were kings of the Lacedæmonians.

Agis was of the royal family of Eurypon, son of Eudamidas, and the sixth in descent from Agesilaus, who made the expedition into Asia, and was the greatest man of his time in Greece. Agesilaus left behind him a son called Archidamus, the same who was slain at Mandonium, in Italy, by the Messapians, and who was then succeeded by his eldest son Agis. He being killed by Antipater near Megalopolis, and leaving no issue, was succeeded by his brother Eudamidas; he by a son called Archidamus; and Archidamus by another Eudamidas, the father of this Agis of whom we now treat.

Leonidas, son of Cleonymus, was of the other royal house of the Agiadæ, and the eighth in descent from Pausanias, who defeated Mardonius in the battle of Platæa. Pausanias was succeeded by a son called Plistoanax; and he by another Pausanias who was banished, and lived as a private man at Tegea, while his eldest son, Agesipolis, reigned in his place. He, dying without issue, was succeeded by a younger brother, called Cleombrotus, who left two sons; the elder was Agesipolis, who reigned but a short time, and died without issue; the younger, who then became king, was called Cleomenes, and had also two sons, Acrotatus and Cleonymus. The first died before his father, but left a son called Areus, who succeeded, and being slain at Corinth, left the kingdom to his son Acrotatus. This Acrotatus was defeated, and slain near Megalopolis, in a battle against the tyrant Aristodemus; he left his wife big with child, and on her being delivered of a son, Leonidas, son of the above-named Cleonymus, was made his guardian, and as the young king died before becoming a man, he succeeded in the kingdom.

Leonidas was a king not particularly suitable to his people. For though there were at that time at Sparta a general decline in manners, yet a greater revolt from the old habits appeared in him than in others. For having lived a long time among the great lords of Persia, and been a follower of King Seleucus, he unadvisedly thought to imitate, among Greek institutions and in a lawful government, the pride and assumption usual in those courts.

Agis, on the contrary, in fineness of nature and elevation of mind, not only far excelled Leonidas, but in a manner all the kings that had reigned since the great Agesilaus. For though he had been bred very tenderly, in abundance and even in luxury, by his mother Agesistrata and his grandmother Archidamia, who were the wealthiest of the Lacedæmonians, yet, before the age of twenty, he renounced all indulgence in pleasures. Withdrawing himself as far as possible from the gaiety and ornament which seemed becoming to the grace of his person, he made it his pride to appear in the coarse Spartan coat. In his meals, his bathings, and in all his exercises, he followed the old Laconian usage, and was often heard to say, he had no desire for the place of king, if he did not hope by means of that authority to restore their ancient laws and discipline.

The Lacedæmonians might date the beginning of their corruption from their conquest of Athens, and the influx of gold and silver among them that thence ensued. Yet, nevertheless, the number of houses which Lycurgus appointed being still maintained, and the law remaining in force by which every one was obliged to leave his lot or portion of land entirely to his son, a kind of order and equality was thereby preserved, which still in some degree sustained the state amidst its errors in other respects. But one Epitadeus happening to be ephor, a man of great influence, and of a wilful, violent spirit, on some occasion of a quarrel with his son, proposed a decree, that all men should have liberty to dispose of their land by gift in their lifetime, or by their last will and testament. This being promoted by him to satisfy a passion of revenge, and through covetousness consented to by others, and thus enacted for a law, was the ruin of the best state of the commonwealth. For the rich men without scruple drew the estate into their own hands, excluding the rightful heirs from their succession; and all the wealth being centred upon the few, the generality were poor and miserable. Honourable pursuits, for which there was no longer leisure, were neglected; the state was filled with sordid business, and with hatred and envy of the rich. There did not remain above seven hundred of the old Spartan families, of which, perhaps, one hundred might have estate in land, the rest were destitute alike of wealth and of honour, were tardy and unperforming in the defence of their country against its enemies abroad, and eagerly watched the opportunity for change and revolution at home.

Agis, therefore, believing it a glorious action, as in truth it was, to equalise and repeople the state, began to sound the inclinations of the citizens. He found the young men disposed beyond his expectation; they were eager to enter with him upon the contest in the cause of virtue, and to fling aside, for freedom's sake, their old manner of life, as readily as the wrestler does his garment. But the old men, habituated and more confirmed in their vices, were most of them as alarmed at the very name of Lycurgus, as a fugitive slave to be brought back before his offended master. These men could not endure to hear Agis continually deploring the present state of Sparta, and wishing she might be restored to her ancient glory. But on the other side, Lysander, the son of Libys, Mandroclidas, the son of Ecphanes, together with Agesilaus, not only approved his design, but assisted and confirmed him in it. Lysander had a great authority and credit with the people; Mandroclidas was esteemed the ablest Greek of his time to manage an affair and put it in train, and, joined with skill and cunning, had a great degree of boldness. Agesilaus was the king's uncle, by the mother's side; an eloquent man, but covetous and voluptuous, who was not moved by considerations of public good, but rather seemed to be persuaded in it by his son Hippomedon, whose courage and signal actions in war had gained him a high esteem and great influence among the young men of Sparta, though indeed the true motive was, that he had many debts, and hoped by this means to be freed from them.

As soon as Agis had prevailed with his uncle, he endeavoured by his mediation to gain his mother also, who had many friends and followers, and a number of persons in her debt in the city, and took a considerable part in public affairs. At the first proposal she was very averse, and strongly advised her son not to engage in so difficult and so unprofitable an enterprise. But Agesilaus endeavoured to possess her, that the thing was not so difficult as she imagined, and that it might, in all likelihood, redound to the advantage of her family; while the king, her son, besought her not for money's sake to decline assisting his hopes of glory. He told her he could not pretend to equal other kings in riches, the very followers and menials of the satraps and stewards of Seleucus or Ptolemy abounding more in wealth than all the Spartan kings put together; but if by contempt of wealth and pleasure, by simplicity and magnanimity, he could surpass their luxury and abundance; if he could restore their former equality to the Spartans, then he should be a great king indeed. In conclusion, the mother and the grandmother also were so taken, so carried away with the inspiration, as it were, of the young man's noble and generous ambition, that they not only consented, but were ready on all occasions to spur him on to a perseverance, and not only sent to speak on his behalf with the men with whom they had an interest, but addressed the other women also, knowing well that the Lacedæmonian wives had always a great power with their husbands, who used to impart to them their state affairs with greater freedom than the women would communicate with the men in the private business of their families. Which was indeed one of the greatest obstacles to this design; for the money of Sparta being most of it in the women's hands, it was their interest to oppose it, not only as depriving them of those superfluous trifles, in which, through want of better knowledge and experience, they placed their chief felicity, but also because they knew their riches were the main support of their power and credit.

Those, therefore, who were of this faction had recourse to Leonidas, representing to him how it was his part, as the elder and more experienced, to put a stop to the ill-advised projects of a rash young man. Leonidas, though of himself sufficiently inclined to oppose Agis, durst not openly, for fear of the people, who were manifestly desirous of this change; but underhand he did all he could to discredit and thwart the project, and to prejudice the chief magistrates against him, and on all occasions craftily insinuated that it was at the price of letting him usurp arbitrary power that Agis thus proposed to divide the property of the rich among the poor, and that the object of these measures for cancelling debts and dividing the lands, was not to furnish Sparta with citizens, but purchase him a tyrant's body guard.

Agis, nevertheless, little regarding these rumours, procured Lysander's election as ephor; and then took the first occasion of proposing through him his Rhetra to the council, the chief articles of which were these: That every one should be free from their debts: all the lands to be divided into equal portions, those that lay betwixt the watercourse near Pellene and Mount Taygetus, and as far as the cities of Malea and Sellasia, into four thousand five hundred lots, the remainder into fifteen thousand; these last to be shared out among those of the country people who were fit for service as heavy-armed soldiers, the first among the natural-born Spartans, and their number also should be supplied from any among the country people or strangers who had received the proper breeding of freemen, and were of vigorous body and of age for military service. All these were to be divided into fifteen companies, some of four hundred, and some of two, with a diet and discipline agreeable to the laws of Lycurgus.

This decree being proposed in the council of Elders, met there with opposition; so that Lysander immediately convoked the great assembly of the people, to whom he, Mandroclidas, and Agesilaus made orations exhorting them that they would not suffer the majesty of Sparta to remain abandoned to contempt, to gratify a few rich men, who lorded it over them; but that they should call to mind the oracles in old times which had forewarned them to beware of the love of money, as the great danger and probable ruin of Sparta, and, moreover, those recently brought from the temple of Pasiphae. This was a famous temple and oracle at Thalamæ; and this Pasiphae, some say, was one of the daughters of Atlas, who had by Jupiter a son called Ammon; others are of opinion it was Cassandra, the daughter of King Priam, who dying in this place, was called Pasiphae, as the *revealer* of oracles to *all* men. Phylarchus says, that this was Daphne, the daughter of Amyclas, who, flying from Apollo, was transformed into a laurel, and honoured by that god with the gift of prophecy. But be it as it will, it is certain the people were made to apprehend that this oracle had commanded them to return to their former state of equality settled by Lycurgus. As soon as these had done speaking, Agis stood up, and after a few words, told them he would make the best contribution in his power to the new legislation, which was proposed for their advantage. In the first place, he would divide among them all his patrimony, which was of large extent in tillage and pasture; he would also give six hundred talents in ready money, and his mother, grandmother, and his other friends and relations, who were the richest of the Lacedæmonians, were ready to follow his example.

The people were transported with admiration of the young man's generosity, and with joy that, after three hundred years' interval, at last there had appeared a king worthy of Sparta. But, on the other side, Leonidas was now more than ever averse, being sensible that he and his friends would be obliged to contribute with their riches, and yet all the honour and obligation would redound to Agis. He asked him then before them all, whether Lycurgus were not in his opinion a wise man, and a lover of his country. Agis answering he was, "And when did Lycurgus," replied Leonidas, "cancel debts, or admit strangers to citizenship,he who thought the commonwealth not secure unless from time to time the city was cleared of all strangers?" To this Agis replied, "It is no wonder that Leonidas, who was brought up and married abroad, and has children by a wife taken out of a Persian court, should know little of Lycurgus or his laws. Lycurgus took away both debts and loans, by taking away money; and objected indeed to the presence of men who were foreign to the manners and customs of the country, not in any case from an ill-will to their persons, but lest the example of their lives and conduct should infect the city with the love of riches, and of delicate and luxurious habits. For it is well known that he himself gladly kept Terpander, Thales, and Pherecydes though they were strangers, because he perceived they were in their poems and in their philosophy of the same mind with him. And you that are wont to praise Ecprepes, who, being ephor, cut with his hatchet two of the nine strings from the instrument of Phrynis the musician, and to commend those who afterwards imitated him, in cutting the strings of Timotheus's harp, with what face can you blame us for designing to cut off superfluity and luxury and display from the commonwealth? Do you think those men were so concerned only about a lute-string, or intended anything else than to check in music that same excess and extravagance which rule in our present lives and manners, and have disturbed and destroyed all the harmony and order of our city?"

From this time forward, as the common people followed Agis, so the rich men adhered to Leonidas. They besought him not to forsake their cause; and with persuasions and entreaties so far prevailed with the council of Elders, whose power consisted in preparing all laws before they were proposed to the people, that the designed Rhetra was rejected, though but by only one vote. Whereupon Lysander, who was still ephor, resolving to be revenged on Leonidas, drew up an information against him, grounded on two old laws: the one forbids any of the blood of Hercules to raise up children by a foreign woman, and the other makes it capital for a Lacedæmonian to leave his country to settle among foreigners. Whilst he set others on to manage this accusation, he with his colleagues went *to observe the sign*, which was a custom they had, and performed in this manner. Every ninth year, the ephors, choosing a starlight night, when there is neither cloud nor moon, sit down together in quiet and silence, and watch the sky. And if they chance to see the shooting of a star, they presently pronounce their king guilty of some offence against the gods, and thereupon he is immediately suspended from all exercise of regal power, till he is relieved by an oracle from Delphi or Olympia.

Lysander, therefore, assured the people he had seen a star shoot, and at the same time Leonidas was cited to answer for himself. Witnesses were produced to testify he had married an Asian woman, bestowed on him by one of King Seleucus's lieutenants: that he had two children by her, but she so disliked and hated him, that against his wishes, flying from her, he was in a manner forced to return to Sparta, where his predecessor dying without issue, he took upon him the government. Lysander, not content with this, persuaded also Cleombrotus to lay claim to the kingdom. He was of the royal family, and son-in-law to Leonidas; who, fearing now the event of this process, fled as a suppliant to the temple of Minerva of the Brazen House, together with his daughter, the wife of Cleombrotus; for she in this occasion resolved to leave her husband, and to follow her father. Leonidas being again cited, and not appearing, they pronounced a sentence of deposition against him, and made Cleombrotus king in his place.

Soon after this revolution, Lysander, his year expiring, went out of his office, and new ephors were chosen, who gave Leonidas assurance of safety, and cited Lysander and Mandroclidas to answer for having, contrary to law, cancelled debts, and designed a new division of lands. They, seeing themselves in danger, had recourse to the two kings, and represented to them how necessary it was for their interest and safety to act with united authority, and bid defiance to the ephors. For, indeed, the power of the ephors, they said, was only grounded on the dissensions of the kings, it being their privilege, when the kings differed in opinion, to add their suffrage to whichever they judged to have given the best advice; but when the two kings were unanimous, none ought or durst resist their authority, the magistrate whose office it was to stand as umpire when they were at variance, had no call to interfere when they were of one mind. Agis and Cleombrotus, thus persuaded, went together with their friends into the market-place, where removing the ephors from their seats, they placed others in their room, of whom Agesilaus was one; proceeding then to arm a company of young men, and releasing many out of prison; so that those of the contrary faction began to be in great fear of their lives; but there was no blood spilt. On the contrary, Agis, having notice that Agesilaus had ordered a company of soldiers to lie in wait for Leonidas, to kill him as he fled to Tegea, immediately sent some of his followers to defend him, and to convey him safely into that city.

Thus far all things proceeded prosperously, none daring to oppose; but through the sordid weakness of one man, these promising beginnings were blasted, and a most noble and truly Spartan purpose overthrown and ruined by the love of money. Agesilaus, as we said, was much in debt, though in possession of one of the largest and best estates in land; and while he gladly joined in this design to be quit of his debts, he was not at all willing to part with his land. Therefore he persuaded Agis, that if both these things should be put in execution at the same time, so great and so sudden an alteration might cause some dangerous commotion; but if debts were in the first place cancelled, the rich men would afterwards more easily be prevailed with to part with their land. Lysander, also, was of the same opinion, being deceived in like manner by the craft of Agesilaus; so that all men were presently commanded to bring in their bonds, or deeds of obligation, by the Lacedæmonians called *Claria,* into the marketplace, where being laid together in a heap, they set fire to them. The wealthy, money-lending people, one may easily imagine, beheld it with a heavy heart; but Agesilaus told them scoffingly, his eyes had never seen so bright and so pure a flame.

And now the people pressed earnestly for an immediate division of lands; the kings also had ordered it should be done; but Agesilaus, sometimes pretending one difficulty, and sometimes another, delayed the execution, till an occasion happened to call Agis to the wars. The Achæans, in virtue of a defensive treaty of alliance, sent to demand succours, as they expected every day that Ætolians would attempt to enter Peloponnesus, from the territory of Megara. They had sent Aratus, their general, to collect forces to hinder this incursion. Aratus wrote to the ephors, who immediately gave order that Agis should hasten to their assistance with the Lacedæmonian auxiliaries. Agis was extremely pleased to see the zeal and bravery of those who went with him upon this expedition. They were for the most part young men, and poor; and being just released from their debts and set at liberty, and hoping on their return to receive each man his lot of land, they followed their king with wonderful alacrity. The cities through which they passed were in admiration to see how they marched from one end of Peloponnesus to the other, without the least disorder, and, in a manner, without being heard. It gave the Greeks occasion to discourse with one another, how great might be the temperance and modesty of a Laconian army in old time, under their famous captains Agesilaus, Lysander, or Leonidas, since they saw such discipline and exact obedience under a leader who perhaps was the youngest man in all the army. They saw also how he was himself content to fare hardly, ready to undergo any labours, and not to be distinguished by pomp or richness of habit or arms from the meanest of his soldiers; and to people in general it was an object of regard and admiration. But rich men viewed the innovation with dislike and alarm, lest haply the example might spread, and work changes to their prejudice in their own countries as well.

Agis joined Aratus near the city of Corinth, where it was still a matter of debate whether or no it were expedient to give the enemy battle. Agis, on this occasion, showed great forwardness and resolution, yet without temerity or presumption. He declared it was his opinion they ought to fight, thereby to hinder the enemy from passing the gates of Peloponnesus, but nevertheless he would submit to the judgment of Aratus, not only as the elder and more experienced captain, but as he was general of the Achæans, whose forces he would not pretend to command, but was only come thither to assist them. I am not ignorant that Baton of Sinope relates it in another manner; he says, Aratus would have fought, and that Agis was against it; but it is certain he was mistaken, not having read what Aratus himself wrote in his own justification, that knowing the people had well-nigh got in their harvest, he thought it much better to let the enemy pass than put all to the hazard of a battle. And, therefore, giving thanks to the confederates for their readiness, he dismissed them. And Agis, not without having gained a great deal of honour, returned to Sparta, where he found the people in disorder, and a new revolution imminent, owing to the ill-government of Agesilaus.

For he, being now one of the ephors, and freed from the fear which formerly kept him in some restraint, forbore no kind of oppression which might bring in gain. Among other things, he exacted a thirteenth month's tax, whereas the usual cycle required at this time no such addition to the year. For these and other reasons fearing those whom he injured, and knowing how he was hated by the people, he thought it necessary to maintain a guard, which always accompanied him to the magistrate's office. And presuming now on his power, he was grown so insolent, that of the two kings, the one he openly contemned, and if he showed any respect towards Agis, would have it thought rather an effect of his near relationship, than any duty or submission to the royal authority. He gave it out also that he was to continue ephor the ensuing year.

His enemies, therefore, alarmed by this report, lost no time in risking an attempt against him; and openly bringing back Leonidas from Tegea, re-established him in the kingdom, to which even the people, highly incensed for having been defrauded in the promised division of lands, willingly consented. Agesilaus himself would hardly have escaped their fury, if his son, Hippomedon, whose manly virtues made him dear to all, had not saved him out of their hands, and then privately conveyed him from the city.

During the commotion, the two kings fled, Agis to the temple of the Brazen House, and Cleombrotus to that of Neptune. For Leonidas was more incensed against his son-in-law; and leaving Agis alone, went with his soldiers to Cleombrotus's sanctuary, and there with great passion reproached him for having, though he was son-in-law, conspired with his enemies, usurped his throne, and forced him from his country. Cleombrotus, having little to say for himself, sat silent. His wife, Chilonis, the daughter of Leonidas, had chosen to follow her father in his sufferings; for when Cleombrotus usurped the kingdom, she forsook him, and wholly devoted herself to comfort her father in his affliction; whilst he still remained in Sparta, she remained also, as a suppliant, with him, and when he fled, she fled with him, bewailing his misfortune, and extremely displeased with Cleombrotus. But now, upon this turn of fortune, she changed in like manner, and was seen sitting now, as a suppliant, with her husband, embracing him with her arms, and having her two little children beside her. All men were full of wonder at the piety and tender affection of the young woman, who pointing to her robes and her hair, both alike neglected and unattended to, said to Leonidas, "I am not brought, my father, to this condition you see me in, on account of the present misfortunes of Cleombrotus; my mourning habit is long since familiar to me. It was put on to condole with you in your banishment; and now you are restored to your country, and to your kingdom, must I still remain in grief and misery? Or would you have me attired in my royal ornaments, that I may rejoice with you, when you have killed, within my arms, the man to whom you gave me for a wife? Either Cleombrotus must appease you by mine and my children's tears, or he must suffer a punishment greater than you propose for his faults, and shall see me, whom he loves so well, die before him. To what end should I live, or how shall I appear among the Spartan women, when it shall so manifestly be seen, that I have not been able to move to compassion either a husband or a father? I was born, it seems, to participate in the ill-fortune and in the disgrace, both as a wife and a daughter, of those nearest and dearest to me. As for Cleombrotus, I sufficiently surrendered any honourable plea on his behalf, when I forsook him to follow you; but you yourself offer the fairest excuse for his proceedings, by showing to the world that for the sake of a kingdom, it is just to kill a son-in-law, and be regardless of a daughter." Chilonis, having ended this lamentation, rested her face on her husband's head, and looked round with her weeping and woebegone eyes upon those who stood before her.

Leonidas, touched with compassion, withdrew a while to advise with his friends; then returning, bade Cleombrotus leave the sanctuary and go into banishment; Chilonis, he said, ought to stay with him, it not being just she should forsake a father whose affection had granted to her intercession the life of her husband. But all he could say would not prevail. She rose up immediately, and taking one of her children in her arms, gave the other to her husband; and making her reverence to the altar of the goddess, went out and followed him. So that, in a word, if Cleombrotus were not utterly blinded by ambition, he must surely choose to be banished with so excellent a woman rather than without her to possess a kingdom.

Cleombrotus thus removed, Leonidas proceeded also to displace the ephors, and to choose others in their room; then he began to consider how he might entrap Agis. At first, he endeavoured by fair means to persuade him to leave the sanctuary, and partake with him in the kingdom. The people, he said, would easily pardon the errors of a young man, ambitious of glory, and deceived by the craft of Agesilaus. But finding Agis was suspicious, and not to be prevailed with to quit his sanctuary, he gave up that design; yet what could not then be effected by the dissimulation of an enemy, was soon after brought to pass by the treachery of friends.

Amphares, Damochares, and Arcesilaus often visited Agis, and he was so confident of their fidelity that after a while he was prevailed on to accompany them to the baths, which were not far distant, they constantly returning to see him safe again in the temple. They were all three his familiars; and Amphares had borrowed a great deal of plate and rich household stuff from Agesistrata, and hoped if he could destroy her and the whole family, he might peaceably enjoy those goods. And he, it is said, was the readiest of all to serve the purposes of Leonidas, and being one of the ephors, did all he could to incense the rest of his colleagues against Agis. These men, therefore, finding that Agis would not quit his sanctuary, but on occasion would venture from it to go to the bath, resolved to seize him on the opportunity thus given them. And one day as he was returning, they met and saluted him as formerly, conversing pleasantly by the way, and jesting, as youthful friends might, till coming to the turning of a street which led to the prison, Amphares, by virtue of his office, laid his hand on Agis, and told him, "You must go with me, Agis, before the other ephors, to answer for your misdemeanours." At the same time Damochares, who was a tall, strong man, drew his cloak tight round his neck, and dragged him after by it, whilst the others went behind to thrust him on. So that none of Agis's friends being near to assist him, nor any one by, they easily got him into the prison, where Leonidas was already arrived, with a company of soldiers, who strongly guarded all the avenues; the ephors also came in, with as many of the Elders as they knew to be true to their party, being desirous to proceed with some semblance of justice. And thus they bade him give an account of his actions. To which Agis, smiling at their dissimulation, answered not a word. Amphares told him it was more seasonable to weep, for now the time was come in which he should be punished for his presumption. Another of the ephors, as though he would be more favourable, and offering as it were an excuse, asked him whether he was not forced to what he did by Agesilaus and Lysander. But Agis answered, he had not been constrained by any man, nor had any other intent in what he did but only to follow the example of Lycurgus, and to govern conformably to his laws. The same ephor asked him whether now at least he did not repent his rashness. To which the young man answered that though he were to suffer the extremest penalty for it, yet he could never repent of so just and so glorious a design. Upon this they passed sentence of death on him, and bade the officers carry him to the Dechas, as it is called, a place in the prison where they strangle malefactors. And when the officers would not venture to lay hands on him, and the very mercenary soldiers declined it, believing it an illegal and a wicked act to lay violent hands on a king, Damochares, threatening and reviling them for it, himself thrust him into the room.

For by this time the news of his being seized had reached many parts of the city, and there was a concourse of people with lights and torches about the prison gates, and in the midst of them the mother and the grandmother of Agis, crying out with a loud voice that their king ought to appear, and to be heard and judged by the people. But this clamour, instead of preventing, hastened his death; his enemies fearing, if the tumult should increase, he might be rescued during the night out of their hands.

Agis, being now at the point to die, perceived one of the officers bitterly bewailing his misfortune; "Weep not, friend," said he, "for me, who die innocent, by the lawless act of wicked men. My condition is much better than theirs." As soon as he had spoken these words, not showing the least sign of fear, he offered his neck to the noose.

Immediately after he was dead, Amphares went out of the prison gate, where he found Agesistrata, who, believing him still the same friend as before, threw herself at his feet. He gently raised her up, and assured her, she need not fear any further violence or danger of death for her son, and that if she pleased she might go in and see him. She begged her mother might also have the favour to be admitted, and he replied, nobody should hinder it. When they were entered, he commanded the gate should again be locked, and Archidamia, the grandmother, to be first introduced. She was now grown very old, and had lived all her days in the highest repute among her fellows. As soon as Amphares thought she was despatched, he told Agesistrata she might now go in if she pleased. She entered, and beholding her son's body stretched on the ground, and her mother hanging by the neck, the first thing she did was, with her own hands, to assist the officers in taking down the body; then covering it decently, she laid it out by her son's, whom then embracing and kissing his cheeks, "O my son," said she, "it was thy too great mercy and goodness which brought thee and us to ruin." Amphares, who stood watching behind the door, on hearing this, broke in, and said angrily to her, "Since you approve so well of your son's actions, it is fit you should partake in his reward." She, rising up to offer herself to the noose, said only, "I pray that it may redound to the good of Sparta."

The three bodies being now exposed to view, and the fact divulged, no fear was strong enough to hinder the people from expressing their abhorrence of what was done, and their detestation of Leonidas and Amphares, the contrivers of it. So wicked and barbarous an act had never been committed in Sparta since first the Dorians inhabited Peloponnesus; the very enemies in war, they said, were always cautious in spilling the blood of a Lacedæmonian king, insomuch that in any combat they would decline, and endeavour to avoid them, from feelings of respect and reverence for their station. And certainly we see that in the many battles fought betwixt the Lacedæmonians and the other Greeks, up to the time of Philip of Macedon, not one of their kings was ever killed, except Cleombrotus by a javelin-wound at the battle of Leuctra. I am not ignorant that the Messenians affirm, Theopompus was also slain by their Aristomenes; but the Lacedæmonians deny it, and say he was only wounded.

Be it as it will, it is certain at least that Agis was the first king put to death in Lacedæmon by the ephors, for having undertaken a design noble in itself and worthy of his country, at a time of life when men's errors usually meet with an easy pardon. And if errors he did commit, his enemies certainly had less reason to blame him than had his friends for that gentle and compassionate temper which made him save the life of Leonidas and believe in other men's professions.

CLEOMENES

THUS fell Agis. His brother Archidamus was too quick for Leonidas, and saved himself by a timely retreat. But his wife, then mother of a young child, he forced from her own house, and compelled Agiatis, for that was her name, to marry his son Cleomenes, though at that time too young for a wife, because he was unwilling that any one else should have her, being heiress to her father Gylippus's great estate; in person the most youthful and beautiful woman in all Greece and well-conducted in her habits of life. And therefore, they say, she did all she could that she might not be compelled to this new marriage. But being thus united to Cleomenes, she indeed hated Leonidas, but to the youth showed herself a kind and obliging wife. He, as soon as they came together, began to love her very much, and the constant kindness that she still retained for the memory of Agis brought somewhat of the like feeling in the young man for him, so that he would often inquire of her concerning what had passed, and attentively listen to the story of Agis's purpose and design. Now Cleomenes had a generous and great soul; he was as temperate and moderate in his pleasures as Agis, but not so scrupulous, circumspect, and gentle. There was something of heat and passion always goading him on, and an impetuosity and violence in his eagerness to pursue anything which he thought good and just. To have men obey him of their own free-will, he conceived to be the best discipline; but likewise, to subdue resistance, and force them to the better course was, in his opinion, commendable and brave.

This disposition made him dislike the management of the city. The citizens lay dissolved in supine idleness and pleasures, the king let everything take its own way, thankful if nobody gave him any disturbance, nor called him away from the enjoyment of his wealth and luxury. The public interest was neglected, and each man intent upon his private gain. It was dangerous, now Agis was killed, so much as to name such a thing as the exercising and training of their youth: and to speak of the ancient temperance, endurance, and equality, was a sort of treason against the state. It is said also that Cleomenes, whilst a boy, studied philosophy under Sphærus, the Borystenite, who crossed over to Sparta, and spent some time and trouble in instructing the youth. Sphærus was one of the first of Zeno the Citiean's scholars, and it is likely enough that he admired the manly temper of Cleomenes and inflamed his generous ambition. The ancient Leonidas, as story tells, being asked what manner of poet he thought Tyrtæus, replied, "Good to whet young men's courage;" for being filled with a divine fury by his poems, they rushed into any danger. And so the Stoic philosophy is a dangerous incentive to strong and fiery dispositions, but where it combines with a grave and gentle temper, is most successful in leading it to its proper good.

Upon the death of his father Leonidas, he succeeded, and observing the citizens of all sorts to be debauched, the rich neglecting the public good, and intent on their private gain and pleasure, and the poor distressed in their own homes, and therefore without either spirit for war or ambition to be trained up as Spartans, that he had only the name of king, and the ephors all the power, he was resolved to change the posture of affairs. He had a friend whose name was Xenares, his lover (such an affection the Spartans express by the term, being *inspired,* or *imbreathed* with); him he sounded, and of him he would commonly inquire what manner of king Agis was, by what means and by what assistance he began and pursued his designs. Xenares, at first, willingly complied with his request, and told him the whole story, with all the particular circumstances of the actions. But when he observed Cleomenes to be extremely affected at the relation, and more than ordinarily taken with Agis's new model of the government, and begging a repetition of the story, he at first severely chid him, told him he was frantic, and at last left off all sort of familiarity and intercourse, yet he never told any man the cause of their disagreement, but would only say, Cleomenes knew very well. Cleomenes, finding Xenares averse to his designs, and thinking all others to be of the same disposition, consulted with none, but contrived the whole business by himself. And considering that it would be easier to bring about an alteration when the city was at war than when in peace, he engaged the commonwealth in a quarrel with the Achæans, who had given them fair occasions to complain. For Aratus, a man of the greatest power amongst all the Achæans, designed from the very beginning to bring all the Peloponnesians into one common body. And to effect this was the one object of all his many commanderships and his long political course; as he thought this the only means to make them a match for their foreign enemies. Pretty nearly all the rest agreed to his proposals, only the Lacedæmonians, the Eleans, and as many of the Arcadians as inclined to the Spartan interest, remained unpersuaded. And so as soon as Leonidas was dead, he began to attack the Arcadians, and wasted those especially that bordered on Achæa; by this means designing to try the inclinations of the Spartans, and despising Cleomenes as a youth, and of no experience in affairs of state or war. Upon this, the ephors sent Cleomenes to surprise the Athenæum, near Belbina, which is a pass commanding an entrance into Laconia, and was then the subject of litigation with the Megalopolitans. Cleomenes possessed himself of the place, and fortified it, at which action Aratus showed no public resentment, but marched by night to surprise Tegea and Orchomenus. The design failed, for those that were to betray the cities into his hands turned afraid, so Aratus retreated, imagining that his design had been undiscovered. But Cleomenes wrote a sarcastic letter to him, and desired to know as from a friend, whither he intended to march at night; and Aratus answering, that having heard of his design to fortify Belbina, he meant to march thither to oppose him, Cleomenes rejoined that he did not dispute it, but begged to be informed, if he might be allowed to ask the question, why he carried those torches and ladders with him.

Aratus laughing at the jest, and asking what manner of youth this was, Damocrates, a Spartan exile, replied, "If you have any designs upon the Lacedæmonians, begin before this young eagle's talons are grown." Presently after this, Cleomenes, encamping in Arcadia with a few horse and three hundred foot, received orders from the ephors, who feared to engage in the war, commanding him to return home; but when upon his retreat Aratus took Caphyæ, they commissioned him again. In this expedition he took Methydrium, and overran the country of the Argives; and the Achæans, to oppose him, came out with an army of twenty thousand foot and one thousand horse, under the command of Aristomachus. Cleomenes faced them at Pallantium, and offered battle, but Aratus, being cowed by his bravery, would not suffer the general to engage, but retreated, amidst the reproaches of the Achæans and the derision and scorn of the Spartans, who were not above five thousand. Cleomenes, encouraged by this success, began to speak boldly among the citizens, and reminding them of a sentence of one of their ancient kings, said, it was in vain now that the Spartans asked not how many their enemies were, but where they were. After this, marching to the assistance of the Eleans, whom the Achæans were attacking, falling upon the enemy in their retreat near the Lycæum, he put their whole army to flight, taking a great number of captives, and leaving many dead upon the place; so that it was commonly reported amongst the Greeks that Aratus was slain. But Aratus, making the best advantage of the opportunity, immediately after the defeat marched to Mantinea, and before anybody suspected it, took the city, and put a garrison into it. Upon this, the Lacedæmonians being quite discouraged, and opposing Cleomenes's designs of carrying on the war, he now exerted himself to have Archidamus, the brother of Agis, sent for from Messene, as he, of the other family, had a right to the kingdom; and besides, Cleomenes thought that the power of the ephors would be reduced, when the kingly state was thus filled up, and raised to its proper position. But those that were concerned in the murder of Agis, perceiving the design, and fearing that upon Archidamus's return that they should be called to an account, received him on his coming privately into town, and joined in bringing him home, and presently after murdered him. Whether Cleomenes was against it, as Phylarchus thinks, or whether he was persuaded by his friends, or let him fall into their hands, is uncertain; however, they were most blamed, as having forced his consent.

He, still resolving to new model the state, bribed the ephors to send him out to war; and won the affections of many others by means of his mother Cratesiclea, who spared no cost and was very zealous to promote her son's ambition; and though of herself she had no inclination to marry, yet for his sake she accepted, as her husband, one of the chiefest citizens for wealth and power. Cleomenes, marching forth with the army now under his command, took Leuctra, a place belonging to Megalopolis; and the Achæans quickly coming up to resist him with a good body of men commanded by Aratus, in a battle under the very walls of the city, some part of his army was routed. But whereas Aratus had commanded the Achæans not to pass a deep watercourse, and thus put a stop to the pursuit, Lydiadas, the Megalopolitan, fretting at the orders, and encouraging the horse which he led, and following the routed enemy, got into a place full of vines, hedges, and ditches; and being forced to break his ranks, began to retire in disorder. Cleomenes, observing the advantage, commanded the Tarentines and Cretans to engage him, by whom, after a brave defence, he was routed and slain. The Lacedæmonians, thus encouraged, fell with a great shout upon the Achæans, and routed their whole army. Of the slain, who were very many, the rest Cleomenes delivered up, when the enemy petitioned for them; but the body of Lydiadas he commanded to be brought to him; and then putting on it a purple robe, and a crown upon its head, sent a convoy with it to the gates of Megalopolis. This is that Lydiadas who resigned his power as tyrant, restored liberty to the citizens, and joined the city to the Achæan interest.

Cleomenes, being very much elated by this success, and persuaded that if matters were wholly at his disposal he should soon be too hard for the Achæans, persuaded Megistonus, his mother's husband, that it was expedient for the state to shake off the power of the ephors, and to put all their wealth into one common stock for the whole body; thus Sparta, being restored to its old equality, might aspire again to the command of all Greece. Megistonus liked the design, and engaged two or three more of his friends. About that time, one of the ephors, sleeping in Pasiphaes temple dreamed a very surprising dream; for he thought he saw the four chairs removed out of the place where the ephors used to sit and do the business of their office, and one only set there; and whilst he wondered, he heard a voice out of the temple, saying, "This is best for Sparta." The person telling Cleomenes this dream, he was a little troubled at first, fearing that he used this as a trick to sift him, upon some suspicion of his design, but when he was satisfied that the relator spoke truth, he took heart again. And carrying with him those whom he thought would be most against his project, he took Heræa and Alsæa two towns in league with the Achæans, furnished Orchomenus with provisions, encamped before Mantinea, and with long marches up and down so harassed the Lacedæmonians that many of them at their own request were left behind in Arcadia, while he with the mercenaries went on toward Sparta, and by the way communicated his design to those whom he thought fitted for his purpose, and marched slowly, that he might catch the ephors at supper.

When he was come near the city, he sent Euryclidas to the public table, where the ephors supped, under pretence of carrying some message from him from the army; Therycion, Phœbis, and two of those who had been bred up with Cleomenes, whom they call *mothaces*, followed with a few soldiers; and whilst Euryclidas was delivering his message to the ephors, they ran upon them with their drawn swords, and slew them. The first of them, Agylæus, on receiving the blow, fell, and lay as dead; but in a little time quietly raising himself, and drawing himself out of the room, he crept, without being discovered, into a little building which was dedicated to Fear, and which always used to be shut, but then by chance was open; and being got in, he shut the door, and lay close. The other four were killed, and above ten more that came to their assistance; to those that were quiet they did no harm, stopped none that fled from the city and spared Agylæus when he came out of the temple the next day.

The Lacedæmonians have not only sacred places dedicated to Fear, but also to Death, Laughter, and the like Passions. Now they worship Fear, not as they do supernatural powers which they dread, esteeming it hurtful, but thinking their polity is chiefly kept up by fear. Therefore the ephors, Aristotle is my author, when they entered upon their government, made proclamation to the people, that they should shave their mustaches and be obedient to the laws, that the laws might not be hard upon them, making, I suppose, this trivial injunction to accustom their youth to obedience even in the smallest matters. And the ancients, I think, did not imagine bravery to be plain fearlessness, but a cautious fear of blame and disgrace. For those that show most timidity towards the laws are most bold against their enemies; and those are least afraid of any danger who are most afraid of a just reproach. Therefore it was well said that—

"A reverence still attends on fear;"

and by Homer,—

"Feared you shall be, dear father, and revered;"

and again,—

"In silence fearing those that bore the sway;"

for the generality of men are most ready to reverence those whom they fear. And, therefore, the Lacedæmonians placed the temple of Fear by the Syssitium of the ephors, having raised that magistracy to almost royal authority.

The next day, Cleomenes proscribed eighty of the citizens whom he thought necessary to banish, and removed all the seats of the ephors, except one, in which he himself designed to sit and give audience; and calling the citizens together he made an apology for his proceedings, saying, that by Lycurgus the counsel of Elders was joined to the kings, and that that model of government had continued a long time, and no other sort of magistrates had been wanted. But afterwards, in the long war with the Messenians, when the kings, having to command the army, found no time to administer justice, they chose some of their friends, and left them to determine the suits of the citizens in their stead. These were called ephors, and at first behaved themselves as servants to the kings; but afterwards, by degrees, they appropriated the power to themselves, and erected a distinct magistracy. An evidence of the truth of this was the custom still observed by the kings, who, when the ephors send for them, refuse, upon the first and the second summons, to go, but upon the third rise up and attend them. And Asteropus, the first that raised the ephors to that height of power, lived a great many years after their institution. So long, therefore, he continued, as they contained themselves within their own proper sphere, it had been better to bear with them than to make a disturbance. But that an upstart introduced power should so far subvert the ancient form of government as to banish some kings, murder others, without hearing their defence, and threaten those who desired to see the best and most divine constitution restored in Sparta, was not to be borne. Therefore, if it had been possible for him without bloodshed to free Lacedæmon from those foreign plagues, luxury, sumptuosity, debts, and usury, and from those yet more ancient evils, poverty and riches, he should have thought himself the happiest king in the world, to have succeeded, like an expert physician, in curing the diseases of his country without pain. But now, in this necessity, Lycurgus's example favoured his proceedings, who being neither king nor magistrate, but a private man, and aiming at the kingdom, came armed into the market-place, so that King Charillus fled in alarm to the altar. He, being a good man, and a lover of his country, readily concurred in Lycurgus's designs, and admitted the revolution in the state. But, by his own actions, Lycurgus had nevertheless borne witness that it was difficult to change the government without force and fear, in the use of which he himself, he said, had been so moderate as to do no more than put out of the way those who opposed themselves to Sparta's happiness and safety. For the rest of the nation, he told them, the whole land was now their common property; debtors should be cleared of their debts, and examination made of those who were not citizens, that the bravest men might thus be made free Spartans, and give aid in arms to save the city, and "we," he said, "may no longer see Laconia, for want of men to defend it, wasted by the Ætolians and Illyrians."

Then he himself first, with his step-father, Megistonus, and his friends, gave up all their wealth into one public stock, and all the other citizens followed the example. The land was divided, and every one that he had banished had a share assigned him; for he promised to restore all as soon as things were settled and in quiet. And completing the number of citizens out of the best and most promising of the country people, he raised a body of four thousand men; and instead of a spear, taught them to use a *sarissa*, with both hands, and to carry their shields by a band, and not by a handle, as before. After this he began to consult about the education of the youth, and the Discipline, as they call it; most of the particulars of which Sphærus, being then at Sparta, assisted in arranging; and in a short time the schools of exercise and the common tables recovered their ancient decency and order, a few out of necessity, but the most voluntarily, returning to that generous and Laconic way of living. And, that the name of monarch might give them no jealousy, he made Euclidas, his brother, partner in the throne; and that was the only time that Sparta had two kings of the same family.

Then, understanding that the Achæans and Aratus imagined that this change had disturbed and shaken his affairs, and that he would not venture out of Sparta and leave the city now unsettled in the midst of so great an alteration, he thought it great and serviceable to his designs to show his enemies the zeal and forwardness of his troops. And, therefore, making an incursion into the territories of Megalopolis, he wasted the country far and wide, and collected considerable booty. And at last, taking a company of actors as they were travelling from Messene, and building a theatre in the enemy's country, and offering a prize of forty minæ in value, he sat spectator a whole day; not that he either desired or needed such amusement, but wishing to show his disregard for his enemies, and by a display of his contempt, to prove the extent of his superiority to them. For his alone, of all the

Greek or royal armies, had no stage-players, no jugglers, no dancing or singing women attending it but was free from all sorts of looseness, wantonness, and festivity, the young men being for the most part at their exercises, and the old men giving them lessons, or, at leisure times, diverting themselves with their native jests, and quick Laconian answers; the good results of which we have noticed in the life of Lycurgus.

He himself instructed all by his example; he was a living pattern of temperance before every man's eyes; and his course of living was neither more stately, nor more expensive, nor in any way more pretentious, than that of his people. And this was a considerable advantage to him in his designs on Greece. For men when they waited upon other kings did not so much admire their wealth, costly furniture, and numerous attendance, as they hated their pride and state, their difficulty of access, and imperious answers to their addresses. But when they came to Cleomenes, who was both really a king and bore that title, and saw no purple, no robes of state upon him, no couches and litters about him for his ease, and that he did not receive requests and return answers after a long delay and difficulty, through a number of messengers and door-keepers, or by memorials, but that he rose and came forward in any dress he might happen to be wearing, to meet those that came to wait upon him, stayed, talked freely and affably with all that had business, they were extremely taken, and won to his service. and professed that he alone was the true son of Hercules. His common every-day's meal was in an ordinary room, very sparing, and after the Laconic manner; and when he entertained ambassadors, or strangers, two more couches were added, and a little better dinner provided by his servants, but no savouring sauces or sweetmeats; only the dishes were larger, and the wine more plentiful. For he reproved one of his friends for entertaining some strangers with nothing but barley bread and black broth, such diet as they usually had in their *phiditia;* saying that upon such occasions, and when they entertained strangers, it was not well to be too exact Laconians. After the table was removed, a stand was brought in with a brass vessel full of wine, two silver bowls, which held about a pint apiece, a few silver cups, of which he that pleased might drink, but wine was not urged on any of the guests. There was no music, nor was any required; for he entertained the company himself, sometimes asking questions, sometimes telling stories; and his conversation was neither too grave or disagreeably serious, nor yet in any way rude or ungraceful in its pleasantry. For he thought those ways of entrapping men by gifts and presents, which other kings use, dishonest and artificial; and it seemed to him to be the most noble method, and most suitable to a king, to win the affections of those that came near him, by personal intercourse and agreeable conversation, since between a friend and a mercenary the only distinction is, that we gain the one by one's character and conversation, the other by one's money.

The Mantineans were the first that requested his aid; and when he entered their city by night, they aided him to expel the Achæan garrison, and put themselves under his protection. He restored them their polity and laws, and the same day marched to Tegea; and a little while after, fetching a compass through Arcadia, he made a descent upon Pheræ, in Achæa, intending to force Aratus to a battle, or bring him into disrepute for refusing to engage, and suffering him to waste the country. Hyperbatas at that time was general, but Aratus had all the power amongst the Achæans, marching forth with their whole strength, and encamping in Dymæ, near the Hecatombæum, Cleomenes came up, and thinking it not advisable to pitch between Dymæ, a city of the enemies, and the camp of the Achæans, he boldly dared the Achæans, and forced them to a battle, and routing their phalanx, slew a great many in the fight, and took many prisoners, and thence marching to Langon, and driving out the Achæan garrison, he restored the city to the Eleans.

The affairs of the Achæans being in this unfortunate condition, Aratus, who was wont to take the office every other year, refused the command, though they entreated and urged him to accept it. And this was ill-done, when the storm was high, to put the power out of his own hands, and set another to the helm. Cleomenes at first proposed fair and easy conditions by his ambassadors to the Achæans, but afterwards he sent others, and required the chief command to be settled upon him; in other matters offering to agree to reasonable terms, and to restore their captives and their country. The Achæans were willing to come to an agreement upon those terms, and invited Cleomenes to Lerna, where an assembly was to be held; but it happened that Cleomenes, hastily marching on, and drinking water at a wrong time, brought up a quantity of blood and lost his voice; therefore being unable to continue his journey, he sent the chiefest of the captives to the Achæans, and, putting off the meeting for some time, retired to Lacedæmon.

This ruined the affairs of Greece, which was just beginning in some sort to recover from its disasters, and to show some capability of delivering itself from the insolence and rapacity of the Macedonians. For Aratus (whether fearing or distrusting Cleomenes, or envying his unlooked-for success, or thinking it a disgrace for him who had commanded thirty-three years to have a young man succeed to all his glory and his power, and be head of that government which he had been raising and settling so many years), first endeavoured to keep the Achæans from closing with Cleomenes ; but when they would not hearken to him, fearing Cleomenes' daring spirit, and thinking the Lacedæmonians' proposals to be very reasonable, who designed only to reduce Peloponnesus to its own model, upon this he took his last refuge in an action which was unbecoming any of the Greeks, most dishonourable to him, and most unworthy his former bravery and exploits. For he called Antigonus into Greece and filled Peloponnesus with Macedonians, whom he himself, when a youth, having beaten their garrison out of the castle of Corinth, had driven from the same country. And there had been constant suspicion and variance between him and all the kings, and of Antigonus, in particular, he has said a thousand dishonourable things in the commentaries he has left behind him. And though he declares himself how he suffered considerable losses, and underwent great dangers, that he might free Athens from the garrison of the Macedonians, yet, afterwards, he brought the very same men armed into his own country, and his own house, even to the women's apartment. He would not endure that one of the family of Hercules, and king of Sparta, and one that reformed the polity of his country, as it were, from a disordered harmony, and returned it to the plain Doric measure and rule of life of Lycurgus, should be styled head of the Tritæans and Sicyonians; and whilst he fled the barley-cake and coarse coat, and, which were his chief accusations against Cleomenes, the extirpation of wealth and reformation of poverty, he basely subjected himself, together with Achæa, to the diadem and purple, to the imperious commands of the Macedonians and their satraps. That he might not seem to be under Cleomenes, he offered sacrifices, called Antigonea, in honour of Antigonus, and sang pæans himself, with a garland on his head, to the praise of a wasted, consumptive Macedonian. I write this not out of any design to disgrace Aratus, for in many things he showed himself a true lover of Greece, and a great man, but out of pity to the weakness of human nature, which, in characters like this, so worthy and in so many ways disposed to virtue, cannot maintain its honours unblemished by some envious fault.

The Achæans meeting again in assembly at Argas, and Cleomenes having come from Tegea, there were great hopes that all differences would be composed. But Aratus, Antigonus and he having already agreed upon the chief articles of their league, fearing that Cleomenes would carry all before him, and either win or force the multitude to comply with his commands, proposed that, having three hundred hostages put into his hands, he should come alone into the town, or bring his army to the place of exercise, called the Cyllarabium, outside the city, and treat there.

Cleomenes, hearing this, said that he was unjustly dealt with; for they ought to have told him so plainly at first, and not now he was come even to their doors, show their jealousy and deny him admission. And writing a letter to the Achæans about the same subject, the greatest part of which was an accusation of Aratus, while Aratus, on the other side, spoke violently against him to the assembly, he hastily dislodged, and sent a trumpeter to denounce war against the Achæans, not to Argos, but to Ægium, as Aratus writes, that he might not give them notice enough to make provision for their defence. There had also been a movement among the Achæans themselves, and the cities were eager for revolt; the common people expecting a division of the land, and a release from their debts, and the chief men being in many places ill-disposed to Aratus, and some of them angry and indignant with him for having brought the Macedonians into Peloponnesus. Encouraged by these misunderstandings, Cleomenes invaded Achæa, and first took Pellene by surprise, and beat out the Achæan garrison, and afterwards brought over Pheneus and Pentelleum to his side. Now the Achæans, suspecting some treacherous designs at Corinth and Sicyon, sent their horse and mercenaries out of Argos, to have an eye upon those cities, and they themselves went to Argos to celebrate the Nemean games. Cleomenes, advertised of this march, and hoping, as it afterwards fell out, that upon an unexpected advance to the city, now busied in the solemnity of the games, and thronged with numerous spectators, he should raise a considerable terror and confusion amongst them by night, marched with his army to the walls, and taking the quarter of the town called Aspis, which lies above the theatre, well fortified, and hard to be approached, he so terrified them that none offered to resist, but they agreed to accept a garrison, to give twenty citizens for hostages, and to assist the Lacedæmonians, and that he should have the chief command.

This action considerably increased his reputation and his power; for the ancient Spartan kings, though they in many ways endeavoured to effect it, could never bring Argos to be permanently theirs. And Pyrrhus, the most experienced captain, though he entered the city by force, could not keep possession, but was slain himself, with a considerable part of his army. Therefore they admired the despatch and contrivance of Cleomenes; and those that before derided him, for imitating, as they said, Solon and Lycurgus, in releasing the people from their debts, and in equalising the property of the citizens, were now fain to admit that this was the cause of the change in the Spartans. For before they were very low in the world, and so unable to secure their own, that the Ætolians, invading Laconia. brought away fifty thousand slaves; so that one of the elder Spartans is reported to have said, that they had done Laconia a kindness by unburdening it; and yet a little while after, by merely recurring once again to their native customs, and re-entering the track of the ancient discipline, they were able to give, as though it had been under the eyes and conduct of Lycurgus himself, the most signal instances of courage and obedience, raising

Sparta to her ancient place as the commanding state of Greece, and recovering all Peloponnesus.

When Argos was captured, and Cleonæ and Phlius came over. as they did at once, to Cleomenes, Aratus was at Corinth, searching after some who were reported to favour the Spartan interest. The news, being brought to him, disturbed him very much; for he perceived the city inclining to Cleomenes, and willing to be rid of the Achæans. Therefore he summoned the citizens to meet in the Council Hall, and slipping away without being observed to the gate, he mounted his horse that had been brought for him thither, and fled to Sicyon. And the Corinthians made such haste to Cleomenes at Argos, that, as Aratus says, striving who should be first there, they spoiled all their horses; he adds that Cleomenes was very angry with the Corinthians for letting him escape; and that Megistonus came from Cleomenes to him, desiring him to deliver up the castle at Corinth, which was then garrisoned by the Achæans, and offered him a considerable sum of money, and that he answered that matters were not now in his power, but he in theirs. Thus Aratus himself writes. But Cleomenes, marching from Argos, and taking in the Trœzenians, Epidaurians, and Hermioneans, came to Corinth, and blocked up the castle, which the Achæans would not surrender; and sending for Aratus's friends and stewards, committed his house and estate to their care and management; and sent Tritymallus, the Messenian, to him a second time, desiring that the castle might be equally garrisoned by the Spartans and Achæans, and promising to Aratus himself double the pension that he received from King Ptolemy. But Aratus, refusing the conditions, and sending his own son with the other hostages to Antigonus, and persuading the Achæans to make a decree for delivering the castle into Antigonus's hands, upon this Cleomenes invaded the territory of the Sicyonians, and by a decree of the Corinthians, accepted Aratus's estate as a gift.

In the meantime Antigonus, with a great army, was passing Geranea; and Cleomenes, thinking it more advisable to fortify and garrison, not the isthmus, but the mountains called Onea, and by a war of posts and positions to weary the Macedonians, rather than to venture a set battle with the highly disciplined phalanx, put his design into execution, and very much distressed Antigonus. For he had not brought victuals sufficient for his army; nor was it easy to force a way through whilst Cleomenes guarded the pass. He attempted by night to pass through Lechæum, but failed and lost some men; so that Cleomenes and his army were mightily encouraged, and so flushed with the victory, that they went merrily to supper; and Antigonus was very much dejected, being driven, by the necessity he was in, to most unpromising attempts. He was proposing to march to the promontory of Heræum, and thence transport his army in boats to Sicyon, which would take up a great deal of time, and require much preparation and means. But when it was now evening, some of Aratus's friends came from Argos by sea, and invited him to return, for the Argives would revolt from Cleomenes. Aristoteles was the man that wrought the revolt, and he had no hard task to persuade the common people; for they were all angry with Cleomenes for not releasing them from their debts as they expected. Accordingly, obtaining fifteen hundred of Antigonus's soldiers, Aratus sailed to Epidaurus; but Aristoteles, not staying for his coming, drew out the citizens, and fought against the garrison of the castle; and Timoxenus, with the Achæans from Sicyon, came to his assistance.

Cleomenes heard the news about the second watch of the night, and sending for Megistonus, angrily commanded him to go and set things right at Argos. Megistonus had passed his word for the Argives' loyalty, and had persuaded him not to banish the suspected. Therefore, despatching him with two thousand soldiers, he himself kept watch upon Antigonus, and encouraged the Corinthians, pretending that there was no great matter in the commotions at Argos, but only a little disturbance raised by a few inconsiderable persons. But when Megistonus, entering Argos, was slain, and the garrison could scarce hold out, and frequent messengers came to Cleomenes for succours, he fearing lest the enemy, having taken Argos, should shut up the passes and securely waste Laconia, and besiege Sparta itself, which he had left without forces, dislodged from Corinth, and immediately lost that city; for Antigonus entered it and garrisoned the town. He turned aside from his direct march, and assaulting the walls of Argos, endeavoured to carry it by a sudden attack; and then, having collected his forces from their march, breaking into the Aspis, he joined the garrison, which still held out against the Achæans; some parts of the city he scaled and took, and his Cretan archers cleared the streets. But when he saw Antigonus with his phalanx descending from the mountains into the plain, and the horse on all sides entering the city, he thought it impossible to maintain his post, and, gathering together all his men, came safely down and made his retreat under the walls, having in so short a time possessed himself of great power, and in one journey, so to say, having made himself master of all Peloponnesus, and now lost all again in as short a time. For some of his allies at once withdrew and forsook him, and others not long after put their cities under Antigonus's protection. His hopes thus defeated, as he was leading back the relics of his forces, messengers from Lacedæmon met him in the evening at Tegea, and brought him news of as great a misfortune as that which he had lately suffered, and this was the death of his wife, to whom he was so attached, and thought so much of her, that even in his most successful expeditions, when he was most prosperous, he could not refrain, but would every now and then come home to Sparta, to visit Agiatis.

This news afflicted him extremely, and he grieved, as a young man would do, for the loss of a very beautiful and excellent wife; yet he did not let his passion disgrace him or impair the greatness of his mind, but keeping his usual voice, his countenance, and his habit, he gave necessary orders to his captains, and took the precautions required for the safety of Tegea. Next morning he came to Sparta, and having at home, with his mother and children, bewailed the loss, and finished his mourning, he at once devoted himself to the public affairs of the state.

Now Ptolemy, the king of Egypt, promised him assistance, but demanded his mother and children for hostages. This, for some considerable time, he was ashamed to discover to his mother; and though he often went to her on purpose, and was just upon the discourse, yet he still refrained, and kept it to himself; so that she began to suspect, and asked his friends, whether Cleomenes had something to say to her, which he was afraid to speak. At last, Cleomenes venturing to tell her, she laughed aloud, and said, "Was this the thing that you had so often a mind to tell me, and were afraid? Make haste and put me on ship-board, and send this carcase where it may be most serviceable to Sparta, before age destroys it unprofitably here." Therefore, all things being provided for the voyage, they went by land to Tænarus, and the army waited on them. Cratesiclea, when she was ready to go on board, took Cleomenes aside into Neptune's temple, and embracing him, who was much dejected and extremely discomposed, she said, "Go to, King of Sparta; when we come forth at the door, let none see us weep, or show any passion that is unworthy of Sparta, for that alone is in our own power; as for success or disappointment, those wait on us as the deity decrees." Having thus said and composed her countenance, she went to the ship with her little grandson, and bade the pilot put at once out to sea. When she came to Egypt, and understood that Ptolemy entertained proposals and overtures of peace from Antigonus, and that Cleomenes, though the Achæans invited and urged him to an agreement, was afraid, for her sake, to come to any, without Ptolemy's consent, she wrote to him, advising him to do that which was most becoming and most profitable for Sparta, and not, for the sake of an old woman and a little child, stand always in fear of Ptolemy. This character she maintained in her misfortunes.

Antigonus, having taken Tegea, and plundered Orchomenus and Mantinea, Cleomenes was shut up within the narrow bounds of Laconia; and making such of the helots as could pay five Attic pounds free of Sparta, and, by that means, getting together five hundred talents, and arming two thousand after the Macedonian fashion, that he might make a body fit to oppose Antigonus's Leucaspides, he undertook a great and unexpected enterprise. Megalopolis was at that time a city of itself as great and as powerful as Sparta, and had the forces of the Achæans and of Antigonus encamping beside it; and it was chiefly the Megalopolitans' doing, that Antigonus had been called in to assist the Achæans. Cleomenes, resolving to snatch the city (no other word so well suits so rapid and so surprising an action), ordered his men to take five days' provision, and marched to Sellasia, as if he intended to ravage the country of the Argives; but from thence making a descent into the territories of Megalopolis, and refreshing his army about Rhœteum, he suddenly took the road by Helicus, and advanced directly upon the city. When he was not far off the town, he sent Panteus, with two regiments, to surprise a portion of the wall between two towers, which he learnt to be the most unguarded quarter of the Megalopolitans' fortifications, and with the rest of his forces he followed leisurely. Panteus not only succeeded at that point, but finding a great part of the wall without guards, he at once proceeded to pull it down in some places and make openings through it in others, and killed all the defenders that he found. Whilst he was thus busied, Cleomenes came up to him, and was got with his army within the city, before the Megalopolitans knew of the surprise. When, after some time, they learned their misfortune, some left the town immediately, taking with them what property they could; others armed and engaged the enemy; and though they were not able to beat them out, yet they gave their citizens time and opportunity safely to retire, so that there were not above one thousand persons taken in the town, all the rest flying, with their wives and children, and escaping to Messene. The greater number, also, of those that armed and fought the enemy were saved, and very few taken, amongst whom were Lysandridas and Thearidas, two men of great power and reputation amongst the Megalopolitans; and therefore the soldiers, as soon as they were taken, brought them to Cleomenes. And Lysandridas, as soon as he saw Cleomenes afar off, cried out, "Now, King of Sparta, it is in your power, by doing a most kingly and a nobler action than you have already performed, to purchase the greatest glory." And Cleomenes, guessing at his meaning, replied, "What, Lysandridas, you will not surely advise me to restore your city to you again?" "It is that which I mean," Lysandridas replied; "and I advise you not to ruin so brave a city, but to fill it with faithful and steadfast friends and allies, by restoring their country to the Megalopolitans, and being the saviour of so considerable a people." Cleomenes paused a while, and then said: "It is very hard to trust so far in these matters; but with us let profit always yield to glory." Having said this, he sent the two men to Messene with a herald from himself, offering the Megalopolitans their city again, if they would forsake the Achæan interest, and be on his side. But though Cleomenes made these generous and humane proposals, Philopœmen would not suffer them to break their league with the Achæans; and accusing Cleomenes to the people, as if his design was not to restore the city, but to take the citizens too, he forced Thearidas and Lysandridas to leave Messene.

This was that Philopœmen who was afterwards chief of the Achæans and a man of the greatest reputation amongst the Greeks, as I have related in his own life. This news coming to Cleomenes, though he had before taken strict care that the city should not be plundered, yet then, being in anger, and out of all patience, he despoiled the place of all the valuables, and sent the statues and pictures to Sparta; and demolishing a great part of the city, he marched away for fear of Antigonus and the Achæans; but they never stirred, for they were at Ægium, at a council of war. There Aratus mounted the speaker's place, and wept a long while, holding his mantle before his face; and at last, the company being amazed, and commanding him to speak, he said, "Megalopolis is destroyed by Cleomenes." The assembly instantly dissolved, the Achæans being astounded at the suddenness and greatness of the loss; and Antigonus, intending to send speedy succours, when he found his forces gather very slowly out of their winter-quarters, sent them orders to continue there still; and he himself marched to Argos with a small body of men. And now the second enterprise of Cleomenes, though it had the look of a desperate and frantic adventure, yet in Polybius's opinion, was done with mature deliberation and great foresight. For knowing very well that the Macedonians were dispersed into their winter-quarters, and that Antigonus with his friends and a few mercenaries about him wintered in Argos, upon these considerations he invaded the country of the Argives, hoping to shame Antigonus to a battle upon unequal terms, or else if he did not dare to fight, to bring him into disrepute with the Achæans. And this accordingly happened. For Cleomenes wasting, plundering, and spoiling the whole country, the Argives, in grief and anger at the loss, gathered in crowds at the king's gates, crying out that he should either fight, or surrender his command to better and braver men. But Antigonus, as became an experienced captain, accounting it rather dishonourable foolishly to hazard his army and quit his security, than merely to be railed at by other people, would not march out against Cleomenes, but stood firm to his convictions. Cleomenes, in the meantime, brought his army up to the very walls, and having without opposition spoiled the country, and insulted over his enemies, drew off again.

A little while after, being informed that Antigonus designed a new advance to Tegea, and thence to invade Laconia, he rapidly took his soldiers, and marching by a side-road, appeared early in the morning before Argos, and wasted the fields about it. The corn he did not cut down, as is usual, with reaping hooks and knives, but beat it down with great wooden staves made like broadswords, as if, in mere contempt and wanton scorn, while travelling on his way, without any effort or trouble, he spoiled and destroyed their harvest. Yet when his soldiers would have set Cyllabaris, the exercise ground, on fire, he stopped the attempt, as if he felt that the mischief he had done at Megalopolis had been the effects of his passion rather than his wisdom. And when Antigonus, first of all, came hastily back to Argos, and then occupied the mountains and passes with his posts, he professed to disregard and despise it all; and sent heralds to ask for the keys of the temple of Juno, as though he proposed to offer sacrifice there and then return. And with this scornful pleasantry upon Antigonus, having sacrificed to the goddess under the walls of the temple, which was shut, he went to Phlius; and from thence driving out those that garrisoned Oligyrtus, he marched down to Orchomenus. And these enterprises not only encouraged the citizens, but made him appear to the very enemies to be a man worthy of high command, and capable of great things. For with the strength of one city, not only to fight the power of the Macedonians and all the Peloponnesians, supported by all the royal treasures, not only to preserve Laconia from being spoiled, but to waste the enemy's country, and to take so many and such considerable cities, was an argument of no common skill and genius for command.

But he that first said that money was the sinews of affairs, seems especially in that saying to refer to war. Demades, when the Athenians had voted that their galleys should be launched and equipped for action, but could produce no money, told them, "The baker was wanted first, and the pilot after." And the old Archidamus, in the beginning of the Peloponnesian war, when the allies desired that the amount of their contributions should be determined, is reported to have answered, that war cannot be fed upon so much a day. For as wrestlers, who have thoroughly trained and disciplined their bodies, in time tire down and exhaust the most agile and most skilful combatant, so Antigonus, coming to the war with great resources to spend from, wore out Cleomenes, whose poverty made it difficult for him to provide the merest sufficiency of pay for the mercenaries, or of provisions for the citizens. For, in all other respects, time favoured Cleomenes; for Antigonus's affairs at home began to be disturbed. For the barbarians wasted and overran Macedonia whilst he was absent, and at that particular time a vast army of Illyrians had entered the country; to be freed from whose devastations, the Macedonians sent for Antigonus, and the letters had almost been brought to him before the battle was fought; upon the receipt of which he would at once have marched away home, and left the Achæans to look to themselves. But Fortune, that loves to determine the greatest affairs by a minute, in this conjuncture showed such an exact niceness of time, that immediately after the battle in Sellasia was over, and Cleomenes had lost his army and his city, the messengers came up and called for Antigonus. And this above everything made Cleomenes's misfortune to be pitied; for if he had gone on retreating and had forborne fighting two days longer, there had been no need of hazarding a battle; since upon the departure of the Macedonians, he might have had what conditions he pleased from the Achæans. But now, as was said before, for want of money, being necessitated to trust everything to arms, he was forced with twenty thousand (such is Polybius's account), to engage thirty thousand. And approving himself an admirable commander in this difficulty, his citizens showing an extraordinary courage, and his mercenaries bravery enough, he was overborne by the different way of fighting, and the weight of the heavy-armed phalanx. Phylarchus also affirms that the treachery of some about him was the chief cause of Cleomenes's ruin.

For Antigonus gave orders that the Illyrians and Acarnanians should march round by a secret way, and encompass the other wing, which Euclidas, Cleomenes's brother, commanded; and then drew out the rest of his forces to the battle. And Cleomenes, from a convenient rising, viewing his order, and not seeing any of the Illyrians and Acarnanians, began to suspect that Antigonus had sent them upon some such design; and calling for Damoteles, who was at the head of those specially appointed to such ambush duty, he bade him carefully to look after and discover the enemy's designs upon his rear. But Damoteles, for some say Antigonus had bribed him, telling him that he should not be solicitous about that matter, for all was well enough, but mind and fight those that met him in the front, he was satisfied, and advanced against Antigonus; and by the vigorous charge of his Spartans, made the Macedonian phalanx give ground, and pressed upon them with great advantage about half a mile; but then making a stand, and seeing the danger which the surrounding wing, commanded by his brother Euclidas, was in, he cried out, "Thou art lost, dear brother, thou art lost, thou brave example to our Spartan youth and theme of our matron's songs." And Euclidas's wing being cut in pieces, and the conquerors from that part falling upon him, he perceived his soldiers to be disordered, and unable to maintain the fight, and therefore provided for his own safety. There fell, we are told, in the battle, besides many of the mercenary soldiers, all the Spartans, six thousand in number, except two hundred.

When Cleomenes came into the city, he advised those citizens that he met to receive Antigonus; and as for himself, he said, which should appear most advantageous to Sparta, whether his life or death, that he would choose. Seeing the women running out to those that had fled with him, taking their arms, and bringing drink to them, he entered into his own house, and his servant, who was a freeborn woman, taken from Megalopolis after his wife's death, offering, as usual, to do the service he needed on returning from war, though he was very thirsty, he refused to drink, and though very weary to sit down; but in his corselet as he was, he laid his arm sideway against a pillar, and leaning his forehead upon his elbow, he rested his body a little while, and ran over in his thoughts all the courses he could take; and then with his friends set out at once for Gythium; where, finding ships which had been got ready for this very purpose, they embarked. Antigonus, taking the city, treated the Lacedæmonians courteously, and in no way offering any insult or offence to the dignity of Sparta, but permitting them to enjoy their own laws and polity, and sacrificing to the gods, dislodged the third day. For he heard that there was a great war in Macedonia, and that the country was devastated by the barbarians. Besides, his malady had now thoroughly settled into a consumption and continual catarrh. Yet he still kept up, and managed to return and deliver his country, and meet there a most glorious death, in a great defeat and vast slaughter of the barbarians. As Phylarchus says, and as is probable in itself, he broke a blood-vessel by shouting in the battle itself. In the schools we used to be told that, after the victory was won, he cried out for joy, "O glorious day! " and presently bringing up a quantity of blood, fell into a fever, which never left him till his death. And thus much concerning Antigonus.

Cleomenes, sailing from Cythera, touched at another island called Ægialia, whence as he was about to depart for Cyrene, one of his friends, Therycion by name, a man of a noble spirit in all enterprises, and bold and lofty in his talk, came privately to him, and said thus: "Sir, death in battle, which is the most glorious, we have let go; though all heard us say that Antigonus should never tread over the King of Sparta, unless dead. And now that course which is next in honour and virtue is presented to us. Whither do we madly sail, flying the evil which is near, to seek that which is at a distance? For if it is not dishonourable for the race of Hercules to serve the successors of Philip and Alexander, we shall save a long voyage by delivering ourselves up to Antigonus, who, probably, is as much better than Ptolemy, as the Macedonians are better than the Egyptians; but if we think it mean to submit to those whose arms have conquered us, why should we choose him for our master, by whom we have not yet been beaten? Is it to acknowledge two superiors instead of one, whilst we run away from Antigonus, and flatter Ptolemy? Or, is it for your mother's sake that you retreat to Egypt? It will indeed be a very fine and very desirable sight for her to show her son to Ptolemy's women, now changed from a prince into an exile and a slave. Are we not still masters of our own swords? And whilst we have Laconia in view, shall we not here free ourselves from this disgraceful misery, and clear ourselves to those who at Sellasia died for the honour and defence of Sparta? Or, shall we sit lazily in Egypt, inquiring what news from Sparta, and whom Antigonus hath been pleased to make governor of Lacedæmon?" Thus spoke Therycion; and this was Cleomenes's reply: "By seeking death, you coward, the most easy and most ready refuge, you fancy that you shall appear courageous and brave, though this flight is baser than the former. Better men than we have given way to their enemies, having been betrayed by fortune, or oppressed by multitude; but he that gives way under labour or distresses, under the ill-opinions or reports of men, yields the victory to his own effeminacy. For a voluntary death ought not to be chosen as a relief from action, but as an exemplary action itself; and it is base either to live or to die only to ourselves. That death to which you now invite us, is proposed only as a release from our present miseries, but carries nothing of nobleness or profit in it. And I think it becomes both me and you not to despair of our country; but when there are no hopes of that left, those that have an inclination may quickly die." To this Therycion returned no answer; but as soon as he had an opportunity of leaving Cleomenes's company, went aside on the seashore, and ran himself through.

But Cleomenes sailed from Ægialia, landed in Libya, and, being honourably conducted through the king's country, came to Alexandria. When he was first brought to Ptolemy, no more than common civilities and usual attentions were paid him; but when, upon trial, he found him a man of deep sense and great reason, and that his plain Laconic way of conversation carried with it a noble and becoming grace, that he did nothing unbecoming his birth, nor bent under fortune, and was evidently a more faithful counsellor than those who made it their business to please and flatter, he was ashamed, and repented that he had neglected so great a man, and suffered Antigonus to get so much power and reputation by ruining him. He now offered him many marks of respect and kindness, and gave him hopes that he would furnish him with ships and money to return to Greece, and would reinstate him in his kingdom. He granted him a yearly pension of four-and-twenty talents; a little part of which sum supplied his and his friends' thrifty temperance; and the rest was employed in doing good offices to, and in relieving the necessities of, the refugees that had fled from Greece, and retired into Egypt.

But the elder Ptolemy dying before Cleomenes's affairs had received a full dispatch, and the successor being a loose, voluptuous, and effeminate prince, under the power of his pleasures and his women, his business was neglected. For the king was so besotted with his women and his wine, that the employments of his most busy and serious hours consisted at the utmost in celebrating religious feasts in his palace, carrying a timbrel, and taking part in the show; while the greatest affairs of state were managed by Agathoclea, the king's mistress, her mother, and the pimp Œnanthes. At the first, indeed, they seemed to stand in need of Cleomenes; for Ptolemy, being afraid of his brother Magas, who by his mother's means had a great interest among the soldiers, gave Cleomenes a place in his secret councils, and acquainted him with the design of taking off his brother. He, though all were for it, declared his opinion to the contrary, saying, "The king, if it were possible, should have more brothers for the better security and stability of his affairs." And Sosibius, the greatest favourite, replying that they were not secure of the mercenaries whilst Magas was alive, Cleomenes returned, that he need not trouble himself about that matter; for amongst the mercenaries there were above three thousand Peloponnesians, who were his fast friends, and whom he could command at any time with a nod. This discourse made Cleomenes for the present to be looked upon as a man of great influence and assured fidelity; but afterwards, Ptolemy's weakness increasing his fear, and he, as it usually happens, where there is no judgment and wisdom, placing his security in general distrust and suspicion, it rendered Cleomenes suspected to the courtiers, as having too much interest with the mercenaries; and many had this saying in their mouths, that he was a lion amidst a flock of sheep. For, in fact, such he seemed to be in the court, quietly watching and keeping his eye upon all that went on.

He therefore gave up all thought of asking for ships and soldiers from the king. But receiving news that Antigonus was dead, that the Achæans were engaged in a war with the Ætolians, and that the affairs of Peloponnesus, being now in very great distraction and disorder, required and invited his assistance, he desired leave to depart only with his friends, but could not obtain that, the king not so much as hearing his petition, being shut up amongst his women, and wasting his hours in bacchanalian rites and drinking parties. But Sosibius, the chief minister and counsellor of state, thought that Cleomenes, being detained against his will, would grow ungovernable and dangerous, and yet that it was not safe to let him go, being an aspiring, daring man, and well acquainted with the diseases and weakness of the kingdom. For neither could presents and gifts conciliate or content him; but even as Apis, while living in all possible plenty and apparent delight, yet desires to live as nature would provide for him, to range at liberty, and bound about the fields, and can scarce endure to be under the priests' keeping, so he could not brook their courtship and soft entertainment, but sat like Achilles—

"and languished far,
Desiring battle and the shout of war."

His affairs standing in this condition, Nicagoras, the Messenian, came to Alexandria, a man that deeply hated Cleomenes, yet pretended to be his friend; for he had formerly sold Cleomenes a fair estate, but never received the money because Cleomenes was either unable as it may be, or else, by reason of his engagement in the wars and other distractions, had no opportunity to pay him. Cleomenes, seeing him landing, for he was then walking upon the quay, kindly saluted him, and asked what business brought him to Egypt. Nicagoras returned his compliment, and told him that he came to bring some excellent war-horses to the king. And Cleomenes, with a smile, subjoined, "I could wish you had rather brought young boys and music-girls; for those now are the king's chief occupation." Nicagoras at the moment smiled at the conceit, but a few days after, he put Cleomenes in mind of the estate that he had bought of him, and desired his money, protesting that he would not have troubled him, if his merchandise had turned out as profitable as he had thought it would. Cleomenes replied, that he had nothing left of all that had been given him. At which answer, Nicagoras, being nettled, told Sosibius Cleomenes's scoff upon the king. He was delighted to receive the information; but desiring to have some greater reason to excite the king against Cleomenes, persuaded Nicagoras to leave a letter written against Cleomenes, importing that he had a design, if he could have gotten ships and soldiers, to surprise Cyrene. Nicagoras wrote such a letter, and left Egypt. Four days after, Sosibius brought the letter to Ptolemy, pretending it was just then delivered him, and excited the young man's fear and anger; upon which it was agreed that Cleomenes should be invited into a large house, and treated as formerly, but not suffered to go out again.

This usage was grievous to Cleomenes, and another incident that occurred made him feel his hopes to be yet more entirely overcast. Ptolemy, the son of Chrysermas, a favourite of the king's, had always shown civility to Cleomenes; there was a considerable intimacy between them, and they had been used to talk freely together about the state. He, upon Cleomenes's desire, came to him, and spoke to him in fair terms, softening down his suspicions and excusing the king's conduct. But as he went out again, not knowing that Cleomenes followed him to the door, he severely reprimanded the keepers for their carelessness in looking after "so great and so furious a wild beast." This Cleomenes himself heard, and retiring before Ptolemy perceived it, told his friends what had been said. Upon this they cast off all former hopes and determined for violent proceedings, resolving to be revenged on Ptolemy for his base and unjust dealing, to have satisfaction for the affronts, to die as it became Spartans, and not stay till, like fatted sacrifices, they were butchered. For it was both grievous and dishonourable for Cleomenes, who had scorned to come to terms with Antigonus, a brave warrior, and a man of action, to wait an effeminate king's leisure, till he should lay aside his timbrel and end his dance, and then kill him.

These courses being resolved on, and Ptolemy happening at the same time to make a progress to Canopus, they first spread abroad a report that his freedom was ordered by the king, and, it being the custom for the king to send presents and an entertainment to those whom he would free, Cleomenes's friends made that provision, and sent it into the prison, thus imposing upon the keepers, who thought it had been sent by the king. For he sacrificed, and gave them large portions, and with a garland upon his head, feasted and made merry with his friends. It is said that he began the action sooner than he designed, having understood that a servant who was privy to the plot had gone out to visit a mistress that he loved. This made him afraid of a discovery; and therefore, as soon as it was full noon, and all the keepers sleeping off their wine, he put on his coat, and opening his seam to bare his right shoulder, with his drawn sword in his hand, he issued forth, together with his friends provided in the same manner, making thirteen in all. One of them, by name Hippitas, was lame, and followed the first onset very well, but when he presently perceived that they were more slow in their advances for his sake, he desired them to run him through and not ruin their enterprise by staying for a useless, unprofitable man. By chance an Alexandrian was then riding by the door; him they threw off, and setting Hippitas on horseback, ran through the streets, and proclaimed liberty to the people. But they, it seems, had courage enough to praise and admire Cleomenes's daring, but not one had the heart to follow and assist him. Three of them fell on Ptolemy, the son of Chrysermas, as he was coming out of the palace, and killed him. Another Ptolemy, the officer in charge of the city, advancing against them in a chariot, they set upon, dispersed his guards and attendants, and pulling him out of the chariot, killed him upon the place. Then they made toward the castle, designing to break open the prison, release those who were confined, and avail themselves of their numbers; but the keepers were too quick for them, and secured the passages. Being baffled in this attempt, Cleomenes with his company roamed about the city, none joining with him, but all retreating from and flying his approach. Therefore, despairing of success, and saying to his friends, that it was no wonder that women ruled over men that were afraid of liberty, he bade them all die as bravely as became his followers and their own past actions. This said, Hippitas was first, as he desired, run through by one of the younger men, and then each of them readily and resolutely fell upon his own sword, except Fanteus, the same who first surprised Megalopolis. This man, being of a very handsome person, and a great lover of the Spartan discipline, the king had made his dearest friend; and he now bade him, when he had seen him and the rest fallen, die by their example. Fanteus walked over them as they lay, and pricked every one with his dagger, to try whether any was alive; when he pricked Cleomenes in the ankle, and saw him turn upon his back, he kissed him, sat down by him, and when he was quite dead, covered up the body, and then killed himself over it.

Thus fell Cleomenes, after the life which we have narrated, having been King of Sparta sixteen years. The news of their fall being noised through the city, Cratesiclea, though a woman of a great spirit, could not bear up against the weight of this affliction; but embracing Cleomenes's children, broke out into lamentations. But the eldest boy, none suspecting such a spirit in a child, threw himself headlong from the top of the house. He was bruised very much, but not killed by the fall, and was taken up crying, and expressing his resentment for not being permitted to destroy himself. Ptolemy, as soon as an account of the action was brought him, gave order that Cleomenes's body should be flayed and hung up, and that his children, mother, and the women that were with her, should be killed. Amongst these was Panteus's wife, a beautiful and noble-looking woman, who had been but lately married, and suffered these disasters in the height of her love. Her parents would not have her embark with Panteus so shortly after they were married, though she eagerly desired it, but shut her up, and kept her forcibly at home. But a few days after she procured a horse and a little money, and escaping by night, made speed to Tænarus, where she embarked for Egypt, came to her husband, and with him cheerfully endured to live in a foreign country. She gave her hand to Cratesiclea, as she was going with the soldiers to execution, held up her robe, and begged her to be courageous; who of herself was not in the least afraid of death, and desired nothing else but only to be killed before the children. When they were come to the place of execution, the children were first killed before Cratesiclea's eyes, and afterwards she herself, with only these words in her mouth, "O children, whither are you gone?" But Panteus's wife, fastening her dress close about her, and being a strong woman, in silence and perfect composure, looked after every one that was slain, and laid them decently out as far as circumstances would permit; and after all were killed, rearraying her dress, and drawing her clothes close about her, suffering none to come near or be an eye-witness of her fall, besides the executioner, she courageously submitted to the stroke, and wanted nobody to look after her or wind her up after she was dead. Thus in her death the modesty of her mind appeared, and set that guard upon her body which she always kept when alive. And she, in the declining age of the Spartans, showed that women were no unequal rivals of the men, and was an instance of a courage superior to the affronts of fortune.

A few days after, those that watched the hanging body of Cleomenes, saw a large snake winding about his head, and covering his face, so that no bird of prey would fly at it. This made the king superstitiously afraid, and set the women upon several expiations, as if he had been some extraordinary being, and one beloved by the gods, that had been slain. And the Alexandrians made processions to the place, and gave Cleomenes the title of hero, and son of the gods, till the philosophers satisfied them by saying, that as oxen breed bees, putrifying horses breed wasps, and beetles rise from the carcasses of dead asses, so the humours and juices of the marrow of a man's body, coagulating, produce serpents. And this the ancients observing, appropriate a serpent, rather than any other creature, to heroes.

TIBERIUS GRACCHUS

HAVING completed the first two narratives, we now may proceed to take a view of misfortunes, not less remarkable, in the Roman couple, and with the lives of Agis and Cleomenes, compare these of Tiberius and Caius. They were the sons of Tiberius Gracchus, who though he had been once censor, twice consul, and twice had triumphed, yet was more renowned and esteemed for his virtue than his honours. Upon this account, after the death of Scipio who overthrew Hannibal, he was thought worthy to match with his daughter Cornelia, though there had been no friendship or familiarity between Scipio and him, but rather the contrary. There is a story told that he once found in his bed-chamber a couple of snakes, and that the soothsayers, being consulted concerning the prodigy, advised that he should neither kill them both nor let them both escape; adding, that if the male serpent was killed, Tiberius should die, and if the female, Cornelia. And that therefore Tiberius, who extremely loved his wife, and thought, besides, that it was much more his part, who was an old man, to die, than it was hers, who as yet was but a young woman, killed the male serpent, and let the female escape; and soon after himself died, leaving behind him twelve children borne to him by Cornelia.

Cornelia, taking upon herself all the care of the household and the education of her children, approved herself so discreet a matron, so affectionate a mother, and so constant and noble-spirited a widow, that Tiberius seemed to all men to have done nothing unreasonable in choosing to die for such a woman; who, when King Ptolemy himself proffered her his crown, and would have married her, refused it, and chose rather to live a widow. In this state she continued, and lost all her children, except one daughter, who was married to Scipio the younger, and two sons, Tiberius and Caius, whose lives we are now writing.

These she brought up with such care, that though they were without dispute in natural endowments and dispositions the first among the Romans of their time, yet they seemed to owe their virtues even more to their education than to their birth. And as, in the statues and pictures made of Castor and Pollux, though the brothers resemble one another, yet there is a difference to be perceived in their countenances, between the one, who delighted in the cestus, and the other, that was famous in the course, so between these two noble youths, though there was a strong general likeness in their common love of fortitude and temperance, in their liberality, their eloquence, and their greatness of mind, yet in their actions and administrations of public affairs, a considerable variation showed itself. It will not be amiss before we proceed to mark the difference between them.

Tiberius, in the form and expression of his countenance, and in his gesture and motion, was gentle and composed; but Caius, earnest and vehement. And so in their public speeches to the people, the one spoke in a quiet, orderly manner, standing throughout on the same spot; the other would walk about on the hustings, and in the heat of his orations pull his gown off his shoulders, and was the first of all the Romans that used such gestures; as Cleon is said to have been the first orator among the Athenians that pulled off his cloak and smote his thigh, when addressing the people. Caius's oratory was impetuous and passionate, making everything tell to the utmost, whereas Tiberius was gentle and persuasive, awakening emotions of pity. His diction was pure and carefully correct, while that of Caius was vehement and rich. So likewise in their way of living and at their tables, Tiberius was frugal and plain, Caius, compared with other men, temperate and even austere, but contrasting with his brother in a fondness for new fashions and rarities, as appears in Drusus's charge against him, that he had bought some silver dolphins, to the value of twelve hundred and fifty drachmas for every pound weight.

The same difference that appeared in their diction was observable also in their tempers. The one was mild and reasonable, the other rough and passionate, and to that degree, that often, in the midst of speaking, he was so hurried away by his passion against his judgment, that his voice lost its tone, and he began to pass into mere abusive talking, spoiling his whole speech. As a remedy to this excess, he made use of an ingenious servant of his, one Licinius, who stood constantly behind him with a sort of pitch-pipe, or instrument to regulate the voice by, and whenever he perceived his master's tone alter and break with anger, he struck a soft note with his pipe, on hearing which Caius immediately checked the vehemence of his passion and his voice, grew quieter, and allowed himself to be recalled to temper. Such are the differences between the two brothers; but their valour in war against their country's enemies, their justice in the government of its subjects, their care and industry in office, and their self-command in all that regarded their pleasures, were equally remarkable in both.

Tiberius was the elder by nine years; owing to which their actions as public men were divided by the difference of the times in which those of the one and those of the other were performed. And one of the principal causes of the failure of their enterprises was this interval between their careers, and the want of combination of their efforts. The power they would have exercised, had they flourished both together, could scarcely have failed to overcome all resistance. We must therefore give an account of each of them singly, and first of the eldest.

Tiberius, immediately on his attaining manhood, had such a reputation that he was admitted into the college of the augurs, and that in consideration more of his early virtue than of his noble birth. This appeared by what Appius Claudius did, who, though he had been consul and censor, and was now the head of the Roman senate, and had the highest sense of his own place and merit, at a public feast of the augurs, addressed himself openly to Tiberius, and with great expressions of kindness, offered him his daughter in marriage. And when Tiberius gladly accepted, and the agreement had thus been completed, Appius returning home, no sooner had reached his door, but he called to his wife and cried out in a loud voice, "O Antistia, I have contracted our daughter Claudia to a husband." She, being amazed, answered, "But why so suddenly, or what means this haste? Unless you have provided Tiberius Gracchus for her husband." I am not ignorant that some apply this story to Tiberius, the father of the Gracchi, and Scipio Africanus; but most relate it as we have done. And Polybius writes, that after the death of Scipio Africanus, the nearest relations of Cornelia, preferring Tiberius to all other competitors, gave her to him in marriage, not having been engaged or promised to any one by her father.

This young Tiberius, accordingly, serving in Africa under the younger Scipio, who had married his sister, and living there under the same tent with him, soon learned to estimate the noble spirit of his commander, which was so fit to inspire strong feelings of emulation in virtue and desire to prove merit in action, and in a short time he excelled all the young men of the army in obedience and courage; and he was the first that mounted the enemy's wall, as Fannius says, who writes that he himself climbed up with him, and was partaker in the achievement. He was regarded, while he continued with the army, with great affection; and left behind him on his departure a strong desire for his return.

After that expedition, being chosen paymaster, it was his fortune to serve in the war against the Numantines, under the command of Caius Mancinus, the consul, a person of no bad character, but the most unfortunate of all the Roman generals. Notwithstanding, amidst the greatest misfortunes, and in the most unsuccessful enterprises, not only the discretion and valour of Tiberius, but also, which was still more to be admired, the great respect and honour which he showed for his general, were most eminently remarkable; though the general himself, when reduced in straits, forgot his own dignity and office. For being beaten in various great battles, he endeavoured to dislodge by night and leave his camp; which the Numantines perceiving, immediately possessed themselves of his camp, and pursuing that part of the forces which was in flight, slew those that were in the rear, hedged the whole army in on every side, and forced them into difficult ground, whence there could be no possibility of an escape. Mancinus, despairing to make his way through by force, sent a messenger to desire a truce and conditions of peace. But they refused to give their confidence to any one except Tiberius, and required that he should be sent to treat with them. This was not only in regard to the young man's own character, for he had a great reputation amongst the soldiers, but also in remembrance of his father Tiberius, who, in his command against the Spaniards, had reduced great numbers of them to subjection, but granted a peace to the Numantines, and prevailed upon the Romans to keep it punctually and inviolably.

Tiberius was accordingly despatched to the enemy, whom he persuaded to accept of several conditions, and he himself complied with others; and by this means, it is beyond a question, that he saved twenty thousand of the Roman citizens, besides attendants and camp followers. However, the Numantines retained posession of all the property they had found and plundered in the encampment; and amongst other things were Tiberius's books of accounts, containing the whole transactions of his quæstorship, which he was extremely anxious to recover. And therefore, when the army were already upon their march, he returned to Numantia, accompanied with only three or four of his friends; and making his application to the officers of the Numantines, he entreated that they would return him his books, lest his enemies should have it in their power to reproach him with not being able to give an account of the moneys intrusted to him. The Numantines joyfully embraced this opportunity of obliging him, and invited him into the city; as he stood hesitating, they came up and took him by the hands, and begged that he would no longer look upon them as enemies, but believe them to be his friends, and treat them as such. Tiberius thought it well to consent, desirous as he was to have his books returned, and was afraid lest he should disoblige them by showing any distrust. As soon as he entered into the city, they first offered him food, and made every kind of entreaty that he would sit down and eat something in their company. Afterwards they returned his books, and gave him the liberty to take whatever he wished for in the remaining spoils. He, on the other hand, would accept of nothing but some frankincense, which he used in his public sacrifices, and bidding them farewell with every expression of kindness, departed.

When he returned to Rome, he found the whole transaction censured and reproached, as a proceeding that was base and scandalous to the Romans. But the relations and friends of the soldiers, forming a large body among the people, came flocking to Tiberius, whom they acknowledged as the preserver of so many citizens, imputing to the general all the miscarriages which had happened. Those who cried out against what had been done, urged for imitation the example of their ancestors, who stripped and handed over to the Samnites not only the generals who had consented to the terms of release, but also all the quæstors, for example, and tribunes, who had in any way implicated themselves in the agreement, laying the guilt of perjury and breach of conditions on their heads. But, in this affair, the populace, showing an extraordinary kindness and affection for Tiberius, indeed voted that the consul should be stripped and put in irons, and so delivered to the Numantines; but, for the sake of Tiberius, spared all the other officers. It may be probable, also, that Scipio, who at that time was the greatest and most powerful man among the Romans, contributed to save him, though indeed he was also censured for not protecting Mancinus too, and that he did not exert himself to maintain the observance of the articles of peace which had been agreed upon by his kinsman and friend Tiberius. But it may be presumed that the difference between them was for the most part due to ambitious feelings, and to the friends and reasoners who urged on Tiberius, and, as it was, it never amounted to anything that might not have been remedied, or that was really bad. Nor can I think that Tiberius would ever have met with his misfortunes, if Scipio had been concerned in dealing with his measures; but he was away fighting at Numantia when Tiberius, upon the following occasion, first came forward as a legislator.

Of the land which the Romans gained by conquest from their neighbours, part they sold publicly, and turned the remainder into common; this common land they assigned to such of the citizens as were poor and indigent, for which they were to pay only a small acknowledgment into the public treasury. But when the wealthy men began to offer larger rents, and drive the poorer people out, it was enacted by law that no person whatever should enjoy more than five hundred acres of ground. This act for some time checked the avarice of the richer, and was of great assistance to the poorer people, who retained under it their respective proportions of ground, as they had been formerly rented by them. Afterwards the rich men of the neighbourhood contrived to get these lands again into their possession, under other people's names, and at last would not stick to claim most of them publicly in their own. The poor, who were thus deprived of their farms, were no longer either ready, as they had formerly been, to serve in war or careful in the education of their children; insomuch that in a short time there were comparatively few freemen remaining in all Italy, which swarmed with workhouses full of foreign-born slaves. These the rich men employed in cultivating their ground of which they dispossessed the citizens. Caius Lælius, the intimate friend of Scipio, undertook to reform this abuse; but meeting with opposition from men of authority, and fearing a disturbance, he soon desisted, and received the name of the Wise or the Prudent, both which meanings belong to the Latin word *Sapiens.*

But Tiberius, being elected tribune of the people, entered upon that design without delay, at the instigation, as is most commonly stated, of Diophanes, the rhetorician, and Blossius, the philosopher. Diophanes was a refugee from Mitylene, the other was an Italian, of the city of Cuma, and was educated there under Antipater of Tarsus, who afterwards did him the honour to dedicate some of his philosophical lectures to him.

Some have also charged Cornelia, the mother of Tiberius, with contributing towards it, because she frequently upbraided her sons, that the Romans as yet rather called her the daughter of Scipio, than the mother of the Gracchi. Others again say that Spurius Postumius was the chief occasion. He was a man of the same age with Tiberius, and his rival for reputation as a public speaker; and when Tiberius, at his return from the campaign, found him to have got far beyond him in fame and influence, and to be much looked up to, he thought to outdo him, by attempting a popular enterprise of this difficulty and of such great consequence. But his brother Caius has left it us in writing, that when Tiberius went through Tuscany to Numantia, and found the country almost depopulated, there being hardly any free husbandmen or shepherds, but for the most part only barbarian, imported slaves, he then first conceived the course of policy which in the sequel proved so fatal to his family. Though it is also most certain that the people themselves chiefly excited his zeal and determination in the prosecution of it, by setting up writings upon the porches, walls, and monuments, calling upon him to reinstate the poor citizens in their former possessions.

However, he did not draw up his law without the advice and assistance of those citizens that were then most eminent for their virtue and authority; amongst whom were Crassus, the high-priest, Mucius Scævola, the lawyer, who at that time was consul, and Claudius Appius, his father-in-law. Never did any law appear more moderate and gentle, especially being enacted against such great oppression and avarice. For they who ought to have been severely punished for transgressing the former laws, and should at least have lost all their titles to such lands which they had unjustly usurped, were notwithstanding to receive a price for quitting their unlawful claims, and giving up their lands to those fit owners who stood in need of help. But though this reformation was managed with so much tenderness that, all the former transactions being passed over, the people were only thankful to prevent abuses of the like nature for the future, yet, on the other hand, the moneyed men, and those of great estates, were exasperated, through their covetous feelings against the law itself, and against the lawgiver, through anger and party-spirit. They therefore endeavoured to seduce the people, declaring that Tiberius was designing a general redivision of lands, to overthrow the government, and put all things into confusion.

But they had no success. For Tiberius, maintaining an honourable and just cause, and possessed of eloquence sufficient to have made a less creditable action appear plausible, was no safe or easy antagonist, when, with the people crowding around the hustings, he took his place, and spoke in behalf of the poor. "The savage beasts," said he, "in Italy, have their particular dens, they have their places of repose and refuge; but the men who bear arms, and expose their lives for the safety of their country, enjoy in the meantime nothing more in it but the air and light; and, having no houses or settlements of their own, are constrained to wander from place to place with their wives and children." He told them that the commanders were guilty of a ridiculous error, when, at the head of their armies, they exhorted the common soldiers to fight for their sepulchres and altars; when not any amongst so many Romans is possessed of either altar or monument, neither have they any houses of their own, or hearths of their ancestors to defend. They fought indeed and were slain, but it was to maintain the luxury and the wealth of other men. They were styled the masters of the world, but in the meantime had not one foot of ground which they could call their own. An harangue of this nature, spoken to an enthusiastic and sympathising audience, by a person of commanding spirit and genuine feelings, no adversaries at that time were competent to oppose. Forbearing, therefore, all discussion and debate, they addressed themselves to Marcus Octavius, his fellow-tribune, who being a young man of a steady, orderly character, and an intimate friend of Tiberius, upon this account declined at first the task of opposing him; but at length, over-persuaded with the repeated importunities of numerous considerable persons, he was prevailed upon to do so, and hindered the passing of the law; it being the rule that any tribune has a power to hinder an act, and that all the rest can effect nothing, if only one of them dissents. Tiberius, irritated at these proceedings, presently laid aside this milder bill, but at the same time preferred another; which, as it was more grateful to the common people, so it was much more severe against the wrongdoers, commanding them to make an immediate surrender of all lands which, contrary to former laws, had come into their possession. Hence there arose daily contentions between him and Octavius in their orations. However, though they expressed themselves with the utmost heat and determination, they yet were never known to descend to any personal reproaches, or in their passion to let slip any indecent expressions, so as to derogate from one another.

For not alone—

"In revellings and Bacchic play,"

but also in contentions and political animosities, a noble nature and a temperate education stay and compose the mind. Observing that Octavius himself was an offender against this law, and detained a great quantity of ground from the commonalty, Tiberius desired him to forbear opposing him any further, and proffered, for the public good, though he himself had but an indifferent estate, to pay a price for Octavius's share at his own cost and charges. But upon the refusal of this proffer by Octavius, he then interposed an edict, prohibiting all magistrates to exercise their respective functions, till such time as the law was either ratified or rejected by public votes. He further sealed up the gates of Saturn's temple, so that the treasurers could neither take any money out from thence, nor put any in. He threatened to impose a severe fine upon those of the prætors who presumed to disobey his commands, insomuch that all the officers, for fear of this penalty, intermitted the exercise of their several jurisdictions. Upon this the rich proprietors put themselves into mourning, and went up and down melancholy and dejected; they entered also into a conspiracy against Tiberius, and procured men to murder him; so that he also, with all men's knowledge, whenever he went abroad, took with him a sword-staff, such as robbers use, called in Latin a *dolo*.

When the day appointed was come, and the people summoned to give their votes, the rich men seized upon the voting urns and carried them away by force; thus all things were in confusion. But when Tiberius's party appeared strong enough to oppose the contrary faction, and drew together in a body, with the resolution to do so, Manlius and Fulvius, two of the consular quality, threw themselves before Tiberius, took him by the hand, and, with tears in their eyes, begged of him to desist. Tiberius, considering the mischiefs that were all but now occurring, and having a great respect for two such eminent persons, demanded of them what they would advise him to do. They acknowledged themselves unfit to advise in a matter of so great importance, but earnestly entreated him to leave it to the determination of the senate. But when the senate assembled, and could not bring the business to any result, through the prevalence of the rich faction, he then was driven to a course neither legal nor fair, and proposed to deprive Octavius of his tribuneship, it being impossible for him in any other way to get the law brought to the vote. At first he addressed him publicly, with entreaties couched in the kindest terms, and taking him by his hands, besought him, that now, in the presence of all the people, he would take this opportunity to oblige them, in granting only that request which was in itself so just and reasonable, being but a small recompense in regard of those many dangers and hardships which they had undergone for the public safety. Octavius, however, would by no means be persuaded to compliance; upon which Tiberius declared openly, that, seeing they two were united in the same office, and of equal authority, it would be a difficult matter to compose their difference on so weighty a matter without a civil war; and that the only remedy which he knew must be the deposing one of them from their office. He desired, therefore, that Octavius would summon the people to pass their verdict upon him first, averring that he would willingly relinquish his authority if the citizens desired it. Octavius refused; and Tiberius then said he would himself put to the people the question of Octavius's deposition, if upon mature deliberation he did not alter his mind; and after this declaration he adjourned the assembly till the next day.

When the people were met together again, Tiberius placed himself in the rostra, and endeavoured a second time to persuade Octavius. But all being to no purpose, he referred the whole matter to the people, calling on them to vote at once, whether Octavius should be deposed or not; and when seventeen of the thirty-five tribes had already voted against him, and there wanted only the votes of one tribe more for his final deprivation, Tiberius put a short stop to the proceedings, and once more renewed his importunities; he embraced and kissed him before all the assembly, begging with all the earnestness imaginable, that he would neither suffer himself to incur the dishonour, nor him to be reputed the author and promoter of so odious a measure. Octavius, we are told, did seem a little softened and moved with these entreaties; his eyes filled with tears, and he continued silent for a considerable time. But presently looking towards the rich men and proprietors of estates, who stood gathered in a body together, partly for shame, and partly for fear of disgracing himself with them, he boldly bade Tiberius use any severity he pleased. The law for his deprivation being thus voted, Tiberius ordered one of his servants, whom he had made a freeman, to remove Octavius from the rostra, employing his own domestic freed servants in the stead of the public officers. And it made the action seem all the sadder, that Octavius was dragged out in such an ignominious manner. The people immediately assaulted him, whilst the rich men ran in to his assistance. Octavius, with some difficulty, was snatched away and safely conveyed out of the crowd; though a trusty servant of his, who had placed himself in front of his master that he might assist his escape, in keeping off the multitude, had his eyes struck out, much to the displeasure of Tiberius, who ran with all haste, when he perceived the disturbance, to appease the rioters.

This being done, the law concerning the lands was ratified and confirmed, and three commissioners were appointed, to make a survey of the grounds, and see the same equally divided. These were Tiberius himself, Claudius Appius, his father-in-law, and his brother, Caius Gracchus, who at this time was not at Rome, but in the army under the command of Scipio Africanus before Numantia. These things were transacted by Tiberius without any disturbance, none daring to offer any resistance to him; besides which, he gave the appointment as tribune in Octavius's place, not to any person of distinction, but to a certain Mucius, one of his own clients. The great men of the city were therefore utterly offended, and, fearing lest he grew yet more popular, they took all opportunities of affronting him publicly in the senate house. For when he requested, as was usual, to have a tent provided at the public charge for his use, while dividing the lands, though it was a favour commonly granted to persons employed in business of much less importance, it was peremptorily refused to him; and the allowance made him for his daily expenses was fixed to nine obols only. The chief promoter of these affronts was Publius Nasica, who openly abandoned himself to his feelings of hatred against Tiberius, being a large holder of the public lands, and not a little resenting now to be turned out of them by force. The people, on the other hand, were still more and more excited, insomuch that a little after this, it happening that one of Tiberius's friends died suddenly, and his body being marked with malignant-looking spots, they ran, in a tumultuous manner, to his funeral, crying aloud that the man was poisoned. They took the bier upon their shoulders, and stood over it, while it was placed on the pile, and really seemed to have fair grounds for their suspicion of foul play. For the body burst open, and such a quantity of corrupt humours issued out, that the funeral fire was extinguished, and when it was again kindled, the wood still would not burn; insomuch that they were constrained to carry the corpse to another place, where with much difficulty it took fire. Besides this, Tiberius, that he might incense the people yet more, put himself into mourning, brought his children amongst the crowd, and entreated the people to provide for them and their mother, as if he now despaired of his own security.

About this time king Attalus, surnamed Philometor, died, and Eudemus, a Pergamenian, brought his last will to Rome, by which he had made the Roman people his heirs. Tiberius, to please the people, immediately proposed making a law, that all the money which Attalus left should be distributed amongst such poor citizens as were to be sharers of the public lands, for the better enabling them to proceed in stocking and cultivating their ground; and as for the cities that were in the territories of Attalus, he declared that the disposal of them did not at all belong to the senate, but to the people, and that he himself would ask their pleasure herein. By this he offended the senate more than ever he had done before, and Pompeius stood up and acquainted them that he was the next neighbour to Tiberius, and so had the opportunity of knowing that Eudemus, the Pergamenian, had presented Tiberius with a royal diadem and a purple robe, as before long he was to be king of Rome. Quintus Metellus also upbraided him, saying, that when his father was censor, the Romans, whenever he happened to be going home from a supper, used to put out all their lights, lest they should be seen to have indulged themselves in feasting and drinking at unseasonable hours, whereas now the most indigent and audacious of the people were found with their torches at night, following Tiberius home. Titus Annius, a man of no great repute for either justice or temperance, but famous for his skill in putting and answering questions, challenged Tiberius to the proof by wager, declaring him to have deposed a magistrate who by law was sacred and inviolable. Loud clamour ensued, and Tiberius, quitting the senate hastily, called together the people, and summoning Annius to appear, was proceeding to accuse him. But Annius, being no great speaker, nor of any repute compared to him, sheltered himself in his own particular art, and desired that he might propose one or two questions to Tiberius before he entered upon the chief argument. This liberty being granted, and silence proclaimed, Annius proposed his question. "If you," said he, "had a design to disgrace and defame me, and I should apply myself to one of your colleagues for redress, and he should come forward to my assistance, would you for that reason fall into a passion, and depose him?" Tiberius, they say, was so much disconcerted at this question, that, though at other times his assurance as his readiness of speech was always remarkable, yet now he was silent and made no reply.

For the present he dismissed the assembly. But beginning to understand that the course he had taken with Octavius had created offence even among the populace as well as the nobility, because the dignity of the tribunes seemed to be violated, which had always continued till that day sacred and honourable, he made a speech to the people in justification of himself; out of which it may not be improper to collect some particulars, to give an impression of his force and persuasiveness in speaking. "A tribune," he said, "of the people, is sacred indeed, and ought to be inviolable, because in a manner consecrated to be the guardian and protector of them; but if he degenerate so far as to oppress the people, abridge their powers, and take away their liberty of voting, he stands deprived by his own act of honours and immunities, by the neglect of the duty for which the honour was bestowed upon him. Otherwise we should be under the obligation to let a tribune do this pleasure, though he should proceed to destroy the capitol or set fire to the arsenal. He who should make these attempts would be a bad tribune. He who assails the power of the people is no longer a tribune at all. Is it not inconceivable that a tribune should have power to imprison a consul, and the people have no authority to degrade him when he uses that honour which he received from them, to their detriment? For the tribunes, as well as the consuls, hold office by the people's votes. The kingly government, which comprehends all sorts of authority in itself alone, is moreover elevated by the greatest and most religious solemnity imaginable into a condition of sanctity. But the citizens, notwithstanding this, deposed Tarquin, when he acted wrongfully; and for the crime of one single man, the ancient government under which Rome was built was abolished for ever. What is there in all Rome so sacred and venerable as the vestal virgins, to whose care alone the preservation of the eternal fire is committed? yet if one of these transgress she is buried alive; the sanctity which for the gods' sakes is allowed them, is forfeited when they offend against the gods. So likewise a tribune retains not his inviolability, which for the people's sake was accorded to him, when he offends against the people, and attacks the foundations of that authority from whence he derived his own. We esteem him to be legally chosen tribune who is elected only by the majority of votes; and is not therefore the same person much more lawfully degraded when, by a general consent of them all, they agreed to depose him? Nothing is so sacred as religious offerings; yet the people were never prohibited to make use of them, but suffered to remove and carry them wherever they pleased; so likewise, as it were some sacred present, they have lawful power to transfer the tribuneship from one man's hands to another's. Nor can that authority be thought inviolable and irremovable which many of those who have held it, have of their own act surrendered and desired to be discharged from."

These were the principal heads of Tiberius's apology. But his friends, apprehending the dangers which seemed to threaten him, and the conspiracy that was gathering head against him, were of opinion that the safest way would be for him to petition that he might be continued tribune for the year ensuing. Upon this consideration he again endeavoured to secure the people's good-will with fresh laws, making the years of serving in the war fewer than formerly, granting liberty of appeal from the judges to the people, and joining to the senators, who were judges at that time, an equal number of citizens of the horsemen's degree, endeavouring as much as in him lay to lessen the power of the senate, rather from passion and partisanship than from any rational regard to equity and the public good. And when it came to the question whether these laws should be passed, and they perceived that the opposite party were strongest, the people as yet being not got together in a full body, they began first of all to gain time by speeches in accusation of some of their fellow-magistrates and at length adjourned the assembly till the day following.

Tiberius then went down into the market-place amongst the people, and made his addresses to them humbly and with tears in his eyes; and told them he had just reason to suspect that his adversaries would attempt in the night-time to break open his house and murder him. This worked so strongly with the multitude, that several of them pitched tents round about his house, and kept guard all night for the security of his person. By break of day came one of the soothsayers, who prognosticate good or bad success by the pecking of fowls, and threw them something to eat. The soothsayer used his utmost endeavours to fright the fowls out of their coop; but none of them except one would venture out, which fluttered with his left wing, and stretched out its leg, and ran back again into the coop, without eating anything. This put Tiberius in mind of another ill-omen which had formerly happened to him. He had a very costly headpiece, which he made use of when he engaged in any battle, and into this piece of armour two serpents crawled, laid eggs, and brought forth young ones. The remembrance of which made Tiberius more concerned now than otherwise he would have been. However, he went towards the capitol as soon as he understood that the people were assembled there; but before he got out of the house he stumbled upon the threshold with such violence, that he broke the nail of his great toe, insomuch that blood gushed out of his shoes. He was not gone very far before he saw two ravens fighting on the top of a house which stood on his left hand as he passed along; and though he was surrounded with a number of people, a stone struck from its place by one of the ravens, fell just at his foot. This even the boldest men about him felt as a check. But Blossius of Cuma, who was present, told him that it would be a shame and an ignominious thing for Tiberius, who was a son of Gracchus, the grandson of Scipio Africanus, and the protector of the Roman people to refuse, for fear of a silly bird, to answer when his countrymen called to him; and that his adversaries would represent it not as a mere matter for their ridicule, but would declaim about it to the people as the mark of a tyrannical temper, which felt a pride in taking liberties with the people. At the same time several messengers came also from his friends, to desire his presence at the capitol, saying that all things went there according to expectation. And indeed Tiberius's first entrance there was in every way successful; as soon as ever he appeared, the people welcomed him with loud acclamations, and as he went up to his place, they repeated their expressions of joy, and gathered in a body around him, so that no one who was not well known to be his friend might approach. Mucius then began to put the business again to the vote; but nothing could be performed in the usual course and order, because of the disturbance caused by those who were on the outside of the crowd, where there was a struggle going on with those of the opposite party, who were pushing on and trying to force their way in and establish themselves among them.

Whilst things were in this confusion, Flavius Flaccus, a senator, standing in a place where he could be seen, but at such a distance from Tiberius that he could not make him hear, signified to him by motions of his hand, that he wished to impart something of consequence to him in private. Tiberius ordered the multitude to make way for him, by which means, though not without some difficulty, Flavius got to him, and informed him that the rich men, in a sitting of the senate, seeing they could not prevail upon the consul to espouse their quarrel, had come to a final determination amongst themselves that he should be assassinated, and to that purpose had a great number of their friends and servants ready armed to accomplish it. Tiberius no sooner communicated this confederacy to those about him, but they immediately tucked up their gowns, broke the halberts which the officers used to keep the crowd off into pieces, and distributed them among themselves, resolving to resist the attack with these. Those who stood at a distance wondered, and asked what was the occasion; Tiberius, knowing that they could not hear him at that distance, lifted his hand to his head wishing to intimate the great danger which he apprehended himself to be in. His adversaries, taking notice of that action, ran off at once to the senate house, and declared that Tiberius desired the people to bestow a crown upon him, as if this were the meaning of his touching his head. This news created general confusion in the senators, and Nasica at once called upon the consul to punish this tyrant, and defend the government. The consul mildly replied, that he would not be the first to do any violence;

and as he would not suffer any freeman to be put to death, before sentence had lawfully passed upon him, so neither would he allow any measure to be carried into effect, if by persuasion or compulsion on the part of Tiberius the people had been induced to pass an unlawful vote. But Nasica, rising from his seat, "Since the consul," said he, "regards not the safety of the commonwealth, let every one who will defend the laws, follow me." He then, casting the skirt of his gown over his head, hastened to the capitol; those who bore him company, wrapped their gowns also about their arms, and forced their way after him. And as they were persons of the greatest authority in the city, the common people did not venture to obstruct their passing, but were rather so eager to clear the way for them, that they tumbled over one another in haste. The attendants they brought with them had furnished themselves with clubs and staves from their houses, and they themselves picked up the feet and other fragments of stools and chairs, which were broken by the hasty flight of the common people. Thus armed, they made towards Tiberius, knocking down those whom they found in front of him, and those were soon wholly dispersed and many of them slain. Tiberius tried to save himself by flight. As he was running, he was stopped by one who caught hold of him by the gown; but he threw it off, and fled in his under-garment only. And stumbling over those who before had been knocked down, as he was endeavouring to get up again, Publius Satureius, a tribune, one of his colleagues, was observed to give him the first fatal stroke, by hitting him upon the head with the foot of a stool. The second blow was claimed, as though it had been a deed to be proud of, by Lucius Rufus. And of the rest there fell above three hundred killed by clubs and staves only, none by an iron weapon.

This, we are told, was the first sedition amongst the Romans, since the abrogation of kingly government, that ended in the effusion of blood. All former quarrels which were neither small nor about trivial matters, were always amicably composed, by mutual concessions on either side, the senate yielding for fear of the commons, and the commons out of respect to the senate. And it is probable indeed that Tiberius himself might then have been easily induced, by mere persuasion, to give way, and certainly, if attacked at all, must have yielded without any recourse to violence and bloodshed, as he had not at that time above three thousand men to support him. But it is evident, that this conspiracy was fomented against him, more out of the hatred and malice which the rich men had to his person, than for the reasons which they commonly pretended against him. In testimony of which, we may adduce the cruelty and unnatural insults which they used to his dead body. For they would not suffer his own brother, though he earnestly begged the favour, to bury him in the night, but threw him, together with the other corpses, into the river. Neither did their animosity stop here; for they banished some of his friends without legal process, and slew as many of the others as they could lay their hands on; amongst whom Diophanes, the orator, was slain, and one Caius Villius cruelly murdered by being shut up in a large tun with vipers and serpents. Blossius of Cuma, indeed, was carried before the consuls, and examined touching what had happened, and freely confessed that he had done, without scruple, whatever Tiberius bade him. "What," cried Nasica "then if Tiberius had bidden you burn the capitol, would you have burnt it?" His first answer was, that Tiberius never would have ordered any such thing; but being pressed with the same question by several, he declared, "If Tiberius had commanded it, it would have been right for me to do it; for he never would have commanded it, if it had not been for the people's good." Blossius at this time was pardoned, and afterwards went away to Aristonicus in Asia, and when Aristonicus was overthrown and ruined, killed himself.

The senate, to soothe the people after these transactions, did not oppose the division of the public lands, and permitted them to choose another commissioner in the room of Tiberius. So they elected Publius Crassus, who was Gracchus's near connection, as his daughter Licinia was married to Caius Gracchus; although Cornelius Nepos says, that it was not Crassus's daughter whom Caius married, but Brutus's, who triumphed for his victories over the Lusitanians: but most writers state it as we have done. The people, however, showed evident marks of their anger at Tiberius's death; and were clearly waiting only for the opportunity to be revenged, and Nasica was already threatened with an impeachment. The senate, therefore, fearing lest some mischief should befall him, sent him ambassador into Asia, though there was no occasion for his going thither. For the people did not conceal their indignation, even in the open streets, but railed at him, whenever they met him abroad calling him a murderer and a tyrant, one who had polluted the most holy and religious spot in Rome with the blood of a sacred and inviolable magistrate. And so Nasica left Italy, although he was bound, being the chief priest, to officiate in all principal sacrifices. Thus wandering wretchedly and ignominiously from one place to another, he died in a short time after, not far from Pergamus. It is no wonder that the people had such an aversion to Nasica, when even Scipio Africanus, though so much and so deservedly beloved by the Romans, was in danger of quite losing the good opinion which the people had of him, only for repeating, when the news of Tiberius's death was first brought to Numantia, the verse out of Homer—

"Even so perish all who do the same."

And afterwards, being asked by Caius and Fulvius, in a great assembly, what he thought of Tiberius's death, he gave an answer adverse to Tiberius's public actions. Upon which account, the people thenceforth used to interrupt him when he spoke, which, until that time, they had never done, and he, on the other hand, was induced to speak ill of the people. But of this the particulars are given in the life of Scipio.

CAIUS GRACCHUS

CAIUS GRACCHUS at first, either for fear of his brother's enemies, or designing to render them more odious to the people, absented himself from the public assemblies, and lived quietly in his own house, as if he were not only reduced for the present to live unambitiously, but was disposed in general to pass his life in inaction. And some indeed, went so far as to say that he disliked his brother's measures, and had wholly abandoned the defence of them. However, he was not but very young, being not so old as Tiberius by nine years; and he was not yet thirty when he was slain.

In some little time, however, he quietly let his temper appear, which was one of an utter antipathy to a lazy retirement and effeminacy, and not the least likely to be contented with a life of eating, drinking, and money-getting. He gave great pains to the study of eloquence, as wings upon which he might aspire to public business; and it was very apparent that he did not intend to pass his days in obscurity. When Vettius, a friend of his, was on his trial, he defended his cause, and the people were in an ecstasy, and transported with joy, finding him master of such eloquence that the other orators seemed like children in comparison, and jealousies and fears on the other hand began to be felt by the powerful citizens; and it was generally spoken of amongst them that they must hinder Caius from being made tribune.

But soon after, it happened that he was elected quæstor, and obliged to attend Orestes, the consul, into Sardinia. This, as it pleased his enemies, so it was not ungrateful to him, being naturally of a warlike character, and as well trained in the art of war as in that of pleading. And, besides, as yet he very much dreaded meddling with state affairs, and appearing publicily in the rostra, which, because of the importunity of the people and his friends, he could not otherwise avoid than by taking this journey. He was therefore most thankful for the opportunity of absenting himself. Notwithstanding which, it is the prevailing opinion that Caius was a far more thorough demagogue, and more ambitious than ever Tiberius had been, of popular applause; yet it is certain that he was borne rather by a sort of necessity than by any purpose of his own into public business. And Cicero, the orator, relates, that when he declined all such concerns, and would have lived privately, his brother appeared to him in a dream, and calling him by his name, said, "Why do you tarry, Caius? There is no escape; one life and one death is appointed for us both, to spend the one and to meet the other in the service of the people."

Caius was no sooner arrived in Sardinia, but he gave exemplary proofs of his high merit; he not only excelled all the young men of his age in his actions against his enemies, in doing justice to his inferiors, and in showing all obedience and respect to his superior officer; but likewise in temperance, frugality, and industry, he surpassed even those who were much older than himself. It happened to be a sharp and sickly winter in Sardinia, insomuch that the general was forced to lay an imposition upon several towns to supply the soldiers with necessary clothes. The cities sent to Rome, petitioning to be excused from that burden; the senate found their request reasonable, and ordered the general to find some other way of new clothing the army. While he was at a loss what course to take in this affair, the soldiers were reduced to great distress; but Caius went from one city to another, and by his mere representations he prevailed with them, that of their own accord they clothed the Roman army. This again being reported to Rome, and seeming to be only an intimation of what was to be expected of him as a popular leader hereafter, raised new jealousies amongst the senators. And, besides, there came ambassadors out of Africa from King Micipsa, to acquaint the senate that their master, out of respect to Caius Gracchus, had sent a considerable quantity of corn to the general in Sardinia; at which the senators were so much offended, that they turned the ambassadors out of the senate house, and made an order that the soldiers should be relieved by sending others in their room; but that Orestes should continue at his post, with whom Caius, also, as they presumed, being his quæstor, would remain. But he, finding how things were carried, immediately in anger took ship for Rome, where his unexpected appearance obtained him the censure not only of his enemies, but also of the people; who thought it strange that a quæstor should leave before his commander. Nevertheless, when some accusation upon this ground was made against him to the censors, he desired leave to defend himself, and did it so effectually, that, when he ended, he was regarded as one who had been very much injured. He made it then appear that he had served twelve years in the army, whereas others are obliged to serve only ten; that he had continued quæstor to the general three years, whereas he might by law have returned at the end of one year; and alone of all who went on the expedition, he had carried out a full and had brought home an empty purse, while others, after drinking up the wine they had carried out with them, brought back the wine-jars filled again with gold and silver from the war.

After this they brought other accusations and writs against him, for exciting insurrection amongst the allies, and being engaged in the conspiracy that was discovered about Fregellæ. But having cleared himself of every suspicion, and proved his entire innocence, he now at once came forward to ask for the tribuneship; in which, though he was universally opposed by all persons of distinction, yet there came such infinite numbers of people from all parts of Italy to vote for Caius, that lodgings for them could not be supplied in the city; and the Field being not large enough to contain the assembly, there were numbers who climbed upon the roofs and the tilings of the houses to use their voices in his favour. However, the nobility so far forced the people to their pleasure and disappointed Caius's hope, that he was not returned the first, as was expected, but the fourth tribune. But when he came to the execution of his office, it was seen presently who was really first tribune, as he was a better orator than any of his contemporaries, and the passion with which he still lamented his brother's death made him the bolder in speaking. He used on all occasions to remind the people of what had happened in that tumult, and laid before them the examples of their ancestors, how they declared war against the Faliscans, only for giving scurrilous language to one Genucius, a tribune of the people; and sentenced Caius Veturius to death, for refusing to give way in the forum to a tribune; "Whereas," said he, "these men did, in the presence of you all, murder Tiberius with clubs, and dragged the slaughtered body through the middle of the city, to be cast into the river. Even his friends, as many as could be taken, were put to death immediately, without any trial, notwithstanding that just and ancient custom, which has always been observed in our city, that whenever any one is accused of a capital crime, and does not make his personal appearance in court, a trumpeter is sent in the morning to his lodging, to summon him by sound of trumpet to appear; and before this ceremony is performed, the judges do not proceed to the vote; so cautious and reserved were our ancestors about business of life and death."

Having moved the people's passion with such addresses (and his voice was of the loudest and strongest), he proposed two laws. The first was, that whoever was turned out of any public office by the people, should be thereby rendered incapable of bearing any office afterwards; the second, that if any magistrate condemn a Roman to be banished without a legal trial, the people be authorized to take cognisance thereof.

One of these laws was manifestly levelled at Marcus Octavius, who, at the instigation of Tiberius, had been deprived of his tribuneship. The other touched Popilius, who, in his prætorship, had banished all Tiberius's friends;

whereupon Popilius, being unwilling to stand the hazard of a trial, fled out of Italy. As for the former law, it was withdrawn by Caius himself, who said he yielded in the case of Octavius, at the request of his mother Cornelia. This was very acceptable and pleasing to the people, who had a great veneration for Cornelia, not more for the sake of her father than for that of her children; and they afterwards erected a statue of brass in honour of her, with this inscription, *Cornelia, the mother of the Gracchi.* There are several expressions recorded, in which he used her name perhaps with too much rhetoric, and too little self-respect, in his attacks upon his adversaries. "How," said he, "dare you presume to reflect upon Cornelia, the mother of Tiberius?" And because the person who made the reflections had been suspected of effeminate courses, "With what face," said he, "can you compare Cornelia with yourself? Have you brought forth children as she has done? And yet all Rome knows that she has refrained from the conversation of men longer than you yourself have done." Such was the bitterness he used in his language; and numerous similar expressions might be adduced from his written remains.

Of the laws which he now proposed, with the object of gratifying the people and abridging the power of the senate, the first was concerning the public lands, which were to be divided amongst the poor citizens; another was concerning the common soldiers, that they should be clothed at the public charge, without any diminution of their pay, and that none should be obliged to serve in the army who was not full seventeen years old; another gave the same right to all the Italians in general, of voting at elections, as was enjoyed by the citizens of Rome; a fourth related to the price of corn, which was to be sold at a lower rate than formerly to the poor; and a fifth regulated the courts of justice, greatly reducing the power of the senators. For hitherto, in all causes, senators only sat as judges, and were therefore much dreaded by the Roman knights and the people. But Caius joined three hundred ordinary citizens of equestrian rank with the senators, who were three hundred likewise in number, and ordained that the judicial authority should be equally invested in the six hundred. While he was arguing for the ratification of this law, his behaviour was observed to show in many respects unusual earnestness, and whereas other popular leaders had always hitherto, when speaking, turned their faces towards the senate house, and the place called the comitium, he, on the contrary, was the first man that in his harangue to the people turned himself the other way, towards them, and continued after that time to do so. An insignificant movement and change of posture, yet it marked no small revolution in state affairs, the conversion, in a manner, of the whole government from an aristocracy to a democracy, his action intimating that public speakers should address themselves to the people, not the senate.

When the commonalty ratified this law, and gave him power to select those of the knights whom he approved of, to be judges, he was invested with a sort of a kingly power, and the senate itself submitted to receive his advice in matters of difficulty; nor did he advise anything that might derogate from the honour of that body. As, for example, his resolution about the corn which Fabius the proprætor sent from Spain, was very just and honourable; for he persuaded the senate to sell the corn, and return the money to the same provinces which had furnished them with it; and also that Fabius should be censured for rendering the Roman government odious and insupportable. This got him extraordinary respect and favour among the provinces. Besides all this, he proposed measures for the colonisation of several cities, for making roads, and for building public granaries; of all which works he himself undertook the management and superintendence, and was never wanting to give necessary orders for the despatch of all these different and great undertakings; and that with such wonderful expedition and diligence, as if he had been but engaged upon one of them; insomuch that all persons, even those who hated or feared him, stood amazed to see what a capacity he had for effecting and completing all he undertook. As for the people themselves, they were transported at the very sight, when they saw him surrounded with a crowd of contractors, artificers, public deputies, military officers, soldiers, and scholars. All these he treated with an easy familiarity, yet without abandoning his dignity in his gentleness; and so accommodated his nature to the wants and occasions of every one who addressed him, that those were looked upon as no better than envious detractors, who had represented him as a terrible, assuming, and violent character. He was even a greater master of the popular leader's art in his common talk and his actions, than he was in his public addresses.

His most especial exertions were given to constructing the roads, which he was careful to make beautiful and pleasant, as well as convenient. They were drawn by his directions through the fields, exactly in a straight line, partly paved with hewn stone, and partly laid with solid masses of gravel. When he met with any valleys or deep watercourses crossing the line, he either caused them to be filled up with rubbish, or bridges to be built over them, so well levelled, that all being of an equal height on both sides, the work presented one uniform and beautiful prospect. Besides this, he caused the roads to be all divided into miles (each mile containing little less than eight furlongs), and erected pillars of stone to signify the distance from one place to another. He likewise placed other stones at small distances from one another, on both sides of the way, by the help of which travellers might get easily on horseback without wanting a groom.

For these reasons, the people highly extolled him, and were ready upon all occasions to express their affection towards him. One day, in an oration to them, he declared that he had only one favour to request, which if they granted, he should think the greatest obligation in the world; yet if it were denied, he would never blame them for the refusal. This expression made the world believe that his ambition was to be consul; and it was generally expected that he wished to be both consul and tribune at the same time. When the day for election of consuls was at hand, and all in great expectation, he appeared in the Field with Caius Fannius, canvassing together with his friends for his election. This was of great effect in Fannius's favour. He was chosen consul, and Caius elected tribune the second time, without his own seeking or petitioning for it, but at the voluntary motion of the people. But when he understood that the senators were his declared enemies, and that Fannius himself was none of the most zealous of friends, he began again to rouse the people with other new laws. He proposed that a colony of Roman citizens might be sent to re-people Tarentum and Capua, and that the Latins should enjoy the same privileges with the citizens of Rome. But the senate, apprehending that he would at last grow too powerful and dangerous, took a new and unusual course to alienate the people's affections from him, by playing the demagogue in opposition to him, and offering favours contrary to all good policy. Livius Drusus was fellow-tribune with Caius, a person of as good a family and as well educated as any amongst the Romans, and noways inferior to those who for their eloquence and riches were the most honoured and most powerful men of that time. To him, therefore, the chief senators made their application, exhorting him to attack Caius, and join in their confederacy against him; which they designed to carry on, not by using any force, or opposing the common people, but by gratifying and obliging them with such unreasonable things as otherwise they would have felt it honourable for them to incur the greatest unpopularity in resisting.

Livius offered to serve the senate with his authority in this business and proceeded accordingly to bring forward such laws as were in reality neither honourable nor advantageous for the public; his whole design being to outdo Caius in pleasing and cajoling the populace (as if it had been in some comedy), with obsequious flattery and every kind of gratifications; the senate thus letting it be seen plainly that they were not angry with Caius's public measures, but only desirous to ruin him utterly, or at least to lessen his reputation. For when Caius proposed the settlement of only two colonies, and mentioned the better class of citizens for that purpose, they accused him of abusing the people; and yet, on the contrary, were pleased with Drusus, when he proposed the sending out of twelve colonies each to consist of three thousand persons, and those, too, the most needy that he could find. When Caius divided the public land amongst the poor citizens, and charged them with a small rent, annually to be paid into the exchequer, they were angry at him, as one who sought to gratify the people only for his own interest; yet afterwards they commended Livius, though he exempted them from paying even that little acknowledgment. They were displeased with Caius for offering the Latins an equal right with the Romans of voting at the election of magistrates; but when Livius proposed that it might not be lawful for a Roman captain to scourge a Latin soldier, they promoted the passing of that law. And Livius, in all his speeches to the people, always told them that he proposed no laws but such as were agreeable to the senate, who had a particular regard to the people's advantage. And this truly was the only point in all his proceedings which was of any real service, as it created more kindly feelings towards the senate in the people; and whereas they formerly suspected and hated the principal senators, Livius appeased and mitigated this perverseness and animosity, by his profession that he had done nothing in favour and for the benefit of the commons without their advice and approbation.

But the greatest credit which Drusus got for kindness and justice towards the people was, that he never seemed to propose any law for his own sake, or his own advantage; he committed the charge of seeing the colonies rightly settled to other commissioners; neither did he ever concern himself with the distribution of the moneys; whereas Caius always took the principal part in any important transactions of this kind. Rubrius, another tribune of the people, had proposed to have Carthage again inhabited, which had been demolished by Scipio, and it fell to Caius's lot to see this performed, and for that purpose he sailed to Africa. Drusus took this opportunity of his absence to insinuate himself still more into the people's affections, which he did chiefly by accusing Fulvius, who was a particular friend to Caius, and was appointed a commissioner with him for the division of the lands. Fulvius was a man of a turbulent spirit; and notoriously hated by the senate; and besides, he was suspected by others to have fomented the difference between the citizens and their confederates, and underhand to be inciting the Italians to rebel; though there was little other evidence of the truth of these accusations than his being an unsettled character and of a well-known seditious temper. This was one principal cause of Caius's ruin; for part of the envy which fell upon Fulvius was extended to him. And when Scipio Africanus died suddenly, and no cause of such an unexpected death could be assigned, only some marks of blows upon his body seemed to intimate that he had suffered violence, as is related in the history of his life, the greatest part of the odium attached to Fulvius, because he was his enemy, and that very day had reflected upon Scipio in a public address to the people. Nor was Caius himself clear from suspicion. However, this great outrage, committed too upon the person of the greatest and most considerable man in Rome, was never either punished or inquired into thoroughly, for the populace opposed and hindered any judicial investigation, for fear that Caius should be implicated in the charge if proceedings were carried on. This, however, had happened some time before.

But in Africa, where at present Caius was engaged in the re-peopling of Carthage, which he named Junonia, many ominous appearances, which presaged mischief, are reported to have been sent from the gods. For a sudden gust of wind falling upon the first standard, and the standard-bearer holding it fast, the staff broke; another sudden storm blew away the sacrifices, which were laid upon the altars, and carried them beyond the bounds laid out for the city, and the wolves came and carried away the very marks that were set up to show the boundary. Caius, notwithstanding all this, ordered and despatched the whole business in the space of seventy days, and then returned to Rome, understanding how Fulvius was prosecuted by Drusus, and that the present juncture of affairs would not suffer him to be absent. For Lucius Opimius, one who sided with the nobility, and was of no small authority in the senate, who had formerly sued to be consul, but was repulsed by Caius's interest, at the time when Fannius was elected, was in a fair way now of being chosen consul, having a numerous company of supporters. And it was generally believed, if he did obtain it, that he would wholly ruin Caius, whose power was already in a declining condition; and the people were not so apt to admire his actions as formerly, because there were so many others who every day contrived new ways to please them, with which the senate readily complied.

After his return to Rome, he quitted his house on the Palatine Mount, and went to live near the market-place, endeavouring to make himself more popular in those parts, where most of the humble and poorer citizens lived. He then brought forward the remainder of his proposed laws, as intending to have them ratified by the popular vote; to support which a vast number of people collected from all quarters. But the senate persuaded Fannius, the consul, to command all persons who were not born Romans to depart the city. A new and unusual proclamation was thereupon made, prohibiting any of the allies or Confederates to appear at Rome during that time. Caius, on the contrary, published an edict, accusing the consul for what he had done, and setting forth to the Confederates, that if they would continue upon the place, they might be assured of his assistance and protection. However, he was not so good as his word; for though he saw one of his own familiar friends and companions dragged to prison by Fannius's officers, he, notwithstanding, passed by without assisting him; either because he was afraid to stand the test of his power, which was already decreased, or because, as he himself reported, he was unwilling to give his enemies an opportunity, which they very much desired, of coming to actual violence and fighting. About that time there happened likewise a difference between him and his fellow-officers upon this occasion. A show of gladiators was to be exhibited before the people in the market-place, and most of the magistrates erected scaffolds round about, with an intention of letting them for advantage. Caius commanded them to take down their scaffolds, that the poor people might see the sport without paying anything. But nobody obeying these orders of his, he gathered together a body of labourers, who worked for him, and overthrew all the scaffolds the very night before the contest was to take place. So that by the next morning the market-place was cleared, and the common people had an opportunity of seeing the pastime. In this, the populace thought he had acted the part of a man; but he much disobliged the tribunes his colleagues, who regarded it as a piece of violent and presumptuous interference.

This was thought to be the chief reason that he failed of being the third time elected tribune; not but that he had the most votes, but because his colleagues out of revenge caused false returns to be made. But as to this matter there was a controversy. Certain it is, he very much resented this repulse, and behaved with unusual arrogance towards some of his adversaries who were joyful at his defeat, telling them that all this was but a false sardonic mirth, as they little knew how much his actions threw them into obscurity.

As soon as Opimius also was chosen consul, they presently cancelled several of Caius's laws, and especially called in question his proceedings at Carthage, omitting nothing that was likely to irritate him, that from some effect of his passion they might find out a tolerable pretence to put him to death. Caius at first bore these things very patiently; but afterwards, at the instigation of his friends, especially Fulvius, he resolved to put himself at the head of a body of supporters, to oppose the consul by force. They say also that on this occasion his mother, Cornelia, joined in the sedition, and assisted him by sending privately several strangers into Rome, under pretence as if they came to be hired there for harvest-men; for that intimations of this are given in her letters to him. However, it is confidently affirmed by others that Cornelia did not in the least approve of these actions.

When the day came in which Opimius designed to abrogate the laws of Caius, both parties met very early at the capitol; and the consul having performed all the rites usual in their sacrifices, one Quintus Antyllius, an attendant on the consul, carrying out the entrails of the victim, spoke to Fulvius, and his friends who stood about him, "Ye factious citizens, make way for honest men." Some report that, besides this provoking language, he extended his naked arm towards them, as a piece of scorn and contempt. Upon this he was presently killed with the strong stiles which are commonly used in writing, though some say that on this occasion they had been manufactured for this purpose only. This murder caused a sudden consternation in the whole assembly, and the heads of each faction had their different sentiments about it. As for Caius, he was much grieved, and severely reprimanded his own party, because they had given their adversaries a reasonable pretence to proceed against them, which they had so long hoped for. Opimius, immediately seizing the occasion thus offered, was in great delight, and urged the people to revenge; but there happening a great shower of rain on a sudden, it put an end to the business of that day.

Early the next morning, the consul summoned the senate, and whilst he advised with the senators in the senate-house, the corpse of Antyllius was laid upon a bier, and brought through the market-place there exposed to open view, just before the senate-house, with a great deal of crying and lamentation. Opimius was not at all ignorant that this was designed to be done; however, he seemed to be surprised, and wondered what the meaning of it should be; the senators, therefore, presently went out to know the occasion of it, and, standing about the corpse, uttered exclamations against the inhuman and barbarous act. The people, meantime, could not but feel resentment and hatred for the senators, remembering how they themselves had not only assassinated Tiberius Gracchus, as he was executing his office in the very capitol, but had also thrown his mangled body into the river; yet now they could honour with their presence and their public lamentations in the forum the corpse of an ordinary hired attendant (who, though he might perhaps die wrongfully, was, however, in a great measure the occasion of it himself), by these means hoping to undermine him who was the only remaining defender and safeguard of the people.

The senators, after some time, withdrew, and presently ordered that Opimius, the consul, should be invested with extraordinary power to protect the commonwealth and suppress all tyrants. This being decreed, he presently commanded the senators to arm themselves, and the Roman knights to be in readiness very early the next morning, and every one of them to be attended with two servants well armed. Fulvius, on the other side, made his preparations and collected the populace. Caius at that time returning from the market-place, made a stop just before his father's statue, and fixing his eyes for some time upon it, remained in a deep contemplation; at length he sighed, shed tears, and departed. This made no small impression upon those who saw it, and they began to upbraid themselves that they should desert and betray so worthy a man as Caius. They therefore went directly to his house, remaining there as a guard about it all night, though in a different manner from those who were a guard to Fulvius; for they passed away the night with shouting and drinking, and Fulvius himself, being the first to get drunk, spoke and acted many things very unbecoming a man of his age and character. On the other side, the party which guarded Caius, were quiet and diligent, relieving one another by turns, and forecasting, as in a public calamity, what the issue of things might be. As soon as daylight appeared, they roused Fulvius, who had not yet slept off the effects of his drinking; and having armed themselves with the weapons hung up in his house, that were formerly taken from the Gauls, whom he conquered in the time of his consulship, they presently, with threats and loud acclamations, made their way towards the Aventine Mount.

Caius could not be persuaded to arm himself, but put on his gown, as if he had been going to the assembly of the people, only with this difference, that under it he had then a short dagger by his side. As he was going out, his wife came running to him at the gate, holding him with one hand, and with the other a young child of his. She bespoke him: "Alas, Caius, I do not now part with you to let you address the people either as a tribune or a lawgiver, nor as if you were going to some honourable war, when, though you might perhaps have encountered that fate which all must some time or other submit to, yet you had left me this mitigation of my sorrow, that my mourning was respected and honoured. You go now to expose your person to the murderers of Tiberius, unarmed indeed, and rightly so, choosing rather to suffer the worst of injuries than do the least yourself. But even your very death at this time will not be serviceable to the public good. Faction prevails; power and arms are now the only measures of justice. Had your brother fallen before Numantia, the enemy would have given back what then had remained of Tiberius; but such is my hard fate, that I probably must be an humble suppliant to the floods or the waves, that they would somewhere restore to me your relics; for since Tiberius was not spared, what trust can we place either on the laws, or in the gods?" Licinia, thus bewailing, Caius, by degrees getting loose from her embraces, silently withdrew himself, being accompanied by his friends; she, endeavouring to catch him by the gown, fell prostrate upon the earth, lying there for some time speechless. Her servants took her up for dead, and conveyed her to her brother Crassus.

Fulvius, when the people were gathered together in a full body, by the advice of Caius sent his youngest son into the market-place, with a herald's rod in his hand. He, being a very handsome youth, and modestly addressing himself, with tears in his eyes and a becoming bashfulness, offered proposals of agreement to the consul and the whole senate. The greatest part of the assembly were inclinable to accept of the proposals; but Opimius said, that it did not become them to send messengers and capitulate with the senate, but to surrender at discretion to the laws, like loyal citizens, and endeavour to merit their pardon by submission. He commanded the youth not to return, unless they would comply with these conditions. Caius, as it is reported, was very forward to go and clear himself before the senate; but none of his friends consenting to it, Fulvius sent his son a second time to intercede for them, as before. But Opimius, who was resolved that a battle should ensue, caused the youth to be apprehended and committed into custody; and then with a company of his foot-soldiers and some Cretan archers set upon the party under Fulvius. These archers did such execution, and inflicted so many wounds, that a rout and flight quickly ensued. Fulvius fled into an obscure bathing-house; but shortly after being discovered, he and his eldest son were slain together. Caius was not observed to use any violence against any one; but extremely disliking all these outrages, retired to Diana's temple. There he attempted to kill himself, but was hindered by his faithful friends, Pomponius and Licinius; they took his sword away from him, and were very urgent that he would endeavour to make his escape. It is reported that, falling upon his knee and lifting up his hands, he prayed the goddess that the Roman people, as a punishment for their ingratitude and treachery, might always remain in slavery. For as soon as a proclamation was made of a pardon, the greater part openly deserted him.

Caius, therefore, endeavoured now to make his escape, but was pursued so close by his enemies, as far as the wooden bridge, that from thence he narrowly escaped. There his two trusty friends begged of him to preserve his own person by flight, whilst they in the meantime would keep their post, and maintain the passage; neither could their enemies, until they were both slain, pass the bridge. Caius had no other companion in his flight but one Philocrates, a servant of his. As he ran along, everybody encouraged him, and wished him success, as standers-by may do to those who are engaged in a race, but nobody either lent him any assistance, or would furnish him with a horse, though he asked for one; for his enemies had gained ground, and got very near him. However, he had still time enough to hide himself in a little grove, consecrated to the Furies. In that place, his servant Philocrates having first slain him, presently afterwards killed himself also, and fell dead upon his master. Though some affirm it for a truth, that they were both taken alive by their enemies, and that Philocrates embraced his master so close, that they could not wound Caius until his servant was slain.

They say that when Caius's head was cut off, and carried away by one of his murderers, Septimuleius, Opimius's friend, met him, and forced it from him; because, before the battle began, they had made proclamation, that whoever should bring the head either of Caius or Fulvius, should, as a reward, receive its weight in gold. Septimuleius, therefore, having fixed Caius's head upon the top of his spear, came and presented it to Opimius. They presently brought the scales, and it was found to weigh above seventeen pounds. But in this affair, Septimuleius gave as great signs of his knavery as he had done before of his cruelty; for having taken out the brains, he had filled the skull with lead. There were others who brought the head of Fulvius, too, but, being mean, inconsiderable persons, were turned away without the promised reward. The bodies of these two persons, as well as of the rest who were slain, to the number of three thousand men, were all thrown into the river; their goods were confiscated, and their widows forbidden to put themselves into mourning. They dealt even more severely with Licinia, Caius's wife, and deprived her even of her jointure; and as in addition still to all their inhumanity, they barbarously murdered Fulvius's youngest son; his only crime being, not that he took up arms against them, or that he was present in the battle, but merely that he had come with articles of agreement; for this he was first imprisoned, then slain.

But that which angered the common people most was, that at this time, in memory of his success, Opimius built the Temple of Concord, as if he gloried and triumphed in the slaughter of so many citizens. Somebody in the night time, under the inscription of the temple added this verse:—

"Folly and Discord Concord's temple built."

Yet this Opimius, the first who, being consul, presumed to usurp the power of a dictator, condemning, without any trial, with three thousand other citizens, Caius Gracchus and Fulvius Flaccus, one of whom had triumphed and been consul, the other far excelled all his contemporaries in virtue and honour, afterwards was found incapable of keeping his hands from thieving: and when he was sent ambassador to Jugurtha, King of Numidia, he was there corrupted by presents, and at his return, being shamefully convicted of it, lost all his honours, and grew old amidst the hatred and the insults of the people; who, though humble, and affrighted at the time, did not fail before long to let everybody see what respect and veneration they had for the memory of the Gracchi. They ordered their statues to be made and set up in public view; they consecrated the places where they were slain, and thither brought the first-fruits of everything, according to the season of the year, to make their offerings. Many came likewise thither to their devotions, and daily worshipped there, as at the temple of the gods.

It is reported that as Cornelia, their mother, bore the loss of her two sons with a noble and undaunted spirit, so, in reference to the holy places in which they were slain, she said, their dead bodies were well worthy of such sepulchres. She removed afterwards, and dwelt near the place called Misenum, not at all altering her former way of living. She had many friends, and hospitably received many strangers at her house; many Greeks and learned men were continually about her; nor was there any foreign prince but received gifts from her and presented her again. Those who were conversant with her, were much interested, when she pleased to entertain them with her recollections of her father Scipio Africanus, and of his habits and way of living. But it was most admirable to hear her make mention of her sons, without any tears or sign of grief, and give the full account of all their deeds and misfortunes, as if she had been relating the history of some ancient heroes. This made some imagine, that age, or the greatness of her afflictions, had made her senseless and devoid of natural feelings. But they who so thought were themselves more truly insensible not to see how much a noble nature and education avail to conquer any affliction; and though fortune may often be more successful, and may defeat the efforts of virtue to avert misfortunes, it cannot, when we incur them, prevent our hearing them reasonably.

THE COMPARISON OF TIBERIUS AND CAIUS GRACCHUS WITH AGIS AND CLEOMENES

HAVING given an account severally of these persons, it remains only that we should take a view of them in comparison with one another.

As for the Gracchi, the greatest detractors and their worst enemies could not but allow that they had a genius to virtue beyond all other Romans, which was improved also by a generous education. Agis and Cleomenes may be supposed to have had stronger natural gifts, since, though they wanted all the advantages of good education, and were bred up in those very customs, manners, and habits of living which had for a long time corrupted others, yet they were public examples of temperance and frugality. Besides, the Gracchi, happening to live when Rome had her greatest repute for honour and virtuous actions, might justly have been ashamed, if they had not also left to the next generation the noble inheritance of the virtues of their ancestors. Whereas the other two had parents of different morals, and though they found their country in a sinking condition, and debauched, yet that did not quench their forward zeal to what was just and honourable.

The integrity of the two Romans, and their superiority to money, was chiefly remarkable in this: that in office and the administration of public affairs, they kept themselves from the imputation of unjust gain; whereas Agis might justly be offended if he had only that mean commendation given him, that he took nothing wrongfully from any man, seeing he distributed his own fortunes which, in ready money only, amounted to the value of six hundred talents, amongst his fellow-citizens. Extortion would have appeared a crime of a strange nature to him, who esteemed it a piece of covetousness to possess, though never so justly gotten, greater riches than his neighbours.

Their political actions, also, and the state revolutions they attempted, were very different in magnitude. The chief things in general that the two Romans commonly aimed at, were the settlement of cities and mending of highways; and, in particular, the boldest design which Tiberius is famed for, was the recovery of the public lands; and Caius gained his greatest reputation by the addition, for the exercise of judiciary powers, of three hundred of the order of knights to the same number of senators. Whereas the alteration which Agis and Cleomenes made was in a quite different kind. They did not set about removing partial evils and curing petty incidents of disease, which would have been (as Plato says) like cutting off one of the Hydra's heads, the very means to increase the number; but they instituted a thorough reformation, such as would free the country from all its grievances, or rather, to speak more truly, they reversed that former change which had been the cause of all their calamities; and so restored their city to its ancient state.

However, this must be confessed in the behalf of the Gracchi, that their undertakings were always opposed by men of the greatest influence. On the other side, those things which were first attempted by Agis, and afterwards consummated by Cleomenes, were supported by the great and glorious precedent of those ancient laws concerning frugality and levelling which they had themselves received upon the authority of Lycurgus, and he had instituted on that of Apollo. It is also further observable, that from the actions of the Gracchi, Rome received no additions to her former greatness; whereas, under the conduct of Cleomenes, Greece presently saw Sparta exert her sovereign power over all Peloponnesus, and contest the supreme command with the most powerful princes of the time; success in which would have freed Greece from Illyrian and Gaulish violence, and placed her once again under the orderly rule of the sons of Hercules.

From the circumstances of their deaths, also, we may infer some difference in the quality of their courage. The Gracchi, fighting with their fellow citizens, were both slain as they endeavoured to make their escape; Agis willingly submitted to his fate, rather than any citizen should be in danger of his life. Cleomenes, being shamefully and unjustly treated, made an effort toward revenge, but failing of that, generously fell by his own hand.

On the other side it must be said, that Agis never did a great action worthy a commander, being prevented by an untimely death. And as for those heroic actions of Cleomenes, we may justly compare with them that of Tiberius, when he was the first who attempted to scale the walls of Carthage, which was no mean exploit. We may add the peace which he concluded with the Numantines, by which he saved the lives of twenty thousand Romans, who otherwise had certainly been cut off. And Caius, not only at home, but in war in Sardinia, displayed distinguished courage. So that their early actions were no small argument that afterwards they might have rivalled the best of the Roman commanders, if they had not died so young.

In civil life, Agis showed a lack of determination; he let himself be baffled by the craft of Agesilaus, disappointed the expectations of the citizens as to the division of the lands, and generally left all the designs, which he had deliberately formed and publicly announced, unperformed and unfulfilled through a young man's want of resolution. Cleomenes, on the other hand, proceeded to effect the revolution with only too much boldness and violence, and unjustly slew the Ephors whom he might, by superiority in arms, have gained over to his party, or else might easily have banished, as he did several others of the city. For to use the knife, unless in the extremest necessity, is neither good surgery nor wise policy, but in both cases mere unskilfulness; and in the latter, unjust as well as unfeeling. Of the Gracchi, neither the one nor the other was the first to shed the blood of his fellow-citizens; and Caius is reported to have avoided all manner of resistance, even when his life was aimed at, showing himself always valiant against a foreign enemy, but wholly inactive in a sedition. This was the reason that he went from his own house unarmed, and withdrew when the battle began, and in all respects showed himself anxious rather not to do any harm to others, than not to suffer any himself. Even the very flight of the Gracchi must not be looked upon as an argument of their mean spirit, but an honourable retreat from endangering of others. For if they had stayed, they must either have yielded to those who assailed them, or else have fought them in their own defence.

The greatest crime that can be laid to Tiberius's charge was the deposing of his fellow tribune, and seeking afterwards a second tribuneship for himself. As for the death of Antyllius, it is falsely and unjustly attributed to Caius, for he was slain unknown to him and much to his grief. On the contrary, Cleomenes (not to mention the murder of the Ephors) set all the slaves at liberty, and governed by himself alone in reality, having a partner only for show; having made choice of his brother Euclidas, who was one of the same family. He prevailed upon Archidamus, who was the right heir to the kingdom of the other line, to venture to return home from Messene; but after his being slain, by not doing anything to revenge his death, confirmed the suspicion that he was privy to it himself. Lycurgus, whose example he professed to imitate, after he had voluntarily settled his kingdom upon Charillus, his brother's son, fearing lest, if the youth should chance to die by accident, he might be suspected for it, travelled a long time, and would not return again to Sparta until Charillus had a son, and an heir to his kingdom. But we have indeed no other Grecian who is worthy to be compared with Lycurgus, and it is clear enough that in the public measures of Cleomenes various acts of considerable audacity and lawlessness may be found.

Those, therefore, who incline to blame their characters may observe, that the two Grecians were disturbers even from their youth, lovers of contest, and aspirants to despotic power; that Tiberius and Caius by nature had an excessive desire after glory and honours. Beyond this, their enemies could find nothing to bring against them; but as soon as the contention began with their adversaries, their heat and passions would so far prevail beyond their natural temper, that by them, as by ill winds, they were driven afterwards to all their rash undertakings. What could be more just and honourable than their first design, had not the power and the faction of the rich, by endeavouring to abrogate that law, engaged them both in those fatal quarrels, the one, for his own preservation, the other, to revenge his brother's death, who was murdered without any law or justice?

From the account, therefore, which has been given, you yourself may perceive the difference; which if it were to be pronounced of every one singly, I should affirm Tiberius to have excelled them all in virtue; that young Agis had been guilty of the fewest misdeeds; and that in action and boldness Caius came far short of Cleomenes.

DEMOSTHENES

WHOEVER it was, Sosius, that wrote the poem in honour of Alcibiades, upon his winning the chariot-race at the Olympian Games, whether it were Euripides, as is most commonly thought, or some other person, he tells us that to a man's being happy it is in the first place requisite he should be born in "some famous city." But for him that would attain to true happiness, which for the most part is placed in the qualities and disposition of the mind, it is, in my opinion, of no other disadvantage to be of a mean, obscure country, than to be born of a small or plain-looking woman. For it were ridiculous to think that Iulis, a little part of Ceos, which itself is no great island, and Ægina, which an Athenian once said ought to be removed, like a small eyesore, from the port of Piræus, should breed good actors and poets, and yet should never be able to produce a just, temperate, wise, and high-minded man. Other arts, whose end it is to acquire riches or honour, are likely enough to wither and decay in poor and undistinguished towns; but virtue, like a strong and durable plant, may take root and thrive in any place where it can lay hold of an ingenuous nature, and a mind that is industrious. I, for my part, shall desire that for any deficiency of mine in right judgment or action, I myself may be, as in fairness, held accountable, and shall not attribute it to the obscurity of my birthplace.

But if any man undertake to write a history that has to be collected from materials gathered by observation and the reading of works not easy to be got in all places, nor written always in his own language, but many of them foreign and dispersed in other hands, for him, undoubtedly, it is in the first place and above all things most necessary to reside in some city of good note, addicted to liberal arts, and populous; where he may have plenty of all sorts of books, and upon inquiry may hear and inform himself of such particulars as, having escaped the pens of writers, are more faithfully preserved in the memories of men, lest his work be deficient in many things, even those which it can least dispense with.

But for me, I live in a little town, where I am willing to continue, lest it should grow less; and having had no leisure, while I was in Rome and other parts of Italy, to exercise myself in the Roman language, on account of public business and of those who came to be instructed by me in philosophy, it was very late, and in the decline of my age, before I applied myself to the reading of Latin authors. Upon which that which happened to me may seem strange, though it be true; for it was not so much by the knowledge of words that I came to the understanding of things, as by my experience of things I was enabled to follow the meaning of words. But to appreciate the graceful and ready pronunciation of the Roman tongue, to understand the various figures and connection of words, and such other ornaments, in which the beauty of speaking consists, is, I doubt not, an admirable and delightful accomplishment; but it requires a degree of practice and study which is not easy, and will better suit those who have more leisure, and time enough yet before them for the occupation.

And so in this fifth book of my Parallel Lives, in giving an account of Demosthenes and Cicero, my comparison of their natural dispositions and their characters will be formed upon their actions and their lives as statesmen, and I shall not pretend to criticise their orations one against the other, to show which of the two was the more charming or the more powerful speaker. For there, as Ion says—

"We are but like a fish upon dry land;"

a proverb which Cæcilius perhaps forgot, when he employed his always adventurous talents in so ambitious an attempt as a comparison of Demosthenes and Cicero; and, possibly, if it were a thing obvious and easy for every man to *know himself*, the precept had not passed for an oracle.

The divine power seems originally to have designed Demosthenes and Cicero upon the same plan, giving them many similarities in their natural characters, as their passion for distinction and their love of liberty in civil life, and their want of courage in dangers and war, and at the same time also to have added many accidental resemblances. I think there can hardly be found two other orators, who, from small and obscure beginnings, became so great and mighty; who both contested with kings and tyrants; both lost their daughters, were driven out of their country, and returned with honour; who, flying from thence again, were both seized upon by their enemies, and at last ended their lives with the liberty of their countrymen. So that if we were to suppose there had been a trial of skill between nature and fortune, as there is sometimes between artists, it would be hard to judge whether that succeeded best in making them alike in their dispositions and manners, or this in the coincidences of their lives. We will speak of the eldest first.

Demosthenes, the father of Demosthenes, was a citizen of good rank and quality, as Theopompus informs us, surnamed the Sword-maker, because he had a large workhouse, and kept servants skilful in that art at work. But of that which Æschines the orator said of his mother, that she was descended of one Gylon, who fled his country upon an accusation of treason, and of a barbarian woman, I can affirm nothing, whether he spoke true, or slandered and maligned her. This is certain, that Demosthenes, being as yet but seven years old, was left by his father in affluent circumstances, the whole value of his estate being little short of fifteen talents, and that he was wronged by his guardians, part of his fortune being embezzled by them, and the rest neglected; insomuch that even his teachers were defrauded of their salaries. This was the reason that he did not obtain the liberal education that he should have had; besides that, on account of weakness and delicate health, his mother would not let him exert himself, and his teachers forbore to urge him. He was meagre and sickly from the first, and hence had his nickname of Batalus given him, it is said, by the boys, in derision of his appearance; Batalus being, as some tell us, a certain enervated flute-player, in ridicule of whom Antiphanes wrote a play. Others speak of Batalus as a writer of wanton verses and drinking songs. And it would seem that some part of the body, not decent to be named, was at that time called *batalus* by the Athenians. But the name of Argas which also they say was a nickname of Demosthenes, was given him for his behaviour, as being savage and spiteful, *argas* being one of the poetical words for a snake; or for his disagreeable way of speaking, Argas being the name of a poet who composed very harshly and disagreeably. So much, as Plato says, for such matters.

The first occasion of his eager inclination to oratory, they say, was this. Callistratus, the orator, being to plead in open court for Oropus, the expectation of the issue of that cause was very great, as well for the ability of the orator, who was then at the height of his reputation, as also for the fame of the action itself. Therefore, Demosthenes, having heard the tutors and school-masters agreeing among themselves to be present at this trial, with much importunity persuades his tutor to take him along with him to the hearing; who, having some acquaintance with the doorkeepers, procured a place where the boy might sit unseen, and hear what was said. Callistratus having got the day, and being much admired, the boy began to look upon his glory with a kind of emulation, observing how he was courted on all hands, and attended on his way by the multitude; but his wonder was more than all excited by the power of his eloquence, which seemed able to subdue and win over anything. From this time, therefore, bidding farewell to other sorts of learning and study, he now began to exercise himself, and to take pains in declaiming, as one that meant to be himself also an orator. He made use of Isæus as his guide to the art of speaking, though Isocrates at that time was giving lessons; whether, as some say, because he was an orphan, and was not able to pay Isocrates his appointed fee of ten minæ, or because he preferred Isæus's speaking, as being more businesslike and effective in actual use. Hermippus says that he met with certain memoirs without any author's name, in which it was written that Demosthenes was a scholar to Plato, and learnt much of his eloquence from him; and he also mentions Ctesibius, as reporting from Callias of Syracuse and some others, that Demosthenes secretly obtained a knowledge of the systems of Isocrates and Alcidamas, and mastered them thoroughly.

As soon, therefore, as he was grown up to man's estate, he began to go to law with his guardians, and to write orations against them; who, in the meantime, had recourse to various subterfuges and pleas for new trials, and Demosthenes, though he was thus, as Thucydides says, taught his business in dangers, and by his own exertions was successful in his suit, was yet unable for all this to recover so much as a small fraction of his patrimony.

He only attained some degree of confidence in speaking, and some competent experience in it. And having got a taste of the honour and power which are acquired by pleadings, he now ventured to come forth, and to undertake public business. And, as it is said of Laomedon, the Orchomenian, that, by advice of his physician, he used to run long distances to keep off some disease of his spleen, and by that means having, through labour and exercise, framed the habit of his body, he betook himself to the great garland games, and became one of the best runners at the long race; so it happened to Demosthenes, who, first venturing upon oratory for the recovery of his own private property, by this acquired ability in speaking, and at length, in public business, as it were in the great games, came to have the pre-eminence of all competitors in the assembly. But when he first addressed himself to the people, met with great discouragements, and was derided for his strange and uncouth style, which was cumbered with long sentences and tortured with formal arguments to a most harsh and disagreeable excess. Besides, he had, it seems, a weakness in his voice, a perplexed and indistinct utterance and a shortness of breath, which, by breaking and disjointing his sentences, much obscured the sense and meaning of what he spoke. So that in the end being quite disheartened, he forsook the assembly; and as he was walking carelessly and sauntering about the Piræus, Eunomus, the Thriasian, then a very old man, seeing him, upbraided him, saying that his diction was very much like that of Pericles, and that he was wanting to himself through cowardice and meanness of spirit, neither bearing up with courage against popular outcry, nor fitting his body for action, but suffering it to languish through mere sloth and negligence.

Another time, when the assembly had refused to hear him, and he was going home with his head muffled up, taking it very heavily, they relate that Satyrus, the actor, followed him, and being his familiar acquaintance, entered into conversation with him. To whom, when Demosthenes bemoaned himself, that having been the most industrious of all the pleaders, and having almost spent the whole strength and vigour of his body in that employment, he could not yet find any acceptance with the people, that drunken sots, mariners, and illiterate fellows were heard, and had the hustings for their own, while he himself was despised, "You say true, Demosthenes," replied Satyrus, "but I will quickly remedy the cause of all this, if you will repeat to me some passage out of Euripides or Sophocles." Which when Demosthenes had pronounced, Satyrus presently taking it up after him, gave the same passage, in his rendering of it, such a new form, by accompanying it with the proper mien and gesture, that to Demosthenes it seemed quite another thing. By this, being convinced how much grace and ornament language acquires from action, he began to esteem it a small matter, and as good as nothing for a man to exercise himself in declaiming, if he neglected enunciation and delivery. Hereupon he built himself a place to study in under ground (which was still remaining in our time), and hither he would come constantly every day to form his action and to exercise his voice; and here he would continue, oftentimes without intermission, two or three months together, shaving one half of his head, that so for shame he might not go abroad, though he desired it ever so much.

Nor was this all, but he also made his conversation with people abroad his common speech, and his business, subservient to his studies, taking from hence occasions and arguments as matter to work upon. For as soon as he was parted from his company, down he would go at once into his study, and run over everything in order that had passed, and the reasons that might be alleged for and against it. Any speeches, also, that he was present at, he would go over again with himself, and reduce into periods; and whatever others spoke to him, or he to them, he would correct, transform, and vary several ways. Hence it was that he was looked upon as a person of no great natural genius, but one who owed all the power and ability he had in speaking to labour and industry. Of the truth of which it was thought to be no small sign that he was very rarely heard to speak upon the occasion, but though he were by name frequently called upon by the people, as he sat in the assembly, yet he would not rise unless he had previously considered the subject, and came prepared for it. So that many of the popular pleaders used to make it a jest against him; and Pytheas once, scoffing at him, said that his arguments smelt of the lamp. To which Demosthenes gave the sharp answer, "It is true, indeed, Pytheas, that your lamp and mine are not conscious of the same things." To others, however, he would not much deny it, but would admit frankly enough, that he neither entirely wrote his speeches beforehand, nor yet spoke wholly extempore. And he would affirm that it was the more truly popular act to use premeditation, such preparation being a kind of respect to the people; whereas, to slight and take no care how what is said is likely to be received by the audience, shows something of an oligarchical temper, and is the course of one that intends force rather than persuasion. Of his want of courage and assurance to speak offhand, they make it also another argument that, when he was at a loss and discomposed, Demades would often rise up on the sudden to support him, but he was never observed to do the same for Demades.

Whence then, may some say, was it, that Æschines speaks of him as a person so much to be wondered at for his boldness in speaking? Or, how could it be, when Python, the Byzantine, with so much confidence and such a torrent of words inveighed against the Athenians, that Demosthenes alone stood up to oppose him? Or when Lamarchus, the Myrinæan, had written a panegyric upon King Philip and Alexander, in which he uttered many things in reproach of the Thebans and Chalcidians, and at the Olympic Games recited it publicly, how was it that he, rising up, and recounting historically and demonstratively what benefits and advantages all Greece had received from the Thebans and Chalcidians, and, on the contrary, what mischiefs the flatterers of the Macedonians had brought upon it, so turned the minds of all that were present that the sophist, in alarm at the outcry against him, secretly made his way out of the assembly? But Demosthenes, it should seem, regarded other points in the character of Pericles to be unsuited to him; but his reserve and his sustained manner, and his forbearing to speak on the sudden, or upon every occasion, as being the things to which principally he owed his greatness, these he followed, and endeavoured to imitate, neither wholly neglecting the glory which present occasion offered, nor yet willing too often to expose his faculty to the mercy of chance. For, in fact, the orations which were spoken by him had much more of boldness and confidence in them than those that he wrote, if we may believe Eratosthenes, Demetrius the Phalerian, and the Comedians. Eratosthenes says that often in his speaking he would be transported into a kind of ecstasy, and Demetrius, that he uttered the famous metrical adjuration to the people—

"By the earth, the springs, the rivers, and the streams,"

as a man inspired and beside himself. One of the comedians calls him a *rhopoperperethras*, and another scoffs at him for his use of antithesis:—

"And what he took, took back; a phrase to please,
The very fancy of Demosthenes."

Unless, indeed, this also is meant by Antiphanes for a jest upon the speech on Halonesus, which Demosthenes advised the Athenians not to *take* at Philip's hands, but to *take back*.

All, however, used to consider Demades, in the mere use of his natural gifts, an orator impossible to surpass, and that in what he spoke on the sudden, he excelled all the study and preparation of Demosthenes. And Ariston, the Chian, has recorded a judgment which Theophrastus passed upon the orators; for being asked what kind of orator he accounted Demosthenes, he answered, "Worthy of the city of Athens;" and then what he thought of Demades, he answered, "Above it." And the same philosopher reports that Polyeuctus, the Sphettian, one of the Athenian politicians about that time, was wont to say that Demosthenes was the greatest orator, but Phocion the ablest, as he expressed the most sense in the fewest words. And, indeed, it is related that Demosthenes himself, as often as Phocion stood up to plead against him, would say to his acquaintance, "Here comes the knife to my speech." Yet it does not appear whether he had this feeling for his powers of speaking, or for his life and character, and meant to say that one word or nod from a man who was really trusted would go further than a thousand lengthy periods from others.

Demetrius, the Phalerian, tells us that he was informed by Demosthenes himself, now grown old, that the ways he made use of to remedy his natural bodily infirmities and defects were such as these; his inarticulate and stammering pronunciation he overcame and rendered more distinct by speaking with pebbles in his mouth; his voice he disciplined by declaiming and reciting speeches or verses when he was out of breath, while running or going up steep places; and that in his house he had a large looking-glass, before which he would stand and go through his exercises. It is told that some one once came to request his assistance as a pleader, and related how he had been assaulted and beaten. "Certainly," said Demosthenes, "nothing of the kind can have happened to you." Upon which the other, raising his voice, exclaimed loudly, "What, Demosthenes, nothing has been done to me?" "Ah," replied Demosthenes, "now I hear the voice of one that has been injured and beaten." Of so great consequence towards the gaining of belief did he esteem the tone and action of the speaker. The action which he used himself was wonderfully pleasing to the common people, but by well-educated people, as, for example, by Demetrius, the Phalerian, it was looked upon as mean, humiliating, and unmanly. And Hermippus says of Æsion, that, being asked his opinion concerning the ancient orators, and those of his own time, he answered that it was admirable to see with what composure and in what high style they addressed themselves to the people; but that the orations of Demosthenes, when they are read, certainly appear to be superior in point of construction, and more effective. His written speeches, beyond all question, are characterised by austere tone and by their severity. In his extempore retorts and rejoinders, he allowed himself the use of jest and mockery. When Demades said, "Demosthenes teach me! So might the sow teach Minerva!" he replied, "Was it this Minerva, that was lately found playing the harlot in Collytus?" When a thief, who had the nickname of the Brazen, was attempting to upbraid him for sitting up late, and writing by candle-light, "I know very well," said he, "that you had rather have all lights out; and wonder not, O ye men of Athens, at the many robberies which are committed, since we have thieves of brass and walls of clay." But on these points, though we have much more to mention, we will add nothing at present. We will proceed to take an estimate of his character from his actions and his life as a statesmen.

His first entering into public business was much about the time of the Phocian war, as himself affirms, and may be collected from his Philippic orations. For of these, some were made after that action was over, and the earliest of them refer to its concluding events. It is certain that he engaged in the accusation of Midias when he was but two-and-thirty years old, having as yet no interest or reputation as a politician. And this it was, I consider, that induced him to withdraw the action, and accept a sum of money as a compromise. For of himself—

"He was no easy or good-natured man,"

but of a determined disposition, and resolute to see himself righted; however, finding it a hard matter and above his strength to deal with Midias, a man so well secured on all sides with money, eloquence, and friends, he yielded to the entreaties of those who interceded for him. But had he seen any hopes or possibility of prevailing, I cannot believe that three thousand drachmas could have taken off the edge of his revenge. The object which he chose for himself in the commonwealth was noble and just, the defence of the Grecians against Philip; and in this he behaved himself so worthily that he soon grew famous, and excited attention everywhere for his eloquence and courage in speaking. He was admired through all Greece, the King of Persia courted him, and by Philip himself he was more esteemed than all the other orators. His very enemies were forced to confess that they had to do with a man of mark; for such a character even Æschines and Hyperides give him, where they accuse and speak against him.

So that I cannot imagine what ground Theopompus had to say that Demosthenes was of a fickle, unsettled disposition, and could not long continue firm either to the same men or the same affairs; whereas the contrary is most apparent, for the same party and post in politics which he held from the beginning, to these he kept constant to the end; and was so far from leaving them while he lived that he chose rather to forsake his life than his purpose. He was never heard to apologise for shifting sides like Demades, who would say he often spoke against himself, but never against the city; nor as Melanopus, who, being generally against Callistratus, but being often bribed off with money, was wont to tell the people, "The man indeed is my enemy, but we must submit for the good of our country;" nor again as Nicodemus, the Messenian, who having first appeared on Cassander's side, and afterwards taken part with Demetrius, said the two things were not in themselves contrary, it being always most advisable to obey the conqueror. We have nothing of this kind to say against Demosthenes, as one who would turn aside or prevaricate, either in word or deed. There could not have been less variation in his public acts if they had all been played, so to say, from first to last, from the same score. Panætius, the philosopher, said that most of his orations are so written as if they were to prove this one conclusion, that what is honest and virtuous is for itself only to be chosen; as that of the Crown, that against Aristocrates, that for the Immunities, and the Philippics; in all which he persuades his fellow-citizens to pursue not that which seems most pleasant, easy, or profitable; but declares, over and over again, that they ought in the first place to prefer that which is just and honourable before their own safety and preservation. So that if he had kept his hands clean, if his courage for the wars had been answerable to the generosity of his principles, and the dignity of his orations, he might deservedly have his name placed, not in the number of such orators as Mærocles, Polyeuctus, and Hyperides, but in the highest rank with Cimon, Thucydides, and Pericles.

Certainly amongst those who were contemporary with him, Phocion, though he appeared on the less commendable side in the commonwealth, and was counted as one of the Macedonian party, nevertheless, by his courage and his honesty, procured himself a name not inferior to these of Ephialtes, Aristides, and Cimon. But Demosthenes, being neither fit to be relied on for courage in arms, as Demetrius says, nor on all sides inaccessible to bribery (for how invincible soever he was against the gifts of Philip and the Macedonians, yet elsewhere he lay open to assault, and was overpowered by the gold which came down from Susa and Ecbatana), was therefore esteemed better able to recommend than to imitate the virtues of past times. And yet (excepting only Phocion), even in his life and manners, he far surpassed the other orators of his time. None of them addressed the people so boldly; he attacked the faults, and opposed himself to the unreasonable desires of the multitude, as may be seen in his orations. Theopompus writes, that the Athenians having by name selected Demosthenes, and called upon him to accuse a certain person, he refused to do it; upon which the assembly being all in an uproar, he rose up and said, "Your counsellor, whether you will or no, O ye men of Athens, you shall always have me; but a sycophant or false accuser, though you would have me, I shall never be." And his conduct in the case of Antiphon was perfectly aristocratical ; whom, after he had been acquitted in the assembly, he took and brought before the court of Areopagus, and, setting at naught the displeasure of the people, convicted him there of having promised Philip to burn the arsenal; whereupon the man was condemned by that court, and suffered for it. He accused, also, Theoris, the priestess, amongst other misdemeanours, of having instructed and taught the slaves to deceive and cheat their masters, for which the sentence of death was passed upon her, and she was executed.

The oration which Apollodorus made use of, and by it carried the cause against Timotheus, the general, in an action of debt, it is said was written for him by Demosthenes; as also those against Phormion and Stephanus, in which latter case he was thought to have acted dishonourably, for the speech which Phormion used against Apollodorus was also of his making; he, as it were, having simply furnished two adversaries out of the same shop with weapons to wound one another. Of his orations addressed to the public assemblies, that against Androtion, and those against Timocrates and Aristocrates, were written for others, before he had come forward himself as a politician. They were composed, it seems, when he was but seven or eight and twenty years old. That against Aristogiton, and that for the Immunities, he spoke himself, at the request, as he says, of Ctesippus, the son of Chabrias, but, as some say, out of courtship to the young man's mother. Though, in fact, he did not marry her, for his wife was a woman of Samos, as Demetrius, the Magnesian, writes, in his book on Persons of the same Name. It is not certain whether his oration against Æschines, for Misconduct as Ambassador, was ever spoken; although Idomeneus says that Æschines wanted only thirty voices to condemn him. But this seems not to be correct, at least so far as may be conjectured from both their orations concerning the Crown; for in these, neither of them speaks clearly or directly of it, as a cause that ever came to trial. But let others decide this controversy.

It was evident, even in time of peace, what course Demosthenes would steer in the commonwealth; for whatever was done by the Macedonian, he criticised and found fault with, and upon all occasions was stirring up the people of Athens, and inflaming them against him. Therefore, in the court of Philip, no man was so much talked of, or of so great account as he; and when he came thither, one of the ten ambassadors who were sent into Macedonia, though all had audience given them, yet his speech was answered with most care and exactness. But in other respects, Philip entertained him not so honourably as the rest, neither did he show him the same kindness and civility with which he applied himself to the party of Æschines and Philocrates. So that, when the others commended Philip for his able speaking, his beautiful person, nay, and also for his good companionship in drinking, Demosthenes could not refrain from cavilling at these praises; the first, he said, was a quality which might well enough become a rhetorician, the second a woman, and the last was only the property of a sponge; no one of them was the proper commendation of a prince.

But when things came at last at war, Philip on the one side being not able to live in peace, and the Athenians, on the other side, being stirred up by Demosthenes, the first action he put them upon was the reducing of

Eubœa, which, by the treachery of the tyrants, was brought under subjection to Philip. And on his proposition, the decree was voted, and they crossed over thither and chased the Macedonians out of the island. The next was the relief of the Byzantines and Perinthians, whom the Macedonians at that time were attacking. He persuaded the people to lay aside their enmity against these cities, to forget the offences committed by them in the Confederate War, and to send them such succours as eventually saved and secured them. Not long after, he undertook an embassy through the states of Greece, which he solicited and so far incensed against Philip that, a few only excepted, he brought them all into a general league. So that, besides the forces composed of the citizens themselves, there was an army consisting of fifteen thousand foot and two thousand horse, and the money to pay these strangers was levied and brought in with great cheerfulness. On which occasion it was, says Theophrastus, on the allies requesting that their contributions for the war might be ascertained and stated, Crobylus, the orator, made use of the saying, "War can't be fed at so much a day." Now was all Greece up in arms, and in great expectation what would be the event. The Eubœans, the Achæns, the Corinthians, the Megarians, the Leucadians, and Corcyræans, their people and their cities, were all joined together in a league. But the hardest task was yet behind, left for Demosthenes, to draw the Thebans into this confederacy with the rest. Their country bordered next upon Attica, they had great forces for the war, and at that time they were accounted the best soldiers of all Greece, but it was no easy matter to make them break with Philip, who, by many good offices, had so lately obliged them in the Phocian war; especially considering how the subjects of dispute and variance between the two cities were continually renewed and exasperated by petty quarrels, arising out of the proximity of their frontiers.

But after Philip, being now grown high and puffed up with his good success at Amphissa, on a sudden surprised Elatea and possessed himself of Phocis, and the Athenians were in a great consternation, none durst venture to rise up to speak, no one knew what to say, all were at a loss, and the whole assembly in silence and perplexity, in this extremity of affairs Demosthenes was the only man who appeared, his counsel to them being alliance with the Thebans. And having in other ways encouraged the people, and, as his manner was, raised their spirits up with hopes, he, with some others, was sent ambassador to Thebes. To oppose him, as Marsyas says, Philip also sent thither his envoys, Amyntas and Clearchus, two Macedonians, besides Daochus, a Thessalian, and Thrasydæus. Now the Thebans, in their consultations, were well enough aware what suited best with their own interest, but every one had before his eyes the terrors of war, and their losses in the Phocian troubles were still recent: but such was the force and power of the orator, fanning up, as Theopompus says, their courage, and firing their emulation, that, casting away every thought of prudence, fear, or obligation, in a sort of divine possession, they chose the path of honour, to which his words invited them. And this success, thus accomplished by an orator, was thought to be so glorious and of such consequence, that Philip immediately sent heralds to treat and petition for a peace: all Greece was aroused, and up in arms to help. And the commanders-in-chief, not only of Attica, but of Bœotia, applied themselves to Demosthenes, and observed his directions. He managed all the assemblies of the Thebans, no less than those of the Athenians; he was beloved both by the one and by the other, and exercised the same supreme authority with both; and that not by unfair means, or without just cause, as Theopompus professes, but indeed it was no more than was due to his merit.

But there was, it would seem, some divinely ordered fortune, commissioned, in the revolution of things, to put a period at this time to the liberty of Greece, which opposed and thwarted all their actions, and by many signs foretold what should happen. Such were the sad predictions uttered by the Pythian priestess, and this old oracle cited out of the Sibyl's verses:—

> "The battle on Thermodon that shall be
> Safe at a distance I desire to see,
> Far, like an eagle, watching in the air,
> Conquered shall weep, and conqueror perish there."

This Thermodon, they say, is a little rivulet here in our country in Chæronea, running into the Cephisus. But we know of none that is so called at the present time; and can only conjecture that the streamlet which is now called Hæmon, and runs by the Temple of Hercules, where the Grecians were encamped, might perhaps in those days be called Thermodon, and after the fight, being filled with blood and dead bodies, upon this occasion, as we guess, might change its old name for that which it now bears. Yet Duris says that this Thermodon was no river, but that some of the soldiers, as they were pitching their tents and digging trenches about them, found a small stone statue, which, by the inscription, appeared to be the figure of Thermodon, carrying a wounded Amazon in his arms; and that there was another oracle current about it, as follows:—

> "The battle on Thermodon that shall be,
> Fail not, black raven, to attend and see;
> The flesh of men shall there abound for thee."

In fine, it is not easy to determine what is the truth. But of Demosthenes it is said that he had such great confidence in the Grecian forces, and was so excited by the sight of the courage and resolution of so many brave men ready to engage the enemy, that he would by no means endure they should give any heed to oracles, or hearken to prophecies, but gave out that he suspected even the prophetess herself, as if she had been tampered with to speak in favour of Philip. The Thebans he put in mind of Epaminondas, the Athenians of Pericles, who always took their own measures and governed their actions by reason, looking upon things of this kind as mere pretexts for cowardice. Thus far, therefore, Demosthenes acquitted himself like a brave man. But in the fight he did nothing honourable, nor was his performance answerable to his speeches. For he fled, deserting his place disgracefully, and throwing away his arms, not ashamed, as Pytheas observed, to belie the inscription written on his shield, in letters of gold, "With good fortune."

In the meantime Philip, in the first moment of victory, was so transported with joy, that he grew extravagant, and going out after he had drunk largely to visit the dead bodies, he chanted the first words of the decree that had been passed on the motion of Demosthenes—

"The motion of Demosthenes, Demosthenes's son,"

dividing it metrically into feet, and marking the beats.

But when he came to himself, and had well considered the danger he was lately under, he could not forbear from shuddering at the wonderful ability and power of an orator who had made him hazard his life and empire on the issue of a few brief hours. The fame of it also reached even to the court of Persia, and the king sent letters to his lieutenants commanding them to supply Demosthenes with money, and to pay every attention to him, as the only man of all the Grecians who was able to give Philip occupation and find employment for his forces near home, in the troubles of Greece. This afterwards came to the knowledge of Alexander, by certain letters of Demosthenes which he found at Sardis, and by other papers of the Persian officers, stating the large sums which had been given him.

At this time, however, upon the ill-success which now happened to the Grecians, those of the contrary faction in the commonwealth fell foul upon Demosthenes and took the opportunity to frame several informations and indictments against him. But the people not only acquitted him of these accusations, but continued towards him their former respect, and still invited him, as a man that meant well, to take a part in public affairs. Insomuch that when the bones of those who had been slain at Chæronea were brought home to be solemnly interred, Demosthenes was the man they chose to make the funeral oration. They did not show, under the misfortunes which befell them, a base or ignoble mind, as Theopompus writes in his exaggerated style, but on the contrary, by the honour and respect paid to their counsellor, they made it appear that they were noway dissatisfied with the counsels he had given them. The speech, therefore, was spoken by Demosthenes. But the subsequent decrees he would not allow to be passed in his own name, but made use of those of his friends, one after another, looking upon his own as unfortunate and inauspicious; till at length he took courage again after the death of Philip, who did not long outlive his victory at Chæronea. And this, it seems, was that which was foretold in the last verse of the oracle—

> "Conquered shall weep, and conqueror perish there."

Demosthenes had secret intelligence of the death of Philip, and laying hold of this opportunity to prepossess the people with courage and better hopes for the future, he came into the assembly with a cheerful countenance, pretending to have had a dream that presaged some great good fortune for Athens; and, not long after, arrived the messengers who brought the news of Philip's death. No sooner had the people received it, but immediately they offered sacrifice to the gods, and decreed that Pausanias should be presented with a crown. Demosthenes appeared publicly in a rich dress, with a chaplet on his head, though it were but the seventh day since the death of his daughter, as is said by Æschines, who upbraids him upon this account, and rails at him as one void of natural affection towards his children. Whereas, indeed, he rather betrays himself to be of a poor, low spirit, and effeminate mind, if he really means to make wailings and lamentation the only signs of a gentle and affectionate nature, and to condemn those who bear such accidents with more temper and less passion. For my own part, I cannot say that the behaviour of the Athenians on this occasion was wise or honourable, to crown themselves with garlands and to sacrifice to the gods for the death of a prince who, in the midst of his success and victories, when they were a conquered people, had used them with so much clemency and humanity. For besides provoking fortune, it was a base thing, and unworthy in itself, to make him a citizen of Athens, and pay him honours while he lived, and yet as soon as he fell by another's hand, to set no bounds to their jollity, to insult over him dead, and to sing triumphant songs of victory, as if by their own valour they had vanquished him. I must at the same time commend the behaviour of Demosthenes, who, leaving tears and lamentations and domestic sorrows to the women, made it his business to attend to the interests of the commonwealth. And I think it the duty of him who would be accounted to have a soul truly valiant, and fit for government, that, standing always firm to the common good, and letting private griefs and troubles find their compensation in public blessings, he should maintain the dignity of his character and station, much more than actors who represent the persons of kings and tyrants, who, we see, when they either laugh or weep on the stage, follow, not their own private inclinations, but the course consistent with the subject and with their position. And if, moreover, when our neighbour is in misfortune, it is not our duty to forbear offering any consolation, but rather to say whatever may tend to cheer him, and to invite his attention to any agreeable objects, just as we tell people who are troubled with sore eyes to withdraw their sight from bright and offensive colours to green, and those of a softer mixture, from whence can a man seek, in his own case, better arguments of consolation for afflictions in his family, than from the prosperity of his country, by making public and domestic chances count, so to say, together, and the better fortune of the state obscure and conceal the less happy circumstances of the individual. I have been induced to say so much, because I have known many readers melted by Æschines's language into a soft and unmanly tenderness.

But now to turn to my narrative. The cities of Greece were inspirited once more by the efforts of Demosthenes to form a league together. The Thebans, whom he had provided with arms, set upon their garrison, and slew many of them; the Athenians made preparations to join their forces with them; Demosthenes ruled supreme in the popular assembly, and wrote letters to the Persian officers who commanded under the king in Asia, inciting them to make war upon the Macedonian, calling him child and simpleton. But as soon as Alexander had settled matters in his own country, and came in person with his army into Bœotia, down fell the courage of the Athenians, and Demosthenes was hushed; the Thebans, deserted by them, fought by themselves, and lost their city. After which, the people of Athens, all in distress and great perplexity, resolved to send ambassadors to Alexander, and amongst others, made choice of Demosthenes for one; but his heart failing him for fear of the king's anger, he returned back from Cithæron, and left the embassy. In the meantime, Alexander sent to Athens, requiring ten of their orators to be delivered up to him, as Idomeneus and Duris have reported, but as the most and best historians say, he demanded these eight only,—Demosthenes, Polyeuctus, Ephialtes, Lycurgus, Mœrocles, Demon, Callisthenes, and Charidemus. It was upon this occasion that Demosthenes related to them the fable in which the sheep are said to deliver up their dogs to the wolves; himself and those who with him contended for the people's safety being, in his comparison, the dogs that defended the flock, and Alexander "the Macedonian arch-wolf." He further told them, "As we see corn-masters sell their whole stock by a few grains of wheat which they carry about with them in a dish, as a sample of the rest, so you by delivering up us, who are but a few, do at the same time unawares surrender up yourselves all together with us;" so we find it related in the history of Aristobulus, the Cassandrian. The Athenians were deliberating, and at a loss what to do, when Demades, having agreed with the persons whom Alexander had demanded, for five talents, undertook to go ambassador, and to intercede with the king for them; and, whether it was that he relied on his friendship and kindness, or that he hoped to find him satiated, as a lion glutted with slaughter, he certainly went, and prevailed with him both to pardon the men, and to be reconciled to the city.

So he and his friends, when Alexander went away, were great men, and Demosthenes was quite put aside. Yet when Agis, the Spartan, made his insurrection, he also for a short time attempted a movement in his favour; but he soon shrunk back again, as the Athenians would not take any part in it, and, Agis being slain, the Lacedæmonians were vanquished. During this time it was that the indictment against Ctesiphon, concerning the crown, was brought to trial. The action was commenced a little before the battle in Chæronea, when Chærondas was archon, but it was not proceeded with till about ten years after, Aristophon being then archon. Never was any public cause more celebrated than this, alike for the fame of the orators, and for the generous courage of the judges, who, though at that time the accusers of Demosthenes were in the height of power, and supported by all the favour of the Macedonians, yet would not give judgment against him, but acquitted him so honourably, that Æschines did not obtain the fifth part of their suffrages on his side, so that, immediately after he left the city, and spent the rest of his life in teaching rhetoric about the island of Rhodes, and upon the continent in Ionia.

It was not long after that Harpalus fled from Alexander, and came to Athens out of Asia; knowing himself guilty of many misdeeds into which his love of luxury had led him, and fearing the king, who was now grown terrible even to his best friends. Yet this man had no sooner addressed himself to the people, and delivered up his goods, his ships, and himself to their disposal, but the other orators of the town had their eyes quickly fixed upon his money, and came in to his assistance, persuading the Athenians to receive and protect their suppliant. Demosthenes at first gave advice to chase him out of the country, and to beware lest they involved their city in a war upon an unnecessary and unjust occasion. But some few days after, as they were taking an account of the treasure, Harpalus, perceiving how much he was pleased with a cup of Persian manufacture, and how curiously he surveyed the sculpture and fashion of it, desired him to poise it in his hand, and consider the weight of the gold. Demosthenes, being amazed to feel how heavy it was, asked him what weight it *came to.* "To you," said Harpalus, smiling, "it shall *come with* twenty talents." And presently after, when night drew on, he sent him the cup with so many talents. Harpalus, it seems, was a person of singular skill to discern a man's covetousness by the air of his countenance, and the look and movements of his eyes. For Demosthenes could not resist the temptation, but admitting the present, like an armed garrison, into the citadel of his house, he surrendered himself up to the interest of Harpalus. The next day, he came into the assembly with his neck swathed about with wool and rollers, and when they called on him to rise up and speak, he made signs as if he had lost his voice. But the wits, turning the matter to ridicule, said that certainly the orator had been seized that night with no other than a silver quinsy. And soon after, the people, becoming aware of the bribery, grew angry, and would not suffer him to speak, or make any apology for himself, but ran him down with noise; and one man stood up, and cried out, "What, ye men of Athens, will you not hear the cup-bearer?" So at length they banished Harpalus out of the city; and fearing lest they should be called to account for the treasure which the orators had purloined, they made a strict inquiry, going from house to house; only Callicles, the son of Arrhenidas, who was newly married, they would not suffer to be searched, out of respects, as Theopompus writes, to the bride, who was within.

Demosthenes resisted the inquisition, and proposed a decree to refer the business to the court of Areopagus, and to punish those whom that court should find guilty. But being himself one of the first whom the court condemned, when he came to the bar, he was fined fifty talents, and committed to prison; where, out of shame of the crime for which he was condemned, and through the weakness of his body, growing incapable of supporting the confinement, he made his escape, by the carelessness of some and by the contrivance of others of the citizens. We are told, at least, that he had not fled far from the city when, finding that he was pursued by some of those who had been his adversaries, he endeavoured to hide himself. But when they called him by his name, and coming up nearer to him, desired he would accept from them some money which they had brought from home as a provision for his journey, and to that purpose only had followed him, when they entreated him to take courage, and to bear up against his misfortune, he burst out into much greater lamentation, saying, "But how is it possible to support myself under so heavy an affliction, since I leave a city in which I have such enemies, as in any other it is not easy to find friends." He did not show much fortitude in his banishment, spending his time for the most part in Ægina and Trœzen, and, with tears in his eyes, looking towards the country of Attica. And there remain upon record some sayings of his, little resembling those sentiments of generosity and bravery which he used to express when he had the management of the commonwealth. For, as he was departing out of the city, it is reported, he lifted up his hands towards the Acropolis, and said, "O Lady Minerva, how is it that thou takest delight in three such fierce untractable beasts, the owl, the snake, and the people?" The young men that came to visit and converse with him, he deterred from meddling with state affairs, telling them, that if at first two ways had been proposed to him, the one leading to the speaker's stand and the assembly, the other going direct to destruction, and he could have foreseen the many evils which attend those who deal in public business, such as fears, envies, calumnies, and contentions, he would certainly have taken that which led straight on to his death.

But now happened the death of Alexander, while Demosthenes was in this banishment which we have been speaking of. And the Grecians were once again up in arms, encouraged by the brave attempts of Leosthenes, who was then drawing a circumvallation about Antipater, whom he held close besieged in Lamia. Pytheas, therefore, the orator, and Callimedon, called the Crab, fled from Athens, and taking sides with Antipater, went about with his friends and ambassadors to keep the Grecians from revolting and taking part with the Athenians. But, on the other side, Demosthenes, associating himself with the ambassadors that came from Athens, used his utmost endeavours and gave them his best assistance in persuading the cities to fall unanimously upon the Macedonians, and to drive them out of Greece. Phylarchus says that in Arcadia there happened a rencounter between Pytheas and Demosthenes, which came at last to downright railing, while the one pleaded for the Macedonians, and the other for the Grecians. Pytheas said, that as we always suppose there is some disease in the family to which they bring asses' milk, so wherever there comes an embassy from Athens that city must needs be indisposed. And Demosthenes answered him, retorting the comparison: "Asses' milk is brought to restore health and the Athenians come for the safety and recovery of the sick." With this conduct the people of Athens were so well pleased that they decreed the recall of Demosthenes from banishment. The decree was brought in by Demon the Pæanian, cousin to Demosthenes. So they sent him a ship to Ægina, and he landed at the port of Piræus, where he was met and joyfully received by all the citizens, not so much as an archon or a priest staying behind. And Demetrius, the Magnesian, says that he lifted up his hands towards heaven, and blessed this day of his happy return, as far more honourable than that of Alcibiades; since he was recalled by his countrymen, not through any force or constraint put upon them, but by their own good-will and free inclinations. There remained only his pecuniary fine, which, according to law, could not be remitted by the people. But they found out a way to elude the law. It was a custom with them to allow a certain quantity of silver to those who were to furnish and adorn the altar for the sacrifice of Jupiter Soter. This office, for that turn, they bestowed on Demosthenes, and for the performance of it ordered him fifty talents, the very sum in which he was condemned.

Yet it was no long time that he enjoyed his country after his return, the attempts of the Greeks being soon all utterly defeated. For the battle of Cranon happened in Metagitnion, in Boëdromion the garrison entered into Munychia, and in the Pyanepsion following died Demosthenes after this manner.

Upon the report that Antipater and Craterus were coming to Athens, Demosthenes with his party took their opportunity to escape privily out of the city; but sentence of death was, upon the motion of Demades, passed upon them by the people. They dispersed themselves, flying some to one place, some to another; and Antipater sent about his soldiers into all quarters to apprehend them. Archias was their captain, and was thence called the exile-hunter. He was a Thurian born, and is reported to have been an actor of tragedies, and they say that Polus, of Ægina, the best actor of his time, was his scholar; but Hermippus reckons Archias among the disciples of Lacritus, the orator, and Demetrius says he spent some time with Anaximenes. This Archias finding Hyperides the orator, Aritonicus of Marathon, and Himeræus, the brother of Demetrius the Phalerian, in Ægina, took them by force out of the temple of Æcus, whither they were fled for safety, and sent them to Antipater, then at Cleonæ, where they were all put to death; and Hyperides, they say, had his tongue cut out.

Demosthenes, he heard, had taken sanctuary at the temple of Neptune in Calauria and, crossing over thither in some light vessels, as soon as he had landed himself, and the Thracian spearmen that came with him, he endeavoured to persuade Demosthenes to accompany him to Antipater, as if he should meet with no hard usage from him. But Demosthenes, in his sleep the night before, had a strange dream. It seemed to him that he was acting a tragedy, and contended with Archias for the victory; and though he acquitted himself well, and gave good satisfaction to the spectators, yet for want of better furniture and provision for the stage, he lost the day. And so, while Archias was discoursing to him with many expressions of kindness, he sate still in the same posture, and looking up steadfastly upon him, "O Archias," said he, "I am as little affected by your promises now as I used formerly to be by your acting." Archias at this beginning to grow angry and to threaten him, "Now," said Demosthenes, "you speak like the genuine Macedonian oracle; before you were but acting a part. Therefore forbear only a little, while I write a word or two home to my family." Having thus spoken, he withdrew into the temple and taking a scroll as if he meant to write, he put the reed into his mouth, and biting it as he was wont to do when he was thoughtful or writing, he held it there some time. Then he bowed down his head and covered it. The soldiers that stood at the door, supposing all this to proceed from want of courage and fear of death, in derision called him effeminate, and faint-hearted, and coward. And Archias drawing near, desired him to rise up, and repeating the same kind of thing he had spoken before, he once more promised to make his peace with Antipater. But Demosthenes, perceiving that now the poison had pierced, and seized his vitals, uncovered his head, and fixing his eyes upon Archias, "Now," said he, "as soon as you please, you may commence the part of Creon in the tragedy, and cast out this body of mine unburied. But, O gracious Neptune, I, for my part while I am yet alive will rise up and depart out of this sacred place; though Antipater and the Macedonians have not left so much as thy temple unpolluted." After he had thus spoken and desired to be held up, because already he began to tremble and stagger, as he was going forward, and passing by the altar, he fell down, and with a groan gave up the ghost.

Ariston says that he took the poison out of a reed, as we have shown before. But Pappus, a certain historian whose history was recovered by Hermippus, says, that as he fell near the altar, there was found in his scroll this beginning only of a letter, and nothing more, "Demosthenes to Antipater." And that when his sudden death was much wondered at, the Thracians who guarded the doors reported that he took the poison into his hand out of a rag, and put it in his mouth, and that they imagined it had been gold which he swallowed, but the maid that served him, being examined by the followers of Archias, affirmed that he had worn it in a bracelet for a long time, as an amulet. And Eratosthenes also says that he kept the poison in a hollow ring, and that that ring was the bracelet which he wore about his arm. There are various other statements made by the many authors who have related the story, but there is no need to enter into their discrepancies; yet I must not omit what is said by Demochares the relation of Demosthenes, who is of opinion it was not by the help of poison that he met with so sudden and so easy a death, but that by the singular favour and providence of the gods he was thus rescued from the cruelty of the Macedonians. He died on the sixteenth of Pyanepsion, the most sad and solemn day of the Thesmophoria, which the women observe by fasting in the temple of the goddess.

Soon after his death, the people of Athens bestowed on him such honours as he had deserved. They erected his statue of brass; they decreed that the eldest of his family should be maintained in the Prytaneum; and on the base of his statue was engraven the famous inscription—

"Had you for Greece been strong, as wise you were,
The Macedonian had not conquered her."

For it is simply ridiculous to say, as some have related, that Demosthenes made these verses himself in Calauria, as he was about to take the poison.

A little before he went to Athens, the following incident was said to have happened. A soldier, being summoned to appear before his superior officer, and answer to an accusation brought against him, put that little gold which he had into the hands of Demosthenes's statue. The fingers of this statue were folded one within another, and near it grew a small plane-tree, from which many leaves, either accidently blown thither by the wind, or placed so on purpose by the man himself, falling together and lying round about the gold, concealed it for a long time. In the end, the soldier returned and found his treasure entire, and the fame of this incident was spread abroad. And many ingenious persons of the city competed with each other, on this occasion, to vindicate the integrity of Demosthenes in several epigrams which they made on the subject.

As for Demades, he did not long enjoy the new honours he now came in for, divine vengeance for the death of Demosthenes pursuing him into Macedonia, where he was justly put to death by those whom he had basely flattered. They were weary of him before, but at this time the guilt he lay under was manifest and undeniable. For some of his letters were intercepted, in which he had encouraged Perdiccas to fall upon Macedonia, and to save the Grecians, who, he said, hung only by an old rotten thread, meaning Antipater. Of this he was accused by Dinarchus, the Corinthian, and Cassander was so enraged, that he first slew his son in his bosom, and then gave orders to execute him; who might now at last, by his own extreme misfortunes, learn the lesson that traitors who made sale of their country sell themselves first; a truth which Demosthenes had often foretold him and he would never believe. Thus, Sosius, you have the life of Demosthenes from such accounts as we have either read or heard concerning him.

CICERO

It is generally said, that Helvia, the mother of Cicero, was both wellborn and lived a fair life; but of his father nothing is reported but in extremes. For whilst some would have him the son of a fuller, and educated in that trade, others carry back the origin of his family to Tullus Attius, an illustrious king of the Volscians, who waged war not without honour against the Romans. However, he who first of that house was surnamed Cicero seems to have been a person worthy to be remembered; since those who succeeded him not only did not reject, but were fond of that name, though vulgarly made a matter of reproach. For the Latins call a vetch *Cicer*, and a nick or dent at the tip of his nose, which resembled the opening in a vetch, gave him the surname of *Cicero.*

Cicero, whose story I am writing, is said to have replied with spirit to some of his friends, who recommended him to lay aside or change the name when he first stood for office and engaged in politics, that he would make it his endeavour to render the name of Cicero more glorious than that of the Scauri and Catuli. And when he was quæstor in Sicily, and was making an offering of silver plate to the gods, and had inscribed his two names, Marcus and Tullius, instead of the third, he jestingly told the artificer to engrave the figure of a vetch by them. Thus much is told us about his name.

Of his birth it is reported that his mother was delivered, without pain or labour, on the third of the new Calends, the same day on which now the magistrates of Rome pray and sacrifice for the emperor. It is said, also, that a vision appeared to his nurse, and foretold the child she then suckled should afterwards become a great benefit to the Roman states. To such presages, which might in general be thought mere fancies and idle talk, he himself ere long gave the credit of true prophecies. For as soon as he was of an age to begin to have lessons, he became so distinguished for his talent, and got such a name and reputation among the boys, that their fathers would often visit the school that they might see young Cicero, and might be able to say that they themselves had witnessed the quickness and readiness in learning for which he was renowned. And the more rude among them used to be angry with their children, to see them, as they walked together, receiving Cicero with respect into the middle place. And being, as Plato would have the scholar-like and philosophical temper, eager for every kind of learning, and indisposed to no description of knowledge or instruction, he showed, however, a more peculiar propensity to poetry; and there is a poem now extant made by him when a boy, in tetrameter verse, called Pontius Glaucus. And afterwards, when he applied himself more curiously to these accomplishments, he had the name of being not only the best orator, but also the best poet of Rome. And the glory of his rhetoric still remains, notwithstanding the many new modes in speaking since his time; but his verses are forgotten and out of all repute, so many ingenious poets have followed him.

Leaving his juvenile studies, he became an auditor of Philo the Academic, whom the Romans, above all the other scholars of Clitomachus, admired for his eloquence and loved for his character. He also sought the company of the Mucii, who were eminent statesmen and leaders in the senate, and acquired from them a knowledge of the laws. For some short time he served in arms under Sylla, in the Marsian war. But perceiving the commonwealth running into factions, and from faction all things tending to an absolute monarchy, he betook himself to a retired and contemplative life, and conversing with the learned Greeks, devoted himself to study, till Sylla had obtained the government, and the commonwealth was in some kind of settlement.

At this time, Chrysogonus, Sylla's emancipated slave, having laid an information about an estate belonging to one who was said to have been put to death by proscription, had bought it himself for two thousand drachmas. And when Roscius, the son and heir of the dead, complained, and demonstrated the estate to be worth two hundred and fifty talents, Sylla took it angrily to have his actions questioned, and preferred a process against Roscius for the murder of his father, Chrysogonus managing the evidence. None of the advocates durst assist him, but, fearing the cruelty of Sylla, avoided the cause. The young man, being thus deserted, came for refuge to Cicero. Cicero's friends encouraged him, saying he was not likely ever to have a fairer and more honourable introduction to public life; he therefore undertook the defence, carried the cause, and got much renown for it.

But fearing Sylla, he travelled into Greece, and gave it out that he did so for the benefit of his health. And indeed he was lean and meagre, and had such a weakness in his stomach that he could take nothing but a spare and thin diet, and that not till late in the evening. His voice was loud and good, but so harsh and unmanaged that in vehemence and heat of speaking he always raised it to so high a tone that there seemed to be reason to fear about his health.

When he came to Athens he was a hearer of Antiochus of Ascalon, with whose fluency and elegance of diction he was much taken, although he did not approve of his innovations in doctrine. For Antiochus had now fallen off from the New Academy, as they call it, and forsaken the sect of Carneades, whether that he was moved by the argument of manifestness and the senses, or, as some say, had been led by feelings of rivalry and opposition to the followers of Clitomachus and Philo to change his opinions, and in most things to embrace the doctrine of the Stoics. But Cicero rather affected and adhered to the doctrines of the New Academy; and purposed with himself, if he should be disappointed of any employment in the commonwealth, to retire hither from pleading and political affairs, and to pass his life with quiet in the study of philosophy.

But after he had received the news of Sylla's death, and his body, strengthened again by exercise, was come to a vigorous habit, his voice managed and rendered sweet and full to the ear and pretty well brought into keeping with his general constitution, his friends at Rome earnestly soliciting him by letters, and Antiochus also urging him to return to public affairs, he again prepared for use his orator's instrument of rhetoric, and summoned into action his political faculties, diligently exercising himself in declamations and attending the most celebrated rhetoricians of the time. He sailed from Athens for Asia and Rhodes. Amongst the Asian masters, he conversed with Xenocles of Adramyttium, Dionysius of Magnesia, and Menippus of Caria; at Rhodes, he studied oratory with Apollonius, the son of Molon, and philosophy with Posidonius. Apollonius, we are told, not understanding Latin, requested Cicero to declaim in Greek. He complied willingly, thinking that his faults would thus be better pointed out to him. And after he finished, all his other hearers were astonished, and contended who should praise him most, but Apollonius, who had shown no signs of excitement whilst he was hearing him, so also now, when it was over, sate musing for some considerable time, without any remark. And when Cicero was discomposed at this, he said, "You have my praise and admiration, Cicero, and Greece my pity and commiseration, since those arts and that eloquence which are the only glories that remain to her, will now be transferred by you to Rome."

And now when Cicero, full of expectation, was again bent upon political affairs, a certain oracle blunted the edge of his inclination; for consulting the god of Delphi how he should attain most glory, the Pythoness answered, by making his own genius and not the opinion of the people the guide of his life; and therefore at first he passed his time in Rome cautiously, and was very backward in pretending to public offices, so that he was at that time in little esteem, and had got the names, so readily given by low and ignorant people in Rome, of Greek and Scholar. But when his own desire of fame and the eagerness of his father and relations had made him take in earnest to pleading, he made no slow or gentle advance to the first place, but shone out in full lustre at once, and far surpassed all the advocates of the bar. At first, it is said, he, as well as Demosthenes, was defective in his delivery, and on that account paid much attention to the instructions, sometimes of Roscius the comedian, and sometimes of Æsop the tragedian. They tell of this Æsop, that whilst he was representing on the theatre Atreus deliberating the revenge of Thyestes, he was so transported beyond himself in the heat of action, that he struck with his sceptre one of the servants, who was running across the stage, so violently that he laid him dead upon the place. And such afterwards was Cicero's delivery that it did not a little contribute to render his eloquence persuasive. He used to ridicule loud speakers, saying that they shouted because they could not speak, like lame men who get on horseback because they cannot walk. And his readiness and address in sarcasm, and generally in witty sayings, was thought to suit a pleader very well, and to be highly attractive, but his using it to excess offended many, and gave him the repute of ill-nature.

He was appointed quæstor in a great scarcity of corn and had Sicily for his province, where though at first he displeased many, by compelling them to send in their provisions to Rome, yet after they had had experience of his care, justice, and clemency, they honoured him more than ever they did any of their governors before. It happened, also, that some young Romans of good and noble families charged with neglect of discipline and misconduct in military service, were brought before the prætor in Sicily. Cicero undertook their defence, which he conducted admirably, and got them acquitted. So returning to Rome with a great opinion of himself for these things, a ludicrous incident befell him, as he tells us himself. Meeting an eminent citizen in Campania, whom he accounted his friend, he asked him what the Romans said and thought of his actions, as if the whole city had been filled with the glory of what he had done. His friend asked him in reply, "Where is it you have been, Cicero?" This for the time utterly mortified and cast him down to perceive that the report of his actions had sunk into the city of Rome as into an immense ocean, without any visible effect or result in reputation. And afterwards considering with himself that the glory he contended for was an infinite thing, and that there was no fixed end nor measure in its pursuit, he abated much of his ambitious thoughts. Nevertheless, he was always excessively pleased with his own praise, and continued to the very last to be passionately fond of glory; which often interfered with the prosecution of his wisest resolutions.

On beginning to apply himself more resolutely to public business, he remarked it as an unreasonable and absurd thing that artificers, using vessels and instruments inanimate, should know the name, place, and use of every one of them, and yet the statesman, whose instruments for carrying out public measures are men, should be negligent and careless in the knowledge of persons. And so he not only acquainted himself with the names, but also knew the particular place where every one of the more eminent citizens dwelt, what lands he possessed, the friends he made use of, and those that were of his neighbourhood, and when he travelled on any road in Italy, he could readily name and show the estates and seats of his friends and acquaintance. Having so small an estate, though a sufficient competency for his own expenses, it was much wondered at that he took neither fees nor gifts from his clients, and more especially that he did not do so when he undertook the prosecution of Verres. This Verres, who had been prætor of Sicily, and stood charged by the Sicilians of many evil practices during his government there, Cicero succeeded in getting condemned, not by speaking, but in a manner by holding his tongue. For the prætors, favouring Verres, had deferred the trial by several adjournments to the last day, in which it was evident there could not be sufficient time for the advocates to be heard, and the cause brought to an issue. Cicero, therefore, came forward, and said there was no need of speeches; and after producing and examining witnesses, he required the judges to proceed to sentence. However, many witty sayings are on record, as having been used by Cicero on the occasion. When a man named Cæcilius, one of the freed slaves, who was said to be given to Jewish practices, would have put by the Sicilians, and undertaken the prosecution of Verres himself, Cicero asked, "What has a Jew to do with swine?" *verres* being the Roman word for a boar. And when Verres began to reproach Cicero with effeminate living, "You ought," replied he, "to use this language at home, to your sons;" Verres having a son who had fallen into disgraceful courses. Hortensius the orator, not daring directly to undertake the defence of Verres, was yet persuaded to appear for him at the laying on of the fine, and received an ivory sphinx for his reward; and when Cicero in some passage of the speech, obliquely reflected on him, and Hortensius told him he was not skilful in solving riddles, "No," said Cicero, "and yet you have the sphinx in your house!"

Verres was thus convicted; though Cicero, who set the fine at seventy-five myriads, lay under the suspicion of being corrupted by bribery to lessen the sum. But the Sicilians, in testimony of their gratitude, came and brought him all sorts of presents from the island, when he was ædile; of which he made no private profit himself, but used their generosity only to reduce the public price of provisions.

He had a very pleasant seat at Arpi, he had also a farm near Naples, and another about Pompeii, but neither of any great value. The portion of his wife, Terentia, amounted to ten myriads, and he had a bequest valued at nine myriads of denarii; upon these he lived in a liberal but temperate style with the learned Greeks and Romans that were his familiars. He rarely, if at any time, sat down to meat till sunset, and that not so much on account of business, as for his health and the weakness of his stomach. He was otherwise in the care of his body nice and delicate, appointing himself, for example, a set number of walks and rubbings. And after this manner managing the habit of his body, he brought it in time to be healthful, and capable of supporting many great fatigues and trials. His father's house he made over to his brother, living himself near the Palatine hill, that he might not give the trouble of long journeys to those that made suit to him. And, indeed, there were not fewer daily appearing at his door, to do their court to him, than there were that came to Crassus for his riches, or to Pompey for his power amongst the soldiers, these being at that time the two men of the greatest repute and influence in Rome. Nay, even Pompey himself used to pay court to Cicero, and Cicero's public actions did much to establish Pompey's authority and reputation in the state.

Numerous distinguished competitors stood with him for the prætor's office; but he was chosen before them all, and managed the decision of causes with justice and integrity. It is related that Licinius Macer, a man himself of great power in the city, and supported also by the assistance of Crassus, was accused before him of extortion, and that, in confidence on his own interest and the diligence of his friends, whilst the judges were debating about the sentence, he went to his house, where hastily trimming his hair and putting on a clean gown as already acquitted, he was setting off again to go to the Forum; but at his hall door meeting Crassus, who told him that he was condemned by all the votes, he went in again, threw himself upon his bed, and died immediately. This verdict was considered very creditable to Cicero, as showing his careful management of the courts of justice. On another occasion, Vatinius, a man of rude manners and often insolent in court to the magistrates, who had large swellings on his neck, came before his tribunal and made some request, and on Cicero's desiring further time to consider it, told him that he himself would have made no question about it had he been prætor. Cicero, turning quickly upon him, answered, "But I, you see, have not the neck that you have."

When there were but two or three days remaining in his office, Manilius was brought before him, and charged with peculation. Manilius had the good opinion and favour of the common people, and was thought to be prosecuted only for Pompey's sake, whose particular friend he was. And therefore, when he asked a space of time before his trial, and Cicero allowed him but one day, and that the next only, the common people grew highly offended, because it had been the custom of the prætors to allow ten days at least to the accused; and the tribunes of the people, having called him before the people and accused him, he, desiring to be heard, said, that as he had always treated the accused with equity and humanity, as far as the law allowed, so he thought it hard to deny the same to Manilius, and that he had studiously appointed that day of which alone, as prætor, he was master, and that it was not the part of those that were desirous to help him to cast the judgment of his cause upon another prætor. These things being said made a wonderful change in the people, and commending him much for it they desired that he himself would undertake the defence of Manilius; which he willingly consented to, and that principally for the sake of Pompey, who was absent. And, accordingly, taking his place before the people again, he delivered a bold invective upon the oligarchical party and on those who were jealous of Pompey.

Yet he was preferd to the consulship no less by the nobles than the common people, for the good of the city; and both parties jointly assisted his promotion, upon the following reasons. The change of government made by Sylla, which at first seemed a senseless one, by time and usage had now come to be considered by the people no unsatisfactory settlement. But there were some that endeavoured to alter and subvert the whole present state of affairs, not from any good motives, but for their own private gain; and Pompey being at this time employed in the wars with the kings of Pontus and Armenia, there was no sufficient force at Rome to suppress any attempts at a revolution. These people had for their head a man of bold, daring, and restless character, Lucius Catiline, who was accused, besides other great offences, of deflowering his virgin daughter, and killing his own brother; for which latter crime, fearing to be prosecuted at law, he persuaded Sylla to set him down, as though he were yet alive, amongst those that were to be put to death by proscription. This man the profligate citizens choosing for their captain, gave faith to one another, amongst other pledges, by sacrificing a man, and eating of his flesh; and a great part of the young men of the city were corrupted by him, he providing for every one pleasures, drink, and women, and profusely supplying the expense of these debauches. Etruria, moreover, had all been excited to revolt, as well as a great part of Gaul within the Alps. But Rome itself was in the most dangerous inclination to change on account of the unequal distribution of wealth and property, those of highest rank and greatest spirit having impoverished themselves by shows, entertainments, ambition of offices, and sumptuous buildings, and the riches of the city having thus fallen into the hands of mean and low-born persons. So that there wanted but a slight impetus to set all in motion, it being in the power of every daring man to overturn a sickly commonwealth.

Catiline, however, being desirous of procuring a strong position to carry out his designs, stood for the consulship, and had great hopes of success, thinking he should be appointed with Caius Antonius as his colleague, who was a man fit to lead neither in a good cause nor in a bad one, but might be a valuable accession to another's power. These things the greatest part of the good and honest citizens apprehending, put Cicero upon standing for the consulship; whom the people readily receiving, Catiline was put by, so that he and Caius Antonius were chosen, although amongst the competitors he was the only man descended from a father of the equestrian and not of the senatorial order.

Though the designs of Catiline were not yet publicly known, yet considerable preliminary troubles immediately followed upon Cicero's entrance upon the consulship. For, on the one side, those who were disqualified by the laws of Sylla from holding any public offices, being neither inconsiderable in power nor in number, came forward as candidates and caressed the people for them; speaking many things truly and justly against the tyranny of Sylla, only that they disturbed the government at an improper and unseasonable time; on the other hand, the tribunes of the people proposed laws to the same purpose, constituting a commission of ten persons, with unlimited powers, in whom as supreme governors should be vested the right of selling the public lands of all Italy and Syria and Pompey's new conquest, of judging and banishing whom they pleased, of planting colonies, of taking moneys out of the treasury, and of levying and paying what soldiers should be thought needful. And several of the nobility favoured this law, but especially Caius Antonius, Cicero's colleague, in hopes of being one of the ten. But what gave the greatest fear to the nobles was, that he was thought privy to the conspiracy of Catiline, and not to dislike it because of his great debts.

Cicero, endeavouring in the first place to provide a remedy against this danger, procured a decree assigning to him the province of Macedonia, he himself declining that of Gaul, which was offered to him. And this piece of favour so completely won over Antonius, that he was ready to second and respond to, like a hired player, whatever Cicero said for the good of the country. And now, having made his colleague thus tame and tractable, he could with greater courage attack the conspirators. And, therefore, in the senate, making an oration against the law of the ten commissioners, he so confounded those who proposed it, that they had nothing to reply. And when they again endeavoured, and, having prepared things beforehand, had called the consuls before the assembly of the people, Cicero, fearing nothing, went first out, and commanded the senate to follow him, and not only succeeded in throwing out the law, but so entirely overpowered the tribunes by his oratory, that they abandoned all thought of their other projects.

For Cicero, it may be said, was the one man, above all others who made the Romans feel how great a charm eloquence lends to what is good, and how invincible justice is, if it be well spoken; and that it is necessary for him who would dexterously govern a commonwealth, in action, always to prefer that which is honest before that which is popular, and in speaking, to free the right and useful measure from everything that may occasion offence. An incident occurred in the theatre, during his consulship, which showed what his speaking could do. For whereas formerly the knights of Rome were mingled in the theatre with the common people, and took their places among them as it happened, Marcus Otho, when he was prætor, was the first who distinguished them from the other citizens and appointed them a proper seat, which they still enjoy as their special place in the theatre. This the common people took as an indignity done to them, and, therefore, when Otho appeared in the theatre they hissed him; the knights, on the contrary, received him with loud clapping. The people repeated and increased their hissing; the knights continued their clapping. Upon this, turning upon one another, they broke out into insulting words, so that the theatre was in great disorder. Cicero being informed of it, came himself to the theatre, and summoning the people into the temple of Bellona, he so effectually chid and chastised them for it, that again returning into the theatre they received Otho with loud applause, contending with the knights who should give him the greatest demonstrations of honour and respect.

The conspirators with Catiline, at first cowed and disheartened, began presently to take courage again. And assembling themselves together, they exhorted one another boldly to undertake the design before Pompey's return, who, as it was said, was now on his march with his forces for Rome. But the old soldiers of Sylla were Catiline's chief stimulus to action. They had been disbanded all about Italy, but the greatest number and the fiercest of them lay scattered among the cities of Etruria entertaining themselves with dreams of new plunder and rapine amongst the hoarded riches of Italy. These, having for their leader Manlius, who had served with distinction in the wars under Sylla, joined themselves to Catiline and came to Rome to assist him with their suffrages at the election. For he again pretended to the consulship, having resolved to kill Cicero in a tumult at the elections. Also, the divine powers seemed to give intimation of the coming troubles, by earthquakes, thunderbolts, and strange appearances. Nor was human evidence wanting certain enough in itself, though not sufficient for the conviction of the noble and powerful Catiline. Therefore Cicero, deferring the day of election, summoned Catiline into the senate, and questioned him as to the charges made against him. Catiline, believing there were many in the senate desirous of change, and to give a specimen of himself to the conspirators present, returned an audacious answer, "What harm," said he, "when I see two bodies, the one lean and consumptive with a head, the other great and strong without one, if I put a head to that body which wants one?" This covert representation of the senate and the people excited yet greater apprehensions in Cicero. He put on armour, and was attended from his house by the noble citizens in a body; and a number of the young men went with him into the Plain. Here, designedly letting his tunic slip partly off from his shoulders, he showed his armour underneath, and discovered his danger to the spectators; who, being much moved at it, gathered round about him for his defence. At length, Catiline was by a general suffrage again put by, and Silanus and Murena chosen consuls.

Not long after this, Catiline's soldiers got together in a body in Etruria, and began to form themselves into companies, the day appointed for the design being near at hand. About midnight, some of the principal and most powerful citizens of Rome, Marcus Crassus, Marcus Marcellus, and Scipio Metellus went to Cicero's house, where, knocking at the gate, and calling up the porter, they commanded him to awake Cicero, and tell him they were there. The business was this: Crassus's porter after supper had delivered to him letters brought by an unknown person. Some of them were directed to others, but one to Crassus, without a name; this only Crassus read, which informed him that there was a great slaughter intended by Catiline, and advised him to leave the city. The others he did not open, but went with them immediately to Cicero, being affrighted at the danger, and to free himself of the suspicion he lay under for his familiarity with Catiline. Cicero, considering the matter, summoned the senate at break of day. The letters he brought with him, and delivered them to those to whom they were directed, commanding them to read them publicly; they all alike contained an account of the conspiracy. And when Quintus Arrius a man of prætorian dignity, recounted to them how soldiers were collecting in companies in Etruria, and Manlius stated to be in motion with a large force, hovering about those cities, in expectation of intelligence from Rome, the senate made a decree to place all in the hands of the consuls, who should undertake the conduct of everything, and do their best to save the state. This was not a common thing, but only done by the senate in case of imminent danger.

After Cicero had received this power, he committed all affairs outside to Quintus Metellus, but the management of the city he kept in his own hands. Such a numerous attendance guarded him every day when he went abroad, that the greatest part of the market-place was filled with his train when he entered it. Catiline, impatient of further delay, resolved himself to break forth and go to Manlius, but he commanded Marcius and Cethegus to take their swords, and go early in the morning to Cicero's gates, as if only intending to salute him, and then to fall upon him and slay him. This a noble lady, Fulvia, coming by night, discovered to Cicero, bidding him beware of Cethegus and Marcius. They came by break of day and being denied entrance, made an outcry and disturbance at the gates, which excited all the more suspicion. But Cicero, going forth, summoned the senate into the temple of Jupiter Stator, which stands at the end of the Sacred Street, going up to the Palatine. And when Catiline with others of his party also came, as intending to make his defence, none of the senators would sit by him, but all of them left the bench where he had placed himself. And when he began to speak, they interrupted him with outcries. At length Cicero, standing up, commanded him to leave the city, for since one governed the commonwealth with words, the other with arms, it was necessary there should be a wall betwixt them. Catiline, therefore, immediately left the town, with three hundred armed men; and assuming, as if he had been a magistrate, the rods, axes, and military ensigns, he went to Manlius, and having got together a body of near twenty thousand men, with these he marched to the several cities, endeavouring to persuade or force them to revolt. So it being now come to open war, Antonius was sent forth to fight him.

The remainder of those in the city whom he had corrupted, Cornelius Lentulus kept together and encouraged. He had the surname Sura, and was a man of a noble family, but a dissolute liver, who for his debauchery was formerly turned out of the senate, and was now holding the office of prætor for the second time, as the custom is with those who desire to regain the dignity of senator. It is said that he got the surname Sura upon this occasion; being quæstor in the time of Sylla, he had lavished away and consumed a great quantity of the public moneys, at which Sylla being provoked, called him to give an account in the senate; he appeared with great coolness and contempt, and said he had no account to give, but they might take this, holding up the calf of his leg, as boys do at ball, when they have missed. Upon which he was surnamed *Sura*, *sura* being the Roman word for the calf of the leg. Being at another time prosecuted at law, and having bribed some of the judges, he escaped only by two votes and complained of the needless expense he had gone to in paying for a second, as one would have sufficed to acquit him. This man, such in his own nature, and now inflamed by Catiline, false prophets and fortune-tellers had also corrupted with vain hopes, quoting to him fictitious verses and oracles, and proving from the Sibylline prophecies that there were three of the name Cornelius designed by fate to be monarchs of Rome; two of whom, Cinna and Sylla, had already fulfilled the decree, and that divine fortune was now advancing with the gift of monarchy for the remaining third Cornelius; and that therefore he ought by all means to accept it, and not lose opportunity by delay, as Catiline had done.

Lentulus, therefore, designed no mean or trivial matter, for he had resolved to kill the whole senate, and as many other citizens as he could, to fire the city, and spare nobody, except only Pompey's children, intending to seize and keep them as pledges of his reconciliation with Pompey. For there was then a common and strong report that Pompey was on his way homeward from his great expedition. The night appointed for the design was one of the Saturnalia; swords, flax, and sulphur they carried and hid in the house of Cethegus; and providing one hundred men, and dividing the city into as many parts, they had allotted to every one singly his proper place, so that in a moment, many kindling the fire, the city might be in a flame all together. Others were appointed to stop up the aqueducts, and to kill those who should endeavour to carry water to put it out. Whilst these plans were preparing, it happened there were two ambassadors from the Allobroges staying in Rome; a nation at that time in a distressed condition, and very uneasy under the Roman government. These Lentulus and his party judging useful instruments to move and seduce Gaul to revolt, admitted into the conspiracy and they gave them letters to their own magistrates, and letters to Catiline; in those they promised liberty, in these they exhorted Catiline to set all slaves free, and to bring them along with him to Rome. They sent also to accompany them to Catiline, one Titus, a native of Croton, who was to carry those letters to him.

These counsels of inconsidering men, who conversed together over wine and with women, Cicero watched with sober industry and forethought, and with most admirable sagacity, having several emissaries abroad, who observed and traced with him all that was done, and keeping also a secret correspondence with many who pretended to join in the conspiracy. He thus knew all the discourse which passed betwixt them and the strangers; and lying in wait for them by night, he took the Crotonian with his letters, the ambassadors of the Allobroges acting secretly in concert with him.

By break of day, he summoned the senate into the temple of Concord, where he read the letters and examined the informers. Junius Silanus further stated that several persons had heard Cethegus say that three consuls and four prætors were to be slain. Piso, also, a person of consular dignity, testified other matters of the like nature; and Caius Sulpicius, one of the praetors, being sent to Cethegus's house, found there a quantity of darts and of armour, and a still greater number of swords and daggers, all recently whetted. At length, the senate decreeing indemnity to the Crotonian upon his confession of the whole matter, Lentulus was convicted, abjured his office (for he was then praetor), and put off his robe edged with purple in the senate, changing it for another garment more agreeable to his present circumstances. He thereupon, with the rest of his confederates present, was committed to the charge of the prætors in free custody.

It being evening, and the common people in crowds expecting without, Cicero went forth to them, and told them what was done, and then, attended by them, went to the house of a friend and near neighbour; for his own was taken up by the women who were celebrating with secret rites the feast of the goddess whom the Romans call the Good, and the Greeks the Women's goddess. For a sacrifice is annually performed to her in the consul's house, either by his wife or mother, in the presence of the vestal virgins. And having got into his friend's house privately, a few only being present, he began to deliberate how he should treat these men. The severest, and the only punishment fit for such heinous crimes, he was somewhat shy and fearful of inflicting, as well from the clemency of his nature, as also lest he should be thought to exercise his authority too insolently, and to treat too harshly men of the noblest birth and most powerful friendships in the city; and yet, if he should use them more mildly, he had a dreadful prospect of danger from them. For there was no likelihood, if they suffered less than death, they would be reconciled, but rather, adding new rage to their former wickedness, they would rush into every kind of audacity, while he himself, whose character for courage already did not stand very high with the multitude, would be thought guilty of the greatest cowardice and want of manliness.

Whilst Cicero was doubting what course to take, a portent happened to the women in their sacrificing. For on the altar, where the fire seemed wholly extinguished, a great and bright flame issued forth from the ashes of the burnt wood; at which others were affrighted, but the holy virgins called to Terentia, Cicero's wife, and bade her haste to her husband, and command him to execute what he had resolved for the good of his country, for the goddess had sent a great light to the increase of his safety and glory. Terentia, therefore, as she was otherwise in her own nature neither tender-hearted nor timorous, but a woman eager for distinction (who, as Cicero himself says, would rather thrust herself into his public affairs, than communicate her domestic matters to him), told him these things, and excited him against the conspirators. So also did Quintus his brother, and Publius Nigidius, one of his philosophical friends, whom he often made use of in his greatest and most weighty affairs of state.

The next day, a debate arising in the senate about the punishment of the men, Silanus, being the first who was asked his opinion, said it was fit they should be all sent to the prison, and there suffer the utmost penalty. To him all consented in order till it came to Caius Cæsar, who was afterwards dictator. He was then but a young man, and only at the outset of his career, but had already directed his hopes and policy to that course by which he afterwards changed the Roman state into a monarchy. Of this others foresaw nothing; but Cicero had seen reason for strong suspicion, though without obtaining any sufficient means of proof. And there were some indeed that said that he was very near being discovered, and only just escaped him; others are of opinion that Cicero voluntarily overlooked and neglected the evidence against him, for fear of his friends and power; for it was very evident to everybody that if Cæsar was to be accused with the conspirators, they were more likely to be saved with him, than he to be punished with them.

When, therefore, it came to Cæsar's turn to give his opinion, he stood up and proposed that the conspirators should not be put to death, but their estates confiscated, and their persons confined in such cities in Italy as Cicero should approve, there to be kept in custody till Catiline was conquered. To this sentence, as it was the most moderate, and he that delivered it a most powerful speaker, Cicero himself gave no small weight, for he stood up and, turning the scale on either side, spoke in favour partly of the former, partly of Cæsar's sentence. And all Cicero's friends, judging Cæsar's sentence most expedient for Cicero, because he would incur the less blame if the conspirators were not put to death, chose rather the latter; so that Silanus, also changing his mind, retracted his opinion, and said he had not declared for capital, but only the utmost punishment, which to a Roman senator is imprisonment. The first man who spoke against Cæsar's motion was Catulus Lutatius. Cato followed, and so vehemently urged in his speech the strong suspicion against Cæsar himself, and so filled the senate with anger and resolution, that a decree was passed for the execution of the conspirators. But Cæsar opposed the confiscation of their goods, not thinking it fair that those who rejected the mildest part of his sentence should avail themselves of the severest. And when many insisted upon it, he appealed to the tribunes, but they would do nothing; till Cicero himself yielding, remitted that part of the sentence.

After this, Cicero went out with the senate to the conspirators; they were not all together in one place, but the several prætors had them, some one, some another, in custody. And first he took Lentulus from the Palatine, and brought him by the Sacred Street, through the middle of the marketplace, a circle of the most eminent citizens encompassing and protecting him. The people, affrighted at what was doing, passed along in silence, especially the young men; as if, with fear and trembling, they were undergoing a rite of initiation into some ancient sacred mysteries of aristocratic power. Thus passing from the market-place, and coming to the gaol, he delivered Lentulus to the officer, and commanded him to execute him; and after him Cethegus, and so all the rest in order, he brought and delivered up to execution. And when he saw many of the conspirators in the market-place, still standing together in companies, ignorant of what was done, and waiting for the night, supposing the men were still alive and in a possibility of being rescued, he called out in a loud voice, and said, "*They did live;*" for so the Romans, to avoid inauspicious language, name those that are dead.

It was now evening, when he returned from the market-place to his own house, the citizens no longer attending him with silence, nor in order, but receiving him, as he passed, with acclamations and applauses, and saluting him as the saviour and founder of his country. A bright light shone through the streets from the lamps and torches set up at the doors, and the women showed lights from the tops of the houses, to honour Cicero, and to behold him returning home with a splendid train of the most principal citizens; amongst whom were many who had conducted great wars, celebrated triumphs, and added to the possessions of the Roman empire, both by sea and land. These, as they passed along with him, acknowledged to one another, that though the Roman people were indebted to several officers and commanders of that age for riches, spoils, and power, yet to Cicero alone they owed the safety and security of all these, for delivering them from so great and imminent a danger. For though it might seem no wonderful thing to present the design, and punish the conspirators, yet to defeat the greatest of all conspiracies with so little disturbance, trouble, and commotion, was very extraordinary. For the greater part of those who had flocked in to Catiline, as soon as they heard the fate of Lentulus and Cethegus, left and forsook him, and he himself, with his remaining forces, joining battle with Antonius, was destroyed with his army.

And yet there were some who were very ready both to speak ill of Cicero, and to do him hurt for these actions; and they had for their leaders some of the magistrates of the ensuing year, as Cæsar, who was one of the prætors, and Metellus and Bestia, the tribunes. These, entering upon their office some few days before Cicero's consulate expired, would not permit him to make any address to the people, but throwing the benches before the rostra, hindered his speaking, telling him he might, if he pleased, make the oath of withdrawal from office, and then come down again. Cicero, accordingly, accepting the conditions, came forward to make his withdrawal; and silence being made, he recited his oath, not in the usual, but in a new and peculiar form, namely, that he had saved his country and preserved the empire; the truth of which oath all the people confirmed with theirs. Cæsar and the tribunes, all the more exasperated by this, endeavoured to create him further trouble, and for this purpose proposed a law for calling Pompey home with his army, to put an end to Cicero's usurpation. But it was a very great advantage for Cicero and the whole commonwealth that Cato was at that time one of the tribunes. For he, being of equal power with the rest and of greater reputation, could oppose their designs. He easily defeated their other projects, and in an oration to the people so highly extolled Cicero's consulate, that the greatest honours were decreed him, and he was publicly declared the Father of his Country, which title he seems to have obtained, the first man who did so, when Cato gave it to him in this address to the people.

At this time, therefore, his authority was very great in the city; but he created himself much envy, and offended very many, not by any evil action, but because he was always lauding and magnifying himself. For neither senate, nor assembly of the people, nor court of judicature could meet, in which he was not heard to talk of Catiline and Lentulus. Indeed, he also filled his books and writings with his own praises, to such an excess as to render a style, in itself most pleasant and delightful, nauseous and irksome to his hearers; this ungrateful humour like a disease, always cleaving to him. Nevertheless, though he was intemperately fond of his own glory, he was very free from envying others, and was, on the contrary, most liberally profuse in commending both the ancients and his contemporaries, as any one may see in his writings. And many such sayings of his are also remembered; as that he called Aristotle a river of flowing gold, and said of Plato's Dialogues, that if Jupiter were to speak, it would be in language like theirs. He used to call Theophrastus his special luxury. And being asked which of Demosthenes's orations he liked best, he answered, the longest. And yet some affected imitators of Demosthenes have complained of some words that occur in one of his letters, to the effect that Demosthenes sometimes falls asleep in his speeches; forgetting the many high encomiums he continually passes upon him, and the compliment he paid him when he named the most elaborate of all his orations, those he wrote against Antony, Philippics. And as for the eminent men of his own time, either in eloquence or philosophy, there was not one of them whom he did not, by writing or speaking favourably of him, render more illustrious. He obtained of Cæsar, when in power, the Roman citizenship for Cratippus, the Peripatetic, and got the court of Areopagus, by public decree, to request his stay at Athens, for the instruction of their youth and the honour of their city. There are letters extant from Cicero to Herodes, and others to his son in which he recommends the study of philosophy under Cratippus. There is one in which he blames Gorgias, the rhetorician, for enticing his son into luxury and drinking, and, therefore, forbids him his company. And this, and one other to Pelops, the Byzantine, are the only two of his Greek epistles which seem to be written in anger. In the first, he justly reflects on Gorgias, if he were what he was thought to be, a dissolute and profligate character; but in the other, he rather meanly expostulates and complains with Pelops for neglecting to procure him a decree of certain honours from the Byzantines.

Another illustration of his love of praise is the way in which sometimes, to make his orations more striking, he neglected decorum and dignity. When Munatius, who had escaped conviction by his advocacy, immediately prosecuted his friend Sabinus, he said in the warmth of his resentment, "Do you suppose you were acquitted for your own merits, Munatius, and was it not that I so darkened the case, that the court could not see your guilt?" When from the rostra he had made a eulogy on Marcus Crassus, with much applause, and within a few days after again as publicly reproached him, Crassus called to him, and said, "Did not you yourself two days ago, in this same place, commend me?" "Yes," said Cicero, "I exercised my eloquence in declaiming upon a bad subject." At another time, Crassus had said that no one of his family had ever lived beyond sixty years of age, and afterwards denied it, and asked, "What should put it into my head to say so?" "It was to gain the people's favour," answered Cicero; "you knew how glad they would be to hear it." When Crassus expressed admiration of the Stoic doctrine, that *the good man is always rich*, "Do you not mean," said Cicero, "their doctrine that *all things belong to the wise?*" Crassus being generally accused of covetousness. One of Crassus's sons, who was thought so exceedingly like a man of the name of Axius as to throw some suspicion on his mother's honour, made a successful speech in the senate. Cicero, on being asked how he liked it, replied with the Greek words *Axios Crassou.*

When Crassus was about to go into Syria, he desired to leave Cicero rather his friend than his enemy, and, therefore, one day saluting him, told him he would come and sup with him, which the other as courteously received. Within a few days after, on some of Cicero's acquaintances interceding for Vatinius, as desirous of reconciliation and friendship, for he was then his enemy, "What," he replied, "does Vatinius also wish to come and sup with me?" Such was his way with Crassus. When Vatinius, who had swellings in his neck, was pleading a cause he called him the *tumid* orator; and having been told by some one that Vatinius was dead, on hearing, presently after, that he was alive, "May the rascal perish," said he, "for his news not being true."

Upon Cæsar's bringing forward a law for the division of the lands in Campania amongst the soldiers, many in the senate opposed it; amongst the rest, Lucius Gellius, one of the oldest men in the house, said it should never pass whilst he lived. "Let us postpone it," said Cicero, "Gellius does not ask us to wait long." There was a man of the name of Octavius, suspected to be of African descent. He once said, when Cicero was pleading, that he could not hear him; "Yet there are holes" said Cicero, "in your ears." When Metellus Nepos told him that he had ruined more as a witness than he had saved as an advocate, "I admit," said Cicero, "that I have more truth than eloquence." To a young man who was suspected of having given a poisoned cake to his father, and who talked largely of the invectives he meant to deliver against Cicero, "Better these," replied he, "than your cakes." Publius Sextius, having amongst others retained Cicero as his advocate in a certain cause, was yet desirous to say all for himself, and would not allow anybody to speak for him; when he was about to receive his acquittal from the judges, and the ballots were passing, Cicero called to him, "Make haste, Sextius, and use your time; to-morrow you will be nobody." He cited Publius Cotta to bear testimony in a certain cause, one who affected to be thought a lawyer, though ignorant and unlearned; to whom, when he had said, "I know nothing of the matter," he answered "You think, perhaps, we ask you about a point of law." To Metellus Nepos, who, in a dispute between them, repeated several times, "Who was your father, Cicero?" he replied, "Your mother has made the answer to such a question in your case more difficult;" Nepos's mother having been of ill-repute. The son, also, was of a giddy, uncertain temper. At one time he suddenly threw up his office of tribune, and sailed off into Syria to Pompey; and immediately after, with as little reason, came back again. He gave his tutor, Philagrus, a funeral with more than necessary attention, and then set up the stone figure of a crow over his tomb. "This," said Cicero, "is really appropriate; as he did not teach you to speak, but to fly about." When Marcus Appius, in the opening of some speech in a court of justice said that his friend had desired him to employ industry, eloquence, and fidelity in that cause, Cicero answered "And how have you had the heart not to accede to any one of his requests?"

To use this sharp raillery against opponents and antagonists in judicial pleading seems allowable rhetoric. But he excited much ill-feeling by his readiness to attack any one for the sake of a jest. A few anecdotes of this kind may be added. Marcus Aquinius, who had two sons-in-law in exile, received from him the name of King Adrastus. Lucius Cotta, an intemperate lover of wine, was censor when Cicero stood for the consulship. Cicero, being thirsty at the election, his friends stood round about him while he was drinking. "You have reason to be afraid," he said, "lest the censor should be angry with me for drinking water." Meeting one day Voconius with his three very ugly daughters, he quoted the verse—

"He reared a race without Apollo's leave."

When Marcus Gellius, who was reputed the son of a slave, had read several letters in the senate with a very shrill and loud voice, "Wonder not," said Cicero, "he comes of the criers." When Faustus Sylla, the son of Sylla the dictator, who had, during his dictatorship, by public bills proscribed and condemned so many citizens, had so far wasted his estate, and got into debt, that he was forced to publish his bills of sale, Cicero told him that he liked these bills much better than those of his father. By this habit he made himself odious with many people.

But Clodius's faction conspired against him upon the following occasion. Clodius was a member of a noble family, in the flower of his youth, and of a bold and resolute temper. He, being in love with Pompeia, Cæsar's wife, got privately into his house in the dress and attire of a music-girl; the women being at that time offering there the sacrifice which must not be seen by men, and there was no man present. Clodius, being a youth and beardless, hoped to get to Pompeia among the women without being taken notice of. But coming into a great house by night, he missed his way in the passages, and a servant belonging to Aurelia, Cæsar's mother, spying him wandering up and down, inquired his name. Thus being necessitated to speak, he told her he was seeking for one of Pompeia's maids, Abra by name; and she, perceiving it not to be a woman's voice, shrieked out, and called in the women; who shutting the gates, and searching every place, at length found Clodius hidden in the chamber of the maid with whom he had come in. This matter being much talked about, Cæsar put away his wife, Pompeia, and Clodius was prosecuted for profaning the holy rites.

Cicero was at this time his friend, for he had been useful to him in the conspiracy of Catiline, as one of his forwardest assistants and protectors. But when Clodius rested his defence upon this point, that he was not then at Rome, but at a distance in the country, Cicero testified that he had come to his house that day, and conversed with him on several matters; which thing was indeed true, although Cicero was thought to testify it not so much for the truth's sake as to preserve his quiet with Terentia his wife. For she bore a grudge against Clodius on account of his sister Clodia's wishing, as it was alleged, to marry Cicero, and having employed for this purpose the intervention of Tullus, a very intimate friend of Cicero's; and his frequent visits to Clodia, who lived in their neighbourhood, and the attentions he paid to her had excited Terentia's suspicions, and, being a woman of a violent temper and having the ascendant over Cicero, she urged him on to taking a part against Clodius, and delivering his testimony. Many other good and honest citizens also gave evidence against him, for perjuries, disorders, bribing the people, and debauching women. Lucullus proved, by his women-servants, that he had debauched his youngest sister when she was Lucullus's wife; and there was a general belief that he had done the same with his two other sisters, Tertia, whom Marcius Rex, and Clodia, whom Metellus Celer had married; the latter of whom was called Quadrantia, because one of her lovers had deceived her with a purse of small copper money instead of silver, the smallest copper coin being called a *quadrant*. Upon this sister's account, in particular, Clodius's character was attacked. Notwithstanding all this, when the common people united against the accusers and witnesses and the whole party, the judges were affrighted, and a guard was placed about them for their defence; and most of them wrote their sentences on the tablets in such a way that they could not well be read. It was decided, however, that there was a majority for his acquittal, and bribery was reported to have been employed; in reference to which Catulus remarked, when he next met the judges, "You were very right to ask for a guard, to prevent your money being taken from you." And when Clodius upbraided Cicero that the judges had not believed his testimony, "Yes," said he, "five-and-twenty of them trusted me and condemned you, and the other thirty did not trust you, for they did not acquit you till they had got your money."

Cæsar, though cited, did not give his testimony against Clodius, and declared himself not convinced of his wife's adultery, but that he had put her away because it was fit that Cæsar's house should not be only free of the evil fact, but of the fame too.

Clodius, having escaped this danger, and having got himself chosen one of the tribunes, immediately attacked Cicero, heaping up all matters and inciting all persons against him. The common people he gained over with popular laws; to each of the consuls he decreed large provinces, to Piso, Macedonia, and to Gabinius, Syria; he made a strong party among the indigent citizens, to support him in his proceedings, and had always a body of armed slaves about him. Of the three men then in greatest power, Crassus was Cicero's open enemy, Pompey indifferently made advances to both, and Cæsar was going with an army into Gaul. To him, though not his friend (what had occurred in the time of the conspiracy having created suspicions between them), Cicero applied, requesting an appointment as one of his lieutenants in the province. Cæsar accepted him, and Clodius, perceiving that Cicero would thus escape his tribunician authority, professed to be inclinable to a reconciliation, laid the greatest fault upon Terentia, made always a favourable mention of him, and addressed him with kind expressions, as one who felt no hatred or ill-will, but who merely wished to urge his complaints in a moderate and friendly way. By these artifices, he so freed Cicero of all his fears, that he resigned his appointment to Cæsar, and betook himself again to political affairs. At which Caesar, being exasperated, joined the party of Clodius against him, and wholly alienated Pompey from him; he also himself declared in a public assembly of the people, that he did not think Lentulus and Cethegus, with their accomplices, were fairly and legally put to death without being brought to trial. And this, indeed, was the crime charged upon Cicero, and this impeachment he was summoned to answer. And so, as an accused man, and in danger for the result, he changed his dress, and went round with his hair untrimmed, in the attire of a suppliant, to beg the people's grace. But Clodius met him in every corner, having a band of abusive and daring fellows about him, who derided

Cicero for his change of dress and his humiliation, and often, by throwing dirt and stones at him, interrupted his supplication to the people.

However, first of all, almost the whole equestrian order changed their dress with him, and no less than twenty thousand young gentlemen followed him with their hair untrimmed, and supplicating with him to the people. And then the senate met, to pass a decree that the people should change their dress as in time of public sorrow. But the consuls opposing it, and Clodius with armed men besetting the senate-house, many of the senators ran out, crying out and tearing their clothes. But this sight moved neither shame nor pity; Cicero must either fly or determine it by the sword with Clodius. He entreated Pompey to aid him, who was on purpose gone out of the way, and was staying at his country-house in the Alban hills; and first he sent his son-in-law Piso to intercede with him, and afterwards set out to go himself. Of which Pompey being informed, would not stay to see him, being ashamed at the remembrance of the many conflicts in the commonwealth which Cicero had undergone in his behalf, and how much of his policy he had directed for his advantage. But being now Cæsar's son-in-law, at his instance he had set aside all former kindness, and, slipping out at another door, avoided the interview. Thus being forsaken by Pompey, and left alone to himself, he fled to the consuls. Gabinius was rough with him, as usual, but Piso spoke more courteously, desiring him to yield and give place for a while to the fury of Clodius, and to await a change of times, and to be now, as before, his country's saviour from the peril of these troubles and commotions which Clodius was exciting.

Cicero, receiving this answer, consulted with his friends. Lucullus advised him to stay, as being sure to prevail at last; others to fly, because the people would soon desire him again, when they should have enough of the rage and madness of Clodius. This last Cicero approved. But first he took a statue of Minerva, which had been long set up and greatly honoured in his house, and carrying it to the capitol, there dedicated it, with the inscription, "To Minerva, Patroness of Rome." And receiving an escort from his friends, about the middle of the night he left the city and went by land through Lucania, intending to reach Sicily.

But as soon as it was publicly known that he was fled, Clodius proposed to the people a decree of exile, and by his own order interdicted him fire and water, prohibiting any within five hundred miles in Italy to receive him into their houses. Most people, out of respect for Cicero, paid no regard to this edict, offering him every attention, and escorting him on his way. But at Hipponium, a city of Lucania now called Vibo, one Vibius, a Sicilian by birth, who, amongst many other instances of Cicero's friendship, had been made head of the state engineers when he was consul, would not receive him into his house, sending him word he would appoint a place in the country for his reception. Caius Vergilius, the prætor of Sicily, who had been on the most intimate terms with him, wrote to him to forbear coming into Sicily. At these things Cicero, being disheartened, went to Brundusium, whence putting forth with a prosperous wind, a contrary gale blowing from the sea carried him back to Italy the next day. He put again to sea, and having reached Dyrrachium, on his coming to shore there, it is reported that an earthquake and a convulsion in the sea happened at the same time, signs which the diviners said intimated that his exile would not be long, for these were prognostics of change. Although many visited him with respect, and the cities of Greece contended which should honour him most, he yet continued disheartened and disconsolate, like an unfortunate lover, often casting his looks back upon Italy; and, indeed, he was become so poor-spirited, so humiliated and dejected by his misfortunes, as none could have expected in a man who had devoted so much of his life to study and learning. And yet he often desired his friends not to call him orator, but philosopher, because he had made philosophy his business, and had only used rhetoric as an instrument for attaining his objects in public life. But the desire of glory has great power in washing the tinctures of philosophy out of the souls of men, and in imprinting the passions of the common people, by custom and conversation, in the minds of those that take a part in governing them, unless the politician be very careful so to engage in public affairs as to interest himself only in the affairs themselves, but not participate in the passions that are consequent to them.

Clodius, having thus driven away Cicero, fell to burning his farms and villas, and afterwards his city house, and built on the site of it a temple to Liberty. The rest of his property he exposed to sale by daily proclamation, but nobody came to buy. By these courses he became formidable to the noble citizens, and being followed by the commonalty, whom he had filled with insolence and licentiousness, he began at last to try his strength against Pompey, some of whose arrangements in the countries he conquered, he attacked. The disgrace of this made Pompey begin to reproach himself for his cowardice in deserting Cicero, and changing his mind, he now wholly set himself with his friends to contrive his return. And when Clodius opposed it, the senate made a vote that no public measure should be ratified or passed by them till Cicero was recalled. But when Lentulus was consul, the commotions grew so high upon this matter, that the tribunes were wounded in the Forum, and Quintus, Cicero's brother, was left as dead, lying unobserved amongst the slain. The people began to change in their feelings, and Annius Milo, one of their tribunes, was the first who took confidence to summon Clodius to trial for acts of violence. Many of the common people out of the neighbouring cities formed a party with Pompey, and he went with them, and drove Clodius out of the Forum, and summoned the people to pass their vote. And, it is said, the people never passed any suffrage more unanimously than this. The senate, also, striving to outdo the people, sent letters of thanks to those cities which had received Cicero with respect in his exile, and decreed that his house and his country-places, which Clodius had destroyed, should be rebuilt at the public charge.

Thus Cicero returned sixteen months after his exile, and the cities were so glad, and people so zealous to meet him, that what he boasted of afterwards, that Italy had brought him on her shoulders home to Rome, was rather less than the truth. And Crassus himself, who had been his enemy before his exile, went then voluntarily to meet him, and was reconciled, to please his son Publius, as he said, who was Cicero's affectionate admirer.

Cicero had not been long at Rome when, taking the opportunity of Clodius's absence, he went with a great company to the capitol, and there tore and defaced the tribunician tables, in which were recorded the acts done in the time of Clodius. And on Clodius calling him in question for this, he answered that he, being of the patrician order, had obtained the office of tribune against law, and therefore nothing done by him was valid. Cato was displeased at this, and opposed Cicero, not that he commended Clodius, but rather disapproved of his whole administration; yet, he contended, it was an irregular and violent course for the senate to vote the illegality of so many decrees and acts, including those of Cato's own government in Cyprus and at Byzantium. This occasioned a breach between Cato and Cicero, which, though it came not to open enmity, yet made a more reserved friendship between them.

After this, Milo killed Clodius, and, being arraigned for the murder, he procured Cicero as his advocate. The senate, fearing lest the questioning of so eminent and high-spirited a citizen as Milo might disturb the peace of the city, committed the superintendence of this and of the other trials to Pompey, who should undertake to maintain the security alike of the city and of the courts of justice. Pompey, therefore, went in the night, and occupying the high grounds about it, surrounded the Forum with soldiers. Milo, fearing lest Cicero, being disturbed by such an unusual sight, should conduct his cause the less successfully, persuaded him to come in a litter into the Forum, and there repose himself till the judges were set and the court filled. For Cicero, it seems, not only wanted courage in arms, but, in his speaking also, began with timidity, and in many cases scarcely left off trembling and shaking when he had got thoroughly into the current and the substance of his speech. Being to defend Licinius Murena against the prosecution of Cato, and being eager to outdo Hortensius, who had made his plea with great applause, he took so little rest that night, and was so disordered with thought and overwatching, that he spoke much worse than usual. And so now, on quitting his litter to commence the cause of Milo, at the sight of Pompey, posted as it were, and encamped with his troops above, and seeing arms shining round about the Forum, he was so confounded that he could hardly begin his speech for the trembling of his body and hesitance of his tongue; whereas Milo, meantime, was bold and intrepid in his demeanour, disdaining either to let his hair grow or to put on the mourning habit. And this, indeed, seems to have been one principal cause of his condemnation. Cicero, however, was thought not so much to have shown timidity for himself, as anxiety about his friend.

He was made one of the priests, whom the Romans call Augurs, in the room of Crassus the younger, dead in Parthia. Then he was appointed by lot to the province of Cilicia, and set sail thither with twelve thousand foot and two thousand six hundred horse. He had orders to bring back Cappadocia to its allegiance to Ariobarzanes, its king; which settlement he effected very completely without recourse to arms. And perceiving the Cilicians, by the great loss the Romans had suffered in Parthia, and the commotions in Syria, to have become disposed to attempt a revolt, by a gentle course of government he soothed them back into fidelity. He would accept none of the presents that were offered him by the kings; he remitted the charge of public entertainments, but daily at his own house received the ingenious and accomplished persons of the province, not sumptuously, but liberally. His house had no porter, nor was he ever found in bed by any man, but early in the morning, standing or walking before his door, he received those who came to offer their salutations. He is said never once to have ordered any of those under his command to be beaten with rods, or to have their garments rent. He never gave contumelious language in his anger, nor inflicted punishment with reproach. He detected an embezzlement, to a large amount, in the public money, and thus relieved the cities from their burdens, at the same time that he allowed those who made restitution to retain without further punishment their rights as citizens. He engaged too, in war, so far as to give a defeat to the banditti who infested Mount Amanus, for which he was saluted by his army Imperator. To Cæcilius, the orator, who asked him to send him some panthers from Cilicia, to be exhibited on the theatre at Rome, he wrote, in commendation of his own actions, that there were no panthers in Cilicia, for they were all fled to Caria, in anger that in so general a peace they had become the sole objects of attack. On leaving his province, he touched at Rhodes, and tarried for some length of time at Athens, longing much to renew his old studies. He visited the eminent men of learning, and saw his former friends and companions; and after receiving in Greece the honours that were due to him, returned to the city, where everything was now just as it were in a flame, breaking out into a civil war.

When the senate would have decreed him a triumph, he told them he had rather, so differences were accommodated, follow the triumphal chariot of Cæsar. In private, he gave advice to both, writing many letters to Cæsar, and personally entreating Pompey; doing his best to soothe and bring to reason both the one and the other. But when matters became incurable and Cæsar was approaching Rome, and Pompey durst not abide it, but, with many honest citizens, left the city, Cicero as yet did not join in the flight, and was reputed to adhere to Cæsar. And it is very evident he was in his thoughts much divided, and wavered painfully between both, for he writes in his epistles, "To which side should I turn? Pompey has the fair and honourable plea for war; and Cæsar, on the other hand, has managed his affairs better, and is more able to secure himself and his friends. So that I know whom I should fly, not whom I should fly to." But when Trebatius, one of Caesar's friends, by letter signified to him that Cæsar thought it was his most desirable course to join his party, and partake his hopes, but if he considered himself too old a man for this, then he should retire into Greece, and stay quietly there, out of the way of either party, Cicero, wondering that Cæsar had not written himself, gave an angry reply, that he should not do anything unbecoming his past life. Such is the account to be collected from his letters.

But as soon as Cæsar was marched into Spain, he immediately sailed away to join Pompey. And he was welcomed by all but Cato; who, taking him privately, chid him for coming to Pompey. As for himself, he said, it had been indecent to forsake that part in the commonwealth which he had chosen from the beginning; but Cicero might have been more useful to his country and friends, if, remaining neuter, he had attended and used his influence to moderate the result, instead of coming hither to make himself, without reason or necessity, an enemy to Cæsar, and a partner in such great dangers.

By this language, partly, Cicero's feelings were altered, and partly, also, because Pompey made no great use of him. Although, indeed, he was himself the cause of it, by his not denying that he was sorry he had come, by his depreciating Pompey's resources, finding fault underhand with his counsels, and continually indulging in jests and sarcastic remarks on his fellow-soldiers. Though he went about in the camp with a gloomy and melancholy face himself, he was always trying to raise a laugh in others, whether they wished it or not. It may not be amiss to mention a few instances. To Domitius, on his preferring to a command one who was no soldier, and saying, in his defence, that he was a modest and prudent person, he replied, "Why did not you keep him for a tutor for your children?" On hearing Theophanes, the Lesbian, who was master of the engineers in the army, praised for the admirable way in which he had consoled the Rhodians for the loss of their fleet, "What a thing it is," he said, "to have a Greek in command !" When Cæsar had been acting successfully, and in a manner blockading Pompey, Lentulus was saying it was reported that Cæsar's friends were out of heart; "Because," said Cicero, "they do not wish Cæsar well." To one Marcius, who had just come from Italy, and told them that there was a strong report at Rome that Pompey was blocked up, he said, "And you sailed hither to see it with your own eyes." To Nonius, encouraging them after a defeat to be of good hope, because there were seven eagles still left in Pompey's camp, "Good reason for encouragement," said Cicero, "if we were going to fight with jackdaws." Labienus insisted on some prophecies to the effect that Pompey would gain the victory; "Yes," said Cicero; "and the first step in the campaign has been losing our camp."

After the battle of Pharsalia was over, at which he was not present for want of health, and Pompey was fled, Cato, having considerable forces and a great fleet at Dyrrachium, would have had Cicero commander-in-chief, according to law and the precedence of his consular dignity. And on his refusing the command, and wholly declining to take part in their plans for continuing the war, he was in the greatest danger of being killed, young Pompey and his friends calling him traitor, and drawing their swords upon him; only that Cato interposed, and hardly rescued and brought him out of the camp.

Afterwards, arriving at Brundusium, he tarried there some time in expectation of Cæsar, who was delayed by his affairs in Asia and Egypt. And when it was told him that he was arrived at Tarentum, and was coming thence by land to Brundusium, he hastened towards him, not altogether without hope, and yet in some fear of making experiment of the temper of an enemy and conqueror in the presence of many witnesses. But there was no necessity for him either to speak or do anything unworthy of himself; for Cæsar, as soon as he saw him coming a good way before the rest of the company, came down to meet him, saluted him, and, leading the way, conversed with him alone for some furlongs. And from that time forward he continued to treat him with honour and respect, so that, when Cicero wrote an oration in praise of Cato, Cæsar in writing an answer to it, took occasion to commend Cicero's own life and eloquence, comparing him to Pericles and Theramenes. Cicero's oration was called Cato; Cæsar's, anti-Cato.

So also it is related that when Quintus Ligarius was prosecuted for having been in arms against Cæsar, and Cicero had undertaken his defence, Cæsar said to his friends, "Why might we not as well once more hear a speech from Cicero? Ligarius, there is no question, is a wicked man and an enemy." But when Cicero began to speak, he wonderfully moved him, and proceeded in his speech with such varied pathos, and such a charm of language, that the colour of Cæsar's countenance often changed, and it was evident that all the passions of his soul were in commotion. At length, the orator touching upon the Pharsalian battle, he was so affected that his body trembled, and some of the papers he held dropped out of his hands. And thus he was overpowered, and acquitted Ligarius.

Henceforth, the commonwealth being changed into a monarchy, Cicero withdrew himself from public affairs, and employed his leisure in instructing those young men that would, in philosophy; and by the near intercourse he thus had with some of the noblest and highest in rank, he again began to possess great influence in the city. The work and object to which he set himself was to compose and translate philosophical dialogues and to render logical and physical terms into the Roman idiom. For he it was, as it is said, who first or principally gave Latin names to *phantasia*, *syncatathesis*, *epokhe*, *catalepsis*, *atamon*, *ameres*, *kenon*, and other such technical terms, which, either by metaphors or other means of accommodation, he succeeded in making intelligible and expressible to the Romans. For his recreation, he exercised his dexterity in poetry, and when he was set to it would make five hundred verses in a night. He spent the greatest part of his time at his country-house near Tusculum. He wrote to his friends that he led the life of Lærtes either jestingly, as his custom was or rather from a feeling of ambition for public employment, which made him impatient under the present state of affairs. He rarely went to the city, unless to pay his court to Cæsar. He was commonly the first amongst those who voted him honours, and sought out new terms of praise for himself and for his actions. As, for example, what he said of the statues of Pompey which had been thrown down, and were afterwards by Cæsar's orders set up again; that Cæsar, by this act of humanity, had indeed set up Pompey's statues, but he had fixed and established his own.

He had a design, it is said, of writing the history of his country, combining with it much of that of Greece, and incorporating in it all the stories and legends of the past that he had collected. But his purposes were interfered with by various public and various private unhappy occurrences and misfortunes; for most of which he was himself in fault. For first of all, be put away his wife Terentia, by whom he had been neglected in the time of the war, and sent away destitute of necessaries for his journey; neither did he find her kind when he returned into Italy, for she did not join him at Brundusium, where he stayed a long time, nor would allow her young daughter, who undertook so long a journey, decent attendance, or the requisite expenses; besides, she left him a naked and empty house, and yet had involved him in many and great debts. These were alleged as the fairest reasons for the divorce. But Terentia, who denied them all, had the most unmistakable defence furnished her by her husband himself, who not long after married a young maiden for the love of her beauty, as Terentia upbraided him; or as Tiro, his emancipated slave, has written, for her riches, to discharge his debts. For the young woman was very rich, and Cicero had the custody of her estate, being left guardian in trust; and being indebted many myriads of money, he was persuaded by friends and relations to marry her, notwithstanding his disparity of age, and to use her money to satisfy his creditors. Antony, who mentions this marriage in his answer to the Philippics, reproaches him for putting away a wife with whom he had lived to old age; adding some happy strokes of sarcasm on Cicero's domestic, inactive, unsoldier-like habits. Not long after this marriage, his daughter died in childbed at Lentulus's house, to whom she had been married after the death of Piso, her former husband. The philosophers from all parts came to comfort Cicero; for his grief was so excessive, that he put away his new-married wife, because she seemed to be pleased at the death of Tullia. And thus stood Cicero's domestic affairs at this time.

He had no concern in the design that was now forming against Cæsar, although, in general, he was Brutus's most principal confidant, and one who was as aggrieved at the present, and as desirous of the former state of public affairs, as any other whatsoever. But they feared his temper, as wanting courage, and his old age, in which the most daring dispositions are apt to be timorous.

As soon, therefore, as the act was committed by Brutus and Cassius, and the friends of Cæsar were got together, so that there was fear the city would again be involved in a civil war, Antony, being consul, convened the senate, and made a short address recommending concord. And Cicero following with various remarks such as the occasion called for, persuaded the senate to imitate the Athenians, and decree an amnesty for what had been done in Cæsar's case, and to bestow provinces on Brutus and Cassius. But neither of these things took effect. For as soon as the common people, of themselves inclined to pity, saw the dead body of Cæsar borne through the market-place, and Antony showing his clothes filled with blood, and pierced through in every part with swords, enraged to a degree of frenzy, they made a search for the murderers, and with firebrands in their hands ran to their houses to burn them. They, however, being forewarned, avoided this danger; and expecting many more and greater to come, they left the city.

Antony on this was at once in exultation, and every one was in alarm with the prospect that he would make himself sole ruler, and Cicero in more alarm than any one. For Antony, seeing his influence reviving in the commonwealth and knowing how closely he was connected with Brutus, was ill-pleased to have him in the city. Besides, there had been some former jealousy between them, occasioned by the difference of their manners. Cicero, fearing the event, was inclined to go as lieutenant with Dolabella into Syria. But Hirtius and Pansa, consuls elect as successors of Antony, good men and lovers of Cicero, entreated him not to leave them, undertaking to put down Antony if he would stay in Rome. And he, neither distrusting wholly, nor trusting them, let Dolabella go without him, promising Hirtius that he would go and spend his summer at Athens, and return again when he entered upon his office. So he set out on his journey; but some delay occurring in his passage, new intelligence, as often happens, came suddenly from Rome, that Antony had made an astonishing change, and was doing all things and managing all public affairs at the will of the senate, and that there wanted nothing but his presence to bring things to a happy settlement. And therefore, blaming himself for his cowardice, he returned again to Rome, and was not deceived in his hopes at the beginning. For such multitudes flocked out to meet him, that the compliments and civilities which were paid him at the gates, and at his entrance into the city, took up almost one whole day's time.

On the morrow, Antony convened the senate, and summoned Cicero thither. He came not, but kept his bed, pretending to be ill with his journey; but the true reason seemed the fear of some design against him, upon a suspicion and intimation given him on his way to Rome. Antony, however, showed great offence at the affront, and sent soldiers, commanding them to bring him or burn his house; but many interceding and supplicating for him, he was contented to accept sureties. Ever after, when they met, they passed one another with silence, and continued on their guard, till Cæsar, the younger, coming from Apollonia, entered on the first Cæsar's inheritance, and was engaged in a dispute with Antony about two thousand five hundred myriads of money, which Antony detained from the estate.

Upon this, Philippus, who married the mother, and Marcellus, who married the sister of young Cæsar, came with the young man to Cicero, and agreed with him that Cicero should give them the aid of his eloquence and political influence with the senate and people, and Cæsar give Cicero the defence of his riches and arms. For the young man had already a great party of the soldiers of Cæsar about him. And Cicero's readiness to join him was founded, it is said, on some yet stronger motives; for it seems, while Pompey and Cæsar were yet alive, Cicero, in his sleep, had fancied himself engaged in calling some of the sons of the senators into the capitol, Jupiter being about, according to the dream, to declare one of them the chief ruler of Rome. The citizens, running up with curiosity, stood about the temple, and the youths, sitting in their purple-bordered robes, kept silence. On a sudden the doors opened, and the youths, arising one by one in order, passed round the god, who reviewed them all, and, to their sorrow, dismissed them; but when this one was passing by, the god stretched forth his right hand and said, "O ye Romans, this young man, when he shall be lord of Rome, shall put an end to all your civil wars." It is said that Cicero formed from his dream a distinct image of the youth, and retained it afterwards perfectly, but did not know who it was. The next day, going down into the Campus Martius, he met the boys returning from their gymnastic exercises, and the first was he, just as he had appeared to him in his dream. Being astonished at it, he asked him who were his parents. And it proved to be this young Cæsar, whose father was a man of no great eminence, Octavius, and his mother, Attia, Cæsar's sister's daughter; for which reason, Cæsar, who had no children, made him by will the heir of his house and property. From that time, it is said that Cicero studiously noticed the youth whenever he met him, and he as kindly received the civility; and by fortune he happened to be born when Cicero was consul.

These were the reasons spoken of; but it was principally Cicero's hatred of Antony, and a temper unable to resist honour, which fastened him to Cæsar, with the purpose of getting the support of Cæsar's power for his own public designs. For the young man went so far in his court to him, that he called him Father; at which Brutus was so highly displeased, that, in his epistles to Atticus, he reflected on Cicero saying, it was manifest, by his courting Cæsar for fear of Antony, he did not intend liberty to his country, but an indulgent master to himself. Notwithstanding, Brutus took Cicero's son, then studying philosophy at Athens, gave him a command, and employed him in various ways, with a good result. Cicero's own power at this time was at the greatest height in the city, and he did whatsoever he pleased; he completely overpowered and drove out Antony, and sent the two consuls, Hirtius and Pansa, with an army, to reduce him; and, on the other hand, persuaded the senate to allow Cæsar the lictors and ensigns of a prætor, as though he were his country's defender. But after Antony was defeated in battle, and the consuls slain, the armies united, and ranged themselves with Cæsar. And the senate, fearing the young man, and his extraordinary fortune, endeavoured, by honours and gifts, to call off the soldiers from him, and to lessen his power; professing there was no further need of arms now Antony was put to flight.

This giving Cæsar an affright, he privately sends some friends to entreat and persuade Cicero to procure the consular dignity for them both together; saying he should manage the affairs as he pleased, should have the supreme power, and govern the young man who was only desirous of name and glory. And Cæsar himself confessed that, in fear of ruin, and in danger of being deserted, he had seasonably made use of Cicero's ambition, persuading him to stand with him, and to accept the offer of his aid and interest for the consulship.

And now, more than at any other time, Cicero let himself be carried away and deceived, though an old man, by the persuasion of a boy. He joined him in soliciting votes, and procured the good-will of the senate, not without blame at the time on the part of his friends; and he, too, soon enough after, saw that he had ruined himself, and betrayed the liberty of his country. For the young man, once established, and possessed of the office of consul, bade Cicero farewell; and, reconciling himself to Antony and Lepidus, joined his power with theirs, and divided the government, like a piece of property, with them. Thus united, they made a schedule of above two hundred persons who were to be put to death. But the greatest contention in all their debates was on the question of Cicero's case. Antony would come to no conditions, unless he should be the first man to be killed. Lepidus held with Antony, and Cæsar opposed them both. They met secretly and by themselves, for three days together, near the town of Bononia. The spot was not far from the camp, with a river surrounding it. Cæsar, it is said, contended earnestly for Cicero the first two days; but on the third day he yielded, and gave him up. The terms of their mutual concessions were these: that Cæsar should desert Cicero, Lepidus his brother Paulus, and Antony, Lucius Cæsar, his uncle by his mother's side. Thus they let their anger and fury take from them the sense of humanity, and demonstrated that no beast is more savage than man when possessed with power answerable to his rage.

Whilst these things were contriving, Cicero was with his brother at his country-house near Tusculum; whence, hearing of the proscriptions, they determined to pass to Astura, a villa of Cicero's near the sea, and to take shipping from thence for Macedonia to Brutus, of whose strength in that province news had already been heard. They travelled together in their separate litters, overwhelmed with sorrow; and often stopping on the way till their litters came together, condoled with one another. But Quintus was the more disheartened when he reflected on his want of means for his journey; for, as he said, he had brought nothing with him from home. And even Cicero himself had but a slender provision. It was judged, therefore, most expedient that Cicero should make what haste he could to fly, and Quintus return home to provide necessaries, and thus resolved, they mutually embraced, and parted with many tears.

Quintus, within a few days after, betrayed by his servants to those who came to search for him, was slain, together with his young son. But Cicero was carried to Astura, where finding a vessel, he immediately went on board her, and sailed as far as Circæum with a prosperous gale; but when the pilots resolved immediately to set sail from thence, whether fearing the sea, or not wholly distrusting the faith of Cæsar, he went on shore, and passed by land a hundred furlongs, as if he was going for Rome. But losing resolution and changing his mind, he again returned to the sea, and there spent the night in fearful and perplexed thoughts. Sometimes he resolved to go into Cæsar's house privately, and there kill himself upon the altar of his household gods, to bring divine vengeance upon him; but the fear of torture put him off this course. And after passing through a variety of confused and uncertain counsels, at last he let his servants carry him by sea to Capitæ, where he had a house, an agreeable place to retire to in the heat of summer, when the Etesian winds are so pleasant.

There was at that place a chapel of Apollo, not far from the seaside, from which a flight of crows rose with a great noise, and made towards Cicero's vessel, as it rowed to land, and lighting on both sides of the yard, some croaked, others pecked the ends of the ropes. This was looked upon by all as an ill-omen; and, therefore, Cicero went again ashore, and entering his house, lay down upon his bed to compose himself to rest. Many of the crows settled about the window, making a dismal cawing; but one of them alighted upon the bed where Cicero lay covered up, and with its bill by little and little pecked off the clothes from his face. His servants, seeing this, blamed themselves that they should stay to be spectators of their master's murder, and do nothing in his defence, whilst the brute creatures came to assist and take care of him in his undeserved affliction; and therefore, partly by entreaty, partly by force, they took him up, and carried him in his litter towards the seaside.

But in the meantime the assassins were come with a band of soldiers, Herennius, a centurion, and Popillius, a tribune, whom Cicero had formerly defended when prosecuted for the murder of his father. Finding the doors shut, they broke them open, and Cicero not appearing, and those within saying they knew not where he was, it is stated that a youth, who had been educated by Cicero in the liberal arts and sciences, an emancipated slave of his brother Quintus, Philologus by name, informed the tribune that the litter was on its way to the sea through the close and shady walks. The tribune, taking a few with him, ran to the place where he was to come out. And Cicero, perceiving Herennius running in the walks, commanded his servants to set down the litter; and stroking his chin, as he used to do, with his left hand, he looked steadfastly upon his murderers, his person covered with dust, his beard and hair untrimmed, and his face worn with his troubles. So that the greatest part of those that stood by covered their faces whilst Herennius slew him. And thus was he murdered, stretching forth his neck out of the litter, being now in his sixty-fourth year. Herennius cut off his head, and, by Antony's command, his hands also, by which his Philippics were written; for so Cicero styled those orations he wrote against Antony, and so they are called to this day.

When these members of Cicero were brought to Rome, Antony was holding an assembly for the choice of public officers; and when he heard it, and saw them, he cried out, "Now let there be an end of our proscriptions." He commanded his head and hands to be fastened up over the rostra, where the orators spoke; a sight which the Roman people shuddered to behold, and they believed they saw there, not the face of Cicero, but the image of Antony's own soul. And yet amidst these actions he did justice in one thing, by delivering up Philologus to Pomponia, the wife of Quintus; who, having got his body into her power, besides other grievous punishments, made him cut off his own flesh by pieces, and roast and eat it; for so some writers have related. But Tiro, Cicero's emancipated slave, has not so much as mentioned the treachery of Philologus.

Some long time after, Cæsar, I have been told, visiting one of his daughter's sons, found him with a book of Cicero's in his hand. The boy for fear endeavoured to hide it under his gown; which Cæsar perceiving, took it from him, and, turning over a great part of the book standing, gave it him again, and said, "My child, this was a learned man, and a lover of his country." And immediately after he had vanquished Antony, being then consul, he made Cicero's son his colleague in the office; and under that consulship the senate took down all the statues of Antony, and abolished all the other honours that had been given him, and decreed that none of that family should thereafter bear the name of Marcus; and thus the final acts of the punishment of Antony were, by the divine powers, devolved upon the family of Cicero.

THE COMPARISON OF DEMOSTHENES AND CICERO

THESE are the most memorable circumstances recorded in history of Demosthenes and Cicero which have come to our knowledge. But omitting an exact comparison of their respective faculties in speaking, yet thus much seems fit to be said; that Demosthenes, to make himself a master in rhetoric, applied all the faculties he had, natural or acquired, wholly that way that he far surpassed in force and strength of eloquence all his contemporaries in political and judicial speaking, in grandeur and majesty all the panegyrical orators, and in accuracy and science all the logicians and rhetoricians of his day; that Cicero was highly educated, and by his diligent study became a most accomplished general scholar in all these branches, having left behind him numerous philosophical treatises of his own on Academic principles; as, indeed, even in his written speeches, both political and judicial, we see him continually trying to show his learning by the way. And one may discover the different temper of each of them in their speeches. For Demosthenes's oratory was without all embellishment and jesting, wholly composed for real effect and seriousness; not smelling of the lamp, as Pytheas scoffingly said, but of the temperance, thoughtfulness, austerity, and grave earnestness of his temper. Whereas Cicero's love of mockery often ran him into scurrility; and in his love of laughing away serious arguments in judicial cases by jests and facetious remarks, with a view to the advantage of his clients, he paid too little regard to what was decent: saying, for example, in his defence of Cælius, that he had done no absurd thing in such plenty and affluence to indulge himself in pleasures, it being a kind of madness not to enjoy the things we possess, especially since the most eminent philosophers have asserted pleasures to be the chiefest good. So also we are told that when Cicero, being consul, undertook the defence of Murena against Cato's prosecution, by way of bantering Cato, he made a long series of jokes upon the absurd *paradoxes,* as they are called, of the Stoic set; so that a loud laughter passing from the crowd to the judges, Cato, with a quiet smile, said to those that sat next him, "My friends, what an amusing consul we have."

And, indeed, Cicero was by natural temper very much disposed to mirth and pleasantry, and always appeared with a smiling and serene countenance. But Demosthenes had constant care and thoughtfulness in his look, and a serious anxiety, which he seldom, if ever, laid aside; and therefore, was accounted by his enemies, as he himself confessed, morose and ill-mannered.

Also, it is very evident, out of their several writings, that Demosthenes never touched upon his own praises but decently and without offence when there was need of it, and for some weightier end; but upon other occasions modestly and sparingly. But Cicero's immeasurable boasting of himself in his orations argues him guilty of an uncontrollable appetite for distinction, his cry being evermore that arms should give place to the gown, and the soldier's laurel to the tongue. And at last we find him extolling not only his deeds and actions, but his orations also, as well those that were only spoken, as those that were published; as if he were engaged in a boyish trial of skill, who should speak best, with the rhetoricians, Isocrates and Anaximenes, not as one who could claim the task to guide and instruct the Roman nation, the—

"Soldier full-armed, terrific to the foe."

It is necessary, indeed, for a political leader to be an able speaker; but it is an ignoble thing for any man to admire and relish the glory of his own eloquence. And, in this matter, Demosthenes had a more than ordinary gravity and magnificence of mind, accounting his talent in speaking nothing more than a mere accomplishment and matter of practice, the success of which must depend greatly on the good-will and candour of his hearers, and regarding those who pride themselves on such accounts to be men of a low and petty disposition.

The power of persuading and governing the people did, indeed, equally belong to both, so that those who had armies and camps at command stood in need of their assistance; as Charas, Diopithes, and Leosthenes of Demosthenes's, Pompey and young Cæsar of Cicero's, as the latter himself admits in his Memoirs addressed to Agrippa and Mæcenas. But what are thought and commonly said most to demonstrate and try the tempers of men, namely, authority and place, by moving every passion, and discovering every frailty, these are things which Demosthenes never received; nor was he ever in a position to give such proof of himself, having never obtained any eminent office, nor led any of those armies into the field against Philip which he raised by his eloquence. Cicero, on the other hand, was sent quæstor into Sicily, and proconsul into Cilicia and Cappadocia, at a time when avarice was at the height, and the commanders and governors who were employed abroad, as though they thought it a mean thing to steal, set themselves to seize by open force; so that it seemed no heinous matter to take bribes, but he that did it most moderately was in good esteem. And yet he, at this time, gave the most abundant proofs alike of his contempt of riches and of his humanity and good-nature. And at Rome, when he was created consul in name, but indeed received sovereign and dictatorial authority against Catiline and his conspirators, he attested the truth of Plato's prediction, that then the miseries of states would be at an end when, by a happy fortune, supreme power, wisdom, and justice should be united in one.

It is said, to the reproach of Demosthenes, that his eloquence was mercenary; that he privately made orations for Phormion and Apollodorus, though adversaries in the same cause; that he was charged with moneys received from the King of Persia, and condemned for bribes from Harpalus. And should we grant that all those (and they are not few) who have made these statements against him have spoken what is untrue, yet that Demosthenes was not the character to look without desire on the presents offered him out of respect and gratitude by royal persons, and that one who lent money on maritime usury was likely to be thus indifferent, is what we cannot assert. But that Cicero refused, from the Sicilians when he was quæstor, from the King of Cappadocia when he was proconsul, and from his friends at Rome when he was in exile, many presents, though urged to receive them, has been said already.

Moreover, Demosthenes's banishment was infamous, upon conviction for bribery; Cicero's very honourable, for ridding his country of a set of villains. Therefore, when Demosthenes fled his country, no man regarded it; for Cicero's sake the senate changed their habit, and put on mourning, and would not be persuaded to make any act before Cicero's return was decreed. Cicero, however, passed his exile idly in Macedonia. But the very exile of Demosthenes made up a great part of the services he did for his country; for he went through the cities of Greece, and everywhere, as we have said, joined in the conflict on behalf of the Grecians; driving out the Macedonian ambassadors, and approving himself a much better citizen than Themistocles and Alcibiades did in the like fortune. And, after his return, he again devoted himself to the same public service and continued firm to his opposition to Antipater and the Macedonians. Whereas Lælius reproached Cicero in the senate for sitting silent when Cæsar, a beardless youth, asked leave to come forward, contrary to the law, as a candidate for the consulship; and Brutus, in his epistles, charges him with nursing and rearing a greater and more heavy tyranny than that they had removed.

Finally, Cicero's death excites our pity; for an old man to be miserably carried up and down by his servants, flying and hiding himself from that death which was, in the course of nature, so near at hand; and yet at last to be murdered. Demosthenes, though he seemed at first a little to supplicate, yet, by his preparing and keeping the poison by him, demands our admiration; and still more admirable was his using it. When the temple of the god no longer afforded him a sanctuary, he took refuge, as it were, at a mightier altar, freeing himself from arms and soldiers, and laughing to scorn the cruelty of Antipater.

DEMETRIUS

INGENIOUS men have long observed a resemblance between the arts and the bodily senses. And they were first led to do so, I think, by noticing the way in which, both in the arts and with our senses, we examine opposites. Judgment once obtained, the use to which we put it differs in the two cases. Our senses are not meant to pick out black rather than white, to prefer sweet to bitter, or soft and yielding to hard and resisting objects; all they have to do is to receive impressions as they occur, and report to the understanding the impressions as received. The arts, on the other hand, which reason institutes expressly to choose and obtain some suitable, and to refuse and get rid of some unsuitable object, have their proper concern in the consideration of the former; though, in a casual and contingent way, they must also, for the very rejection of them, pay attention to the latter. Medicine, to produce health, has to examine disease, and music, to create harmony, must investigate discord; and the supreme arts, of temperance, of justice, and of wisdom, as they are acts of judgment and selection, exercised not on good and just and expedient only, but also on wicked, unjust, and inexpedient objects, do not give their commendations to the mere innocence whose boast is its inexperience of evil, and whose truer name is, by their award, simpleness and ignorance of what all men who live aright should know. The ancient Spartans, at their festivals, used to force their Helots to swallow large quantities of raw wine, and then expose them at the public tables, to let the young men see what it is to be drunk. And, though I do not think it consistent with humanity or with civil justice to correct one man's morals by corrupting those of another, yet we may, I think, avail ourselves of the cases of those who have fallen into indiscretions, and have, in high stations, made themselves conspicuous for misconduct; and I shall not do ill to introduce a pair or two of such examples among these biographies, not, assuredly, to amuse and divert my readers, or give variety to my theme, but as Ismenias, the Theban, used to show his scholars good and bad performers on the flute, and to tell them, "You should play like this man," and, "You should not play like that," and as Antigenidas used to say, young people would take greater pleasure in hearing good playing, if first they were set to hear bad, so, in the same manner, it seems to me likely enough that we shall be all the more zealous and more emulous to read, observe, and imitate the better lives, if we are not left in ignorance of the blameworthy and the bad.

For this reason, the following book contains the lives of Demetrius

Poliorcetes and Antonius the Triumvir; two persons who have abundantly justified the words of Plato, that great natures produce great vices as well as virtues. Both alike were amorous and intemperate, warlike and munificent, sumptuous in their way of living and overbearing in their manners. And the likeness of their fortunes carried out the resemblance in their characters. Not only were their lives each a series of great successes and great disasters, mighty acquisitions and tremendous losses of power, sudden overthrows followed by unexpected recoveries, but they died, also, Demetrius in actual captivity to his enemies and Antony on the verge of it.

Antigonus had by his wife, Stratonice, the daughter of Corrhæus, two sons; the one of whom, after the name of his uncle, he called Demetrius, the other had that of his grandfather Philip, and died young. This is the most general account, although some have related that Demetrius was not the son of Antigonus, but of his brother; and that his own father dying young, and his mother being afterwards married to Antigonus, he was accounted to be his son.

Demetrius had not the height of his father Antigonus, though he was a tall man. But his countenance was one of such singular beauty and expression that no painter or sculptor ever produced a good likeness of him. It combined grace and strength, dignity with boyish bloom, and, in the midst of youthful heat and passion, what was hardest of all to represent was a certain heroic look and air of kingly greatness. Nor did his character belie his looks, as no one was better able to render himself both loved and feared. For as he was the most easy and agreeable of companions, and the most luxurious and delicate of princes in his drinking and banqueting and daily pleasures, so in action there was never any one that showed a more vehement persistence, or a more passionate energy. Bacchus, skilled in the conduct of war, and after war in giving peace its pleasures and joys, seems to have been his pattern among the gods.

He was wonderfully fond of his father Antigonus; and the tenderness he had for his mother led him, for her sake, to redouble attentions, which it was evident were not so much owing to fear or duty as to the more powerful motives of inclination. It is reported that, returning one day from hunting, he went immediately into the apartment of Antigonus, who was conversing with some ambassadors, and after stepping up and kissing his father, he sat down by him, just as he was, still holding in his hand the javelins which he had brought with him. Whereupon Antigonus, who had just dismissed the ambassadors with their answer, called out in a loud voice to them, as they were going, "Mention, also, that this is the way in which we two live together;" as if to imply to them that it was no slender mark of the power and security of his government that there was so perfect good understanding between himself and his son. Such an unsociable, solitary thing is power, and so much of jealousy and distrust in it, that the first and greatest of the successors of Alexander could make it a thing of glory in that he was not so afraid of his son as to forbid his standing beside him with a weapon in his hand. And, in fact, among all the successors of Alexander, that of Antigonus was the only house which, for many descents, was exempted from crime of this kind; or to state it exactly, Philip was the only one of this family who was guilty of a son's death. All the other families, we may fairly say, afforded frequent examples of fathers who brought their children, husbands their wives, children their mothers, to untimely ends; and that brothers should put brothers to death was assumed, like the postulate of mathematicians as the common and recognised royal first principle of safety.

Let us here record an example in the early life of Demetrius, showing his natural humane and kindly disposition. It was an adventure which passed betwixt him and Mithridates, the son of Ariobarzanes, who was about the same age with Demetrius, and lived with him, in attendance on Antigonus; and although nothing was said or could be said to his reproach, he fell under suspicion, in consequence of a dream which Antigonus had. Antigonus thought himself in a fair and spacious field, where he sowed golden seed, and saw presently a golden crop come up; of which, however, looking presently again, he saw nothing remain but the stubble, without the ears. And as he stood by in anger and vexation, he heard some voices saying Mithridates had cut the golden harvest and carried it off into Pontus. Antigonus, much discomposed with his dream, first bound his son, by an oath not to speak, and then related it to him, adding that he had resolved, in consequence, to lose no time in ridding himself of Mithridates, and making away with him. Demetrius was extremely distressed; and when the young man came, as usual, to pass his time with him, to keep his oath he forbore from saying a word, but, drawing him aside little by little from the company, as soon as they were by themselves, without opening his lips, with the point of his javelin he traced before him the words "Fly, Mithridates." Mithridates took the hint, and fled by night into Cappadocia, where Antigonus's dream about him was quickly brought to its due fulfilment; for he got possession of a large and fertile territory; and from him descended the line of the kings of Pontus, which, in the eighth generation, was reduced by the Romans. This may serve for a specimen of the early goodness and love of justice that was part of Demetrius's natural character.

But as in the elements of the world, Empedocles tells us, out of liking and dislike, there springs up contention and warfare, and all the more, the closer the contact, or the nearer the approach of the objects, even so the perpetual hostilities among the successors of Alexander were aggravated and inflamed, in particular cases, by juxtaposition of interests and of territories; as, for example, in the case of Antigonus and Ptolemy. News came to Antigonus that Ptolemy had crossed from Cyprus and invaded Syria, and was ravaging the country and reducing the cities. Remaining, therefore, himself in Phrygia, he sent Demetrius, now twenty-two years old, to make his first essay as sole commander in an important charge. He, whose youthful heat outran his experience, advancing against an adversary trained in Alexander's school, and practised in many encounters, incurred a great defeat near the town of Gaza, in which eight thousand of his men were taken and five thousand killed. His own tent, also his money, and all his private effects and furniture, were captured. These, however, Ptolemy sent back, together with his friends, accompanying them with the humane and courteous message, that they were not fighting for anything else but honour and dominion. Demetrius accepted the gift, praying only to the gods not to leave him long in Ptolemy's debt, but to let him have an early chance of doing the like to him. He took his disaster, also with the temper, not of a boy defeated in his attempt, but of an old and long-tried general familiar with reverse of fortune; he busied himself in collecting his men, replenishing his magazines, watching the allegiance of the cities, and drilling his new recruits.

Antigonus received the news of the battle with the remark that Ptolemy had beaten boys and would now have to fight with men. But not to humble the spirit of his son, he acceded to his request, and left him to command on the next occasion.

Not long after, Cilles, Ptolemy's lieutenant, with a powerful army, took the field, and looking upon Demetrius as already defeated by the previous battle, he had in his imagination driven him out of Syria before he saw him. But he quickly found himself deceived; for Demetrius came so unexpectedly upon him that he surprised both the general and his army, making him and seven thousand of the soldiers prisoners of war, and possessing himself of a large amount of treasure. But his joy in the victory was not so much for the prizes he should keep, as for those he could restore; and his thankfulness was less for the wealth and glory than for the means it gave him of requiting his enemy's former generosity. He did not, however, take it into his own hands, but wrote to his father. And on receiving leave to do as he liked, he sent back to Ptolemy Cilles and his friends, loaded with presents. This defeat drove Ptolemy out of Syria, and brought Antigonus from Calænæ to enjoy the victory and the sight of the son who had gained it.

Soon after, Demetrius was sent to bring the Nabathæan Arabs into obedience. And here he got into a district without water, and incurred considerable danger, but by his resolute and composed demeanour he overawed the barbarians, and returned after receiving from them a large amount of booty and seven hundred camels. Not long after, Seleucus, whom Antigonus had formerly chased out of Babylon, but who had afterwards recovered his dominion by his own efforts and maintained himself in it, went with large forces on an expedition to reduce the tribes on the confines of India and the provinces near Mount Caucasus. And Demetrius, conjecturing that he had left Mesopotamia but slenderly guarded in his absence, suddenly passed the Euphrates with his army and made his way into Babylonia unexpectedly; when he succeeded in capturing one of the two citadels, out of which he expelled the garrison of Seleucus, and placed in it seven thousand men of his own. And after allowing his soldiers to enrich themselves with all the spoil they could carry with them out of the country, he retired to the sea, leaving Seleucus more securely master of his dominions than before, as he seemed by this conduct to abandon every claim to a country which he treated like an enemy's. However, by a rapid advance, he rescued Halicarnassus from Ptolemy, who was besieging it. The glory which this act obtained them inspired both the father and son with a wonderful desire for freeing Greece, which Cassander and Ptolemy had everywhere reduced to slavery. No nobler or juster war was undertaken by any of the kings; the wealth they had gained while humbling, with Greek assistance, the barbarians, being thus employed, for honour's sake and good repute, in helping the Greeks. When the resolution was taken to begin their attempt with Athens, one of his friends told Antigonus, if they captured Athens, they must keep it safe in their own hands, as by this gangway they might step out from their ships into Greece when they pleased. But Antigonus would not hear of it; he did not want a better or a steadier gangway than people's good-will; and from Athens, the beacon of the world, the news of their conduct would soon be handed on to all the world's inhabitants. So Demetrius, with a sum of five thousand talents, and a fleet of two hundred and fifty ships, set sail for Athens, where Demetrius the Phalerian was governing the city for Cassander, with a garrison lodged in the port of Munychia. By good fortune and skilful management he appeared before Piræus, on the twenty-sixth of Thargelion, before anything had been heard of him. Indeed, when his ships were seen, they were taken for Ptolemy's and preparations were commenced for receiving them; till at last, the generals discovering their mistake, hurried down, and all was alarm and confusion, and attempts to push forward preparations to oppose the landing of this hostile force. For Demetrius, having found the entrances of the port undefended, stood in directly, and was by this time safely inside, before the eyes of everybody, and made signals from his ship, requesting a peaceful hearing. And on leave being given, he caused a herald with a loud voice to make proclamation that he was come thither by the command of his father, with no other design than what he prayed the gods to prosper with success, to give the Athenians their liberty, to expel the garrison, and to restore the ancient laws and constitution of the country.

The people, hearing this, at once threw down their shields, and clapping their hands, with loud acclamations entreated Demetrius to land, calling him their deliverer and benefactor. And the Phalerian and his party, who saw that there was nothing for it but to receive the conqueror, whether he should perform his promises or not, sent, however, messengers to beg for his protection; to whom Demetrius gave a kind reception, and sent back with them Aristodemus of Miletus, one of his father's friends. The Phalerian, under the change of government, was more afraid of his fellow-citizens than of the enemy; but Demetrius took precautions for him, and out of respect for his reputation and character, sent him with a safe conduct to Thebes, whither he desired to go. For himself, he declared he would not, in spite of all his curiosity, put his foot in the city till he had completed his deliverance by driving out the garrison. So blockading Munychia with a palisade and trench, he sailed off to attack Megara, where also there was one of Cassander's garrisons. But, hearing that Cratesipolis, the wife of Alexander, son of Polysperchon, who was famous for her beauty, was well disposed to see him, he left his troops near Megara, and set out with a few light-armed attendants for Patræ, where she was now staying. And, quitting these also, he pitched his tent apart from everybody, that the woman might pay her visit without being seen. This some of the enemy perceived, and suddenly attacked him; and, in his alarm, he was obliged to disguise himself in a shabby cloak, and run for it, narrowly escaping the shame of being made a prisoner, in reward for his foolish passion. And as it was, his tent and money were taken. Megara, however, surrendered, and would have been pillaged by the soldiers, but for the urgent intercession of the Athenians. The garrison was driven out, and the city restored to independence. While he was occupied in this, he remembered that Stilpo, the philosopher, famous for his choice of a life of tranquillity was residing here. He, therefore, sent for him, and begged to know whether anything belonging to him had been taken. "No," replied Stilpo, "I have not met with any one to take away knowledge." Pretty nearly all the servants in the city had been stolen away; and so, when Demetrius, renewing his courtesies to Stilpo, on taking leave of him, said, "I leave your city, Stilpo, a city of freemen." "Certainly," replied Stilpo, "there is not one serving man left among us all."

Returning from Megara, he sat down before the citadel of Munychia which in a few days he took by assault, and caused the fortifications to be demolished; and thus having accomplished his design, upon the request and invitation of the Athenians he made his entrance into the upper city, where, causing the people to be summoned, he publicly announced to them that their ancient constitution was restored, and that they should receive from his father, Antigonus, a present of one hundred and fifty thousand measures of wheat, and such a supply of timber as would enable them to build a hundred galleys. In this manner did the Athenians recover their popular institutions, after the space of fifteen years from the time of the war of Lamia and the battle before Cranon, during which interval of time the government had been administered nominally as an oligarchy, but really by a single man, Demetrius the Phalerian being so powerful. But the excessive honours which the Athenians bestowed, for these noble and generous acts upon Demetrius, created offence and disgust. The Athenians were the first who gave Antigonus and Demetrius the title of kings, which hitherto they had made it a point of piety to decline, as the one remaining royal honour still reserved for the lineal descendants of Philip and Alexander, in which none but they could venture to participate. Another name which they received from no people but the Athenians was that of the Tutelar Deities and Deliverers. And to enhance this flattery, by a common vote it was decreed to change the style of the city, and not to have the years named any longer from the annual archon; a priest of the two Tutelary Divinities, who was to be yearly chosen, was to have this honour, and all public acts and instruments were to bear their date by his name. They decreed, also, that the figures of Antigonus and Demetrius should be woven, with those of the gods, into the pattern of the great robe. They consecrated the spot where Demetrius first alighted from his chariot, and built an altar there, with the name of the Altar of the Descent of Demetrius. They created two new tribes, calling them after the names of these princes, the Antigonid and the Demetriad; and to the Council, which consisted of five hundred persons, fifty being chosen out of every tribe, they added one hundred more to represent these new tribes. But the wildest proposal was one made by Stratocles, the great inventor of all these ingenious and exquisite compliments, enacting that the members of any deputation that the city should send to Demetrius or Antigonus should have the same title as those sent to Delphi or Olympia for the performance of the national sacrifices in behalf of the state at the great Greek festivals. This Stratocles was, in all respects, an audacious and abandoned character, and seemed to have made it his object to copy, by his buffoonery and impertinence, Cleon's old familiarity with the people. His mistress, Phylacion, one day bringing him a dish of brains and neckbones for his dinner, "Oh," said he, "I am to dine upon the things which we statesmen play at ball with." At another time, when the Athenians received their naval defeat near Amorgos, he hastened home before the news could reach the city, and having a chaplet on his head, came riding through the Ceramicus, announcing that they had won a victory, and moved a vote for thanksgivings to the gods, and a distribution of meat among the people in their tribes. Presently after came those who brought home the wrecks from the battle; and when the people exclaimed at what he had done, he came boldly to face the outcry, and asked what harm there had been in giving them two days' pleasure.

Such was Stratocles. And, "adding flame to fire," as Aristophanes says, there was one who, to outdo Stratocles, proposed that it should be decreed that, whensoever Demetrius should honour their city with his presence, they should treat him with the same show of hospitable entertainment with which Ceres and Bacchus are received; and the citizen who exceeded the rest in the splendour and costliness of his reception should have a sum of money granted him from the public purse to make a sacred offering. Finally, they changed the name of the month of Munychion, and called it Demetrion; they gave the name of the Demetrion to the odd day between the end of the old and the beginning of the new month; and turned the feast of Bacchus, the Dionysia, into the Demetria or feast of Demetrius. Most of these changes were marked by the divine displeasure. The sacred robe, in which, according to their decree, the figures of Demetrius and Antigonus had been woven with those of Jupiter and Minerva, was caught by a violent gust of wind, while the procession was conveying it through the Ceramicus, and was torn from the top to the bottom. A crop of hemlock, a plant which scarcely grew anywhere, even in the country thereabouts, sprang up in abundance round the altars which they had erected to these new divinities. They had to omit the solemn procession at the feast of Bacchus, as upon the very day of its celebration there was such a severe and rigorous frost, coming quite out of its time, that not only the vines and figtrees were killed, but almost all the wheat was destroyed in the blade. Accordingly, Philippides, an enemy to Stratocles, attacked him in a comedy, in the following verses:—

"He for whom frosts that nipped your vines were sent,
And for whose sins the holy robe was rent,
Who grants to men the gods' own honours, he,
Not the poor stage, is now the people's enemy."

Philippides was a great favourite with King Lysimachus, from whom the Athenians received, for his sake, a variety of kindnesses. Lysimachus went so far as to think it a happy omen to meet or see Philippides at the outset of any enterprise or expedition. And, in general, he was well thought of for his own character, as a plain, uninterfering person, with none of the officious, self-important habits of a court. Once, when Lysimachus was solicitous to show him kindness, and asked what he had that he could make him a present of, "Anything," replied Philippides, "but your state secrets." The stage-player, we thought, deserved a place in our narrative quite as well as the public speaker.

But that which exceeded all the former follies and flatteries was the proposal of Dromoclides of Sphettus; who, when there was a debate about sending to the Delphic Oracle to inquire the proper course for the consecration of certain bucklers, moved in the assembly that they should rather send to receive an oracle from Demetrius. I will transcribe the very words of the order, which was in these terms: "May it be happy and propitious. The people of Athens have decreed, that a fit person shall be chosen among the Athenian citizens, who shall be deputed to be sent to the Deliverer and after he hath duly performed the sacrifices, shall inquire of the Deliverer, in what most religious and decent manner he will please to direct, at the earliest possible time, the consecration of the bucklers; and according to the answer the people shall act." With this befooling they completed the perversion of a mind which even before was not so strong or sound as it should have been.

During his present leisure in Athens, he took to wife Eurydice, a descendant of the ancient Miltiades, who had been married to Opheltas, the ruler of Cyrene, and after his death had come back to Athens. The Athenians took the marriage as a compliment and favour to the city. But Demetrius was very free in these matters, and was the husband of several wives at once; the highest place and honour among all being retained by Phila, who was Antipater's daughter, and had been the wife of Craterus, the one of all the successors of Alexander who left behind him the strongest feelings of attachment among the Macedonians. And for these reasons Antigonus had obliged him to marry her, notwithstanding the disparity of their years, Demetrius being quite a youth, and she much older; and when upon that account he made some difficulty in complying, Antigonus whispered in his ear the maxim from Euripides, broadly substituting a new word for the original, *serve*—

> "Natural or not,
> A man must *wed* where profit will be got."

Any respect, however, which he showed either to Phila or to his other wives did not go so far as to prevent him from consorting with any number of mistresses, and bearing, in this respect, the worst character of all the princes of his time.

A summons now arrived from his father, ordering him to go and fight with Ptolemy in Cyprus, which he was obliged to obey, sorry as he was to abandon Greece. And in quitting this nobler and more glorious enterprise, he sent to Cleonides, Ptolemy's general, who was holding garrisons in Sicyon and Corinth, offering him money to let the cities be independent. But on his refusal, he set sail hastily, taking additional forces with him, and made for Cyprus; where, immediately upon his arrival, he fell upon Menelaus, the brother of Ptolemy, and gave him a defeat. But when Ptolemy himself came in person, with large forces both on land and sea, for some little time nothing took place beyond an interchange of menaces and lofty talk. Ptolemy bade Demetrius sail off before the whole armament came up, if he did not wish to be trampled under foot; and Demetrius offered to let him retire, on condition of his withdrawing his garrisons from Sicyon and Corinth. And not they alone, but all the other potentates and princes of the time, were in anxiety for the uncertain impending issue of the conflict; as it seemed evident that the conqueror's prize would be, not Cyprus or Syria, but the absolute supremacy.

Ptolemy had brought a hundred and fifty galleys with him, and gave orders to Menelaus to sally, in the heat of the battle, out of the harbour of Salamis, and attack with sixty ships the rear of Demetrius. Demetrius, however, opposing to these sixty ten of his galleys, which were a sufficient number to block up the narrow entrance of the harbour, and drawing out his land forces along all the headlands running out into sea, went into action with a hundred and eighty galleys, and, attacking with the utmost boldness and impetuosity, utterly routed Ptolemy, who fled with eight ships, the sole remnant of his fleet, seventy having been taken with all their men, and the rest destroyed in the battle; while the whole multitude of attendants, friends, and women, that had followed in the ships of burden, all the arms, treasure, and military engines fell, without exception, into the hands of Demetrius, and were by him collected and brought into the camp. Among the prisoners was the celebrated Lamia, famed at one time for her skill on the flute, and afterwards renowned as a mistress. And although now upon the wane of her youthful beauty, and though Demetrius was much her junior, she exercised over him so great a charm that all other women seemed to be amorous of Demetrius, but Demetrius amorous only of Lamia. After this signal victory, Demetrius came before Salamis; and Menelaus, unable to make any resistance, surrendered himself and all his fleet, twelve hundred horse, and twelve thousand foot, together with the place. But that which added more than all to the glory and splendour of the success was the humane and generous conduct of Demetrius to the vanquished. For, after he had given honourable funerals to the dead, he bestowed liberty upon the living; and that he might not forget the Athenians, he sent them, as a present, complete arms for twelve hundred men.

To carry this happy news, Aristodemus of Miletus, the most perfect flatterer belonging to the court, was despatched to Antigonus; and he, to enhance the welcome message, was resolved, it would appear, to make his most successful effort. When he crossed from Cyprus, he bade the galley which conveyed him to come to anchor off the land; and, having ordered all the ship's crew to remain aboard, he took the boat, and was set ashore alone. Thus he proceeded to Antigonus, who, one may well imagine, was in suspense enough about the issue, and suffered all the anxieties natural to men engaged in so perilous a struggle. And when he heard that Aristodemus was coming alone, it put him into yet greater trouble; he could scarcely forbear from going out to meet him himself; he sent messenger on messenger, and friend after friend, to inquire what news. But Aristodemus, walking gravely and with a settled countenance, without making any answer, still proceeded quietly onward; until Antigonus, quite alarmed and no longer able to refrain, got up and met him at the gate, whither he came with a crowd of anxious followers now collected and running after him. As soon as he saw Antigonus within hearing stretching out his hands, he accosted him with the loud exclamation, "Hail, King Antigonus! we have defeated Ptolemy by sea, and have taken Cyprus and sixteen thousand eight hundred prisoners." "Welcome, Aristodemus," replied Antigonus, "but, as you chose to torture us so long for your good news, you may wait awhile for the reward of it."

Upon this the people around gave Antigonus and Demetrius, for the first time, the title of kings. His friends at once set a diadem on the head of Antigonus; and he sent one presently to his son, with a letter addressed to him as King Demetrius. And when this news was told in Egypt, that they might not seem to be dejected with the late defeat, Ptolemy's followers also took occasion to bestow the style of king upon him; and the rest of the successors of Alexander were quick to follow the example. Lysimachus began to wear the diadem, and Seleucus, who had before received the name in all addresses from the barbarians, now also took it upon him in all business with the Greeks, Cassander still retained his usual superscription in his letters, but others, both in writing and speaking, gave him the royal title. Nor was this the mere accession of a name, or introduction of a new fashion. The men's own sentiments about themselves were disturbed, and their feelings elevated; a spirit of pomp and arrogance passed into their habits of life and conversation, as a tragic actor on the stage modifies, with a change of dress, his steps, his voice, his motions in sitting down, his manner in addressing another. The punishments they inflicted were more violent after they had thus laid aside that modest style under which they formerly dissembled their power, and the influence of which had often made them gentler and less exacting to their subjects. A single flattering voice effected a revolution in the world.

Antigonus, extremely elevated with the success of his arms in Cyprus, under the conduct of Demetrius, resolved to push on his good fortune, and to lead his forces in person against Ptolemy by land whilst Demetrius should coast with a great fleet along the shore, to assist him by sea. The issue of the contest was intimated in a dream which Medius, a friend of Antigonus, had at this time in his sleep. He thought he saw Antigonus and his whole army running, as if it had been a race; that, in the first part of the course, he went off showing great strength and speed; gradually, however, his pace slackened, and at the end he saw him come lagging up, tired and almost breathless and quite spent. Antigonus himself met with many difficulties by land; and Demetrius, encountering a great storm at sea, was driven, with the loss of many of his ships, upon a dangerous coast without a harbour. So the expedition returned without effecting anything. Antigonus, now nearly eighty years old, was no longer well able to go through the fatigues of a marching campaign, though rather on account of his great size and corpulence than from loss of strength; and for this reason he left things to his son, whose fortune and experience appeared sufficient for all undertakings, and whose luxury and expense and revelry gave him no concern. For though in peace he vented himself in pleasures, and, when there was nothing to do, ran headlong into any excesses, in war he was as sober and abstemious as the most temperate character. The story is told that once, after Lamia had gained open supremacy over him, the old man, when Demetrius coming home from abroad began to kiss him with unusual warmth, asked him if he took him for Lamia. At another time, Demetrius, after spending several days in a debauch, excused himself for his absence, by saying he had had a violent flux. "So I heard," replied Antigonus; "was it of Thasian wine, or Chian?" Once he was told his son was ill, and went to see him. At the door he met some young beauty. Going in, he sat down by the bed and took his pulse. "The fever," said Demetrius, "has just left me." "Oh yes," replied the father, "I met it going out at the door." Demetrius's great actions made Antigonus treat him thus easily. The Scythians in their drinking-bouts twang their bows, to keep their courage awake amidst the dreams of indulgence; but he would resign his whole being, now to pleasure, and now to action; and though he never let thoughts of the one intrude upon the pursuit of the other, yet when the time came for preparing for war, he showed as much capacity as any man.

And indeed his ability displayed itself even more in preparing for than in conducting a war. He thought he could never be too well supplied for every possible occasion, and took a pleasure, not to be satiated, in great improvements in ship-building and machines. He did not waste his natural genius and power of mechanical research on toys and idle fancies, turning, painting, and playing on the flute, like some kings, Æropus, for example, King of Macedon, who spent his days in making small lamps and tables; or Attalus Philometor, whose amusement was to cultivate poisons, henbane and hellebore, and even hemlock, aconite, and dorycnium, which he used to sow himself in the royal gardens, and made it his business to gather the fruits and collect the juices in their season. The Parthian kings took a pride in whetting and sharpening with their own hands the points of their arrows and javelins. But when Demetrius played the workman, it was like a king, and there was magnificence in his handicraft. The articles he produced bore marks upon the face of them not of ingenuity only, but of a great mind and a lofty purpose. They were such as a king might not only design and pay for, but use his own hands to make; and while friends might be terrified with their greatness, enemies could be charmed with their beauty; a phrase which is not so pretty to the ear as it is true to the fact. The very people against whom they were to be employed could not forbear running to gaze with admiration upon his galleys of five and six ranges of oars, as they passed along their coasts; and the inhabitants of besieged cities came on their walls to see the spectacles of his famous *City-takers.* Even Lysimachus, of all the kings of his time the greatest enemy of Demetrius, coming to raise the siege of Soli in Cilicia, sent first to desire permission to see his galleys and engines, and, having had his curiosity gratified by a view of them, expressed his admiration and quitted the place. The Rhodians, also, whom he long besieged, begged him, when they concluded a peace, to let them have some of his engines, which they might preserve as a memorial at once of his power and of their own brave resistance.

The quarrel between him and the Rhodians was on account of their being allies to Ptolemy, and in the siege the greatest of all the engines was planted against their walls. The base of it was exactly square, each side containing twenty-four cubits; it rose to a height of thirty-three cubits, growing narrower from the base to the top. Within were several apartments or chambers, which were to be filled with armed men, and in every story the front towards the enemy had windows for discharging missiles of all sorts, the whole being filled with soldiers for every description of fighting. And what was most wonderful was that, notwithstanding its size, when it was moved it never tottered or inclined to one side, but went forward on its base in perfect equilibrium, with a loud noise and great impetus, astounding the minds, and yet at the same time charming the eyes of all the beholders.

Whilst Demetrius was at this same siege, there were brought to him two iron cuirasses from Cyprus, weighing each of them on more than forty pounds, and Zoilus, who had forged them, to show the excellence of their temper, desired that one of them might be tried with a catapult missile, shot out of one of the engines at no greater distance than six-and-twenty paces; and, upon the experiment, it was found that though the dart exactly hit the cuirass, yet it made no greater impression than such a slight scratch as might be made with the point of a style or graver. Demetrius took this for his own wearing, and gave the other to Alcimus the Epirot, the best soldier and strongest man of all his captains, the only one who used to wear armour to the weight of two talents, one talent being the weight which others thought sufficient. He fell during this siege in a battle near the theatre.

The Rhodians made a brave defence, insomuch that Demetrius saw he was making but little progress, and only persisted out of obstinacy and passion; and the rather because the Rhodians, having captured a ship in which some clothes and furniture, with letters from herself, were coming to him from Phila his wife, had sent on everything to Ptolemy, and had not copied the honourable example of the Athenians, who, having surprised an express sent from King Philip, their enemy, opened all the letters he was charged with, excepting only those directed to Queen Olympias, which they returned with the seal unbroken. Yet, although greatly provoked, Demetrius, into whose power it shortly after came to repay the affront, would not suffer himself to retaliate. Protogenes the Caunian had been making them a painting of the story of Ialysus, which was all but completed, when it was taken by Demetrius in one of the suburbs. The Rhodians sent a herald begging him to be pleased to spare the work and not let it be destroyed; Demetrius's answer to which was that he would rather burn the pictures of his father than a piece of art which had cost so much labour. It is said to have taken Protogenes seven years to paint, and they tell us that Apelles, when he first saw it, was struck dumb with wonder, and called it, on recovering his speech, "a great labour and a wonderful success," adding, however, that it had not the graces which carried his own paintings as it were up to the heavens. This picture, which came with the rest in the general mass to Rome, there perished by fire.

While the Rhodians were thus defending their city to the utmost, Demetrius, who was not sorry for an excuse to retire, found one in the arrival of ambassadors from Athens, by whose mediation terms were made that the Rhodians should bind themselves to aid Antigonus and Demetrius against all enemies, Ptolemy excepted.

The Athenians entreated his help against Cassander, who was besieging the city. So he went thither with a fleet of three hundred and thirty ships, and many soldiers; and not only drove Cassander out of Attica, but pursued him as far as Thermopylæ, routed him and became master of Heraclea, which came over to him voluntarily, and of a body of six thousand Macedonians, which also joined him. Returning hence, he gave their liberty to all the Greeks on this side Thermopylæ, and made alliance with the Bœotians, took Cenchræ, and reducing the fortresses of Phyle and Panactum, in which were garrisons of Cassander, restored them to the Athenians. They, in requital, though they had before been so profuse in bestowing honours upon him that one would have thought they had exhausted all the capacities of invention, showed they had still new refinements of adulation to devise for him. They gave him, as his lodging, the back temple in the Parthenon, and here he lived, under the immediate roof, as they meant it to imply, of his hostess, Minerva—no reputable or well-conducted guest to be quartered upon a maiden goddess! When his brother Philip was once put into a house where three young women were living, Antigonus, saying nothing to him, sent for his quartermaster, and told him, in the young man's presence, to find some less crowded lodgings for him.

Demetrius, however, who should, to say the least, have paid the goddess the respect due to an elder sister, for that was the purport of the city's compliment, filled the temple with such pollutions that the place seemed least profaned when his licence confined itself to common women like Chrysis, Lamia, Demo, and Anticyra.

The fair name of the city forbids any further plain particulars; let us only record the severe virtue of the young Damocles, surnamed, and by that surname pointed out to Demetrius, the beautiful; who, to escape importunities, avoided every place of resort, and when at last followed into a private bathing room by Demetrius, seeing none at hand to help or deliver, seized the lid from the cauldron, and, plunging into the boiling water, sought a death untimely and unmerited, but worthy of the country and of the beauty that occasioned it. Not so Cleænetus, the son of Cleomedon, who, to obtain from Demetrius a letter of intercession to the people in behalf of his father, lately condemned in a fine of fifty talents, disgraced himself, and got the city into trouble. In deference to the letter, they remitted the fine, yet they made an edict prohibiting any citizen for the future to bring letters from Demetrius. But being informed that Demetrius resented this as a great indignity, they not only rescinded in alarm the former order, but put some of the proposers and advisers of it to death and banished others, and furthermore enacted and decreed, that whatsoever King Demetrius should in time to come ordain, should be accounted right towards the gods and just towards men; and when one of the better class of citizens said Stratocles must be mad to use such words, Demochares of Leuconoe observed he would be a fool not to be mad. For Stratocles was well rewarded for his flatteries; and the saying was remembered against Demochares, who was soon after sent into banishment. So fared the Athenians, after being relieved of the foreign garrison, and recovering what was called their liberty.

After this Demetrius marched with his forces into Peloponnesus, where he met with none to oppose him, his enemies flying before him, and allowing the cities to join him. He received into friendship all Acte, as it is called, and all Arcadia except Mantinea. He bought the liberty of Argos, Corinth, and Sicyon, by paying a hundred talents to their garrisons to evacuate them. At Argos, during the feast of Juno, which happened at the time, he presided at the games, and, joining in the festivities with the multitude of the Greeks assembled there, he celebrated his marriage with Deidamia, daughter of Æacides, King of the Molossians, and sister of Pyrrhus. At Sicyon he told the people they had put the city just outside of the city, and, persuading them to remove to where they now live, gave their town not only a new site but a new name, Demetrias, after himself. A general assembly met on the Isthmus, where he was proclaimed, by a great concourse of the people, the Commander of Greece, like Philip and Alexander of old; whose superior he, in the present height of his prosperity and power, was willing enough to consider himself; and certainly, in one respect, he outdid Alexander, who never refused their title to other kings, or took on himself the style of king of kings, though many kings received both their title and their authority as such from him; whereas Demetrius used to ridicule those who gave the name of king to any except himself and his father; and in his entertainments was well pleased when his followers, after drinking to him and his father as kings, went on to drink the healths of Seleucus, with the title of Master of the Elephants; of Ptolemy, by the name of High Admiral; of Lysimachus, with the addition of Treasurer; and of Agathocles, with the style of Governor of the Island of Sicily. The other kings merely laughed when they were told of this vanity; Lysimachus alone expressed some indignation at being considered a eunuch, such being usually then selected for the office of treasurer. And, in general, there was a more bitter enmity between him and Lysimachus than with any of the others. Once, as a scoff at his passion for Lamia, Lysimachus said he had never before seen a courtesan act a queen's part; to which Demetrius rejoined that his mistress was quite as honest as Lysimachus's own Penelope.

But to proceed. Demetrius being about to return to Athens, signified by letter to the city that he desired immediate admission to the rites of initiation into the Mysteries, and wished to go through all the stages of the ceremony, from first to last, without delay. This was absolutely contrary to the rules, and a thing which had never been allowed before; for the lesser mysteries were celebrated in the month of Anthesterion, and the great solemnity in Bœdromion, and none of the novices were finally admitted till they had completed a year after this latter. Yet all this notwithstanding, when in the public assembly these letters of Demetrius were produced and read, there was not one single person who had the courage to oppose them, except Pythodorus, the torch-bearer. But it signified nothing, for Stratocles at once proposed that the month of Munychion, then current, should by edict be reputed to be the month of Anthesterion; which being voted and done, and Demetrius thereby admitted to the lesser ceremonies, by another vote they turned the same month of Munychion into the other month of Bœdromion; the celebration of the greater mysteries ensued, and Demetrius was fully admitted. These proceedings gave the comedian, Philippides, a new occasion to exercise his wit upon Stratocles—

"——whose flattering fear
Into one month hath crowded all the year."

And on the vote that Demetrius should lodge in the Parthenon—

"Who turns the temple to a common inn,
And makes the Virgin's house a house of sin."

Of all the disreputable and flagitious acts of which he was guilty in this visit, one that particularly hurt the feelings of the Athenians was that, having given command that they should forthwith raise for his service two hundred and fifty talents, and they to comply with his demands being forced to levy it upon the people with the utmost rigour and severity, when they presented him with the money which they had with such difficulty raised, as if it were a trifling sum, he ordered it to be given to Lamia and the rest of his women, to buy soap. The loss, which was bad enough, was less galling than the shame, and the words more intolerable than the act which they accompanied. Though, indeed, the story is variously reported; and some say it was the Thessalians, and not the Athenians, who were thus treated. Lamia, however, exacted contributions herself to pay for an entertainment she gave to the king, and her banquet was so renowned for its sumptuosity that a description of it was drawn up by the Samian writer, Lynceus. Upon this occasion, one of the comic writers gave Lamia the name of the real *Helepolis;* and Demochares of Soli called Demetrius *Mythus,* because the fable always has its Lamia, and so had he.

And, in truth, his passion for this woman, and the prosperity in which she lived were such as to draw upon him not only the envy and jealousy of all his wives, but the animosity even of his friends. For example, on Lysimachus's showing to some ambassadors from Demetrius the scars of the wounds which he had received upon his thighs and arms by the paws of the lion with which Alexander had shut him up, after hearing his account of the combat, they smiled and answered, that their king, also, was not without his scars, but could show upon his neck the marks of a Lamia, a no less dangerous beast. It was also matter of wonder that, though he had objected so much to Phila on account of her age, he was yet such a slave to Lamia who was so long past her prime. One evening at supper, when she played the flute, Demetrius asked Demo, whom the men called Madness, what she thought of her. Demo answered she thought her an old woman. And when a quantity of sweetmeats were brought in, and the king said again, "See what presents I get from Lamia!" "My old mother," answered Demo, "will send you more, if you will make her your mistress." Another story is told of a criticism passed by Lamia on the famous judgment of Bocchoris. A young Egyptian had long made suit to Thonis, the courtesan, offering a sum of gold for her favour. But before it came to pass, he dreamed one night that he had obtained it, and, satisfied with the shadow, felt no more desire for the substance. Thonis upon this brought an action for the sum. Bocchoris, the judge, on hearing the case, ordered the defendant to bring into court the full amount in a vessel, which he was to move to and fro in his hand, and the shadow of it was to be adjudged to Thonis. The fairness of this sentence Lamia contested, saying the young man's desire might have been satisfied with the dream, but Thonis's desire for the money could not be relieved by the shadow. Thus much for Lamia.

And now the story passes from the comic to the tragic stage in pursuit of the acts and fortunes of its subjects. A general league of the kings, who were now gathering and combining their forces to attack Antigonus, recalled Demetrius from Greece. He was encouraged by finding his father full of a spirit and resolution for the combat that belied his years. Yet it would seem to be true, that if Antigonus could only have borne to make some trifling concessions, and if he had shown any moderation in his passion for empire, he might have maintained for himself till his death and left to his son behind him the first place among the kings. But he was of a violent and haughty spirit; and the insulting words as well as actions in which he allowed himself could not be borne by young and powerful princes, and provoked them into combining against him. Though now when he was told of the confederacy, he could not forbear from saying that this flock of birds would soon be scattered by one stone and a single shout. He took the field at the head of more than seventy thousand foot and of ten thousand horse, and seventy-five elephants. His enemies had sixty-four thousand foot, five hundred more horse than he, elephants to the number of four hundred, and a hundred and twenty chariots. On their near approach to each other, an alteration began to be observable, not in the purposes, but in the presentiments of Antigonus. For whereas in all former campaigns he had ever shown himself lofty and confident, loud in voice and scornful in speech, often by some joke or mockery on the eve of battle expressing his contempt and displaying his composure, he was now remarked to be thoughtful, silent, and retired. He presented Demetrius to the army and declared him his successor; and what every one thought stranger than all was that he now conferred alone in his tent with Demetrius; whereas in former time he had never entered into any secret consultations even with him; but had always followed his own advice, made his resolutions, and then given out his commands. Once when Demetrius was a boy and asked him how soon the army would move, he is said to have answered him sharply, "Are you afraid lest you, of all the army, should not hear the trumpet?"

There were now, however, inauspicious signs, which affected his spirits. Demetrius, in a dream, had seen Alexander completely armed, appear and demand of him what word they intended to give in the time of the battle; and Demetrius answering that he intended the word should be "Jupiter and Victory," "Then," said Alexander, "I will go to your adversaries and find my welcome with them." And on the morning of the combat, as the armies were drawing up, Antigonus, going out of the door of his tent, by some accident or other stumbled and fell flat upon the ground, hurting himself a good deal. And on recovering his feet, lifting up his hands to heaven, he prayed the gods to grant him, "either victory, or death without knowledge of defeat." When the armies engaged, Demetrius, who commanded the greatest and best part of the cavalry, made a charge on Antiochus, the son of Seleucus, and gloriously routing the enemy, followed the pursuit, in the pride and exultation of success, so eagerly, and so unwisely far, that it fatally lost him the day; for when, perceiving his error, he would have come in to the assistance of his own infantry, he was not able, the enemy with their elephants having cut off his retreat. And on the other hand, Seleucus, observing the main battle of Antigonus left naked of their horse, did not charge, but made a show of charging; and keeping them in alarm and wheeling about and still threatening an attack, he gave opportunity for those who wished it to separate and come over to him; which a large body of them did, the rest taking to flight. But the old King Antigonus still kept his post, and when a strong body of the enemies drew up to charge him, and one of those about him cried out to him, "Sir, they are coming upon you," he only replied, "What else should they do? but Demetrius will come to my rescue." And in this hope he persisted to the last, looking out on every side for his son's approach, until he was borne down by a whole multitude of darts, and fell. His other followers and friends fled, and Thorax of Larissa remained alone by the body.

The battle having been thus decided, the kings who had gained the victory, carving up the whole vast empire that had belonged to Demetrius and Antigonus, like a carcass, into so many portions, added these new gains to their former possessions. As for Demetrius, with five thousand foot and four thousand horse, he fled at his utmost speed to Ephesus, where it was the common opinion he would seize the treasures of the temple to relieve his wants; but he, on the contrary, fearing such an attempt on the part of his soldiers, hastened away, and sailed for Greece, his chief remaining hopes being placed in the fidelity of the Athenians, with whom he had left part of his navy and of his treasures and his wife Deidamia. And in their attachment he had not the least doubt but he should in this his extremity find a safe resource. Accordingly when, upon reaching the Cyclades, he was met by ambassadors from Athens, requesting him not to proceed to the city, as the people had passed a vote to admit no king whatever within their walls, and had conveyed Deidamia with honourable attendance to Megara, his anger and surprise overpowered him, and the constancy quite failed him which he had hitherto shown in a wonderful degree under his reverses, nothing humiliating or mean-spirited having as yet been seen in him under all his misfortunes. But to be thus disappointed in the Athenians, and to find the friendship he had trusted prove, upon trial, thus empty and unreal, was a great pang to him. And, in truth, an excessive display of outward honour would seem to be the most uncertain attestation of the real affection of a people for any king or potentate. Such shows lose their whole credit as tokens of affection (which has its virtue in the feelings and moral choice), when we reflect that they may equally proceed from fear. The same decrees are voted upon the latter motive as upon the former. And therefore judicious men do not look so much to statues, paintings, or divine honours that are paid them, as to their own actions and conduct, judging hence whether they shall trust these as a genuine, or discredit them as a forced homage. As in fact nothing is less unusual than for a people, even while offering compliments, to be disgusted with those who accept them greedily, or arrogantly, or without respect to the free-will of the givers.

Demetrius, shamefully used as he thought himself, was in no condition to revenge the affront. He returned a message of gentle expostulation, saying, however, that he expected to have his galleys sent to him, among which was that of thirteen banks of oars. And this being accorded him, he sailed to the Isthmus, and, finding his affairs in very ill condition, his garrisons expelled, and a general secession going on to the enemy, he left Pyrrhus to attend to Greece, and took his course to the Chersonesus, where he ravaged the territories of Lysimachus, and by the booty which he took, maintained and kept together his troops, which were now once more beginning to recover and to show some considerable front. Nor did any of the other princes care to meddle with him on that side; for Lysimachus had quite as little claim to be loved, and was more to be feared for his power. But not long after Seleucus sent to treat with Demetrius for a marriage betwixt himself and Stratonice, daughter of Demetrius by Phila. Seleucus, indeed, had already, by Apama, the Persian, a son named Antiochus, but he was possessed of territories that might well satisfy more than one successor, and he was the rather induced to this alliance with Demetrius, because Lysimachus had just married himself to one daughter of King Ptolemy, and his son Agathocles to another. Demetrius, who looked upon the offer as an unexpected piece of good fortune, presently embarked with his daughter, and with his whole fleet sailed for Syria. Having during his voyage to touch several times on the coast, among other places he landed in part of Cilicia, which by the apportionment of the kings after the defeat of Antigonus was allotted to Plistarchus, the brother of Cassander. Plistarchus, who took this descent of Demetrius upon his coasts as an infraction of his rights, and was not sorry to have something to complain of, hastened to expostulate in person with Seleucus for entering separately into relations with Demetrius, the common enemy, without consulting the other kings.

Demetrius, receiving information of this, seized the opportunity, and fell upon the city of Quinda, which he surprised, and took in it twelve hundred talents still remaining of the treasure. With this prize, he hastened back to his galleys, embarked, and set sail. At Rhosus, where his wife Phila was now with him, he was met by Seleucus, and their communications with each other at once were put on a frank, unsuspecting, and kingly footing. First, Seleucus gave a banquet to Demetrius in his tent in the camp; then Demetrius received him in the ship of thirteen banks of oars. Meetings for amusements, conferences, and long visits for general intercourse succeeded, all without attendants or arms; until at length Seleucus took his leave, and in great state conducted Stratonice to Antioch. Demetrius meantime possessed himself of Cilicia, and sent Phila to her brother Cassander, to answer the complaints of Plistarchus. And here his wife Deidamia came by sea out of Greece to meet him, but not long after contracted an illness, of which she died. After her death, Demetrius, by the mediation of Seleucus, became reconciled to Ptolemy, and an agreement was made that he should marry his daughter Ptolemais. Thus far all was handsomely done on the part of Seleucus. But, shortly after, desiring to have the province of Cilicia from Demetrius for a sum of money, and being refused it, he then angrily demanded of him the cities of Tyre and Sidon, which seemed a mere piece of arbitrary dealing, and, indeed, an outrageous thing that he, who was possessed of all the vast provinces between India and the Syrian sea, should think himself so poorly off as, for the sake of two cities which he coveted, to disturb the peace of his dear connection, already a sufferer under a severe reverse of fortune. However, he did but justify the saying of Plato, that the only certain way to be truly rich is not to have more property, but fewer desires. For whoever is always grasping at more avows that he is still in want, and must be poor in the midst of affluence.

But Demetrius, whose courage did not sink, resolutely sent him answer, that, though he were to lose ten thousand battles like that of Ipsus, he would pay no price for the good-will of such a son-in-law as Seleucus. He reinforced these cities with sufficient garrisons to enable them to make a defence against Seleucus; and, receiving information that Lachares, taking the opportunity of their civil dissensions, had set up himself as a usurper over the Athenians, he imagined that if he made a sudden attempt upon the city, he might now without difficultly get possession of it. He crossed the sea in safety with a large fleet; but passing along the coast of Attica, was met by a violent storm, and lost the greater number of his ships, and a very considerable body of men on board of them. As for him he escaped, and began to make war in a petty manner with the Athenians, but, finding himself unable to effect his design, he sent back orders for raising another fleet, and, with the troops which he had, marched into Peloponnesus and laid siege to the city of Messena. In attacking which place he was in danger of death; for a missile from an engine struck him in the face, and passed through the cheek into his mouth. He recovered, however, and, as soon as he was in a condition to take the field, won over divers cities which had revolted from him, and made an incursion into Attica, where he took Eleusis and Rhamnus, and wasted the country thereabout. And that he might straiten the Athenians by cutting off all manner of provision, a vessel laden with corn bound thither falling into his hands, he ordered the master and the supercargo to be immediately hanged, thereby to strike a terror into others, that so they might not venture to supply the city with provisions. By which means they were reduced to such extremities that a bushel of salt sold for forty drachmas, and a peck of wheat for three hundred. Ptolemy had sent to their relief a hundred and fifty galleys, which came so near as to be seen off Ægina; but this brief hope was soon extinguished by the arrival of three hundred ships, which came to reinforce Demetrius from Cyprus, Peloponnesus, and other places; upon which Ptolemy's fleet took to flight, and Lachares, the tyrant, ran away, leaving the city to its fate.

And now the Athenians, who before had made it capital for any person to propose a treaty or accommodation with Demetrius, immediately opened the nearest gates to send ambassadors to him, not so much out of hopes of obtaining any honourable conditions from his clemency as out of necessity, to avoid death by famine. For among many frightful instances of the distress they were reduced to, it is said that a father and son were sitting in a room together, having abandoned every hope, when a dead mouse fell from the ceiling; and for this prize they leaped up and came to blows. In this famine, it is also related, the philosopher Epicurus saved his own life, and the lives of his scholars, by a small quantity of beans, which he distributed to them daily by number.

In this condition was the city when Demetrius made his entrance and issued a proclamation that all the inhabitants should assemble in the theatre; which being done, he drew up his soldiers at the back of the stage, occupied the stage itself with his guards, and, presently coming in himself by the actors' passages, when the people's consternation had risen to its height, with his first words he put an end to it. Without any harshness of tone or bitterness of words, he reprehended them in a gentle and friendly way, and declared himself reconciled, adding a present of a hundred thousand bushels of wheat, and appointing as magistrates persons acceptable to the people. So Dromoclides, the orator, seeing the people at a loss how to express their gratitude by any words or acclamations, and ready for anything that would outdo the verbal encomiums of the public speakers, came forward, and moved a decree for delivering Piræus and Munychia into the hands of King Demetrius. This was passed accordingly, and Demetrius, of his own motion, added a third garrison, which he placed in the Museum, as a precaution against any new restiveness on the part of the people, which might give him the trouble of quitting his other enterprises.

He had not long been master of Athens before he had formed designs against Lacedæmon; of which Archidamus, the king, being advertised, came out and met him, but he was overthrown in a battle near Mantinea; after which Demetrius entered Laconia, and, in a second battle near Sparta itself, defeated him again with the loss of two hundred Lacedæmonians slain, and five hundred taken prisoners. And now it was almost impossible for the city, which hitherto had never been captured, to escape his arms. But certainly there never was any king upon whom fortune made such short turns, nor any other life or story so filled with her swift and surprising changes, over and over again, from small things to great, from splendour back to humiliation and from utter weakness once more to power and might. They say in his sadder vicissitudes he used sometimes to apostrophise fortune in the words of Æschylus—

> "Thou liftest up, to cast us down again."

And so at this moment, when all things seemed to conspire together to give him his heart's desire of dominion and power, news arrived that Lysimachus had taken all his cities in Asia, that Ptolemy had reduced all Cyprus with the exception of Salamis, and that in Salamis his mother and children were shut up and close besieged; and yet, like the woman in Archilochus—

"Water in one deceitful hand she shows,
While burning fire within her other glows."

The same fortune that drew him off with these disastrous tidings from Sparta, in a moment after opened upon him a new and wonderful prospect, of the following kind. Cassander, King of Macedon, dying, and his eldest son, Philip, who succeeded him, not long surviving his father, the two younger brothers fell at variance concerning the succession. And Antipater having murdered his mother Thessalonica, Alexander, the younger brother, called in to his assistance Pyrrhus out of Epirus, and Demetrius out of the Peloponnese. Pyrrhus arrived first, and, taking in recompense for his succour a large slice of Macedonia, had made Alexander begin to be aware that he had brought upon himself a dangerous neighbour. And, that he might not run a yet worse hazard from Demetrius, whose power and reputation were so great, the young man hurried away to meet him at Dium, whither he, who on receiving his letter had set out on his march was now come. And, offering his greetings and grateful acknowledgments, he at the same time informed him that his affairs no longer required the presence of his ally, thereupon he invited him to supper. There were not wanting some feelings of suspicion on either side already; and when Demetrius was now on his way to the banquet, some one came and told him that in the midst of the drinking he would be killed. Demetrius showed little concern, but, making only a little less haste, he sent to the principal officers of his army commanding them to draw out the soldiers, and make them stand to their arms, and ordered his retinue (more numerous a good deal than that of Alexander) to attend him into the very room of the entertainment, and not to stir from thence till they saw him rise from the table. Thus Alexander's servants, finding themselves overpowered, had not courage to attempt anything. And, indeed, Demetrius gave them no opportunity, for he made a very short visit, and pretending to Alexander that he was not at present in health for drinking wine, left early. And the next day he occupied himself in preparations for departing, telling Alexander he had received intelligence that obliged him to leave, and begging him to excuse so sudden a parting; he would hope to see him further when his affairs allowed him leisure. Alexander was only too glad, not only that he was going, but that he was doing so of his own motion, without any offence, and proposed to accompany him into Thessaly. But when they came to Larissa, new invitations passed between them, new professions of good-will, covering new conspiracies; by which Alexander put himself into the power of Demetrius. For as he did not like to use precautions on his own part, for fear Demetrius should take the hint to use them on his, the very thing he meant to do was first done to him. He accepted an invitation, and came to Demetrius's quarters; and when Demetrius, while they were still supping, rose from the table and went forth, the young man rose also, and followed him to the door, where Demetrius, as he passed through, only said to the guards, "Kill him that follows me," and went on; and Alexander was at once despatched by them, together with such of his friends as endeavoured to come to his rescue, one of whom, before he died, said, "You have been one day too quick for us."

The night following was one, as may be supposed, of disorder and confusion. And with the morning, the Macedonians, still in alarm, and fearful of the forces of Demetrius, on finding no violence offered, but only a message sent from Demetrius desiring an interview and opportunity for explanation of his actions, at last began to feel pretty confident again, and prepared to receive him favourably. And when he came, there was no need of much being said; their hatred of Antipater for his murder of his mother, and the absence of any one better to govern them, soon decided them to proclaim Demetrius King of Macedon. And into Macedonia they at once started and took him. And the Macedonians at home, who had not forgotten or forgiven the wicked deeds committed by Cassander on the family of Alexander, were far from sorry at the change. Any kind recollections that still might subsist of the plain and simple rule of the first Antipater went also to the benefit of Demetrius, whose wife was Phila, his daughter, and his son by her, a boy already old enough to be serving in the army with his father, was the natural successor to the government.

To add to this unexpected good fortune, news arrived that Ptolemy had dismissed his mother and children, bestowing upon them presents and honours; and also that his daughter Stratonice, whom he had married to Seleucus, was remarried to Antiochus, the son of Seleucus, and proclaimed Queen of Upper Asia.

For Antiochus, it appears, had fallen passionately in love with Stratonice, the young queen, who had already made Seleucus the father of a son. He struggled very hard with the beginning of this passion, and at last, resolving with himself that his desires were wholly unlawful, his malady past all cure, and his powers of reason too feeble to act, he determined on death, and thought to bring his life slowly to extinction by neglecting his person and refusing nourishment, under the pretence of being ill. Erasistratus, the physician who attended him, quickly perceived that love was his distemper, but the difficulty was to discover the object. He therefore waited continually in his chamber, and when any of the beauties of the court made their visit to the sick prince, he observed the emotions and alterations in the countenance of Antiochus, and watched for the changes which he knew to be indicative of the inward passions and inclinations of the soul. He took notice that the presence of other women produced no effect upon him; but when Stratonice came, as she often did, alone, or in company with Seleucus, to see him, he observed in him all Sappho's famous symptoms,—his voice faltered, his face flushed up, his eyes glanced stealthily, a sudden sweat broke out on his skin, the beatings of his heart were irregular and violent, and, unable to support the excess of his passion, he would sink into a state of faintness, prostration, and pallor.

Erasistratus, reasoning upon these symptoms, and, upon the probabilities of things, considering that the king's son would hardly, if the object of his passion had been any other, have persisted to death rather than reveal it, felt, however, the difficulty of making a discovery of this nature to Seleucus. But, trusting to the tenderness of Seleucus for the young man, he put on all the assurances he could, and at last, on some opportunity, spoke out and told him the malady was love, a love impossible to gratify or relieve. The king was extremely surprised, and asked, "Why impossible to relieve?" "The fact is," replied Erasistratus, "he is in love with my wife." "How!" said Seleusus, "and will our friend Erasistratus refuse to bestow his wife upon my son and only successor, when there is no other way to save his life?" "You," replied Erasistratus, "who are his father, would not do so, if he were in love with Stratonice." "Ah, my friend," answered Seleucus, "would to heaven any means, human or divine, could but convert his present passion to that; it would be well for me to part not only with Stratonice, but with my empire, to save Antiochus." This he said with the greatest passion, shedding tears as he spoke; upon which Erasistratus, taking him by the hand, replied, "In that case, you have no need of Erasistratus; for you, who are the husband, the father, and the king, are the proper physician for your own family." Seleucus, accordingly, summoning a general assembly of his people, declared to them, that he had resolved to make Antiochus king, and Stratonice queen, of all the provinces of Upper Asia, uniting them in marriage; telling them, that he thought he had sufficient power over the prince's will that he should find in him no repugnance to obey his commands; and for Stratonice, he hoped all his friends would endeavour to make her sensible, if she should manifest any reluctance to such a marriage, that she ought to esteem those things just and honourable which had been determined upon by the king as necessary to the general good. In this manner, we are told, was brought about the marriage of Antiochus and Stratonice.

To return to the affairs of Demetrius. Having obtained the crown of

Macedon, he presently became master of Thessaly also. And holding the greatest part of Peloponnesus, and, on this side of the Isthmus, the cities of Megara and Athens, he now turned his arms against the Bœotians. They at first made overtures for an accommodation; but Cleonymus of Sparta having ventured with some troops to their assistance, and having made his way into Thebes, and Pisis, the Thespian, who was their first man in power and reputation, animating them to make a brave resistance, they broke off the treaty. No sooner, however, had Demetrius begun to approach the walls with his engines, but Cleonymus in affright secretly withdrew; and the Bœtians, finding themselves abandoned, made their submission. Demetrius placed a garrison in charge of their towns, and, having raised a large sum of money from them, he placed Hieronymus, the historian, in the office of governor and military commander over them, and was thought on the whole to have shown great clemency, more particularly to Pisis, to whom he did no hurt, but spoke with him courteously and kindly, and made him chief magistrate of Thespiæ. Not long after, Lysimachus was taken prisoner by Dromichætes, and Demetrius went off instantly in the hopes of possessing himself of Thrace, thus left without a king. Upon this, the Bœotians revolted again, and news also came that Lysimachus had regained his liberty. So Demetrius, turning back quickly and in anger, found on coming up that his son Antigonus had already defeated the Bœotians in battle, and therefore proceeded to lay siege again to Thebes

But understanding that Pyrrhus had made an incursion into Thessaly, and that he was advanced as far as Thermopylæ, leaving Antigonus to continue the siege, he marched with the rest of his army to oppose this enemy. Pyrrhus, however, made a quick retreat. So, leaving ten thousand foot and a thousand horse for the protection of Thessaly, he returned to the siege of Thebes, and there brought up his famous City-taker to the attack, which, however, was so laboriously and so slowly moved on account of its bulk and heaviness, that in two months it did not advance two furlongs. In the meantime the citizens made a stout defence, and Demetrius, out of heat and contentiousness very often, more than upon any necessity, sent his soldiers into danger; until at last Antigonus, observing how many men were losing their lives, said to him, "Why, my father, do we go on letting the men be wasted in this way without any need of it?" But Demetrius, in a great passion, interrupted him: "And you, good sir, why do you afflict yourself for the matter? will dead men come to you for rations?" But that the soldiers might see that he valued his own life at no dearer rate than theirs, he exposed himself freely, and was wounded with a javelin through his neck, which put him into great hazard of his life. But, notwithstanding, he continued the siege, and in conclusion took the town again. And after his entrance, when the citizens were in fear and trembling, and expected all the severities which an incensed conqueror could inflict, he only put to death thirteen and banished some few others, pardoning all the rest. Thus the city of Thebes, which had not yet been ten years restored, in that short space was twice besieged and taken.

Shortly after, the festival of the Pythian Apollo was to be celebrated, and the Ætolians having blocked up all the passages to Delphi, Demetrius held the games and celebrated the feast at Athens, alleging it was great reason those honours should be paid in that place, Apollo being the paternal god of the Athenian people, and the reputed first founder of their race.

From thence Demetrius returned to Macedon, and as he not only was of a restless temper himself, but saw also that the Macedonians were ever the best subjects when employed in military expeditions, but turbulent and desirous of change in the idleness of peace, he led them against the Ætolians, and, having wasted their country, he left Pantauchus with a great part of his army to complete the conquest, and with the rest he marched in person to find out Pyrrhus, who in like manner was advancing to encounter him. But so it fell out, that by taking different ways the two armies did not meet; but whilst Demetrius entered Epirus, and laid all waste before him, Pyrrhus fell upon Pantauchus, and in a battle in which the two commanders met in person and wounded each other, he gained the victory, and took five thousand prisoners, besides great numbers slain in the field. The worst thing, however, for Demetrius was that Pyrrhus had excited less animosity as an enemy than admiration as a brave man. His taking so large a part with his own hand in the battle had gained him the greatest name and glory among the Macedonians. Many among them began to say that this was the only king in whom there was any likeness to be seen of the great Alexander's courage; the other kings, and particularly Demetrius, did nothing but personate him, like actors on a stage, in his pomp and outward majesty. And Demetrius truly was a perfect play and pageant, with his robes and diadems, his gold-edged purple and his hats with double streamers, his very shoes being of the richest purple felt, embroidered over in gold. One robe in particular, a most superb piece of work, was long in the loom in preparation for him, in which was to be wrought the representation of the universe and the celestial bodies. This, left unfinished when his reverse overtook him, not any one of the kings of Macedon, his successors, though divers of them haughty enough, ever presumed to use.

But it was not this theatric pomp alone which disgusted the Macedonians, but his profuse and luxurious way of living; and, above all, the difficulty of speaking with him or of obtaining access to his presence. For either he would not be seen at all, or, if he did give audience, he was violent and overbearing. Thus he made the envoys of the Athenians, to whom yet he was more attentive than to all the other Grecians, wait two whole years before they could obtain a hearing. And when the Lacedæmonians sent a single person on an embassy to him, he held himself insulted, and asked angrily whether it was the fact that the Lacedæmonians had sent but one ambassador. "Yes," was the happy reply he received, "one ambassador to one king."

Once when in some apparent fit of a more popular and acceptable temper he was riding abroad, a number of people came up and presented their written petitions. He courteously received all these, and put them up in the skirt of his cloak, while the poor people were overjoyed, and followed him close. But when he came upon the bridge of the river Axius, shaking out his cloak, he threw all into the river. This excited very bitter resentment among the Macedonians, who felt themselves to be not governed, but insulted. They called to mind what some of them had seen, and others had heard related of King Philip's unambitious and open, accessible manners. One day when an old woman had assailed him several times in the road, and importuned him to hear her after he had told her he had no time, "If so," cried she, "you have no time to be a king." And this reprimand so stung the king that, after thinking of it a while, he went back into the house, and setting all other matters apart, for several days together he did nothing else but receive, beginning with the old woman, the complaints of all that would come. And to do justice, truly enough, might well be called a king's first business. "Mars," as says Timotheus, "is the tyrant;" but Law, in Pindar's words, the king of all. Homer does not say that kings received at the hands of Jove besieging engines or ships of war, but sentences of justice, to keep and observe; nor is it the most warlike, unjust, and murderous, but the most righteous of kings, that has from him the name of Jupiter's "familiar friend" and scholar. Demetrius's delight was the title most unlike the choice of the king of gods. The divine names were those of the Defender and Keeper, his was that of the Besieger of Cities. The place of virtue was given by him to that which, had he not been as ignorant as he was powerful, he would have known to be vice, and honour by his act was associated with crime. While he lay dangerously ill at Pella, Pyrrhus pretty nearly overran all Macedon, and advanced as far as the city of Edessa. On recovering his health, he quickly drove him out, and came to terms with him, being desirous not to employ his time in a string of petty local conflicts with a neighbour, when all his thoughts were fixed upon another design. This was no less than to endeavour the recovery of the whole empire which his father had possessed; and his preparations were suitable to his hopes and the greatness of the enterprise. He had arranged for the levying of ninety-eight thousand foot and nearly twelve thousand horse; and he had a fleet of five hundred galleys on the stocks, some building at Athens, others at Corinth and Chalcis, and in the neighbourhood of Pella. And he himself was passing evermore from one to another of these places, to give his directions and his assistance to the plans, while all that saw were amazed, not so much at the number, as at the magnitude of the works. Hitherto, there had never been seen a galley with fifteen or sixteen ranges of oars. At a later time, Ptolemy Philopator built one of forty rows, which was two hundred and eighty cubits in length and the height of her to the top of her stern, forty-eight cubits; she had four hundred sailors and four thousand rowers, and afforded room besides for very near three thousand soldiers to fight on her decks. But this, after all, was for show, and not for service, scarcely differing from a fixed edifice ashore, and was not to be moved without extreme toil and peril; whereas these galleys of Demetrius were meant quite as much for fighting as for looking at, were not the less serviceable for their magnificence, and were as wonderful for their speed and general performance as for their size.

These mighty preparations against Asia, the like of which had not been made since Alexander first invaded it, united Seleucus, Ptolemy, and Lysimachus in a confederacy for their defence. They also despatched ambassadors to Pyrrhus, to persuade him to make a diversion by attacking Macedonia; he need not think there was any validity in a treaty which Demetrius had concluded, not as an engagement to be at peace with him, but as a means of enabling himself to make war first upon the enemy of his choice. So when Pyrrhus accepted their proposals, Demetrius, still in the midst of his preparations, was encompassed with war on all sides. Ptolemy, with a mighty navy, invaded Greece; Lysimachus entered Macedonia upon the side of Thrace, and Pyrrhus, from the Epirot border, both of them spoiling and wasting the country. Demetrius, leaving his son to look after Greece, marched to the relief of Macedon, and first of all to oppose Lysimachus. On his way, he received the news that Pyrrhus had taken the city Berœa; and the report quickly getting out among the soldiers, all discipline at once was lost, and the camp was filled with lamentations and tears, anger and execrations on Demetrius; they would stay no longer, they would march off, as they said, to take care of their country, friends, and families; but in reality the intention was to revolt to Lysimachus. Demetrius, therefore, thought it his business to keep them as far away as he could from Lysimachus, who was their own countryman, and for Alexander's sake kindly looked upon by many; they would be ready to fight with Pyrrhus, a new comer and a foreigner, whom they could hardly prefer to himself. But he found himself under a great mistake in these conjectures. For when he advanced and pitched his camp near, the old admiration for Pyrrhus's gallantry in arms revived again; and as they had been used from time immemorial to suppose that the best king was he that was the bravest soldier, so now they were also told of his generous usage of his prisoners, and, in short, they were eager to have any one in the place of Demetrius, and well pleased that the man should be Pyrrhus. At first, some straggling parties only deserted, but in a little time the whole army broke out into a universal mutiny, insomuch that at last some of them went up and told him openly that if he consulted his own safety he were best to make haste to be gone, for that the Macedonians were resolved no longer to hazard their lives for the satisfaction of his luxury and pleasure. And this was thought fair and moderate language, compared with the fierceness of the rest. So, withdrawing into his tent, and, like an actor rather than a real king, laying aside his stage-robes of royalty, he put on some common clothes and stole away. He was no sooner gone but the mutinous army were fighting and quarrelling for the plunder of his tent, but Pyrrhus, coming immediately, took possession of the camp without a blow, after which he, with Lysimachus, parted the realm of Macedon betwixt them, after Demetrius had securely held it just seven years.

As for Demetrius, being thus suddenly despoiled of everything, he retired to Cassandrea. His wife Phila, in the passion of her grief, could not endure to see her hapless husband reduced to the condition of a private and banished man. She refused to entertain any further hope, and resolving to quit a fortune which was never permanent except for calamity, took poison and died. Demetrius, determining still to hold on by the wreck, went off to Greece, and collected his friends and officers there. Menelaus, in the play of Sophocles, to give an image of his vicissitudes of estate, says—

> "For me, my destiny, alas, is found
> Whirling upon the gods' swift wheel around,
> And changing still, and as the moon's fair frame
> Cannot continue for two nights the same,
> But out of shadow first a crescent shows,
> Thence into beauty and perfection grows,
> And when the form of plenitude it wears,
> Dwindles again, and wholly disappears."

The simile is yet truer of Demetrius and the phases of his fortunes, now on the increase, presently on the wane, now filling up and now falling away. And so, at this time of apparent entire obscuration and extinction, his light again shone out, and accessions of strength, little by little, came in to fulfil once more the measure of his hope. At first he showed himself in the garb of a private man, and went about the cities without any of the badges of a king. One who saw him at Thebes applied to him, not inaptly, the lines of Euripides—

"Humbled to man, laid by the godhead's pride,
He comes to Dirce and Ismenus's side."

But ere long his expectations had re-entered the royal track, and he began once more to have about him the body and form of empire. The Thebans received back, as his gift, their ancient constitution. The Athenians had deserted him. They displaced Diphilus, who was that year the priest of the two Tutelar Deities, and restored the archons, as of old, to mark the year; and on hearing that Demetrius was not so weak as they had expected, they sent into Macedonia to beg the protection of Pyrrhus. Demetrius, in anger, marched to Athens, and laid close siege to the city. In this distress, they sent out to him Crates the philosopher, a person of authority and reputation, who succeeded so far, that what with his entreaties and the solid reasons which he offered, Demetrius was persuaded to raise the siege; and, collecting all his ships, he embarked a force of eleven thousand men with cavalry, and sailed away to Asia, to Caria and Lydia, to take those provinces from Lysimachus. Arriving at Miletus, he was met there by Eurydice, the sister of Phila, who brought along with her Ptolemais, one of her daughters by King Ptolemy, who had before been affianced to Demetrius, and with whom he now consummated his marriage. Immediately after, he proceeded to carry out his project, and was so fortunate in the beginning that many cities revolted to him; others, as particularly Sardis, he took by force; and some generals of Lysimachus, also, came over to him with troops and money. But when Agathocles, the son of Lysimachus, arrived with an army, he retreated into Phrygia, with an intention to pass into Armenia, believing that, if he could once plant his foot in Armenia, he might set Media in revolt, and gain a position in Upper Asia, where a fugitive commander might find a hundred ways of evasion and escape. Agathocles pressed hard upon him, and many skirmishes and conflicts occurred, in which Demetrius had still the advantage; but Agathocles straitened him much in his forage, and his men showed a great dislike to his purpose, which they suspected, of carrying them far away into Armenia and Media. Famine also pressed upon them, and some mistake occurred in their passage of the river Lycus, in consequence of which a large number were swept away and drowned. Still, however, they could pass their jests, and one of them fixed upon Demetrius's tent-door a paper with the first verse, slightly altered, of the Œdipus:—

"Child of the blind old man, Antigonus,
Into what country are you bringing us?"

But at last, pestilence, as is usual when armies are driven to such necessities as to subsist upon any food they can get, began to assail them as well as famine. So that, having lost eight thousand of his men, with the rest he retreated and came to Tarsus, and because that city was within the dominions of Seleucus, he was anxious to prevent any plundering, and wished to give no sort of offence to Seleucus. But when he perceived it was impossible to restrain the soldiers in their extreme necessity, Agathocles also having blocked up all the avenues of Mount Taurus, he wrote a letter to Seleucus, bewailing first all his own sad fortunes, and proceeding with entreaties and supplications for some compassion on his part towards one nearly connected with him, who was fallen into such calamities as might extort tenderness and pity from his very enemies.

These letters so far moved Seleucus, that he gave orders to the governors of those provinces that they should furnish Demetrius with all things suitable to his royal rank, and with sufficient provisions for his troops. But Patrocles, a person whose judgment was greatly valued, and who was a friend highly trusted by Seleucus, pointed out to him the expense of maintaining such a body of soldiers was the least important consideration, but that it was contrary to all policy to let Demetrius stay in the country, since he, of all the kings of his time, was the most violent, and most addicted to daring enterprises; and he was now in a condition which might tempt persons of the greatest temper and moderation to unlawful and desperate attempts. Seleucus, excited by this advice, moved with a powerful army towards Cilicia; and Demetrius, astonished at this sudden alteration, betook himself for safety to the most inaccessible places of Mount Taurus; from whence he sent envoys to Seleucus, to request from him that he would permit him the liberty to settle with his army somewhere among the independent barbarian tribes, where he might be able to make himself a petty king, and end his life without further travel and hardship; or, if he refused him this, at any rate to give his troops food during the winter, and not expose him in this distressed and naked condition to the fury of his enemies.

But Seleucus, whose jealousy made him put an ill-construction on all he said, sent him answer, that he would permit him to stay two months and no longer in Cataonia, provided he presently sent him the principal of his friends as hostages for his departure then; and, in the meantime, he fortified all the passages into Syria. So that Demetrius, who saw himself thus like a wild beast, in the way to be encompassed on all sides in the toils, was driven in desperation to his defence, overran the country, and in several engagements in which Seleucus attacked him, had the advantage of him. Particularly, when he was once assailed by the scythed chariots, he successfully avoided the charge and routed his assailants, and then, expelling the troops that were in guard of the passes, made himself master of the roads leading into Syria. And now, elated himself, and finding his soldiers also animated by these successes, he was resolved to push at all, and to have one deciding blow for the empire with Seleucus; who indeed was in considerable anxiety and distress, being averse to any assistance from Lysimachus, whom he both mistrusted and feared, and shrinking from a battle with Demetrius, whose desperation he knew, and whose fortune he had so often seen suddenly pass from the lowest to the highest.

But Demetrius, in the meanwhile, was taken with a violent sickness, from which he suffered extremely himself, and which ruined all his prospects. His men deserted to the enemy, or dispersed. At last, after forty days, he began to be so far recovered as to be able to rally his remaining forces, and marched as if he directly designed for Cilicia; but in the night, raising his camp without sound of trumpet, he took a countermarch, and, passing the mountain Amanus, he ravaged all the lower country as far as Cyrrhestica.

Upon this, Seleucus advancing towards him and encamping at no great distance, Demetrius set his troops in motion to surprise him by night. And almost to the last moment Seleucus knew nothing, and was lying asleep. Some deserter came with the tidings just so soon that he had time to leap, in great consternation, out of bed, and give the alarm to his men. And as he was putting on his boots to mount his horse, he bade the officers about him look well to it, for they had to meet a furious and terrible wild beast. But Demetrius, by the noise he heard in the camp, finding they had taken the alarm, drew off his troops in haste. With the morning's return he found Seleucus pressing hard upon him; so, sending one of his officers against the other wing, he defeated those that were opposed to himself. But Seleucus, lighting from his horse, pulling off his helmet, and taking a target, advanced to the foremost ranks of the mercenary soldiers, and, showing them who he was, bade them come over and join him, telling them that it was for their sakes only that he had so long forborne coming to extremities. And thereupon, without a blow more, they saluted Seleucus as their king and passed over.

Demetrius, who felt that this was his last change of fortune, and that he had no more vicissitudes to expect, fled to the passes of Amanus, where, with a very few friends and followers, he threw himself into a dense forest, and there waited for the night, purposing, if possible, to make his escape towards Caunus, where he hoped to find his shipping ready to transport him. But upon inquiry, finding that they had not provisions even for that one day, he began to think of some other project. Whilst he was yet in doubt, his friend Sosigenes arrived, who had four hundred pieces of gold about him, and, with this relief, he again entertained hopes of being able to reach the coast, and, as soon as it began to be dark, set forward towards the passes.

But, perceiving by the fires that the enemies had occupied them, he gave up all thought of that road, and retreated to his old station in the wood, but not with all his men; for some had deserted, nor were those that remained as willing as they had been. One of them, in fine, ventured to speak out, and say that Demetrius had better give himself up to Seleucus; which Demetrius overhearing, drew out his sword, and would have passed it through his body, but that some of his friends interposed and prevented the attempt, persuading him to do as had been said. So at last he gave way, and sent to Seleucus, to surrender himself at discretion.

Seleucus, when he was told of it, said it was not Demetrius's good fortune that had found out this means for his safety, but his own, which had added to his other honours the opportunity of showing his clemency and generosity. And forthwith he gave order to his domestic officers to prepare a royal pavilion, and all things suitable to give him a splendid reception and entertainment. There was in the attendance of Seleucus one Apollonides, who formerly had been intimate with Demetrius. He was, therefore, as the fittest person, despatched from the king to meet Demetrius, that he might feel himself more at his ease, and might come with the confidence of being received as a friend and relative. No sooner was this message known, but the courtiers and officers, some few at first, and afterwards almost the whole of them, thinking Demetrius would presently become of great power with the king, hurried off, vying who should be foremost to pay him their respects. The effect of which was that compassion was converted into jealousy, and ill-natured, malicious people could the more easily insinuate to Seleucus that he was giving way to an unwise humanity, the very first sight of Demetrius having been the occasion of a dangerous excitement in the army. So, whilst Apollonides, in great delight, and after him many others, were relating to Demetrius the kind expressions of Seleucus, and he, after so many troubles and calamities, if indeed he had still any sense of his surrender of himself being a disgrace, had now, in confidence on the good hopes held out to him, entirely forgotten all such thoughts, Pausanias with a guard of a thousand horse and foot came and surounded him; and, dispersing the rest that were with him, carried him not to the presence of Seleucus, but to the Syrian Chersonese, where he was committed to the safe custody of a strong guard. Sufficient attendance and liberal provisions were here allowed him, space for riding and walking, a park with game for hunting, those of his friends and companions in exile who wished it had permission to see him, and messages of kindness, also, from time to time, were brought him from Seleucus, bidding him fear nothing, and intimating that, as soon as Antiochus and Stratonice should arrive, he would receive his liberty.

Demetrius, however, finding himself in this condition, sent letters to those who were with his son, and to his captains and friends at Athens and Corinth, that they should give no manner of credit to any letters written to them in his name, though they were sealed with his own signet, but that, looking upon him as if he were already dead, they should maintain the cities and whatever was left of his power for Antigonus, as his successor. Antigonus received the news of his father's captivity with great sorrow; he put himself into mourning and wrote letters to the rest of the kings, and to Seleucus himself, making entreaties, and offering not only to surrender whatever they had left, but himself to be a hostage for his father. Many cities also and princes joined in interceding for him; only Lysimachus sent and offered a large sum of money to Seleucus to take away his life. But he, who had always shown his aversion to Lysimachus before, thought him only the greater barbarian and monster for it. Nevertheless, he still protracted the time, reserving the favour, as he professed, for the intercession of Antiochus and Stratonice.

Demetrius, who had sustained the first stroke of his misfortune, in time grew so familiar with it, that, by continuance, it became easy. At first he persevered one way or other in taking exercise, in hunting, so far as he had means, and in riding. Little by little, however, after a while, he let himself grow indolent and indisposed for them, and took to dice and drinking, in which he passed most of his time, whether it were to escape the thoughts of his present condition, with which he was haunted when sober, and to drown reflection in drunkenness, or that he acknowledged to himself that this was the real happy life he had long desired and wished for, and had foolishly let himself be seduced away from it by a senseless and vain ambition, which had only brought trouble to himself and others; that highest good which he had thought to obtain by arms and fleets and soldiers he had now discovered unexpectedly in idleness, leisure, and repose. As, indeed, what other end or period is there of all the wars and dangers which hapless princes run into, whose misery and folly it is, not merely that they make luxury and pleasure, instead of virtue and excellence, the object of their lives, but that they do not so much as know where this luxury and pleasure are to be found?

Having thus continued three years a prisoner in Chersonesus, for want of exercise, and by indulging himself in eating and drinking, he fell into a disease, of which he died at the age of fifty-four. Seleucus was ill spoken of, and was himself greatly grieved, that he had yielded so far to his suspicions, and had let himself be so much outdone by the barbarian Dromichætes of Thrace, who had shown so much humanity and such a kingly temper in his treatment of his prisoner Lysimachus.

There was something dramatic and theatrical in the very funeral ceremonies with which Demetrius was honoured. For his son Antigonus, understanding that his remains were coming over from Syria, went with all his fleet to the islands to meet them. They were there presented to him in a golden urn, which he placed in his largest admiral galley. All the cities where they touched in their passage sent chaplets to adorn the urn, and deputed certain of their citizens to follow in mourning, to assist at the funeral solemnity. When the fleet approached the harbour of Corinth, the urn, covered with purple, and a royal diadem upon it, was visible upon the poop, and a troop of young men attended in arms to receive it at landing. Xenophantus, the most famous musician of the day, played on the flute his most solemn measure, to which the rowers, as the ship came in, made loud response, their oars, like the funeral beating of the breast, keeping time with the cadences of the music. But Antigonus, in tears and mourning attire, excited among the spectators gathered on the shore the greatest sorrow and compassion. After crowns and other honours had been offered at Corinth, the remains were conveyed to Demetrias, a city to which Demetrius had given his name, peopled from the inhabitants of small villages of Iolcus.

Demetrius left no other children by his wife Phila but Antigonus and Stratonice, but he had two other sons, both of his own name, one surnamed the Thin, by an Illyrian mother, and one who ruled in Cyrene, by Ptolemais. He had also, by Deidamia, a son, Alexander, who lived and died in Egypt; and there are some who say that he had a son by Eurydice, named Corrhabus. His family was continued in a succession of kings down to Perseus, the last, from whom the Romans took Macedonia.

And now, the Macedonian drama being ended, let us prepare to see the Roman.

ANTONY

THE grandfather of Antony was the famous pleader, whom Marius put to death for having taken part with Sylla. His father was Antony, surnamed of Crete, not very famous or distinguished in public life, but a worthy good man, and particularly remarkable for his liberality, as may appear from a single example. He was not very rich, and was for that reason checked in the exercise of his good nature by his wife. A friend that stood in need of money came to borrow of him. Money he had none, but he bade a servant bring him water in a silver basin, with which, when it was brought, he wetted his face, as if he meant to shave, and, sending away the servant upon another errand, gave his friend the basin, desiring him to turn it to his purpose. And when there was, afterwards, a great inquiry for it in the house, and his wife was in a very ill humour, and was going to put the servants one by one to the search, he acknowledged what he had done, and begged her pardon.

His wife was Julia, of the family of the Cæsars, who, for her discretion and fair behaviour, was not inferior to any of her time. Under her, Antony received his education, she being, after the death of his father, remarried to Cornelius Lentulus, who was put to death by Cicero for having been of Catiline's conspiracy. This, probably, was the first ground and occasion of that mortal grudge that Antony bore Cicero. He says, even, that the body of Lentulus was denied burial, till, by application made to Cicero's wife, it was granted to Julia. But this seems to be a manifest error, for none of those that suffered in the consulate of Cicero had the right of burial denied them. Antony grew up a very beautiful youth, but by the worst of misfortunes, he fell into the acquaintance and friendship of Curio, a man abandoned to his pleasures, who, to make Antony's dependence upon him a matter of greater necessity, plunged him into a life of drinking and dissipation, and led him through a course of such extravagance that he ran, at that early age, into debt to the amount of two hundred and fifty talents. For this sum Curio became his surety; on hearing which, the elder Curio, his father, drove Antony out of his house. After this, for some short time he took part with Clodius, the most insolent and outrageous demagogue of the time, in his course of violence and disorder; but getting weary, before long, of his madness, and apprehensive of the powerful party forming against him, he left Italy and travelled into Greece, where he spent his time in military exercises and in the study of eloquence. He took most to what was called the Asiatic taste in speaking, which was then at its height, and was, in many ways, suitable to his ostentatious, vaunting temper, full of empty flourishes and unsteady efforts for glory.

After some stay in Greece, he was invited by Gabinius, who had been consul, to make a campaign with him in Syria, which at first he refused, not being willing to serve in a private character, but receiving a commission to command the horse, he went along with him. His first service was against Aristobulus, who had prevailed with the Jews to rebel. Here he was himself the first man to scale the largest of the works, and beat Aristobulus out of all of them; after which he routed, in a pitched battle, an army many times over the number of his, killed almost all of them and took Aristobulus and his son prisoners. This war ended, Gabinius was solicited by Ptolemy to restore him to his kingdom of Egypt, and a promise made of ten thousand talents reward. Most of the officers were against this enterprise, and Gabinius himself did not much like it, though sorely tempted by the ten thousand talents. But Antony, desirous of brave actions, and willing to please Ptolemy, joined in persuading Gabinius to go. And whereas all were of opinion that the most dangerous thing before them was the march to Pelusium, in which they would have to pass over a deep sand, where no fresh water was to be hoped for, along the Acregma and the Serbonian marsh (which the Egyptians call Typhon's breathing-hole, and which is, in probability, water left behind by, or making its way through from, the Red Sea, which is here divided from the Mediterranean by a narrow isthmus), Antony, being ordered thither with the horse, not only made himself master of the passes, but won Pelusium itself, a great city, took the garrison prisoners, and by this means rendered the march secure to the army, and the way to victory not difficult for the general to pursue. The enemy also reaped some benefit of his eagerness for honour. For when Ptolemy, after he had entered Pelusium, in his rage and spite against the Egyptians, designed to put them to the sword, Antony withstood him, and hindered the execution. In all the great and frequent skirmishes and battles he gave continual proofs of his personal valour and military conduct; and once in particular, by wheeling about and attacking the rear of the enemy, he gave the victory to the assailants in the front, and received for this service signal marks of distinction. Nor was his humanity towards the deceased Archelaus less taken notice of. He had been formerly his guest and acquaintance, and, as he was now compelled, he fought him bravely while alive, but on his death, sought out his body and buried it with royal honours. The consequence was that he left behind him a great name among the Alexandrians, and all who were serving in the Roman army looked upon him as a most gallant soldier.

He had also a very good and noble appearance; his beard was well grown, his forehead large, and his nose aquiline, giving him altogether a bold, masculine look that reminded people of the faces of Hercules in paintings and sculptures. It was, moreover, an ancient tradition, that the Antonys were descended from Hercules, by a son of his called Anton; and this opinion he thought to give credit to by the similarity of his person just mentioned, and also by the fashion of his dress. For, whenever he had to appear before large numbers, he wore his tunic girt low about the hips, a broadsword on his side, and over all a large coarse mantle. What might seem to some very insupportable, his vaunting, his raillery, his drinking in public, sitting down by the men as they were taking their food, and eating, as he stood, off the common soldiers' tables, made him the delight and pleasure of the army. In love affairs, also, he was very agreeable: he gained many friends by the assistance he gave them in theirs, and took other people's raillery upon his own with good-humour. And his generous ways, his open and lavish hand in gifts and favours to his friends and fellow-soldiers, did a great deal for him in his first advance to power, and after he had become great, long maintained his fortunes, when a thousand follies were hastening their overthrow. One instance of his liberality I must relate. He had ordered payment to one of his friends of twenty-five myriads of money or *decies*, as the Romans call it, and his steward wondering at the extravagance of the sum, laid all the silver in a heap, as he should pass by. Antony, seeing the heap, asked what it meant; his steward replied, "The money you have ordered to be given to your friend." So, perceiving the man's malice, said he, "I thought the *decies* had been much more; 'tis too little; let it be doubled." This, however, was at a later time.

When the Roman state finally broke up into two hostile factions, the aristocratical party joining Pompey, who was in the city, and the popular side seeking help from Cæsar, who was at the head of an army in Gaul, Curio, the friend of Antony, having changed his party and devoted himself to Cæsar, brought over Antony also to his service. And the influence which he gained with the people by his eloquence and by the money which was supplied by Cæsar, enabled him to make Antony, first, tribune of the people, and then, augur. And Antony's accession to office was at once of the greatest advantage to Cæsar. In the first place, he resisted the consul Marcellus, who was putting under Pompey's orders the troops who were already collected, and was giving him power to raise new levies; he, on the other hand, making an order that they should be sent into Syria to reinforce Bibulus, who was making war with the Parthians, and that no one should give in his name to serve under Pompey. Next, when the senators would not suffer Cæsar's letters to be received or read in the senate, by virtue of his office he read them publicly, and succeeded so well, that many were brought to change their mind; Cæsar's demands, as they appeared in what he wrote, being but just and reasonable. At length, two questions being put in the senate, the one, whether Pompey should dismiss his army, the other, if Cæsar his, some were for the former, for the latter all, except some few, when Antony stood up and put the question, if it would be agreeable to them that both Pompey and Cæsar should dismiss their armies. This proposal met with the greatest approval, they gave him loud acclamations, and called for it to be put to the vote. But when the consuls would not have it so, Cæsar's friends again made some few offers, very fair and equitable, but were strongly opposed by Cato, and Antony himself was commanded to leave the senate by the consul Lentulus. So, leaving them with execrations, and disguising himself in a servant's dress, hiring a carriage with Quintus Cassius, he went straight away to Cæsar, declaring at once, when they reached the camp, that affairs at Rome were conducted without any order or justice, that the privilege of speaking in the senate was denied the tribunes, and that he who spoke for common fair dealing was driven out and in danger of his life.

Upon this, Cæsar set his army in motion, and marched into Italy, and for this reason it is that Cicero writes in his Philippics that Antony was as much the cause of the civil war as Helen was of the Trojan. But this is but a calumny. For Cæsar was not of so slight or weak a temper as to suffer himself to be carried away, by the indignation of the moment, into a civil war with his country, upon the sight of Antony and Cassius seeking refuge in his camp meanly dressed and in a hired carriage, without ever having thought of it or taken any such resolution long before. This was to him, who wanted a pretence of declaring war, a fair and plausible occasion; but the true motive that led him was the same that formerly led Alexander and Cyrus against all mankind, the unquenchable thirst of empire, and the distracted ambition of being the greatest man in the world, which was impracticable for him, unless Pompey were put down. So soon, then, as he had advanced and occupied Rome, and driven Pompey out of Italy, he proposed first to go against the legions that Pompey had in Spain, and then cross over and follow him with the fleet that should be prepared during his absence, in the meantime leaving the government of Rome to Lepidus, as prætor, and the command of the troops and of Italy to Antony, as tribune of the people. Antony was not long in getting the hearts of the soldiers, joining with them in their exercises, and for the most part living amongst them and making them presents to the utmost of his abilities; but with all others he was unpopular enough. He was too lazy to pay attention to the complaints of persons who were injured; he listened impatiently to petitions; and he had an ill name for familiarity with other people's wives. In short, the government of Cæsar (which, so far as he was concerned himself, had the appearance of anything rather than a tyranny) got a bad repute through his friends. And of these friends, Antony, as he had the largest trust, and committed the greatest errors, was thought the most deeply in fault.

Cæsar, however, at his return from Spain, overlooked the charges against him, and had no reason ever to complain, in the employments he gave him in the war, of any want of courage, energy, or military skill. He himself, going aboard at Brundusium, sailed over the Ionian Sea with a few troops and sent back the vessels with orders to Antony and Gabinius to embark the army, and come over with all speed to Macedonia. Gabinius, having no mind to put to sea in the rough, dangerous weather of the winter season, was for marching the army round by the long land route; but Antony, being more afraid lest Cæsar might suffer from the number of his enemies, who pressed him hard, beat back Libo, who was watching with a fleet at the mouth of the haven of Brundusium, by attacking his galleys with a number of small boats, and gaining thus an opportunity, put on board twenty thousand foot and eight hundred horse, and so set out to sea. And, being espied by the enemy and pursued, from this danger he was rescued by a strong south wind, which sprang up and raised so high a sea that the enemy's galleys could make little way. But his own ships were driving before it upon a lee shore of cliffs and rocks running sheer to the water, where there was no hope of escape, when all of a sudden the wind turned about to southwest, and blew from land to the main sea, where Antony, now sailing in security, saw the coast all covered with the wreck of the enemy's fleet. For hither the galleys in pursuit had been carried by the gale, and not a few of them dashed to pieces. Many men and much property fell into Antony's hands; he took also the town of Lissus, and, by the seasonable arrival of so large a reinforcement, gave Cæsar great encouragement.

There was not one of the many engagements that now took place one after another in which he did not signalise himself; twice he stopped the army in its full flight, led them back to a charge, and gained the victory. So that now without reason his reputation, next to Cæsar's, was greatest in the army. And what opinion Cæsar himself had of him well appeared when, for the final battle in Pharsalia, which was to determine everything, he himself chose to lead the right wing, committing the charge of the left to Antony, as to the best officer of all that served under him. After the battle, Cæsar, being created dictator, went in pursuit of Pompey, and sent Antony to Rome, with the character of Master of the Horse, who is in office and power next to the dictator, when present, and in his absence the first, and pretty nearly indeed the sole magistrate. For on the appointment of a dictator, with the one exception of the tribunes, all other magistrates cease to exercise any authority in Rome.

Dolabella, however, who was tribune, being a young man and eager for change, was now for bringing in a general measure for cancelling debts, and wanted Antony, who was his friend, and forward enough to promote any popular project, to take part with him in this step. Asinius and Trebellius were of the contrary opinion, and it so happened, at the same time, Antony was crossed by a terrible suspicion that Dolabella was too familiar with his wife; and in great trouble at this, he parted with her (she being his cousin, and daughter to Caius Antonius, colleague of Cicero), and, taking part with Asinius, came to open hostilities with Dolabella, who had seized on the forum, intending to pass his law by force. Antony, backed by a vote of the senate that Dolabella should be put down by force of arms, went down and attacked him, killing some of his, and losing some of his own men; and by this action lost his favour with the commonalty, while with the better class and with all well-conducted people his general course of life made him, as Cicero says, absolutely odious, utter disgust being excited by his drinking bouts at all hours, his wild expenses, his gross amours, the day spent in sleeping or walking off his debauches, and the night in banquets and at theatres, and in celebrating the nuptials of some comedian or buffoon. It is related that, drinking all night at the wedding of Hippias, the comedian, on the morning, having to harangue the people, he came forward, overcharged as he was, and vomited before them all, one of his friends holding his gown for him. Sergius, the player, was one of the friends who could do most with him; also Cytheris, a woman of the same trade, whom he made much of, and who, when he went his progress, accompanied him in a litter, and had her equipage not in anything inferior to his mother's; while every one, moreover, was scandalized at the sight of the golden cups that he took with him, fitter for the ornaments of a procession than the uses of a journey, at his having pavilions set up, and sumptuous morning repasts laid out by river sides and in groves, at his having chariots drawn by lions, and common women and singing girls quartered upon the houses of serious fathers and mothers of families. And it seemed very unreasonable that Cæsar, out of Italy, should lodge in the open field, and, with great fatigue and danger, pursue the remainder of a hazardous war, whilst others, by favour of his authority, should insult the citizens with their impudent luxury.

All this appears to have aggravated party quarrels in Rome, and to have encouraged the soldiers in acts of licence and rapacity. And, accordingly, when Cæsar came home, he acquitted Dolabella, and, being created the third time consul, took not Antony, but Lepidus, for his colleague. Pompey's house being offered for sale, Antony bought it, and when the price was demanded of him, loudly complained. This, he tells us himself, and because he thought his former services had not been recompensed as they deserved, made him not follow Cæsar with the army into Libya. However, Cæsar, by dealing gently with his errors, seems to have succeeded in curing him of a good deal of his folly and extravagance. He gave up his former courses, and took a wife, Fulvia, the widow of Clodius the demagogue, a woman not born for spinning or housewifery, nor one that could be content with ruling a private husband, but prepared to govern a first magistrate, or give orders to a commander-in-chief. So that Cleopatra had great obligations to her for having taught Antony to be so good a servant, he coming to her hands tame and broken into entire obedience to the commands of a mistress. He used to play all sorts of sportive, boyish tricks, to keep Fulvia in good humour. As, for example, when Cæsar, after his victory in Spain, was on his return, Antony, among the rest, went out to meet him; and, a rumour being spread that Cæsar was killed and the enemy marching into Italy, he returned to Rome, and, disguising himself, came to her by night muffled up as a servant that brought letters from Antony. She, with great impatience, before she received the letter, asks if Antony were well, and instead of an answer he gives her the letter; and, as she was opening it, took her about the neck and kissed her. This little story, of many of the same nature, I give as a specimen.

There was nobody of any rank in Rome that did not go some days' journey to meet Cæsar on his return from Spain; but Antony was the best received of any, admitted to ride the whole journey with him in his carriage, while behind came Brutus Albinus and Octavian, his niece's son, who afterwards bore his name and reigned so long over the Romans. Cæsar being created, the fifth time, consul, without delay chose Antony for his colleague, but designing himself to give up his own consulate to Dolabella, he acquainted the senate with his resolution. But Antony opposed it with all his might, saying much that was bad against Dolabella, and receiving the like language in return, till Cæsar could bear with the indecency no longer, and deferred the matter to another time. Afterwards, when he came before the people to proclaim Dolabella, Antony cried out that the auspices were unfavourable, so that at last Cæsar, much to Dolabella's vexation, yielded and gave it up. And it is credible that Cæsar was about as much disgusted with the one as the other. When some one was accusing them both to him, "It is not," said he, "these well-fed, long-haired men that I fear, but the pale and the hungry-looking;" meaning Brutus and Cassius, by whose conspiracy he afterwards fell.

And the fairest pretext for that conspiracy was furnished, without his meaning it, by Antony himself. The Romans were celebrating their festival, called the Lupercalia, when Cæsar, in his triumphal habit, and seated above the rostra in the market-place, was a spectator of the sports. The custom is, that many young noblemen and of the magistracy, anointed with oil and having straps of hide in their hands, run about and strike, in sport, at every one they meet. Antony was running with the rest; but, omitting the old ceremony, twining a garland of bay round a diadem, he ran up to the rostra, and, being lifted up by his companions, would have put it upon the head of Cæsar, as if by that ceremony he was declared king. Cæsar seemingly refused, and drew aside to avoid it, and was applauded by the people with great shouts. Again Antony pressed it, and again he declined its acceptance. And so the dispute between them went on for some time, Antony's solicitations receiving but little encouragement from the shouts of a few friends, and Cæsar's refusal being accompanied with the general applause of the people; a curious thing enough, that they should submit with patience to the fact, and yet at the same time dread the name as the destruction of their liberty. Cæsar, very much discomposed at what had passed, got up from his seat, and, laying bare his neck, said he was ready to receive a stroke, if any one of them desired to give it. The crown was at last put on one of his statues, but was taken down by some of the tribunes, who were followed home by the people with shouts of applause. Cæsar, however, resented it, and deposed them.

These passages gave great encouragement to Brutus and Cassius, who, in making choice of trusty friends for such an enterprise, were thinking to engage Antony. The rest approved, except Trebonius, who told them that Antony and he had lodged and travelled together in the last journey they took to meet Cæsar, and that he had let fall several words, in a cautious way, on purpose to sound him; that Antony very well understood him, but did not encourage it; however, he had said nothing of it to Cæsar, but had kept the secret faithfully. The conspirators then proposed that Antony should die with him, which Brutus would not consent to, insisting that an action undertaken in defence of right and the laws must be maintained unsullied, and pure of injustice. It was settled that Antony, whose bodily strength and high office made him formidable, should, at Cæsar's entrance into the senate, when the deed was to be done, be amused outside by some of the party in a conversation about some pretended business.

So when all was proceeded with, according to their plan, and Cæsar had fallen in the senate-house, Antony, at the first moment, took a servant's dress, and hid himself. But, understanding that the conspirators had assembled in the Capitol, and had no further design upon any one, he persuaded them to come down, giving them his son as a hostage. That night Cassius supped at Antony's house, and Brutus with Lepidus. Antony then convened the senate, and spoke in favour of an act of oblivion, and the appointment of Brutus and Cassius to provinces. These measures the senate passed; and resolved that all Cæsar's acts should remain in force. Thus Antony went out of the senate with the highest possible reputation and esteem; for it was apparent that he had prevented a civil war, and had composed, in the wisest and most statesmanlike way, questions of the greatest difficulty and embarrassment. But these temperate counsels were soon swept away by the tide of popular applause, and the prospect, if Brutus were overthrown, of being without doubt the ruler-in-chief. As Cæsar's body was conveying to the tomb, Antony, according to the custom, was making his funeral oration in the market-place, and perceiving the people to be infinitely affected with what he had said, he began to mingle with his praises language of commiseration, and horror at what had happened, and, as he was ending his speech, he took the under-clothes of the dead, and held them up, showing them stains of blood and the holes of the many stabs, calling those that had done this act villains and bloody murderers. All which excited the people to such indignation, that they would not defer the funeral, but, making a pile of tables and forms in the very market-place, set fire to it; and every one, taking a brand, ran to the conspirators' houses, to attack them.

Upon this, Brutus and his whole party left the city, and Cæsar's friends joined themselves to Antony. Calpurnia, Cæsar's wife, lodged with him the best part of the property to the value of four thousand talents; he got also into his hands all Cæsar's papers wherein were contained journals of all he had done, and draughts of what he designed to do, which Antony made good use of; for by this means he appointed what magistrates he pleased, brought whom he would into the senate, recalled some from exile, freed others out of prison, and all this as ordered so by Cæsar. The Romans, in mockery, gave those who were thus benefited the name of Charonites, since, if put to prove their patents, they must have recourse to the papers of the dead. In short, Antony's behaviour in Rome was very absolute, he himself being consul and his two brothers in great place; Caius, the one, being prætor, and Lucius, the other, tribune of the people.

While matters went thus in Rome, the young Cæsar, Cæsar's niece's son, and by testament left his heir, arrived at Rome from Apollonia, where he was when his uncle was killed. The first thing he did was to visit Antony, as his father's friend. He spoke to him concerning the money that was in his hands, and reminded him of the legacy Cæsar had made of seventy-five drachmas of every Roman citizen. Antony, at first, laughing at such discourse from so young a man, told him he wished he were in his health, and that he wanted good counsel and good friends to tell him the burden of being executor to Cæsar would sit very uneasy upon his young shoulders. This was no answer to him; and, when he persisted in demanding the property, Antony went on treating him injuriously both in word and deed, opposed him when he stood for the tribune's office, and, when he was taking steps for the dedication of his father's golden chair, as had been enacted, he threatened to send him to prison if he did not give over soliciting the people. This made the young Cæsar apply himself to Cicero, and all those that hated Antony; by them he was recommended to the senate, while he himself courted the people, and drew together the soldiers from their settlements, till Antony got alarmed, and gave him a meeting in the Capitol, where, after some words, they came to an accommodation.

That night Antony had a very unlucky dream, fancying that his right hand was thunderstruck. And, some few days after, he was informed that Cæsar was plotting to take his life. Cæsar explained, but was not believed, so that the breach was now made as wide as ever; each of them hurried about all through Italy to engage, by great offers, the old soldiers that lay scattered in their settlements, and to be the first to secure the troops that still remained undischarged. Cicero was at this time the man of greatest influence in Rome. He made use of all his art to exasperate the people against Antony, and at length persuaded the senate to declare him a public enemy, to send Cæsar the rods and axes and other marks of honour usually given to prætors, and to issue orders to Hirtius and Pansa, who were the consuls, to drive Antony out of Italy. The armies engaged near Modena, and Cæsar himself was present and took part in the battle. Antony was defeated, but both the consuls were slain. Antony, in his flight, was overtaken by distresses of every kind, and the worst of all of them was famine. But it was his character in calamities to be better than at any other time. Antony, in misfortune, was most nearly a virtuous man. It is common enough for people, when they fall into great disasters, to discern what is right, and what they ought to do; but there are but few who in such extremities have the strength to obey their judgment, either in doing what it approves or avoiding what it condemns; and a good many are so weak as to give way to their habits all the more, and are incapable of using their minds. Antony, on this occasion, was a most wonderful example to his soldiers. He, who had just quitted so much luxury and sumptuous living, made no difficulty now of drinking foul water and feeding on wild fruits and roots. Nay, it is related they ate the very bark of trees, and, in passing over the Alps, lived upon creatures that no one before had ever been willing to touch.

The design was to join the army on the other side the Alps, commanded by Lepidus, who he imagined would stand his friend, he having done him many good offices with Cæsar. On coming up and encamping near at hand, finding he had no sort of encouragement offered him, he resolved to push his fortune and venture all. His hair was long and disordered, nor had he shaved his beard since his defeat; in this guise, and with a dark coloured cloak flung over him, he came into the trenches of Lepidus, and began to address the army. Some were moved at his habit, others at his words, so that Lepidus, not liking it, ordered the trumpets to sound, that he might be heard no longer. This raised in the soldiers yet a greater pity, so that they resolved to confer secretly with him, and dressed Lælius and Clodius in women's clothes, and sent them to see him. They advised him without delay to attack Lepidus's trenches, assuring him that a strong party would receive him, and, if he wished it, would kill Lepidus. Antony, however, had no wish for this, but next morning marched his army to pass over the river that parted the two camps. He was himself the first man that stepped in, and, as he went through towards the other bank, he saw Lepidus's soldiers in great numbers reaching out their hands to help him, and beating down the works to make him way. Being entered into the camp, and finding himself absolute master, he nevertheless treated Lepidus with the greatest civility, and gave him the title of Father, when he spoke to him, and though he had everything at his own command, he left him the honour of being called the general. This fair usage brought over to him Munatius Plancus, who was not far off with a considerable force. Thus in great strength he repassed the Alps, leading with him into Italy seventeen legions and ten thousand horse, besides six legions which he left in garrison under the command of Varius, one of his familiar friends and boon companions, whom they used to call by the nickname of Cotylon.

Cæsar, perceiving that Cicero's wishes were for liberty, had ceased to pay any further regard to him, and was now employing the mediation of his friends to come to a good understanding with Antony. They both met together with Lepidus in a small island, where the conference lasted three days. The empire was soon determined of, it being divided amongst them as if it had been their paternal inheritance. That which gave them all the trouble was to agree who should be put to death, each of them desiring to destroy his enemies and to save his friends. But, in the end, animosity to those they hated carried the day against respect for relations and affection for friends; and Cæsar sacrificed Cicero to Antony, Antony gave up his uncle Lucius Cæsar, and Lepidus received permission to murder his brother Paulus, or, as others say, yielded his brother to them. I do not believe anything ever took place more truly savage or barbarous than this composition, for, in this exchange of blood for blood, they were equally guilty of the lives they surrendered and of those they took; or, indeed, more guilty in the case of their friends, for whose deaths they had not even the justification of hatred. To complete the reconciliation, the soldiery, coming about them, demanded that confirmation should be given to it by some alliance of marriage; Cæsar should marry Clodia, the daughter of Fulvia, wife to Antony. This also being agreed to, three hundred persons were put to death by proscription. Antony gave orders to those that were to kill Cicero to cut off his head and right hand, with which he had written his invectives against him; and, when they were brought before him, he regarded them joyfully, actually bursting out more than once into laughter, and, when he had satiated himself with the sight of them, ordered them to be hung up above the speaker's place in the forum, thinking thus to insult the dead, while in fact he only exposed his own wanton arrogance, and his unworthiness to hold the power that fortune had given him. His uncle, Lucius Cæsar, being closely pursued, took refuge with his sister, who, when the murderers had broken into her house and were pressing into her chamber, met them at the door, and spreading out hands, cried out several times. "You shall not kill

Lucius Cæsar till you first despatch me who gave your general his birth;" and in this manner she succeeded in getting her brother out of the way, and saving his life.

This triumvirate was very hateful to the Romans, and Antony most of all bore the blame, because he was older than Cæsar, and had greater authority than Lepidus, and withal he was no sooner settled in his affairs, but he turned to his luxurious and dissolute way of living. Besides the ill reputation he gained by his disadvantage to him his living in the house of Pompey the Great, who had been as much admired for his temperance and his sober, citizen-like habits of life, as ever he was for having triumphed three times. They could not without anger see the doors of that house shut against magistrates, officers, and envoys, who were shamefully refused admittance, while it was filled inside with players, jugglers, and drunken flatterers, upon whom were spent the greatest part of the wealth which violence and cruelty procured. For they did not limit themselves to the forfeiture of the estates of such as were proscribed, defrauding the widows and families, nor were they contented with laying on every possible kind of tax and imposition; but hearing that several sums of money were, as well by strangers as citizens of Rome, deposited in the hands of the vestal virgins, they went and took the money away by force. When it was manifest that nothing would ever be enough for Antony, Cæsar at last called for a division of property. The army was also divided between them, upon their march into Macedonia to make war with Brutus and Cassius, Lepidus being left with the command of the city.

However, after they had crossed the sea and engaged in operations of war, encamping in front of the enemy, Antony opposite Cassius, and Cæsar opposite Brutus, Cæsar did nothing worth relating, and all the success and victory were Antony's. In the first battle, Cæsar was completely routed by Brutus, his camp taken, he himself very narrowly escaping by flight. As he himself writes in his Memoirs, he retired before the battle, on account of a dream which one of his friends had. But Antony, on the other hand, defeated Cassius; though some have written that he was not actually present in the engagement, and only joined afterwards in the pursuit. Cassius was killed, at his own entreaty and order, by one of his most trusted freedmen, Pindarus, not being aware of Brutus's victory. After a few days' interval, they fought another battle, in which Brutus lost the day, and slew himself; and Cæsar being sick, Antony had almost all the honour of the victory. Standing over Brutus's dead body, he uttered a few words of reproach upon him for the death of his brother Caius, who had been executed by Brutus's order in Macedonia in revenge of Cicero; but, saying presently that Hortensius was most to blame for it, he gave order for his being slain upon his brother's tomb, and, throwing his own scarlet mantle, which was of great value, upon the body of Brutus, he gave charge to one of his own freedmen to take care of his funeral. This man, as Antony came to understand, did not leave the mantle with the corpse, but kept both it and a good part of the money that should have been spent in the funeral for himself; for which he had him put to death.

But Cæsar was conveyed to Rome, no one expecting that he would long survive. Antony, purposing to go to the eastern provinces to lay them under contribution, entered Greece with a large force. The promise had been made that every common soldier should receive for his pay five thousand drachmas; so it was likely there would be need of pretty severe taxing and levying to raise money. However, to the Greeks he showed at first reason and moderation enough: he gratified his love of amusement by hearing the learned men dispute, by seeing the games, and undergoing initiation; and in judicial matters he was equitable, taking pleasure in being styled a lover of Greece, but, above all, in being called a lover of Athens, to which city he made very considerable presents. The people of Megara wished to let him know that they also had something to show him, and invited him to come and see their senate-house. So he went and examined it, and on their asking him how he liked it, told them it was not very large, but extremely *ruinous.*" At the same time, he had a survey made of the temple of the Pythian Apollo as if he had designed to repair it, and indeed he had declared to the senate his intention so to do.

However, leaving Lucius Censorinus in Greece, he crossed over into Asia, and there laid his hands on the stores of accumulated wealth, while kings waited at his door, and queens were rivalling one another, who should make him the greatest presents or appear most charming in his eyes. Thus, whilst Cæsar in Rome was wearing out his strength amidst seditions and wars, Antony, with nothing to do amidst the enjoyments of peace, let his passions carry him easily back to the old course of life that was familiar to him. A set of harpers and pipers, Anaxenor and Xuthus, the dancing-man, Metrodorus, and a whole Bacchic rout of the like Asiatic exhibitors, far outdoing in licence and buffoonery the pests that had followed him out of Italy, came in and possessed the court; the thing was past patience, wealth of all kinds being wasted on objects like these. The whole of Asia was like the city in Sophocles, loaded, at one time—

"——with incense in the air,
Jubilant songs, and outcries of despair."

When he made his entry into Ephesus, the women met him dressed up like Bacchantes, and the men and boys like satyrs and fauns, and throughout the town nothing was to be seen but spears wreathed about with ivy, harps, flutes, and psalteries, while Antony in their songs was Bacchus, the Giver of Joy, and the Gentle. And so indeed he was to some but to far more the Devourer and the Savage; for he would deprive persons of worth and quality of their fortunes to gratify villains and flatterers, who would sometimes beg the estates of men yet living, pretending they were dead, and, obtaining a grant, take possession. He gave his cook the house of a Magnesian citizen, as a reward for a single highly successful supper, and, at last, when he was proceeding to lay a second whole tribute on Asia, Hybreas, speaking on behalf of the cities, took courage, and told him broadly, but aptly enough for Antony's taste, "if you can take two yearly tributes, you can doubtless give us a couple of summers and a double harvest time;" and put it to him in the plainest and boldest way, that Asia had raised two hundred thousand talents for his service: "If this has not been paid to you, ask your collectors for it; if it has, and is all gone, we are ruined men." These words touched Antony to the quick, who was simply ignorant of most things that were done in his name; not that he was so indolent, as he was prone to trust frankly in all about him. For there was much simplicity in his character; he was slow to see his faults, but when he did see them, was extremely repentant, and ready to ask pardon of those he had injured; prodigal in his acts of reparation, and severe in his punishments, but his generosity was much more extravagant than his severity; his raillery was sharp and insulting, but the edge of it was taken off by his readiness to submit to any kind of repartee; for he was as well contented to be rallied, as he was pleased to rally others. And this freedom of speech was, indeed, the cause of many of his disasters. He never imagined those who used so much liberty in their mirth would flatter or deceive him in business of consequence, not knowing how common it is with parasites to mix their flattery with boldness, as confectioners do their sweetmeats with something biting, to prevent the sense of satiety. Their freedoms and impertinences at table were designed expressly to give to their obsequiousness in council the air of being not complaisance, but conviction.

Such being his temper, the last and crowning mischief that could befall him came in the love of Cleopatra, to awaken and kindle to fury passions that as yet lay still and dormant in his nature, and to stifle and finally corrupt any elements that yet made resistance in him of goodness and a sound judgment. He fell into the snare thus. When making preparation for the Parthian war, he sent to command her to make her personal appearance in Cilicia, to answer an accusation, that she had given great assistance, in the late wars, to Cassius. Dellius, who was sent on this message, had no sooner seen her face, and remarked her adroitness and subtlety in speech, but he felt convinced that Antony would not so much as think of giving any molestation to a woman like this; on the contrary, she would be the first in favour with him. So he set himself at once to pay his court to the Egyptian, and gave her his advice, "to go," in the Homeric style, to Cilicia, "in her best attire," and bade her fear nothing from Antony, the gentlest and kindest of soldiers. She had some faith in the words of Dellius, but more in her own attractions; which, having formerly recommended her to Cæsar and the young Cnæus Pompey, she did not doubt might prove yet more successful with Antony. Their acquaintance was with her when a girl, young and ignorant of the world, but she was to meet Antony in the time of life when women's beauty is most splendid, and their intellects are in full maturity. She made great preparation for her journey, of money, gifts, and ornaments of value, such as so wealthy a kingdom might afford, but she brought with her her surest hopes in her own magic arts and charms.

She received several letters, both from Antony and from his friends, to summon her, but she took no account of these orders; and at last, as if in mockery of them, she came sailing up the river Cydnus, in a barge with gilded stern and outspread sails of purple, while oars of silver beat time to the music of flutes and fifes and harps. She herself lay all along under a canopy of cloth of gold, dressed as Venus in a picture; and beautiful young boys, like painted Cupids, stood on each side to fan her. Her maids were dressed like sea nymphs and graces, some steering at the rudder, some working at the ropes. The perfumes diffused themselves from the vessel to the shore, which was covered with multitudes, part following the galley up the river on either bank, part running out of the city to see the sight. The market-place was quite emptied, and Antony at last was left alone sitting upon the tribunal; while the word went through all the multitude, that Venus was come to feast with Bacchus, for the common good of Asia. On her arrival, Antony sent to invite her to supper. She thought it fitter he should come to her; so, willing to show his good-humour and courtesy, he complied, and went. He found the preparations to receive him magnificent beyond expression, but nothing so admirable as the great number of lights; for on a sudden there was let down altogether so great a number of branches with lights in them so ingeniously disposed, some in squares, and some in circles, that the whole thing was a spectacle that has seldom been equalled for beauty.

The next day, Antony invited her to supper, and was very desirous to outdo her as well in magnificence as contrivance; but he found he was altogether beaten in both, and was so well convinced of it that he was himself the first to jest and mock at his poverty of wit and his rustic awkwardness. She, perceiving that his raillery was broad and gross, and savoured more of the soldier than the courtier, rejoined in the same taste, and fell into it at once, without any sort of reluctance or reserve. For her actual beauty, it is said, was not in itself so remarkable that none could be compared with her, or that no one could see her without being struck by it, but the contact of her presence, if you lived with her, was irresistible; the attraction of her person, joining with the charm of her conversation, and the character that attended all she said or did, was something bewitching. It was a pleasure merely to hear the sound of her voice, with which, like an instrument of many strings, she could pass from one language to another; so that there were few of the barbarian nations that she answered by an interpreter; to most of them she spoke herself, as to the Æthiopians, Troglodytes, Hebrews, Arabians, Syrians, Medes, Parthians, and many others, whose language she had learnt; which was all the more surprising because most of the kings, her predecessors, scarcely gave themselves the trouble to acquire the Egyptian tongue, and several of them quite abandoned the Macedonian.

Antony was so captivated by her that, while Fulvia his wife maintained his quarrels in Rome against Cæsar by actual force of arms, and the Parthian troops, commanded by Labienus (the king's generals having made him commander-in-chief), were assembled in Mesopotamia, and ready to enter Syria, he could yet suffer himself to be carried away by her to Alexandria, there to keep holiday, like a boy, in play and diversion, squandering and fooling away in enjoyments that most costly, as Antiphon says, of all valuables, time. They had a sort of company, to whicb they gave a particular name, calling it that of the Inimitable Livers. The members entertained one another daily in turn, with an extravagance of expenditure beyond measure or belief. Philotas, a physician of Amphissa, who was at that time a student of medicine in Alexandria, used to tell my grandfather Lamprias that, having some acquaintance with one of the royal cooks, he was invited by him, being a young man, to come and see the sumptuous preparations for supper. So he was taken into the kitchen, where he admired the prodigious variety of all things; but particularly, seeing eight wild boars roasting whole, says he, "Surely you have a great number of guests." The cook laughed at his simplicity, and told him there were not above twelve to sup, but that every dish was to be served up just roasted to a turn, and if anything was but one minute ill-timed, it was spoiled; "And," said he, "maybe Antony will sup just now, maybe not this hour, maybe he will call for wine, or begin to talk, and will put it off. So that," he continued, "it is not one, but many suppers must be had in readiness, as it is impossible to guess at his hour." This was Philotas's story; who related besides, that he afterwards came to be one of the medical attendants of Antony's eldest son by Fulvia, and used to be invited pretty often, among other companions, to his table, when he was not supping with his father. One day another physician had talked loudly, and given great disturbance to the company, whose mouth Philotas stopped with this sophistical syllogism: "In some states of fever the patient should take cold water; every one who has a fever is in some state of fever; therefore in a fever cold water should always be taken." The man was quite struck dumb, and Antony's son, very much pleased, laughed aloud, and said, "Philotas, I make you a present of all you see there," pointing to a sideboard covered with plate. Philotas thanked him much, but was far enough from ever imagining that a boy of his age could dispose of things of that value. Soon after, however, the plate was all brought to him, and he was desired to get his mark upon it; and when he put it away from him, and was afraid to accept the present. "What ails the man?" said he that brought it; "do you know that he who gives you this is Antony's son, who is free to give it, if it were all gold? but if you will be advised by me, I would counsel you to accept of the value in money from us; for there may be amongst the rest some antique or famous piece of workmanship, which Antony would be sorry to part with." These anecdotes, my grandfather told us, Philotas used frequently to relate.

To return to Cleopatra; Plato admits four sorts of flattery, but she had a thousand. Were Antony serious or disposed to mirth, she had at any moment some new delight or charm to meet his wishes; at every turn she was upon him, and let him escape her neither by day nor by night. She played at dice with him, drank with him, hunted with him; and when he exercised in arms, she was there to see. At night she would go rambling with him to disturb and torment people at their doors and windows, dressed like a servant-woman, for Antony also went in servant's disguise, and from these expeditions he often came home very scurvily answered, and sometimes even beaten severely, though most people guessed who it was. However, the Alexandrians in general liked it all well enough, and joined good-humouredly and kindly in his frolic and play, saying they were much obliged to Antony for acting his tragic parts at Rome, and keeping his comedy for them. It would be trifling without end to be particular in his follies, but his fishing must not be forgotten. He went out one day to angle with Cleopatra, and, being so unfortunate as to catch nothing in the presence of his mistress, he gave secret orders to the fishermen to dive under water, and put fishes that had been already taken upon his hooks; and these he drew so fast that the Egyptian perceived it. But, feigning great admiration, she told everybody how dexterous Antony was, and invited them next day to come and see him again. So, when a number of them had come on board the fishing-boats, as soon as he had let down his hook, one of her servants was beforehand with his divers, and fixed upon his hook a salted fish from Pontus. Antony, feeling his line give, drew up the prey, and when, as may be imagined, great laughter ensued, "Leave," said Cleopatra, "the fishing-rod, general, to us poor sovereigns of Pharos and Canopus; your game is cities, provinces, and kingdoms."

Whilst he was thus diverting himself and engaged in this boy's play, two despatches arrived; one from Rome, that his brother Lucius and his wife Fulvia, after many quarrels among themselves, had joined in war against Cæsar, and having lost all, had fled out of Italy; the other bringing little better news, that Labienus, at the head of the Parthians, was overrunning Asia, from Euphrates and Syria as far as Lydia and Ionia. So, scarcely at last rousing himself from sleep, and shaking off the fumes of wine, he set out to attack the Parthians, and went as far as Phœnicia; but, upon the receipt of lamentable letters from Fulvia, turned his course with two hundred ships to Italy. And, in his way, receiving such of his friends as fled from Italy, he was given to understand that Fulvia was the sole cause of the war, a woman of a restless spirit and very bold, and withal her hopes were that commotions in Italy would force Antony from Cleopatra. But it happened that Fulvia, as she was coming to meet her husband, fell sick by the way, and died at Sicyon, so that an accommodation was the more easily made. For when he reached Italy, and Cæsar showed no intention of laying anything to his charge, and he on his part shifted the blame of everything on Fulvia, those that were friends to them would not suffer that the time should be spent in looking narrowly into the plea, but made a reconciliation first, and then a partition of the empire between them, taking as their boundary the Ionian Sea, the eastern provinces falling to Antony, to Cæsar the western, and Africa being left to Lepidus. And an agreement was made that everyone in their turn, as they thought fit, should make their friends consuls, when they did not choose to take the offices themselves.

These terms were well approved of, but yet it was thought some closer tie would be desirable; and for this, fortune offered occasion. Cæsar had an elder sister, not of the whole blood, for Attia was his mother's name, hers Ancharia. This sister, Octavia, he was extremely attached to, as indeed she was, it is said, quite a wonder of a woman. Her husband, Caius Marcellus, had died not long before, and Antony was now a widower by the death of Fulvia; for, though he did not disavow the passion he had for Cleopatra, yet he disowned anything of marriage, reason as yet, upon this point, still maintaining the debate against the charms of the Egyptian. Everybody concurred in promoting this new alliance, fully expecting that with the beauty, honour, and prudence of Octavia, when her company should, as it was certain it would, have engaged his affections, all would be kept in the safe and happy course of friendship. So, both parties being agreed, they went to Rome to celebrate the nuptials, the senate dispensing with the law by which a widow was not permitted to marry till ten months after the death of her husband.

Sextus Pompeius was in possession of Sicily, and with his ships, under the command of Menas, the pirate, and Menecrates, so infested the Italian coast that no vessels durst venture into those seas. Sextus had behaved with much humanity towards Antony, having received his mother when she fled with Fulvia, and it was therefore judged fit that he also should be received into the peace. They met near the promontory of Misenum, by the mole of the port, Pompey having his fleet at anchor close by, and Antony and Cæsar their troops drawn up all along the shore. There it was concluded that Sextus should quietly enjoy the government of Sicily and Sardinia, he conditioning to scour the seas of all pirates, and to send so much corn every year to Rome.

This agreed on, they invited one another to supper, and by lot it fell to Pompey's turn to give the first entertainment, and Antony, asking where it was to be, "There," said he, pointing to the admiral-galley, a ship of six banks of oars, "that is the only house that Pompey is heir to of his father's." And this he said, reflecting upon Antony, who was then in possession of his father's house. Having fixed the ship on her anchors, and formed a bridgeway from the promontory to conduct on board of her, he gave them a cordial welcome. And when they began to grow warm, and jests were passing freely on Antony and Cleopatra's loves, Menas, the pirate, whispered Pompey, in the ear, "Shall I," said he, "cut the cables, and make you master not of Sicily only and Sardinia, but of the whole Roman empire?" Pompey, having considered a little while, returned him answer, "Menas, this might have been done without acquainting me; now we must rest content; I do not break my word." And so, having been entertained by the other two in their turns, he set sail for Sicily.

After the treaty was completed, Antony despatched Ventidius into Asia, to check the advance of the Parthians, while he, as a compliment to Cæsar, accepted the office of priest to the deceased Cæsar. And in any state affair and matter of consequence, they both behaved themselves with much consideration and friendliness for each other. But it annoyed Antony that in all their amusements, on any trial of skill or fortune, Cæsar should be constantly victorious. He had with him an Egyptian diviner, one of those who calculate nativities, who, either to make his court to Cleopatra, or that by the rules of his art he found it to be so, openly declared to him that though the fortune that attended him was bright and glorious, yet it was overshadowed by Cæsar's; and advised him to keep himself as far distant as he could from that young man; "for your Genius," said he, "dreads his; when absent from him yours is proud and brave, but in his presence unmanly and dejected;" and incidents that occurred appeared to show that the Egyptian spoke truth. For whenever they cast lots for any playful purpose, or threw dice, Antony was still the loser; and repeatedly, when they fought gamecocks or quails, Cæsar's had the victory. This gave Antony a secret displeasure, and made him put the more confidence in the skill of his Egyptian. So, leaving the management of his home affairs to Cæsar, he left Italy, and took Octavia, who had lately borne him a daughter, along with him into Greece.

Here, whilst he wintered in Athens, he received the first news of Ventidius's successes over the Parthians, of his having defeated them in a battle, having slain Labienus and Pharnapates, the best general their king, Hyrodes, possessed. For the celebrating of which he made public feast through Greece, and for the prizes which were contested at Athens he himself acted as steward, and, leaving at home the ensigns that are carried before the general, he made his public appearance in a gown and white shoes, with the steward's wands marching before; and he performed his duty in taking the combatants by the neck, to part them, when they had fought enough.

When the time came for him to set out for the war, he took a garland from the sacred olive, and, in obedience to some oracle, he filled a vessel with the water of the Clepsydra to carry along with him. In this interval, Pacorus, the Parthian king's son, who was marching into Syria with a large army, was met by Ventidius, who gave him battle in the country of Cyrrhestica, slew a large number of his men, and Pacorus among the first. This victory was one of the most renowned achievements of the Romans, and fully avenged their defeats under Crassus, the Parthians being obliged, after the loss of three battles successively, to keep themselves within the bounds of Media and Mesopotamia. Ventidius was not willing to push his good fortune further, for fear of raising some jealousy in Antony, but turning his arms against those that had quitted the Roman interest, he reduced them to their former obedience. Among the rest, he besieged Antiochus, King of Commagene, in the city of Samosata, who made an offer of a thousand talents for his pardon, and a promise of submission to Antony's commands. But Ventidius told him that he must send to Antony, who was already on his march, and had sent word to Ventidius to make no terms with Antiochus, wishing that at any rate this one exploit might be ascribed to him, and that people might not think that all his successes were won by his lieutenants. The siege, however, was long protracted; for when those within found their offers refused, they defended themselves stoutly, till, at last, Antony, finding he was doing nothing, in shame and regret for having refused the first offer, was glad to make an accommodation with Antiochus for three hundred talents. And, having given some orders for the affairs of Syria, he returned to Athens; and, paying Ventidius the honours he well deserved, dismissed him to receive his triumph. He is the only man that has ever yet triumphed for victories obtained over the Parthians; he was of obscure birth, but, by means of Antony's friendship, obtained an opportunity of showing his capacity, and doing great things; and his making such glorious use of it gave new credit to the current observation about Cæsar and Antony, that they were more fortunate in what they did by their lieutenants than in their own persons. For Sossius, also, had great success, and Canidius, whom he left in Armenia, defeated the people there, and also the kings of the Albanians and Iberians, and marched victorious as far as Caucasus, by which means the fame of Antony's arms had become great among the barbarous nations.

He, however, once more, upon some unfavourable stories, taking offence against Cæsar, set sail with three hundred ships for Italy, and, being refused admittance to the port of Brundusium, made for Tarentum. There his wife Octavia, who came from Greece with him, obtained leave to visit her brother, she being then great with child, having already borne her husband a second daughter; and as she was on her way she met Caesar, with his two friends Agrippa and Mæcenas, and, taking these two aside, with great entreaties and lamentations she told them, that of the most fortunate woman upon earth, she was in danger of becoming the most unhappy; for as yet every one's eyes were fixed upon her as the wife and sister of the two great commanders, but, if rash counsels should prevail, and war ensue, "I shall be miserable," said she, "without redress; for on what side soever victory falls, I shall be sure to be a loser." Cæsar was overcome by these entreaties, and advanced in a peaceable temper to Tarentum, where those that were present beheld a most stately spectacle; a vast army drawn up by the shore, and as great a fleet in the harbour, all without the occurrence of any act of hostility; nothing but the salutations of friends, and other expressions of joy and kindness, passing from one armament to the other. Antony first entertained Cæsar, this also being a concession on Cæsar's part to his sister; and when at length an agreement was made between them, that Cæsar should give Antony two of his legions to serve him in the Parthian war, and that Antony should in return leave with him a hundred armed galleys, Octavia further obtained of her husband, besides this, twenty light ships for her brother, and of her brother, a thousand foot for her husband. So, having parted good friends, Cæsar went immediately to make war with Pompey to conquer Sicily. And Antony, leaving in Cæsar's charge his wife and children, and his children by his former wife Fulvia, set sail for Asia.

But the mischief that thus long had lain still, the passion for Cleopatra, which better thoughts had seemed to have lulled and charmed into oblivion, upon his approach to Syria gathered strength again, and broke out into a flame. And, in fine, like Plato's restive and rebellious horse of the human soul, flinging off all good and wholesome counsel, and breaking fairly loose, he sends Fonteius Capito to bring Cleopatra into Syria. To whom at her arrival he made no small or trifling present, Phœnicia, Cœle-Syria, Cyprus, great part of Cilicia, that side of Judæa which produces balm, that part of Arabia where the Nabathæans extend to the outer sea; profuse gifts which much displeased the Romans. For although he had invested several private persons in great governments and kingdoms, and bereaved many kings of theirs, as Antigonus of Judæa, whose head he caused to be struck off (the first example of that punishment being inflicted on a king), yet nothing stung the Romans like the shame of these honours paid to Cleopatra. Their dissatisfaction was augmented also by his acknowledging as his own the twin children he had by her, giving them the name of Alexander and Cleopatra, and adding, as their surnames, the titles of Sun and Moon. But he, who knew how to put a good colour on the most dishonest action, would say that the greatness of the Roman empire consisted more in giving than in taking kingdoms, and that the way to carry noble blood through the world was by begetting in every place a new line and series of kings; his own ancestor had thus been born of Hercules; Hercules had not limited his hopes of progeny to a single womb, nor feared any law like Solon's or any audit of procreation, but had freely let nature take her will in the foundation and first commencement of many families.

After Phraates had killed his father Hyrodes, and taken possession of his kingdom, many of the Parthians left their country; among the rest Monæses, a man of great distinction and authority, sought refuge with Antony, who, looking on his case as similar to that of Themistocles, and likening his own opulence and magnanimity to those of the former Persian kings, gave him three cities, Larissa, Arethusa, and Hierapolis, which was formerly called Bambyce. But when the King of Parthia soon recalled him, giving him his word and honour for his safety, Antony was not unwilling to give him leave to return, hoping thereby to surprise Phraates, who would believe that peace would continue; for he only made the demand of him that he should send back the Roman ensigns which were taken when Crassus was slain, and the prisoners that remained yet alive. This done, he sent Cleopatra to Egypt, and marched through Arabia and Armenia; and, when his forces came together, and were joined by those of his confederate kings (of whom there were very many, and the most considerable, Artavasdes, King of Armenia, who came at the head of six thousand horse and seven thousand foot), he made a general muster. There appeared sixty thousand Roman foot, ten thousand horse, Spaniards and Gauls, who counted as Romans; and, of other nations, horse and foot thirty thousand. And these great preparations, that put the Indians beyond Bactria into alarm, and made all Asia shake, were all we are told rendered useless to him because of Cleopatra. For, in order to pass the winter with her, the war was pushed on before its due time; and all he did was done without perfect consideration, as by a man who had no power of control over his faculties, who, under the effect of some drug or magic, was still looking back elsewhere, and whose object was much more to hasten his return than to conquer his enemies.

For, first of all, when he should have taken up his winter-quarters in Armenia, to refresh his men, who were tired with long marches, having come at least eight thousand furlongs, and then having taken the advantage in the beginning of the spring to invade Media, before the Parthians were out of winter-quarters, he had not patience to expect his time, but marched into the province of Atropatene, leaving Armenia on the left hand, and laid waste all that country. Secondly, his haste was so great that he left behind the engines absolutely required for any siege which followed the camp in three hundred waggons, and, among the rest, a ram eighty feet long; none of which was it possible, if lost or damaged, to repair or to make the like, as the provinces of the Upper Asia produce no trees long or hard enough for such uses. Nevertheless, he left them all behind, as a mere impediment to his speed, in the charge of a detachment under the command of Statianus, the waggon officer. He himself laid siege to Phraata, a principal city of the King of Media, wherein were that king's wife and children. And when actual need proved the greatness of his error, in leaving the siege-train behind him, he had nothing for it but to come up and raise a mound against the walls, with infinite labour and great loss of time. Meantime Phraates, coming down with a large army, and hearing that the waggons were left behind with the battering engines, sent a strong party of horse, by which Statianus was surprised, he himself and ten thousand of his men slain, the engines all broken in pieces, many taken prisoners, and among the rest King Polemon.

This great miscarriage in the opening of the campaign much discouraged Antony's army, and Artavasdes, King of Armenia, deciding that the Roman prospects were bad, withdrew with all his forces from the camp, although he had been the chief promoter of the war. The Parthians, encouraged by their success, came up to the Romans at the siege, and gave them many affronts; upon which Antony, fearing that the despondency and alarm of his soldiers would only grow worse if he let them lie idle, taking all the horse, ten legions, and three prætorian cohorts of heavy infantry, resolved to go out and forage, designing by this means to draw the enemy with more advantage to a battle. To effect this, he marched a day's journey from his camp, and finding the Parthians hovering about, in readiness to attack him while he was in motion, he gave orders for the signal of battle to be hung out in the encampment, but, at the same time, pulled down the tents, as if he meant not to fight, but to lead his men home again; and so he proceeded to lead them past the enemy, who were drawn up in a half-moon, his orders being that the horse should charge as soon as the legions were come up near enough to second them. The Parthians, standing still while the Romans marched by them, were in great admiration of their army, and of the exact discipline it observed, rank after rank passing on at equal distances in perfect order and silence, their pikes all ready in their hands. But when the signal was given, and the horse turned short upon the Parthians, and with loud cries charged them, they bravely received them, though they were at once too near for bowshot; but the legions coming up with loud shouts and rattling of their arms so frightened their horses and indeed the men themselves, that they kept their ground no longer. Antony pressed them hard, in great hopes that this victory should put an end to the war; the foot had them in pursuit for fifty furlongs, and the horse for thrice that distance, and yet, the advantage summed up, they had but thirty prisoners, and there were but fourscore slain. So that they were all filled with dejection and discouragement, to consider that when they were victorious, their advantages were so small, and that when they were beaten, they lost so great a number of men as they had done when the carriages were taken.

The next day, having put the baggage in order, they marched back to the camp before Phraata, in the way meeting with some scattering troops of the enemy, and, as they marched further, with greater parties, at length with the body of the enemy's army, fresh and in good order, who defied them to battle, and charged them on every side, and it was not without great difficulty that they reached the camp. There Antony, finding that his men had in a panic deserted the defence of the mound, upon a sally of the Medes, resolved to proceed against them by decimation, as it is called, which is done by dividing the soldiers into tens, and, out of every ten, putting one to death, as it happens by lot. The rest he gave orders should have, instead of wheat, their rations of corn in barley.

The war was now become grievous to both parties, and the prospect of its continuance yet more fearful to Antony, in respect that he was threatened with famine; for he could no longer forage without wounds and slaughter. And Phraates, on the other side, was full of apprehension that if the Romans were to persist in carrying on the siege, the autumnal equinox being past and the air already closing in for cold, he should be deserted by his soldiers, who would suffer anything rather than wintering in open field. To prevent which, he had recourse to the following deceit: he gave orders to those of his men who had made most acquaintance among the Roman soldiers, not to pursue too close when they met them foraging, but to suffer them to carry off some provision; moreover, that they should praise their valour, and declare that it was not without just reason that their king looked upon the Romans as the bravest men in the world. This done, upon further opportunity, they rode nearer in, and, drawing up their horses by the men, began to revile Antony for his obstinacy; that whereas Phraates desired nothing more than peace, and an occasion to show how ready he was to save the lives of so many brave soldiers, he, on the contrary, gave no opening to any friendly offers, but sat awaiting the arrival of the two fiercest and worst enemies, winter and famine, from whom it would be hard for them to make their escape, even with all the good-will of the Parthians to help them. Antony, having these reports from many hands, began to indulge the hope; nevertheless, he would not send any message to the Parthian till he had put the question to these friendly talkers, whether what they said was said by order of their king. Receiving answer that it was, together with new encouragement to believe them, he sent some of his friends to demand once more the standards and prisoners, lest if he should ask nothing, he might be supposed to be too thankful to have leave to retreat in quiet. The Parthian king made answer that, as for the standards and prisoners, he need not trouble himself: but if he thought fit to retreat, he might do it when he pleased, in peace and safety. Some few days, therefore, being spent in collecting the baggage he set out upon his march. On which occasion, though there was no man of his time like him for addressing a multitude, or for carrying soldiers with him by the force of words, out of shame and sadness he could not find in his heart to speak himself but employed Domitius Ænobarbus. And some of the soldiers resented it, as an undervaluing of them; but the greater number saw the true cause, and pitied it, and thought it rather a reason why they on their side should treat their general with more respect and obedience than ordinary.

Antony had resolved to return by the same way he came, which was through a level country clear of all trees; but a certain Mardian came to him (one that was very conversant with the manners of the Parthians, and whose fidelity to the Romans had been tried at the battle where the machines were lost), and advised him to keep the mountains close on his right hand, and not to expose his men, heavily armed, in a broad, open, riding country, to the attacks of a numerous army of light horse and archers; that

Phraates with fair promises had persuaded him from the siege on purpose that he might with more ease cut him off in his retreat; but if so he pleased, he would conduct him by a nearer route, on which moreover he should find the necessaries for his army in greater abundance. Antony upon this began to consider what was best to be done; he was unwilling to seem to have any mistrust of the Parthians after their treaty; but, holding it to be really best to march his army the shorter and more inhabited way, he demanded of the Mardian some assurance of his faith, who offered himself to be bound until the army came safe into Armenia. Two days he conducted the army bound, and, on the third, when Antony had given up all thought of the enemy, and was marching at his ease in no very good order, the Mardian, perceiving the bank of the river broken down, and the water let out and overflowing the road by which they were to pass, saw at once that this was the handiwork of the Parthians, done out of mischief, and to hinder their march: so he advised Antony to be upon his guard, for that the enemy was nigh at hand. And no sooner had he begun to put his men in order, disposing the slingers and dart-men in convenient intervals for sallying out, but the Parthians came pouring in on all sides, fully expecting to encompass them, and throw the whole army into disorder. They were at once attacked by the light troops, whom they galled a good deal with their arrows; but being themselves as warmly entertained with the slings and darts, and many wounded, they made their retreat. Soon after, rallying up afresh, they were beat back by a battalion of Gallic horse, and appeared no more that day.

By their manner of attack Antony, seeing what to do, not only placed the slings and darts as a rear guard, but also lined both flanks with them, and so marched in a square battle, giving order to the horse to charge and beat off the enemy, but not to follow them far as they retired. So that the Parthians, not doing more mischief for the four ensuing days than they received, began to abate in their zeal, and, complaining that the winter season was much advanced, pressed for returning home.

But, on the fifth day, Flavius Gallus, a brave and active officer, who had a considerable command in the army, came to Antony, desiring of him some light infantry out of the rear, and some horse out of the front, with which he would undertake to do some considerable service. Which when he had obtained, he beat the enemy back, not withdrawing, as was usual, at the same time, and retreating upon the mass of the heavy infantry, but maintaining his own ground, and engaging boldly. The officers who commanded in the rear, perceiving how far he was getting from the body of the army, sent to warn him back, but he took no notice of them. It is said that Titius the quæstor snatched the standards and turned them round, upbraiding Gallus with thus leading so many brave men to destruction.

But when he on the other side reviled him again, and commanded the men that were about him to stand firm, Titius made his retreat, and Gallus, charging the enemies in the front, was encompassed by a party that fell upon his rear, which at length perceiving, he sent a messenger to demand succour. But the commanders of the heavy infantry, Canidius amongst others, a particular favourite of Antony's, seem here to have committed a great oversight. For, instead of facing about with the whole body, they sent small parties, and, when they were defeated, they still sent out small parties, so that by their bad management the rout would have spread through the whole army, if Antony himself had not marched from the van at the head of the third legion, and, passing this through among the fugitives, faced the enemies, and hindered them from any further pursuit.

In this engagement were killed three thousand, five thousand were carried back to the camp wounded, amongst the rest Gallus, shot through the body with four arrows, of which wounds he died. Antony went from tent to tent to visit and comfort the rest of them, and was not able to see his men without tears and a passion of grief. They, however, seized his hand with joyful faces, bidding him go and see to himself and not be concerned about them, calling him their emperor and their general, and saying that if he did well they were safe. For, in short, never in all these times can history make mention of a general at the head of a more splendid army; whether you consider strength and youth, or patience and sufferance in labours and fatigues; but as for the obedience and affectionate respect they bore their general, and the unanimous feeling amongst small and great alike, officers and common soldiers, to prefer his good opinion of them to their very lives and being, in this part of military excellence it was not possible that they could have been surpassed by the very Romans of old. For this devotion, as I have said before, there were many reasons, as the nobility of his family, his eloquence, his frank and open manners, his liberal and magnificent habits, his familiarity in talking with everybody, and, at this time particularly, his kindness in visiting and pitying the sick, joining in all their pains, and furnishing them with all things necessary, so that the sick and wounded were even more eager to serve than those that were whole and strong.

Nevertheless, this last victory had so encouraged the enemy that, instead of their former impatience and weariness, they began soon to feel contempt for the Romans, staying all night near the camp, in expectation of plundering their tents and baggage, which they concluded they must abandon; and in the morning new forces arrived in large masses, so that their number was grown to be not less, it is said, than forty thousand horse; and the king had sent the very guards that attended upon his own person, as to a sure and unquestioned victory, for he himself was never present in any fight. Antony, designing to harangue the soldiers, called for a mourning habit that he might move them the more, but was dissuaded by his friends; so he came forward in the general's scarlet cloak, and addressed them, praising those that had gained the victory, and reproaching those that had fled, the former answering him with promises of success, and the latter excusing themselves, and telling him they were ready to undergo decimation, or any other punishment he should please to inflict upon them, only entreating that he would forget and not discompose himself with their faults. At which he lifted up his hands to heaven, and prayed the gods that, if to balance the great favours he had received of them any judgment lay in store, they would pour it upon his head alone, and grant his soldiers victory.

The next day they took better order for their march, and the Parthians, who thought they were marching rather to plunder than to fight, were much taken aback, when they came up and were received with a shower of missiles, to find the enemy not disheartened, but fresh and resolute. So that they themselves began to lose courage. But at the descent of a hill where the Romans were obliged to pass, they got together, and let fly their arrows upon them as they moved slowly down. But the full-armed infantry, facing round, received the light troops within; and those in the first rank knelt on one knee, holding their shields before them, the next rank holding theirs over the first, and so again others over these, much like the tiling of a house, or the rows of seats in a theatre, the whole affording sure defence against arrows, which glanced upon them without doing any harm. The Parthians, seeing the Romans down upon their knees, could not imagine but that it must proceed from weariness; so that they laid down their bows, and, taking their spears, made a fierce onset, when the Romans, with a great cry, leaped upon their feet, striking hand to hand with their javelins, slew the foremost, and put the rest to flight. After this rate it was every day, and the trouble they gave made the marches short; in addition to which famine began to be felt in the camp, for they could get but little corn, and that which they got they were forced to fight for; and, besides this, they were in want of implements to grind it and make bread. For they had left almost all behind, the baggage horses being dead or otherwise employed in carrying the sick and wounded. Provision was so scarce in the army that an Attic quart of wheat sold for fifty drachmas, and barley loaves for their weight in silver. And when they tried vegetables and roots, they found such as are commonly eaten very scarce, so that they were constrained to venture upon any they could get, and, among others they chanced upon an herb that was mortal, first taking away all sense and understanding. He that had eaten of it remembered nothing in the world, and employed himself only in moving great stones from one place to another, which he did with as much earnestness and industry as if it had been a business of the greatest consequence. Through all the camp there was nothing to be seen but men grubbing upon the ground at stones, which they carried from place to place. But in the end they threw up bile and died, as wine, moreover, which was the one antidote, failed. When Antony saw them die so fast, and the Parthians still in pursuit, he was heard to exclaim several times over, "O, the Ten Thousand!" as if in admiration of the retreat of the Greeks, with Xenophon, who, when they had a longer journey to make from Babylonia, and a more powerful enemy to deal with, nevertheless came home safe.

The Parthians, finding that they could not divide the Roman army, nor break the order of their battle, and that withal they had been so often worsted, once more began to treat the foragers with professions of humanity; they came up to them with their bows unbent, telling them that they were going home to their houses; that this was the end of their retaliation, and that only some Median troops would follow for two or three days, not with any design to annoy them, but for the defence of some of the villages further on. And, saying this, they saluted them and embraced them with a great show of friendship. This made the Romans full of confidence again, and Antony, on hearing of it, was more disposed to take the road through the level country, being told that no water was to be hoped for on that through the mountains. But while he was preparing thus to do, Mithridates came into the camp, a cousin to Monæses, of whom we related that he sought refuge with the Romans, and received in gift from Antony three cities. Upon his arrival, he desired somebody might be brought to him that could speak Syriac or Parthian. One Alexander, of Antioch, a friend of Antony's, was brought to him, to whom the stranger, giving his name, and mentioning Monæses as the person who desired to do the kindness, put the question, did he see that high range of hills, pointing at some distance. He told him, yes. "It is there," said he, "the whole Parthian army lie in wait for your passage; for the great plains come immediately up to them, and they expect that, confiding in their promises, you will leave the way of the mountains, and take the level route. It is true that in passing over the mountains you will suffer the want of water, and the fatigue to which you have become familiar, but if you pass through the plains, Antony must expect the fortune of Crassus."

This said, he departed. Antony, in alarm calling his friends in council, sent for the Mardian guide, who was of the same opinion. He told them that, with or without enemies, the want of any certain track in the plain, and the likelihood of their losing their way, were quite objection enough; the other route was rough and without water, but then it was but for a day.

Antony, therefore, changing his mind, marched away upon this road that night, commanding that every one should carry water sufficient for his own use; but most of them being unprovided with vessels, they made shift with their helmets, and some with skins. As soon as they started, the news of it was carried to the Parthians, who followed them, contrary to their custom, through the night, and at sunrise attacked the rear, which was tired with marching and want of sleep, and not in condition to make any considerable defence. For they had got through two hundred and forty furlongs that night, and at the end of such a march to find the enemy at their heels put them out of heart. Besides, having to fight for every step of the way increased their distress from thirst. Those that were in the van came up to a river, the water of which was extremely cool and clear, but brackish and medicinal, and, on being drunk, produced immediate pains in the bowels and a renewed thirst. Of this the Mardian had forewarned them, but they could not forbear, and, beating back those that opposed them, they drank of it. Antony ran from one place to another, begging they would have a little patience, that not far off there was a river of wholesome water, and that the rest of the way was so difficult for the horse that the enemy could pursue them no further; and, saying this, he ordered to sound a retreat to call those back that were engaged, and commanded the tents should be set up, that the soldiers might at any rate refresh themselves in the shade.

But the tents were scarce well put up, and the Parthians beginning, according to their custom, to withdraw, when Mithridates came again to them, and informed Alexander, with whom he had before spoken, that he would do well to advise Antony to stay where he was no longer than needs he must, that, after having refreshed his troops, he should endeavour with all diligence to gain the next river, that the Parthians would not cross it, but so far they were resolved to follow them. Alexander made his report to Antony, who ordered a quantity of gold plate to be carried to Mithridates, who, taking as much as he could well hide under his clothes, went his way. And, upon this advice, Antony, while it was yet day, broke up his camp, and the whole army marched forward without receiving any molestation from the Parthians, though that night by their own doing was in effect the most wretched and terrible that they passed. For some of the men began to kill and plunder those whom they suspected to have any money, ransacked the baggage, and seized the money there. In the end, they laid hands on Antony's own equipage, and broke all his rich tables and cups, dividing the fragments amongst them. Antony, hearing such a noise and such a stirring to and fro all through the army, the belief prevailing that the enemy had routed and cut off a portion of the troops, called for one of his freedmen, then serving as one of his guards, Rhamnus by name, and made him take an oath that whenever he should give him orders he would run his sword through his body and cut off his head, that he might not fall alive into the hands of the Parthians, nor, when dead, be recognised as the general. While he was in this consternation, and all his friends about him in tears, the Mardian came up and gave them all new life. He convinced them, by the coolness and humidity of the air, which they could feel in breathing it, that the river which he had spoken of was now not far off, and the calculation of the time that had been required to reach it came, he said, to the same result, for the night was almost spent. And, at the same time, others came with information that all the confusion in the camp proceeded only from their own violence and robbery among themselves. To compose this tumult, and bring them again into some order after their distraction, he commanded the signal to be given for a halt.

Day began to break, and quiet and regularity were just reappearing, when the Parthian arrows began to fly among the rear, and the light-armed troops were ordered out to battle. And, being seconded by the heavy infantry, who covered one another as before described with their shields, they bravely received the enemy, who did not think convenient to advance any further, while the van of the army, marching forward leisurely in this manner, came in sight of the river, and Antony, drawing up the cavalry on the banks to confront the enemy, first passed over the sick and wounded. And, by this time, even those who were engaged with the enemy had opportunity to drink at their ease; for the Parthians, on seeing the river, unbent their bows, and told the Romans they might pass over freely, and made them great compliments in praise of their valour. Having crossed without molestation, they rested themselves awhile, and presently went forward, not giving perfect credit to the fair words of their enemies. Six days after this last battle, they arrived at the river Araxes, which divides Media and Armenia, and seemed, both by its deepness and the violence of the current, to be very dangerous to pass. A report, also, had crept in amongst them, that the enemy was in ambush, ready to set upon them as soon as they should be occupied with their passage. But when they were got over on the other side, and found themselves in Armenia, just as if land was now sighted after a storm at sea, they kissed the ground for joy, shedding tears and embracing each other in their delight. But taking their journey through a land that abounded in all sorts of plenty, they ate, after their long want, with that excess of everything they met with that they suffered from dropsies and dysenteries.

Here Antony, making a review of his army, found that he had lost twenty thousand foot and four thousand horse, of which the better half perished, not by the enemy, but by diseases. Their march was of twenty-seven days from Phraata, during which they had beaten the Parthians in eighteen battles, though with little effect or lasting result, because of their being so unable to pursue. By which it is manifest that it was Artavasdes who lost Antony the benefit of the expedition. For had the sixteen thousand horsemen whom he led away, out of Media, armed in the same style as the Parthians, and accustomed to their manner of fight, been there to follow the pursuit when the Romans put them to flight, it is impossible they could have rallied so often after their defeats, and reappeared again as they did to renew their attacks. For this reason, the whole army was very earnest with Antony to march into Armenia to take revenge. But he, with more reflection, forbore to notice the desertion, and continued all his former courtesies, feeling that the army was wearied out, and in want of all manner of necessaries. Afterwards, however, entering Armenia, with invitations and fair promises he prevailed upon Artavasdes to meet him, when he seized him, bound him, and carried him to Alexandria, and there led him in a triumph; one of the things which most offended the Romans, who felt as if all the honours and solemn observances of their country were, for Cleopatra's sake, handed over to the Egyptians.

This, however was at an after time. For the present, marching his army in great haste in the depth of winter through continual storms of snow, he lost eight thousand of his men, and came with much diminished numbers to a place called the White Village, between Sidon and Berytus, on the seacoast, where he waited for the arrival of Cleopatra. And, being impatient of the delay she made, he bethought himself of shortening the time in wine and drunkenness, and yet could not endure the tediousness of a meal, but would start from table and run to see if she were coming. Till at last she came into port, and brought with her clothes and money for the soldiers. Though some say that Antony only received the clothes from her and distributed his own money in her name.

A quarrel presently happened between the King of Media and Phraates of Parthia, beginning, it is said, about the division of the booty that was taken from the Romans, and creating great apprehension in the Median lest he should lose his kingdom. He sent, therefore, ambassadors to Antony, with offers of entering into a confederate war against Phraates. And Antony, full of hopes at being thus asked, as a favour, to accept that one thing, horse and archers, the want of which had hindered his beating the Parthians before, began at once to prepare for a return to Armenia, there to join the Medes on the Araxes, and begin the war afresh. But Octavia, in Rome, being desirous to see Antony, asked Cæsar's leave to go to him; which he gave her, not so much, say most authors, to gratify his sister, as to obtain a fair pretence to begin the war upon her dishonourable reception. She no sooner arrived at Athens, but by letters from Antony she was informed of his new expedition, and his will that she should await him there. And, though she were much displeased, not being ignorant of the real reason of this usage, yet she wrote to him to know to what place he would be pleased she should send the things she had brought with her for his use; for she had brought clothes for his soldiers, baggage, cattle, money, and presents for his friends and officers, and two thousand chosen soldiers sumptuously armed, to form prætorian cohorts. This message was brought from Octavia to Antony by Niger, one of his friends, who added to it the praises she deserved so well. Cleopatra, feeling her rival already, as it were, at hand, was seized with fear, lest if to her noble life and her high alliance, she once could add the charm of daily habit and affectionate intercourse, she should become irresistible, and be his absolute mistress forever. So she feigned to be dying for love of Antony, bringing her body down by slender diet; when he entered the room, she fixed her eyes upon him in a rapture, and when he left, seemed to languish and half faint away. She took great pains that he should see her in tears, and, as soon as he noticed it, hastily dried them up and turned away, as if it were her wish that he should know nothing of it. All this was acting while he prepared for Media; and Cleopatra's creatures were not slow to forward the design, upbraiding Antony with his unfeeling, hard-hearted temper, thus letting a woman perish whose soul depended upon him and him alone. Octavia, it was true, was his wife, and had been married to him because it was found convenient for the affairs of her brother that it should be so, and she had the honour of the title; but Cleopatra, the sovereign queen of many nations, had been contented with the name of his mistress, nor did she shun or despise the character whilst she might see him, might live with him, and enjoy him; if she were bereaved of this, she would not survive the loss. In fine, they so melted and unmanned him that, fully believing she would die if he forsook her, he put off the war and returned to Alexandria, deferring his Median expedition until next summer, though news came of the Parthians being all in confusion with intestine disputes. Nevertheless, he did some time after go into that country, and made an alliance with the King of Media, by marriage of a son of his by Cleopatra to the king's daughter, who was yet very young; and so returned, with his thoughts taken up about the civil war.

When Octavia returned from Athens, Cæsar, who considered she had been injuriously treated, commanded her to live in a separate house; but she refused to leave the house of her husband, and entreated him, unless he had already resolved, upon other motives, to make war with Antony, that he would on her account let it alone; it would be intolerable to have it said of the two greatest commanders in the world that they had involved the Roman people in a civil war, the one out of passion for, the other out of resentment about, a woman. And her behaviour proved her words to be sincere. She remained in Antony's house as if he were at home in it, and took the noblest and most generous care, not only of his children by her, but of those by Fulvia also. She received all the friends of Antony that came to Rome to seek office or upon any business, and did her utmost to prefer their requests to Cæsar; yet this her honourable deportment did but, without her meaning it, damage the reputation of Antony; the wrong he did to such a woman made him hated. Nor was the division he made among his sons at Alexandria less unpopular; it seemed a theatrical piece of insolence and contempt of his country. For assembling the people in the exercise ground, and causing two golden thrones to be placed on a platform of silver, the one for him and the other for Cleopatra, and at their feet lower thrones for their children, he proclaimed Cleopatra Queen of Egypt, Cyprus, Libya, and Cœle-Syria, and with her conjointly Cæsarion, the reputed son of the former Cæsar, who left Cleopatra with child. His own sons by Cleopatra were to have the style of king of kings; to Alexander he gave Armenia and Media, with Parthia, so soon as it should be overcome; to Ptolemy, Phœnicia, Syria, and Cilicia. Alexander was brought out before the people in Median costume, the tiara and upright peak, and Ptolemy, in boots and mantle and Macedonian cap done about with the diadem; for this was the habit of the successors of Alexander, as the other was of the Medes and Armenians. And as soon as they had saluted their parents, the one was received by a guard of Macedonians, the other by one of Armenians. Cleopatra was then, as at other times when she appeared in public, dressed in the habit of the goddess Isis, and gave audience to the people under the name of the New Isis.

Cæsar, relating these things in the senate, and often complaining to the people, excited men's minds against Antony, and Antony also sent messages of accusation against Cæsar. The principal of his charges were these: first, that he had not made any division with him of Sicily, which was lately taken from Pompey; secondly, that he had retained the ships he had lent him for the war; thirdly, that, after deposing Lepidus, their colleague, he had taken for himself the army, governments, and revenues formerly appropriated to him; and lastly, that he had parcelled out almost all Italy amongst his own soldiers, and left nothing for his. Cæsar's answer was as follows: that he had put Lepidus out of government because of his own misconduct; that what he had got in war he would divide with Antony, so soon as Antony gave him a share of Armenia; that Antony's soldiers had no claims in Italy, being in possession of Media and Parthia, the acquisitions which their brave actions under their general had added to the Roman empire.

Antony was in Armenia when this answer came to him, and immediately sent Canidius with sixteen legions towards the sea; but he, in the company of Cleopatra, went to Ephesus, whither ships were coming in from all quarters to form the navy, consisting, vessels of burden included, of eight hundred vessels, of which Cleopatra furnished two hundred, together with twenty thousand talents, and provision for the whole army during the war. Antony, on the advice of Domitius and some others, bade Cleopatra return into Egypt, there to expect the event of the war; but she, dreading some new reconciliation by Octavia's means, prevailed with Canidius, by a large sum of money, to speak in her favour with Antony, pointing out to him that it was not just that one that bore so great a part in the charge of the war should be robbed of her share of glory in the carrying it on; nor would it be politic to disoblige the Egyptians, who were so considerable a part of his naval forces; nor did he see how she was inferior in prudence to any of the kings that were serving with him; she had long governed a great kingdom by herself alone, and long lived with him, and gained experience in public affairs. These arguments (so the fate that destined all to Cæsar would have it) prevailed; and when all their forces had met, they sailed together to Samos, and held high festivities. For, as it was ordered that all kings, princes, and governors, all nations and cities within the limits of Syria, the Mæotid Lake, Armenia, and Illyria, should bring or cause to be brought all munitions necessary for war, so was it also proclaimed that all stage-players should make their appearance at Samos; so that, while pretty nearly the whole world was filled with groans and lamentations, this one island for some days resounded with piping and harping, theatres filling, and choruses playing. Every city sent an ox as its contribution to the sacrifice, and the kings that accompanied Antony competed who should make the most magnificent feasts and the greatest presents; and men began to ask themselves, what would be done to celebrate the victory, when they went to such an expense of festivity at the opening of the war.

This over, he gave Priene to his players for a habitation, and set sail for Athens, where fresh sports and play-acting employed him. Cleopatra, jealous of the honours Octavia had received at Athens (for Octavia was much beloved by the Athenians), courted the favour of the people with all sorts of attentions. The Athenians, in requital, having decreed her public honours, deputed several of the citizens to wait upon her at her house; amongst whom went Antony as one, he being an Athenian citizen, and he it was that made the speech. He sent orders to Rome to have Octavia removed out of his house. She left it, we are told, accompanied by all his children, except the eldest by Fulvia, who was then with his father, weeping and grieving that she must be looked upon as one of the causes of the war. But the Romans pitied, not so much her, as Antony himself, and more particularly those who had seen Cleopatra, whom they could report to have no way the advantage of Octavia either in youth or in beauty.

The speed and extent of Antony's preparations alarmed Cæsar, who feared he might be forced to fight the decisive battle that summer. For he wanted many necessaries, and the people grudged very much to pay the taxes; freemen being called upon to pay a fourth part of their incomes, and freed slaves an eighth of their property, so that there were loud outcries against him, and disturbances throughout all Italy. And this is looked upon as one of the greatest of Antony's oversights, that he did not then press the war. For he allowed time at once for Cæsar to make his preparations and for the commotions to pass over. For while people were having their money called for, they were mutinous and violent; but, having paid it, they held their peace. Titius and Plancus, men of consular dignity and friends to Antony, having been ill-used by Cleopatra, whom they had most resisted in her design of being present in the war, came over to Cæsar and gave information of the contents of Antony's will, with which they were acquainted. It was deposited in the hands of the vestal virgins, who refused to deliver it up, and sent Cæsar word, if he pleased, he should come and seize it himself, which he did. And, reading it over to himself, he noted those places that were most for his purpose, and, having summoned the senate, read them publicly. Many were scandalised at the proceeding, thinking it out of reason and equity to call a man to account for what was not to be until after his death. Cæsar specially pressed what Antony said in his will about his burial; for he had ordered that even if he died in the city of Rome, his body, after being carried in state through the forum, should be sent to Cleopatra at Alexandria. Calvisius, a dependant of Cæsar's, urged other charges in connection with Cleopatra against Antony; that he had given her the library of Pergamus, containing two hundred thousand distinct volumes; that at a great banquet, in the presence of many guests, he had risen up and rubbed her feet, to fulfil some wager or promise ; that he had suffered the Ephesians to salute her as their queen; that he had frequently at the public audience of kings and princes received amorous messages written in tablets made of onyx and crystal, and read them openly on the tribunal; that when Furnius, a man of great authority and eloquence among the Romans, was pleading, Cleopatra happening to pass by in her chair, Antony started up and left them in the middle of their cause, to follow at her side and attend her home.

Calvisius, however, was looked upon as the inventor of most of these stories. Antony's friends went up and down the city to gain him credit, and sent one of themselves, Geminius, to him, to beg him to take heed and not allow himself to be deprived by vote of his authority, and proclaimed a public enemy to the Roman state. But Geminius no sooner arrived in Greece but he was looked upon as one of Octavia's spies; at their suppers he was made a continual butt for mockery, and was put to sit in the least honourable places; all of which he bore very well, seeking only an occasion of speaking with Antony. So at supper, being told to say what business he came about, he answered he would keep the rest for a soberer hour, but one thing he had to say, whether full or fasting, that all would go well if Cleopatra would return to Egypt. And on Antony showing his anger at it, "You have done well, Geminius," said Cleopatra, "to tell your secret without being put to the rack." So Geminius, after a few days, took occasion to make his escape and go to Rome. Many more of Antony's friends were driven from him by the insolent usage they had from Cleopatra's flatterers, amongst whom were Marcus Silanus and Dellius the historian. And Dellius says he was afraid of his life, and that Glaucus, the physician, informed him of Cleopatra's design against him. She was angry with him for having said that Antony's friends were served with sour wine, while at Rome Sarmentus, Cæsar's little page (his *delicia*, as the Romans call it), drank Falernian.

As soon as Cæsar had completed his preparations, he had a decree made declaring war on Cleopatra, and depriving Antony of the authority which he had let a woman exercise in his place. Cæsar added that he had drunk potions that had bereaved him of his senses, and that the generals they would have to fight with would be Mardion the eunuch, Pothinus, Iras, Cleopatra's hairdressing girl, and Charmion, who were Antony's chief state-councillors.

These prodigies are said to have announced the war. Pisaurum, where Antony had settled a colony, on the Adriatic sea, was swallowed up by an earthquake; sweat ran from one of the marble statues of Antony at Alba for many days together, and though frequently wiped off, did not stop. When he himself was in the city of Patræ, the temple of Hercules was struck by lightning, and, at Athens, the figure of Bacchus was torn by a violent wind out of the Battle of the Giants, and laid flat upon the theatre; with both which deities Antony claimed connection, professing to be descended from Hercules, and from his imitating Bacchus in his way of living having received the name of young Bacchus. The same whirlwind at Athens also brought down, from amongst many others which were not disturbed, the colossal statues of Fumenes and Attalus, which were inscribed with Antony's name. And in Cleopatra's admiral-galley, which was called the Antonias, a most inauspicious omen occurred. Some swallows had built in the stern of the galley, but other swallows came, beat the first away, and destroyed their nests.

When the armaments gathered for the war, Antony had no less than five hundred ships of war, including numerous galleys of eight and ten banks of oars, as richly ornamented as if they were meant for a triumph. He had a hundred thousand foot and twelve thousand horse. He had vassal kings attending, Bocchus of Libya, Tarcondemus of the Upper Cilicia, Archelaus of Cappadocia, Philadelphus of Paphlagonia, Mithridates of Commagene, and Sadalas of Thrace; all these were with him in person. Out of Pontus Polemon sent him considerable forces, as did also Malchus from Arabia, Herod the Jew, and Amyntas, King of Lycaonia and Galatia; also the Median king sent some troops to join him. Cæsar had two hundred and fifty galleys of war, eighty thousand foot, and horse about equal to the enemy. Antony's empire extended from Euphrates and Armenia to the Ionian sea and the Illyrians; Caesar's, from Illyria to the westward ocean, and from the ocean all along the Tuscan and Sicilian sea. Of Africa, Cæsar had all the coast opposite to Italy, Gaul, and Spain, as far as the Pillars of Hercules, and Antony the provinces from Cyrene to Æthiopia.

But so wholly was he now the mere appendage to the person of Cleopatra that, although he was much superior to the enemy in land-forces, yet, out of complaisance to his mistress, he wished the victory to be gained by sea, and that, too, when he could not but see how, for want of sailors, his captains, all through unhappy Greece, were pressing every description of men, common travellers and ass-drivers, harvest labourers and boys, and for all this the vessels had not their complements, but remained, most of them, il-manned and badly rowed. Cæsar, on the other side, had ships that were built not for size or show, but for service, not pompous galleys, but light, swift, and perfectly manned; and from his headquarters at Tarentum and Brundusium he sent messages to Antony not to protract the war, but come out with his forces; he would give him secure roadsteads and ports for his fleet, and, for his land army to disembark and pitch their camp, he would leave him as much ground in Italy, inland from the sea, as a horse could traverse in a single course. Antony, on the other side, with the like bold language, challenged him to a single combat, though he were much the older; and, that being refused, proposed to meet him in the Pharsalian fields, where Cæsar and Pompey had fought before. But whilst Antony lay with his fleet near Actium, where now stands Nicopolis, Cæsar seized his opportunity and crossed the Ionian sea, securing himself at a place in Epirus called the Ladle. And when those about Antony were much disturbed, their land forces being a good way off, "Indeed," said Cleopatra, in mockery, "we may well be frightened if Cæsar has got hold of the Ladle!"

On the morrow, Antony, seeing the enemy sailing up, and fearing lest his ships might be taken for want of the soldiers to go on board of them, armed all the rowers, and made a show upon the decks of being in readiness to fight; the oars were mounted as if waiting to be put in motion, and the vessels themselves drawn up to face the enemy on either side of the channel of Actium, as though they were properly manned and ready for an engagement. And Cæsar, deceived by this stratagem, retired. He was also thought to have shown considerable skill in cutting off the water from the enemy by some lines of trenches and forts, water not being plentiful anywhere else, nor very good. And again, his conduct to Domitius was generous, much against the will of Cleopatra. For when he had made his escape in a little boat to Cæsar, having then a fever upon him, although Antony could not but resent it highly, yet he sent after him his whole equipage with his friends and servants; and Domitius, as if he would give a testimony to the world how repentant he had become on his desertion and treachery being thus manifest, died soon after. Among the kings, also, Amyntas and Deiotarus went over to Cæsar. And the fleet was so unfortunate in everything that was undertaken, and so unready on every occasion, that Antony was driven again to put his confidence in the land forces. Canidius, too, who commanded the legions, when he saw how things stood, changed his opinion, and now was of advice that Cleopatra should be sent back, and that, retiring into Thrace or Macedonia, the quarrel should be decided in a land fight. For Dicomes, also, the King of the Getæ, promised to come and join him with a great army, and it would not be any kind of disparagement to him to yield the sea to Cæsar, who, in the Sicilian wars, had had such long practice in shipfighting; on the contrary, it would be simply ridiculous for Antony, who was by land the most experienced commander living, to make no use of his well-disciplined and numerous infantry, scattering and wasting his forces by parcelling them out in the ships. But for all this, Cleopatra prevailed that a sea-fight should determine all, having already an eye to flight, and ordering all her affairs, not so as to assist in gaining a victory, but to escape with the greatest safety from the first commencement of a defeat.

There were two long walls, extending from the camp to the station of the ships, between which Antony used to pass to and fro without suspecting any danger. But Cæsar, upon the suggestion of a servant that it would not be difficult to surprise him, laid an ambush, which, rising up somewhat too hastily, seized the man that came just before him, he himself escaping narrowly by flight.

When it was resolved to stand to a fight at sea, they set fire to all the Egyptian ships except sixty; and of these the best and largest, from ten banks down to three, he manned with twenty thousand full-armed men and two thousand archers. Here it is related that a foot captain, one that had

fought often under Antony, and had his body all mangled with wounds, exclaimed, "O my general, what have our wounds and swords done to displease you, that you should give your confidence to rotten timbers? Let Egyptians and Phœnicians contend at sea, give us the land, where we know well how to die upon the spot or gain the victory." To which he answered nothing, but, by his look and motion of his hand seeming to bid him be of good courage, passed forwards, having already, it would seem, no very sure hopes, since when the masters proposed leaving the sails behind them, he commanded they should be put aboard, "For we must not," said he, "let one enemy escape."

That day and the three following the sea was so rough they could not engage. But on the fifth there was a calm, and they fought; Antony commanding with Publicola the right, and Cœlius the left squadron, Marcus Octavius and Marcus Insteius the centre. Cæsar gave the charge of the left to Agrippa, commanding in person on the right. As for the land forces, Canidius was general for Antony, Taurus for Cæsar; both armies remaining drawn up in order along the shore. Antony in a small boat went from one ship to another, encouraging his soldiers, and bidding them stand firm and fight as steadily on their large ships as if they were on land. The masters he ordered that they should receive the enemy lying still as if they were at anchor, and maintain the entrance of the port, which was a narrow and difficult passage. Of Cæsar they relate that, leaving his tent and going round, while it was yet dark, to visit the ships, he met a man driving an ass, and asked him his name. He answered him that his own name was "Fortunate, and my ass," says he, "is called Conqueror." And afterwards, when he disposed the beaks of the ships in that place in token of his victory, the statue of this man and his ass in bronze were placed amongst them. After examining the rest of his fleet, he went in a boat to the right wing, and looked with much admiration at the enemy lying perfectly still in the straits, in all appearance as if they had been at anchor. For some considerable length of time he actually thought they were so, and kept his own ships at rest, at a distance of about eight furlongs from them. But about noon a breeze sprang up from the sea, and Antony's men, weary of expecting the enemy so long, and trusting to their large tall vessels, as if they had been invincible, began to advance the left squadron. Cæsar was overjoyed to see them move, and ordered his own right squadron to retire, that he might entice them out to sea as far as he could, his design being to sail round and round, and so with his light and well-manned galleys to attack these huge vessels, which their size and their want of men made slow to move and difficult to manage.

When they engaged, there was no charging or striking of one ship by another, because Antony's, by reason of their great bulk, were incapable of

the rapidity required to make the stroke effectual, and on the other side, Cæsar's durst not charge head to head on Antony's, which were all armed with solid masses and spikes of brass; nor did they like even to run in on their sides, which were so strongly built with great squared pieces of timber, fastened together with iron bolts, that their vessels' beaks would easily have been shattered upon them. So that the engagement resembled a land fight, or, to speak yet more properly, the attack and defence of a fortified place; for there were always three or four vessels of Cæsar's about one of Antony's, pressing them with spears, javelins, poles, and several inventions of fire, which they flung among them, Antony's men using catapults also, to pour down missiles from wooden towers. Agrippa drawing out the squadron under his command to outflank the enemy, Publicola was obliged to observe his motions, and gradually to break off from the middle squadron, where some confusion and alarm ensued, while Arruntius engaged them. But the fortune of the day was still undecided, and the battle equal, when on a sudden Cleopatra's sixty ships were seen hoisting sail and making out to sea in full flight, right through the ships that were engaged. For they were placed behind the great ships, which, in breaking through, they put into disorder. The enemy was astonished to see them sailing off with a fair wind towards Peloponnesus. Here it was that Antony showed to all the world that he was no longer actuated by the thoughts and motives of a commander or a man, or indeed by his own judgment at all, and what was once said as a jest, that the soul of a lover lives in some one else's body, he proved to be a serious truth. For, as if he had been born part of her, and must move with her wheresoever she went, as soon as he saw her ship sailing away, he abandoned all that were fighting and spending their lives for him, and put himself aboard a galley of five banks of oars, taking with him only Alexander of Syria and Scellias, to follow her that had so well begun his ruin and would hereafter accomplish it.

She, perceiving him to follow, gave the signal to come aboard. So, as soon as he came up with them, he was taken into the ship. But without seeing her or letting himself be seen by her, he went forward by himself, and sat alone, without a word, in the ship's prow, covering his face with his two hands. In the meanwhile, some of Cæsar's light Liburnian ships, that were in pursuit, came in sight. But on Antony's commanding to face about, they all gave back except Eurycles the Laconian, who pressed on, shaking a lance from the deck, as if he meant to hurl it at him. Antony, standing at the prow, demanded of him, "Who is this that pursues Antony?" "I am," said he, "Eurycles, the son of Lachares, armed with Cæsar's fortune to revenge my father's death." Lachares had been condemned for a robbery, and beheaded by Antony's orders. However, Eurycles did not at-

tack Antony, but ran with his full force upon the other admiral-galley (for there were two of them), and with the blow turned her round, and took both her and another ship, in which was a quantity of rich plate and furniture. So soon as Eurycles was gone, Antony returned to his posture and sate silent, and thus he remained for three days, either in anger with Cleopatra, or wishing not to upbraid her, at the end of which they touched at Tænarus. Here the women of their company succeeded first in bringing them to speak, and afterwards to eat and sleep together. And, by this time, several of the ships of burden and some of his friends began to come in to him from the rout, bringing news of his fleet's being quite destroyed, but that the land forces, they thought, still stood firm. So that he sent messengers to Canidius to march the army with all speed through Macedonion into Asia. And, designing himself to go from Tænarus into Africa, he gave one of the merchant ships, laden with a large sum of money, and vessels of silver and gold of great value, belonging to the royal collections, to his friends, desiring them to share it amongst them, and provide for their own safety. They refusing his kindness with tears in their eyes, he comforted them with all the goodness and humanity imaginable, entreating them to leave him, and wrote letters in their behalf to Theophilus, his steward, at Corinth, that he would provide for their security, and keep them concealed till such time as they could make their peace with Cæsar. This Theophilus was the father of Hipparchus, who had such interest with Antony, who was the first of all his freedmen that went over to Cæsar, and who settled afterwards at Corinth. In this posture were affairs with Antony.

But at Actium, his fleet, after a long resistance to Cæsar, and suffering the most damage from a heavy sea that set in right ahead, scarcely at four in the afternoon, gave up the contest, with the loss of not more than five thousand killed, but of three hundred ships taken, as Cæsar himself has recorded. Only a few had known of Antony's flight; and those who were told of it could not at first give any belief to so incredible a thing as that a general who had nineteen entire legions and twelve thousand horse upon the seashore, could abandon all and fly away; and he, above all, who had so often experienced both good and evil fortune, and had in a thousand wars and battles been inured to changes. His soldiers, however, would not give up their desires and expectations, still fancying he would appear from some part or other, and showed such a generous fidelity to his service that, when they were thoroughly assured that he was fled in earnest, they kept themselves in a body seven days, making no account of the messages that Cæsar sent to them. But at last, seeing that Canidius himself, who commanded them, was fled from the camp by night, and that all their officers had quite abandoned them, they gave way, and made their submission to the conqueror. After this, Cæsar set sail for Athens, where he made a settlement with Greece, and distributed what remained of the provision of co that Antony had made for his army among the cities, which were in a miserable condition, despoiled of their money, their slaves, their horses, and beasts of service. My great-grandfather Nicharchus used to relate that the whole body of the people of our city were put in requisition to carry each one a certain measure of corn upon their shoulders to the seaside near Anticyra, men standing by to quicken them with the lash. They had made one journey of the kind, but when they had just measured out the corn, and were putting it on their backs for a second, news came of Antony's defeat, and so saved Chæronea, for all Antony's purveyors and soldiers fled upon the news, and left them to divide the corn among themselves.

When Antony came into Africa, he sent on Cleopatra from Parcetonium into Egypt, and stayed himself in the most entire solitude that he could desire, roaming and wandering about with only two friends, one a Greek, Aristocrates, a rhetorician, and the other a Roman, Lucilius, of whom we have elsewhere spoken, how, at Philippi, to give Brutus time to escape, he suffered himself to be taken by the pursuers, pretending he was Brutus. Antony gave him his life, and on this account he remained true and faithful to him to the last.

But when also the officer who commanded for him in Africa, to whose care he had committed all his forces there, took them over to Cæsar, he resolved to kill himself, but was hindered by his friends. And coming to Alexandria, he found Cleopatra busied in a most bold and wonderful enterprise. Over the small space of land which divides the Red Sea from the sea near Egypt, which may be considered also the boundary between Asia and Africa, and in the narrowest place is not much above three hundred furlongs across, over this neck of land Cleopatra had formed a project of dragging her fleet and setting it afloat in the Arabian Gulf, thus with her soldiers and her treasure to secure herself a home on the other side, where she might live in peace far away from war and slavery. But the first galleys which were carried over being burnt by the Arabians of Petra, and Antony not knowing but that the army before Actium still held together, she desisted from her enterprise, and gave orders for the fortifying all the approaches to Egypt. But Antony, leaving the city and the conversation of his friends, built him a dwelling-place in the water, near Pharos, upon a little mole which he cast up in the sea, and there, secluding himself from the company of mankind, said he desired nothing but to live the life of Timon; as indeed, his case was the same, and the ingratitude and injuries which he suffered from those he had esteemed his friends made him hate and distrust all mankind.

This Timon was a citizen of Athens, and lived much about the Peloponnesian war, as may be seen by the comedies of Aristophanes and Plato, in which he is ridiculed as hater and enemy of mankind. He avoided and repelled the approaches of every one, but embraced with kisses and the greatest show of affection Alcibiades, then in his hot youth. And when Apemantus was astonished, and demanded the reason, he replied that he knew this young man would one day do infinite mischief to the Athenians. He never admitted any one into his company, except at times this Apemantus, who was of the same sort of temper, and was an imitator of his way of life. At the celebration of the festival of flagons, these two kept the feast together, and Apemantus, saying to him, "What a pleasant party, Timon!" "It would be," he answered, "if you were away." One day he got up in a full assembly on the speaker's place, and when there was a dead silence and great wonder at so unusual a sight, he said, "Ye men of Athens, I have a little plot of ground, and in it grows a fig-tree, on which many citizens have been pleased to hang themselves; and now, having resolved to build in that place, I wish to announce it publicly, that any of you who may be desirous may go and hang yourselves before I cut it down." He died and was buried at Halæ, near the sea, where it so happened that, after his burial, a land-slip took place on the point of the shore, and the sea, flowing in, surrounded his tomb, and made it inaccessible to the foot of man. It bore this inscription:—

"Here am I laid, my life of misery done.
Ask not my name, I curse you every one."

And this epitaph was made by himself while yet alive; that which is more generally known is by Callimachus:—

"Timon, the misanthrope, am I below.
Go, and revile me, traveller, only go."

Thus much of Timon, of whom much more might be said. Canidius now came, bringing word in person of the loss of the army before Actium. Then he received news that Herod of Judæa was gone over to Cæsar with some legions and cohorts, and that the other kings and princes were in like manner deserting him, and that, out of Egypt, nothing stood by him. All this, however, seemed not to disturb him, but, as if he were glad to put away all hope, that with it he might be rid of all care, and leaving his habitation by the sea, which he called the Timoneum, he was received by Cleopatra in the palace, and set the whole city into a course of feasting, drinking, and presents. The son of Cæsar and Cleopatra was registered among the youths, and Antyllus, his own son by Fulvia, received the gown without the purple border given to those that are come of age; in honour of which the citizens of Alexandria did nothing but feast and revel for many days. They themselves broke up the Order of the Inimitable Livers, and constituted another in its place, not inferior in splendour, luxury, and sumptuosity, calling it that of the Diers Together. For all those that said they would die with Antony and Cleopatra gave in their names, for the present passing their time in all manner of pleasures and a regular succession of banquets. But Cleopatra was busied in making a collection of all varieties of poisonous drugs, and, in order to see which of them were the least painful in the operation, she had them tried upon prisoners condemned to die. But, finding that the quick poisons always worked with sharp pains, and that the less painful were slow, she next tried venomous animals, and watching with her own eyes whilst they were applied, one creature to the body of another. This was her daily practice, and she pretty well satisfied herself that nothing was comparable to the bite of the asp, which, without convulsion or groaning, brought on a heavy drowsiness and lethargy, with a gentle sweat on the face, the senses being stupefied by degrees; the patient, in appearance, being sensible of no pain, but rather troubled to be disturbed or awakened like those that are in a profound natural sleep.

At the same time, they sent ambassadors to Cæsar into Asia, Cleopatra asking for the kingdom of Egypt for her children, and Antony, that he might have leave to live as a private man in Egypt, or, if that were thought too much, that he might retire to Athens. In lack of friends, so many having deserted, and others not being trusted, Euphronius, his son's tutor, was sent on this embassy. For Alexas of Laodicea, who, by the recommendation of Timagenes, became acquainted with Antony at Rome, and had been more powerful with him than any Greek, and was, of all the instruments which Cleopatra made use of to persuade Antony, the most violent, and the chief subverter of any good thoughts that from time to time might rise in his mind in Octavia's favour, had been sent before to dissuade Herod from desertion; but betraying his master, stayed with him and, confiding in Herod's interest, had the boldness to come into Cæsar's presence. Herod, however, was not able to help him, for he was immediately put in chains and sent into his own country, where, by Cæsar's orders, he was put to death. This reward of his treason Alexas received while Antony was yet alive.

Cæsar would not listen to any proposals for Antony, but he made answer to Cleopatra, that there was no reasonable favour which she might not expect, if she put Antony to death, or expelled him from Egypt. He sent back with the ambassadors his own freedman, Thyrsus, a man of understanding, and not at all ill-qualified for conveying the messages of a youthful general to a woman so proud of her charms and possessed with the opinion of the power of her beauty. But by the long audiences he received from her, and the special honours which she paid him, Antony's jealousy began to be awakened; he had him seized, whipped, and sent back; writing Cæsar word that the man's busy, impertinent ways had provoked him; in his circumstances he could not be expected to be very patient: "But if it offends you," he added, "you have got my freedman, Hipparchus, with you; hang him up and scourge him to make us even." But Cleopatra after this, to clear herself, and to allay his jealousies, paid him all the attentions imaginable. When her own birthday came, she kept it as was suitable to their fallen fortunes; but his was observed with the utmost prodigality of splendour and magnificence, so that many of the guests sat down in want, and went home wealthy men. Meantime, continual letters came to Cæsar from Agrippa, telling him his presence was extremely required at Rome.

And so the war was deferred for a season. But, the winter being over, he began his march, he himself by Syria, and his captains through Africa. Pelusium being taken, there went a report as if it had been delivered up to Cæsar by Seleucus, not without the consent of Cleopatra; but she, to justify herself, gave up into Antony's hands the wife and children of Seleucus to be put to death. She had caused to be built, joining to the temple of Isis, several tombs and monuments of wonderful height, and very remarkable for the workmanship; thither she removed her treasure, her gold, silver, emeralds, pearls, ebony, ivory, cinnamon, and, after all, a great quantity of torchwood and tow. Upon which Cæsar began to fear lest she should, in a desperate fit, set all these riches on fire; and, therefore, while he was marching toward the city with his army, he omitted no occasion of giving her new assurances of his good intentions. He took up his position in the Hippodrome, where Antony made a fierce sally upon him, routed the horse, and beat them back into their trenches, and so returned with great satisfaction to the palace, where, meeting Cleopatra, armed as he was, he kissed her, and commended to her favour one of his men, who had most signalised himself in the fight, to whom she made a present of a breastplate and helmet of gold; which he having received went that very night and deserted to Cæsar.

After this, Antony sent a new challenge to Cæsar to fight him hand-to-hand; who made him answer that he might find several other ways to end his life; and he, considering with himself that he could not die more honourably than in battle, resolved to make an effort both by land and sea. At supper, it is said, he bade his servants help him freely, and pour him out wine plentifully, since to-morrow, perhaps, they should not do the same, but be servants to a new master, whilst he should lie on the ground, a dead corpse, and nothing. His friends that were about him wept to hear him talk so; which he perceiving, told them he would not lead them to a battle in which he expected rather an honourable death than either safety or victory. That night, it is related, about the middle of it, when the whole city was in a deep silence and general sadness, expecting the event of the next day, on a sudden was heard the sound of all sorts of instruments, and voices singing in tune, and the cry of a crowd of people shouting and dancing, like a troop of bacchanals on its way. This tumultuous procession seemed to take its course right through the middle of the city to the gate nearest the enemy; here it became the loudest, and suddenly passed out. People who reflected considered this to signify that Bacchus, the god whom Antony had always made it his study to copy and imitate, had now forsaken him.

As soon as it was light, he marched his infantry out of the city, and posted them upon a rising ground, from whence he saw his fleet make up to the enemy. There he stood in expectation of the event; but as soon as the fleets came near to one another, his men saluted Cæsar's with their oars; and on their responding, the whole body of the ships, forming into a single fleet, rowed up direct to the city. Antony had no sooner seen this, but the horse deserted him, and went over to Cæsar; and his foot being defeated, he retired into the city, crying out that Cleopatra had betrayed him to the enemies he had made for her sake. She, being afraid lest in his fury and despair he might do her a mischief, fled to her monument, and letting down the falling doors, which were strong with bars and bolts, she sent messengers who should tell Antony she was dead. He, believing it, cried out, "Now, Antony, why delay longer? Fate has snatched away the only pretext for which you could say you desired yet to live." Going into his chamber, and there loosening and opening his coat of armour, "I am not," said he, "troubled, Cleopatra, to be at present bereaved of you, for I shall soon be with you; but it distresses me that so great a general should be found of a tardier courage than a woman." He had a faithful servant, whose name was Eros; he had engaged him formerly to kill him when he should think it necessary, and now he put him to his promise. Eros drew his sword, as designing to kill him, but, suddenly turning round, he slew himself. And as he fell dead at his feet, "It is well done, Eros," said Antony; "you show your master how to do what you had not the heart to do yourself;" and so he ran himself into the belly, and laid himself upon the couch. The wound, however, was not immediately mortal; and the flow of blood ceasing when he lay down, presently he came to himself, and entreated those that were about him to put him out of his pain; but they all fled out of the chamber, and left him crying out and struggling, until Diomede, Cleopatra's secretary, came to him, having orders from her to bring him into the monument.

When he understood she was alive, he eagerly gave order to the servants to take him up, and in their arms was carried to the door of the building. Cleopatra would not open the door, but, looking from a sort of window, she let down ropes and cords, to which Antony was fastened; and she and her two women the only persons she had allowed to enter the monument, drew him up. Those that were present say that nothing was ever more sad than this spectacle, to see Antony, covered all over with blood and just expiring, thus drawn up, still holding up his hands to her, and lifting up his body with the little force he had left. As, indeed, it was no easy task for the women; and Cleopatra, with all her force, clinging to the rope, and straining with her head to the ground, with difficulty pulled him up, while those below encouraged her with their cries, and joined in all her efforts and anxiety. When she had got him up, she laid him on the bed, tearing all her clothes, which she spread upon him; and, beating her breast with her hands, lacerating herself, and disfiguring her own face with the blood from his wounds, she called him her lord, her husband, her emperor, and seemed to have pretty nearly forgotten all her own evils, she was so intent upon his misfortunes. Antony, stopping her lamentations as well as he could, called for wine to drink, either that he was thirsty, or that he imagined that it might put him the sooner out of pain. When he had drunk, he advised her to bring her own affairs, so far as might be honourably done, to a safe conclusion, and that, among all the friends of Cæsar, she should rely on Proculeius; that she should not pity him in this last turn of fate, but rather rejoice for him in remembrance of his past happiness, who had been of all men the most illustrious and powerful, and in the end had fallen not ignobly, a Roman by a Roman overcome.

Just as he breathed his last, Proculeius arrived from Cæsar; for when Antony gave himself his wound, and was carried in to Cleopatra, one of his guards, Dercetæus, took up Antony's sword and hid it; and, when he saw his opportunity, stole away to Cæsar, and brought him the first news of Antony's death, and withal showed him the bloody sword. Cæsar, upon this, retired into the inner part of his tent, and giving some tears to the death of one that had been nearly allied to him in marriage, his colleague in empire, and companion in so many wars and dangers, he came out to his friends, and, bringing with him many letters, he read to them with how much reason and moderation he had always addressed himself to Antony, and in return what overbearing and arrogant answers he received. Then he sent Proculeius to use his utmost endeavours to get Cleopatra alive into his power; for he was afraid of losing a great treasure, and, besides, she would be no small addition to the glory of his triumph. She, however, was careful not to put herself in Proculeius's power; but from within her monument, he standing on the outside of a door, on the level of the ground, which was strongly barred, but so that they might well enough hear one another's voice, she held a conference with him; she demanding that her kingdom might be given to her children, and he binding her to be of good courage, and trust Cæsar in everything.

Having taken particular notice of the place, he returned to Cæsar, and Gallus was sent to parley with her the second time; who, being come to the door, on purpose prolonged the conference, while Proculeius fixed his scaling-ladders in the window through which the women had pulled up Antony. And so entering, with two men to follow him, he went straight down to the door where Cleopatra was discoursing with Gallus. One of the two women who were shut up in the monument with her cried out, "Miserable Cleopatra, you are taken prisoner!" Upon which she turned quick, and, looking at Proculeius, drew out her dagger which she had with her to stab herself. But Proculeius ran up quickly, and seizing her with both his hands, "For shame," said he, "Cleopatra; you wrong yourself and Cæsar much, who would rob him of so fair an occasion of showing his clemency, and would make the world believe the most gentle of commanders to be a faithless and implacable enemy." And so, taking the dagger out of her hand, he also shook her dress to see if there were any poison hid in it. After this, Cæsar sent Epaphroditus, one of his freedmen, with orders to treat her with all the gentleness and civility possible, but to take the strictest precautions to keep her alive.

In the meanwhile, Cæsar made his entry into Alexandria, with Areius the philosopher at his side, holding him by the hand and talking with him; desiring that all his fellow-citizens should see what honour was paid to him, and should look up to him accordingly from the very first moment. Then, entering the exercise ground, he mounted a platform erected for the purpose, and from thence commanded the citizens (who, in great fear and consternation, fell prostrate at his feet) to stand up, and told them that he freely acquitted the people of all blame, first, for the sake of Alexander, who built their city, then for the city's sake itself, which was so large and beautiful; and, thirdly, to gratify his friend Areius.

Such great honour did Areius receive from Cæsar; and by his intercession many lives were saved, amongst the rest that of Philostratus, a man, of all the professors of logic that ever were, the most ready in extempore speaking, but quite destitute of any right to call himself one of the philosophers of the Academy. Cæsar, out of disgust at his character, refused all attention to his entreaties. So, growing a long white beard, and dressing himself in black, he followed behind Areius, shouting out the verse,

"The wise, if they are wise, will save the wise."

Which Cæsar hearing, gave him his pardon, to prevent rather any odium that might attach to Areius, than any harm that Philostratus might suffer.

Of Antony's children, Antyllus, his son by Fulvia, being betrayed by his tutor, Theodorus, was put to death; and while the soldiers were cutting off his head, his tutor contrived to steal a precious jewel which he wore about his neck, and put it in his pocket, and afterwards denied the fact, but was convicted and crucified. Cleopatra's children, with their attendants, had a guard set on them, and were treated very honourably. Cæsarion, who was reputed to be the son of Cæsar the Dictator, was sent by his mother, with a great sum of money, through Æthiopia, to pass into India; but his tutor, a man named Rhodon, about as honest as Theodorus, persuaded him to turn back, for that Cæsar designed to make him king. Cæsar consulting what was best to be done with him, Areius we are told, said,

"Too many *Cæsars* are not well."

So, afterwards, when Cleopatra was dead he was killed.

Many kings and great commanders made petition to Cæsar for the body of Antony, to give him his funeral rites; but he would not take away his corpse from Cleopatra by whose hands he was buried with royal splendour and magnificence, it being granted to her to employ what she pleased on his funeral. In this extremity of grief and sorrow, and having inflamed and ulcerated her breasts with beating them, she fell into a high fever, and was very glad of the occasion, hoping, under this pretext, to abstain from food, and so to die in quiet without interference. She had her own physician, Olympus, to whom she told the truth, and asked his advice and help to put an end to herself, as Olympus himself has told us, in a narrative which he wrote of these events. But Cæsar, suspecting her purpose, took to menacing language about her children, and excited her fears for them, before which engines her purpose shook and gave way, so that she suffered those about her to give her what meat or medicine they pleased.

Some few days after, Cæsar himself came to make her a visit and comfort her. She lay then upon her pallet-bed in undress, and, on his entering, sprang up from off her bed, having nothing on but the one garment next her body, and flung herself at his feet, her hair and face looking wild and disfigured, her voice quivering, and her eyes sunk in her head. The marks of the blows she had given herself were visible about her bosom, and altogether her whole person seemed no less afflicted than her soul. But, for all this, her old charm, and the boldness of her youthful beauty, had not wholly left her, and, in spite of her present condition, still sparkled from within, and let itself appear in all the movements of her countenance. Cæsar, desiring her to repose herself, sat down by her; and, on this opportunity, she said something to justify her actions, attributing what she had done to the necessity she was under, and to her fear of Antony; and when Cæsar, on each point, made his objections, and she found herself confuted, she broke off at once into language of entreaty and deprecation, as if she desired nothing more than to prolong her life. And at last, having by her a list of her treasure, she gave it into his hands; and when Seleucus, one of her stewards, who was by, pointed out that various articles were omitted, and charged her with secreting them, she flew up and caught him by the hair, and struck him several blows on the face. Cæsar smiling and withholding her, "Is it not very hard, Cæsar," said she, "when you do me the honour to visit me in this condition I am in, that I should be accused by one of my own servants of laying by some women's toys, not meant to adorn, be sure, my unhappy self, but that I might have some little present by me to make your Octavia and your Livia, that by their intercession I might hope to find you in some measure disposed to mercy?" Cæsar was pleased to hear her talk thus, being now assured that she was desirous to live. And, therefore, letting her know that the things she had laid by she might dispose of as she pleased, and his usage of her should be honourable above her expectation, he went away, well satisfied that he had overreached her, but, in fact, was himself deceived.

There was a young man of distinction among Cæsar's companions named Cornelius Dolabella. He was not without a certain tenderness for Cleopatra, and sent her word privately, as she had besought him to do, that Cæsar was about to return through Syria, and that she and her children were to be sent on within three days. When she understood this, she made her request to Cæsar that he would be pleased to permit her to make oblations to the departed Antony; which being granted, she ordered herself to be carried to the place where he was buried, and there, accompanied by her women, she embraced his tomb with tears in her eyes, and spoke in this manner: "O, dearest Antony," said she, "it is not long since that with these hands I buried you; then they were free, now I am a captive, and pay these last duties to you with a guard upon me, for fear that my just griefs and sorrows should impair my servile body, and make it less fit to appear in their triumph over you. No further offerings or libations expect from me; these are the last honours that Cleopatra can pay your memory, for she is to be hurried away far from you. Nothing could part us whilst we lived, but death seems to threaten to divide us. You, a Roman born, have found a grave in Egypt; I, an Egyptian, am to seek that favour, and none but that, in your country. But if the gods below, with whom you now are, either can or will do anything (since those above have betrayed us), suffer not your living wife to be abandoned; let me not be led in triumph to your shame, but hide me and bury me here with you, since, amongst all my bitter misfortunes, nothing has afflicted me like this brief time that I have lived away from you."

Having made these lamentations, crowning the tomb with garlands and kissing it, she gave orders to prepare her a bath, and, coming out of the bath, she lay down and made a sumptuous meal. And a country fellow brought her a little basket, which the guards intercepting and asking what it was, the fellow put the leaves which lay uppermost aside, and showed them it was full of figs; and on their admiring the largeness and beauty of the figs, he laughed, and invited them to take some, which they refused, and, suspecting nothing, bade him carry them in. After her repast, Cleopatra sent to Cæsar a letter which she had written and sealed; and, putting everybody out of the monument but her two women, she shut the doors. Cæsar, opening her letter, and finding pathetic prayers and entreaties that she might be buried in the same tomb with Antony, soon guessed what was doing. At first he was going himself in all haste, but, changing his mind, he sent others to see. The thing had been quickly done. The messengers came at full speed, and found the guards apprehensive of nothing; but on opening the doors they saw her stone-dead, lying upon a bed of gold, set out in all her royal ornaments. Iras, one of her women, lay dying at her feet, and Charmion, just ready to fall, scarce able to hold up her head, was adjusting her mistress's diadem. And when one that came in said angrily, "Was this well done of your lady, Charmion?" "Extremely well," she answered, "and as became the descendant of so many kings;" and as she said this, she fell down dead by the bedside.

Some relate that an asp was brought in amongst those figs and covered with the leaves, and that Cleopatra had arranged that it might settle on her before she knew, but, when she took away some of the figs and saw it, she said, "So here it is," and held out her bare arm to be bitten. Others say that it was kept in a vase, and that she vexed and pricked it with a golden spindle till it seized her arm. But what really took place is known to no one, since it was also said that she carried poison in a hollow bodkin, about which she wound her hair; yet there was not so much as a spot found, or any symptom of poison upon her body, nor was the asp seen within the monument; only something like the trail of it was said to have been noticed on the sand by the sea, on the part towards which the building faced and where the windows were. Some relate that two faint puncture-marks were found on Cleopatra's arm, and to this account Cæsar seems to have given credit; for in his triumph there was carried a figure of Cleopatra, with an asp clinging to her. Such are the various accounts. But Cæsar, though much disappointed by her death, yet could not but admire the greatness of her spirit, and gave order that her body should be buried by Antony with royal splendour and magnificence. Her women also, received honourable burial by his directions. Cleopatra had lived nine-and-thirty years, during twenty-two of which she had reigned as queen, and for fourteen had been Antony's partner in his empire. Antony, according to some authorities, was fifty-three, according to others, fifty-six years old. His statues were all thrown down, but those of Cleopatra were left untouched; for Archibius, one of her friends, gave Cæsar two thousand talents to save them from the fate of Antony's.

Antony left by his three wives seven children, of whom only Antyllus the eldest, was put to death by Cæsar; Octavia took the rest, and brought them up with her own. Cleopatra, his daughter by Cleopatra, was given in marriage to Juba, the most accomplished of kings; and Antony, his son by Fulvia, attained such high favour that, whereas Agrippa was considered to hold the first place with Cæsar, and the sons of Livia the second, the third, without dispute, was possessed by Antony. Octavia, also, having had by her first husband, Marcellus, two daughters, and one son named Marcellus, this son Cæsar adopted, and gave him his daughter in marriage; as did Octavia one of the daughters to Agrippa. But Marcellus dying almost immediately after his marriage, she, perceiving that her brother was at a loss to find elsewhere any sure friend to be his son-in-law, was the first to recommend that Agrippa should put away her daughter and marry Julia. To this Cæsar first, and then Agrippa himself, gave assent; so Agrippa married Julia, and Octavia, receiving her daughter, married her to the young Antony. Of the two daughters whom Octavia had borne to Antony, the one was married to Domitius Ahenobarbus; and the other, Antonia, famous for her beauty and discretion, was married to Drusus, the son of Livia, and step-son to Cæsar. Of these parents were born Germanicus and Claudius. Claudius reigned later; and of the children of Germanicus, Caius, after a reign of distinction, was killed with his wife and child; Agrippina, after bearing a son Lucius Domitius, to Ahenobarbus, was married to Claudius Cæsar, who adopted Domitius, giving him the name of Nero Germanicus. He was emperor in our time, and put his mother to death, and with his madness and folly came not far from ruining the Roman empire, being Antony's descendant in the fifth generation.

THE COMPARISON OF DEMETRIUS AND ANTONY

As both are great examples of the vicissitudes of fortune, let us first consider in what way they attained their power and glory. Demetrius hired a kingdom already won for him by Antigonus, the most powerful of the Successors, who, before Demetrius grew to be a man, traversed with his armies and subdued the greater part of Asia. Antony's father was well enough in other respects, but was no warrior, and could bequeath no great legacy of reputation to his son, who had the boldness, nevertheless, to take upon him the government, to which birth give him no claim, which had been held by Cæsar, and became the inheritor of his great labours. And such power did he attain, with only himself to thank for it, that, in a division of the whole empire into two portions, he took and received the nobler one; and, absent himself, by his mere subalterns and lieutenants often defeated the Parthians, and drove the barbarous nations of the Caucasus back to the Caspian Sea. Those very things that procured him ill-repute bear witness to his greatness. Antigonus considered Antipater's daughter Phila, in spite of the disparity of her years, an advantageous match for Demetrius. Antony was thought disgraced by his marriage with Cleopatra, a queen superior in power and glory to all, except Arsaces, who were kings in her time. Antony was so great as to be thought by others worthy of higher things than his own desires.

As regards the right and justice of their aims at empire, Demetrius need not be blamed for seeking to rule a people that had always had a king to rule them. Antony, who enslaved the Roman people, just liberated from the rule of Cæsar, followed a cruel and tyrannical object. His greatest and most illustrious work, his successful war with Brutus and Cassius, was done to crush the liberties of his country and of his fellow-citizens. Demetrius, till he was driven to extremity, went on, without intermission, maintaining liberty in Greece, and expelling the foreign garrisons from the cities; not like Antony, whose boast was to have slain in Macedonia those who had set up liberty in Rome. As for the profusion and magnificence of his gifts, one point for which Antony is lauded, Demetrius so far outdid them that what he gave to his enemies was far more than Antony ever gave to his friends. Antony was renowned for giving Brutus honourable burial; Demetrius did so to all the enemy's dead, and sent the prisoners back to Ptolemy with money and presents.

Both were insolent in prosperity, and abandoned themselves to luxuries and enjoyments. Yet it cannot be said that Demetrius, in his revellings and dissipations, ever let slip the time for action; pleasures with him attended only the superabundance of his ease, and his Lamia, like that of the fable, belonging only to his playful, half-waking, half-sleeping hours. When war demanded his attention, his spear was not wreathed with ivy, nor his helmet redolent of unguents; he did not come out to battle from the women's chamber, but, hushing the bacchanal shouts and putting an end to the orgies, he became at once, as Euripides calls it, "the minister of the unpriestly Mars;" and, in short, he never once incurred disaster through indolence or self-indulgence. Whereas Antony, like Hercules in the picture where Omphale is seen removing his club and stripping him of his lion's skin, was over and over again disarmed by Cleopatra, and beguiled away, while great actions and enterprises of the first necessity fell, as it were, from his hands, to go with her to the seashore of Canopus and Taphosiris, and play about. And in the end, like another Paris, he left the battle to fly to her arms; or rather, to say the truth, Paris fled when he was already beaten; Antony fled first, and, following Cleopatra, abandoned his victory.

There was no law to prevent Demetrius from marrying several wives; from the time of Philip and Alexander it had become usual with Macedonian kings, and he did no more than was done by Lysimachus and Ptolemy. And those he married he treated honourably. But Antony, first of all, in marrying two wives at once, did a thing which no Roman had ever allowed himself; and then he drove away his lawful Roman wife to please the foreign and unlawful woman. And so Demetrius incurred no harm at all; Antony procured his ruin by his marriage. On the other hand, no licentious act of Antony's can be charged with that impiety which marks those of Demetrius. Historical writers tell us that the very dogs are excluded from the whole Acropolis because of their gross, uncleanly habits. The very Parthenon itself saw Demetrius consorting with harlots and debauching free women of Athens. The vice of cruelty, also, remote as it seems from the indulgence of voluptuous desires, must be attributed to him, who, in the pursuit of his pleasures, allowed or, to say more truly, compelled the death of the most beautiful and most chaste of the Athenians, who found no way but this to escape his violence. In one word, Antony himself suffered by his excesses, and other people by those of Demetrius.

In his conduct to his parents, Demetrius was irreproachable. Antony gave up his mother's brother, in order that he might have leave to kill Cicero, this itself being so cruel and shocking an act that Antony would hardly be forgiven if Cicero's death had been the price of this uncle's safety. In respect of breaches of oaths and treaties, the seizure of Artabazes, and the assassination of Alexander, Antony may urge the plea which no one denies to be true, that Artabazes first abandoned and betrayed him in Media;

Demetrius is alleged by many to have invented false pretexts for his act, and not to have retaliated for injuries, but to have accused one whom he injured himself.

The achievements of Demetrius are all his own work. Antony's noblest and greatest victories were won in his absence by his lieutenants. For their final disasters they have both only to thank themselves; not, however, in an equal degree. Demetrius was deserted, the Macedonians revolted from him; Antony deserted others, and ran away while men were fighting for him at the risk of their lives. The fault to be found with the one is that he had thus entirely alienated the affections of his soldiers; the other's condemnation is that he abandoned so much love and faith as he still possessed. We cannot admire the death of either, but that of Demetrius excites our greater contempt. He let himself become a prisoner, and was thankful to gain a three years' accession of life in captivity. He was tamed like a wild beast by his belly, and by wine; Antony took himself out of the world in a cowardly, pitiful, and ignoble manner, but still in time to prevent the enemy having his person in their power.

DION

IF it be true, Sosius Senecio, that, as Simonides tells us—

"Of the Corinthians Troy does not complain"

for having taken part with the Achæans in the siege, because the Trojans also had Corinthians (Glaucus, who sprang from Corinth) fighting bravely on their side, so also it may be fairly said that neither Romans nor Greeks can quarrel with the Academy, each nation being equally represented in the following pair of lives, which will give an account of Brutus and of Dion,—Dion, who was Plato's own hearer, and Brutus, who was brought up in his philosophy. They came from one and the self-same school, where they had been trained alike to run the race of honour; nor need we wonder that in the performance of actions often most nearly allied and akin, they both bore evidence to the truth of what their guide and teacher said, that, without the concurrence of power and success, with justice and prudence, public actions do not attain their proper, great, and noble character. For as Hippomachus the wrestling-master affirmed, he could distinguish his scholars at a distance, though they were but carrying meat from the shambles, so it is very probable that the principles of those who have had the same good education should appear with a resemblance in all their actions, creating in them a certain harmony and proportion, at once agreeable and becoming.

We may also draw a close parallel of the lives of the two men from their fortunes, wherein chance, even more than their own designs, made them nearly alike. For they were both cut off by an untimely death, not being able to accomplish those ends which through many risks and difficulties they aimed at. But, above all, this is most wonderful; that by preternatural interposition both of them had notice given of their approaching death by an unpropitious form, which visibly appeared to them. Although there are people who utterly deny any such thing, and say that no man in his right senses ever yet saw any supernatural phantom or apparition, but that children only, and silly women, or men disordered by sickness, in some aberration of the mind or distemperature of the body, have had empty and extravagant imaginations, whilst the real evil genius, superstition, was in themselves. Yet if Dion and Brutus, men of solid understanding, and philosophers, not to be easily deluded by fancy or discomposed by any sudden apprehension, were thus affected by visions that they forthwith declared to their friends what they had seen, I know not how we can avoid admitting again the utterly exploded opinion of the oldest times, that evil and beguiling spirits, out of envy to good men, and a desire of impeding their good deeds, make efforts to excite in them feelings of terror and distraction, to make them shake and totter in their virtue, lest by a steady and unbiased perseverance they should obtain a happier condition than these beings after death. But I shall leave these things for another opportunity, and in this twelfth book of the lives of great men compared one with another, begin with his who was the elder.

Dionysius the First, having possessed himself of the government, at once took to wife the daughter of Hermocrates, the Syracusan. She, in an outbreak which the citizens made before the new power was well settled, was abused in such a barbarous and outrageous manner that for shame she put an end to her own life. But Dionysius, when he was re-established and confirmed in his supremacy, married two wives together, one named Doris, of Locri, the other Aristomache, a native of Sicily, and daughter of Hipparinus, a man of the first quality in Syracuse, and colleague with Dionysius when he was first chosen general with unlimited powers for the war. It is said he married them both in one day, and no one ever knew which of the two he first made his wife; and ever after he divided his kindness equally between them, both accompanying him together at his table, and in his bed by turns. Indeed, the Syracusans were urgent that their own countrywoman might be preferred before the stranger; but Doris, to compensate her for her foreign extraction, had the good fortune to be the mother of the son and heir of the family, whilst Aristomache continued a long time without issue, though Dionysius was very desirous to have children by her, and, indeed, caused Doris's mother to be put to death, laying to her charge that she had given drugs to Aristomache to prevent her being with child.

Dion, Aristomache's brother, at first found an honourable reception for his sister's sake; but his own worth and parts soon procured him a nearer place in his brother-in-law's affection, who, among other favours, gave special command to his treasurers to furnish Dion with whatever money he demanded, only telling him on the same day what they had delivered out. Now, though Dion was before reputed a person of lofty character, of a noble mind, and daring courage, yet these excellent qualifications all received a great development from the happy chance which conducted Plato into Sicily; not assuredly by any human device or calculation, but some supernatural power, designing that this remote cause should hereafter occasion the recovery of the Sicilians' lost liberty and the subversion of the tyrannical government, brought the philosopher out of Italy to Syracuse, and made acquaintance between him and Dion. Dion was, indeed, at this time extremely young in years, but of all the scholars that attended Plato he was the quickest and aptest to learn, and the most prompt and eager to practise, the lessons of virtue, as Plato himself reports of him and his own actions sufficiently testify. For though he had been bred up under a tyrant in habits of submission, accustomed to a life on the one hand of servility and intimidation, and yet on the other of vulgar display and luxury, the mistaken happiness of people that knew no better thing than pleasure and self-indulgence, yet, at the first taste of reason and a philosophy that demands obedience to virtue, his soul was set in a flame, and in the simple innocence of youth, concluding, from his own disposition, that the same reason would work the same effects upon Dionysius, he made it his business, and at length obtained the favour of him, at a leisure hour, to hear Plato.

At this their meeting, the subject-matter of their discourse in general was human virtue, but, more particularly, they disputed concerning fortitude, which Plato proved tyrants, of all men, had the least pretence to; and thence proceeding to treat of justice, asserted the happy estate of the just and the miserable condition of the unjust; arguments which Dionysius would not hear out, but, feeling himself, as it were, convicted by his words, and much displeased to see the rest of the auditors full of admiration for the speaker and captivated with his doctrine, at last, exceedingly exasperated, he asked the philosopher in a rage, what business he had in Sicily. To which Plato answered, "I came to seek a virtuous man." "It seems, then," replied Dionysius, "you have lost your labour." Dion, supposing that this was all, and that nothing further could come of his anger, at Plato's request, conveyed him aboard a galley, which was conveying Pollis, the Spartan, into Greece. But Dionysius privately dealt with Pollis, by all means to kill Plato in the voyage; if not, to be sure to sell him for a slave: he would, of course, take no harm of it, being the same just man as before; he would enjoy that happiness, though he lost his liberty. Pollis, therefore, it is stated, carried Plato to Ægina, and there sold him; the Æginetans, then at war with Athens, having made a decree that whatever Athenian was taken on their coasts should forthwith be exposed to sale. Notwithstanding, Dion was not in less favour and credit with Dionysius than formerly, but was intrusted with the most considerable employments, and sent on important embassies to Carthage, in the management of which he gained very great reputation. Besides, the usurper bore with the liberty he took to speak his mind freely, he being the only man who, upon any occasion, durst boldly say what he thought, as, for example, in the rebuke he gave him about Gelon. Dionysius was ridiculing Gelon's government, and, alluding to his name, said he had been the laughingstock of Sicily. While others seemed to admire and applaud the quibble, Dion very warmly replied, "Nevertheless, it is certain that you are sole governor here, because you were trusted for Gelon's sake; but for your sake no man will ever hereafter be trusted again." For, indeed, Gelon had made a monarchy appear the best, whereas Dionysius had convinced men that it was the worst of governments.

Dionysius had three children by Doris, and by Aristomache four, two of which were daughters, Sophrosyne and Arete. Sophrosyne was married to his son Dionysius; Arete, to his brother Thearides, after whose death Dion received his niece Arete to wife. Now when Dionysius was sick and like to die, Dion endeavoured to speak with him in behalf of the children he had by Aristomache, but was still prevented by the physicians, who wanted to ingratiate themselves with the next successor, who also, as Timæus reports, gave him a sleeping potion which he asked for, which produced an insensibility only followed by his death.

Nevertheless, at the first council which the young Dionysius held with his friends, Dion discoursed so well of the present state of affairs that he made all the rest appear in their politics but children, and in their votes rather slaves than counsellors, who timorously and disingenuously advised what would please the young man, rather than what would advance his interest. But that which startled them most was the proposal he made to avert the imminent danger they feared of a war with the Carthaginians, undertaking, if Dionysius wanted peace, to sail immediately over into Africa, and conclude it there upon honourable terms; but, if he rather preferred war, then he would fit out and maintain at his own cost and charges fifty galleys ready for the service.

Dionysius wondered much at his greatness of mind, and received his offer with satisfaction. But the other courtiers, thinking his generosity reflected upon them, and jealous of being lessened by his greatness, from hence took all occasions by private slanders to render him obnoxious to the young man's displeasure; as if he designed, by his power at sea, to surprise the government, and by the help of those naval forces confer the supreme authority upon his sister Aristomache's children. But, indeed, the most apparent and the strongest grounds for dislike and hostility existed already in the difference of his habits, and his reserved and separate way of living. For they, who, from the beginning by flatteries and all unworthy artifices, courted the favour and familiarity of the prince, youthful and voluptuously bred, ministered to his pleasures, and sought how to find him daily some new amours and occupy him in vain amusements, with wine or with women, and in other dissipations; by which means, the tyranny, like iron softened in the fire, seemed, indeed, to the subject, to be more moderate and gentle, and to abate somewhat of its extreme severity; the edge of it being blunted, not by the clemency, but rather the sloth and degeneracy of the sovereign, whose dissoluteness, gaining ground daily, and growing upon him, soon weakened and broke those "adamantine chains," with which his father, Dionysius, said he had left the monarchy fastened and secured. It is reported of him that, having begun a drunken debauch, he continued it ninety days without intermission; in all which time no person on business was allowed to appear, nor was any serious conversation heard at court, but drinking, singing, dancing, and buffoonery reigned there without control.

It is likely then they had little kindness for Dion, who never indulged himself in any youthful pleasure or diversion. And so his very virtues were the matter of their calumnies, and were represented under one or other plausible name as vices; they called his gravity pride, his plain-dealing self-will, the good advice he gave was all construed into reprimand, and he was censured for neglecting and scorning those in whose misdemeanours he declined to participate. And to say the truth, there was in his natural character something stately, austere, reserved, and unsociable in conversation, which made his company unpleasant and disagreeable not only to the young tyrant, whose ears had been corrupted by flatteries; many also of Dion's own intimate friends, though they loved the integrity and generosity of his temper, yet blamed his manner, and thought he treated those with whom he had to do less courteously and affably than became a man engaged in civil business. Of which Plato also afterwards wrote to him; and, as it were, prophetically advised him carefully to avoid an arbitrary temper, whose proper helpmate was a solitary life. And, indeed, at this very time, though circumstances made him so important, and in the danger of the tottering government he was recognised as the only or the ablest support of it, yet he well understood that he owed not his high position to any good-will or kindness, but to the mere necessities of the usurper.

And, supposing the cause of this to be ignorance and want of education, he endeavoured to induce the young man into a course of liberal studies, and to give him some knowledge of moral truths and reasonings, hoping he might thus lose his fear of virtuous living, and learn to take pleasure in laudable actions. Dionysius, in his own nature, was not one of the worst kind of tyrants, but his father, fearing that if he should come to understand himself better, and converse with wise and reasonable men, he might enter into some design against him, and dispossess him of his power, kept him closely shut up at home; where, for want of other company, and ignorant how to spend his time better, he busied himself in making little chariots, candlesticks, stools, tables, and other things of wood. For the elder Dionysius was so diffident and suspicious, and so continually on his guard against all men, that he would not so much as let his hair be trimmed with any barber's or haircutter's instruments, but made one of his artificers singe him with a live coal. Neither were his brother or his son allowed to come into his apartment in the dress they wore, but they, as all others, were stript to their skins by some of the guard, and, after being seen naked, put on other clothes before they were admitted into the presence. When his brother Leptines was once describing the situation of a place, and took a javelin from one of the guard to draw the plan of it, he was extremely angry with him, and had the soldier who gave him the weapon put to death. He declared the more judicious his friends were the more he suspected them; because he knew that, were it in their choice, they would rather be tyrants themselves than the subjects of a tyrant. He slew Marsyas, one of his captains whom he had preferred to a considerable command, for dreaming that he killed him: without some previous waking thought and purpose of the kind, he could not, he supposed, have had that fancy in his sleep. So timorous was he, and so miserable a slave to his fears, yet very angry with Plato, because he would not allow him to be the valiantest man alive.

Dion, as we said before, seeing the son thus deformed and spoilt in character for want of teaching, exhorted him to study, and to use all his entreaties to persuade Plato, the first of philosophers, to visit him in Sicily, and when he came, to submit himself to his direction and advice; by whose instructions he might conform his nature to the truths of virtue and, living after the likeness of the Divine and glorious Model of Being, out of obedience to whose control the general confusion is changed into the beautiful order of the universe, so he in like manner might be the cause of great happiness to himself and to all his subjects, who, obliged by his justice and moderation, would then willingly pay him obedience as their father, which now grudgingly, and upon necessity, they are forced to yield him as their master. Their usurping tyrant he would then no longer be, but their lawful king. For fear and force, a great navy and standing army of ten thousand hired barbarians are not, as his father had said, the adamantine chains which secure the regal power, but the love, zeal, and affection inspired by clemency and justice; which, though they seem more pliant than the stiff and hard bonds of severity, are nevertheles the strongest and most durable ties to sustain a lasting government. Moreover, it is mean and dishonourable that a ruler, while careful to be splendid in his dress, and luxurious and magnificent in his habitation, should, in reason and power of speech, make no better show than the commonest of his subjects, nor have the princely palace of his mind adorned according to his royal dignity.

Dion frequently entertaining the king upon this subject, and, as occasion offered, repeating some of the philosopher's sayings, Dionysius grew impatiently desirous to have Plato's company, and to hear him discourse. Forthwith, therefore, he sent letter upon letter to him to Athens, to which Dion added his entreaties; also several philosophers of the Pythagorean sect from Italy sent their recommendations, urging him to come and obtain a hold upon this pliant, youthful soul, which his solid and weighty reasonings might steady, as it were, upon the seas of absolute power and authority. Plato, as he tells us himself, out of shame more than any other feeling, lest it should seem that he was all mere theory, and that of his own good-will he would never venture into action, hoping withal, that if he could work a cure upon one man, the head and guide of the rest, he might remedy the distempers of the whole island of Sicily, yielded to their requests.

But Dion's enemies, fearing an alteration in Dionysius, persuaded him to recall from banishment Philistus, a man of learned education, and at the same time of great experience in the ways of tyrants, and who might serve as a counterpoise to Plato and his philosophy. For Philistus from the beginning had been a great instrument in establishing the tyranny, and for a long time had held the office of captain of the citadel. There was a report that he had been intimate with the mother of Dionysius the first, and not without his privity. And when Leptines, having two daughters by a married woman who he had debauched, gave one of them in marriage to Philistus, without acquainting Dionysius, he, in great anger, put Leptines's mistress in prison, and banished Philistus from Sicily. Whereupon, he fled to some of his friends on the Adriatic coast, in which retirement and leisure it is probable he wrote the greatest part of his history; for he returned not into his country during the reign of that Dionysius.

But after his death, as is just related, Dion's enemies occasioned him to be recalled home, as fitted for their purpose, and a firm friend to the arbitrary government. And this, indeed, immediately upon his return he set himself to maintain; and at the same time various calumnies and accusations against Dion were by others brought to the king: as that he held correspondence with Theodotes and Heraclides, to subvert the government; as, doubtless, it is likely enough, that Dion had entertained hopes, by the coming of Plato, to mitigate the rigid and despotic severity of the tyranny, and to give Dionysius the character of a fair and lawful governor; and had determined, if he should continue averse to that, and were not to be reclaimed, to depose him, and restore the commonwealth to the Syracusans; not that he approved a democratic government, but thought it altogether preferable to a tyranny, when a sound and good aristocracy could not be procured.

This was the state of affairs when Plato came into Sicily, who, at his first arrival, was received with wonderful demonstration of kindness and respect. For one of the royal chariots, richly ornamented, was in attendance to receive him when he came on shore; Dionysius himself sacrificed to the gods in thankful acknowledgment for the great happiness which had befallen his government. The citizens, also, began to entertain marvellous hopes of a speedy reformation, when they observed the modesty which now ruled in the banquets, and the general decorum which prevailed in all the court, their tyrant himself also behaving with gentleness and humanity in all their matters of business that came before him. There was a general passion for reasoning and philosophy, insomuch that the very palace, it is reported, was filled with dust by the concourse of the students in mathematics who were working their problems there. Some few days after, it was the time of one of the Syracusan sacrifices, and when the priest, as he was wont, prayed for the long and safe continuance of the tyranny, Dionysius, it is said, as he stood by, cried out, "Leave off praying for evil upon us." This sensibly vexed Philistus and his party, who conjectured, that if Plato, upon such brief acquaintance, had so far transformed and altered the young man's mind, longer converse and greater intimacy would give him such influence and authority that it would be impossible to withstand him.

Therefore, no longer privately and apart, but jointly and in public, all of them, they began to slander Dion, noising it about that he had charmed and bewitched Dionysius by Plato's sophistry, to the end that when he was persuaded voluntarily to part with his power, and lay down his authority, Dion might take it up, and settle it upon his sister Aristomache's children. Others professed to be indignant that the Athenians, who formerly had come to Sicily with a great fleet and a numerous land army, and perished miserably without being able to take the city of Syracuse, should now, by means of one sophister, overturn the sovereignty of Dionysius; inveighing him to cashier his guard of ten thousand lances, dismiss a navy of four hundred galleys, disband an army of ten thousand horse and many times over that number of foot, and go seek in the schools an unknown and imaginary bliss, and learn by the mathematics how to be happy; while, in the meantime, the substantial enjoyments of absolute power, riches, and pleasure would be handed over to Dion and his sister's children.

By these means, Dion began to incur at first suspicion, and by degrees more apparent displeasure and hostility. A letter, also, was intercepted and brought to the young prince which Dion had written to the Carthaginian agents, advising them that, when they treated with Dionysius concerning the peace, they should not come to their audience without communicating with him: they would not fail to obtain by this means all that they wanted. When Dionysius had shown this to Philistus, and consulted with him, as Timæus relates, about it, he overreached Dion by a feigned reconciliation, professing, after some fair and reasonable expression of his feelings, that he was at friends with him, and thus, leading him alone to the seaside, under the castle wall, he showed him the letter, and taxed him with conspiring with the Carthaginians against him. And when Dion essayed to speak in his own defence, Dionysius suffered him not; but immediately forced him aboard a boat, which lay there for that purpose, and commanded the sailors to set him ashore on the coast of Italy.

When this was publicly known, and was thought very hard usage, there was much lamentation in the tyrant's own household on account of the women, but the citizens of Syracuse encouraged themselves, expecting that for his sake some disturbance would ensue; which, together with the mistrust others would now feel, might occasion a general change and revolution in the state. Dionysius seeing this, took alarm, and endeavoured to pacify the women and others of Dion's kindred and friends, assuring them that he had not banished, but only sent him out of the way for a time, for fear of his own passion, which might be provoked some day by Dion's self-will into some act which he should be sorry for. He gave also two ships to his relations, with liberty to send into Peloponnesus for him whatever of his property or servants they thought fit.

Dion was very rich, and had his house furnished with little less than royal splendour and magnificence. These valuables his friends packed up and conveyed to him, besides many rich presents which were sent him by the women and his adherents. So that, so far as wealth and riches went, he made a noble appearance among the Greeks, and they might judge, by the affluence of the exile, what was the power of the tyrant.

Dionysius immediately removed Plato into the castle, designing, under colour of an honourable and kind reception, to set a guard upon him, lest he should follow Dion, and declare to the world, in his behalf, how injuriously he had been dealt with. And, moreover, time and conversation (as wild beasts by use grow tame and tractable) had brought Dionysius to endure Plato's company and discourse, so that he began to love the philosopher, but with such an affection as had something of the tyrant in it, requiring of Plato that he should, in return of his kindness, love him only, and attend to him above all other men; being ready to permit to his care the chief management of affairs, and even the government, too, upon condition that he would not prefer Dion's friendship before his. This extravagant affection was a great trouble to Plato, for it was accompanied with petulant and jealous humours, like the fond passions of those that are desperately in love; frequently he was angry and fell out with him, and presently begged and entreated to be friends again. He was beyond measure desirous to be Plato's scholar, and to proceed in the study of philosophy, and yet he was ashamed of it with those who spoke against it and professed to think it would ruin him.

But a war about this time breaking out, he sent Plato away, promising him in the summer to recall Dion, though in this he broke his word at once; nevertheless, he remitted to him his revenues, desiring Plato to excuse him as to the time appointed, because of the war, but, as soon as he had settled a peace, he would immediately send for Dion, requiring him in the interim to be quiet, and not raise any disturbance, nor speak ill of him among the Grecians. This Plato endeavoured to effect, by keeping Dion with him in the academy, and busying him in philosophical studies.

Dion sojourned in the Upper Town of Athens, with Callippus, one of his acquaintance; but for his pleasure he bought a seat in the country, which afterwards, when he went into Sicily, he gave to Speusippus, who had been his most frequent companion while he was at Athens, Plato so arranging it, with the hope that Dion's austere temper might be softened by agreeable company, with an occasional mixture of seasonable mirth. For Speusippus was of the character to afford him this; we find him spoken of in Timon's Silli, as "good at a jest." And Plato himself, as it happened, being called upon to furnish a chorus of boys, Dion took upon him the ordering and management of it, and defrayed the whole expense, Plato giving him this opportunity to oblige the Athenians, which was likely to procure his friend more kindness than himself credit. Dion went also to see several other cities, visiting the noblest and most statesmanlike persons in Greece, and joining in their recreations and entertainments in their times of festival. In all which, no sort of vulgar ignorance, or tyrannic assumption, or luxuriousness was remarked in him; but, on the contrary, a great deal of temperance, generosity, and courage, and a wellbecoming taste for reasoning and philosophic discourses. By which means he gained the love and admiration of all men, and in many cities had public honours decreed him; the Lacedæmonians making him a citizen of Sparta, without regard to the displeasure of Dionysius, though at that time he was aiding them in their wars against the Thebans.

It is related that once, upon invitation, he went to pay a visit to Ptœodorus, the Megarian, a man, it would seem, of wealth and importance; and when, on account of the concourse of people about his door, and the press of business, it was very troublesome and difficult to get access to him, turning about to his friends, who seemed concerned and angry at it, "What reason," said he, "have we to blame Ptœodorus, when we ourselves used to do no better when we were at Syracuse?"

After some little time, Dionysius, envying Dion, and jealous of the favour and interest he had among the Grecians, put a stop upon his incomes, and no longer sent him his revenues, making his own commissioners trustees of the estate. But, endeavouring to obviate the ill-will and discredit which, upon Plato's account, might accrue to him among the philosophers, he collected in his court many reputed learned men; and ambitiously desiring to surpass them in their debates, he was forced to make use, often incorrectly, of arguments he had picked up from Plato. And now he wished for his company again, repenting he had not made better use of it when he had it, and had given no greater heed to his admirable lessons. Like a tyrant, therefore, inconsiderate in his desires, headstrong and violent in whatever he took a will to, on a sudden he was eagerly set on the design of recalling him, and left no stone unturned, but addressed himself to Archytas, the Pythagorean (his acquaintance and friendly relations with whom owed their origin to Plato), and persuaded him to stand as surety for his engagements, and to request Plato to revisit Sicily.

Archytas, therefore, sent Archedemus and Dionysius some galleys, with divers friends, to entreat his return; moreover, he wrote to him himself expressly and in plain terms, that Dion must never look for any favour or kindness if Plato would not be prevailed with to come into Sicily; but if Plato did come Dion should be assured of whatever he desired. Dion also received letters full of solicitations from his sister and his wife, urging him to beg Plato to gratify Dionysius in this request, and not give him an excuse for further ill-doing. So that, as Plato says to himself, the third time he set sail for the Strait of Scylla—

"Venturing again Charybdis's dangerous gulf."

This arrival brought great joy to Dionysius, and no less hopes to the Sicilians, who were earnest in their prayers and good wishes that Plato might get the better of Philistus, and philosophy triumph over tyranny. Neither was he unbefriended by the women, who studied to oblige him and he had with Dionysius that peculiar credit which no man else ever obtained, namely, liberty to come into his presence without being examined or searched. When he would have given him a considerable sum of money, and, on several repeated occasions, made fresh offers, which Plato as often declined, Aristippus, the Cyranaean, then present, said that Dionysius was very safe in his munificence, he gave little to those who were ready to take all they could get, and a great deal to Plato, who would accept of nothing.

After the first compliments of kindness were over, when Plato began to discourse of Dion, he was at first diverted by excuses for delay, followed soon after by complaints and disgusts, though not as yet observable to others, Dionysius endeavouring to conceal them, and, by other civilities and honourable usage, to draw him off from his affection to Dion. And for some time Plato himself was careful not to let anything of this dishonesty and breach of promise appear, but bore with it, and dissembled his annoyance. While matters stood thus between them, and, as they thought, they were unobserved and undiscovered, Helicon, the Cyzicenian, one of Plato's followers, foretold an eclipse of the sun, which happened according to his prediction; for which he was much admired by the tyrant, and rewarded with a talent of silver; whereupon Aristippus, jesting with some others of the philosophers, told them, he also could predict something extraordinary; and on their entreating him to declare it, "I foretell," said he, "that before long there will be a quarrel between Dionysius and Plato."

At length, Dionysius made sale of Dion's estate, and converted the money to his own use, and removed Plato from an apartment he had in the gardens of the palace to lodgings among the guards he kept in pay, who from the first had hated Plato, and sought opportunity to make away with him, supposing he advised Dionysius to lay down the government and disband his soldiers.

When Archytas understood the danger he was in, he immediately sent a galley with messengers to demand him of Dionysius; alleging that he stood engaged for his safety, upon the confidence of which Plato had come to Sicily. Dionysius, to palliate his secret hatred, before Plato came away, treated him with great entertainments and all seeming demonstrations of kindness, but could not forbear breaking out one day into the expression, "No doubt, Plato, when you are at home among the philosophers, your companions, you will complain of me, and reckon up a great many of my faults." To which Plato answered with a smile, "The Academy will never, I trust, be at such a loss for subjects to discuss as to seek one in you." Thus, they say, Plato was dismissed; but his own writings do not altogether agree with this account.

Dion was angry at all this, and not long after declared open enmity to Dionysius, on hearing what had been done with his wife; on which matter Plato, also, had had some confidential correspondence with Dionysius. Thus it was. After Dion's banishment, Dionysius, when he sent Plato back, had desired him to ask Dion privately, if he would be averse to his wife's marrying another man. For there went a report, whether true, or raised by Dion's enemies, that his marriage was not pleasing to him, and that he lived with his wife on uneasy terms. When Plato therefore came to Athens, and had mentioned the subject to Dion, he wrote a letter to Dionysius speaking of other matters openly, but on this in language expressly designed to be understood by him alone, to the effect that he had talked with Dion about the business, and that it was evident he would highly resent the affront, if it should be put into execution. At that time, therefore, while there were yet great hopes of an accommodation, he took no new steps with his sister, suffering her to live with Dion's child. But when things were come to that pass, that no reconciliation could be expected, and Plato, after his second visit, was again sent away in displeasure, he then forced Arete, against her will, to marry Timocrates, one of his favourites; in this action coming short even of his father's justice and lenity; for he, when Polyxenus, the husband of his sister, Theste, became his enemy, and fled in alarm out of Sicily, sent for his sister, and taxed her, that, being privy to her husband's flight, she had not declared it to him. But the lady, confident and fearless, made him this reply: "Do you believe me, brother, so bad a wife, or so timorous a woman, that having known my husband's flight, I would not have borne his company, and shared his fortunes? I knew nothing of it; since otherwise it had been my better lot to be called the wife of the exile Polyxenus than the sister of the tyrant Dionysius." It is said, he admired her free and ready answer, as did the Syracusans also her courage and virtue, insomuch that she retained her dignity and princely retinue after the dissolution of the tyranny, and when she died, the citizens, by public decree, attended the solemnity of her funeral. And the story, though a digression from the present purpose, was well worth the telling.

From this time, Dion set his mind upon warlike measures; with which Plato, out of respect for past hospitalities, and because of his age, would have nothing to do. But Speusippus and the rest of his friends assisted and encouraged him, bidding him deliver Sicily, which with lift-up hands implored his help, and with open arms was ready to receive him. For when Plato was staying at Syracuse, Speusippus, being oftener than he in company with the citizens, had more thoroughly made out how they were inclined; and though at first they had been on their guard, suspecting his bold language, as though he had been set on by the tyrant to trepan them, yet at length they trusted him. There was but one mind and one wish or prayer among them all, that Dion would undertake the design, and come, though without either navy, men, horse, or arms; that he would simply put himself aboard any ship, and lend the Sicilians his person and name against Dionysius. This information from Speusippus encouraged Dion, who, concealing his real purpose, employed his friends privately to raise what men they could; and many statesmen and philosophers were assisting him, as, for instance, Eudemus the Cyprian, on whose death Aristotle wrote his Dialogue of the Soul, and Timonides the Leucadian. They also engaged on his side Miltas the Thessalian, who was a prophet, and had studied in the Academy. But of all that were banished by Dionysius, who were not fewer than a thousand, five and twenty only joined in the enterprise; the rest were afraid, and abandoned it. The rendezvous was in the island Zacynthus, where a small force of not quite eight hundred men came together, all of them, however, persons already distinguished in plenty of previous hard service, their bodies well trained and practised, and their experience and courage amply sufficient to animate and embolden to action the numbers whom Dion expected to join in Sicily.

Yet these men, when they first understood the expedition was against Dionysius, were troubled and disheartened, blaming Dion, that, hurried on like a madman by mere passion and despair, he rashly threw both himself and them into certain ruin. Nor were they less angry with their commanders and muster-masters that they had not in the beginning let them know the design. But when Dion in his address to them had set forth the unsafe and weak condition of arbitrary government, and declared that he carried them rather for commanders than soldiers, the citizens of Syracuse and the rest of the Sicilians having been long ready for a revolt, and when, after him, Alcimenes, an Achæan of the highest birth and reputation, who accompanied the expedition, harangued them to the same effect, they were contented.

It was now the middle of summer, and the Etesian winds blowing steadily on the seas, the moon was at the full, when Dion prepared a magnificent sacrifice to Apollo, and with great solemnity marched his soldiers to the temple in all their arms and accoutrements. And after the sacrifice, he feasted them all in the race-course of the Zacynthians, where he had made provisions for their entertainment. And when here they beheld with wonder the quantity and the richness of the gold and silver plate, and the tables laid to entertain them, all far exceeding the fortunes of a private man, they concluded with themselves that a man now past the prime of life, who was master of so much treasure, would not engage himself in so hazardous an enterprise without good reason of hope, and certain and sufficient assurances of aid from friends over there. Just after the libations were made, and the accompanying prayers offered, the moon was eclipsed; which was no wonder to Dion, who understood the revolutions of eclipses, and the way in which the moon is overshadowed and the earth interposed between her and the sun. But because it was necessary that the soldiers, who were surprised and troubled at it, should be satisfied and encouraged, Miltas the diviner, standing up in the midst of the assembly, bade them be of good cheer, and expect all happy success, for that the divine powers foreshowed that something at present glorious and resplendent should be eclipsed and obscured; nothing at this time being more splendid than the sovereignty of Dionysius, their arrival in Sicily should dim this glory, and extinguish this brightness. Thus Miltas, in public, descanted upon the incident. But concerning a swarm of bees which settled on the poop of Dion's ship, he privately told him and his friends that he feared the great actions they were like to perform, though for a time they should thrive and flourish, would be of short continuance, and soon suffer a decay. It is reported, also, that many prodigies happened to Dionysius at that time. An eagle, snatching a javelin from one of the guard, carried it aloft, and from thence let it fall into the sea. The water of the sea that washed the castle walls was for a whole day sweet and potable, as many that tasted it experienced. Pigs were farrowed perfect in all their other parts, but without ears. This the diviners declared to portend revolt and rebellion, for that the subjects would no longer give ear to the commands of their superiors. They expounded the sweetness of the water to signify to the Syracusans a change from hard and grievous times into easier and more happy circumstances. The eagle being the bird of Jupiter, and the spear an emblem of power and command, this prodigy was to denote that the chief of the gods designed the end and dissolution of the present government. These things Theopompus relates in his history.

Two ships of burden carried all Dion's men; a third vessel, of no great size, and two galleys of thirty oars attended them. In addition to his soldiers' own arms, he carried two thousand shields, a very great number of darts and lances, and abundant stores of all manner of provisions, that there might be no want of anything in their voyage; their purpose being to keep out at sea during the whole voyage, and use the winds, since all the land was hostile to them, and Philistus, they had been told, was in Iapygia with a fleet, looking out for them. Twelve days they sailed with a fresh and gentle breeze; on the thirteenth, they made Pachynus, the Sicilian cape. There Protus, the chief pilot, advised them to land at once and without delay, for if they were forced again from the shore, and did not take advantage of the headland, they might ride out at sea many nights and days, waiting for a southerly wind in the summer season. But Dion, fearing a descent too near his enemies, and desirous to begin at a greater distance, and further on in the country, sailed on past Pachynus. They had not gone far, before stress of weather, the wind blowing hard at north, drove the fleet from the coast; and it being now about the time that Arcturus rises, a violent storm of wind and rain came on, with thunder and lightning; the mariners were at their wits' end, and ignorant what course they ran, until on a sudden they found they were driving with the sea on Cercina, the island on the coast of Africa, just where it is most craggy and dangerous to run upon. Upon the cliffs there they escaped narrowly of being forced and staved to pieces; but, labouring hard at their oars, with much difficulty they kept clear until the storm ceased. Then, lighting by chance upon a vessel, they understood they were upon the Heads, as it is called, of the Great Syrtis; and when they were now again disheartened by a sudden calm, and beating to and fro without making any way, a soft air began to blow from the land, when they expected anything rather than wind from the south, and scarce believed the happy change of their fortune. The gale gradually increasing, and beginning to blow fresh, they clapped on all their sails, and, praying to the gods, put out again into the open seas, steering right from Africa for Sicily. And, running steady before the wind, the fifth day they arrived at Minoa, a little town of Sicily, in the dominion of the Carthaginians, of which Synalus, an acquaintance and friend of Dion's, happened at that time to be governor; who, not knowing it was Dion and his fleet, endeavoured to hinder his men from landing; but they rushed on shore with their swords in their hands, not slaying any of their opponents (for this Dion had forbidden, because of his friendship with the Carthaginians), but forced them to retreat, and, following close, pressed in a body with them into the place, and took it. As soon as the two commanders met, they mutually saluted each other; Dion delivered up the place again to Synalus, without the least damage done to any one therein, and Synalus quartered and entertained the soldiers, and supplied Dion with what he wanted.

They were most of all encouraged by the happy accident of Dionysius absence at this nick of time; for it appeared that he was lately gone with eighty sail of ships to Italy. Therefore, when Dion was desirous that the soldiers should refresh themselves there, after their tedious and troublesome voyage, they would not be prevailed with, but earnest to make the best use of that opportunity, they urged Dion to lead them straight on to Syracuse. Leaving, therefore, their baggage, and the arms they did not use, Dion desired Synalus to convey them to him as he had occasion, and marched directly to Syracuse.

The first that came in to him upon his march were two hundred horse of the Agrigentines who were settled near Ecnomum, and, after them, the Geloans. But the news soon flying to Syracuse, Timocrates, who had married Dion's wife, the sister of Dionysius, and was the principal man among his friends now remaining in the city, immediately despatched a courier to Dionysius, with letters announcing Dion's arrival; while he himself took all possible care to prevent any stir or tumult in the city, where all were in great excitement, but as yet continued quiet, fearing to give too much credit to what was reported. A very strange accident happened to the messenger who was sent with the letters; for being arrived in Italy, as he travelled through the land of Rhegium, hastening to Dionysius at Caulonia, he met one of his acquaintance, who was carrying home part of a sacrifice. He accepted a piece of the flesh, which his friend offered him, and proceeded on his journey with all speed; having travelled a good part of the night, and being, through weariness, forced to take a little rest, he laid himself down in the next convenient place he came to, which was in a wood near the road. A wolf, scenting the flesh, came and seized it as it lay fastened to the letter-bag, and with the flesh carried away the bag also, in which were the letters to Dionysius. The man, awaking and missing his bag, sought for it up and down a great while, and, not finding it, resolved not to go to the king without his letters, but to conceal himself, and keep out of the way.

Dionysius, therefore, came to hear of the war in Sicily from other hands, and that a good while after. In the meantime, as Dion proceeded in his march, the Camarineans joined his forces, and the country people in the territory of Syracuse rose and joined him in a large body. The Leontines and Campanians, who, with Timocrates, guarded the Epipolæ, receiving a false alarm which was spread on purpose by Dion, as if he intended to attack their cities first, left Timocrates, and hastened off to carry succour to their own homes. News of which being brought to Dion, where he lay near Macrze, he raised his camp by night, and came to the river Anapus which is distant from the city about ten furlongs; there he made a halt, and sacrificed by the river, offering vows to the rising sun. The soothsayers declared that the gods promised him victory; and they that were present, seeing him assisting at the sacrifice with a garland on his head, one and all crowned themselves with garlands. There were about five thousand that had joined his forces in their march; who, though but ill-provided, with such weapons as came next to hand, made up by zeal and courage for the want of better arms; and when once they were told to advance, as if Dion were already conqueror, they ran forward with shouts and acclamations, encouraging each other with the hopes of liberty.

The most considerable men and better sort of the citizens of Syracuse, clad all in white, met him at the gates. The populace set upon all that were of Dionysius's party, and principally searched for those they called setters or informers, a number of wicked and hateful wretches, who made it their business to go up and down the city, thrusting themselves into all companies, that they might inform Dionysius what men said, and how they stood affected. These were the first that suffered, being beaten to death by the crowd.

Timocrates, not being able to force his way to the garrison that kept the castle, took horse, and fled out of the city, filling all the places where he came with fear and confusion, magnifying the amount of Dion's forces that he might not be supposed to have deserted his charge without good reason for it. By this time, Dion was come up, and appeared in the sight of the people; he marched first in a rich suit of arms, and by him on one hand his brother, Megacles, on the other, Callippus the Athenian, crowned with garlands. Of the foreign soldiers, a hundred followed as his guard, and their several officers led the rest in good order; the Syracusans looking on and welcoming them, as if they believed the whole to be a sacred and religious procession, to celebrate the solemn entrance, after an absence of forty-eight years, of liberty and popular government.

Dion entered by the Menitid gate, and having by sound of trumpet quieted the noise of the people, he caused proclamation to be made, that Dion and Megacles, who were come to overthrow the tyrannical government, did declare the Syracusans and all other Sicilians to be free from the tyrant. But, being desirous to harangue the people himself, he went up through the Achradina. The citizens on each side the way brought victims for sacrifice, set out their tables and goblets, and as he passed by each door threw flowers and ornaments upon him, with vows and acclamations, honouring him as a god. There was under the castle and the Pentapyla a lofty and conspicuous sun-dial, which Dionysius had set up. Getting up upon the top of that, he made an oration to the people, calling upon them to maintain and defend their liberty; who, with great expressions of joy and acknowledgment, created Dion and Megacles generals, with plenary powers, joining in commission with them, at their desire and entreaty, twenty colleagues, of whom half were of those that had returned with them out of banishment. It seemed also to the diviners a most happy omen that Dion, when he made his address to the people, had under his feet the stately monument which Dionysius had been at such pains to erect; but because it was a sun-dial on which he stood when he was made general, they expressed some fears that the great actions he had performed might be subject to change, and admit some rapid turn and declination of fortune.

After this, Dion, taking the Epipolæ, released the citizens who were imprisoned there, and then raised a wall to invest the castle. Seven days after,

Dionysius arrived by sea, and got into the citadel, and about the same time came carriages, bringing the arms and ammunition which Dion had left with Synalus. These he distributed among the citizens; and the rest that wanted furnished themselves as well as they could, and put themselves in the condition of zealous and serviceable men-at-arms.

Dionysius sent agents, at first privately, to Dion, to try what terms they could make with him. But he declaring that any overtures they had to make must be made in public to the Syracusans as a free people, envoys now went and came between the tyrant and the people, with fair proposals, and assurances that they should have abatements of their tributes and taxes, and freedom from the burdens of military expeditions, all which should be made according to their own approbation and consent with him. The Syracusans laughed at these offers, and Dion returned answer to the envoys, that Dionysius must not think to treat with them upon any other terms but resigning the government; which if he would actually do, he would not forget how nearly he was related to him, or be wanting to assist him in procuring oblivion for the past, and whatever else was reasonable and just. Dionysius seemed to consent to this, and sent his agents again, desiring some of the Syracusans to come into the citadel and discuss with him in person the terms to which on each side they might be willing, after fair debate, to consent. There were, therefore, some deputed, such as Dion approved of; and the general rumour from the castle was, that Dionysius would voluntarily resign his authority, and rather do it himself as his own good deed than let it be the act of Dion. But this profession was a mere trick to amuse the Syracusans. For he put the deputies that were sent to him in custody, and by break of day, having first to encourage his men made them drink plentifully of raw wine, he sent the garrison of mercenaries out to make a sudden sally against Dion's works. The attack was quite unexpected, and the barbarians set to work boldly with loud cries to pull down the cross-wall, and assailed the Syracusans so furiously that they were not able to maintain their post. Only a party of Dion's hired soldiers, on first taking the alarm, advanced to the rescue; neither did they at first know what to do, or how to employ the aid they brought, not being able to hear the commands of their officers, amidst the noise and confusion of the Syracusans, who fled from the enemy and ran in among them, breaking through their ranks, until Dion, seeing none of his orders could be heard, resolved to let them see by example what they ought to do, and charged into the thickest of the enemy. The fight about him was fierce and bloody, he being as well known by the enemy as by his own party, and all running with loud cries to the quarters where he fought. Though his time of life was no longer that of the bodily strength and agility for such a combat, still his determination and courage were sufficient to maintain him against all that attacked him; but, while bravely driving them back, he was wounded in the hand with a lance, his body armour also had been much battered, and was scarcely any longer serviceable to protect him, either against missiles or blows hand-to-hand. Many spears and javelins had passed into it through the shield, and, on these being broken back, he fell to the ground, but was immediately rescued, and carried off by his soldiers. The command-in-chief he left to Timonides, and, mounting a horse, rode about the city, rallying the Syracusans that fled; and, ordering up a detachment of the foreign soldiers out of Achradina, where they were posted on guard, he brought them as a fresh reserve, eager for battle, upon the tired and failing enemy, who were already well inclined to give up their design. For having hopes at their first sally to take the whole city, when beyond their expectation they found themselves engaged with bold and practised fighters, they fell back towards the castle. As soon as they gave ground, the Greek soldiers pressed the harder upon them, till they turned and fled within the walls. There were lost in this action seventy-four of Dion's men, and a very great number of the enemy. This being a signal victory, and principally obtained by the valour of the foreign soldiers, the Syracusans rewarded them in honour of it with a hundred minæ, and the soldiers on their part presented Dion with a crown of gold.

Soon after, there came heralds from Dionysius bringing Dion letters from the women of his family, and one addressed outside, "To his father, from Hipparinus;" this was the name of Dion's son, though Timæus says, he was, from his mother Arete's name, called Aretæus; but I think credit is rather to be given to Timonides's report, who was his father's fellow-soldier and confidant. The rest of the letters were read publicly, containing many solicitations and humble requests of the women; that professing to be from his son, the heralds would not have them open publicly, but Dion, putting force upon them, broke the seal. It was from Dionysius, written in the terms of it to Dion, but in effect to the Syracusans, and so worded that, under a plausible justification of himself and entreaty to him, means were taken for rendering him suspected by the people. It reminded him of the good service he had formerly done the usurping government, it added threats to his dearest relations, his sister, son, and wife, if he did not comply with the contents, also passionate demands mingled with lamentations, and, most to the purpose of all, urgent recommendations to him not to destroy the government, and put the power into the hands of men who always hated him, and would never forget their old piques and quarrels; let him take the sovereignty himself, and so secure the safety of his family and his friends.

When this letter was read, the Syracusans were not, as they should have been, transported with admiration at the unmovable constancy and magnanimity of Dion, who withstood all his dearest interests to be true to virtue and justice, but, on the contrary, they saw in this their reason for fearing and suspecting that he lay under an invincible necessity to be favourable to Dionysius; and they began, therefore, to look out for other leaders, and the rather because to their great joy they received the news that Heraclides was on his way. This Heraclides was one of those whom Dionysius had banished, a very good soldier, and well known for the commands he had formerly had under the tyrant; yet a man of no constant purpose, of a fickle temper, and least of all to be relied upon when he had to act with a colleague in any honourable command. He had had a difference formerly with Dion in Peloponnesus, and had resolved, upon his own means, with what ships and soldiers he had, to make an attack upon Dionysius. When he arrived at Syracuse, with seven galleys and three small vessels, he found Dionysius already close besieged, and the Syracusans high and proud of their victories. Forthwith, therefore, he endeavoured by all ways to make himself popular; and, indeed, he had in him naturally something that was very insinuating and taking with a populace that loves to be courted. He gained his end, also, the easier, and drew the people over to his side, because of the dislike they had taken to Dion's grave and stately manner, which they thought overbearing and assuming; their successes having made them so careless and confident that they expected popular arts and flatteries from their leaders before they had in reality secured a popular government.

Getting, therefore, together in an irregular assembly, they chose Heraclides their admiral; but when Dion came forward, and told them that conferring this trust upon Heraclides was in effect to withdraw that which they had granted him, for he was no longer their generalissimo if another had the command of the navy, they repealed their order, and, though much against their wills, cancelled the new appointment. When this business was over, Dion invited Heraclides to his house, and pointed out to him, in gentle terms, that he had not acted wisely or well to quarrel with him upon a punctilio of honour, at a time when the least false step might be the ruin of all; and then, calling a fresh assembly of the people, he there named Heraclides admiral, and prevailed with the citizens to allow him a life-guard, as he himself had.

Heraclides openly professed the highest respect for Dion, and made him great acknowledgments for this favour, attending him with all deference, as ready to receive his commands; but underhand he kept up his dealings with the populace and the unrulier citizens, unsettling their minds and disturbing them with his complaints, and putting Dion into the utmost perplexity and disquiet. For if he advised to give Dionysius leave to quit the castle, he would be exposed to the imputation of sparing and protecting him; if, to avoid giving offence or suspicion, he simply continued the siege, they would say he protracted the war to keep his office of general the longer and overawe the citizens.

There was one Sosis, notorious in the city for his bad conduct and his impudence, yet a favourite with the people, for the very reason that they liked to see it made a part of popular privileges to carry free speech to this excess of licence. This man, out of a design against Dion, stood up one day in an assembly, and, having sufficiently railed at the citizens as a set of fools that could not see how they had made an exchange of a dissolute and drunken for a sober and watchful despotism, and thus having publicly declared himself Dion's enemy, took his leave. The next day he was seen running through the streets, as if he fled from some that pursued him, almost naked, wounded in the head, and bloody all over. In this condition, getting people about him in the market-place, he told them that he had been assaulted by Dion's men; and, to confirm what he said, showed them the wounds he had received in his head. And a good many took his part, exclaiming loudly against Dion for his cruel and tyrannical conduct, stopping the mouths of the people by bloodshed and peril of life. Just as an assembly was gathering in this unsettled and tumultuous state of mind, Dion came before them, and made it appear how this Sosis was brother to one of Dionysius's guard, and that he was set on by him to embroil the city in tumult and confusion; Dionysius having now no way left for his security but to make his advantage of their dissensions and distractions. The surgeons, also, having searched the wound, found it was rather raised than cut with a downright blow; for the wounds made with a sword are, from their mere weight, most commonly deepest in the middle, but this was very slight, and all along of an equal depth; and it was not one continued wound, as if cut at once, but several incisions, in all probability made at several times, as he was able to endure the pain. There were credible persons, also, who brought a razor, and showed it in the assembly, stating that they met Sosis, running in the street, all bloody, who told them that he was flying from Dion's soldiers, who had just attacked and wounded him; they ran at once to look after them, and met no one, but spied this razor lying under a hollow stone near the place from which they observed he came.

Sosis was now likely to come by the worst of it. But, when to back all this, his own servants came in, and gave evidence that he had left his house alone before break of day, with the razor in his hand, Dion's accusers withdrew themselves, and the people by a general vote condemned Sosis to die, being once again well satisfied with Dion and his proceedings.

Yet they were still as jealous as before of his soldiers, and the rather because the war was now carried on principally by sea; Philistus being come from Iapygia with a great fleet to Dionysius's assistance. They supposed, therefore, that there would be no longer need of the soldiers, who were all landsmen and armed accordingly; these were rather, indeed, they thought, in a condition to be protected by themselves, who were seamen, and had their power in their shipping. Their good opinion of themselves was also much enhanced by an advantage they got in an engagement by sea, in which they took Philistus prisoner, and used him in a barbarous and cruel manner. Ephorus relates that when he saw his ship was taken, he slew himself. But Timonides, who was with Dion from the very first, and was present at all the events as they occurred, writing to Speusippus the philosopher, relates the story thus: that Philistus's galley running aground, he was taken prisoner alive, and first disarmed, then stripped of his corselet, and exposed naked, being now an old man, to every kind of contumely; after which they cut off his head, and gave his body to the boys of the town, bidding them drag it through the Achradina, and then throw it into the Quarries. Timæus, to increase the mockery, adds further, that the boys tied him by his lame leg, and so drew him through the streets, while the Syracusans stood by laughing and jesting at the sight of that very man thus tied and dragged about by the leg, who had told Dionysius that, so far from flying on horseback from Syracuse, he ought to wait till he should be dragged out by the heels. Philistus, however, has stated that this was said to Dionysius by another, and not by himself.

Timæus avails himself of this advantage, which Philistus truly enough affords against himself in his zealous and constant adherence to the tyranny, to vent his own spleen and malice against him. They, indeed, who were injured by him at the time, are perhaps excusable, if they carried their resentment to the length of indignities to his dead body; but they who write history afterwards, and were noways wronged by him in his lifetime, and have received assistance from his writings, in honour should not with opprobrious and scurrilous language upbraid him for those misfortunes which may well enough befall even the best of men. On the other side, Ephorus is as much out of the way in his encomiums. For, however ingenious he is in supplying unjust acts and wicked conduct with fair and worthy motives, and in selecting decorous and honourable terms, yet when he does his best, he does not himself stand clear of the charge of being the greatest lover of tyrants, and the fondest admirer of luxury and power and rich estates and alliances of marriage with absolute princes. He that neither praises Philistus for his conduct, nor insults over his misfortunes, seems to me to take the fittest course.

After Philistus's death, Dionysius sent to Dion, offering to surrender the castle, all the arms, provisions, and garrison soldiers, with full pay for them for five months, demanding in return that he might have safe conduct to go unmolested into Italy, and there to continue, and also to enjoy the revenues of Gyarta, a large and fruitful territory belonging to Syracuse, reaching from the seaside to the middle of the country. Dion rejected these proposals, and referred him to the Syracusans. They, hoping in a short time to take Dionysius alive, dismissed his ambassadors summarily. But he, leaving his eldest son, Apollocrates, to defend the castle, and putting on board his ships the persons and the property that he set most value upon, took the opportunity of a fair wind, and made his escape, undiscovered by the admiral Heraclides and his fleet.

The citizens loudly exclaimed against Heraclides for this neglect; but he got one of their public speakers, Hippo by name, to go among them, and make proposals to the assembly for a redivision of lands, alleging that the first beginning of liberty was equality, and that poverty and slavery were inseparable companions. In support of this, Heraclides spoke, and used the faction in favour of it to overpower Dion, who opposed it; and in fine, he persuaded the people to ratify it by their vote, and further to decree that the foreign soldiers should receive no pay, and that they would elect new commanders, and so be rid of Dion's oppression. The people, attempting, as it were, after their long sickness of despotism, all at once to stand on their legs, and to do their part, for which they were yet unfit, of freemen, stumbled in all their actions; and yet hated Dion, who, like a good physician, endeavoured to keep the city to a strict and temperate regimen.

When they met in the assembly to choose their commanders, about the middle of summer, unusual and terrible thunders, with other inauspicious appearances, for fifteen days together, dispersed the people, deterring them, on grounds of religious fear, from creating new generals. But, at last, the popular leaders, having found a fair and clear day, and having got their party together, were proceeding to an election, when a draught-ox, who was used to the crowd and noise of the streets, but for some reason or other grew unruly to his driver, breaking from his yoke, ran furiously into the theatre where they were assembled, and set the people flying and running in all directions before him in the greatest disorder and confusion; and from thence went on, leaping and rushing about, over all that part of the city which the enemies afterwards made themselves masters of. However, the Syracusans, not regarding all this, elected five-and-twenty captains, and, among the rest, Heraclides, and underhand tampered with Dion's men, promising, if they would desert him, and enlist themselves in their service, to make them citizens of Syracuse, with all the privileges of natives. But they would not hear the proposals, but, to show their fidelity and courage, with their swords in their hands, placing Dion for his security in the midst of their battalion, conveyed him out of the city, not offering violence to any one, but upbraiding those they met with their baseness and ingratitude. The citizens, seeing they were but few, and did not offer any violence, despised them; and, supposing that with their large numbers they might with ease overpower and cut them off before they got out of the city, fell upon them in the rear.

Here Dion was in a great strait, being necessitated either to fight against his own countrymen or tamely suffer himself and his faithful soldiers to be cut in pieces. He used many entreaties to the Syracusans, stretching out his hands towards the castle that was full of their enemies, and showing them the soldiers, who in great numbers appeared on the walls and watched what was doing. But when no persuasions could divert the impulse of the multitude, and the whole mass, like the sea in a storm, seemed to be driven before the breath of the demagogues, he commanded his men, not to charge them, but to advance with shouts and clashing of their arms; which being done, not a man of them stood his ground; all fled at once through the streets, though none pursued them. For Dion immediately commanded his men to face about, and led them towards the city of the Leontines.

The very women laughed at the new captains for this retreat; so, to redeem their credit, they bid the citizens arm themselves again, and followed after Dion, and came up with him as he was passing a river. Some of the light-horse rode up and began to skirmish. But when they saw Dion no more tame and calm, and no signs in his face of any fatherly tenderness towards his countrymen, but with an angry countenance, as resolved not to suffer their indignities any longer, bidding his men face round and form in their ranks for the onset, they presently turned their backs more basely than before, and fled to the city, with the loss of some few of their men.

The Leontines received Dion very honourably, gave money to his men, and made them free of their city; sending envoys to the Syracusans, to require them to do the soldiers justice, who, in return, sent back other agents to accuse Dion. But when a general meeting of the confederates met in the town of the Leontines, and the matter was heard and debated, the Syracusans were held to be in fault. They, however, refused to stand to the award of their allies, following their own conceit, and making it their pride to listen to no one, and not to have any commanders but those who would fear and obey the people.

About this time, Dionysius sent in a fleet, under the command of Nypsius the Neapolitan, with provisions and pay for the garrison. The Syracusans fought him, had the better, and took four of his ships; but they made very ill use of their good success, and for want of good discipline, fell in their joy to drinking and feasting in an extravagant manner, with so little regard to their main interest that, when they thought themselves sure of taking the castle, they actually lost their city. Nypsius, seeing the citizens in this general disorder, spending day and night in their drunken singing and revelling, and their commanders well pleased with the frolic, or at least not daring to try and give any orders to men in their drink, took advantage of this opportunity, made a sally, and stormed their works; and having made his way through these, let his barbarians loose upon the city, giving up it and all that were in it to their pleasure.

The Syracusans quickly saw their folly and misfortune, but could not, in the distraction they were in, so soon redress it. The city was in actual process of being sacked, the enemy putting the men to the sword, demolishing the fortifications, and dragging the women and children, with lamentable shrieks and cries, prisoners into the castle. The commanders, giving all for lost, were not able to put the citizens in any tolerable posture of defence, finding them confusedly mixed up and scattered among the enemy. While they were in this condition, and the Achradina in danger to be taken, every one was sensible who he was in whom all their remaining hopes rested, but no man for shame durst name Dion, whom they had so ungratefully and foolishly dealt with. Necessity at last forcing them, some of the auxiliary troops and horsemen cried out, "Send for Dion and his Peloponnesians from the Leontines." No sooner was the venture made and the name heard among the people, but they gave a shout for joy, and, with tears in their eyes, wished him there, that they might once again see that leader at the head of them, whose courage and bravery in the worst of dangers they well remembered, calling to mind not only with what an undaunted spirit he always behaved himself, but also with what courage and confidence he inspired them when he led them against the enemy. They immediately, therefore, despatched Archonides and Telesides of the confederate troops, and of the horsemen Hellanicus and four others. These, traversing the road between at their horses' full speed, reached the town of the Leontines in the evening. The first thing they did was to leap from their horses and fall at Dion's feet, relating with tears the sad condition the Syracusans were in. Many of the Leontines and Peloponnesians began to throng about them, guessing by their speed and the manner of their address that something extraordinary had occurred.

Dion at once led the way to the assembly, and the people being gathered together in a very little time, Archonides and Hellanicus and the others came in among them, and in short declared the misery and distress of the Syracusans, begging the foreign soldiers to forget the injuries they had received, and assist the afflicted, who had suffered more for the wrong they had done than they themselves who received it would (had it been in their power) have inflicted upon them. When they had made an end there was a profound silence in the theatre; Dion then stood up, and began to speak, but tears stopped his words; his soldiers were troubled at his grief, but bade him take good courage and proceed. When he had recovered himself a little, therefore, "Men of Peloponnesus," he said, "and of the confederacy, I asked for your presence here, that you might consider your own interests. For myself, I have no interests to consult while Syracuse is perishing, and though I may not save it from destruction, I will nevertheless hasten thither, and be buried in the ruins of my country. Yet if you can find in your hearts to assist us, the most inconsiderate and unfortunate of men, you may to your eternal honour again retrieve this unhappy city. But if the Syracusans can obtain no more pity nor relief from you, may the gods reward you for what you have formerly valiantly done for them, and for your kindness to Dion, of whom speak hereafter as one who deserted you not when you were injured and abused, nor afterwards forsook his fellow-citizens in their afflictions and misfortunes."

Before he had yet ended his speech, the soldiers leapt up, and with a great shout testified their readiness for the service, crying out, to march immediately to the relief of the city. The Syracusan messengers hugged and embraced them, praying the gods to send down blessings upon Dion and the Peloponnesians. When the noise was pretty well over, Dion gave orders that all should go to their quarters to prepare for their march, and having refreshed themselves, came ready armed to their rendezvous in the place where they now were, resolving that very night to attempt the rescue.

Now at Syracuse, Dionysius's soldiers, as long as day continued, ransacked the city, and did all the mischief they could; but when night came on, they retired into the castle, having lost some few of their number. At which the factious ringleaders taking heart, and hoping the enemy would rest content with what they had done and make no further attempt upon them, persuaded the people again to reject Dion, and, if he came with the foreign soldiers, not to admit him; advising them not to yield, as inferior to them in point of honour and courage, but to save their city and defend their liberties and properties themselves. The populace, therefore, and their leaders, sent messengers to Dion to forbid him to advance, while the noble citizens and the horse sent others to him to desire him to hasten his march; for which reason he slacked his pace, yet did not remit his advance. And in the course of the night, the faction that was against him set a guard upon the gates of the city to hinder him from coming in. But Nypsius made another sally out of the castle with a far greater number of men, and those far more bold and eager than before, who quite ruined what of the rampart was left standing, and fell in, pell-mell, to sack and ravage the city. The slaughter was now very great, not only of the men, but of the women, also, and children; for they regarded not so much the plunder, as to destroy and kill all they met. For Dionysius, despairing to regain the kingdom, and mortally hating the Syracusans, resolved to bury his lost sovereignty in the ruin and desolation of Syracuse. The soldiers, therefore, to anticipate Dion's succours, resolved upon the most complete and ready way of destruction, to lay the city in ashes, firing all at hand with torches and lamps, and at distance with flaming arrows, shot from their bows. The citizens fled every way before them; they who, to avoid the fire, forsook their houses, were taken in the streets and put to the sword; they who betook themselves for refuge into the houses were forced out again by the flames, many buildings being now in a blaze, and many falling in ruins upon them as they fled past.

This fresh misfortune by general consent opened the gates for Dion. He had given up his rapid advance, when he received advice that the enemies were retreated into the castle, but, in the morning, some horse brought him the news of another assault, and, soon after, some of those who before opposed his coming fled now to him, to entreat him he would hasten his relief. The pressure increasing, Heraclides sent his brother, and after him his uncle, Theodotes, to beg him to help them; for that now they were not able to resist any longer; he himself was wounded, and the greatest part of the city either in ruins or in flames. When Dion met this sad news, he was about sixty furlongs distant from the city. When he had acquainted the soldiers with the exigency, and exhorted them to behave themselves like men, the army no longer marched but ran forwards, and by the way were met by messengers upon messengers entreating them to make haste. By the wonderful eagerness of the soldiers, and their extraordinary speed, Dion quickly came to the city, and entered what is called the Hecatompedon, sending his light-armed men at once to charge the enemy, that, seeing them, the Syracusans might take courage. In the meantime, he drew up in good order his full-armed men and all the citizens that came in and joined him; forming his battalions deep, and distributing his officers in many separate commands, that he might be able to attack from many quarters at once, and so be more alarming to the enemy.

So, having made his arrangements and offered vows to the gods, when he was seen in the streets advancing at the head of his men to engage the enemy, a confused noise of shouts, congratulations, vows, and prayers was raised by the Syracusans, who now called Dion their deliverer and tutelar deity, and his soldiers their friends, brethren, and fellow-citizens. And, indeed, at that moment, none seemed to regard themselves, or value their safeties, but to be concerned more for Dion's life than for all their own together, as he marched at the head of them to meet the danger, through blood and fire and over heaps of dead bodies that lay in his way.

And indeed the posture of the enemy was in appearance terrible; for they were flushed and ferocious with victory, and had posted themselves very advantageously along the demolished works, which made the access to them very hazardous and difficult. Yet that which disturbed Dion's soldiers most was the apprehension they were in of the fire, which made their march very troublesome and difficult; for the houses being in flames on all sides, they were met everywhere with the blaze, and, treading upon burning ruins and every minute in danger of being overwhelmed with falling houses, through clouds of ashes and smoke they laboured hard to keep their order and maintain their ranks. When they came near to the enemy, the approach was so narrow and uneven that but few of them could engage at a time; but at length, with loud cheers and much zeal on the part of the Syracusans, encouraging them and joining with them, they beat off Nypsius's men, and put them to flight. Most of them escaped into the castle, which was near at hand; all that could not get in were pursued and picked up here and there by the soldiers, and put to the sword. The present exigency, however, did not suffer the citizens to take immediate benefit of their victory in such mutual congratulations and embraces as became so great a success; for now all were busily employed to save what houses were left standing, labouring hard all night, and scarcely so could master the fire.

The next day, not one of the popular haranguers durst stay in the city, but all of them, knowing their own guilt, by their flight confessed it, and secured their lives. Only Heraclides and Theodotes went voluntarily and surrendered themselves to Dion, acknowledging that they had wronged him, and begging he would be kinder to them than they had been just to him, adding how much it would become him who was master of so many excellent accomplishments to moderate his anger and be generously compassionate to ungrateful men, who were here before him, making their confession that, in all the matter of their former enmity and rivalry against him they were now absolutely overcome by his virtue. Though they thus humbly addressed him, his friends advised him not to pardon these turbulent and ill-conditioned men, but to yield them to the desires of his soldiers, and utterly root out of the commonwealth the ambitious affectation of popularity, a disease as pestilent and pernicious as the passion for tyranny itself. Dion endeavoured to satisfy them, telling them that other generals exercised and trained themselves for the most part in the practices of war and arms; but that he had long studied in the Academy how to conquer anger, and not let emulation and envy conquer him; that to do this it is not sufficient that a man be obliging and kind to his friends, and those that have deserved well of him, but, rather, gentle and ready to forgive in the case of those who do wrong; that he wished to let the world see that he valued not himself so much upon excelling Heraclides in ability and conduct, as he did in outdoing him in justice and clemency; herein to have the advantage is to excel indeed; whereas the honour of success in war is never entire; fortune will be sure to dispute it, though no man should pretend to have a claim. What if Heraclides be perfidious, malicious, and base, must Dion therefore sully or injure his virtue by passionate concern for it? For, though the laws determine it juster to revenge an injury than to do an injury, yet it is evident that both, in the nature of things, originally proceed from the same deficiency and weakness. The malicious humour of men, though perverse and refractory, is not so savage and invincible but it may be wrought upon by kindness, and altered by repeated obligations. Dion, making use of these arguments, pardoned and dismissed Heraclides and Theodotes.

And now, resolving to repair the blockade about the castle, he commanded all the Syracusans to cut each man a stake and bring it to the works; and then, dismissing them to refresh themselves, and take their rest, he employed his own men all night, and by morning had finished his line of palisade; so that both the enemy and the citizens wondered, when day returned, to see the work so far advanced in so short a time. Burying, therefore, the dead, and redeeming the prisoners, who were near two thousand, he called a public assembly, where Heraclides made a motion that Dion should be declared general, with full powers at land and sea. The better citizens approved well of it, and called on the people to vote it so. But the mob of sailors and handicraftsmen would not yield that Heraclides should lose his command of the navy; believing him, if otherwise an ill man, at any rate to be more citizen-like than Dion, and readier to comply with the people. Dion therefore submitted to them in this, and consented Heraclides should continue admiral. But when they began to press the project of the redistribution of lands and houses, he not only opposed it, but repealed all the votes they had formerly made upon that account, which sensibly vexed them. Heraclides, therefore, took a new advantage of him, and, being at Messene, harangued the soldiers and ships' crews that sailed with him, accusing Dion that he had a design to make himself absolute. And yet at the same time he held private correspondence for a treaty with Dionysius by means of Pharax the Spartan. Which, when the noble citizens of Syracuse had intimation of, there arose a sedition in the army, and the city was in great distress and want of provisions; and Dion now knew not what course to take, being also blamed by all his friends for having thus fortified against himself such a perverse and jealous and utterly corrupted man as Heraclides was.

Pharax at this time lay encamped at Neapolis, in the territory of Agrigentum. Dion, therefore, led out the Syracusans, but with an intent not to engage him till he saw a fit opportunity. But Heraclides and his seamen exclaimed against him, that he had delayed fighting on purpose that he might the longer continue his command; so that, much against his will, he was forced to an engagement and was beaten, his loss, however, being inconsiderable, and that occasioned chiefly by the dissension that was in the army. He rallied his men, and, having put them in good order and encouraged them to redeem their credit, resolved upon a second battle. But in the evening, he received advice that Heraclides with his fleet was on his way to Syracuse, with the purpose to possess himself of the city and keep him and his army out. Instantly, therefore, taking with him some of the strongest and most active of his men, he rode off in the dark, and about nine the next morning was at the gates, having ridden seven hundred furlongs that night. Heraclides, though he strove to make all the speed he could, yet, coming too late, tacked and stood out again to sea; and, being unresolved what course to steer, accidentally he met Gæsylus the Spartan, who told him he was come from Lacedæmon to head the Sicilians, as Gylippus had formerly done. Heraclides was only too glad to get hold of him, and fastening him as it might be a sort of amulet to himself, he showed him to the confederates, and sent a herald to Syracuse to summon them to accept the Spartan general. Dion returned answer that they had generals enough, and, if they wanted a Spartan to command them, he could supply that office, being himself a citizen of Sparta. When Gæsylus saw this, he gave up all pretensions, and sailed in to Dion, and reconciled Heraclides to him, making Heraclides swear the most solemn oaths to perform what he engaged, Gæsylus himself also undertaking to maintain Dion's right and inflict chastisement on Heraclides if he broke his faith.

The Syracusans then laid up their navy, which was at present a great charge and of little use to them, but an occasion of differences and dissensions among the generals, and pressed on the siege, finishing the wall of blockade with which they invested the castle. The besieged, seeing no hopes of succour and their provisions failing, began to mutiny; so that the son of Dionysius, in despair of holding out longer for his father, capitulated, and articled with Dion to deliver up the castle with all the garrison soldiers and ammunition; and so, taking his mother and sisters and manning five galleys, he set out to go to his father, Dion seeing him safely out, and scarce a man in all the city not being there to behold the sight, as indeed they called even on those that were not present, out of pity, that they could not be there, to see this happy day and the sun shining on a free Syracuse. And as this expulsion of Dionysius is even now always cited as one of the greatest and most remarkable examples of fortune's vicissitudes, how extraordinary may we imagine their joy to have been, and how entire their satisfaction, who had totally subverted the most potent tyranny that ever was by very slight and inconsiderable means!

When Apollocrates was gone, and Dion coming to take possession of the castle, the women could not stay while he made his entry, but ran to meet him at the gate. Aristomache led Dion's son, and Arete followed after weeping, fearful and dubious how to salute or address her husband, after living with another man. Dion first embraced his sister, then his son; when Aristomache bringing Arete to him, "O Dion," said she, "your banishment made us all equally miserable; your return and victory has cancelled all sorrows, excepting this poor sufferer's, whom I, unhappy, was compelled to be another's while you were yet alive. Fortune has now given you the sole disposal of us; how will you determine concerning her hard fate? In what relation must she salute you, as her uncle, or as her husband?" This speech of Aristomache's brought tears from Dion, who with great affection embraced his wife, gave her his son, and desired her to retire to his own house, where he continued to reside when he had delivered up the castle to the Syracusans.

For though all things had now succeeded to his wish, yet he desired not to enjoy any present advantage of his good fortune, except to gratify his friends, reward his allies, and bestow upon his companions of former time in Athens, and the soldiers that had served him, some special mark of kindness and honour, striving herein to outdo his very means in his generosity. As for himself, he was content with a very frugal and moderate competency, and was indeed the wonder of all men, that when not only Sicily and Carthage, but all Greece looked to him as in the height of prosperity, and no man living greater than he, no general more renowned for valour and success, yet in his guard, his attendance, his table, he seemed as if he rather commoned with Plato in the Academy than lived among hired captains and paid soldiers, whose solace of their toils and dangers it is to eat and drink their fill, and enjoy themselves plentifully every day. Plato indeed wrote to him that the eyes of all the world were now upon him; but it is evident that he himself had fixed his eye upon one place in one city, the Academy, and considered that the spectators and judges there regarded not great actions, courage, or fortune, but watched to see how temporately and wisely he could use his prosperity, how evenly he could behave himself in the high condition he now was in. Neither did he remit anything of his wonted stateliness in conversation or serious charge to the people; he made it rather a point to maintain it, notwithstanding that a little condescension and obliging civility were very necessary for his present affairs; and Plato, as we said before, rebuked him, and wrote to tell him that self-will keeps house with solitude. But certainly his natural temperament was one that could not bend to complaisance; and, besides, he wished to work the Syracusans back the other way, out of their present excess of license and caprice.

Heraclides began again to set up against him, and, being invited by Dion to make one of the Council, refused to come, saying he would give his opinion as a private citizen in the public assembly. Next he complained of Dion because he had not demolished the citadel, and because he had hindered the people from throwing down Dionysius's tomb and doing despite to the dead; moreover, he accused him for sending to Corinth for counsellors and assistants in the government, thereby neglecting and slighting his fellow-citizens. And indeed he had sent messages for some Corinthians to come to him, hoping by their means and presence the better to settle that constitution he intended; for he designed to suppress the unlimited democratic government, which indeed is not a government, but, as Plato calls it, a market-place of governments, and to introduce and establish a mixed polity, on a Spartan and Cretan model, between a commonwealth and a monarchy, wherein an aristocratic body should preside, and determine all matters of greatest consequence; for he saw also that the Corinthians were chiefly governed by something like an oligarchy, and the people but little concerned in public business.

Now knowing that Heraclides would be his most considerable adversary, and that in all ways he was a turbulent, fickle, and factious man, he gave way to some whom formerly he hindered when they designed to kill him, who, breaking in, murdered Heraclides in his own house. His death was much resented by the citizens. Nevertheless, when Dion made him a splendid funeral, followed the dead body with all his soldiers, and then addressed them, they understood that it would have been impossible to have kept the city quiet, as long as Dion and Heraclides were competitors in the government.

Dion had a friend called Callippus, an Athenian, who, Plato says, first made acquaintance and afterwards obtained familiarity with him, not from any connection with his philosophic studies, but on occasion afforded by the celebration of the mysteries, and in the way of ordinary society. This man went with him in all his military service, and was in great honour and esteem; being the first of his friends who marched by his side into Syracuse, wearing a garland upon his head, having behaved himself very well in all the battles, and made himself remarkable for his gallantry. He, finding that Dion's principal and most considerable friends were cut off in the war, Heraclides now dead, and the people without a leader, and that the soldiers had a great kindness for him, like a perfidious and wicked villain, in hopes to get the chief command of Sicily as his reward for the ruin of his friend and benefactor, and, as some say, being also bribed by the enemy with twenty talents to destroy Dion, inveigled and engaged several of the soldiers in a conspiracy against him, taking this cunning and wicked occasion for his plot. He daily informed Dion of what he heard or what he feigned the soldiers said against him; whereby he gained that credit and confidence, that he was allowed by Dion to consort privately with whom he would, and talk freely against him in any company, that he might discover who were his secret and factious maligners. By this means, Callippus in a short time got together a cabal of all the seditious malcontents in the city; and if any one who would be drawn in advised Dion that he was tampered with, he was not troubled or concerned at, believing Callippus did it in compliance with his directions.

While this conspiracy was afoot, a strange and dreadful apparition was seen by Dion. As he sat one evening in a gallery in his house, alone and thoughtful, hearing a sudden noise he turned about, and saw at the end of the colonnade, by clear daylight, a tall woman, in her countenance and garb like one of the tragical Furies, with a broom in her hand, sweeping the floor. Being amazed and extremely affrighted, he sent for some of his friends, and told them what he had seen, entreating them to stay with him and keep him company all night; for he was excessively discomposed and alarmed, fearing that if he were left alone the spectre would again appear to him. He saw it no more. But a few days after, his only son, being almost grown up to man's estate, upon some displeasure and pet he had taken upon a childish and frivolous occasion, threw himself headlong from the top of the house and broke his neck.

While Dion was under this affliction, Callippus drove on his conspiracy, and spread a rumour among the Syracusans that Dion, being now childless, was resolved to send for Dionysius's son, Apollocrates, who was his wife's nephew and sister's grandson, and make him his heir and successor. By this time, Dion and his wife and sister began to suspect what was doing, and from all hands information came to them of the plot. Dion being troubled, it is probable, for Heraclides's murder, which was like to be a blot and stain upon his life and actions, in continual weariness and vexation, he had rather die a thousand times, and open his breast himself to the assassin, than live not only in fear of his enemies but suspicion of his friends. But Callippus, seeing the women very inquisitive to search to the bottom of the business, took alarm, and came to them, utterly denying it with tears in his eyes, and offering to give them whatever assurances of his fidelity they desired. They required that he should take the Great Oath, which was after this manner. The juror went into the sanctuary of Ceres and Proserpine, where, after the performance of some ceremonies, he was clad in the purple vestment of the goddess, and, holding a lighted torch in his hand, took his oath. Callippus did as they required, and forswore the fact. And indeed he so little valued the goddesses that he stayed but till the very festival of Proserpine, by whom he had sworn, and on that very day committed his intended murder; as truly he might well enough disregard the day, since he must at any other time as impiously offend her, when he who had acted as her initiating priest should shed the blood of her worshipper.

There were a great many in the conspiracy; and as Dion was at home with several of his friends in a room with tables for entertainment in it, some of the conspirators beset the house around, others secured the doors and windows. The actual intended murderers were some Zacynthians, who went inside in their under-dresses without swords. Those outside shut the doors upon them and kept them fast. The murderers fell on Dion, endeavouring to stifle and crush him; then, finding they were doing nothing, they called for a sword, but none durst open the door. There were a great many within with Dion, but every one was for securing himself, supposing that by letting him lose his life he should save his own, and therefore no man ventured to assist him. When they had waited a good while, at length Lycon the Syracusan reached a short sword in at the window to one of the Zacynthians, and thus, like a victim at a sacrifice, this long time in their power and trembling for the blow, they killed him. His sister, and wife big with child, they hurried to prison, who, poor lady, in her unfortunate condition was there brought to bed of a son, which, by the consent of the keepers, they intended to bring up, the rather because Callippus began already to be embroiled in troubles.

After the murder of Dion, he was in great glory, and had the sole government of Syracuse in his hands; and to that effect wrote to Athens, a place which, next the immortal gods, being guilty of such an abominable crime, he ought to have regarded with shame and fear. But true it is, what is said of that city, that the good men she breeds are the most excellent, and the bad the most notorious; as their country also produces the most delicious honey and the most deadly hemlock. Callippus, however, did not long continue to scandalise fortune and upbraid the gods with his prosperity, as though they connived at and bore with the wretched man, while he purchased riches and power by heinous impieties, but quickly received the punishment he deserved. For, going to take Catana, he lost Syracuse; whereupon they report he said, he had lost a city and got a bauble. Then attempting Messene, he had most of his men cut off, and, among the rest, Dion's murderers. When no city in Sicily would admit him, but all hated and abhorred him, he went into Italy and took Rhegium; and there, being in distress and not able to maintain his soldiers, he was killed by Leptines and Polysperchon, and, as fortune would have it, with the same sword by which Dion was murdered, which was known by the size, being but short, as the Spartan swords, and the workmanship of it very curious and artificial. Thus Callippus received the reward of his villainies.

When Aristomache and Arete were released out of prison, Hicetes, one of Dion's friends, took them to his house, and seemed to intend to entertain them well and like a faithful friend. Afterwards, being persuaded by Dion's enemies, he provided a ship and pretended to send them into Peloponnesus, but commanded the sailors, when they came out to sea, to kill them and throw them overboard. Others say that they and the little boy were thrown alive into the sea. This man also escaped not the due recompense of his wickedness, for he was taken by Timoleon and put to death, and the Syracusans, to revenge Dion, slew his two daughters: of all which I have given a more particular account in the life of Timoleon.

MARCUS BRUTUS

Marcus Brutus was descended from that Junius Brutus to whom the ancient Romans erected a statue of brass in the capitol among the images of their kings with a drawn sword in his hand, in remembrance of his courage and resolution in expelling the Tarquins and destroying the monarchy. But that ancient Brutus was of a severe and inflexible nature, like steel of too hard a temper, and having never had his character softened by study and thought, he let himself be so far transported with his rage and hatred against tyrants that, for conspiring with them, he proceeded to the execution even of his own sons. But this Brutus, whose life we now write, having to the goodness of his disposition added the improvements of learning and the study of philosophy, and having stirred up his natural parts, of themselves grave and gentle, by applying himself to business and public affairs, seems to have been of a temper exactly framed for virtue; insomuch that they who were most his enemies upon account of his conspiracy against Cæsar, if in that whole affair there was any honourable or generous part, referred it wholly to Brutus, and laid whatever was barbarous and cruel to the charge of Cassius, Brutus's connection and familiar friend, but not his equal in honesty and pureness of purpose. His mother, Servilia, was of the family of Servilius Ahala, who when Spurius Mælius worked the people into a rebellion and designed to make himself king, taking a dagger under his arm, went forth into the market-place, and upon pretence of having some private business with him, came up close to him, and, as he bent his head to hear what he had to say, struck him with his dagger and slew him. And thus much, as concerns his descent by the mother's side, is confessed by all; but as for his father's family, they who for Cæsar's murder bore any hatred or ill-will to Brutus say that he came not from that Brutus who expelled the Tarquins, there being none of his race left after the execution of his two sons; but that his ancestor was a plebeian, son of one Brutus, a steward, and only rose in the latest times to office or dignity in the commonwealth. But Posidonius the philosopher writes that it is true indeed what the history relates, that two of the sons of Brutus who were of men's estate were put to death, but that a third, yet an infant, was left alive, from whom the family was propagated down to Marcus Brutus; and further, that there were several famous persons of this house in his time whose looks very much resembled the statue of Junius Brutus. But of this subject enough.

Cato the philosopher was brother to Servilia, the mother of Brutus, and he it was whom of all the Romans his nephew most admired and studied to imitate, and he afterwards married his daughter Porcia. Of all the sects of the Greek philosophers, though there was none of which he had not been a hearer, and in which he had not made some proficiency, yet he chiefly esteemed the Platonists; and not much approving of the modern and middle Academy, as it is called, he applied himself to the study of the ancient. He was all his lifetime a great admirer of Antiochus of the city of Ascalon, and took his brother Aristus into his own house for his friend and companion, a man for his learning inferior indeed to many of the philosophers, but for the evenness of his temper and steadiness of his conduct equal to the best. As for Empylus, of whom he himself and his friends often make mention in their epistles, as one that lived with Brutus, he was a rhetorician, and has left behind him a short but well-written history of the death of Cæsar, entitled Brutus.

In Latin, he had by exercise attained a sufficient skill to be able to make public addresses and to plead a cause; but in Greek, he must be noted for affecting the sententious and short Laconic way of speaking in sundry passages of his epistles; as when, in the beginning of the war, he wrote thus to the Pergamenians: "I hear you have given Dolabella money; if willingly, you must own you have injured me; if unwillingly, show it by giving willingly to me." And another time to the Samians: "Your counsels are remiss and your performances slow; what think ye will be the end?" And of the Patareans thus: "The Xanthians, suspecting my kindness, have made their country the grave of their despair; the Patareans, trusting themselves to me, enjoy in all points their former liberty; it is in your power to choose the judgment of the Patareans on the pretence of the Xanthians." And this is the style for which some of his letters are to be noted.

When he was but a very young man, he accompanied his uncle Cato to Cyprus, when he was sent there against Ptolemy. But when Ptolemy killed himself, Cato, being by some necessary business detained in the isle of Rhodes, had already sent one of his friends, named Canidius, to take into his care and keeping the treasure of the king; but presently, not feeling sure of his honesty, he wrote to Brutus to sail immediately for Cyprus out of Pamphylia, where he then was staying to refresh himself, being but just recovered of a fit of sickness. He obeyed his orders, but with a great deal of unwillingness, as well out of respect to Canidius, who was thrown out of this employment by Cato with so much disgrace, as also because he esteemed such a commission mean and unsuitable to him, who was in the prime of his youth, and given to books and study. Nevertheless, applying himself to the business, he behaved himself so well in it that he was highly commended by Cato, and having turned all the goods of Ptolemy into ready money, he sailed with the greatest part of it in his own ship to Rome.

But upon the general separation into two factions, when, Pompey and Cæsar taking up arms against one another, the whole empire was turned into confusion, it was commonly believed that he would take Cæsar's side; for his father in past time had been put to death by Pompey. But he, thinking it his duty to prefer the interest of the public to his own private feelings, and judging Pompey's to be the better cause, took part with him; though formerly he used not so much as to salute or take any notice of Pompey, if he happened to meet him, esteeming it a pollution to have the least conversation with the murderer of his father. But now, looking upon him as the general of his country, he placed himself under his command, and set sail for Cilicia in quality of lieutenant to Sestius, who had the government of that province. But finding no opportunity there of doing any great service, and hearing that Pompey and Cæsar were now near one another and preparing for the battle upon which all depended, he came of his own accord to Macedonia to partake in the danger. At his coming it is said that Pompey was so surprised and so pleased that, rising from his chair in the sight of all who were about him, he saluted and embraced him, as one of the chiefest of his party. All the time that he was in the camp, excepting that which he spent in Pompey's company, he employed in reading and in study, which he did not neglect even the day before the great battle. It was the middle of summer, and the heat was very great, the camp having been pitched near some marshy ground, and the people that carried Brutus's tent were a long while before they came. Yet though upon these accounts he was extremely harassed and out of order, having scarcely by the middle of the day anointed himself and eaten a sparing meal, whilst most others were either laid to sleep or taken up with the thoughts and apprehensions of what would be the issue of the fight, he spent his time until the evening in writing an epitome of Polybius.

It is said that Cæsar had so great a regard for him that he ordered his commanders by no means to kill Brutus in the battle, but to spare him, if possible, and bring him safe to him, if he would willingly surrender himself; but if he made any resistance, to suffer him to escape rather than do him any violence. And this he is believed to have done out of a tenderness to Servilia, the mother of Brutus; for Cæsar had, it seems, in his youth been very intimate with her, and she passionately in love with him; and, considering that Brutus was born about that time in which their loves were at the highest, Cæsar had a belief that he was his own child. The story is told that, when the great question of the conspiracy of Catiline, which had like to have been the destruction of the commonwealth, was debated in the senate, Cato and Cæsar were both standing up, contending together on the decision to be come to; at which time a little note was delivered to Cæsar from without, which he took and read silently to himself. Upon this, Cato cried out aloud, and accused Cæsar of holding correspondence with and receiving letters from the enemies of the commonwealth; and when many other senators exclaimed against it, Cæsar delivered the note as he had received it to Cato, who reading it found it to be a love-letter from his own sister Servilia, and threw it back again to Cæsar with the words, "Keep it, you drunkard," and returned to the subject of the debate. So public and notorious was Servilia's love to Cæsar.

After the great overthrow at Pharsalia, Pompey himself having made his escape to the sea, and Cæsar's army storming the camp, Brutus stole privately out by one of the gates leading to marshy ground full of water and covered with reeds, and, travelling through the night, got safe to Larissa. From Larissa he wrote to Cæsar who expressed a great deal of joy to hear that he was safe, and, bidding him come, not only forgave him freely, but honoured and esteemed him among his chiefest friends. Now when nobody could give any certain account which way Pompey had fled, Cæsar took a little journey along with Brutus, and tried what was his opinion herein, and after some discussion which passed between them, believing that Brutus's conjecture was the right one, laying aside all other thoughts, he set out directly to pursue him towards Egypt. But Pompey, having reached Egypt, as Brutus guessed his design was to do, there met his fate.

Brutus in the meantime gained Cæsar's forgiveness for his friend Cassius; and pleading also in defence of the king of the Lybians, though he was overwhelmed with the greatness of the crimes alleged against him, yet by his entreaties and deprecations to Cæsar in his behalf, he preserved to him a great part of his kingdom. It is reported that Cæsar, when he first heard Brutus speak in public, said to his friends, "I know not what this young man intends, but, whatever he intends, he intends vehemently." For his natural firmness of mind, not easily yielding, or complying in favour of every one that entreated his kindness, once set into action upon motives of right reason and deliberate moral choice, whatever direction it thus took, it was pretty sure to take effectively, and to work in such a way as not to fail in its object. No flattery could ever prevail with him to listen to unjust petitions: and he held that to be overcome by the importunities of shameless and fawning entreaties, though some compliment it with the name of modesty and bashfulness, was the worst disgrace a great man could suffer. And he used to say that he always felt as if they who could deny nothing could not have behaved well in the flower of their youth.

Cæsar, being about to make his expedition into Africa against Cato and Scipio, committed to Brutus the government of Cisalpine Gaul, to the great happiness and advantage of that province. For while people in other provinces were in distress with the violence and avarice of their governors, and suffered as much oppression as if they had been slaves and captives of war, Brutus, by his easy government, actually made them amends for their calamities under former rulers, directing moreover all their gratitude for his good deeds to Cæsar himself; insomuch that it was a most welcome and pleasant spectacle to Cæsar, when in his return he passed through Italy, to see the cities that were under Brutus's command, and Brutus himself increasing his honour and joining agreeably in his progress.

Now several prætorships being vacant, it was all men's opinion that that of the chiefest dignity, which is called the prætorship of the city, would be conferred either upon Brutus or Cassius; and some say that, there having been some little difference upon former accounts between them, this competition set them much more at variance, though they were connected in their families, Cassius having married Junia, the sister of Brutus. Others say that the contention was raised between them by Caesar's doing, who had privately given each of them such hopes of his favour as led them on, and provoked them at last into this open competition and trial of their interest. Brutus had only the reputation of his honour and virtue to oppose to the many and gallant actions performed by Cassius against the Parthians. But Cæsar, having heard each side, and deliberating about the matter among his friends, said, "Cassius has the stronger plea, but we must let Brutus be first prætor." So another prætorship was given to Cassius; the gaining of which could not so much oblige him, as he was incensed for the loss of the other. And in all other things Brutus was partaker of Cæsar's power as much as he desired: for he might, if he had pleased, have been the chief of all his friends, and had authority and command beyond them all, but Cassius and the company he met with him drew him off from Cæsar. Indeed, he was not yet wholly reconciled to Cassius, since that competition which was between them: but yet he gave ear to Cassius's friends, who were perpetually advising him not to be so blind as to suffer himself to be softened and won over by Cæsar, but to shun the kindness and favours of a tyrant, which they intimated that Cæsar showed him, not to express any honour to his merit or virtue, but to unbend his strength, and undermine his vigour of purpose.

Neither was Caesar wholly without suspicion of him, nor wanted informers that accused Brutus to him; but he feared, indeed, the high spirit and the great character and the friends that he had, but thought himself secure in his moral disposition. When it was told him that Antony and Dolabella designed some disturbance, "It is not," said he, "the fat and the long-haired men that I fear, but the pale and the lean," meaning Brutus and Cassius. And when some maligned Brutus to him, and advised him to beware of him, taking hold of his flesh with his hand, "What," he said, "do you think that Brutus will not wait out the time of this little body?" as if he thought none so fit to succeed him in his power as Brutus. And indeed it seems to be without doubt that Brutus might have been the first man in the commonwealth, if he had had patience but a little time to be second to Caesar, and would have suffered his power to decline after it was come to its highest pitch, and the fame of his great actions to die away by degrees. But Cassius, a man of a fierce disposition, and one that out of private malice, rather than love of the public, hated Cæsar, not the tyrant, continually fired and stirred him up. Brutus felt the rule an oppression, but Cassius hated the ruler; and, among other reasons on which he grounded his quarrel against Cæsar, the loss of his lions which he had procured when he was ædile-elect was one; for Cæsar, finding these in Megara, when that city was taken by Calenus, seized them to himself. These beasts, they say, were a great calamity to the Megarians; for, when their city was just taken, they broke open the lions' dens, and pulled off their chains and let them loose that they might run upon the enemy that was entering the city; but the lions turned upon them themselves, and tore to pieces a great many unarmed persons running about, so that it was a miserable spectacle even to their enemies to behold.

And this, some say, was the chief provocation that stirred up Cassius to conspire against Cæsar; but they are much in the wrong. For Cassius had from his youth a natural hatred and rancour against the whole race of tyrants, which he showed when he was but a boy, and went to the same school with Faustus, the son of Sylla; for, on his boasting himself amongst the boys, and extolling the sovereign power of his father, Cassius rose up and struck him two or three boxes on the ear; which when the guardians and relations of Faustus designed to inquire into and to prosecute, Pompey forbade them, and, sending for both the boys together, examined the matter himself. And Cassius is then reported to have said thus, "Come, then, Faustus, dare to speak here those words that provoked me, that I may strike you again as I did before." Such was the disposition of Cassius.

But Brutus was roused up and pushed on to the undertaking by many persuasions of his familiar friends, and letters and invitations from unknown citizens. For under the statue of his ancestor Brutus, that overthrew the kingly government, they wrote the words, "O that we had a Brutus now!" and, "O that Brutus were alive!" And Brutus's own tribunal, on which he sat as prætor, was filled each morning with writings such as these: "You are asleep, Brutus," and, "You are not a true Brutus." Now the flatterers of Cæsar were the occasion of all this, who, among other invidious honours which they strove to fasten upon Cæsar, crowned his statues by night with diadems, wishing to incite the people to salute him king instead of dictator. But quite the contrary came to pass, as I have more particularly related in the life of Cæsar.

When Cassius went about soliciting friends to engage in this design against Cæsar, all whom he tried readily consented, if Brutus would be head of it; for their opinion was that the enterprise wanted not hands or resolution, but the reputation and authority of a man such as he was, to give as it were the first religious sanction, and by his presence, if by nothing else, to justify the undertaking; that without him they should go about this action with less heart, and should lie under greater suspicions when they had done it; for if their cause had been just and honourable, people would be sure that Brutus would not have refused it. Cassius, having considered these things with himself, went to Brutus and made him the first visit after their falling out; and after the compliments of reconciliation had passed, and former kindnesses were renewed between them, he asked him if he designed to be present on the calends of March, for it was discoursed, he said, that Cæsar's friends intended then to move that he might be made king. When Brutus answered, that he would not be there, "But what," says Cassius, "if they should send for us?" "It will be my business, then," replied Brutus, "not to hold my peace, but to stand up boldly, and die for the liberty of my country." To which Cassius with some emotion answered, "But what Roman will suffer you to die? What, do you not know yourself, Brutus? Or do you think that those writings that you find upon your prætor's seat were put there by weavers and shopkeepers, and not by the first and most powerful men of Rome? From other prætors, indeed, they expect largesses and shows and gladiators, but from you they claim, as an hereditary debt, the extirpation of tyranny; they are all ready to suffer anything on your account, if you will but show yourself such as they think you are and expect you should be." Which said, he fell upon Brutus, and embraced him; and after this, they parted each to try their several friends.

Among the friends of Pompey there was one Caius Ligarius, whom Cæsar had pardoned, though accused for having been in arms against him. This man, not feeling so thankful for having been forgiven as he felt oppressed by that power which made him need a pardon, hated Cæsar, and was one of Brutus's most intimate friends. Him Brutus visited, and finding him sick, "O Ligarius," says he, "what a time you have found out to be sick in!" At which words Ligarius, raising himself and leaning on his elbow, took Brutus by the hand, and said, "But, O Brutus, if you are on any design worthy of yourself, I am well."

From this time they tried the inclinations of all their acquaintances that they durst trust, and communicated the secret to them, and took into the design not only their familiar friends, but as many as they believed bold and brave and despisers of death. For which reason they concealed the plot from Cicero, though he was very much trusted and as well beloved by them all, lest, to his own disposition, which was naturally timorous, adding now the weariness and caution of old age, by his weighing, as he would do, every particular, that he might not make one step without the greatest security, he should blunt the edge of their forwardness and resolution in a business which required all the despatch imaginable. As indeed there were also two others that were companions of Brutus, Statilius the Epicurean, and Favonius the admirer of Cato, whom he left but for this reason: as he was conversing one day with them, trying them at a distance, and proposing some such question to be disputed of as among philosophers, to see what opinion they were of, Favonius declared his judgment to be that a civil war was worse than the most illegal monarchy; and Statilius held, that to bring himself into troubles and danger upon the account of evil or foolish men did not become a man that had any wisdom or discretion. But Labeo, who was present, contradicted them both; and Brutus, as if it had been an intricate dispute, and difficult to be decided, held his peace for that time, but afterwards discovered the whole design to Labeo, who readily undertook it. The next thing that was thought convenient was to gain the other Brutus, surnamed Albinus, a man of himself of no great bravery or courage, but considerable for the number of gladiators that he was maintaining for a public show, and the great confidence that Cæsar put in him. When Cassius and Labeo spoke with him concerning the matter, he gave them no answer; but, seeking an interview with Brutus himself alone, and finding that he was their captain, he readily consented to partake in the action. And among the others, also, the most and best were gained by the name of Brutus. And, though they neither gave nor took any oath of secrecy, nor used any other sacred rite to assure their fidelity to each other, yet all kept their design so close, were so wary, and held it so silently among themselves that, though by prophecies and apparitions and signs in the sacrifices the gods gave warning of it, yet could it not be believed.

Now Brutus, feeling that the noblest spirits of Rome for virtue, birth, or courage were depending upon him, and surveying with himself all the circumstances of the dangers they were to encounter, strove indeed, as much as possible, when abroad, to keep his uneasiness of mind to himself, and to compose his thoughts; but at home, and especially at night, he was not the same man, but sometimes against his will his working care would make him start out of his sleep, and other times he was taken up with further reflection and consideration of his difficulties, so that his wife that lay with him could not choose but take notice that he was full of unusual trouble, and had in agitation some dangerous and perplexing question. Porcia, as was said before, was the daughter of Cato, and Brutus, her cousin-german, had married her very young, though not a maid, but after the death of her former husband, by whom she had one son, that was named Bibulus; and there is a little book, called Memoirs of Brutus, written by him, yet extant. This Porcia, being addicted to philosophy, a great lover of her husband, and full of an understanding courage, resolved not to inquire into Brutus's secrets before she had made this trial of herself. She turned all her attendants out of her chamber, and taking a little knife, such as they use to cut nails with, she gave herself a deep gash in the thigh; upon which followed a great flow of blood, and soon after, violent pains and a shivering fever, occasioned by the wound. Now when Brutus was extremely anxious and afflicted for her, she, in the height of all her pain, spoke thus to him: "I, Brutus, being the daughter of Cato, was given to you in marriage, not like a concubine, to partake only in the common intercourse of bed and board, but to bear a part in all your good and all your evil fortunes; and for your part, as regards your care for me, I find no reason to complain; but from me, what evidence of my love, what satisfaction can you receive, if I may not share with you in bearing your hidden griefs, nor to be admitted to any of your counsels that require secrecy and trust? I know very well that women seem to be of too weak a nature to be trusted with secrets; but certainly, Brutus, a virtuous birth and education, and the company of the good and honourable, are of some force to the forming our manners; and I can boast that I am the daughter of Cato, and the wife of Brutus, in which two titles though before I put less confidence, yet now I have tried myself, and find that I can bid defiance to pain." Which words having spoken, she showed him her wound, and related to him the trial that she had made of her constancy; at which he being astonished, lifted up his hands to heaven, and begged the assistance of the gods in his enterprise, that he might show himself a husband worthy of such a wife as Porcia. So then he comforted his wife.

But a meeting of the senate being appointed, at which it was believed that Cæsar would be present, they agreed to make use of that opportunity; for then they might appear all together without suspicion; and, besides, they hoped that all the noblest and leading men of the commonwealth, being then assembled as soon as the great deed was done, would immediately stand forward and assert the common liberty. The very place too where the senate was to meet seemed to be by divine appointment favourable to their purpose. It was a portico, one of those joining the theatre, with a large recess, in which there stood a statue of Pompey, erected to him by the commonwealth, when he adorned that part of the city with the porticos and the theatre. To this place it was that the senate was summoned for the middle of March (the Ides of March is the Roman name for the day); as if some more than human power were leading the man thither, there to meet his punishment for the death of Pompey.

As soon as it was day, Brutus, taking with him a dagger, which none but his wife knew of, went out. The rest met together at Cassius's house, and brought forth his son that was that day to put on the manly gown, as it is called, into the forum; and from thence, going all to Pompey's porch, stayed there, expecting Cæsar to come without delay to the senate. Here it was chiefly that any one who had known what they had purposed, would have admired the unconcerned temper and the steady resolution of these men in their most dangerous undertaking; for many of them, being prætors, and called upon by their office to judge and determine causes, did not only hear calmly all that made application to them and pleaded against each other before them, as if they were free from all other thoughts, but decided causes with as much accuracy and judgment as they had heard them with attention and patience. And when one person refused to stand to the award of Brutus, and with great clamour and many attestations appealed to Cæsar, Brutus, looking round about him upon those that were present, said, "Cæsar does not hinder me, nor will he hinder me, from doing according to the laws."

Yet there were many unusual accidents that disturbed them and by mere chance were thrown in their way. The first and chiefest was the long stay of Cæsar, though the day was spent, and he being detained at home by his wife, and forbidden by the soothsayers to go forth, upon some defect that appeared in his sacrifice. Another was this: There came a man up to Casca, one of the company, and, taking him by the hand, "You concealed," said he, "the secret from us, but Brutus has told me all." At which words when Casca was surprised, the other said laughing, "How came you to be so rich of a sudden, that you should stand to be chosen ædile?" So near was Casca to let out the secret, upon the mere ambiguity of the other's expression. Then Popilius Lenæs, a senator, having saluted Brutus and Cassius more earnestly than usual, whispered them softly in the ear, and said, "My wishes are with you, that you may accomplish what you design, and I advise you to make no delay, for the thing is now no secret." This said, he departed, and left them in great suspicion that the design had taken wind. In the meanwhile, there came one in haste from Brutus's house and brought him news that his wife was dying. For Porcia, being extremely disturbed with expectation of the event, and not able to bear the greatness of her anxiety, could scarce keep herself within doors; and at every little noise or voice she heard, starting up suddenly, like those possessed with the bacchic frenzy, she asked every one that came in from the forum what Brutus was doing, and sent one messenger after another to inquire. At last, after long expectation and waiting, the strength of her constitution could hold out no longer; her mind was overcome with her doubts and fears, and she lost the control of herself, and began to faint away. She had not time to betake herself to her chamber, but, sitting as she was amongst her women, a sudden swoon and a great stupor seized her, and her colour changed, and her speech was quite lost. At this sight her women made a loud cry, and many of the neighbours running to Brutus's door to know what was the matter, the report was soon spread abroad that Porcia was dead; though with her women's help she recovered in a little while, and came to herself again. When Brutus received this news, he was extremely troubled, not without reason, yet was not so carried away by his private grief as to quit his public purpose.

For now news was brought that Cæsar was coming, carried in a litter. For, being discouraged by the ill-omens that attended his sacrifice, he had determined to undertake no affairs of any great importance that day, but to defer them till another time, excusing himself that he was sick. As soon as he came out of his litter, Popilius Lænas, he who but a little before had wished Brutus good success in his undertaking, coming up to him, conversed a great while with him, Cæsar standing still all the while, and seeming to be very attentive. The conspirators (to give them this name), not being able to hear what he said, but guessing by what themselves were conscious of that this conference was the discovery of their treason, were again disheartened, and, looking upon one another, agreed from each other's countenances that they should not stay to be taken, but should all kill themselves. And now when Cassius and some others were laying hands upon their daggers under their robes, and were drawing them out, Brutus, viewing narrowly the looks and gesture of Lænas, and finding that he was earnestly petitioning and not accusing, said nothing, because there were many strangers to the conspiracy mingled amongst them, but by a cheerful countenance encouraged Cassius. And after a little while, Lenas, having kissed Cæsar's hand, went away, showing plainly that all his discourse was about some particular business relating to himself.

Now when the senate was gone in before to the chamber where they were to sit, the rest of the company placed themselves close about Cæsar's chair, as if they had some suit to make to him, and Cassius, turning his face to Pompey's statue, is said to have invoked it, as if it had been sensible of his prayers. Trebonius, in the meanwhile, engaged Antony's attention at the door, and kept him in talk outside. When Cæsar entered, the whole senate rose up to him. As soon as he was sat down, the men all crowded round about him, and set Tillius Cimber, one of their own number, to intercede in behalf of his brother that was banished; they all joined their prayers with his, and took Cæsar by the hand, and kissed his head and his breast. But he putting aside at first their supplications, and afterwards, when he saw they would not desist, violently rising up, Tillius with both hands caught hold of his robe and pulled it off from his shoulders, and Casca, that stood behind him, drawing his dagger, gave him the first, but a slight wound, about the shoulder. Cæsar snatching hold of the handle of the dagger, and crying out aloud in Latin, "Villain Casca, what do you?" he, calling in Greek to his brother, bade him come and help. And by this time, finding himself struck by a great many hands, and looking around about him to see if he could force his way out, when he saw Brutus with his dagger drawn against him, he let go Casca's hand, that he had hold of, and covering his head with his robe, gave up his body to their blows. And they so eagerly pressed towards the body, and so many daggers were hacking together, that they cut one another; Brutus, particularly, received a wound in his hand, and all of them were besmeared with the blood.

Cæsar being thus slain, Brutus, stepping forth into the midst, intended to have made a speech, and called back and encouraged the senators to stay; but they all affrighted ran away in great disorder, and there was a great confusion and press at the door, though none pursued or followed. For they had come to an express resolution to kill nobody beside Cæsar, but to call and invite all the rest to liberty. It was indeed the opinion of all the others, when they consulted about the execution of their design, that it was necessary to cut off Antony with Cæsar, looking upon him as an insolent man, an affecter of monarchy, and one that, by his familiar intercourse, had gained a powerful interest with the soldiers. And this they urged the rather, because at that time to the natural loftiness and ambition of his temper there was added the dignity of being counsel and colleague to Cæsar. But Brutus opposed this consul, insisting first upon the injustice of it, and afterwards giving them hopes that a change might be worked in Antony. For he did not despair but that so highly gifted and honourable a man, and such a lover of glory as Antony, stirred up with emulation of their great attempt, might, if Cæsar were once removed, lay hold of the occasion to be joint restorer with them of the liberty of his country. Thus did Brutus save Antony's life. But he, in the general consternation, put himself into a plebeian habit, and fled. But Brutus and his party marched up to the capitol, in their way showing their hands all bloody, and their naked swords, and proclaiming liberty to the people. At first all places were filled with cries and shouts; and the wild running to and fro, occasioned by the sudden surprise and passion that every one was in, increased the tumult in the city. But no other bloodshed following, and no plundering of the goods in the streets, the senators and many of the people took courage and went up to the men in the capitol; and a multitude being gathered together, Brutus made an oration to them, very popular, and proper for the state that affairs were then in. Therefore, when they applauded his speech, and cried out to him to come down, they all took confidence and descended into the forum; the rest promiscuously mingled with one another, but many of the most eminent persons, attending Brutus, conducted him in the midst of them with great honour from the capitol, and placed him in the rostra. At the sight of Brutus, the crowd, though consisting of a confused mixture and all disposed to make a tumult, were struck with reverence, and expected what he would say with order and with silence, and, when he began to speak, heard him with quiet and attention. But that all were not pleased with this action they plainly showed when, Cinna beginning to speak and accuse Cæsar, they broke out into a sudden rage, and railed at him in such language that the whole party thought fit again to withdraw to the capitol. And there Brutus, expecting to be besieged, dismissed the most eminent of those that had acccompanied them thither, not thinking it just that they who were not partakers of the fact should share in the danger.

But the next day, the senate being assembled in the temple of the Earth, and Antony and Plancus and Cicero having made orations recommending concord in general and an act of oblivion, it was decreed that the men should not only be put out of all fear or danger, but that the consuls should see what honours and dignities were proper to be conferred upon them. After which done, the senate broke up; and, Antony having sent his son as an hostage to the capitol, Brutus and his company came down, and mutual salutes and invitations passed amongst them, the whole of them being gathered together. Antony invited and entertained Cassius, Lepidus did the same to Brutus, and the rest were invited and entertained by others, as each of them had acquaintance or friends. And as soon as it was day, the senate met again, and voted thanks to Antony for having stifled the beginning of a civil war; afterwards Brutus and his associates that were present received encomiums, and had provinces assigned and distributed among them. Crete was allotted to Brutus, Africa to Cassius, Asia to Trebonius, Bithynia to Cimber, and to the other Brutus Gaul about the Po.

After these things, they began to consider of Cæsar's will, and the ordering of his funeral. Antony desired that the will might be read, and that the body should not have a private or dishonourable interment, lest that should further exasperate the people. This Cassius violently opposed, but Brutus yielded to it, and gave leave; in which he seems to have a second time committed a fault. For as before in sparing the life of Antony he could not be without some blame from his party, as thereby setting up against the conspiracy a dangerous and difficult enemy, so now, in suffering him to have the ordering of the funeral, he fell into a total and irrevocable error. For first, it appearing by the will that Cæsar had bequeathed to the Roman people seventy-five drachmas a man, and given to the public his gardens beyond Tiber (where now the temple of Fortune stands), the whole city was fired with a wonderful affection for him, and a passionate sense of the loss of him. And when the body was brought forth into the forum, Antony, as the custom was, making a funeral oration in the praise of Cæsar, and finding the multitude moved with his speech, passing into the pathetic tone, unfolded the bloody garment of Cæsar, showed them in how many places it was pierced, and the number of his wounds. Now there was nothing to be seen but confusion, some cried out to kill the murderers, others (as was formerly done when Clodius led the people) tore away the benches and tables out of the shops round about, and, heaping them altogether, built a great funeral pile, and having put the body of Cæsar upon it, set it on fire, the spot where this was done being moreover surrounded with a great many temples and other consecrated places, so that they seemed to burn the body in a kind of sacred solemnity. As soon as the fire flamed out, the multitude, flocking in some from one part and some from another, snatched the brands that were half burnt out of the pile, and ran about the city to fire the houses of the murderers of Cæsar. But they, having beforehand well fortified themselves, repelled this danger.

There was, however, a kind of poet, one Cinna, not at all concerned in the guilt of the conspiracy, but on the contrary one of Cæsar's friends. This man dreamed that he was invited to supper by Cæsar, and that he declined to go, but that Cæsar entreated and pressed him to it very earnestly; and at last, taking him by the hand, led him into a very deep and dark place, whither he was forced against his will to follow in great consternation and amazement. After this vision, he had a fever the most part of the night; nevertheless in the morning, hearing that the body of Cæsar was to be carried forth to be interred, he was ashamed not to be present at the solemnity, and came abroad and joined the people, when they were already infuriated by the speech of Antony. And perceiving him, and taking him not for that Cinna who indeed he was, but for him that a little before in a speech to the people had reproached and inveighed against Cæsar, they fell upon him and tore him to pieces.

This action chiefly, and the alteration that Antony had wrought, so alarmed Brutus and his party that for their safety they retired from the city. The first stay they made was at Antium, with a design to return again as soon as the fury of the people had spent itself and was abated, which they expected would soon and easily come to pass in an unsettled multitude, apt to be carried away with any sudden and impetuous passion, especially since they had the senate favourable to them; which, though it took no notice of those that had torn Cinna to pieces, yet made a strict search and apprehended in order to punishment those that had assaulted the houses of the friends of Brutus and Cassius. By this time, also, the people began to be dissatisfied with Antony, who they perceived was setting up a kind of monarchy for himself; they longed for the return of Brutus, whose presence they expected and hoped for at the games and spectacles which he, as prætor, was to exhibit to the public. But he, having intelligence that many of the old soldiers that had borne arms under Cæsar, by whom they had had lands and cities given them, lay in wait for him, and by small parties at a time had stolen into the city, would not venture to come himself; however, in his absence there were most magnificent and costly shows exhibited to the people; for, having brought up a great number of all sorts of wild beasts, he gave order that not any of them should be returned or saved, but that all should be spent freely at the public spectacles. He himself made a journey to Naples to procure a considerable number of players, and hearing of one Canutius that was very much praised for his acting upon the stage, he wrote to his friends to use all their entreaties to bring him to Rome (for, being a Grecian, he could not be compelled); he wrote also to Cicero, begging him by no means to omit being present at the shows.

This was the posture of affairs when another sudden alteration was made upon the young Cæsar's coming to Rome. He was son to the niece of Cæsar, who adopted him, and left him his heir by his will. At the time when Cæsar was killed, he was following his studies at Apollonia, where he was expecting also to meet Cæsar on his way to the expedition which he had determined on against the Parthians; but, hearing of his death, he immediately came to Rome, and to ingratiate himself with the people, taking upon himself the name of Cæsar, and punctually distributing among the citizens the money that was left them by the will, he soon got the better of Antony; and by money and largesses, which he liberally dispersed amongst the soldiers, he gathered together and brought over to his party a great number of those that had served under Cæsar. Cicero himself, out of the hatred which he bore to Antony, sided with young Cæsar; which Brutus took so ill that he treated with him very sharply in his letters, telling him that he perceived Cicero could well enough endure a tyrant, but was afraid that he who hated him should be the man; that in writing and speaking so well of Cæsar, he showed that his aim was to have an easy slavery. "But our forefathers," said Brutus, "could not brook even gentle masters." Further he added, that for his own part he had not as yet fully resolved whether he should make war or peace; but that as to one point he was fixed and settled, which was, never to be a slave; that he wondered Cicero should fear the dangers of a civil war, and not be much more afraid of a dishonourable and infamous peace; that the very reward that was to be given him for subverting Antony's tyranny was the privilege of establishing Cæsar as tyrant in his place. This is the tone of Brutus's first letters to Cicero.

The city being now divided into two factions, some betaking themselves to Cæsar and others to Antony, the soldiers selling themselves, as it were, by public outcry, and going over to him that would give them most, Brutus began to despair of any good event of such proceedings, and, resolving to leave Italy, passed by land through Lucania and came to Elea by the seaside. From hence it was thought convenient that Porcia should return to Rome. She was overcome with grief to part from Brutus, but strove as much as was possible to conceal it; but, in spite of all her constancy, a picture which she found there accidentally betrayed it. It was a Greek subject, Hector parting from Andromache when he went to engage the Greeks, giving his young son Astyanax into her arms, and she fixing her eyes upon him. When she looked at this piece, the resemblance it bore to her own condition made her burst into tears, and several times a day she went to see the picture, and wept before it. Upon this occasion, when Acilius, one of Brutus's friends, repeated out of Homer the verses, where Andromache speaks to Hector:—

"But Hector, you
To me are father and are mother too,
My brother, and my loving husband true."

Brutus, smiling, replied, "But I must not answer Porcia, as Hector did Andromache:—

"'Mind you your loom, and to your maids give law.'

"For though the natural weakness of her body hinders her from doing what only the strength of men can perform, yet she has a mind as valiant and as active for the good of her country as the best of us." This narrative is in the memoirs of Brutus written by Bibulus, Porcia's son.

Brutus took ship from hence, and sailed to Athens, where he was received by the people with great demonstrations of kindness, expressed in their acclamation and the honours that were decreed him. He lived there with a private friend, and was a constant auditor of Theomnestus, the Academic, and Cratippus, the Peripatetic, with whom he so engaged in philosophical pursuits that he seemed to have laid aside all thoughts of public business, and to be wholly at leisure for study. But all this while, being unsuspected, he was secretly making preparations for war; in order to which he sent Herostratus into Macedonia to secure the commanders there to his side, and he himself won over and kept at his disposal all the young Romans that were then students at Athens. Of this number was Cicero's son whom he everywhere highly extols, and says that whether sleeping or waking he could not choose but admire a young man of so great a spirit and such a hater of tyranny.

At length he began to act openly, and to appear in public business, and, being informed that there were several Roman ships full of treasure that in their course from Asia were to come that way, and that they were commanded by one of his friends, he went to meet him about Carystus. Finding him there, and having persuaded him to deliver up the ships, he made a more than usually splendid entertainment, for it happened also to be his birthday. Now when they came to drink, and were filling their cups with hopes for victory to Brutus and liberty to Rome, Brutus, to animate them the more, called for a larger bowl, and holding it in his hand, on a sudden, upon no occasion or forethought, pronounced aloud this verse:—

"But fate my death and Leto's son have wrought."

And some writers add that in the last battle which he fought at Philippi, the word that he gave to his soldiers was Apollo, and from thence conclude that this sudden unaccountable exclamation of his was a presage of the overthrow that he suffered there.

Antistius, the commander of these ships, at his parting, gave him fifty thousand myriads of the money that he was conveying to Italy; and all the soldiers yet remaining of Pompey's army, who after their general's defeat wandered about Thessaly, readily and joyfully flocked together to join him. Besides this, he took from Cinna five hundred horse that he was carrying to Dolabella into Asia. After that, he sailed to Demetrias, and there seized a great quantity of arms that had been provided by the command of the deceased Cæsar for the Parthian war, and were now to be sent to Antony. Then Macedonia was put into his hands and delivered up by Hortensius the prætor, and all the kings and potentates round about came and offered their services. So when news was brought that Caius, the brother of Antony, having passed over from Italy, was marching on directly to join the forces that Vatinius commanded in Dyrrhachium and Apollonia, Brutus resolved to anticipate him, and to seize them first, and in all haste moved forwards with those that he had about him. His march was very difficult, through rugged places and in a great snow, but so swift that he left those that were to bring his provisions for the morning meal a great way behind. And now, being very near to Dyrrhachium, with fatigue and cold he fell into the distemper called Bulimia. This is a disease that seizes both men and cattle after much labour, and especially in a great snow; whether it is caused by the natural heat when the body is seized with cold, being forced all inwards, and consuming at once all the nourishment laid in, or whether the sharp and subtle vapour which comes from the snow as it dissolves cuts the body, as it were, and destroys the heat which issues through the pores; for the sweatings seem to arise from the heat meeting with the cold, and being quenched by it on the surface of the body. But this I have in another place discussed more at large.

Brutus growing very faint, and there being none in the whole army that had anything for him to eat, his servants were forced to have recourse to the enemy, and, going as far as to the gates of the city, begged bread of the sentinels that were upon duty. As soon as they heard of the condition of Brutus, they came themselves, and brought both meat and drink along with them; in return for which Brutus, when he took the city, showed the greatest kindness, not to them only, but to all the inhabitants, for their sakes. Caius Antonius, in the meantime, coming to Apollonia, summoned all the soldiers that were near that city to join him there; but finding that they nevertheless went all to Brutus, and suspecting that even those of Apollonia were inclined to the same party, he quitted that city, and came to Buthrotum, having first lost three cohorts of his men, that in their march thither were cut to pieces by Brutus. After this, attempting to make himself master of some strong places about Byllis which the enemy had first seized, he was overcome in a set battle by young Cicero, to whom Brutus gave the command, and whose conduct he made use of often and with much success. Caius himself was surprised in a marshy place, at a distance from his support; and Brutus having him in his power would not suffer his soldiers to attack, but manœuvring about the enemy with his horse, gave command that none of them should be killed, for that in a little time they would all be of his side; which accordingly came to pass, for they surrendered both themselves and their general. So that Brutus had by this time a very great and considerable army. He showed all marks of honour and esteem to Caius for a long time, and left him the use of the ensigns of his office, though, as some report, he had several letters from Rome, and particularly from Cicero, advising him to put him to death. But at last, perceiving that he began to corrupt his officers, and was trying to raise a mutiny amongst the soldiers, he put him aboard a ship and kept him close prisoner. In the meantime, the soldiers that had been corrupted by Caius retired to Apollonia, and sent word to Brutus, desiring him to come to them thither. He answered that this was not the custom of the Romans, but that it became those who had offended to come themselves to their general and beg forgiveness of their offences; which they did, and accordingly received their pardon.

As he was preparing to pass into Asia, tidings reached him of the alteration that had happened at Rome; where the young Cæsar, assisted by the senate, in opposition to Antony, and having driven his competitor out of Italy, had begun himself to be very formidable, suing for the consulship contrary to law, and maintaining large bodies of troops of which the commonwealth had no manner of need. And then, perceiving that the senate, dissatisfied with the proceedings, began to cast their eyes abroad upon Brutus, and decreed and confirmed the government of several provinces to him, he had taken the alarm. Therefore despatching messengers to Antony, he desired that there might be a reconciliation, and a friendship between them. Then, drawing all his forces about the city, he made himself to be chosen consul, though he was but a boy, being scarce twenty years old, as he himself writes in his memoirs. At the first entry upon the consulship he immediately ordered a judicial process to be issued out against Brutus and his accomplices for having murdered a principal man of the city, holding the highest magistracies of Rome, without being heard or condemned; and appointed Lucius Cornificus to accuse Brutus, and Marcus Agrippa to accuse Cassius. None appearing to the accusation, the judges were forced to pass sentence and condemn them both. It is reported that when the crier from the tribunal, as the custom was, with a loud voice cried Brutus to appear, the people groaned audibly, and the noble citizens hung down their heads for grief. Publicus Silicius was seen to burst out into tears, which was the cause that not long after he was put down in the list of those that were proscribed. After this, the three men, Cæsar, Antony, and Lepidus, being perfectly reconciled, shared the provinces among themselves, and made up the catalogue of proscription, wherein were set those that were designed for slaughter, amounting to two hundred men, in which number Cicero was slain.

The news being brought to Brutus in Macedonia, he was under a compulsion, and sent orders to Hortensius that he should kill Caius Antonius in revenge of the death of Cicero his friend, and Brutus his kinsman, who also was proscribed and slain. Upon this account it was that Antony, having afterwards taken Hortensius in the battle of Philippi, slew him upon his brother's tomb. But Brutus expresses himself as more ashamed for the cause of Cicero's death than grieved for the misfortune of it, and says he cannot help accusing his friends at Rome, that they were slaves more through their own doing than that of those who now were their tyrants; they could be present and see and yet suffer those things which even to hear related ought to them to have been insufferable.

Having made his army, that was already very considerable, pass into Asia, he ordered a fleet to be prepared in Bithynia and about Cyzicus. But going himself through the country by land, he made it his business to settle and confirm all the cities, and gave audience to the princes of the parts through which he passed. And he sent orders into Syria to Cassius to come to him, and leave his intended journey into Egypt; letting him understand that it was not to gain an empire for themselves, but to free their country, that they went thus wandering about and had got an army together whose business it was to destroy the tyrants; that therefore, if they remembered and resolved to persevere in their first purpose, they ought not to be too far from Italy, but make what haste they could thither, and endeavour to relieve their fellow-citizens from oppression.

Cassius obeyed his summons, and returned, and Brutus went to meet him; and at Smyrna they met, which was the first time they had seen one another since they parted at the Piræus in Athens, one for Syria, and the other for Macedonia. They were both extremely joyful and had great confidence of their success at the sight of the forces that each of them had got together, since they who had fled from Italy, like the most despicable exiles, without money, without arms, without a ship or a soldier or a city to rely on, in a little time after had met together so well furnished with shipping and money, and an army both of horse and foot, that they were in a condition to contend for the empire of Rome.

Cassius was desirous to show no less respect and honour to Brutus than Brutus did to him; but Brutus was still beforehand with him, coming for the most part to him, both because he was the elder man, and of a weaker constitution than himself. Men generally reckoned Cassius a very expert soldier, but of a harsh and angry nature, and one that desired to command rather by fear than love, though, on the other side, among his familiar acquaintance he would easily give way to jesting and play the buffoon. But Brutus, for his virtue, was esteemed by the people, beloved by his friends, admired by the best men, and hated not by his enemies themselves. For he was a man of a singularly gentle nature, of a great spirit, insensible of the passions of anger or pleasure or covetousness; steady and inflexible to maintain his purpose for what he thought right and honest. And that which gained him the greatest affection and reputation was the entire faith in his intentions. For it had not ever been supposed that Pompey the Great himself, if he had overcome Cæsar, would have submitted his power to the laws, instead of taking the management of the state upon himself, soothing the people with the specious name of consul or dictator, or some other milder title than king. And they were well persuaded that Cassius, being a man governed by anger and passion, and carried often, for his interest's sake, beyond the bounds of justice, endured all these hardships of war and travel and danger most assuredly to obtain dominion to himself, and not liberty to the people. And as for the former disturbers of the peace of Rome, whether a Cinna, a Marius, or a Carbo, it is manifest that they, having set their country as a stake for him that should win, did almost own in express terms that they fought for empire. But even the enemies of Brutus did not, they tell us, lay this accusation to his charge; nay, many heard Antony himself say that Brutus was the only man that conspired against Cæsar out of a sense of the glory and the apparent justice of the action, but that all the rest rose up against the man himself, from private envy and malice of their own. And it is plain by what he writes himself, that Brutus did not so much rely upon his forces, as upon his own virtue. For thus he speaks in a letter to Atticus, shortly before he was to engage with the enemy: that his affairs were in the best state of fortune that he could wish; for that either he should overcome, and restore liberty to the people of Rome, or die, and be himself out of the reach of slavery; that other things being certain and beyond all hazard, one thing was yet in doubt, whether they should live or die free men. He adds further, that Mark Antony had received a just punishment for his folly, who, when he might have been numbered with Brutus and Cassius and Cato, would join himself to Octavius; that though they should not now be both overcome, they soon would fight between themselves. And in this he seems to have been no ill prophet.

Now when they were at Smyrna, Brutus desired of Cassius that he might have part of the great treasure that he had heaped up, because all his own was expended in furnishing out such a fleet of ships as was sufficient to keep the whole interior sea in their power. But Cassius's friends dissuaded him from this; "for," said they, "it is not just that the money which you with so much parsimony keep, and with so much envy have got, should be given to him to be disposed of in making himself popular, and gaining the favour of the soldiers." Notwithstanding this, Cassius gave him a third part of all that he had; and then they parted each to their several commands. Cassius, having taken Rhodes, behaved himself there with no clemency; though at his first entry, when some had called him lord and king, he answered that he was neither king nor lord, but the destroyer and punisher of a king and lord. Brutus, on the other part, sent to the Lycians to demand from them a supply of money and men, but Laucrates, their popular leader, persuaded the cities to resist, and they occupied several little mountains and hills with a design to hinder Brutus's passage. Brutus at first sent out a party of horse which, surprising them as they were eating, killed six hundred of them, and afterward, having taken all their small towns and villages round about, he set all his prisoners free without ransom, hoping to win the whole nation by good-will. But they continued obstinate, taking in anger what they had suffered, and despising his goodness and humanity; until, having forced the most warlike of them into the city of Xanthus, he besieged them there. They endeavoured to make their escape by swimming and diving through the river that flows by the town, but were taken by nets let down for that purpose in the channel, which had little bells at the top, which gave present notice of any that were taken in them. After that, they made a sally in the night, and seizing several of the battering engines, set them on fire; but being perceived by the Romans, were beaten back to their walls, and there being a strong wind, it carried the flames to the battlements of the city with such fierceness that several of the adjoining houses took fire. Brutus, fearing lest the whole city should be destroyed, commanded his own soldiers to assist and quench the fire.

But the Lycians were on a sudden possessed with a strange and incredible desperation; such a frenzy as cannot be better expressed than by calling it a violent appetite to die, for both women and children, the bondmen and the free, those of all ages and of all conditions strove to force away the soldiers that came in to their assistance from the walls; and themselves gathering together reeds and wood, and whatever combustible matter they found, spread the fire over the whole city, feeding it with whatever fuel they could, and by all possible means exciting its fury, so that the flame, having dispersed itself and encircled the whole city, blazed out in so terrible a manner that Brutus, extremely afflicted at their calamity, got on horseback and rode round the walls, earnestly desirous to preserve the city, and stretching forth his hands to the Xanthians, begged of them that they would spare themselves and save the town. Yet none regarded his entreaties, but, by all manner of ways, strove to destroy themselves; not only men and women, but even boys and little children, with a hideous outcry, leaped some into the fire, others from the walls, others fell upon their parents' swords, baring their throats and desiring to be struck. After the destruction of the city, there was found a woman who had hanged herself with her young child hanging from her neck, and the torch in her hand with which she had fired her own house.

It was so tragical a sight that Brutus could not endure to see it, but wept at the very relation of it and proclaimed a reward to any soldier that could save a Xanthian. And it is said that an hundred and fifty only were found, to have their lives saved against their wills. Thus the Xanthians after a long space of years, the fated period of their destruction having, as it were, run its course, repeated by their desperate deed the former calamity of their forefathers, who after the very same manner in the Persian war had fired their city and destroyed themselves.

Brutus, after this, finding the Patareans resolved to make resistance and hold out their city against him, was very unwilling to besiege it, and was in great perplexity lest the same frenzy might seize them too. But having in his power some of their women, who were his prisoners, he dismissed them all without any ransom; who, returning and giving an account to their husbands and fathers, who were of the greatest rank, what an excellent man Brutus was, how temperate and how just, persuaded them to yield themselves and put their city into his hands. From this time all the cities round about came into his power, submitting themselves to him, and found him good and merciful even beyond their hopes. For though Cassius at the same time had compelled the Rhodians to bring in all the silver and gold that each of them privately was possessed of, by which he raised a sum of eight thousand talents, and besides this had condemned the public to pay the sum of five hundred talents more, Brutus, not having taken above a hundred and fifty talents from the Lycians, and having done them no other manner of injury, parted from thence with his army to go into Ionia.

Through the whole course of this expedition, Brutus did many memorable acts of justice in dispensing rewards and punishments to such as had deserved either; but one in particular I will relate, because he himself, and all the noblest Romans, were gratified with it above all the rest. When Pompey the Great, being overthrown from his great power by Cæsar, had fled to Egypt, and landed near Pelusium, the protectors of the young king consulted among themselves what was fit to be done on that occasion, nor could they all agree in the same opinion, some being for receiving him, others for driving him from Egypt. But Theodotus, a Chian by birth, and then attending upon the king as a paid teacher of rhetoric, and for want of better men admitted into the council, undertook to prove to them that both parties were in the wrong, those that counselled to receive Pompey, and those that advised to send him away; that in their present case one thing only was truly expedient, to seize him and to kill him; and ended his argument with the proverb, that "dead men don't bite." The council agreed to his opinion, and Pompey the Great (an example of incredible and unforeseen events) was slain, as the sophister himself had the impudence to boast, through the rhetoric and cleverness of Theodotus. Not long after, when Cæsar came to Egypt, some of the murderers received their just reward and suffered the evil death they deserved. But Theodotus, though he had borrowed on from fortune a little further time for a poor, despicable, and wandering life, yet did not lie hid from Brutus as he passed through Asia; but being seized by him and executed, had his death made more memorable than was his life.

About this time, Brutus sent to Cassius to come to him at the city of Sardis, and, when he was on his journey, went forth with his friends to meet him; and the whole army in array saluted each of them with the name of Imperator. Now (as it usually happens in business of great concern, and where many friends and many commanders are engaged), several jealousies of each other and matters of private accusation having passed between Brutus and Cassius, they resolved, before they entered upon any other business, immediately to withdraw into some apartment; where, the door being shut and they two alone, they began first to expostulate, then to dispute hotly, and accuse each other; and finally were so transported into passion as to fall to hard words, and at last burst out into tears. Their friends who stood without were amazed, hearing them loud and angry, and feared lest some mischief might follow, but yet durst not interrupt them, being commanded not to enter the room. However, Marcus Favonius, who had been an ardent admirer of Cato, and, not so much by his learning or wisdom as by his wild, vehement manner, maintained the character of a philosopher, was rushing in upon them, but was hindered by the attendants. But it was a hard matter to stop Favonius, wherever his wildness hurried him; for he was fierce in all his behaviour, and ready to do anything to get his will. And though he was a senator, yet, thinking that one of the least of his excellences, he valued himself more upon a sort of cynical liberty of speaking what he pleased, which sometimes, indeed, did away with the rudeness and unseasonableness of his addresses with those that would interpret it in jest. This Favonius, breaking by force through those that kept the doors, entered into the chamber, and with a set voice declaimed the verses that Homer makes Nestor use —

"Be ruled, for I am older than ye both."

At this Cassius laughed; but Brutus thrust him out, calling him impudent dog and counterfeit Cynic; but yet for the present they let it put an end to their dispute, and parted. Cassius made a supper that night, and Brutus invited the guests; and when they were set down, Favonius, having bathed, came in among them. Brutus called out aloud and told him he was not invited, and bade him go to the upper couch; but he violently thrust himself in, and lay down on the middle one; and the entertainment passed in sportive talk, not wanting either wit or philosophy.

The next day after, upon the accusation of the Sardians, Brutus publicly disgraced and condemned Lucius Pella, one that had been censor of Rome, and employed in offices of trust by himself, for having embezzled the public money. This action did not a little vex Cassius; for but a few days before, two of his own friends being accused of the same crime, he only admonished them in private, but in public absolved them, and continued them in his service; and upon this occasion he accused Brutus of too much rigour and severity of justice in a time which required them to use more policy and favour. But Brutus bade him remember the Ides of March, the day when they killed Cæsar, who himself neither plundered nor pillaged mankind, but was only the support and strength of those that did; and bade him consider that if there was any colour for justice to be neglected, it had been better to suffer the injustice of Cæsar's friends than to give impunity to their own; "for then," said he, "we would have been accused of cowardice only; whereas now we are liable to the accusation of injustice, after all our pain and dangers which we endure." By which we may perceive what was Brutus's purpose, and the rule of his actions.

About the time that they were going to pass out of Asia into Europe, it is said that a wonderful sign was seen by Brutus. He was naturally given to much watching, and by practice and moderation in his diet had reduced his allowance of sleep to a very small amount of time. He never slept in the daytime, and in the night then only when all his business was finished, and when, every one else being gone to rest, he had nobody to discourse with him. But at this time, the war being begun, having the whole state of it to consider, and being solicitous of the event, after his first sleep which he let himself take after his supper, he spent all the rest of the night in settling his most urgent affairs; which if he could despatch early and so make a saving of any leisure, he employed himself in reading until the third watch, at which time the centurions and tribunes were used to come to him for orders. Thus one night before he passed out of Asia, he was very late all alone in his tent, with a dim light burning by him, all the rest of the camp being hushed and silent; and reasoning about something with himself and very thoughtful, he fancied some one came in, and, looking up towards the door, he saw a terrible and strange appearance of an unnatural and frightful body standing by him without speaking. Brutus boldly asked it, "What are you, of men or gods, and upon what business come to me?" The figure answered,

"I am your evil genius, Brutus; you shall see me at Philippi." To which Brutus, not at all disturbed, replied, "Then I shall see you."

As soon as the apparition vanished, he called his servants to him, who all told him that they had neither heard any voice nor seen any vision. So then he continued watching till the morning, when he went to Cassius, and told him of what he had seen. He, who followed the principles of Epicurus's philosophy, and often used to dispute with Brutus concerning matters of this nature, spoke to him thus upon this occasion: "It is the opinion of our sect, Brutus, that not all that we feel or see is real and true; but that the sense is a most slippery and deceitful thing, and the mind yet more quick and subtle to put the sense in motion and affect it with every kind of change upon no real occasion of fact; just as an impression is made upon wax; and the soul of man, which has in itself both what imprints, and what is imprinted on, may most easily, by its own operations, produce and assume every variety of shape and figure. This is evident from the sudden changes of our dreams; in which the imaginative principle, once started by any trifling matter, goes through a whole series of most diverse emotions and appearances. It is its nature to be ever in motion, and its motion is fantasy or conception. But besides all this, in your case, the body, being tired and distressed with continual toil, naturally works upon the mind and keeps it in an excited and unusual condition. But that there should be any such thing as supernatural beings, or, if there were, that they should have human shape or voice or power that can reach to us, there is no reason for believing; though I confess I could wish that there were such beings, that we might not rely upon our arms only, and our horses and our navy, all which are so numerous and powerful, but might be confident of the assistance of gods also, in this our most sacred and honourable attempt." With such discourses as these Cassius soothed the mind of Brutus. But just as the troops were going on board, two eagles flew and lighted on the first two ensigns, and crossed over the water with them, and never ceased following the soldiers and being fed by them till they came to Philippi, and there, but one day before the fight, they both flew away.

Brutus had already reduced most of the places and people of these parts; but they now marched on as far as to the coast opposite Thasos, and, if there were any city or man of power that yet stood out, brought them all to subjection. At this point Norbanus was encamped, in a place called the Straits, near Symbolum. Him they surrounded in such sort that they forced him to dislodge and quit the place; and Norbanus narrowly escaped losing his whole army, Cæsar by reason of sickness being too far behind; only Antony came to his relief with such wonderful swiftness that Brutus and those with him did not believe when they heard he was come. Cæsar came up ten days after, and encamped over against Brutus, and Antony over against Cassius.

The space between the two armies is called by the Romans the Campi Philippi. Never had two such large Roman armies come together to engage each other. That of Brutus was somewhat less in number than that of Cæsar, but in the splendidness of the men's arms and richness of their equipage it wonderfully exceeded; for most of their arms were of gold and silver, which Brutus had lavishly bestowed among them. For though in other things he had accustomed his commanders to use all frugality and self-control, yet he thought that the riches which soldiers carried about them in their hands and on their bodies would add something of spirit to those that were desirous of glory, and would make those that were covetous and lovers of gain fight the more valiantly to preserve the arms which were their estate.

Cæsar made a view and lustration of his army within his trenches, and distributed only a little corn and but five drachmas to each soldier for the sacrifice they were to make. But Brutus, either pitying this poverty, or disdaining this meanness of spirit in Cæsar, first, as the custom was, made a general muster and lustration of the army in the open field, and then distributed a great number of beasts for sacrifice to every regiment, and fifty drachmas to every soldier; so that in the love of his soldiers and their readiness to fight for him Brutus had much the advantage. But at the time of lustration it is reported that an unlucky omen happened to Cassius; for his lictor, presenting him with a garland that he was to wear at sacrifice, gave it him the wrong way up. Further, it is said that some time before, at a certain solemn procession, a golden image of Victory, which was carried before Cassius, fell down by a slip of him that carried it. Besides this there appeared many birds of prey daily about the camp, and swarms of bees were seen in a place within the trenches, which place the soothsayers ordered shut out from the camp, to remove the superstition which insensibly began to infect even Cassius himself and shake him in his Epicurean philosophy, and had wholly seized and subdued the soldiers; from whence it was that Cassius was reluctant to put all to the hazard of a present battle, but advised rather to draw out the war until further time, considering that they were stronger in money and provisions, but in numbers of men and arms inferior. But Brutus, on the contrary, was still, as formerly, desirous to come with all speed to the decision of a battle; that so he might either restore his country to her liberty, or else deliver from their misery all those numbers of people whom they harassed with the expenses and the service and exactions of the war. And finding also his light-horse in several skirmishes still to have had the better, he was the more encouraged and resolved; and some of the soldiers having deserted and gone to the enemy, and others beginning to accuse and suspect one another, many of Cassius's friends in the council changed their opinions to that of Brutus. But there was one of Brutus's party, named Attellius, who opposed his resolution, advising rather that they should tarry over the winter. And when Brutus asked him in how much better a condition he hoped to be a year after, his answer was, "If I gain nothing else, yet I shall live so much the longer." Cassius was much displeased at this answer; and among the rest, Attellius was had in much disesteem for it. And so it was presently resolved to give battle the next day.

Brutus that night at supper showed himself very cheerful and full of hope, and reasoned on subjects of philosophy with his friends, and afterwards went to his rest. But Messala says that Cassius supped privately with a few of his nearest acquaintance, and appeared thoughtful and silent, contrary to his temper and custom; that after supper he took him earnestly by the hand, and speaking to him, as his manner was when he wished to show affection, in Greek, said, "Bear witness for me, Messala, that I am brought into the same necessity as Pompey the Great was before me, of hazarding the liberty of my country upon one battle; yet ought we to be of courage, relying on our good fortune, which it were unfair to mistrust, though we take evil counsels." These, Messala says, were the last words that Cassius spoke before he bade him farewell; and that he was invited to sup with him the next night, being his birthday.

As soon as it was morning, the signal of battle, the scarlet coat, was set out in Brutus's and Cassius's camps, and they themselves met in the middle space between their two armies. There Cassius spoke thus to Brutus: "Be it as we hope, O Brutus, that this day we may overcome, and all the rest of our time may live a happy life together; but since the greatest of human concerns are the most uncertain, and since it may be difficult for us ever to see one another again, if the battle should go against us, tell me, what is your resolution concerning flight and death?" Brutus answered, "When I was young, Cassius, and unskilful in affairs, I was led, I know not how, into uttering a bold sentence in philosophy, and blamed Cato for killing himself, as thinking it an irreligious act, and not a valiant one among men, to try to evade the divine course of things, and not fearlessly to receive and undergo the evil that shall happen, but run away from it. But now in my own fortunes I am of another mind; for if Providence shall not dispose what we now undertake according to our wishes, I resolve to put no further hopes or warlike preparations to the proof, but will die contented with my fortune. For I already have given up my life to my country on the Ides of March; and have lived since then a second life for her sake, with liberty and honour." Cassius at these words smiled, and, embracing Brutus, said, "With these resolutions let us go on upon the enemy; for either we ourselves shall conquer, or have no cause to fear those that do." After this they discoursed among their friends about the ordering of the battle; and Brutus desired of Cassius that he might command the right wing, though it was thought that this was more fit for Cassius, in regard both of his age and his experience. Yet even in this Cassius complied with Brutus, and placed Messala with the valiantest of all his legions in the same wing, so Brutus immediately drew out his horse, excellently well equipped, and was not long in bringing up his foot after them.

Antony's soldiers were casting trenches from the marsh by which they were encamped across the plain, to cut off Cassius's communications with the sea. Cæsar was to be at hand with his troops to support them, but he was not able to be present himself, by reason of his sickness; and his soldiers, not much expecting that the enemy would come to a set battle, but only make some excursions with their darts and light arms to disturb the men at work in the trenches, and not taking notice of the troops drawn up against them ready to give battle, were amazed when they heard the confused and great outcry that came from the trenches. In the meanwhile Brutus had sent his tickets, in which was the word of battle, to the officers; and himself riding about to all the troops, encouraged the soldiers; but there were but few of them that understood the word before they engaged; the most of them, not staying to have it delivered to them, with one impulse and cry ran upon the enemy. This disorder caused an unevenness in the line, and the legions got severed and divided one from another; that of Messala first, and afterwards the other adjoining, went beyond the left wing of Cæsar; and having just touched the extremity, without slaughtering any great number, passing around that wing, fell directly into Cæsar's camp. Cæsar himself, as his own memoirs tell us, had but just before been conveyed away, Marcus Artorius, one of his friends, having had a dream bidding Cæsar be carried out of the camp. And it was believed that he was slain; for the soldiers had pierced his litter, which was left empty, in many places with their darts and pikes. There was a great slaughter in the camp that was taken; and two thousand Lacedæmonians that were newly come to the assistance of Cæsar were all cut off together.

The rest of the army, that had not gone round, but had engaged the front, easily overthrew them, finding them in great disorder, and slew upon the place three legions; and being carried on with the stream of victory, pursuing those that fled, fell into the camp with them, Brutus himself being there. But they that were conquered took the advantage in their extremity of what the conquerors did not consider. For they fell upon that part of the main body which had been left exposed and separated, where the right wing had broke off from them and hurried away in the pursuit; yet they could not break into the midst of their battle, but were received with strong resistance and obstinacy. Yet they put to flight the left wing, where Cassius commanded, being in great disorder, and ignorant of what had passed on the other wing; and pursuing them to their camp, they pillaged and destroyed it, neither of their generals being present; for Antony, they say, to avoid the fury of the first onset, had retired into the marsh that was hard by; and Cæsar was nowhere to be found after his being conveyed out of the tents; though some of the soldiers showed Brutus their swords bloody, and declared that they had killed him, describing his person and his age. By this time also the centre of Brutus's battle had driven back their opponents with great slaughter; and Brutus was everywhere plainly conqueror, as on the other side Cassius was conquered. And this one mistake was the ruin of their affairs, that Brutus did not come to the relief of Cassius, thinking, that he, as well as himself, was conqueror; and that Cassius did not expect the relief of Brutus, thinking that he too was overcome. For as a proof that the victory was on Brutus's side, Messala urges his taking three eagles and many ensigns of the enemy without losing any of his own. But now, returning from the pursuit after having plundered Cæsar's camp, Brutus wondered that he could not see Cassius's tent standing high, as it was wont, and appearing above the rest, nor other things appearing as they had been; for they had been immediately pulled down and pillaged by the enemy upon their first falling into the camp. But some that had a quicker and longer sight than the rest acquainted Brutus that they saw a great deal of shining armour and silver targets moving to and fro in Cassius's camp, and that they thought, by their number and the fashion of their armour, they could not be those that they left to guard the camp; but yet that there did not appear so great a number of dead bodies thereabouts as it was probable there would have been after the actual defeat of so many legions. This first made Brutus suspect Cassius's misfortune, and, leaving a guard in the enemy's camp, he called back those that were in the pursuit, and rallied them together to lead them to the relief of Cassius, whose fortune had been as follows.

First, he had been angry at the onset that Brutus's soldiers made, without the word of battle or command to charge. Then, after they had overcome, he was as much displeased to see them rush on to the plunder and spoil, and neglect to surround and encompass the rest of the enemy. Besides this, letting himself act by delay and expectation, rather than command, boldly and with a clear purpose, he got hemmed in by the right wing of the enemy, and, his horse making with all haste their escape and flying towards the sea, the foot also began to give way, which he perceiving laboured as much as ever he could to hinder their flight and bring them back; and, snatching an ensign out of the hand of one that fled, he stuck it at his feet, though he could hardly keep even his own personal guard together. So that at last he was forced to fly with a few about him to a little hill that overlooked the plain. But he himself, being weaksighted, discovered nothing, only the destruction of his camp, and that with difficulty. But they that were with him saw a great body of horse moving towards him, the same whom Brutus had sent. Cassius believed these were enemies, and in pursuit of him; however, he sent away Titinius, one of those that were with him, to learn what they were. As soon as Brutus's horse saw him coming, and knew him to be a friend and a faithful servant of Cassius, those of them that were his more familiar acquaintance, shouting out for joy and alighting from their horses, shook hands and embraced him, and the rest rode round about him singing and shouting, through their excess of gladness at the sight of him. But this was the occasion of the greatest mischief that could be. For Cassius really thought that Titinius had been taken by the enemy, and cried out, "Through too much fondness of life, I have lived to endure the sight of my friend taken by the enemy before my face." After which words he retired into an empty tent, taking along with him only Pindarus, one of his freemen, whom he had reserved for such an occasion ever since the disasters in the expedition against the Parthians, when Crassus was slain. From the Parthians he came away in safety; but now, pulling up his mantle over his head, he made his neck bare, and held it forth to Pindarus, commanding him to strike. The head was certainly found lying severed from the body. But no man ever saw Pindarus after, from which some suspected that he had killed his master without his command. Soon after they perceived who the horsemen were, and saw Titinius, crowned with garlands, making what haste he could towards Cassius. But as soon as he understood by the cries and lamentations of his afflicted friends the unfortunate error and death of his general, he drew his sword, and having very much accused and upbraided his own long stay, that had caused it, he slew himself.

Brutus, as soon as he was assured of the defeat of Cassius, made haste to him; but heard nothing of his death till he came near his camp. Then having lamented over his body, calling him "the last of the Romans," it being impossible that the city should ever produce another man of so great a spirit, he sent away the body to be buried at Thasos, lest celebrating his funeral within the camp might breed some disorder. He then gathered the soldiers together and comforted them; and, seeing them destitute of all things necessary, he promised to every man two thousand drachmas in recompense of what he had lost. They at these words took courage, and were astonished at the magnificence of the gift; and waited upon him at his parting with shouts and praises, magnifying him for the only general of all the four who was not overcome in the battle. And indeed the action itself testified that it was not without reason he believed he should conquer; for with a few legions he overthrew all that resisted him; and if all his soldiers had fought, and the most of them had not passed beyond the enemy in pursuit of the plunder, it is very likely that he had utterly defeated every part of them.

There fell of his side eight thousand men, reckoning the servants of the army, whom Brutus calls Briges; and on the other side, Messala says his opinion is that there were slain about twice that number. For which reason they were more out of heart than Brutus, until a servant of Cassius, named Demetrius, came in the evening to Antony, and brought to him the garment which he had taken from the dead body, and his sword; at the sight of which they were so encouraged, that, as soon as it was morning, they drew out their whole force into the field, and stood in battle array. But Brutus found both his camps wavering and in disorder; for his own, being filled with prisoners, required a guard more strict than ordinary over them; and that of Cassius was uneasy at the change of general, besides some envy and rancour, which those that were conquered bore to that part of the army which had been conquerors. Wherefore he thought it convenient to put his army in array, but to abstain from fighting. All the slaves that were taken prisoners, of whom there was a great number that were mixed up, not without suspicion, among the soldiers, he commanded to be slain; but of the freemen and citizens, some he dismissed, saying that among the enemy they were rather prisoners than with him, for with them they were captives and slaves, but with him freemen and citizens of Rome. But he was forced to hide and help them to escape privately, perceiving that his friends and officers were bent upon revenge against them. Among the captives there was one Volumnius, a player, and Sacculio, a buffoon; of these Brutus took no manner of notice, but his friends brought them before him and accused them that even then in that condition they did not refrain from their jests and scurrilous language. Brutus, having his mind taken up with other affairs, said nothing to their accusation; but the judgment of Messala Corvinus was, that they should be whipped publicly upon a stage, and so sent naked to the captains of the enemy, to show them what sort of fellow drinkers and companions they took with them on their campaigns. At this some that were present laughed; and Publius Casca, he that gave the first wound to Cæsar, said, "We do ill to jest and make merry at the funeral of Cassius. But you, O Brutus," he added, "will show what esteem you have for the memory of that general, according as you punish or preserve alive those who will scoff and speak shamefully of him." To this Brutus, in great discomposure, replied, "Why then, Casca, do you ask me about it, and not do yourselves what you think fitting?" This answer of Brutus was taken for his consent to the death of these wretched men; so they were carried away and slain.

After this he gave the soldiers the reward that he had promised them; and having slightly reproved them for having fallen upon the enemy in disorder without the word of battle or command, he promised them, that if they behaved themselves bravely in the next engagement, he would give them up two cities to spoil and plunder, Thessalonica and Lacedæmon. This is the one indefensible thing of all that is found fault with in the life of Brutus; though true it may be that Antony and Cæsar were much more cruel in the rewards that they gave their soldiers after victory; for they drove out, one might almost say, all the old inhabitants of Italy, to put their soldiers in possession of other men's lands and cities. But indeed their only design and end in undertaking the war was to obtain dominion and empire, whereas Brutus, for the reputation of his virtue, could not be permitted either to overcome or save himself but with justice and honour, especially after the death of Cassius, who was generally accused of having been his adviser to some things that he had done with less clemency. But now, as in a ship, when the rudder is broken by a storm, the mariners fit and nail on some other piece of wood instead of it, striving against the danger not well, but as well as in that necessity they can, so Brutus, being at the head of so great an army, in a time of such uncertainty, having no commander equal to his need, was forced to make use of those that he had, and to do and to say many things according to their advice; which was, in effect, whatever might conduce to the bringing of Cassius's soldiers into better order. For they were very headstrong and intractable, bold and insolent in the camp for want of their general, but in the field cowardly and fearful, remembering that they had been beaten.

Neither were the affairs of Cæsar and Antony in any better posture; for they were straitened for provision, and, the camp being in a low ground, they expected to pass a very hard winter. For being driven close upon the marshes, and a great quantity of rain, as is usual in autumn, having fallen after the battle, their tents were all filled with mire and water, which through the coldness of the weather immediately froze. And while they were in this condition, there was news brought to them of their loss at sea. For Brutus's fleet fell upon their ships, which were bringing a great supply of soldiers out of Italy, and so entirely defeated them, that but very few of the men escaped being slain, and they too were forced by famine to feed upon the sails and tackle of the ship. As soon as they heard this, they made what haste they could to come to the decision of a battle, before Brutus should have notice of his good success. For it had so happened that the fight both by sea and land was on the same day, but by some misfortune, rather than the fault of his commanders, Brutus knew not of his victory twenty days after. For had he been informed of this, he would not have been brought to a second battle, since he had sufficient provisions for his army for a long time, and was very advantageously posted, his camp being well sheltered from the cold weather, and almost inaccessible to the enemy, and his being absolute master of the sea, and having at land overcome on that side wherein he himself was engaged, would have made him full of hope and confidence. But it seems the state of Rome not enduring any longer to be governed by many, but necessarily requiring a monarchy, the divine power, that it might remove out of the way the only man that was able to resist him that could control the empire, cut off his good fortune from coming to the ears of Brutus; though it came but a very little too late, for the very evening before the fight, Clodius, a deserter from the enemy, came and announced that Cæsar had received advice of the loss of his fleet, and for that reason was in such haste to come to a battle. But his story met with no credit, nor was he so much as seen by Brutus, being simply set down as one that had no good information, or invented lies to bring himself into favour.

The same night, they say, the vision appeared again to Brutus, in the same shape that it did before, but vanished without speaking. But Publius Volumnius, a philosopher, and one that had from the beginning borne arms with Brutus, makes no mention of this apparition, but says that the first eagle was covered with a swarm of bees, and that there was one of the captains whose arm of itself sweated oil of roses, and, though they often dried and wiped it, yet it would not cease; and that immediately before the battle, two eagles falling upon each other fought in the space between the two armies, that the whole field kept incredible silence and all were intent upon the spectacle, until at last that which was on Brutus's side yielded and fled. But the story of the Ethiopian is very famous, who, meeting the standard-bearer at the opening the gate of the camp, was cut to pieces by the soldiers, that took it for an ill omen.

Brutus, having brought his army into the field and set them in array against the enemy, paused a long while before he would fight; for as he was reviewing the troops, suspicions were excited and informations laid against some of them. Besides, he saw his horse not very eager to begin the action, and waiting to see what the foot would do. Then suddenly Camulatus, a very good soldier, and one whom for his valour he highly esteemed, riding hard by Brutus himself, went over to the enemy, the sight of which grieved Brutus exceedingly. So that partly out of anger, and partly out of fear of some greater treason and desertion, he immediately drew on his forces upon the enemy, the sun now declining, about three of the clock in the afternoon. Brutus on his side had the better, and pressed hard on the left wing, which gave way and retreated; and the horse too fell in together with the foot, when they saw the enemy in disorder. But the other wing, when the officers extended the line to avoid its being encompassed, the numbers being inferior, got drawn out too thin in the centre, and was so weak here that they could not withstand the charge, but at the first onset fled. After defeating these, the enemy at once took Brutus in the rear, who all the while did all that was possible for an expert general and valiant soldier, doing everything in the peril, by counsel and by hand, that might recover the victory. But that which had been his superiority in the first fight was to his prejudice in the second. For in the first, that part of the enemy which was beaten was killed on the spot; but of Cassius's soldiers that fled, few had been slain, and those that escaped, daunted with their defeat, infected the other and larger part of the army with their want of spirit and their disorder. Here Marcus, the son of Cato, was slain, fighting and behaving himself with great bravery in the midst of the youth of the highest rank and greatest valour. He would neither fly nor give the least ground, but still fighting and declaring who he was and naming his father's name, he fell upon a heap of dead bodies of the enemy. And of the rest, the bravest were slain in defending Brutus.

There was in the field one Lucilius, an excellent man and a friend of Brutus, who, seeing some barbarian horse taking no notice of any other in the pursuit, but galloping at full speed after Brutus, resolved to stop them, though with the hazard of his life; and, letting himself fall a little behind, he told them that he was Brutus. They believed him the rather, because he prayed to be carried to Antony, as if he feared Cæsar, but durst trust him. They, overjoyed with their prey, and thinking themselves wonderfully fortunate, carried him along with them in the night, having first sent messengers to Antony of their coming. He was much pleased, and came to meet them; and all the rest that heard that Brutus was taken and brought alive flocked together to see him, some pitying his fortune, others accusing him of a meanness unbecoming his former glory, that out of too much love of life he would be a prey to barbarians. When they came near together, Antony stood still, considering with himself in what manner he should receive Brutus; but Lucilius, being brought up to him, with great confidence said: "Be assured, Antony, that no enemy either has taken or ever shall take Marcus Brutus alive (forbid it, heaven, that fortune should ever so much prevail above virtue!), but he shall be found, alive or dead, as becomes himself. As for me, I am come hither by a cheat that I put upon your soldiers, and am ready, upon this occasion, to suffer any severities you will inflict." All were amazed to hear Lucilius speak these words. But Antony, turning himself to those that brought him, said: "I perceive, my fellow-soldiers, that you are concerned, and take it ill that you have been thus deceived, and think yourselves abused and injured by it; but know that you have met with a booty better than that you sought. For you were in search of an enemy, but you have brought me here a friend. For indeed I am uncertain how I should have used Brutus, if you had brought him alive; but of this I am sure, that it is better to have such men as Lucilius our friends than our enemies." Having said this, he embraced Lucilius, and for the present commended him to the care of one of his friends, and ever after found him a steady and a faithful friend.

Brutus had now passed a little brook, running among trees and under steep rocks, and, it being night, would go no further, but sat down in a hollow place with a great rock projecting before it, with a few of his officers and friends about him. At first, looking up to heaven, that was then full of stars, he repeated two verses, one of which, Volumnius writes, was this:—

"Punish, great Jove, the author of these ills."

The other he says he has forgot. Soon after, naming severally all his friends that had been slain before his face in the battle, he groaned heavily, especially at the mentioning of Flavius and Labeo, the latter his lieutenant, and the other chief officer of his engineers. In the meantime, one of his companions, that was very thirsty and saw Brutus in the same condition, took his helmet and ran to the brook for water, when a noise being heard from the other side of the river, Volumnius, taking Dardanus, Brutus's armour-bearer, with him, went out to see what it was. They returned in a short space, and inquired about the water. Brutus, smiling with much meaning, said to Volumnius. "It is all drunk; but you shall have some more fetched." But he that had brought the first water, being sent again, was in great danger of being taken by the enemy, and having received a wound, with much difficulty escaped.

Now Brutus guessing that not many of his men were slain in the fight, Statyllius undertook to dash through the enemy (for there was no other way), and to see what was become of their camp; and promised, if he found all things there safe, to hold up a torch for a signal, and then return. The torch was held up, Statyllius got safe to the camp; but when after a long time he did not return, Brutus said, "If Statyllius be alive, he will come back." But it happened that in his return he fell into the enemy's hands, and was slain.

The night now being far spent, Brutus, as he was sitting, leaned his head towards his servant, Clitus, and spoke to him; he answered him not, but fell a weeping. After that he drew aside his armour-bearer, Dardanus, and had some discourse with him in private. At last, speaking to Volumnius in Greek, he reminded him of their common studies and former discipline and begged that he would take hold of his sword with him, and help him to thrust it through him. Volumnius put away his request, and several others did the like; and some one saying, that there was no staying there, but they needs must fly, Brutus, rising up, said, "Yes, indeed, we must fly, but not with our feet, but with our hands." Then giving each of them his right hand, with a countenance full of pleasure, he said, that he found an infinite satisfaction in this, that none of his friends had been false to him; that as for fortune, he was angry with that only for his country's sake; as for himself, he thought himself much more happy than they who had overcome, not only as he had been a little time ago, but even now in his present condition; since he was leaving behind him such a reputation of his virtue as none of the conquerors with all their arms and riches should ever be able to acquire, no more than they could hinder posterity from believing and saying, that being unjust and wicked men, they had destroyed the just and the good, and usurped a power to which they had no right. After this, having exhorted and entreated all about him to provide for their own safety, he withdrew from them with two or three only of his peculiar friends; Strato was one of these, with whom he had contracted an acquaintance when they studied rhetoric together. Him he placed next to himself, and, taking hold of the hilt of his sword and directing it with both his hands, fell upon it, and killed himself. But others say, that not he himself, but Strato, at the earnest entreaty of Brutus, turning aside his head, held the sword, upon which he violently throwing himself, it pierced his breast, and he immediately died. This same Strato, Messala, a friend of Brutus, being after reconciled to Cæsar, brought to him once at his leisure, and with tears in his eyes said, "This, O Cæsar, is the man that did the last friendly office to my beloved Brutus." Upon which Cæsar received him kindly; and had good use of him in his labours and his battles at Actium, being one of the Greeks that proved their bravery in his service. It is reported of Messala himself, that, when Cæsar once gave him this commendation, that though he was his fiercest enemy at Philippi in the cause of Brutus, yet he had shown himself his most entire friend in the fight of Actium, he answered, "You have always found me, Cæsar, on the best and justest side."

Brutus's dead body was found by Antony, who commanded the richest purple mantle that he had to be thrown over it, and afterwards the mantle being stolen, he found the thief, and had him put to death. He sent the ashes of Brutus to his mother Servilia. As for Porcia his wife, Nicolaus the philosopher and Valerius Maximus write, that, being desirous to die, but being hindered by her friends, who continually watched her, she snatched some burning charcoal out of the fire, and, shutting it close in her mouth, stifled herself, and died. Though there is a letter current from Brutus to his friends, in which he laments the death of Porcia, and accuses them for neglecting her so that she desired to die rather than languish with her disease. So that it seems Nicolaus was mistaken in the time; for this epistle (if it indeed is authentic and truly Brutus's) gives us to understand the malady and love of Porcia, and the way in which her death occurred.

THE COMPARISON OF DION AND BRUTUS

THERE are noble points in abundance in the characters of these two men, and one to be first mentioned is their attaining such a height of greatness upon such inconsiderable means; and on this score Dion has by far the advantage. For he had no partner to contest his glory, as Brutus had in Cassius, who was not, indeed, his equal in proved virtue and honour, yet contributed quite as much to the service of the war by his boldness, skill, and activity; and some there be who impute to him the rise and beginning of the whole enterprise, saying that it was he who roused Brutus, till then indisposed to stir, into action against Cæsar. Whereas Dion seems of himself to have provided not only arms, ships, and soldiers, but likewise friends and partners for the enterprise. Neither did he, as Brutus, collect money and forces from the war itself, but, on the contrary, laid out of his own substance, and employed the very means of his private sustenance in exile for the liberty of his country. Besides this, Brutus and Cassius, when they fled from Rome, could not live safe or quiet, being condemned to death and pursued, and were thus of necessity forced to take arms and hazard their lives in their own defence, to save themselves, rather than their country. On the other hand, Dion enjoyed more ease, was more safe, and his life more pleasant in his banishment, than was the tyrant's who had banished him, when he flew to action, and ran the risk of all to save Sicily.

Take notice, too, that it was not the same thing for the Sicilians to be freed from Dionysius, and for the Romans to be freed from Cæsar. The former owned himself a tyrant, and vexed Sicily with a thousand oppressions; whereas Cæsar's supremacy, certainly, in the process for attaining it, had inflicted no trouble on its opponents, but, once established and victorious, it had indeed the name and appearance, but fact that was cruel or tyrannical there was none. On the contrary, in the malady of the times and the need of a monarchical government, he might be thought to have been sent as the gentlest physician, by no other than a divine intervention. And thus the common people instantly regretted Cæsar, and grew enraged and implacable against those that killed him. Whereas Dion's chief offence in the eyes of his fellow-citizens was his having let Dionysius escape, and not having demolished the former tyrant's tomb.

In the actual conduct of war, Dion was a commander without fault improving to the utmost those counsels which he himself gave, and where others led him into disaster correcting and turning everything to the best. But Brutus seems to have shown little wisdom in engaging in the final battle, which was to decide everything, and when he failed not to have done his business in seeking a remedy; he gave all up, and abandoned his hopes, not venturing against fortune even as far as Pompey did, when he had still means enough to rely on in his troops, and was clearly master of all the seas with his ships.

The greatest thing charged on Brutus is, that he, being saved by Cæsar's kindness, having saved all the friends whom he chose to ask for, he moreover accounted a friend, and preferred above many, did yet lay violent hands upon his preserver. Nothing like this could be objected against Dion; quite the contrary; whilst he was of Dionysius's family and his friend, he did good service and was useful to him; but driven from his country, wronged in his wife, and his estate lost, he openly entered upon a war just and lawful. Does not, however, the matter turn the other way? For the chief glory of both was their hatred of tyranny, and abhorrence of wickedness. This was unmixed and sincere in Brutus; for he had no private quarrel with Cæsar, but went into the risk singly for the liberty of his country. The other, had he not been privately injured, had not fought. This is plain from Plato's epistles, where it is shown that he was turned out, and did not forsake the court to wage war upon Dionysius. Moreover, the public good made Brutus Pompey's friend (instead of his enemy as he had been) and Cæsar's enemy; since he proposed for his hatred and his friendship no other end and standard but justice. Dion was very serviceable to Dionysius whilst in favour; when no longer trusted, he grew angry and fell to arms. And, for this reason, not even were his own friends all of them satisfied with his undertaking, or quite assured that, having overcome Dionysius, he might not settle the government on himself, deceiving his fellow-citizens by some less obnoxious name than tyranny. But the very enemies of Brutus would say that he had no other end or aim, from first to last, save only to restore to the Roman people their ancient government.

And apart from what has just been said, the adventure against Dionysius was nothing equal with that against Cæsar. For none that was familiarly conversant with Dionysius but scorned him for his life of idle amusement with wine, women, and dice; whereas it required an heroic soul and a truly intrepid and unquailing spirit so much as to entertain the thought of crushing Cæsar, so formidable for his ability, his power, and his fortune, whose very name disturbed the slumbers of the Parthian and Indian kings. Dion was no sooner seen in Sicily but thousands ran in to him and joined him against Dionysius; whereas the renown of Cæsar, even when dead, gave strength to his friends; and his very name so heightened the person that took it, that from a simple boy he presently became the chief of the Romans; and he could use it for a spell against the enmity and power of Antony. If any object that it cost Dion great trouble and difficulties to overcome the tyrant, whereas Brutus slew Cæsar naked and unprovided, yet this itself was the result of the most consummate policy and conduct, to bring it about that a man so guarded around, and so fortified at all points, should be taken naked and unprovided. For it was not on the sudden, nor alone, nor with a few, that he fell upon and killed Cæsar; but after long concerting the plot, and placing confidence in a great many men, not one of whom deceived him. For he either at once discerned the best men, or by confiding in them made them good. But Dion, either making a wrong judgment, trusted himself with ill men, or else by his employing them made ill men of good; either of the two would be a reflection on a wise man. Plato also is severe upon him, for choosing such for friends as betrayed him.

Besides, when Dion was killed, none appeared to revenge his death. Whereas Brutus, even amongst his enemies, had Antony that buried him splendidly; and Cæsar also took care his honours should be preserved. There stood at Milan in Gaul, within the Alps, a brazen statue, which Cæsar in aftertimes noticed (being a real likeness, and a fine work of art), and passing by it presently stopped short, and in the hearing of many commanded the magistrates to come before him. He told them their town had broken their league, harbouring an enemy. The magistrates at first simply denied the thing, and, not knowing what he meant, looked one upon another, when Cæsar, turning towards the statue and gathering his brows, said, "Pray, is not that our enemy who stands there?" They were all in confusion, and had nothing to answer; but he, smiling, much commended the Gauls, as who had been firm to their friends, though in adversity, and ordered that the statue should remain standing as he found it.

ARATUS

THE Philosopher Chrysippus, O Polycrates, quotes an ancient proverb, not as really it should be, apprehending, I suppose, that it sounded too harshly, but so as he thought it would run best, in these words:—

"Who praise their fathers but the generous sons?"

But Dionysodorus the Trœzenian proves him to be wrong, and restores the true reading, which is thus:—

"Who praise their fathers but degenerate sons?"

telling us that the proverb is meant to stop the mouth of those who, having no merit of their own, take refuge in the virtues of their ancestors, and make their advantage of praising them. But, as Pindar hath it—

"He that by nature doth inherit
From ancestors a noble spirit,"

as you do, who made your life the copy of the fairest originals of your family—such, I say, may take great satisfaction in being reminded, both by hearing others speak and speaking themselves, of the best of their progenitors. For they assume not the glory of praises earned by others out of any want of worth of their own, but affiliating their own deeds to those of their ancestors, give them honour as the authors both of their descent and manners. Therefore I have sent to you the life which I have written of your fellow-citizen and forefather, Aratus, to whom you are no discredit in point either of reputation or of authority, not as though you had not been most diligently careful to inform yourself from the beginning concerning his actions, but that your sons, Polycrates and Pythocles, may both by hearing and reading become familiar with those family examples which it behooves them to follow and imitate. It is a piece of self-love, and not of the love of virtue, to imagine one has already attained to what is best.

The city of Sicyon, from the time that it first fell off from the pure and Doric aristocracy (its harmony being destroyed, and a mere series of seditions and personal contests of popular leaders ensuing), continued to be distempered and unsettled, changing from one tyrant to another, until Cleon being slain, Timoclides and Clinias, men of the most repute and power amongst the citizens, were chosen to the magistracy. And the commonwealth now seeming to be in a pretty settled condition, Timoclides died, and Abantidas, the son of Paseas, to possess himself of the tyranny, killed Clinias, and, of his kindred and friends, slew some and banished others. He sought also to kill his son Aratus, whom he left behind him, being but seven years old. This boy in the general disorder getting out of the house with those that fled, and wandering about the city helpless and in great fear, by chance got undiscovered into the house of a woman who was Abantidas's sister, but married to Prophantus, the brother of Clinias, her name being Soso. She, being of a generous temper, and believing the boy had by some supernatural guidance fled to her for shelter, hid him in the house, and at night sent him away to Argos.

Aratus, being thus delivered and secured from this danger, conceived from the first and ever after nourished a vehement and burning hatred against tyrants, which strengthened with his years. Being therefore bred up amongst his father's acquaintance and friends at Argos with a liberal education, and perceiving his body to promise good health and stature, he addicted himself to the exercises of the palæstra, to that degree that he competed in the five games, and gained some crowns; and indeed in his statues one may observe a certain kind of athletic cast, and the sagacity and majesty of his countenance does not dissemble his full diet and the use of the hoe. Whence it came to pass that he less studied eloquence than perhaps became a statesman, and yet he was more accomplished in speaking than many believe, judging by the commentaries which he left behind him, written carelessly and, by the way, as fast as he could do it, and in such words as first came to his mind.

In the course of time, Dinias and Aristoteles the logician killed Abantidas, who used to be present in the market-place at their discussions, and to make one in them; till they taking the occasion, insensibly accustomed him to the practice, and so had opportunity to contrive and execute a plot against him. After him Paseas, the father of Abantidas, taking upon him the government, was assassinated by Nicocles, who himself set up for tyrant. Of him it is related that he was strikingly like Periander, the son of Cypselus, just as it is said that Orontes the Persian bore a great resemblance to Alcmæon, the son of Amphiaraus, and that Lacedæmonian youth, whom Myrsilus relates to have been trodden to pieces by the crowd of those that came to see him upon that report, to Hector.

This Nicocles governed four months, in which, after he had done all kinds of mischief to the city, he very nearly let it fall into the hands of the Ætolians. By this time Aratus, being grown a youth, was in much esteem, both for his noble birth, and his spirit and disposition, which, while neither insignificant nor wanting in energy, were solid, and tempered with a steadiness of judgment beyond his years. For which reason the exiles had their eyes most upon him, nor did Nicocles less observe his motions, but secretly spied and watched him, not out of apprehension of any such considerable or utterly audacious attempt, but suspecting he held correspondence with the kings, who were his father's friends and acquaintance. And, indeed, Aratus first attempted this way; but finding that Antigonus, who had promised fair, neglected him and delayed the time, and that his hopes from Egypt and Ptolemy were long to wait for, he determined to cut off the tyrant by himself.

And first he broke his mind to Aristomachus and Ecdelus, the one an exile of Sicyon, the other, Ecdelus, an Arcadian of Megalopolis, a philosopher, and a man of action, having been the familiar friend of Arcesilaus the Academic at Athens. These readily consenting, he communicated with the other exiles, whereof some few, being ashamed to seem to despair of success, engaged in the design; but most of them endeavoured to divert him from his purpose, as one that for want of experience was too rash and daring.

Whilst he was consulting to seize upon some post in Sicyonia, from whence he might make war upon the tyrant, there came to Argos a certain Sicyonian, newly escaped out of prison, brother to Xenocles, one of the exiles, who, being by him presented to Aratus, informed him that that part of the wall over which he escaped was, inside, almost level with the ground, adjoining a rocky and elevated place, and that from the outside it might be scaled with ladders. Aratus, hearing this, despatches away Xenocles with two of his own servants, Seuthas and Technon, to view the wall, resolving, if possible, secretly and with one risk to hazard all on a single trial, rather than carry on a contest as a private man against a tyrant by long war and open force. Xenocles, therefore, with his companions, returning, having taken the height of the wall, and declaring the place not to be impossible or indeed difficult to get over, but that it was not easy to approach it undiscovered by reason of some small but uncommonly savage and noisy dogs belonging to a gardener hard by, he immediately undertook the business.

Now the preparation of arms gave no jealousy, because robberies and petty forays were at that time common everywhere between one set of people and another; and for the ladders, Euphranor, the machine-maker, made them openly, his trade rendering him unsuspected, though one of the exiles. As for men, each of his friends in Argos furnished him with ten apiece out of those few they had, and he armed thirty of his own servants and hired some few soldiers of Xenophilus, the chief of the robber captains, to whom it was given out that they were to march into the territory of Sicyon to seize the king's stud; most of them were sent before, in small parties, to the tower of Polygnotus, with orders to wait there; Caphisias also was despatched beforehand lightly armed, with four others, who were, as soon as it was dark, to come to the gardener's house, pretending to be travellers, and procuring their lodging there, to shut up him and his dogs; for there was no other way to getting past. And for the ladders, they had been made to take in pieces, and were put into chests, and sent before hidden upon waggons. In the meantime, some of the spies of Nicocles appearing in Argos, and being said to go privately about watching Aratus, he came early in the morning into the market-place, showing himself openly and conversing with his friends; then he anointed himself in the exercise ground, and, taking with him thence some of the young men that used to drink and spend their time with him, he went home; and presently after several of his servants were seen about the market-place, one carrying garlands, another buying flambeaux, and a third speaking to the women that used to sing and play at banquets, all of which things the spies observing were deceived, and said, laughing to one another "Certainly nothing can be more timorous than a tyrant, if Nicocles, being master of so great a city and so numerous a force, stands in fear of a youth that spends what he has to subsist upon in his banishment in pleasures and day-debauches;" and, being thus imposed upon, they returned home.

But Aratus, departing immediately after his morning meal, and coming to his soldiers at Polygnotus's tower, led them to Nemea; where he disclosed to most of them, for the first time, his true design, making them large promises and fair speeches, and marched towards the city, giving for the word Apollo victorious, proportioning his march to the motion of the moon, so as to have the benefit of her light upon the way, and to be in the garden, which was close to the wall, just as she was setting. Here Caphisias came to him, who had not secured the dogs, which had run away before he could catch them, but had only made sure of the gardener. Upon which most of the company being out of heart and desiring to retreat, Aratus encouraged them to go on, promising to retire in case the dogs were too troublesome; at the same time sending forward those that carried the ladders, conducted by Ecdelus and Mnasitheus, he followed them himself leisurely, the dogs already barking very loud and following the steps of Ecdelus and his companion. However, they got to the wall, and reared the ladders with safety. But as the foremost men were mounting them, the captain of the watch that was to be relieved by the morning guard passed on his way with the bell; and there were many lights, and a noise of people coming up. Hearing which, they clapt themselves close to the ladders, and so were unobserved; but as the other watch also was coming up to meet this, they were in extreme danger of being discovered.

But when this also went by without observing them, immediately Mnasitheus and Ecdelus got upon the wall, and, possessing themselves of the approaches inside and out, sent away Technon to Aratus, desiring him to make all the haste he could.

Now there was no great distance from the garden to the wall and to the tower in which latter a large hound was kept. The hound did not hear their steps of himself, whether that he were naturally drowsy, or overwearied the day before, but, the gardener's curs awaking him, he first began to growl and grumble in response, and then as they passed by to bark out aloud. And the barking was now so great, that the sentinel opposite shouted out to the dog's keeper to know why the dog kept such a barking, and whether anything was the matter; who answered, that it was nothing but only that his dog had been set barking by the lights of the watch and the noise of the bell. This reply much encouraged Aratus's soldiers, who thought the dog's keeper was privy to their design, and wished to conceal what was passing, and that many others in the city were of the conspiracy. But when they came to scale the wall, the attempt then appeared both to require time and to be full of danger, for the ladders shook and tottered extremely unless they mounted them leisurely and one by one, and time pressed, for the cocks began to crow, and the country people that used to bring things to the market would be coming to the town directly. Therefore Aratus made haste to get up himself, forty only of the company being already upon the wall, and, staying but for a few more of those that were below, he made straight to the tyrant's house and the general's office, where the mercenary soldiers passed the night, and, coming suddenly upon them, and taking them prisoners without killing any one of them, he immediately sent to all his friends in their houses to desire them to come to him, which they did from all quarters. By this time the day began to break, and the theatre was filled with a multitude that were held in suspense by uncertain reports and knew nothing distinctly of what had happened, until a public crier came forward and proclaimed that Aratus, the son of Clinias, invited the citizens to recover their liberty.

Then at last assured that what they had so long looked for was come to pass, they pressed in throngs to the tyrant's gates to set them on fire. And such a flame was kindled, the whole house catching fire, that it was seen as far as Corinth; so that the Corinthians, wondering what the matter could be, were upon the point of coming to their assistance. Nicocles fled away secretly out of the city by means of certain underground passages, and the soldiers helping the Sicyonians to quench the fire, plundered the house. This Aratus hindered not, but divided also the rest of the riches of the tyrant amongst the citizens. In this exploit, not one of these engaged in it was slain, nor any of the contrary party, fortune so ordering the action as to be clear and free from civil bloodshed. He restored eighty exiles who had been expelled by Nicocles, and no less than five hundred who had been driven out by former tyrants and had endured a long banishment, pretty nearly, by this time, of fifty years' duration. These returning, most of them very poor, were impatient to enter upon their former possessions, and, proceeding to their several farms and houses, gave great perplexity to Aratus, who considered that the city without was envied for its liberty and aimed at by Antigonus, and within was full of disorder and sedition. Wherefore, as things stood, he thought it best to associate it to the Achæan community, and so, although Dorians, they of their own will took upon them the name and citizenship of the Achæns, who at that time had neither great repute nor much power. For the most of them lived in small towns, and their territory was neither large nor fruitful, and the neighbouring sea was almost wholly without a harbour, breaking direct upon a rocky shore. But yet these above others made it appear that the Grecian courage was invincible, whensoever it could only have order and concord within itself and a prudent general to direct it. For though they had scarcely been counted as any part of the ancient Grecian power, and at this time it did not equal the strength of one ordinary city, yet by prudence and unanimity, and because they knew not how to envy and malign, but to obey and follow him amongst them that was most eminent for virtue, they not only preserved their own liberty in the midst of so many great cities, military powers, and monarchies, but went on steadily saving and delivering from slavery great numbers of the Greeks.

As for Aratus, he was in his behaviour a true statesman, high-minded, and more intent upon the public than his private concerns, a bitter hater of tyrants, making the common good the rule and law of his friendships and enmities. So that indeed he seems not to have been so faithful a friend, as he was a reasonable and gentle enemy, ready, according to the needs of the state, to suit himself on occasion to either side; concord between nations, brotherhood between cities, the council and the assembly unanimous in their votes, being the objects above all other blessings to which he was passionately devoted; backward, indeed, and diffident in the use of arms and open force, but in effecting a purpose underhand, and outwitting cities and potentates without observation, most politic and dexterous. Therefore, though he succeeded beyond hope in many enterprises which he undertook, yet he seems to have left quite as many unattempted, though feasible enough, for want of assurance. For it should seem, that as the sight of certain beasts is strong in the night but dim by day, the tenderness of the humours of their eyes not bearing the contact of the light, so there is also one kind of human skill and sagacity which is easily daunted and disturbed in actions done in the open day and before the world, and recovers all its self-possession in secret and covert enterprises; which inequality is occasioned in noble minds for want of philosophy, a mere wild and uncultivated fruit of a virtue without true knowledge coming up; as might be made out by examples.

Aratus, therefore, having associated himself and his city to the Achæns, served in the cavalry, and made himself much beloved by his commanding officers for his exact obedience; for though he had made so large an addition to the common strength as that of his own credit and the power of his country, yet he was as ready as the most ordinary person to be commanded by the Achæan general of the time being, whether he were a man of Dynæ, or of Tritæa, or any yet meaner town than these. Having also a present of five-and-twenty talents sent him from the king, he took them, but gave them all to his fellow-citizens, who wanted money, amongst other purposes, for the redemption of those who had been taken prisoners.

But the exiles being by no means to be satisfied, disturbing continually those that were in possession of their estates, Sicyon was in great danger of falling into perfect desolation; so that, having no hope left but in the kindness of Ptolemy, he resolved to sail to him, and to beg so much money of him as might reconcile all parties. So he set sail from Mothone beyond Malea, designing to make the direct passage. But the pilot not being able to keep the vessel up against a strong wind and high waves that came in from the open sea, he was driven from his course, and with much ado got to shore in Andros, an enemy's land, possessed by Antigonus, who had a garrison there. To avoid which he immediately landed, and, leaving the ship, went up into the country a good way from the sea, having along with him only one friend, called Timanthes; and throwing themselves into some ground thickly covered with wood, they had but an ill night's rest of it. Not long after, the commander of the troops came, and, inquiring for Aratus, was deceived by his servants, who had been instructed to say that he had fled at once over into the island of Eubœa. However, he declared the ship, the property on board of her, and the servants, to be lawful prize, and detained them accordingly. As for Aratus, after some few days in his extremity, by good fortune a Roman ship happened to put in just at the spot in which he made his abode, sometimes peeping out to seek his opportunity, sometimes keeping close. She was bound for Syria; but going aboard, he agreed with the master to land him in Caria. In which voyage he met with no less danger on the sea than before. From Caria being after much time arrived in Egypt, he immediately went to the king, who had a great kindness for him, and had received from him many presents of drawings and paintings out of Greece. Aratus had a very good judgment in them, and always took care to collect and send him the most curious and finished works, especially those of Pamphilus and Melanthus.

For the Sicyonian pieces were still in the height of their reputation, as being the only ones whose colours were lasting; so that Apelles himself, even after he had become well known and admired, went thither, and gave a talent to be admitted into the society of the painters there, not so much to partake of their skill, which he wanted not, but of their credit. And accordingly Aratus, when he freed the city, immediately took down the representations of the rest of the tyrants, but demurred a long time about that of Aristratus, who flourished in the time of Philip. For this Aristratus was painted by Melanthus and his scholars, standing by a chariot, in which a figure of Victory was carried, Apelles himself having had a hand in it, as Polemon the geographer reports. It was an extraordinary piece, and therefore Aratus was fain to spare it for the workmanship, and yet, instigated by the hatred he bore the tyrants, commanded it to be taken down. But Neacles the painter, one of Aratus's friends, entreated him, it is said, with tears in his eyes, to spare it, and, finding he did not prevail with him, told him at last he should carry on his war with the tyrants, but with the tyrants alone: "Let therefore the chariot and the Victory stand, and I will take means for the removal of Aristratus;" to which Aratus consenting, Neacles blotted out Aristratus, and in his place painted a palm-tree, not daring to add anything else of his own invention. The feet of the defaced figure of Aristratus are said to have escaped notice, and to be hid under the chariot. By these means Aratus got favour with the king, who, after he was more fully acquainted with him, loved him so much the more, and gave him for the relief of his city one hundred and fifty talents; forty of which he immediately carried away with him, when he sailed to Peloponnesus, but the rest the king divided into instalments, and sent them to him afterwards at different times.

Assuredly it was a great thing to procure for his fellow-citizens a sum of money, a small portion of which had been sufficient, when presented by a king to other captains and popular leaders, to induce them to turn dishonest, and betray and give away their native countries to him. But it was a much greater, that by means of this money he effected a reconciliation and good understanding between the rich and poor, and created quiet and security for the whole people. His moderation, also, amidst so great power was very admirable. For being declared sole arbitrator and plenipotentiary for settling the questions of property in the case of the exiles, he would not accept the commission alone, but, associating with himself fifteen of the citizens, with great pains and trouble he succeeded in adjusting matters, and established peace and good-will in the city, for which good service, not only all the citizens in general bestowed extraordinary honours upon him, but the exiles, apart by themselves, erecting his statue in brass, inscribed on it these elegiac verses:

"Your counsels, deeds, and skill for Greece in war
Known beyond Hercules's pillars are;
But we this image, O Aratus, gave,

Of you who saved us, to the gods who save,
By you from exile to our homes restored,
That virtue and that justice to record,
To which the blessing Sicyon owes this day
Of wealth that's shared alike, and laws that all obey."

By his success in effecting these things, Aratus secured himself from the envy of his fellow-citizens, on account of the benefits they felt he had done them; but King Antigonus being troubled in his mind about him, and designing either wholly to bring him over to his party, or else to make him suspected by Ptolemy, besides other marks of his favour shown to him, who had little mind to receive them, added this too, that, sacrificing to the gods in Corinth, he sent portions to Aratus at Sicyon, and at the feast, where were many guests, he said openly, "I thought this Sicyonian youth had been only a lover of liberty and of his fellow-citizens, but now I look upon him as a good judge of the manners and actions of kings. For formerly he despised us, and, placing his hopes further off, admired the Egyptian riches, hearing so much of their elephants, fleets, and palaces. But after seeing all these at a nearer distance, perceiving them to be but mere stage show and pageantry, he is now come over to us. And for my part I willingly receive him, and, resolving to make great use of him myself, command you to look upon him as a friend." These words were soon taken hold of by those that envied and maligned him, who strove which of them should, in their letters to Ptolemy, attack him with the worst calumnies, so that Ptolemy sent to expostulate the matter with him; so much envy and ill-will did there always attend the so much contended for, and so ardently and passionately aspired to, friendships of princes and great men.

But Aratus, being now for the first time chosen general of the Achæans, ravaged the country of Locris and Calydon, just over against Achæa, and then went to assist the Bœotians with ten thousand soldiers, but came not up to them until after the battle near Chæronea had been fought, in which they were beaten by the Ætolians, with the loss of Abœocritus the Bœotarch, and a thousand men besides. A year after, being again elected general, he resolved to attempt the capture of the Acro-Corinthus, not so much for the advantage of the Sicyonians or Achæans, as considering that by expelling the Macedonian garrison he should free all Greece alike from a tyranny which oppressed every part of her. Chares, the Athenian, having the good fortune to get the better, in a certain battle, of the king's generals, wrote to the people of Athens that this victory was "sister to that at Marathon." And so may this action be very safely termed sister to those of Pelopidas the Theban and Thrasybulus the Athenian, in which they slew the tyrants; except, perhaps, it exceed them upon this account, that it was not against natural Grecians, but against a foreign and stranger domination. The Isthmus, rising like a bank between the seas, collects into a single spot and compresses together the whole continent of Greece; and Acro-Corinthus, being a high mountain springing up out of the very middle of what here is Greece, whensoever it is held with a garrison, stands in the way and cuts off all Peloponnesus from intercourse of every kind, free passage of men and arms, and all traffic by sea and land, and makes him lord of all that is master of it. Wherefore the younger Philip did not jest, but said very true, when he called the city of Corinth "the fetters of Greece." So that this post was always much contended for, especially by the kings and tyrants; and so vehemently was it longed for by Antigonus, that his passion for it came little short of that of frantic love; he was continually occupied with devising how to take it by surprise from those that were then masters of it, since he despaired to do it by open force.

Therefore Alexander, who held the place, being dead, poisoned by him, as is reported, and his wife Nicæa succeeding in the government and the possession of Acro-Corinthus, he immediately made use of his son, Demetrius, and, giving her pleasing hopes of a royal marriage and of a happy life with a youth, whom a woman now growing old might well find agreeable, with this lure of his son he succeeded in taking her; but the place itself she did not deliver up, but continued to hold it with a very strong garrison, of which he seeming to take no notice, celebrated the wedding in Corinth, entertaining them with shows and banquets every day, as one that had nothing else in his mind but to give himself up for a while to indulgence in pleasure and mirth. But when the moment came, and Amœbeus began to sing in the theatre, he waited himself upon Nicæa to the play, she being carried in a royally decorated chair, extremely pleased with her new honour, not dreaming of what was intended. As soon, therefore, as they were come to the turning which led up to the citadel, he desired her to go on before him to the theatre, but for himself, bidding farewell to the music, farewell to the wedding, he went on faster than one would have thought his age would have admitted to the Acro-Corinthus, and, finding the gate shut, knocked with his staff, commanding them to open, which they within, being amazed, did. And having thus made himself master of the place, he could not contain himself for joy; but, though an old man, and one that had seen so many turns of fortune, he must needs revel it in the open streets and the midst of the market-place, crowned with garlands and attended with flute-women, inviting everybody he met to partake in his festivity. So much more does joy without discretion transport and agitate the mind than either fear or sorrow. Antigonus, therefore, having in this manner possessed himself of Acro-Corinthus, put a garrison into it of those he trusted most, making Persæus the philosopher governor.

Now Aratus, even in the lifetime of Alexander, had made an attempt, but, a confederacy being made between Alexander and the Achæans, he desisted. But now he started afresh, with a new plan of effecting the thing, which was this: there were in Corinth four brothers, Syrians born, one of whom, called Diocles, served as a soldier in the garrison, but the three others, having stolen some gold of the king's, came to Sicyon, to one Ægias, a banker, whom Aratus made use of in his business. To him they immediately sold part of their gold, and the rest, one of them, called Erginus, coming often thither, exchanged by parcels. Becoming, by this means, familiarly acquainted with Ægias, and being by him led into discourses concerning the fortress, he told him that in going up to his brother he had observed, in the face of the rock, a side cleft, leading to that part of the wall of the castle which was lower than the rest. At which Ægias joking with him and saying, "So, you wise man, for the sake of a little gold you have broken into the king's treasure; when you might, if you chose, get money in abundance for a single hour's work, burglary, you know, and treason being punished with the same death." Erginus laughed and told him then, he would break the thing to Diocles (for he did not altogether trust his other brothers), and, returning within a few days, he bargained to conduct Aratus to that part of the wall where it was no more than fifteen feet high, and to do what else should be necessary, together with his brother Diocles.

Aratus, therefore, agreed to give them sixty talents if he succeeded, but if he failed in his enterprise, and yet he and they came off safe, then he would give each of them a house and a talent. Now the threescore talents being to be deposited in the hands of Ægias for Erginus and his partners, and Aratus neither having so much by him, nor willing, by borrowing it from others, to give any one a suspicion of his design, he pawned his plate and his wife's golden ornaments to Ægias for the money. For so high was his temper, and so strong his passion for noble actions, that, even as he had heard that Phocion and Epaminondas were the best and justest of the Greeks, because they refused the greatest presents, and would not surrender their duty for money, so he now chose to be at the expense of this enterprise privately, and to advance all the cost out of his own property, taking the whole hazard on himself for the sake of the rest that did not so much as know what was doing. And who indeed can withhold, even now, his admiration for and his sympathy with the generous mind of one, who paid so largely to purchase so great a risk, and lent out his richest possessions to have an opportunity to expose his own life, by entering among his enemies in the dead of the night, without desiring any other security for them than the hope of a noble success.

Now the enterprise, though dangerous enough in itself, was made much more so by an error happening through mistake in the very beginning. For Technon, one of Aratus's servants, was sent away to Diocles, that they might together view the wall. Now he had never seen Diocles, but made no question of knowing him by the marks Erginus had given him of him, namely, that he had curly hair, a swarthy complexion, and no beard. Being come, therefore, to the appointed place, he stayed waiting for Erginus and Diocles outside the town, in front of the place called Ornis. In the meantime, Dionysius, elder brother to Erginus and Diocles, who knew nothing at all of the matter, but much resembled Diocles, happened to pass by. Technon, upon this likeness, all being in accordance with what he had been told, asked him if he knew Erginus; and on his replying that he was his brother, taking it for granted that he was speaking with Diocles, not so much as asking his name or staying for any other token, he gave him his hand, and began to discourse with him and ask him questions about matters agreed upon with Erginus. Dionysius, cunningly taking the advantage of his mistake, seemed to understand him very well, and returning towards the city, led him on, still talking, without any suspicion. And being now near the gate, he was just about to seize on him, when by chance again Erginus met them, and, apprehending the cheat and the danger, beckoned to Technon to make his escape, and immediately both of them, betaking themselves to their heels, ran away as fast as they could to Aratus, who for all this despaired not, but immediately sent away Erginus to Dionysius to bribe him to hold his tongue. And he not only effected that, but also brought him along with him to Aratus. But when they had him, they no longer left him at liberty, but binding him, they kept him close shut up in a room, whilst they prepared for executing their design.

All things being now ready, he commanded the rest of his forces to pass the night by their arms, and taking with him four hundred chosen men, few of whom knew what they were going about, he led them to the gates by the temple of Juno. It was the midst of summer, and the moon was at full, and the night so clear without any clouds, that there was danger lest the arms glistening in the moonlight should discover them. But as the foremost of them came near the city, a mist came off from the sea, and darkened the city itself and the outskirts about it. Then the rest of them, sitting down, put off their shoes, because men both make less noise and also climb surer if they go up ladders barefooted, but Erginus, taking with him seven young men dressed like travellers, got unobserved to the gate, and killed the sentry with the other guards. And at the same time the ladders were clapped to the walls, and Aratus, having in great haste got up a hundred men, commanded the rest to follow as they could, and immediately drawing up his ladders after him, he marched through the city with his hundred men towards the castle, being already overjoyed that he was undiscovered, and not doubting of the success. But while still they were some way off, a watch of four men came with a light, who did not see them, because they were still in the shade of the moon, but were seen plainly enough themselves as they came on directly towards them. So withdrawing a little way amongst some walls and plots for houses, they lay in wait for them; and three of them they killed. But the fourth, being wounded in the head with a sword, fled, crying out that the enemy was in the city. And immediately the trumpets sounded, and all the city was in an uproar at what had happened, and the streets were full of people running up and down, and many lights were seen shining both below in the town, and above in the castle, and a confused noise was to be heard in all parts.

In the meantime, Aratus was hard at work struggling to get up the rocks, at first slowly and with much difficulty, straying continually from the path, which lay deep, and was overshadowed with the crags, leading to the wall with many windings and turnings; but the moon immediately, and as if by miracle, it is said, dispersing the clouds, shone out and gave light to the most difficult part of the way, until he got to that part of the wall he desired, and there she overshadowed and hid him, the clouds coming together again. Those soldiers whom Aratus had left outside the gate, near Juno's temple, to the number of three hundred, entering the town, now full of tumult and lights, and not knowing the way by which the former had gone, and finding no track of them, slunk aside, and crowded together in one body under a flank of the cliff that cast a strong shadow, and there stood and waited in great distress and perplexity. For, by this time, those that had gone with Aratus were attacked with missiles from the citadel, and were busy fighting, and a sound of cries of battle came down from above, and a loud noise, echoed back and back from the mountain sides, and therefore confused and uncertain whence it proceeded, was heard on all sides. They being thus in doubt which way to turn themselves, Archelaus, the commander of Antigonus's troops, having a great number of soldiers with him, made up towards the castle with great shouts and noise of trumpets to fall upon Aratus's people, and passed by the three hundred, who, as if they had risen out of an ambush, immediately charged him, killing the first they encountered, and so affrighted the rest, together with Archelaus, that they put them to flight and pursued them until they had quite broken and dispersed them about the city. No sooner were these defeated, but Erginus came to them from those that were fighting above, to acquaint them that Aratus was engaged with the enemy, who defended themselves very stoutly, and there was a fierce conflict at the very wall, and need of speedy help. They therefore desired him to lead them on without delay, and, marching up, by their shouts made their friends understand who they were, and encouraged them; and the full moon, shining on their arms, made them, in the long line in which they advanced, appear more in number to the enemy than they were; and the echo of the night multiplied their shouts. In short, falling on with the rest they made the enemy give way, and were masters of the castle and garrison, day now beginning to be bright, and the rising sun shining out upon their success. By this time, also, the rest of his army came up to Aratus from Sicyon, the Corinthians joyfully receiving them at the gates and helping them to secure the king's party.

And now, having put all things into a safe posture, he came down from the castle to the theatre, an infinite number of people crowding thither to see him and to hear what he would say to the Corinthians. Therefore drawing up the Achæans on each side of the stage-passages, he came forward himself upon the stage, with his corselet still on, and his face showing the effects of all his hard work and want of sleep, so that his natural exultation and joyfulness of mind were overborne by the weariness of his body. The people, as soon as he came forth, breaking out into great applauses and congratulations, he took his spear in his right hand, and resting his body upon it with his knee a little bent, stood a good while in that posture, silently receiving their shouts and acclamations, while they extolled his valour and wondered at his fortune; which being over, standing up, he began an oration in the name of the Achæans, suitable to the late action, persuading the Corinthians to associate themselves to the Achæans, and withal delivered up to them the keys of their gates, which had never been in their power since the time of King Philip. Of the captains of Antigonus, he dismissed Archelaus, whom he had taken prisoner, and Theophrastus, who refused to quit his post, he put to death. As for Persæus, when he saw the castle was lost, he had got away to Cenchreæ, where, some time after, discoursing with one that said to him that the wise man only is a true general, "Indeed," he replied, "none of Zeno's maxims once pleased me better than this, but I have been converted to another opinion by the young man of Sicyon." This is told by many of Persæus. Aratus immediately after made himself master of the temple of Juno and haven of Lechæum, seized upon five-and-twenty of the king's ships, together with five hundred horses and four hundred Syrians: these he sold. The Achæans kept guard in the Acro-Corinthus with a body of four hundred soldiers, and fifty dogs with as many keepers.

The Romans, extolling Philopœmen, called him the last of the Grecians, as if no great man had ever since his time been bred amongst them. But I should call this capture of the Acro-Corinthus the last of the Grecian exploits, being comparable to the best of them, both for the daringness of it, and the success, as was presently seen by the consequences. For the Megarians, revolting from Antigonus, joined Aratus, and the Trœzenians and Epidaurians enrolled themselves in the Achæan community, and issuing forth for the first time, he entered Attica, and passing over into Salamis, he plundered the island, turning the Achæan force every way, as if it were just let loose out of prison and set at liberty. All freemen whom he took he sent back to the Athenians without ransom, as a sort of first invitation to them to come over to the league. He made Ptolemy become a confederate of the Achæans, with the privilege of command both by sea and land. And so great was his power with them, that since he could not by law be chosen their general every year, yet every other year he was, and by his counsels and actions was in effect always so. For they perceived that neither riches nor reputation, nor the friendship of kings, nor the private interest of his own country, nor anything else was so dear to him as the increase of the Achæans' power and greatness. For he believed that the cities, weak individually, could be preserved by nothing else but a mutual assistance under the closest bond of the common interest, and, as the members of the body live and breathe by the union of all in a single natural growth, and on the dissolution of this, when once they separate, pine away and putrify, in the same manner are cities ruined by being dissevered, as well as preserved when, as the members of one great body, they enjoy the benefit of that province and counsel that govern the whole.

Now being distressed to see that, whereas the chief neighbouring cities enjoyed their own laws and liberties, the Argives were in bondage, he took counsel for destroying their tyrant, Aristomachus, being very desirous both to pay his debt of gratitude to the city where he had been bred up, by restoring it its liberty, and to add so considerable a town to the Achæans. Nor were there some wanting who had the courage to undertake the thing, of whom Æschylus and Charimenes the soothsayer were the chief. But they wanted swords; for the tyrant had prohibited the keeping of any under a great penalty. Therefore Aratus, having provided some small daggers at Corinth and hidden them in the pack-saddles of some pack-horses that carried ordinary ware, sent them to Argos. But Charimenes letting another person into the design, Æschylus and his partners were angry at it, and henceforth would have no more to do with him, and took their measures by themselves, and Charimenes, on finding this, went, out of anger, and informed against them, just as they were on their way to attack the tyrant; however, the most of them made a shift to escape out of the market-place, and fled to Corinth. Not long after, Aristomachus was slain by some slaves, and Aristippus, a worse tyrant than he, seized the government. Upon this, Aratus, mustering all the Achæans present that were of age, hurried away to the aid of the city, believing that he should find the people ready to join with him. But the greater number being by this time habituated to slavery and content to submit, and no one coming to join him, he was obliged to retire, having moreover exposed the Achæans to the charge of committing acts of hostility in the midst of peace; upon which account they were sued before the Mantineans, and, Aratus not making his appearance, Aristippus gained the cause, and had damages allowed him to the value of thirty minæ. And now hating and fearing Aratus, he sought means to kill him, having the assistance herein of King Antigonus; so that Aratus was perpetually dogged and watched by those that waited for an opportunity to do this service. But there is no such safeguard of a ruler as the sincere and steady good-will of his subjects, for where both the common people and the principal citizens have their fears not of, but for, their governor, he sees with many eyes and hears with many ears whatsoever is doing. Therefore I cannot but here stop short a little in the course of my narrative to describe the manner of life which the so much envied arbitrary power and the so much celebrated and admired pomp and pride of absolute government obliged Aristippus to lead.

For though Antigonus was his friend and ally, and though he maintained numerous soldiers to act as his body-guard, and had not left one enemy of his alive in the city, yet he was forced to make his guards encamp in the colonnade about his house; and for his servants, he turned them all out immediately after supper, and then shutting the doors upon them, he crept up into a small upper chamber, together with his mistress, through a trap-door, upon which he placed his bed, and there slept after such a fashion, as one in his condition can be supposed to sleep, that is, interruptedly and in fear. The ladder was taken away by the woman's mother, and locked up in another room; in the morning she brought it again, and putting it to, called up this brave and wonderful tyrant, who came crawling out like some creeping thing out of its hole. Whereas Aratus, not by force of arms, but lawfully and by his virtue, lived in possession of a firmly settled command, wearing the ordinary coat and cloak, being the common and declared enemy of all tyrants, and has left behind him a noble race of descendants surviving among the Grecians to this day; while those occupiers of citadels and maintainers of body-guards, who made all this use of arms and gates and bolts to protect their lives, in some few cases perhaps escaped like the hare from the hunters; but in no instance have we either house or family, or so much as a tomb to which any respect is shown, remaining to preserve the memory of any one of them.

Against this Aristippus, therefore, Aratus made many open and many secret attempts, whilst he endeavoured to take Argos, though without success; once, particularly, clapping scaling ladders in the night to the walls, he desperately got up upon it with a few of his soldiers, and killed the guards that opposed him. But the day appearing, the tyrant set upon him on all hands, whilst the Argives, as if it had not been their liberty that was contended for, but some Nemean game going on for which it was their privilege to assign the prize, like fair and impartial judges, sat looking on in great quietness. Aratus, fighting bravely, was run through the thigh with a lance, yet he maintained his ground against the enemy till night, and, had he been able to go on and hold out that night also, he had gained his point; for the tyrant thought of nothing but flying, and had already shipped most of his goods. But Aratus, having no intelligence of this, and wanting water, being disabled himself by his wound, retreated with his soldiers.

Despairing henceforth to do any good this way, he fell openly with his army into Argolis, and plundered it, and in a fierce battle with Aristippus near the river Chares, he was accused of having withdrawn out of the fight, and thereby abandoned the victory. For whereas one part of his army had unmistakably got the better, and was pursuing the enemy at a good distance from him, he yet retreated in confusion into his camp, not so much because he was overpressed by those with whom he was engaged, as out of mistrust of success and through a panic fear. But when the other wing, returning from the pursuit, showed themselves extremely vexed, that though they had put the enemy to flight and killed many more of his men than they had lost, yet those that were in a manner conquered should erect a trophy as conquerors, being much ashamed he resolved to fight them again about the trophy, and the next day but one drew up his army to give them battle. But, perceiving that they were reinforced with fresh troops, and came on with better courage than before, he durst not hazard a fight, but retired and sent to request a truce to bury his dead. However, by his dexterity in dealing personally with men and managing political affairs, and by his general favour, he excused and obliterated this fault, and brought in Cleonæ to the Achæan association, and celebrated the Nemean games at Cleonæ, as the proper and more ancient place for them. The games were also celebrated by the Argives at the same time, which gave the first occasion to the violation of the privilege of safe conduct and immunity always granted to those that came to compete for the prizes, the Achæans at that time selling as enemies all those they caught going through their country after joining in the games at Argos. So vehement and implacable a hater was he of the tyrants.

Not long after, having notice that Aristippus had a design upon Cleonæ, but was afraid of him, because he then was staying in Corinth, he assembled an army by public proclamation, and commanding them to take along with them provisions for several days, he marched to Cenchreæ, hoping by this stratagem to entice Aristippus to fall upon Cleonæ, when he supposed him far enough off. And so it happened, for he immediately brought his forces against it from Argos. But Aratus, returning from Cenchræ to Corinth in the dusk of the evening, and setting posts of his troops in all the roads, led on the Achæans, who followed in such good order and with so much speed and alacrity, that they were undiscovered by Aristippus, not only whilst upon their march, but even when they got, still in the night, into Cleonæ, and drew up in order of battle. As soon as it was morning, the gates being opened and the trumpets sounding, he fell upon the enemy with great cries and fury, routed them at once, and kept close in pursuit, following the course which he most imagined Aristippus would choose, there being many turns that might be taken. And so the chase lasted as far as Mycenæ, where the tyrant was slain by a certain Cretan called Tragiscus, as Dinias reports. Of the common soldiers, there fell above fifteen hundred. Yet though Aratus had obtained so great a victory and that too without the loss of a man, he could not make himself master of Argos, nor set it at liberty, because Agias and the younger Aristomachus got into the town with some of the king's forces, and seized upon the government. However, by this exploit he spoiled the scoffs and jests of those that flattered the tyrants, and in their raillery would say that the Achæan general was usually troubled with a looseness when he was to fight a battle, that the sound of a trumpet struck him with a drowsiness and a giddiness, and that when he had drawn up his army and given the word, he used to ask his lieutenants and officers whether there was any further need of his presence now the die was cast, and then went aloof, to await the result at a distance. For indeed these stories were so generally listened to, that, when the philosophers disputed whether to have one's heart beat and to change colour upon any apparent danger be an argument of fear, or rather of some distemperature and chilliness of bodily constitution, Aratus was always quoted as a good general who was always thus affected in time of battle.

Having thus despatched Aristippus, he advised with himself how to overthrow Lydiades, the Megalopolitan, who held usurped power over his country. This person was naturally of a generous temper, and not insensible of true honour, and had been led into this wickedness, not by the ordinary motives of other tyrants, licentiousness and rapacity, but being young, and stimulated with the desire of glory, he had let his mind be unwarily prepossessed with the vain and false applauses given to tyranny, as some happy and glorious thing. But he no sooner seized the government, than he grew weary of the pomp and burden of it. And at once emulating the tranquillity and fearing the policy of Aratus, he took the best resolutions, first, to free himself from hatred and fear, from soldiers and guards, and, secondly, to be the public benefactor of his country. And sending for Aratus, he resigned the government, and incorporated his city into the Achæan community. The Achæans, applauding this generous action, chose him their general; upon which, desiring to outdo Aratus in glory, amongst many other uncalled-for things, he declared war against the Lacedæmonians; which Aratus opposing was thought to do it out of envy; and Lydiades was the second time chosen general, though Aratus acted openly against him, and laboured to have the office conferred upon another. For Aratus himself had the command every other year, as has been said. Lydiades, however, succeeded so well in his pretensions, that he was thrice chosen general, governing alternately, as did Aratus; but at last, declaring himself his professed enemy, and accusing him frequently to the Achæans, he was rejected, and fell into contempt, people now seeing that it was a contest between a counterfeit and a true, unadulterated virtue, and, as Æsop tells us that the cuckoo once, asking the little birds why they flew away from her, was answered, because they feared she would one day prove a hawk, so Lydiades's former tyranny still cast a doubt upon the reality of his change.

But Aratus gained new honour in the Ætolian war. For the Achæans resolving to fall upon the Ætolians on the Megarian confines, and Agis also, the Lacedæmonian king, who came to their assistance with an army, encouraging them to fight, Aratus opposed this determination. And patiently enduring many reproaches, many scoffs and jeerings at his soft and cowardly temper, he would not, for any appearance of disgrace, abandon what he judged to be true common advantage, and suffered the enemy to pass over Geranea into Peloponnesus without a battle. But when, after they passed by, news came that they had suddenly captured Pellene, he was no longer the same man, nor would he hear of any delay, or wait to draw together his whole force, but marched towards the enemy, with such as he had about him, to fall upon them, as they were indeed now much less formidable through the intemperances and disorders committed in their success. For as soon as they entered the city, the common soldiers dispersed and went hither and thither into the houses, quarrelling and fighting with one another about the plunder, and the officers and commanders were running about after the wives and daughters of the Pellenians, on whose heads they put their own helmets, to mark each man his prize, and prevent another from seizing it. And in this posture were they when news came that Aratus was ready to fall upon them. And in the midst of the consternation likely to ensue in the confusion they were in before all of them heard of the danger, the outmost of them, engaging at the gates and in the suburbs with the Achæans, were already beaten and put to flight, and as they came headlong back, filled with their panic those who were collecting and advancing to their assistance.

In this confusion, one of the captives, daughter of Epigethes, a citizen of repute, being extremely handsome and tall, happened to be sitting in the temple of Diana, placed there by the commander of the band of chosen men, who had taken her and put his crested helmet upon her. She, hearing the noise, and running out to see what was the matter, stood in the temple gates, looking down from above upon those that fought, having the helmet upon her head; in which posture she seemed to the citizens to be something more than human, and struck fear and dread into the enemy, who believed it to be a divine apparition; so that they lost all courage to defend themselves. But the Pellenians tell us that the image of Diana stands usually untouched, and when the priestess happens at any time to remove it to some other place, nobody dares look upon it, but all turn their faces from it; for not only is the sight of it terrible and hurtful to mankind, but it makes even the trees, by which it happens to be carried, become barren and cast fruit. This image, therefore, they say, the priestess produced at that time, and holding it directly in the faces of the Ætolians, made them lose their reason and judgment. But Aratus mentions no such thing in his commentaries, but saying that having put to flight the Ætolians, and falling in pell-mell with them into the city, he drove them out by main force, and killed seven hundred of them. And the action was extolled as one of the most famous exploits, and Timanthes the painter made a picture of the battle, giving by his composition a most lively representation of it.

But many great nations and potentates combining against the Achæans, Aratus immediately treated for friendly arrangements with the Ætolians, and, making use of the assistance of Pantaleon, the most powerful man amongst them, he not only made a peace, but an alliance between them and the Achæans. But being desirous to free the Athenians, he got into disgrace and ill-repute among the Achæans, because, notwithstanding the truce and suspension of arms made between them and the Macedonians, he had attempted to take the Piræus. He denies this fact in his commentaries, and lays the blame on Erginus, by whose assistance he took Acro-Corinthus, alleging that he upon his own private account attacked the Piræus, and his ladders happening to break, being hotly pursued, he called out upon Aratus, as if present, by which means deceiving the enemy he got safely off. This excuse, however, sounds very improbable; for it is not in any way likely that Erginus, a private man and a Syrian stranger, should conceive in his mind so great an attempt, without Aratus at his back, to tell him how and when to make it, and to supply him with the means. Nor was it twice or thrice, but very often, that, like an obstinate lover, he repeated his attempts on the Piræus, and was so far from being discouraged by his disappointments, that his missing his hopes but narrowly was an incentive to him to proceed the more boldly in a new trial. One time amongst the rest, in making his escape through the Thrasian plain, he put his leg out of joint, and was forced to submit to many operations with the knife before he was cured, so that for a long time he was carried in a litter to the wars.

And when Antigonus was dead, and Demetrius succeeded him in the kingdom, he was more bent than ever upon Athens, and in general quite despised the Macedonians. And so, being overthrown in battle near Phylacia by Bithys, Demetrius's general, and there being a very strong report that he was either taken or slain, Diogenes, the governor of the Piræus, sent letters to Corinth, commanding the Achæans to quit that city, seeing Aratus was dead. When these letters came to Corinth, Aratus happened to be there in person, so that Diogenes's messengers being sufficiently mocked and derided, were forced to return to their master. King Demetrius himself also sent a ship, wherein Aratus was to be brought to him in chains. And the Athenians, exceeding all possible fickleness of flattery to the Macedonians, crowned themselves with garlands upon the first news of his death. And so in anger he went at once and invaded Attica, and penetrated as far as the Academy, but then suffering himself to be pacified he did no further act of hostility. And the Athenians afterwards, coming to a due sense of his virtue when upon the death of Demetrius they attempted to recover their liberty, called him to their assistance; although at that time another person was general of the Achæans, and he himself had long kept his bed with a sickness, yet rather than fail the city in a time of need, he was carried thither in a litter, and helped to persuade Diogenes the governor to deliver up the Piræus, Munychia, Salamis and Sunium to the Athenians in consideration of a hundred and fifty talents, of which Aratus himself contributed twenty to the city. Upon this, the Æginetans and the Hermionians immediately joined the Achæans, and the greatest part of Arcadia entered their confederacy; and the Macedonians being occupied with various wars upon their own confines and with their neighbours, the Achæan power, the Ætolians also being in alliance with them, rose to great height.

But Aratus, still bent on effecting his old project, and impatient that tyranny should maintain itself in so near a city as Argos, sent to Aristomachus to persuade him to restore liberty to that city, and to associate it to the Achæans, and that, following Lydiades's example, he should rather choose to be the general of a great nation, with esteem and honour, than the tyrant of one city, with continual hatred and danger. Aristomachus slighted not the message, but desired Aratus to send him fifty talents, with which he might pay off the soldiers. In the meantime, whilst the money was providing, Lydiades, being then general, and extremely ambitious that this advantage might seem to be of his procuring for the Achæans, accused Aratus to Aristomachus, as one that bore an irreconcilable hatred to the tyrants, and, persuading him to commit the affair to his management, he presented him to the Achæans. But there the Achæan council gave a manifest proof of the great credit Aratus had with them and the good-will they bore him. For when he, in anger, spoke against Aristomachus's being admitted into the association, they rejected the proposal, but when he was afterwards pacified and came himself and spoke in its favour, they voted everything cheerfully and readily, and decreed that the Argives and Phliasians should be incorporated into their commonwealth, and the next year they chose Aristomachus general. He, being in good credit with the Achæans, was very desirous to invade Laconia and for that purpose sent for Aratus from Athens. Aratus wrote to him to dissuade him as far as he could from that expedition, being very unwilling the Achæans should be engaged in a quarrel with Cleomenes, who was a daring man, and making extraordinary advances to power. But Aristomachus resolving to go on, he obeyed and served in person, on which occasion he hindered Aristomachus from fighting a battle when Cleomenes came upon them at Pallantium; and for this act was accused by Lydiades, and, coming to an open conflict with him in a contest for the office of general, he carried it by the show of hands, and was chosen general the twelfth time.

This year, being routed by Cleomenes, near the Lycæum, he fled, and, wandering out of the way in the night, was believed to be slain; and once more it was confidently reported so throughout all Greece. He, however, having escaped this danger and rallied his forces, was not content to march off in safety, but making a happy use of the present conjuncture, when nobody dreamed of any such thing, he fell suddenly upon the Mantineans, allies of Cleomenes, and, taking the city, put a garrison into it, and made the stranger inhabitants free of the city; procuring, by this means, those advantages for the beaten Achæans, which being conquerors, they would not easily have obtained. The Lacedæmonians again invading the Megalopolitan territories, he marched to the assistance of the city, but refused to give Cleomenes, who did all he could to provoke him to it, any opportunity of engaging him in a battle, nor could be prevailed upon by the Megalopolitans, who urged him to it extremely. For besides that by nature he was ill-suited for set battles, he was then much inferior in numbers, and was to deal with a daring leader, still in the heat of youth, while he himself, now past the prime of courage and come to a chastised ambition, felt it his business to maintain by prudence the glory which he had obtained, and the other was only aspiring to by forwardness and daring.

So that though the light-armed soldiers had sallied out and driven the Lacedæmonians as far as their camp, and had come even to their tents, yet would not Aratus lead his men forward, but, posting himself in a hollow water-course in the way thither, stopped and prevented the citizens from crossing this. Lydiades, extremely vexed at what was going on, and loading Aratus with reproaches, entreated the horse that, together with him, they would second them that had the enemy in chase, and not let a certain victory slip out of their hands, nor forsake him that was going to venture his life for his country. And being reinforced with many brave men that turned after him, he charged the enemy's right wing, and routing it followed the pursuit without measure or discretion, letting his eagerness and hopes of glory tempt him on into broken ground, full of planted fruit-trees and cut up with broad ditches, where, being engaged by Cleomenes, he fell, fighting gallantly the noblest of battles, at the gate of his country. The rest, flying back to their main body and troubling the ranks of the full-armed infantry, put the whole army to the rout. Aratus was extremely blamed, being suspected to have betrayed Lydiades, and was constrained by the Achæans, who withdrew in great anger, to accompany them to Ægium, where they called a council, and decreed that he should no longer be furnished with money, nor have any more soldiers hired for him, but that, if he would make war, he should pay them himself.

This affront he resented so far as to resolve to give up the seal and lay down the office of general; but upon second thoughts he found it best to have patience, and presently marched with the Achæans to Orchomenus and fought a battle with Megistonus, the stepfather of Cleomenes, where he got the victory, killing three hundred men and taking Megistonus prisoner. But whereas he used to be chosen general every other year, when his turn came and he was called to take upon him that charge, he declined it, and Timoxenus was chosen in his stead. The true cause of which was not the pique he was alleged to have taken at the people, but the ill circumstances of the Achæan affairs. For Cleomenes did not now invade them gently and tenderly as hitherto, as one controlled by the civil authorities, but having killed the Ephors, divided the lands, and made many of the stranger residents free of the city, he was responsible to no one in his government; and therefore fell in good earnest upon the Achæans, and put forward his claim to the supreme military command. Wherefore Aratus is much blamed, that in a stormy and tempestuous time, like a cowardly pilot, he should forsake the helm when it was even perhaps his duty to have insisted, whether they would or no, on saving them; or if he thought the Achæan affairs desperate, to have yielded all up to Cleomenes, and not to have let Peloponnesus fall once again into barbarism with Macedonian garrisons, and Acro-Corinthus be occupied with

Illyric and Gaulish soldiers, and, under the specious name of confederates, to have made those masters of the cities whom he had held it his business by arms and by policy to baffle and defeat, and, in the memoirs he left behind him, loaded with reproaches and insults. And say that Cleomenes was arbitrary and tyrannical, yet was he descended from the Heraclidæ, and Sparta was his country, the obscurest citizens of which deserved to be preferred to the generalship before the best of the Macedonians by those that had any regard to the honour of Grecian birth. Besides, Cleomenes sued for that command over the Achæans as one that would return the honour of that title with real kindnesses to the cities; whereas Antigonus, being declared absolute general by sea and land, would not accept the office unless Acro-Corinthus were by special agreement put into his hands, following the example of Æsop's hunter; for he would not get up and ride the Achæans, who desired him so to do, and offered their backs to him by embassies and popular decrees, till, by a garrison and hostages, they had allowed him to bit and bridle them. Aratus exhausts all his powers of speech to show the necessity that was upon him. But Polybius writes, that long before this, and before there was any necessity, apprehending the daring temper of Cleomenes, he communicated secretly with Antigonus, and that he had beforehand prevailed with the Megalopolitans to press the Achæans to crave aid from Antigonus. For they were the most harassed by the war, Cleomenes continually plundering and ransacking their country. And so writes also Phylarchus, who, unless seconded by the testimony of Polybius, would not be altogether credited; for he is seized with enthusiasm when he so much as speaks a word of Cleomenes, and as if he were pleading, not writing a history, goes on throughout defending the one and accusing the other.

The Achæans, therefore, lost Mantinea, which was recovered by Cleomenes, and being beaten in a great fight near Hecatombæum, so general was the consternation, that they immediately sent to Cleomenes to desire him to come to Argos and take the command upon him. But Aratus, as soon as he understood that he was coming, and was got as far as Lerna with his troops, fearing the result, sent ambassadors to him, to request him to come accompanied with three hundred only, as to friends and confederates, and, if he mistrusted anything, he should receive hostages. Upon which Cleomenes, saying this was mere mockery and affront, went away, sending a letter to the Achæans full of reproaches and accusation against Aratus. And Aratus also wrote letters against Cleomenes; and bitter revilings and railleries were current on both hands, not sparing even their marriages and wives. Hereupon Cleomenes sent a herald to declare war against the Achæans, and in the meantime missed very narrowly of taking Sicyon by treachery. Turning off at a little distance, he attacked and took

Pellene which the Achæan general abandoned, and not long after took also Pheneus and Penteleum. Then immediately the Argives voluntarily joined with him, and the Phliasians received a garrison, and in short nothing among all their new acquisitions held firm to the Achæans. Aratus was encompassed on every side with clamour and confusion; he saw the whole of Peloponnesus shaking hands around him, and the cities everywhere set in revolt by men desirous of innovations.

Indeed no place remained quiet or satisfied with the present condition; even amongst the Sicyonians and Corinthians themselves, many were well known to have had private conferences with Cleomenes, who long since, out of desire to make themselves masters of their several cities, had been discontented with the present order of things. Aratus, having absolute power given him to bring these to condign punishment, executed as many of them as he could find at Sicyon, but going about to find them out and punish them at Corinth also, he irritated the people, already unsound in feeling and weary of the Achæan government. So collecting tumultuously in the temple of Apollo, they sent for Aratus, having determined to take or kill him before they broke out into open revolt. He came accordingly, leading his horse in his hand, as if he suspected nothing. Then several leaping up and accusing and reproaching him, with mild words and a settled countenance he bade them sit down, and not stand crying out upon him in a disorderly manner, desiring also, that those that were about the door might be let in, and saying so, he stepped out quietly, as if he would give his horse to somebody. Clearing himself thus of the crowd, and speaking without discomposure to the Corinthians that he met, commanding them to go to Apollo's temple, and being now, before they were aware, got near to the citadel, he leaped upon his horse, and commanding Cleopater, the governor of the garrison, to have a special care of his charge, he galloped to Sicyon, followed by thirty of his soldiers, the rest leaving him and shifting for themselves. And not long after, it being known that he was fled, the Corinthians pursued him, but not overtaking him, they immediately sent for Cleomenes and delivered up the city to him, who, however, thought nothing they could give was so great a gain, as was the loss of their having let Aratus get away. Nevertheless, being strengthened by the accession of the people of the Acte, as it is called, who put their towns into his hands, he proceeded to carry a palisade and lines of circumvallation around the Acro-Corinthus.

But Aratus being arrived at Sicyon, the body of the Achæans there flocked to him, and, in an assembly there held, he was chosen general with absolute power, and he took about him a guard of his own citizens, it being now three-and-thirty years since he first took a part in public affairs among the Achæans, having in that time been the chief man in credit and power of all Greece; but he was now deserted on all hands, helpless and overpowered, drifting about amidst the waves and danger on the shattered hulk of his native city. For the Ætolians, whom he applied to, declined to assist him in his distress, and the Athenians who were well affected to him were diverted from lending him any succour by the authority of Euclides and Micion. Now whereas he had a house and property in Corinth, Cleomenes meddled not with it, nor suffered anybody else to do so, but calling for his friends and agents, he bade them hold themselves responsible to Aratus for everything, as to him they would have to render their account; and privately he sent to him Tripylus, and afterwards Megistonus, his own stepfather, to offer him, besides several other things, a yearly pension of twelve talents, which was twice as much as Ptolemy allowed him, for he gave him six; and all that he demanded was to be declared commander of the Achæans, and together with them to have the keeping of the citadel of Corinth. To which Aratus returning answer that affairs were not so properly in his power as he was in the power of them, Cleomenes, believing this a mere evasion, immediately entered the country of Sicyon, destroying all with fire and sword, and besieged the city three months, whilst Aratus held firm, and was in dispute with himself whether he should call in Antigonus upon condition of delivering up the citadel of Corinth to him; for he would not lend him assistance upon any other terms.

In the meantime the Achæans assembled at Ægium, and called for Aratus; but it was very hazardous for him to pass thither, while Cleomenes was encamped before Sicyon; besides, the citizens endeavoured to stop him by their entreaties, protesting that they would not suffer him to expose himself to so evident danger, the enemy being so near; the women, also, and children hung about him, weeping and embracing him as their common father and defender. But he, having comforted and encouraged them as well as he could, got on horseback, and being accompanied with ten of his friends and his son, then a youth, got away to the seaside, and finding vessels there waiting off the shore, went on board of them and sailed to Ægium to the assembly; in which it was decreed that Antigonus should be called in to their aid, and should have the Acro-Corinthus delivered to him. Aratus also sent his son to him with the other hostages. The Corinthians, extremely angry at this proceeding, now plundered his property, and gave his house as a present to Cleomenes.

Antigonus being now near at hand with his army, consisting of twenty thousand Macedonian foot and one thousand three hundred horse, Aratus, with the members of council, went to meet him by sea, and got, unobserved by the enemy, to Pegæ, having no great confidence either in Antigonus or the Macedonians. For he was very sensible that his own greatness had been made out of the losses he had caused them, and that the first great principle of his public conduct had been hostility to the former Antigonus. But perceiving the necessity that was now upon him, and the pressure of the time, that lord and master of those we call rulers, to be inexorable, he resolved to put all to the venture. So soon, therefore, as Antigonus was told that Aratus was coming up to him, he saluted the rest of the company after the ordinary manner, but him he received at the very first approach with especial honour, and finding him afterwards to be both good and wise, admitted him to his nearer familiarity. For Aratus was not only useful to him in the management of great affairs, but singularly agreeable also as the private companion of a king in his recreations. And therefore, though Antigonus was young, yet as soon as he observed the temper of the man to be proper for a prince's friendship, he made more use of him than of any other, not only of the Achæans, but also of the Macedonians that were about him. So that the thing fell out to him just as the god had foreshown in a sacrifice. For it is related that, as Aratus was not long before offering sacrifice, there were found in the liver two gall-bags inclosed in the same caul of fat; whereupon the soothsayer told him that there should very soon be the strictest friendship imaginable between him and his greatest and most mortal enemies; which prediction he at that time slighted, having in general no great faith in soothsayings and prognostications, but depending most upon rational deliberation. At an after time, however, when, things succeeding well in the war, Antigonus made a great feast at Corinth, to which he invited a great number of guests, and placed Aratus next above him, and presently calling for a coverlet, asked him if he did not find it cold, and on Aratus's answering, "Yes, extremely cold," bade him come nearer, so that when the servants brought the coverlet, they threw it over them both, then Aratus, remembering the sacrifice, fell a laughing, and told the king the sign which had happened to him, and the interpretation of it. But this fell out a good while after.

So Aratus and the king, plighting their faith to each other at Pegæ, immediately marched toward the enemy, with whom they had frequent engagements near the city, Cleomenes maintaining a strong position, and the Corinthians making a very brisk defence. In the meantime Aristoteles the Argive, Aratus's friend, sent privately to him to let him know that he would cause Argos to revolt, if he would come thither in person with some soldiers. Aratus acquainted Antigonus, and taking fifteen hundred men with him, sailed in boats along the shore as quickly as he could from the Isthmus to Epidaurus. But the Argives had not patience till he could arrive, but, making a sudden insurrection, fell upon Cleomenes's soldiers, and drove them into the citadel. Cleomenes having news of this, and fearing lest, if the enemy should possess themselves of Argos, they might cut off his retreat home, leaves the Acro-Corinthus and marches away by night to help his men. He got thither first, and beat off the enemy, but Aratus appearing not long after, and the king approaching with his forces, he retreated to Mantinea, upon which all the cities again came over to the Achæans, and Antigonus took possession of the Acro-Corinthus. Aratus, being chosen general by the Argives, persuaded them to make a present to Antigonus of the property of the tyrants and the traitors. As for Aristomachus, after having put him to the rack in the town of Cenchreæ, they drowned him in the sea; for which, more than anything else, Aratus was reproached, that he could suffer a man to be so lawlessly put to death, who was no bad man, had been one of his long acquaintance, and at his persuasion had abdicated his power and annexed the city to the Achæans.

And already the blame of the other things that were done began to be laid to his account; as that they so lightly gave up Corinth to Antigonus, as if it had been an inconsiderable village; that they had suffered him after first sacking Orchomenus, then to put into it a Macedonian garrison; that they made a decree that no letters nor embassy should be sent to any other king without the consent of Antigonus, that they were forced to furnish pay and provision for the Macedonian soldiers, and celebrated sacrifices, processions, and games in honour of Antigonus, Aratus's citizens setting the example and receiving Antigonus, who was lodged and entertained at Aratus's house. All these things they treated as his fault, not knowing that having once put the reins into Antigonus's hands and let himself be borne by the impetus of regal power, he was no longer master of anything but one single voice, the liberty of which it was not so very safe for him to use. For it was very plain that Aratus was much troubled at several things, as appeared by the business about the statues. For Antigonus replaced the statues of the tyrants of Argos that had been thrown down, and on the contrary threw down the statues of all those that had taken the Acro-Corinthus, except that of Aratus, nor could Aratus, by all his entreaties, dissuade him. Also, the usage of the Mantineans by the Achæans seemed not in accordance with the Grecian feelings and manners. For being master of their city by the help of Antigonus, they put to death the chief and most noted men amongst them; and of the rest, some they sold, others they sent, bound in fetters, into Macedonia, and made slaves of their wives and children; and of the money thus raised, a third part they divided among themselves, and the other two-thirds were distributed among the Macedonians. And this might seem to have been justified by the law of retaliation; for although it be a barbarous thing for men of the same nation and blood thus to deal with one another in their fury, yet necessity makes it, as Simonides says, sweet and something excusable, being the proper thing, in the mind's painful and inflamed condition, to give alleviation and relief. But for what was afterwards done to that city, Aratus cannot be defended on any ground either of reason or necessity. For the Argives having had the city bestowed on them by Antigonus, and resolving to people it, he being then chosen as the new founder, and being general at that time, decreed that it should no longer be called Mantinea, but Antigonea, which name it still bears. So that he may be said to have been the cause that the old memory of the "beautiful Mantinea" has been wholly extinguished and the city to this day has the name of the destroyer and slayer of its citizens.

After this, Cleomenes, being overthrown in a great battle near Sellasia, forsook Sparta and fled into Egypt, and Antigonus, having shown all manner of kindness and fair-dealing to Aratus, retired into Macedonia. There, falling sick, he sent Philip, the heir of the kingdom, into Peloponnesus, being yet scarce a youth, commanding him to follow above all the counsel of Aratus, to communicate with the cities through him, and through him to make acquaintance with the Achæans; and Aratus, receiving him accordingly, so managed him as to send him back to Macedon both well affected to himself and full of desire and ambition to take an honourable part in the affairs of Greece.

When Antigonus was dead, the Ætolians, despising the sloth and negligence of the Achæans, who having learnt to be defended by other men's valour and to shelter themselves under the Macedonian arms, lived in ease and without any discipline, now attempted to interfere in Peloponnesus. And plundering the land of Patræ and Dyme in their way, they invaded Messene and ravaged it; at which Aratus being indignant, and finding that Timoxenus, then general, was hesitating and letting the time go by, being now on the point of laying down his office, in which he himself was chosen to succeed him, he anticipated the proper term by five days, that he might bring relief to the Messenians. And mustering the Achæans, who were both in their persons unexercised in arms and in their minds relaxed and averse to war, he met with a defeat at Caphyæ. Having thus begun the war, as it seemed, with too much heat and passion, he then ran into the other extreme, cooling again and desponding so much that he let pass and overlooked many fair opportunities of advantage given by the Ætolians, and allowed them to run riot, as it were, throughout all Peloponnesus, with all manner of insolence and licentiousness. Wherefore, holding forth their hands once more to the Macedonians, they invited and drew in Philip to intermeddle in the affairs of Greece, chiefly hoping, because of his affection and trust that he felt for Aratus, they should find him easy-tempered, and ready to be managed as they pleased.

But the king, being now persuaded by Apelles, Megaleas, and other courtiers, that endeavoured to ruin the credit Aratus had with him, took the side of the contrary faction and joined them in canvassing to have Eperatus chosen general by the Achæans. But he being altogether scorned by the Achæans, and, for the want of Aratus to help, all things going wrong, Philip saw he had quite mistaken his part, and, turning about and reconciling himself to Aratus, he was wholly his, and his affairs, now going on favourably both for his power and reputation, he depended upon him altogether as the author of all his gains in both respects; Aratus hereby giving a proof to the world that he was as good a nursing father of a kingdom as he had been of a democracy, for the actions of the king had in them the touch and colour of his judgment and character. The moderation which the young man showed to the Lacedæmonians, who had incurred his displeasure, and his affability to the Cretans, by which in a few days he brought over the whole island to his obedience, and his expedition against the Ætolians, so wonderfully successful, brought Philip reputation for hearkening to good advice, and to Aratus for giving it; for which things the king's followers envying him more than ever and finding they could not prevail against him by their secret practices, began openly to abuse and affront him at the banquets and over their wine, with every kind of petulance and impudence; so that once they threw stones at him as he was going back from supper to his tent. At which Philip being much offended, immediately fined them twenty talents, and finding afterwards that they still went on disturbing matters and doing mischief in his affairs, he put them to death.

But with his run of good success, prosperity began to puff him up, and various extravagant desires began to spring and show themselves in his mind; and his natural bad inclinations breaking through the artificial restraints he had put upon them, in a little time laid open and discovered his true and proper character. In the first place, he privately injured the younger Aratus in his wife, which was not known of a good while, because he was lodged and entertained at their house; then he began to be more rough and untractable in the domestic politics of Greece, and showed plainly that he was wishing to shake himself loose of Aratus. This the Messenian affairs first gave occasion to suspect. For they falling into sedition, and Aratus being just too late with his succours, Philip, who got into the city one day before him, at once blew up the flame of contention amongst them, asking privately, on the one hand, the Hessenian generals, if they had not laws whereby to suppress the insolence of the common people, and on the other, the leaders of the people, whether they had not hands to help themselves against their oppressors. Upon which gathering courage, the officers attempted to lay hands on the heads of the people, and they on the other side, coming upon the officers with the multitude, killed them, and very near two hundred persons with them.

Philip having committed this wickedness, and doing his best to set the Messenians by the ears together more than before, Aratus arrived there, and both showed plainly that he took it ill himself, and also he suffered his son bitterly to reproach and revile him. It should seem that the young man had an attachment for Philip, and so at this time one of his expressions to him was, that he no longer appeared to him the handsomest, but the most deformed of all men, after so foul an action. To all which Philip gave him no answer, though he seemed so angry as to make it expected he would, and though several times he cried out aloud while the young man was speaking. But as for the elder Aratus, seeming to take all that he said in good part, and as if he were by nature a politic character and had a good command of himself, he gave him his hand and led him out of the theatre, and carried him with him to the Ithomatas, to sacrifice there to Jupiter, and take a view of the place, for it is a post as fortifiable as the Acro-Corinthus, and, with a garrison in it, quite as strong and as impregnable to the attacks of all around it. Philip therefore went up hither, and having offered sacrifice, receiving the entrails of the ox with both his hands from the priest, he showed them to Aratus and Demetrius the Pharian, presenting them sometimes to the one and sometimes to the other, asking them what they judged, by the tokens in the sacrifice, was to be done with the fort; was he to keep it for himself, or restore it to the Messenians. Demetrius laughed and answered, "If you have in you the soul of a soothsayer, you will restore it, but if of a prince you will hold the ox by both the horns," meaning to refer to Peloponnesus, which would be wholly in his power and at his disposal if he added the Ithomatas to the Acro-Corinthus. Aratus said not a word for a good while; but Philip entreating him to declare his opinion, he said: "Many and great hills are there in Crete, and many rocks in Bœotia and Phocis, and many remarkable strongholds both near the sea and in the midland in Acarnania, and yet all these people obey your orders, though you have not possessed yourself of any one of those places. Robbers nest themselves in rocks and precipices; but the strongest fort a king can have is confidence and affection. These have opened to you the Cretan sea; these make you master of Peloponnesus, and by the help of these, young as you are, are you become captain of the one, and lord of the other." While he was still speaking, Philip returned the entrails to the priest, and drawing Aratus to him by the hand, "Come, then," said he, "let us follow the same course;" as if he felt himself forced by him, and obliged to give up the town.

From this time Aratus began to withdraw from court, and retired by degrees from Philip's company; when he was preparing to march into Epirus, and desired him that he would accompany him thither, he excused himself and stayed at home, apprehending that he should get nothing but discredit by having anything to do with his actions. But then, afterwards, having shamefully lost his fleet against the Romans and miscarried in all his designs, he returned into Peloponnesus, where he tried once more to beguile the Messenians by his artifices, and failing in this, began openly to attack them and to ravage their country, then Aratus fell out with him downright, and utterly renounced his friendship; for he had begun then to be fully aware of the injuries done to his son in his wife, which vexed him greatly, though he concealed them from his son, as he could but know he had been abused, without having any means to revenge himself. For, indeed, Philip seems to have been an instance of the greatest and strangest alteration of character; after being a mild king and modest and chaste youth, he became a lascivious man and most cruel tyrant; though in reality this was not a change of his nature, but a bold unmasking, when safe opportunity came, of the evil inclinations which his fear had for a long time made him dissemble.

For that the respect he at the beginning bore to Aratus had a great alloy of fear and awe appears evidently from what he did to him at last. For being desirous to put him to death, not thinking himself, whilst he was alive, to be properly free as a man, much less at liberty to do his pleasure as king or tyrant, he durst not attempt to do it by open force, but commanded Taurion, one of his captains and familiars, to make him away secretly by poison, if possible, in his absence. Taurion, therefore, made himself intimate with Aratus, and gave him a dose not of your strong and violent poisons, but such as cause gentle, feverish heats at first, and a dull cough, and so by degrees bring on certain death. Aratus perceived what was done to him, but, knowing that it was in vain to make any words of it, bore it patiently and with silence, as if it had been some common and usual distemper. Only once, a friend of his being with him in his chamber, he spat some blood, which his friend observing and wondering at, "These, O Cephalon," said he, "are the wages of a king's love."

Thus died he in Ægium, in his seventeenth generalship. The Achæans were very desirous that he should be buried there with a funeral and monument suitable to his life, but the Sicyonians treated it as a calamity to them if he were interred anywhere but in their city, and prevailed with the Achæans to grant them the disposal of the body.

But there being an ancient law that no person should be buried within the walls of their city, and besides the law also a strong religious feeling about it, they sent to Delphi to ask counsel of the Pythoness, who returned this answer:—

"Sicyon, whom oft he rescued, 'Where,' you say,
'Shall we the relics of Aratus lay?'
The soil that would not lightly o'er him rest,
Or to be under him would feel opprest,
Were in the sight of earth and seas and skies unblest."

This oracle being brought, all the Achæans were well pleased at it, but especially the Sicyonians, who, changing their mourning into public joy, immediately fetched the body from Ægium, and in a kind of solemn procession brought it into the city, being crowned with garlands, and arrayed in white garments, with singing and dancing, and, choosing a conspicuous place, they buried him there, as the founder and saviour of their city. The place is to this day called Aratium, and there they yearly make two solemn sacrifices to him, the one on the day he delivered the city from tyranny, being the fifth of the month Dæsius, which the Athenians call Anthesterion, and this sacrifice they call Soteria; the other in the month of his birth, which is still remembered. Now the first of these was performed by the priest of Jupiter Soter, the second by the priest of Aratus, wearing a band around his head, not pure white, but mingled with purple. Hymns were sung to the harp by the singers of the feasts of Bacchus; the procession was led up by the president of the public exercises, with the boys and young men; these were followed by the councillors wearing garlands, and other citizens such as pleased. Of these observances, some small traces, it is still made a point of religion not to omit, on the appointed days; but the greatest part of the ceremonies have through time and other intervening accidents been disused.

And such, as history tells us, was the life and manners of the elder Aratus. And for the younger, his son, Philip, abominably wicked by nature and a savage abuser of his power, gave him such poisonous medicines, as though they did not kill him indeed, yet made him lose his senses, and run into wild and absurd attempts and desire to do actions and satisfy appetites that were ridiculous and shameful. So that his death, which happened to him while he was yet young and in the flower of his age, cannot be so much esteemed a misfortune as a deliverance and end of his misery. However Philip paid dearly, all through the rest of his life, for these impious violations of friendship and hospitality. For being overcome by the Romans, he was forced to put himself wholly into their hands, and, being deprived of his other dominions and surrendering all his ships except five, he had also to pay a fine of a thousand talents, and to give his son for hostage, and only out of mere pity he was suffered to keep Macedonia and its dependencies; where continually putting to death the noblest of his subjects and the nearest relations he had, he filled the whole kingdom with horror and hatred of him. And whereas amidst so many misfortunes he had but one good chance, which was the having a son of great virtue and merit, him, through jealousy and envy at the honour the Romans had for him, he caused to be murdered, and left his kingdom to Perseus, who, as some say, was not his own child, but supposititious, born of a sempstress Gnathænion. This was he whom Paulus Æmilius led in triumph, and in whom ended the succession of Antigonus's line and kingdom. But the posterity of Aratus continued still in our days at Sicyon and Pellene.

ARTAXERXES

THE first Artaxerxes, among all the kings of Persia the most remarkable for a gentle and noble spirit, was surnamed the Long-handed, his right hand being longer than his left, and was the son of Xerxes. The second, whose story I am now writing, who had the surname of the Mindful, was the grandson of the former, by his daughter Parysatis, who brought Darius four sons, the eldest Artaxerxes, the next Cyrus, and two younger than these, Ostanes and Oxathres. Cyrus took his name of the ancient Cyrus, as he, they say, had his from the sun, which, in the Persian language, is called Cyrus. Artaxerxes was at first called Arsicas; Dinon says Oarses; but it is utterly improbable that Ctesias (however otherwise he may have filled his books with a perfect farrago of incredible and senseless fables) should be ignorant of the name of the king with whom he lived as his physician, attending upon himself, his wife, his mother, and his children.

Cyrus, from his earliest youth, showed something of a headstrong and vehement character; Artaxerxes, on the other side, was gentler in everything, and of a nature more yielding and soft in its action. He married a beautiful and virtuous wife at the desire of his parents, but kept her as expressly against their wishes. For King Darius, having put her brother to death, was purposing likewise to destroy her. But Arsicas, throwing himself at his mother's feet, by many tears, at last, with much ado, persuaded her that they should neither put her to death nor divorce her from him. However, Cyrus was his mother's favourite, and the son whom she most desired to settle in the throne. And therefore, his father Darius now lying ill, he, being sent for from the sea to the court, set out thence with full hopes that by her means he was to be declared the successor to the kingdom. For Parysatis had the specious plea in his behalf, which Xerxes on the advice of Demaratus had of old made use of, that she had borne him Arsicas when he was a subject, but Cyrus, when a king. Notwithstanding, she prevailed not with Darius, but the eldest son, Arsicas, was proclaimed king, his name being changed into Artaxerxes; and Cyrus remained satrap of Lydia, and commander in the maritime provinces.

It was not long after the decease of Darius that the king, his successor, went to Pasargadæ, to have the ceremony of his inauguration consummated by the Persian priests. There is a temple dedicated to a warlike goddess, whom one might liken to Minerva, into which when the royal person to be initiated has passed, he must strip himself of his own robe, and put on that which Cyrus the first wore before he was king; then, having devoured a frail of figs, he must eat turpentine, and drink a cup of sour milk. To which if they superadd any other rites, it is unknown to any but those that are present at them. Now Artaxerxes being about to address himself to this solemnity, Tisaphernes came to him, bringing a certain priest, who, having trained up Cyrus in his youth in the established discipline of Persia, and having taught him the Magian philosophy, was likely to be as much disappointed as any man that his pupil did not succeed to the throne. And for that reason his veracity was the less questioned when he charged Cyrus as though he had been about to lie in wait for the king in the temple, and to assault and assassinate him as he was putting off his garment. Some affirm that he was apprehended upon this impeachment, others that he had entered the temple and was pointed out there, as he lay lurking by the priest. But as he was on the point of being put to death, his mother clasped him in her arms, and, entwining him with the tresses of her hair, joined his neck close to her own, and by her bitter lamentation and intercession to Artaxerxes for him, succeeded in saving his life; and sent him away again to the sea and to his former province. This, however, could no longer content him; nor did he so well remember his delivery as his arrest, his resentment for which made him more eagerly desirous of the kingdom than before.

Some say that he revolted from his brother, because he had not a revenue allowed him sufficient for his daily meals; but this is on the face of it absurd. For had he had nothing else, yet he had a mother ready to supply him with whatever he could desire out of her own means. But the great number of soldiers who were hired from all quarters and maintained, as Xenophon informs us, for his service, by his friends and connections, is in itself a sufficient proof of his riches. He did not assemble them together in a body, desiring as yet to conceal his enterprise; but he had agents everywhere, enlisting foreign soldiers upon various pretences; and, in the meantime, Parysatis, who was with the king, did her best to put aside all suspicions, and Cyrus himself always wrote in a humble and dutiful manner to him, sometimes soliciting favour, and sometimes making countercharges against Tisaphernes, as if his jealousy and contest had been wholly with him. Moreover, there was a certain natural dilatoriness in the king, which was taken by many for clemency. And, indeed, in the beginning of his reign, he did seem really to emulate the gentleness of the first Artaxerxes, being very accessible in his person, and liberal to a fault in the distribution of honours and favours. Even in his punishments, no contumely or vindictive pleasure could be seen; and those who offered him presents were as much pleased with his manner of accepting, as were those who received gifts from him with his graciousness and amiability in giving them. Nor truly was there anything, however inconsiderable, given him, which he did not deign kindly to accept of; insomuch that when one Omises had presented him with a very large pomegranate, "By Mithras," said he, "this man, were he intrusted with it, would turn a small city into a great one."

Once when some were offering him one thing, some another, as he was on a progress, a certain poor labourer, having got nothing at hand to bring him, ran to the river side, and, taking up water in his hands, offered it to him; with which Artaxerxes was so well pleased that he sent him a goblet of gold and a thousand darics. To Euclidas, the Lacedæmonian, who had made a number of bold and arrogant speeches to him, he sent word by one of his officers. "You have leave to say what you please to me, and I, you should remember, may both say and do what I please to you." Teribazus once, when they were hunting, came up and pointed out to the king that his royal robe was torn; the king asked him what he wished him to do; and when Teribazus replied, "May it please you to put on another and give me that," the king did so, saying withal, "I give it you, Teribazus, but I charge you not to wear it." He, little regarding the injunction, being not a bad, but a lightheaded, thoughtless man, immediately the king took it off, put it on, and bedecked himself further with royal golden necklaces and women's ornaments, to the great scandal of everybody, the thing being quite unlawful. But the king laughed and told him, "You have my leave to wear the trinkets as a woman, and the robe of state as a fool." And whereas none usually sat down to eat with the king besides his mother and his wedded wife, the former being placed above, the other below him, Artaxerxes invited also to his table his two younger brothers, Ostanes and Oxathres. But what was the most popular thing of all among the Persians was the sight of his wife Statira's chariot, which always appeared with its curtains down, allowing her country women to salute and approach her, which made the queen a great favourite with the people.

Yet busy, factious men, that delighted in change, professed it to be their opinion that the times needed Cyrus, a man of great spirit, an excellent warrior, and a lover of his friends, and that the largeness of their empire absolutely required a bold and enterprising prince. Cyrus, then, not only relying upon those of his own province near the sea, but upon many of those in the upper countries near the king, commenced the war against him. He wrote to the Lacedæmonians, bidding them come to his assistance and supply him with men, assuring them that to those who came to him on foot he would give horses, and to the horsemen chariots; that upon those who had farms he would bestow villages, and those who were lords of villages he would make so of cities; and that those who would be his soldiers should receive their pay, not by count, but by weight. And among many other high praises of himself, he said he had the stronger soul; was more a philosopher and a better Magian; and could drink and bear more wine than his brother, who, as he averred, was such a coward and so little like a man, that he could neither sit his horse in hunting nor his throne in time of danger. The Lacedæmonians, his letter being read, sent a staff to Clearchus, commanding him to obey Cyrus in all things. So Cyrus marched towards the king, having under his conduct a numerous host of barbarians, and but little less than thirteen thousand stipendiary Grecians; alleging first one cause, then another, for his expedition. Yet the true reason lay not long concealed, but Tisaphernes went to the king in person to declare it. Thereupon, the court was all in an uproar and tumult, the queen-mother bearing almost the whole blame of the enterprise, and her retainers being suspected and accused. Above all, Statira angered her by bewailing the war and passionately demanding where were now the pledges and the intercession which saved the life of him that conspired against his brother; "to the end," she said, "that he might plunge us all into war and trouble." For which words Parysatis hating Statira, and being naturally implacable and savage in her anger and revenge, consulted how she might destroy her. But since Dinon tells us that her purpose took effect in the time of the war, and Ctesias says it was after it, I shall keep the story for the place to which the latter assigns it, as it is very unlikely that he, who was actually present, should not know the time when it happened, and there was no motive to induce him designedly to misplace its date in his narrative of it, though it is not infrequent with him in his history to make excursions from truth into mere fiction and romance.

As Cyrus was upon the march, rumours and reports were brought him, as though the king still deliberated, and were not minded to fight and presently to join battle with him; but to wait in the heart of his kingdom until his forces should have come in thither from all parts of his dominions. He had cut a trench through the plain ten fathoms in breadth, and as many in depth, the length of it being no less than four hundred furlongs. Yet he allowed Cyrus to pass across it, and to advance almost to the city of Babylon. Then Teribazus, as the report goes, was the first that had the boldness to tell the king that he ought not to avoid the conflict, nor to abandon Media, Babylon, and even Susa, and hide himself in Persis, when all the while he had an army many times over more numerous than his enemies, and an infinite company of governors and captains that were better soldiers and politicians than Cyrus. So at last he resolved to fight, as soon as it was possible for him. Making, therefore, his first appearance, all on a sudden, at the head of nine hundred thousand well-marshalled men, he so startled and surprised the enemy, who with the confidence of contempt were marching on their way in no order, and with their arms not ready for use, that Cyrus, in the midst of such noise and tumult, was scarcely able to form them for battle. Moreover, the very manner in which he led on his men, silently and slowly, made the Grecians stand amazed at his good discipline; who had expected irregular shouting and leaping, much confusion and separation between one body of men and another, in so vast a multitude of troops. He also placed the choicest of his armed chariots in the front of his own phalanx over against the Grecian troops, that a violent charge with these might cut open their ranks before they closed with them.

But as this battle is described by many historians, and Xenophon in particular as good as shows it us by eyesight, not as a past event, but as a present action, and by his vivid account makes his hearers feel all the passions and join in all the dangers of it, it would be folly in me to give any larger account of it than barely to mention any things omitted by him which yet deserve to be recorded. The place, then, in which the two armies were drawn out is called Cunaxa, being about five hundred furlongs distant from Babylon. And here Clearchus beseeching Cyrus before the fight to retire behind the combatants, and not expose himself to hazard, they say he replied, "What is this, Clearchus? Would you have me, who aspire to empire, show myself unworthy of it?" But if Cyrus committed a great fault in entering headlong into the midst of danger, and not paying any regard to his own safety, Clearchus was as much to blame, if not more, in refusing to lead the Greeks against the main body of the enemy, where the king stood, and in keeping his right wing close to the river, for fear of being surrounded. For if he wanted, above all other things, to be safe, and considered it his first object to sleep in a whole skin, it had been his best way not to have stirred from home. But, after marching in arms ten thousand furlongs from the seacoast, simply on his choosing, for the purpose of placing Cyrus on the throne, to look about and select a position which would enable him, not to preserve him under whose pay and conduct he was, but himself to engage with more ease and security, seemed much like one that through fear of present dangers had abandoned the purpose of his actions, and been false to the design of his expedition. For it is evident from the very event of the battle that none of those who were in array around the king's person could have stood the shock of the Grecian charge; and had they been beaten out of the field, and Artaxerxes either fled or fallen, Cyrus would have gained by the victory, not only safety, but a crown. And, therefore, Clearchus by his caution must be considered more to blame for the result in the destruction of the life and fortune of Cyrus, than he by his heat and rashness. For had the king made it his business to discover a place, where having posted the Grecians, he might encounter them with the least hazard, he would never have found out any other but that which was most remote from himself and those near him; of his defeat in which he was insensible, and, though Clearchus had the victory, yet Cyrus could not know of it, and could take no advantage of it before his fall. Cyrus knew well enough what was expedient to be done, and commanded Clearchus with his men to take their place in the centre. Clearchus replied that he would take care to have all arranged as was best, and then spoiled all.

For the Grecians, where they were, defeated the barbarians till they were weary, and chased them successfully a very great way. But Cyrus being mounted upon a noble but a headstrong and hard-mouthed horse, bearing the name, as Ctesias tells us, of Pasacas, Artagerses, the leader of the Cadusians, galloped up to him, crying aloud, "O most unjust and senseless of men, who are the disgrace of the honoured name of Cyrus, are you come here leading the wicked Greeks on a wicked journey, to plunder the good things of the Persians, and this with the intent of slaying your lord and brother, the master of ten thousand times ten thousand servants that are better men than you? As you shall see this instant; for you shall lose your head here, before you look upon the face of the king." Which when he had said, he cast his javelin at him. But his coat of mail stoutly repelled it, and Cyrus was not wounded; yet the stroke falling heavy upon him, he reeled under it. Then Artagerses turning his horse, Cyrus threw his weapon, and sent the head of it through his neck near the shoulder bone. So that it is almost universally agreed to by all the authors that Artagerses was slain by him.

But as to the death of Cyrus, since Xenophon, as being himself no eyewitness of it, has stated it simply and in few words, it may not be amiss perhaps to run over on the one hand what Dinon, and on the other, what Ctesias has said of it.

Dinon then affirms that, after the death of Artagerses, Cyrus, furiously attacking the guard of Artaxerxes, wounded the king's horse, and so dismounted him, and when Teribazus had quickly lifted him up upon another, and said to him, "O king, remember this day, which is not one to be forgotten," Cyrus, again spurring up his horse, struck down Artaxerxes. But at the third assault the king being enraged, and saying to those near him that death was more eligible, made up to Cyrus, who furiously and blindly rushed in the face of the weapons opposed to him. So the king struck him with a javelin, as likewise did those that were about him. And thus Cyrus falls, as some say, by the hand of the king; as others by the dart of a Carian, to whom Artaxerxes for a reward of his achievement gave the privilege of carrying ever after a golden cock upon his spear before the first ranks of the army in all expeditions. For the Persians call the men of Caria cocks, because of the crests with which they adorn their helmets.

But the account of Ctesias, to put it shortly, omitting many details, is as follows: Cyrus, after the death of Artagerses, rode up against the king, as he did against him, neither exchanging a word with the other. But Ariæus, Cyrus's friend, was beforehand with him, and darted first at the king, yet wounded him not. Then the king cast his lance at his brother, but missed him, though he both hit and slew Satiphernes, a noble man and a faithful friend to Cyrus. Then Cyrus directed his lance against the king, and pierced his breast with it quite through his armour, two inches deep, so that he fell from his horse with the stroke. At which those that attended him being put to flight and disorder, he, rising with a few, among whom was Ctesias, and making his way to a little hill not far off, rested himself. But Cyrus, who was in the thick enemy, was carried off a great way by the wildness of his horse, the darkness which was now coming on making it hard for them to know him, and for his followers to find him. However, being made elate with victory, and full of confidence and force, he passed through them, crying out, and that more than once, in the Persian language, "Clear the way, villains, clear the way;" which they indeed did, throwing themselves down at his feet. But his tiara dropped off his head, and a young Persian, by name Mithridates, running by, struck a dart into one of his temples near his eye, not knowing who he was; out of which wound much blood gushed, so that Cyrus, swooning and senseless, fell off his horse. The horse escaped, and ran about the field; but the companion of Mithridates took the trappings which fell off, soaked with blood. And as Cyrus slowly began to come to himself, some eunuchs who were there tried to put him on another horse, and so convey him safe away. And when he was not able to ride, and desired to walk on his feet, they led and supported him, being indeed dizzy in the head and reeling, but convinced of his being victorious, hearing, as he went, the fugitives saluting Cyrus as king, and praying for grace and mercy. In the meantime, some wretched, poverty-stricken Caunians, who in some pitiful employment as camp followers had accompanied the king's army, by chance joined these attendants of Cyrus, supposing them to be of their own party. But when, after a while, they made out that their coats over their breastplates were red, whereas all the king's people wore white ones, they knew that they were enemies. One of them, therefore, not dreaming that it was Cyrus, ventured to strike him behind with a dart. The vein under the knee was cut open, and Cyrus fell, and at the same time struck his wounded temple against a stone, and so died. Thus runs Ctesias's account, tardily, with the slowness of a blunt weapon effecting the victim's death.

When he was now dead, Artasyras, the king's eye, passed by on horseback, and, having observed the eunuchs lamenting, he asked the most trusty of them, "Who is this, Pariscas, whom you sit here deploring?" He replied, "Do not you see, O Artasyras, that it is my master, Cyrus?" Then Artasyras wondering, bade the eunuch be of good cheer, and keep the dead body safe. And going in all haste to Artaxerxes, who had now given up all hope of his affairs, and was in great suffering also with his thirst and his wound, he with much joy assured him that he had seen Cyrus dead. Upon this, at first, he set out to go in person to the place, and commanded Artasyras to conduct him where he lay. But when there was a great noise made about the Greeks, who were said to be in full pursuit, conquering and carrying all before them, he thought it best to send a number of persons to see; and accordingly thirty men went with torches in their hands. Meantime, as he seemed to be almost at the point of dying from thirst, his eunuch Satibarzanes ran about seeking drink for him; for the place had no water in it and he was at a good distance from his camp. After a long search he at last met one of those poor Caunian camp-followers, who had in a wretched skin about four pints of foul and stinking water, which he took and gave to the king; and when he had drunk all off, he asked him if he did not dislike the water; but he declared by all the gods that he never so much relished either wine, or water out of the lightest or purest stream. "And therefore," said he, "if I fail myself to discover and reward him who gave it to you, I beg of heaven to make him rich and prosperous."

Just after this, came back the thirty messengers, with joy and triumph in their looks, bringing him the tidings of his unexpected fortune. And now he was also encouraged by the number of soldiers that again began to flock in and gather about him; so that he presently descended into the plain with many lights and flambeaux round about him. And when he had come near the dead body, and, according to a certain law of the Persians, the right hand and head had been lopped off from the trunk, he gave orders that the latter should be brought to him, and, grasping the hair of it, which was long and bushy, he showed it to those who were still uncertain and disposed to fly. They were amazed at it, and did him homage; so that there were presently seventy thousand of them got about him, and entered the camp again with him. He had led out to the fight, as Ctesias affirms, four hundred thousand men. But Dinon and Xenophon aver that there were many more than forty myriads actually engaged. As to the number of the slain, as the catalogue of them was given up to Artaxerxes, Ctesias says, they were nine thousand, but that they appeared to him no fewer than twenty thousand. Thus far there is something to be said on both sides. But it is a flagrant untruth on the part of Ctesias to say that he was sent along with Phalinus the Zacynthian and some others to the Grecians. For Xenophon knew well enough that Ctesias was resident at court; for he makes mention of him, and had evidently met with his writings. And, therefore, had he come, and been deputed the interpreter of such momentous words, Xenophon surely would not have struck his name out of the embassy to mention only Phalinus. But Ctesias, as is evident, being excessively vainglorious and no less a favourer of the Lacedæmonians and Clearchus, never fails to assume to himself some province in his narrative, taking opportunity, in these situations, to introduce abundant high praise of Clearchus and Sparta.

When the battle was over, Artaxerxes sent goodly and magnificent gifts to the son of Artagerses, whom Cyrus slew. He conferred likewise high honours upon Ctesias and others, and, having found out the Caunian who gave him the bottle of water, he made him—a poor, obscure man—a rich and an honourable person. As for the punishments he inflicted upon delinquents, there was a kind of harmony betwixt them and the crimes. He gave order that one Arbaces, a Mede, that had fled in the fight to Cyrus and again at his fall had come back, should, as a mark that he was considered a dastardly and effeminate, not a dangerous or treasonable man, have a common harlot set upon his back, and carry her about for a whole day in the market-place. Another, besides that he had deserted to them, having falsely vaunted that he had killed two of the rebels, he decreed that three needles should be struck through his tongue. And both supposing that with his own hand he had cut off Cyrus, and being willing that all men should think and say so, he sent rich presents to Mithridates, who first wounded him, and charged those by whom he conveyed the gifts to him to tell him, that "the king has honoured you with these his favours, because you found and brought him the horse-trappings of Cyrus."

The Carian, also, from whose wound in the ham Cyrus died, suing for his reward, he commanded those that brought it him to say that "the king presents you with this as a second remuneration of the good news told him; for first Artasyras, and, next to him, you assured him of the decease of Cyrus." Mithridates retired without complaint, though not without resentment. But the unfortunate Carian was fool enough to give way to a natural infirmity. For being ravished with the sight of the princely gifts that were before him, and being tempted thereupon to challenge and aspire to things above him, he deigned not to accept the king's present as a reward for good news, but indignantly crying out and appealing to witnesses, he protested that he, and none but he, had killed Cyrus, and that he was unjustly deprived of the glory. These words, when they came to his ear, much offended the king, so that forthwith he sentenced him to be beheaded. But the queen mother, being in the king's presence, said, "Let not the king so lightly discharge this pernicious Carian; let him receive from me the fitting punishment of what he dares to say." So when the king had consigned him over to Parysatis, she charged the executioners to take up the man, and stretch him upon the rack for ten days, then, tearing out his eyes, to drop molten brass into his ears till he expired.

Mithridates, also, within a short time after, miserably perished by the like folly; for being invited to a feast where were the eunuchs both of the king and of the queen mother, he came arrayed in the dress and the golden ornaments which he had received from the king. After they began to drink, the eunuch that was the greatest in power with Parysatis thus speaks to him: "A magnificent dress, indeed, O Mithridates, is this which the king has given you; the chains and bracelets are glorious, and your scymetar of invaluable worth; how happy has he made you, the object of every eye!" To whom he, being a little overcome with the wine, replied, "What are these things, Sparamizes? Sure I am, I showed myself to the king in that day of trial to be one deserving greater and costlier gifts than these." At which Sparamizes smiling, said, "I do not grudge them to you, Mithridates; but since the Grecians tell us that wine and truth go together, let me hear now, my friend, what glorious or mighty matter was it to find some trappings that had slipped off a horse, and to bring them to the king?" And this he spoke, not as ignorant of the truth, but desiring to unbosom him to the company, irritating the vanity of the man, whom drink had now made eager to talk and incapable of controlling himself. So he forbore nothing, but said out, "Talk you what you please of horse-trappings and such trifles; I tell you plainly, that this hand was the death of Cyrus. For I threw not my darts as Artagerses did, in vain and to no purpose, but only just missing his eye, and hitting him right on the temple, and piercing him through. I brought him to the ground; and of that wound he died." The rest of the company, who saw the end and the hapless fate of Mithridates as if it were already completed, bowed their heads to the ground; and he who entertained them said, "Mithridates, my friend, let us eat and drink now, revering the fortune of our prince, and let us waive discourse which is too weighty for us."

Presently after, Sparamizes told Parysatis what he said, and she told the king, who was greatly enraged at it, as having the lie given him, and being in danger to forfeit the most glorious and most pleasant circumstance of his victory. For it was his desire that every one, whether Greek or barbarian, should believe that in the mutual assaults and conflicts between him and his brother, he, giving and receiving a blow, was himself indeed wounded, but that the other lost his life. And, therefore, he decreed that Mithridates should be put to death in boats; which execution is after the following manner: Taking two boats framed exactly to fit and answer each other, they lay down in one of them the malefactor that suffers, upon his back; then, covering it with the other, and so setting them together that the head, hands, and feet of him are left outside, and the rest of his body lies shut up within, they offer him food, and if he refuse to eat it they force him to do it by pricking his eyes; then, after he has eaten, they drench him with a mixture of milk and honey, pouring it not only into his mouth, but all over his face. They then keep his face continually turned towards the sun: and it becomes completely covered up and hidden by the multitude of flies that settle on it. And as within the boats he does what those that eat and drink must needs do, creeping things and vermin spring out of the corruption and rottenness of the excrement, and these entering into the bowels of him, his body is consumed. When the man is manifestly dead, the uppermost boat being taken off, they find his flesh devoured, and swarms of such noisome creatures preying upon and, as it were, growing to his inwards. In this way Mithridates, after suffering for seventeen days, at last expired.

Masabates, the king's eunuch, who had cut off the hand and head of Cyrus, remained still as a mark for Parysatis's vengeance. Whereas, therefore, he was so circumspect, that he gave her no advantage against him she framed this kind of snare for him. She was a very ingenious woman in other ways, and was an excellent player at dice, and, before the war, had often played with the king. After the war, too, when she had been reconciled to him, she joined readily in all amusements with him, played at dice with him, was his confidant in his love matters, and in every way did her best to leave him as little as possible in the company of Statira, both because she hated her more than any other person, and because she wished to have no one so powerful as herself. And so once when Artaxerxes was at leisure, and inclined to divert himself, she challenged him to play at dice with her for a thousand darics, and purposely let him win them, and paid him down in gold. Yet, pretending to be concerned for her loss, and that she would gladly have her revenge for it, she pressed him to begin a new game for a eunuch; to which he consented. But first they agreed that each of them might except five of their most trusty eunuchs, and that out of the rest of them the loser should yield up any the winner should make choice of. Upon these conditions they played. Thus being bent upon her design, and thoroughly in earnest with her game, and the dice also running luckily for her, when she had got the game, she demanded Masabates, who was not in the number of the five excepted. And before the king could suspect the matter, having delivered him up to the tormentors, she enjoined them to flay him alive, to set his body upon three stakes, and to stretch his skin upon stakes separately from it.

These things being done, and the king taking them ill, and being incensed against her, she with raillery and laughter told him, "You are a comfortable and happy man indeed, if you are so much disturbed for the sake of an old rascally eunuch, when I, though I have thrown away a thousand darics, hold my peace and acquiesce in my fortune." So the king, vexed with himself for having been thus deluded, hushed up all. But Statira both in other matters openly opposed her, and was angry with her for thus, against all law and humanity, sacrificing to the memory of Cyrus the king's faithful friend and eunuch.

Now after that Tisaphernes had circumvented and by a false oath had betrayed Clearchus and the other commanders, and, taking them, had sent them bound in chains to the king, Ctesias says that he was asked by Clearchus to supply him with a comb; and that when he had it, and had combed his head with it, he was much pleased with this good office, and gave him a ring, which might be a token of the obligation to his relatives and friends in Sparta; and that the engraving upon this signet was a set of Caryatides dancing. He tells us that the soldiers, his fellow-captives, used to purloin a part of the allowance of food sent to Clearchus, giving him but little of it; which thing Ctesias says he rectified, causing a better allowance to be conveyed to him, and that a separate share should be distributed to the soldiers by themselves; adding that he ministered to and supplied him thus by the interest and at the instance of Parysatis. And there being a portion of ham sent daily with his other food to Clearchus, she, he says, advised and instructed him, that he ought to bury a small knife in the meat, and thus send it to his friend, and not leave his fate to be determined by the king's cruelty; which he, however, he says, was afraid to do. However, Artaxerxes consented to the entreaties of his mother, and promised her with an oath that he would spare Clearchus; but afterwards, at the instigation of Statira, he put every one of them to death except Menon. And thenceforward, he says, Parysatis watched her advantage against Statira and made up poison for her; not a very probable story, or a very likely motive to account for her conduct, if indeed he means that out of respect to Clearchus she dared to attempt the life of the lawful queen, that was mother of those who were heirs of the empire. But it is evident enough, that this part of his history is a sort of funeral exhibition in honour of Clearchus. For he would have us believe that, when the generals were executed, the rest of them were torn in pieces by dogs and birds; but as for the remains of Clearchus, that a violent gust of wind bearing before it a vast heap of earth, raised a mound to cover his body, upon which, after a short time, some dates having fallen there, a beautiful grove of trees grew up and overshadowed the place, so that the king himself declared his sorrow, concluding that in Clearchus he put to death a man beloved of the gods.

Parysatis, therefore, having from the first entertained a secret hatred and jealousy against Statira, seeing that the power she herself had with Artaxerxes was founded upon feelings of honour and respect for her, but that Statira's influence was firmly and strongly based upon love and confidence, was resolved to contrive her ruin, playing at hazard, as she thought, for the greatest stake in the world. Among her attendant women there was one that was trusty and in the highest esteem with her, whose name was Gigis; who, as Dinon avers, assisted in making up the poison. Ctesias allows her only to have been conscious of it, and that against her will; charging Belitaras with actually giving the drug, whereas Dinon says it was Melantas. The two women had begun again to visit each other and to eat together; but though they had thus far relaxed their former habits of jealousy and variance, still, out of fear and as a matter of caution, they always ate of the same dishes and of the same parts of them. Now there is a small Persian bird, in the inside of which no excrement is found, only a mass of fat, so that they suppose the little creatures lives upon air and dew. It is called *rhyntaces.* Ctesias affirms, that Parysatis, cutting a bird of this kind into two pieces with a knife one side of which had been smeared with the drug, the other side being clear of it, ate the untouched and wholesome part herself, and gave Statira that which was thus infected; but Dinon will not have it to be Parysatis, but Melantas, that cut up the bird and presented the envenomed part of it to Statira, who, dying with dreadful agonies and convulsions, was herself sensible of what had happened to her, and aroused in the king's mind suspicion of his mother, whose savage and implacable temper he knew. And therefore proceeding instantly to an inquest, he seized upon his mother's domestic servants that attended at her table and put them upon the rack. Parysatis kept Gigis at home with her a long time, and though the king commanded her, she would not produce her. But she, at last herself desiring that she might be dismissed to her own home by night, Artaxerxes had intimation of it, and lying in wait for her, hurried her away, and adjudged her to death. Now poisoners in Persia suffer thus by law. There is a broad stone, on which they place the head of the culprit, and then with another stone beat and press it, until the face and the head itself are all pounded to pieces; which was the punishment Gigis lost her life by. But to his mother, Artaxerxes neither said nor did any other hurt, save that he banished and confined her, not much against her will, to Babylon, protesting that while she lived he would not come near that city. Such was the condition of the king's affairs in his own house.

But when all his attempts to capture the Greeks that had come with Cyrus, though he desired to do so no less than he had desired to overcome Cyrus and maintain his throne, proved unlucky, and they, though they had lost both Cyrus and their own generals, nevertheless escaped, as it were, out of his very palace, making it plain to all men that the Persian king and his empire were mighty indeed in gold and luxury and women, but otherwise were a mere show and vain display, upon this all Greece took courage and despised the barbarians; and especially the Lacedæmonians thought it strange if they should not now deliver their countrymen that dwelt in Asia from their subjection to the Persians, nor put an end to the contumelious usage of them. And first having an army under the conduct of Thimbron, then under Dercyllidas, but doing nothing memorable, they at last committed the war to the management of their King Agesilaus, who, when he had arrived with his men in Asia, as soon as he had landed them, fell actively to work, and got himself great renown. He defeated Tisaphernes in a pitched battle, and set many cities in revolt. Upon this, Artaxerxes, perceiving what was his wisest way of waging the war, sent Timocrates the Rhodian into Greece, with large sums of gold, commanding him by a free distribution of it to corrupt the leading men in the cities, and to excite a Greek war against Sparta. So Timocrates following his instructions, the most considerable cities conspiring together, and Peloponnesus being in disorder, the ephors remanded Agesilaus from Asia. At which time, they say, as he was upon his return, he told his friends that Artaxerxes had driven him out of Asia with thirty thousand archers; the Persian coin having an archer stamped upon it.

Artaxerxes scoured the seas, too, of the Lacedæmonians, Conon the Athenian and Pharnabazus being his admirals. For Conon, after the battle of Ægospotami, resided in Cyprus; not that he consulted his own mere security, but looking for a vicissitude of affairs with no less hope than men wait for a change of wind at sea. And perceiving that his skill wanted power, and that the king's power wanted a wise man to guide it, he sent him an account of his projects, and charged the bearer to hand it to the king, if possible, by the mediation of Zeno the Cretan or Polycritus the Mendæan (the former being a dancing-master, the latter a physician), or, in the absence of them both, by Ctesias; who is said to have taken Conon's letter, and foisted into the contents of it a request, that the king would also be pleased to send over Ctesias to him, who was likely to be of use on the sea-coast. Ctesias, however, declares that the king, of his accord, deputed him to his service. Artaxerxes, however, defeating the Lacedæmonians in a sea-fight at Cnidos, under the conduct of Pharnabazus and Conon, after he had stripped them of their sovereignty by sea, at the same time brought, so to say, the whole of Greece over to him, so that upon his own terms he dictated the celebrated peace among them, styled the peace of Antalcidas. This Antalcidas was a Spartan, the son of one Leon, who, acting for the king's interest, induced the Lacadæmonians to covenant to let all the Greek cities in Asia and the islands adjacent to it become subject and tributary to him, peace being upon these conditions established among the Greeks, if indeed the honourable name of peace can fairly be given to what was in fact the disgrace and betrayal of Greece, a treaty more inglorious than had ever been the result of any war to those defeated in it.

And therefore Artaxerxes, though always abominating other Spartans; and looking upon them, as Dinon says, to be the most impudent men living, gave wonderful honour to Antalcidas when he came to him into Persia; so much so that one day, taking a garland of flowers and dipping it in the most precious ointment, he sent it to him after supper, a favour which all were amazed at. Indeed he was a person fit to be thus delicately treated and to have such a crown, who had among the Persians thus made fools of Leonidas and Callicratidas. Agesilaus, it seems, on some one having said "O the deplorable fate of Greece, now that the Spartans turn Medes!" replied, "Nay, rather it is the Medes who become Spartans." But the subtlety of the repartee did not wipe off the infamy of the action. The Lacedæmonians soon after lost their sovereignty in Greece by their defeat at Leuctra; but they had already lost their honour by this treaty. So long then as Sparta continued to be the first state in Greece, Artaxerxes continued to Antalcidas the honour of being called his friend and his guest; but when, routed and humbled at the battle of Leuctra, being under great distress for money, they had despatched Agesilaus into Egypt, and Antalcidas went up to Artaxerxes, beseeching him to supply their necessities, he so despised, slighted, and rejected him, that finding himself, on his return, mocked and insulted by his enemies, and fearing also the ephors, he starved himself to death. Ismenias, also, the Theban, and Pelopidas, who had already gained the victory at Leuctra, arrived at the Persian court; where the latter did nothing unworthy of himself. But Ismenias, being commanded to do obeisance to the king, dropped his ring before him upon the ground, and so, stooping to take it up, made a show of doing him homage. He was so gratified with some secret intelligence which Timagoras the Athenian sent in to him by the hand of his secretary Beluris, that he bestowed upon him ten thousand darics, and because he was ordered, on account of some sickness, to drink cow's milk, there were fourscore milch kine driven after him; also, he sent him a bed, furniture, and servants for it, the Grecians not having skill enough to make it, as also chairmen to carry him, being infirm in body, to the seaside. Not to mention the feast made for him at court, which was so princely and splendid that Ostanes, the king's brother, said to him, "O Timagoras, do not forget the sumptuous table you have sat at here; it was not put before you for nothing;" which was indeed rather a reflection upon his treason than to remind him of the king's bounty. And indeed the Athenians condemned Timagoras to death for taking bribes.

But Artaxerxes gratified the Grecians in one thing in lieu of the many wherewith he plagued them, and that was by taking off Tisaphernes, their most hated and malicious enemy, whom he put to death; Parysatis adding her influence to the charges made against him. For the king did not persist long in his wrath with his mother, but was reconciled to her, and sent for her, being assured that she had wisdom and courage fit for royal power, and there being now no cause discernible but that they might converse together without suspicion or offence. And from thenceforward humouring the king in all things according to his heart's desire, and finding fault with nothing that he did, she obtained great power with him, and was gratified in all her requests. She perceived he was desperately in love with Atossa, one of his own two daughters, and that he concealed and checked his passion chiefly for fear of herself, though, if we may believe some writers, he had privately given way to it with the young girl already. As soon as Parysatis suspected it, she displayed a greater fondness for the young girl than before, and extolled both her virtue and beauty to him, as being truly imperial and majestic. In fine she persuaded him to marry her and declare her to be his lawful wife, overriding all the principles and the laws by which the Greeks hold themselves bound, and regarding himself as divinely appointed for a law to the Persians, and the supreme arbitrator of good and evil. Some historians further affirm, in which number is Heraclides of Cuma, that Artaxerxes married not only this one, but a second daughter also, Amestris, of whom we shall speak by and by. But he so loved Atossa when she became his consort, that when leprosy had run through her whole body, he was not in the least offended at it; but putting up his prayers to Juno for her, to this one alone of all the deities he made obeisance, by laying his hands upon the earth; and his satraps and favourites made such offerings to the goddess by his direction, that all along for sixteen furlongs, betwixt the court and her temple, the road was filled up with gold and silver, purple and horses, devoted to her.

He waged war out of his own kingdom with the Egyptians, under the conduct of Pharnabazus and Iphicrates, but was unsuccessful by reason of their dissensions. In his expedition against the Cadusians, he went himself in person with three hundred thousand footmen and ten thousand horse, and making an incursion into their country, which was so mountainous as scarcely to be passable, and withal very misty, producing no sort of harvest of corn or the like, but with pears, apples, and other treefruits feeding a war-like and valiant breed of men, he unawares fell into great distresses and dangers. For there was nothing to be got, fit for his men to eat, of the growth of that place, nor could anything be imported from any other. All they could do was to kill their beasts of burden, and thus an ass's head could scarcely be bought for sixty drachmas. In short, the king's own table failed; and there were but few horses left; the rest they had spent for food. Then Teribazus, a man often in great favour with his prince for his valour and as often out of it for his buffoonery, and particularly at that time in humble estate and neglected, was the deliverer of the king and his army. There being two kings amongst the Cadusians, and each of them encamping separately, Teribazus, after he had made his application to Artaxerxes and imparted his design to him, went to one of the princes, and sent away his son privately to the other. So each of them deceived his man, assuring him that the other prince had deputed an ambassador to Artaxerxes, suing for friendship and alliance for himself alone; and, therefore, if he were wise, he told him, he must apply himself to his master before he had decreed anything, and he, he said, would lend him his assistance in all things. Both of them gave credit to these words, and because they supposed they were each intrigued against by the other, they both sent their envoys, one along with Teribazus, and the other with his son. All this taking some time to transact, fresh surmises and suspicions of Teribazus were expressed to the king, who began to be out of heart, sorry that he had confided in him, and ready to give ear to his rivals who impeached him. But at last he came, and so did his son, bringing the Cadusian agents along with them, and so there was a cessation of arms and a peace signed with both the princes. And Teribazus, in great honour and distinction, set out homewards in the company of the king; who, indeed, upon this journey made it appear plainly that cowardice and effeminacy are the effects, not of delicate and sumptuous living, as many suppose, but of a base and vicious nature, actuated by false and bad opinions. For notwithstanding his golden ornaments, his robe of state, and the rest of that costly attire, worth no less than twelve thousand talents, with which the royal person was constantly clad, his labours and toils were not a whit inferior to those of the meanest persons in his army. With his quiver by his side and his shield on his arm, he led them on foot, quitting his horse, through craggy and steep ways, insomuch that the sight of his cheerfulness and unwearied strength gave wings to the soldiers, and so lightened the journey, that they made daily marches of above two hundred furlongs.

After they had arrived at one of his own mansions, which had beautiful ornamented parks in the midst of a region naked and without trees, the weather being very cold, he gave full commission to his soldiers to provide themselves with wood by cutting down any, without exception, even the pine and cypress. And when they hesitated and were for sparing them, being large and goodly trees, he, taking up an axe himself, felled the greatest and most beautiful of them. After which his men used their hatchets, and piling up many fires, passed away the night at their ease. Nevertheless, he returned not without the loss of many and valiant subjects, and of almost all his horses. And supposing that his misfortunes and the ill-success of his expedition made him despised in the eyes of his people, he looked jealously on his nobles, many of whom he slew in anger, and yet more out of fear. As, indeed, fear is the bloodiest passion in princes; confidence, on the other hand, being merciful, gentle, and unsuspicious. So we see among wild beasts, the intractable and least tamable are the most timorous and most easily startled; the nobler creatures, whose courage makes them trustful, are ready to respond to the advances of men.

Artaxerxes, now being an old man, perceived that his sons were in controversy about his kingdom, and that they made parties among his favourites and peers. Those that were equitable among them thought it fit, that as he had received it, so he should bequeath it, by right of age, to Darius. The younger brother, Ochus, who was hot and violent, had indeed a considerable number of the courtiers that espoused his interest, but his chief hope was that by Atossa's means he should win his father. For he flattered her with the thoughts of being his wife and partner in the kingdom after the death of Artaxerxes. And truly it was rumoured that already Ochus maintained a too intimate correspondence with her. This, however, was quite unknown to the king; who, being willing to put down in good time his son Ochus's hopes, lest, by his attempting the same things his uncle Cyrus did, wars and contentions might again afflict his kingdom, proclaimed Darius, then twenty-five years old, his successor, and gave him leave to wear the upright hat, as they called it. It was a rule and usage of Persia, that the heir apparent to the crown should beg a boon, and that he that declared him so should give whatever he asked, provided it were within the sphere of his power. Darius therefore requested Aspasia, in former time the most prized of the concubines of Cyrus, and now belonging to the king. She was by birth a Phocæan, of Ionia, born of free parents, and well educated. Once when Cyrus was at supper, she was led in to him with other women, who, when they were sat down by him, and he began to sport and dally and talk jestingly with them, gave way freely to his advances. But she stood by in silence, refusing to come when Cyrus called her, and when his chamberlains were going to force her towards him, said, "Whosoever lays hands on me shall rue it;" so that she seemed to the company a sullen and rude-mannered person. However, Cyrus was well pleased, and laughed, saying to the man that brought the women, "Do you not see to a certainty that this woman alone of all that came with you is truly noble and pure in character?" After which time he began to regard her, and loved her, above all of her sex, and called her the Wise. But Cyrus being slain in the fight, she was taken among the spoils of his camp.

Darius, in demanding her, no doubt much offended his father, for the barbarian people keep a very jealous and watchful eye over their carnal pleasures, so that it is death for a man not only to come near and touch any concubine of his prince, but likewise on a journey to ride forward and pass by the carriages in which they are conveyed. And though, to gratify his passion, he had against all law married his daughter Atossa, and had besides her no less than three hundred and sixty concubines selected for their beauty, yet being importuned for that one by Darius, he urged that she was a free-woman, and allowed him to take her, if she had an inclination to go with him, but by no means to force her away against it. Aspasia, therefore, being sent for, and, contrary to the king's expectation, making choice of Darius, he gave him her indeed, being constrained by law, but when he had done so, a little after he took her from him. For he consecrated her priestess to Diana of Ecbatana, whom they name Anaitis, that she might spend the remainder of her days in strict chastity, thinking thus to punish his son, not rigorously, but with moderation, by a revenge checkered with jest and earnest. But he took it heinously, either that he was passionately fond of Aspasia, or because he looked upon himself as affronted and scorned by his father. Teribazus, perceiving him thus minded, did his best to exasperate him yet further, seeing in his injuries a representation of his own, of which the following is the account: Artaxerxes, having many daughters, promised to give Apama to Pharnabazus to wife, Rhodogune to Orontes, and Amestris to Teribazus; whom alone of the three he disappointed, by marrying Amestris himself. However, to make him amends, he betrothed his youngest daughter Atossa to him. But after he had, being enamoured of her too, as has been said, married her, Teribazus entertained an irreconcilable enmity against him. As indeed he was seldom at any other time steady in his temper, but uneven and inconsiderate; so that whether he were in the number of the choicest favourites of his prince, or whether he were offensive and odious to him, he demeaned himself in neither condition with moderation, but if he was advanced he was intolerably insolent, and in his degradation not submissive and peaceable in his deportment, but fierce and haughty.

And therefore Teribazus was to the young prince flame added upon flame, ever urging him, and saying, that in vain those wear their hats upright who consult not the real success of their affairs, and that he was ill-befriended of reason if he imagined, whilst he had a brother, who, through the women's apartments, was seeking a way to the supremacy, and a father of so rash and fickle a humour, that he should by succession infallibly step up into the throne. For he that out of fondness to an Ionian girl has eluded a law sacred and inviolable among the Persians is not likely to be faithful in the performance of the most important promises. He added, too, that it was not all one for Ochus not to attain to, and for him to be put by his crown; since Ochus as a subject might live happily, and nobody could hinder him; but he, being proclaimed king, must either take up his sceptre or lay down his life. These words presently inflamed Darius: what Sophocles says being indeed generally true:—

"Quick travels the persuasion to what's wrong."

For the path is smooth, and upon an easy descent, that leads us to our own will; and the most part of us desire what is evil through our strangeness to and ignorance of good. And in this case, no doubt, the greatness of the empire and the jealousy Darius had of Ochus furnished Teribazus with material for his persuasions. Nor was Venus wholly unconcerned in the matter, in regard, namely, of his loss of Aspasia.

Darius, therefore, resigned himself up to the dictates of Teribazus; and many now conspiring with them, a eunuch gave information to the king of their plot and the way how it was to be managed, having discovered the certainty of it, that they had resolved to break into his bed-chamber by night, and there to kill him as he lay. After Artaxerxes had been thus advertised, he did not think fit, by disregarding the discovery, to despise so great a danger, nor to believe it when there was little or no proof of it. Thus then he did: he charged the eunuch constantly to attend and accompany the conspirators wherever they were; in the meanwhile, he broke down the party-wall of the chamber behind his bed, and placed a door in it to open and shut, which he covered up with tapestry; so the hour approaching, and the eunuch having told him the precise time in which the traitors designed to assassinate him, he waited for them in his bed, and rose not up till he had seen the faces of his assailants and recognised every man of them. But as soon as he saw them with their swords drawn and coming up to him, throwing up the hanging, he made his retreat into the inner chamber, and, bolting the door, raised a cry. Thus when the murderers had been seen by him, and had attempted him in vain, they with speed went back through the same doors they came in by, enjoining Teribazus and his friends to fly, as their plot had been certainly detected. They, therefore, made their escape different ways; but Teribazus was seized by the king's guards, and after slaying many, while they were laying hold on him, at length being struck through with a dart at a distance, fell. As for Darius, who was brought to trial with his children, the king appointed the royal judges to sit over him, and because he was not himself present, but accused Darius by proxy, he commanded his scribes to write down the opinion of every one of the judges, and show it to him. And after they had given their sentences, all as one man, and condemned Darius to death, the officers seized on him, and hurried him to a chamber not far off. To which place the executioner, when summoned, came with a razor in his hand, with which men of his employment cut off the heads of offenders. But when he saw that Darius was the person thus to be punished he was appalled and started back, offering to go out, as one that had neither power nor courage enough to behead a king; yet at the threats and commands of the judges who stood at the prison door, he returned and grasping the hair of his head and bringing his face to the ground with one hand, he cut through his neck with the razor he had in the other. Some affirm that sentence was passed in the presence of Artaxerxes; that Darius, after he had been convicted by clear evidence, falling prostrate before him, did humbly beg his pardon; that instead of giving it, he rising up in rage and drawing his scymetar, smote him till he had killed him; and then, going forth into the court, he worshipped the sun, and said, "Depart in peace, ye Persians, and declare to your fellow-subjects how the mighty Oromasdes hath dealt out vengeance to the contrivers of unjust and unlawful things."

Such, then, was the issue of this conspiracy. And now Ochus was high in his hopes, being confident in the influence of Atossa; but yet was afraid of Ariaspes, the only male surviving, besides himself, of the legitimate offspring of his father, and of Arsames, one of his natural sons. For indeed Ariaspes was already claimed as their prince by the wishes of the Persians, not because he was the elder brother, but because he excelled Ochus in gentleness, plain dealing, and good-nature; and on the other hand Arsames appeared, by his wisdom, fitted for the throne, and that he was dear to his father Ochus well knew. So he laid snares for them both, and being no less treacherous than bloody, he made use of the cruelty of his nature against Arsames, and of his craft and wiliness against Ariaspes. For he suborned the king's eunuchs and favourites to convey to him menacing and harsh expressions from his father, as though he had decreed to put him to a cruel and ignominious death. When they daily communicated these things as secrets, and told him at one time that the king would do so to him ere long, and at another, that the blow was actually close impending, they so alarmed the young man, struck such a terror into him, and cast such a confusion and anxiety upon his thoughts, that, having prepared some poisonous drugs, he drank them, that he might be delivered from his life. The king, on hearing what kind of death he died, heartily lamented him, and was not without a suspicion of the cause of it. But being disabled by his age to search into and prove it, he was, after the loss of this son, more affectionate than before to Arsames, did manifestly place his greatest confidence in him, and made him privy to his counsels. Whereupon Ochus had no longer patience to defer the execution of his purpose, but having procured Arpates, Teribazus's son, for the undertaking, he killed Arsames by his hand. Artaxerxes at that time had but a little hold on life, by reason of his extreme age, and so, when he heard of the fate of Arsames, he could not sustain it at all, but sinking at once under the weight of his grief and distress, expired, after a life of ninety-four years, and a reign of sixty-two. And then he seemed a moderate and gracious governor, more especially as compared to his son Ochus, who outdid all his predecessors in blood-thirstiness and cruelty.

GALBA

IPHICRATES the Athenian used to say that it is best to have a mercenary soldier fond of money and of pleasures, for thus he will fight the more boldly, to procure the means to gratify his desires. But most have been of opinion, that the body of an army, as well as the natural one, when in its healthy condition, should make no efforts apart, but in compliance with its head. Wherefore they tell us that Paulus Æmilius, on taking command of the forces in Macedonia, and finding them talkative and impertinently busy, as though they were all commanders, issued out his orders that they should have only ready hands and keen swords, and leave the rest to him. And Plato, who can discern no use of a good ruler or general if his men are not on their part obedient and conformable (the virtue of obeying, as of ruling, being, in his opinion, one that does not exist without first a noble nature, and then a philosophic education, where the eager and active powers are allayed with the gentler and humaner sentiments), may claim in confirmation of his doctrine sundry mournful instances elsewhere, and, in particular, the events that followed among the Romans upon the death of Nero, in which plain proofs were given that nothing is more terrible than a military force moving about in an empire upon uninstructed and unreasoning impulses. Demades, after the death of Alexander, compared the

Macedonian army to the Cyclops after his eye was out, seeing their many disorderly and unsteady motions. But the calamities of the Roman government might be likened to the motions of the giants that assailed heaven, convulsed as it was, and distracted, and from every side recoiling, as it were, upon itself, not so much by the ambition of those who were proclaimed emperors, as by the covetousness and licence of the soldiery, who drove commander after commander out, like nails one upon another.

Dionysius, in raillery, said of the Pheræan who enjoyed the government of Thessaly only ten months, that he had been a tragedy-king, but the Cæsars' house in Rome, the Palatium, received in a shorter space of time no less than four emperors, passing, as it were, across the stage, and one making room for another to enter.

This was the only satisfaction of the distressed, that they need not require any other justice on their oppressors, seeing them thus murder each other, and first of all, and that most justly, the one that ensnared them first, and taught them to expect such happy results from a change of emperors, sullying a good word by the pay he gave for its being done and turning revolt against Nero into nothing better than treason.

For, as already related, Nymphidius Sabinus, captain of the guards, together with Tigellinus, after Nero's circumstances were now desperate, and it was perceived that he designed to fly into Egypt, persuaded the troops to declare Galba emperor, as if Nero had been already gone, promising to all the court and prætorian soldiers, as they are called, seven thousand five hundred drachmas apiece, and to those in service abroad twelve hundred and fifty drachmas each; so vast a sum for a largess as it was impossible any one could raise, but he must be infinitely more exacting and oppressive than ever Nero was. This quickly brought Nero to his grave, and soon after Galba too; they murdered the first in expectation of the promised gift, and not long after the other because they did not obtain it from him; and then, seeking about to find some one who would purchase at such a rate, they consumed themselves in a succession of treacheries and rebellions before they obtained their demands. But to give a particular relation of all that passed would require a history in full form; I have only to notice what is properly to my purpose, namely, what the Cæsars did and suffered.

Sulpicius Galba is owned by all to have been the richest private person that ever came to the imperial seat. And besides the additional honour of being of the Servii, he valued himself more especially for his relationship to Catulus, the most eminent citizen of his time both for virtue and renown, however he may have voluntarily yielded to others as regards power and authority. Galba was also akin to Livia, the wife of Augustus, by whose interest he was preferred to the consulship by the emperor. It is said of him that he commanded the troops well in Germany, and, being made proconsul in Libya, gained a reputation that few ever had. But his quiet manner of living and his sparingness in expenses and his disregard of appearances gave him, when he became emperor, an ill-name for meanness, being, in fact, his worn-out credit for regularity and moderation. He was entrusted by Nero with the government of Spain, before Nero had yet learned to be apprehensive of men of great repute. To the opinion, moreover, entertained of his mild natural temper, his old age added a belief that he would never act incautiously. There while Nero's iniquitous agents savagely and cruelly harassed the provinces under Nero's authority, he could afford no succour, but merely offer this only ease and consolation, that he seemed plainly to sympathise, as a fellow-sufferer, with those who were condemned upon suits and sold. And when lampoons were made upon Nero and circulated and sung everywhere about, he neither prohibited them, nor showed any indignation on behalf of the emperor's agents, and for this was the more beloved; as also that he was now well acquainted with them, having been in chief power there eight years at the time when Junius Vindex, general of the forces in Gaul, began his insurrection against Nero. And it is reported that letters came to Galba before it fully broke out into an open rebellion, which he neither seemed to give credit to, nor on the other hand to take means to let Nero know; as other officers did, sending to him the letters which came to them, and so spoiled the design, as much as in them lay, who yet afterwards shared in the conspiracy, and confessed they had been treacherous to themselves as well as him. At last Vindex, plainly declaring war, wrote to Galba, encouraging him to take the government upon him, and give a head to this strong body, the Gaulish provinces, which could already count a hundred thousand men in arms, and were able to arm a yet greater number if occasion were. Galba laid the matter before his friends, some of whom thought it fit to wait, and see what movement there might be and what inclinations displayed at Rome for the revolution. But Titus Vinius, captain of his prætorian guard, spoke thus: "Galba, what means this inquiry? To question whether we shall continue faithful to Nero is, in itself, to cease to be faithful. Nero is our enemy, and we must by no means decline the help of Vindex: or else we must at once denounce him, and march to attack him, because he wishes you to be the governor of the Romans, rather than Nero their tyrant." Thereupon Galba, by an edict, appointed a day when he would receive manumissions, and general rumour and talk beforehand about his purpose brought together a great crowd of men so ready for a change, that he scarcely appeared, stepping up to the tribunal, but they with one consent saluted him emperor. That title he refused at present to take upon him; but after he had a while inveighed against Nero, and bemoaned the loss of the more conspicuous of those that had been destroyed by him, he offered himself and service to his country, not by the titles of Cæsar or emperor, but as the lieutenant of the Roman senate and people.

Now that Vindex did wisely in inviting Galba to the empire, Nero himself bore testimony; who, though he seemed to despise Vindex and altogether to slight the Gauls and their concerns, yet when he heard of Galba (as by chance he had just bathed and sat down to his morning meal), at this news he overturned the table. But the senate having voted Galba an enemy, presently, to make his jest, and likewise to personate a confidence among his friends, "This is a very happy opportunity," he said, "for me, who sadly want such a booty as that of the Gauls, which must all fall in as lawful prize; and Galba's estate I can use or sell at once, he being now an open enemy." And accordingly he had Galba's property exposed to sale, which when Galba heard of, he sequestered all that was Nero's in Spain, and found far readier bidders.

Many now began to revolt from Nero, and pretty nearly all adhered to Galba; only Clodius Macer in Africa, and Virginius Rufus, commander of the German forces in Gaul, followed counsel of their own; yet these two were not of one and the same advice, for Clodius, being sensible of the rapines and murders to which he had been led by cruelty and covetousness, was in perplexity, and felt it was not safe for him either to retain or quit his command. But Virginius, who had the command of the strongest legions, by whom he was many repeated times saluted emperor and pressed to take the title upon him, declared that he neither would assume that honour himself, nor see it given to any other than whom the senate should elect.

These things at first did not a little disturb Galba, but when presently Virginius and Vindex were in a manner forced by their armies, having got the reins, as it were, out of their hands, to a great encounter and battle, in which Vindex, having seen twenty thousand of the Gauls destroyed, died by his own hand, and when the report straight spread abroad, that all desired Virginius, after this great victory, to take the empire upon him, or else they would return to Nero again, Galba, in great alarm at this, wrote to Virginius, exhorting him to join with him for the preservation of the empire and the liberty of the Romans, and so retiring with his friends into Clunia, a town in Spain, he passed away his time, rather repenting his former rashness, and wishing for his wonted ease and privacy, than setting about what was fit to be done.

It was now summer, when on a sudden, a little before dusk, comes a freedman, Icelus by name, having arrived in seven days from Rome; and being informed where Galba was reposing himself in private, he went straight on, and pushing by the servants of the chamber, opened the door and entered the room, and told him, that Nero being yet alive but not appearing, first the army, and then the people and senate, declared Galba emperor; not long after, it was reported that Nero was dead; "but I," said he, "not giving credit to common fame, went myself to the body and saw him lying dead, and only then set out to bring you word." This news at once made Galba great again, and a crowd of people came hastening to the door, all very confident of the truth of his tidings, though the speed of the man was almost incredible. Two days after came Titus Vinius with sundry others from the camp, who gave an account in detail of the orders of the senate, and for this service was considerably advanced. On the freedman, Galba conferred the honour of the gold ring, and Icelus, as he had been before, now taking the name of Marcianus, held the first place of the freedmen.

But at Rome, Nymphidius Sabinus, not gently, and little by little, but at once, and without exception, engrossed all power to himself; Galba, being an old man (seventy-three years of age), would scarcely, he thought, live long enough to be carried in a litter to Rome; and the troops in the city were from old time attached to him, and now bound by the vastness of the promised gift, for which they regarded him as their benefactor, and Galba as their debtor. Thus presuming on his interest, he straightway commanded Tigellinus, who was in joint commission with himself, to lay down his sword; and giving entertainments, he invited the former consuls and commanders, making use of Galba's name for the invitation; but at the same time prepared many in the camp to propose that a request should be sent to Galba that he should appoint Nymphidius sole prefect for life without a colleague. And the modes which the senate took to show him honour and increase his power, styling him their benefactor, and attending daily at his gates, and giving him the compliment of heading with his own name and confirming all their acts, carried him on to a yet greater degree of arrogance, so that in a short time he became an object, not only of dislike, but of terror, to those that sought his favour. When the consuls themselves had despatched their couriers with the decrees of the senate to the emperor, together with the sealed diplomas, which the authorities in all the towns where horses or carriages are changed look at, and on that certificate hasten the courtiers forward with all their means, he was highly displeased that his seal had not been used, and none of his soldiers employed on the errand. Nay, he even deliberated what course to take with the consuls themselves, but upon their submission and apology he was at last pacified. To gratify the people, he did not interfere with their beating to death any that fell into their hands of Nero's party. Amongst others, Spiclus, the gladiator, was killed in the forum by being thrown under Nero's statues, which they dragged about the place over his body. Aponius, one of those who had been concerned in accusations, they knocked to the ground, and drove carts loaded with stones over him. And many others they tore in pieces, some of them no way guilty, insomuch that Mauriscus, a person of great account and character, told the senate that he feared, in a short time, they might wish for Nero again.

Nymphidius, now advancing towards the consummation of his hopes, did not refuse to let it be said that he was the son of Caius Cæsar, Tiberius's successor; who, it is told, was well acquainted with his mother in his early youth, a woman indeed handsome enough, the offspring of Callistus, one of Cæsar's freedmen, and a certain sempstress. But it is plain that Caius's familiarity with his mother was of too late date to give him any pretensions, and it was suspected he might, if he pleased, claim a father in Martianus, the gladiator, whom his mother, Nymphidia, took a passion for, being a famous man in his way, whom also he much more resembled. However, though he certainly owned Nymphidia for his mother, he ascribed meantime the downfall of Nero to himself alone, and thought he was not sufficiently rewarded with the honours and riches he enjoyed (nay, though to all was added the company of Sporus, whom he immediately sent for while Nero's body was yet burning on the pile, and treated as his consort with the name of Poppæa), but he must also aspire to the empire. And at Rome he had friends who took measures for him secretly, as well as some women and some members of the senate also, who worked underhand to assist him. And into Spain he despatched one of his friends, named Gellianus, to view the posture of affairs.

But all things succeeded well with Galba after Nero's death; only Virginius Rufus, still standing doubtful, gave him some anxiety, lest he should listen to the suggestions of some who encouraged him to take the government upon him, having, at present, besides the command of a large and warlike army, the new honours of the defeat of Vindex and the subjugation of one considerable part of the Roman empire, namely, the entire Gaul, which had seemed shaking about upon the verge of open revolt. Nor had any man indeed a greater name and reputation than Virginius, who had taken a part of so much consequence in the deliverance of the empire at once from a cruel tyranny and a Gallic war. But he, standing to his first resolves, reserved to the senate the power of electing an emperor. Yet when it was now manifest that Nero was dead, the soldiers pressed him hard to it, and one of the tribunes, entering his tent with his drawn sword, bade him either take the government or that. But after Fabius Valens, having the command of one legion, had first sworn fealty to Galba, and letters from Rome came with tidings of the resolves of the senate, at last with much ado he persuaded the army to declare Galba emperor. And when Flaccus Hordeonius came by Galba's commission as his successor, he handed over to him his forces, and went himself to meet Galba on his way, and having met him turned back to attend him; in all which no apparent displeasure nor yet honour was shown him. Galba's feelings of respect for him prevented the former; the latter was checked by the envy of his friends, and particularly of Titus Vinius, who, acting in the desire of hindering Virginius's promotion, unwittingly aided his happy genius in rescuing him from those hazards and hardships which other commanders were involved in, and securing him the safe enjoyment of a quiet life and peaceable old age.

Near Narbo, a city in Gaul, the deputation of the senate met Galba, and after they had delivered their compliments, begged him to make what haste he could to appear to the people that impatiently expected him. He discoursed with them courteously and unassumingly, and in his entertainment, though Nymphidius had sent him royal furniture and attendance of Nero's, he put all aside, and made use of nothing but his own, for which he was well spoken of, as one who had a great mind, and was superior to little vanities. But in a short time, Vinius, by declaring to him that these noble, unpompous, citizen-like ways were a mere affectation of popularity and a petty bashfulness at assuming his proper greatness, induced him to make use of Nero's supplies, and in his entertainments not to be afraid of a regal sumptuosity. And in more than one way the old man let it gradually appear that he had put himself under Vinius's disposal.

Vinius was a person of an excessive covetousness, and not quite free from blame in respect to women. For being a young man, newly entered into the service under Calvisius Sabinus, upon his first campaign, he brought his commander's wife, a licentious woman, in a soldier's dress, by night into the camp, and was found with her in the very general's quarters, the *principia*, as the Romans call them. For which insolence Caius Cæsar cast him into prison, from whence he was fortunately delivered by Caius's death. Afterwards, being invited by Claudius Cæsar to supper, he privily conveyed away a silver cup, which Cæsar hearing of, invited him again the next day, and gave order to his servants to set before him no silver plate, but only earthenware. And this offence, through the comic mildness of Cæsar's reprimand, was treated rather as a subject of jest than as a crime. But the acts to which now, when Galba was in his hands and his power was so extensive, his covetous temper led him were the causes, in part, and in part the provocation, of tragical and fatal mischiefs.

Nymphidius became very uneasy upon the return out of Spain of Gellianus, whom he had sent to pry into Galba's actions, understanding that Cornelius Laco was appointed commander of the court guards, and that

Vinius was the great favourite, and that Gellianus had not been able so much as to come nigh, much less have any opportunity to offer any words in private, so narrowly had he been watched and observed. Nymphidius, therefore, called together the officers of the troops, and declared to them that Galba of himself was a good, well-meaning old man, but did not act by his own counsel, and was ill-guided by Vinius and Laco; and lest, before they were aware, they should engross the authority Tigellinus had with the troops, he proposed to them to send deputies from the camp, acquainting him that if he pleased to remove only these two from his counsel and presence, he would be much more welcome to all at his arrival. Wherein, when he saw he did not prevail (it seeming absurd and unmannerly to give rules to an old commander what friends to retain or displace, as if he had been a youth newly taking the reins of authority into his hands), adopting another course, he wrote himself to Galba letters in alarming terms, one while as if the city were unsettled, and had not yet recovered its tranquillity; then that Clodius Macer withheld the cornships from Africa; that the legions in Germany began to be mutinous, and that he heard the like of those in Syria and Judæa. But Galba not minding him much or giving credit to his stories, he resolved to make his attempt beforehand, though Clodius Celsus, a native of Antioch, a person of sense, and friendly and faithful to Nymphidius, told him he was wrong, saying he did not believe one single street in Rome would ever give him the title of Cæsar. Nevertheless many also derided Galba, amongst the rest Mithridates of Pontus, saying, that as soon as this wrinkled, baldheaded man should be seen publicly at Rome, they would think it an utter disgrace even to have had such a Cæsar.

At last it was resolved, about midnight, to bring Nymphidius into the camp, and declare him emperor. But Antonius Honoratus, who was first among the tribunes, summoning together in the evening those under his command, charged himself and them severely with their many and unreasonable turns and alterations, made without any purpose or regard to merit, simply as if some evil genius hurried them from one reason to another. "What though Nero's miscarriages," said he, "gave some colour to your former acts, can you say you have any plea for betraying Galba in the death of a mother, the blood of a wife, or the degradation of the imperial power upon the stage and amongst players? Neither did we desert Nero for all this, until Nymphidius had persuaded us that he had first left us and fled into Egypt. Shall we, therefore, send Galba after, to appease Nero's shade, and, for the sake of making the son of Nymphidia emperor, take off one of Livia's family, as we have already the son of Agrippina? Rather, doing justice on him, let us revenge Nero's death, and show ourselves true and faithful by preserving Galba."

The tribune having ended his harangue, the soldiers assented, and encouraged all they met with to persist in their fidelity to the emperor, and, indeed, brought over the greatest part. But presently hearing a great shout, Nymphidius, imagining, as some say, that the soldiers called for him, or hastening to be in time to check any opposition and gain the doubtful, came on with many lights, carrying in his hand a speech in writing, made by Cingonius Varro, which he had got by heart, to deliver to the soldiers. But seeing the gates of the camp shut up, and large numbers standing armed about the walls, he began to be afraid. Yet drawing nearer he demanded what they meant, and by whose orders they were then in arms; but hearing a general acclamation, all with one consent crying out that Galba was their emperor, advancing towards them, he joined in the cry, and likewise commanded those that followed him to do the same. The guard notwithstanding permitted him to enter the camp only with a few, where he was presently struck with a dart, which Septimius, being before him, received on his shield; others, however, assaulted him with their naked swords, and on his flying, pursued him into a soldier's cabin, where they slew him. And dragging his body thence, they placed a railing about it, and exposed it next day to public view. When Galba heard of the end which Nymphidius had thus come to, he commanded that all his confederates who had not at once killed themselves should immediately be despatched; amongst whom were Cingonius, who made his oration, and Mithridates, formerly mentioned. It was, however, regarded as arbitrary and illegal, and though it might be just, yet by no means popular, to take off men of their rank and equality without a hearing. For every one expected another scheme of government, being deceived, as is usual, by the first plausible pretences; and the death of Petronius Turpilianus, who was of consular dignity, and had remained faithful to Nero, was yet more keenly resented. Indeed, the taking off of Macer in Africa by Trebonius, and Fonteius by Valens in Germany, had a fair pretence, they being dreaded as armed commanders, having their soldiers at their bidding; but why refuse Turpilianus, an old man and unarmed, permission to try to clear himself, if any part of the moderation and equity at first promised were really to come to a performance? Such were the comments to which these actions exposed him. When he came within five-and-twenty furlongs or thereabouts of the city, he happened to light on a disorderly rabble of the seamen, who beset him as he passed. These were they whom Nero made soldiers, forming them into a legion. They so rudely crowded to have their commission confirmed that they did not let Galba either be seen or heard by those that had come out to meet their new emperor; but tumultuously pressed on with loud shouts to have colours to their legion, and quarters assigned them. Galba put them off until another time, which they interpreted as a denial, grew more insolent and mutinous, following and crying out, some with their drawn swords in their hands. Upon seeing which, Galba commanded the horse to ride over them, when they were soon routed, not a man standing his ground, and many of them were slain, both there and in the pursuit; an ill-omen, that Galba should make his first entry through so much blood and among dead bodies. And now he was looked upon with terror and alarm by any one who had entertained contempt of him at the sight of his age and apparent infirmities.

But when he desired presently to let it appear what a change would be made from Nero's profuseness and sumptuosity in giving presents, he much missed his aim, and fell so short of magnificence, that he scarcely came within the limits of decency. When Canus, who was a famous musician, played at supper for him, he expressed his approbation, and bade the bag he brought to him; and taking a few gold pieces, put them in with this remark, that it was out of his own purse, and not on the public account. He ordered the largess which Nero had made to actors and wrestlers and such like to be strictly required again, allowing only the tenth part to be retained; though it turned to very small account, most of those persons expending their daily income as fast as they received it, being rude, improvident livers; upon which he had further inquiry made as to those who had bought or received from them, and called upon these people to refund. The trouble was infinite, the exactions being prosecuted far, touching a great number of persons, bringing disrepute on Galba, and general hatred on Vinius, who made the emperor appear base-hearted and mean to the world, whilst he himself was spending profusely, taking whatever he could get, and selling to any buyer. Hesiod tells us to drink without stinting of—

> "The end and the beginning of the cask."

And Vinius, seeing his patron old and decaying, made the most of what he considered to be at once the first of his fortune and the last of it.

Thus the aged man suffered in two ways, first, through the evil deeds which Vinius did himself, and, next, by his preventing or bringing into disgrace those just acts which he himself designed. Such was the punishing Nero's adherents. When he destroyed the bad, amongst whom were Helius, Polycletus, Petinus, and Patrobius, the people mightily applauded the act, crying out, as they were dragged through the forum, that it was a goodly sight, grateful to the gods themselves, adding, however, that the gods and men alike demanded justice on Tigellinus, the very tutor and prompter of all the tyranny. This good man, however, had taken his measures beforehand, in the shape of a present and a promise to Vinius. Turpilianus could not be allowed to escape with life, though his one and only crime had been that he had not betrayed or shown hatred to such a ruler as Nero. But he who had made Nero what he became, and afterwards deserted and betrayed him whom he had so corrupted, was allowed to survive as an instance that Vinius could do anything, and an advertisement that those that had money to give him need despair of nothing. The people, however, were so possessed with the desire of seeing Tigellinus dragged to execution, that they never ceased to require it at the theatre, and in the race-course, till they were checked by an edict from the emperor himself, announcing that Tigellinus could not live long, being wasted with a consumption, and requesting them not to seek to make his government appear cruel and tyrannical. So the dissatisfied populace were laughed at, and Tigellinus made a splendid feast, and sacrificed in thanksgiving for his deliverance; and after supper, Vinius, rising from the emperor's table, went to revel with Tigellinus, taking his daughter, a widow, with him; to whom Tigellinus presented his compliments, with a gift of twenty-five myriads of money, and bade the superintendent of his concubines take off a rich necklace from her own neck and tie it about hers, the value of it being estimated at fifteen myriads.

After this, even reasonable acts were censured; as, for example, the treatment of the Gauls who had been in the conspiracy with Vindex. For people looked upon their abatement of tribute and admission to citizenship as a piece, not of clemency on the part of Galba, but of money-making on that of Vinius. And thus the mass of the people began to look with dislike upon the government. The soldiers were kept on a while in expectation of the promised donative, supposing that if they did not receive the full, yet they should have at least as much as Nero gave them. But when Galba, on hearing they began to complain, declared greatly, and like a general, that he was used to enlist and not to buy his soldiers, when they heard of this, they conceived an implacable hatred against him; for he did not seem to defraud them merely himself in their present expectations, but to give an ill precedent, and instruct his successors to do the like. This heartburning, however, was as yet at Rome a thing undeclared, and a certain respect for Galba's personal presence somewhat retarded their motions, and took off their edge, and their having no obvious occasion for beginning a revolution curbed and kept under, more or less, their resentments. But those forces that had been formerly under Virginius, and now were under Flaccus in Germany, valuing themselves much upon the battle they had fought with Vindex, and finding now no advantage of it, grew very refractory and intractable towards their officers; and Flaccus they wholly disregarded, being incapacitated in body by unintermitted gout, and, besides, a man of little experience in affairs. So at one of their festivals, when it was customary for the officers of the army to wish all health and happiness to the emperor, the common soldiers began to murmur loudly, and on their officers persisting in the ceremony, responded with the words, "If he deserves it."

When some similar insolence was committed by the legions under Vitellius, frequent letters with the information came to Galba from his agents; and taking alarm at this, and fearing that he might be despised not only for his old age, but also for want of issue, he determined to adopt some young man of distinction, and declare him his successor. There was at this time in the city Marcus Otho, a person of fair extraction, but from his childhood one of the few most debauched, voluptuous, and luxurious livers in Rome. And as Homer gives Paris in several places the title of "fair Helen's love," making a woman's name the glory and addition to his, as if he had nothing else to distinguish him, so Otho was renowned in Rome for nothing more than his marriage with Poppæa, whom Nero had a passion for when she was Crispinus's wife. But being as yet respectful to his own wife, and standing in awe of his mother, he engaged Otho underhand to solicit her. For Nero lived familiarly with Otho, whose prodigality won his favour, and he was well pleased when he took the freedom to jest upon him as mean and penurious. Thus when Nero one day perfumed himself with some rich essence and favoured Otho with a sprinkle of it, he, entertaining Nero next day, ordered gold and silver pipes to disperse the like on a sudden freely, like water, throughout the room. As to Poppæa, he was beforehand with Nero, and first seducing her himself, then, with the hope of Nero's favour, he prevailed with her to part with her husband, and brought her to his own house as his wife, and was not content afterwards to have a share in her, but grudged to have Nero for a claimant, Poppæa herself, they say, being rather pleased than otherwise with this jealousy she sometimes excluded Nero, even when Otho was not present, either to prevent his getting tired with her, or, as some say, not liking the prospect of an imperial marriage, though willing enough to have the emperor as her lover. So that Otho ran the risk of his life, and strange it was he escaped when Nero, for this very marriage, killed his wife and sister. But he was beholden to Seneca's friendship, by whose persuasions and entreaty Nero was prevailed with to despatch him as prætor into Lusitania, on the shores of the Ocean; where he behaved himself very agreeably and indulgently to those he had to govern, well knowing this command was but to colour and disguise his banishment.

When Galba revolted from Nero, Otho was the first governor of any of the provinces that came over to him, bringing all the gold and silver he possessed in the shape of cups and tables, to be coined into money, and also what servants he had fitly qualified to wait upon a prince. In all other points, too, he was faithful to him, and gave him sufficient proof that he was inferior to none in managing public business. And he so far ingratiated himself, that he rode in the same carriage with him during the whole journey, several days together. And in this journey and familiar companionship he won over Vinius also, both by his conversation and presents, but especially by conceding to him the first place, securing the second, by his interest, for himself. And he had the advantage of him in avoiding all odium and jealousy, assisting all petitioners, without asking for any reward, and appearing courteous and of easy access towards all especially to the military men, for many of whom he obtained commands, some immediately from the emperor, others by Vinius's means, and by the assistance of the two favourite freedmen, Icelus and Asiaticus, these being the men in chief power in the court. As often as he entertained Galba, he gave the cohort on duty, in addition to their pay, a piece of gold for every man there, upon pretence of respect to the emperor, while really he undermined him, and stole away his popularity with the soldiers.

So Galba consulting about a successor, Vinius introduced Otho, yet not even this gratis, but upon promise that he would marry his daughter if Galba should make him his adopted son and successor to the empire. But Galba, in all his actions, showed clearly that he preferred the public good before his own private interest, not aiming so much to pleasure himself as to advantage the Romans by his selection. Indeed he does not seem to have been so much as inclined to make choice of Otho had it been but to inherit his own private fortune, knowing his extravagant and luxurious character, and that he was already plunged in debt five thousand myriads deep. So he listened to Vinius, and made no reply, but mildly suspended his determination. Only he appointed himself consul, and Vinius his colleague, and it was the general expectation that he would declare his successor at the beginning of the new year. And the soldiers desired nothing more than that Otho should be the person.

But the forces in Germany broke out into their mutiny whilst he was yet deliberating, and anticipated his design. All the soldiers in general felt much resentment against Galba for not having given them their expected largess, but these troops made a pretence of a more particular concern, that Virginius Rufus was cast off dishonourably, and that the Gauls who had fought with them were well rewarded, while those who had refused to take part with Vindex were punished; and Galba's thanks seemed all to be for him, to whose memory he had done honour after his death with public solemnities as though he had been made emperor by his means only. Whilst these discourses passed openly throughout the army, on the first day of the first month of the year, the Calends, as they call it, of January, Flaccus summoning them to take the usual anniversary oath of fealty to the emperor, they overturned and pulled down Galba's statues, and having sworn in the name of the senate and people of Rome, departed. But the officers now feared anarchy and confusion, as much as rebellion; and one of them came forward and said: "What will become of us, my fellow soldiers, if we neither set up another general, nor retain the present one? This will be not so much to desert from Galba as to decline all subjection and command. It is useless to try and maintain Flaccus Hordeonius, who is but a mere shadow and image of Galba. But Vitellius, commander of the other Germany, is but one day's march distant, whose father was censor and thrice consul, and in a manner co-emperor with Claudius Cæsar; and he himself has the best proof to show of his bounty and largeness of mind, in the poverty with which some reproach him. Him let us make choice of, that all may see we know how to choose an emperor better than either Spaniards or Lusitanians." Which motion whilst some assented to, and others gainsaid, a certain standard-bearer slipped out and carried the news to Vitellius, who was entertaining much company by night. This taking air, soon passed through the troops, and Fabius Valens, who commanded one legion, riding up next day with a large body of horse, saluted Vitellius emperor. He had hitherto seemed to decline it, professing a dread he had to undertake the weight of the government; but on this day, being fortified, they say, by wine and a plentiful noon-day repast, he began to yield, and submitted to take on him the title of Germanicus they gave him, but desired to be excused as to that of Cæsar. And immediately the army under Flaccus also, putting away their fine and popular oaths in the name of the senate, swore obedience to Vitellius as emperor, to observe whatever he commanded.

Thus Vitellius was publicly proclaimed emperor in Germany; which news coming to Galba's ear, he no longer deferred his adoption; yet knowing that some of his friends were using their interest for Dolabella, and the greatest number of them for Otho, neither of whom he approved of, on a sudden, without any one's privity, he sent for Piso, the son of Crassus and Scribonia, whom Nero slew, a young man in general of excellent disposition for virtue, but his most eminent qualities those of steadiness and austere gravity. And so he set out to go to the camp to declare him Cæsar and successor to the empire. But at his very first going forth many signs appeared in the heavens, and when he began to make a speech to the soldiers, partly extempore, and partly reading it, the frequent claps of thunder and flashes of lightning, and the violent storm of rain that burst on both the camp and the city, were plain discoveries that the divine powers did not look with favour or satisfaction on this act of adoption that would come to no good result. The soldiers, also, showed symptoms of hidden discontent, and wore sullen looks, no distribution of money being even now made to them. However, those that were present and observed Piso's countenance and voice could not but feel admiration to see him so little overcome by so great a favour, of the magnitude of which at the same time he seemed not at all insensible. Otho's aspect, on the other hand, did not fail to let many marks appear of his bitterness and anger at his disappointment; since to have been the first man thought of for it, and to have come to the very point of being chosen, and now to be put by, was in his feelings a sign of the displeasure and ill-will of Galba towards him. This filled him with fears and apprehensions, and sent him home with a mind full of various passions, whilst he dreaded Piso, hated Galba, and was full of wrath and indignation against Vinius. And the Chaldeans and soothsayers about him would not permit him to lay aside his hopes or quit his design, chiefly Ptolemæus, insisting much on a prediction he had made, that Nero should not murder Otho, but he himself should die first, and Otho succeed as emperor; for the first proving true, he thought he could not distrust the rest. But none perhaps stimulated him more than those that professed privately to pity his hard fate and compassionate him for being thus ungratefully dealt with by Galba; especially Nymphidius's and Tigellinus's creatures, who, being now cast off and reduced to low estate, were eager to put themselves upon him, exclaiming at the indignity he had suffered, and provoking him to revenge himself.

Amongst these were Viturius and Barbius, the one an *optio*, the other a *tesserarius* (these are men who have the duties of messengers and scouts), with whom Onomastus, one of Otho's freedmen, went to the camp, to tamper with the army, and brought over some with money, others with fair promises, which was no hard matter, they being already corrupted, and only wanting a fair pretence. It had been otherwise more than the work of four days (which elapsed between the adoption and murder), so completely to infect them as to cause a general revolt. On the sixth day ensuing, the eighteenth, as the Romans call it, before the Calends of February, the murder was done. On that day, in the morning, Galba sacrificed in the Falatium in the presence of his friends, when Umbricius, the priest, taking up the entrails, and speaking not ambiguously, but in plain words, said that there were signs of great troubles ensuing, and dangerous snares laid for the life of the emperor. Thus Otho had even been discovered by the finger of the god; being there just behind Galba, hearing all that was said, and seeing what was pointed out to them by Umbricius. His countenance changed to every colour in his fear, and he was betraying no small discomposure, when Onomastus, his freedman, came up and acquainted him that the master builders had come, and were waiting for him at home. Now that was the signal for Otho to meet the soldiers. Pretending then that he had purchased an old house, and was going to show the defects to those that had sold it to him, he departed; and passing through what is called Tiberius's house, he went on into the forum, near the spot where a golden pillar stands, at which all the several roads through Italy terminate.

Here, it is related, no more than twenty-three received and saluted him emperor; so that, although he was not in mind as in body enervated with soft living and effeminacy, being in his nature bold and fearless enough in danger, nevertheless, he was afraid to go on. But the soldiers that were present would not suffer him to recede, but came with their swords drawn around his chair, commanding the bearers to take him up, whom he hastened on, saying several times over to himself, "I am a lost man." Several persons overheard the words, who stood by wondering, rather than alarmed, because of the small number that attempted such an enterprise. But as they marched on through the forum, about as many more met him, and here and there three or four at a time joined in. Thus returning towards the camp, with their bare swords in their hands, they saluted him as Cæsar; whereupon Martialis, the tribune in charge of the watch, who was, they say, noways privy to it, but was simply surprised at the unexpectedness of the thing, and afraid to refuse, permitted him entrance. And after this, no man made any resistance; for they that knew nothing of the design, being purposely encompassed by the conspirators, as they were straggling here and there, first submitted for fear, and afterwards were persuaded into compliance. Tidings came immediately to Galba in the Palatium, whilst the priests were still present and the sacrifices at hand, so that persons who were most entirely incredulous about such things, and most positive in their neglect of them, were astonished, and began to marvel at the divine event. A multitude of all sorts of people now began to run together out of the forum; Vinius and Laco and some of Galba's freedmen drew their swords and placed themselves beside him; Piso went forth and addressed himself to the guards on duty in the court; and Marius Celsus, a brave man, was despatched to the Illyrian legion, stationed in what is called the Vipsanian chamber, to secure them.

Galba now consulting whether he should go out, Vinius dissuaded him, but Celsus and Laco encouraged him by all means to do so, and sharply reprimanded Vinius. But on a sudden a rumour came hot that Otho was slain in the camp; and presently appeared one Julius Atticus, a man of some distinction in the guards, running up with his drawn sword, crying out that he had slain Cæsar's enemy; and pressing through the crowd that stood in his way, he presented himself before Galba with his bloody weapon, who, looking on him, demanded, "Who gave you your orders?" And on his answering that it had been his duty and the obligation of the oath he had taken, the people applauded, giving loud acclamations, and Galba got into his chair and was carried out to sacrifice to Jupiter, and so to show himself publicly. But coming into the forum, there met him there, like a turn of wind, the opposite story, that Otho had made himself master of the camp. And as usual in a crowd of such a size, some called to him to return back, others to move forwards; some encouraged him to be bold and fear nothing, others bade him to be cautious and distrust. And thus whilst his chair was tossed to and fro, as it were on the waves, often tottering, there appeared first horse, and straightway heavy-armed foot, coming through Paulus's court, and all with one accord crying out, "Down with this private man." Upon this, the crowd of people set off running, not to fly and disperse, but to possess themselves of the colonnades and elevated places of the forum, as it might be to get places to see a spectacle. And as soon as Atillius Vergilio knocked down one of Galba's statues, this was taken as the declaration of war, and they sent a discharge of darts upon Galba's litter, and missing their aim, came up and attacked him nearer hand with their naked swords. No man resisted or offered to stand up in his defence, save one only, a centurion, Sempronius Densus, the single man among so many thousands that the sun beheld that day act worthily of the Roman empire, who, though he had never received any favour from Galba, yet out of bravery and allegiance endeavoured to defend the litter. First, lifting up his switch of vine, with which the centurions correct the soldiers when disorderly, he called aloud to the aggressors, charging them not to touch their emperor. And when they came upon him hand-to-hand, he drew his sword, and made a defence for a long time, until at last he was cut under the knees and brought to the ground.

Galba's chair was upset at the spot called the Lacus Curtius, where they ran up and struck at him as he lay in his corselet. He, however, offered his throat, bidding them "Strike, if it be for the Romans' good." He received several wounds on his legs and arms, and at last was struck in the throat, as most say, by one Camurius, a soldier of the fifteenth legion. Some name Terentius, others Lecanius; and there are others that say it was Fabius Fabulus, who it is reported cut off the head and carried it away in the skirt of his coat, the baldness making it a difficult thing to take hold of. But those that were with him would not allow him to keep it covered up, but bade him let every one see the brave deed he had done; so that after a while he stuck upon the lance the head of the aged man that had been their grave and temperate ruler, their supreme priest and consul, and, tossing it up in the air, ran like a bacchanal, twirling and flourishing with it, while the blood ran down the spear. But when they brought the head to Otho, "Fellow-soldiers," he cried out, "this is nothing, unless you show me Piso's too," which was presented him not long after. The young man, retreating upon a wound received, was pursued by one Murcus, and slain at the temple of Vesta. Titus Vinius was also despatched, avowing himself to have been privy to the conspiracy against Galba by calling out that they were killing him contrary to Otho's pleasure. However, they cut off his head, and Laco's too, and brought them to Otho, requesting a boon.

And as Archilochus says—

"When six or seven lie breathless on the ground,
'Twas I, 'twas I, say thousands, gave the wound."

Thus many that had no share in the murder wetted their hands and swords in blood, and came and showed them to Otho, presenting memorials suing for a gratuity. Not less than one hundred and twenty were identified afterwards from their written petitions; all of whom Vitellius sought out and put to death. There came also into the camp Marius Celsus, and was accused by many voices of encouraging the soldiers to assist Galba, and was demanded to death by the multitude. Otho had no desire for this, yet, fearing an absolute denial, he professed that he did not wish to take him off so soon, having many matters yet to learn from him; and so committed him safe to the custody of those he most confided in.

Forthwith a senate was convened, and as if they were not the same men, or had other gods to swear by, they took that oath in Otho's name which he himself had taken in Galba's and had broken; and withal conferred on him the titles of Cæsar and Augustus; whilst the dead carcasses of the slain lay yet in their consular robes in the market-place. As for their heads, when they could make no other use of them, Vinius's they sold to his daughter for two thousand five hundred drachmas; Piso's was begged by his wife, Verania; Galba's they gave to Patrobius's servants; who when they had it, after all sorts of abuse and indignities, tumbled it into the place where those that suffer death by the emperor's orders are usually cast, called Sessorium. Galba's body was conveyed away by Priscus Helvidius by Otho's permission, and buried in the night by Argius, his freedman.

Thus you have the history of Galba, a person inferior to few Romans, either for birth or riches, rather exceeding all of his time in both, having lived in great honour and reputation in the reigns of five emperors, insomuch that he overthrew Nero rather by his fame and repute in the world than by actual force and power. Of all the others that joined in Nero's deposition, some were by general consent regarded as unworthy, others had only themselves to vote them deserving of the empire. To him the title was offered, and by him it was accepted; and simply lending his name to

Vindex's attempt, he gave to what had been called rebellion before, the name of a civil war, by the presence of one that was accounted fit to govern. And therefore, as he considered that he had not so much sought the position as the position had sought him, he proposed to command those whom Nymphidius and Tigellinus had wheedled into obedience no otherwise than Scipio formerly and Fabricius and Camillus had commanded the Romans of their times. But being now overcome with age, he was indeed among the troops and legions an upright ruler upon the antique model; but for the rest, giving himself up to Vinius, Laco, and his freedmen, who make their gain of all things, no otherwise than Nero had done to his insatiate favourites, he left none behind him to wish him still in power, though many to compassionate his death.

OTHO

THE new emperor went early in the morning to the capitol, and sacrificed; and, having commanded Marius Celsus to be brought, he saluted him, and with obliging language desired him rather to forget his accusation than remember his acquittal; to which Celsus answered neither meanly nor ungratefully, that his very crime ought to recommend his integrity, since his guilt had been his fidelity to Galba, from whom he had never received any personal obligations. Upon which, they were both of them admired by those that were present, and applauded by the soldiers.

In the senate, Otho said much in a gentle and popular strain. He was to have been consul for part of that year himself, but he gave the office to Virginius Rufus, and displaced none that had been named for the consulship by either Nero or Galba. Those that were remarkable for their age and dignity he promoted to the priesthoods; and restored the remains of their fortunes, that had not yet been sold, to all those senators that were banished by Nero, and recalled by Galba. So that the nobility and chief of the people, who were at first apprehensive that no human creature, but some supernatural, or penal vindictive power had seized the empire, began now to flatter themselves with hopes of a government that smiled upon them thus early.

Besides, nothing gratified or gained the whole Roman people more than his justice in relation to Tigellinus. It was not seen how he was in fact already suffering punishment, not only by the very terror of retribution which he saw the whole city requiring as a just debt, but with several in curable diseases also; not to mention those unhallowed frightful excesses among impure and prostitute women, to which, at the very close of life, his lewd nature clung, and in them gasped out, as it were, its last; these, in the opinion of all reasonable men, being themselves the extremest punishment, and equal to many deaths. But it was felt like a grievance by people in general that he continued yet to see the light of day, who had been the occasion of the loss of it to so many persons, and such persons, as had died by his means. Wherefore Otho ordered him to be sent for, just as he was contriving his escape of means of some vessels that lay ready for him on the coast near where he lived, in the neighbourhood of Sinuessa. At first he endeavoured to corrupt the messenger, by a large sum of money, to favour his design; but when he found this was to no purpose, he made him as considerable a present as if he had really connived at it, only entreating him to stay till he had shaved; and so took that opportunity, and with his razor despatched himself.

And while giving the people this most righteous satisfaction of their desires, for himself he seemed to have no sort of regard for any private injuries of his own. And at first, to please the populace, he did not refuse to be called Nero in the theatre, and did not interfere when some persons displayed Nero's statues to public view. And Cluvius Rufus says, imperial letters, such as are sent with couriers, went into Spain with the name of Nero affixed adoptively to that of Otho; but as soon he perceived this gave offence to the chief and most distinguished citizens, it was omitted.

After he had begun to model the government in this manner, the paid soldiers began to murmur, and endeavoured to make him suspect and chastise the nobility, either really out of a concern for his safety, or wishing, upon this pretence, to stir up trouble and warfare. Thus, whilst Crispinus, whom he had ordered to bring him the seventeenth cohort from Ostia, began to collect what he wanted after it was dark, and was putting the arms upon the waggons, some of the most turbulent cried out that Crispinus was disaffected, that the senate was practising something against the emperor, and that those arms were to be employed against Cæsar, and not for him. When this report was once set afoot, it got the belief and excited the passions of many; they broke out into violence; some seized the waggons, and others slew Crispinus and two centurions that opposed them; and the whole number of them, arraying themselves in their arms, and encouraging one another to stand by Cæsar, marched to Rome. And hearing there that eighty of the senators were at supper with Otho, they flew into the palace, and declared it was a fair opportunity to take off Cæsar's enemies at one stroke. A general alarm ensued of an immediate coming sack of the city. All were in confusion about the palace, and Otho himself in no small consternation, being not only concerned for the senators (some of whom had brought their wives to supper thither), but also feeling himself to be an object of alarm and suspicion to them, whose eyes he saw fixed on him in silence and terror. Therefore he gave orders to the prefects to address the soldiers and do their best to pacify them, while he bade the guests rise, and leave by another door. They had only just made their way out, when the soldiers rushed into the room, and called out, "Where are Cæsar's enemies?" Then Otho, standing up on his couch, made use both of arguments and entreaties, and by actual tears at last, with great difficulty, persuaded them to desist. The next day he went to the camp, and distributed a bounty of twelve hundred and fifty drachmas a man amongst them; then commended them for the regard and zeal they had for his safety, but told them that there were some who were intriguing among them, who not only accused his own clemency, but had also misrepresented their loyalty; and, therefore, he desired their assistance in doing justice upon them. To which, when they all consented, he was satisfied with the execution of two only, whose deaths he knew would be regretted by no one man in the whole army.

Such conduct, so little expected from him, was regarded by some with gratitude and confidence; others looked upon his behaviour as a course to which necessity drove him, to gain the people to the support of the war. For now there were certain tidings that Vitellius had assumed the sovereign title and authority, and frequent expresses brought accounts of new accessions to him; others, however, came, announcing that the Pannonian, Dalmatian, and Mœsian legions, with their officers, adhered to Otho. Ere long also came favourable letters from Mucianus and Vespasian, generals of two formidable armies, the one in Syria, the other in Judæa, to assure him of their firmness to his interest: in confidence whereof he was so exalted, that he wrote to Vitellius not to attempt anything beyond his post; and offered him large sums of money and a city, where he might live his time out in pleasure and ease. These overtures at first were responded to by Vitellius with equivocating civilities; which soon, however, turned into an interchange of angry words; and letters passed between the two, conveying bitter and shameful terms of reproach, which were not false indeed, for that matter, only it was senseless and ridiculous for each to assail the other with accusations to which both alike must plead guilty. For it were hard to determine which of the two had been most profuse, most effeminate, which was most a novice in military affairs, and most involved in debt through previous want of means.

As to the prodigies and apparitions that happened about this time, there were many reported which none could answer for, or which were told in different ways; but one which everybody actually saw with their eyes, was the statue, in the capitol, of Victory carried in a chariot, with the reins dropped out of her hands, as if she were grown too weak to hold them any longer; and a second, that Caius Cæsar's statue in the island of Tiber, without any earthquake or wind to account for it, turned round from west to east; and this, they say, happened about the time when Vespasian and his party first openly began to put themselves forward. Another incident, which the people in general thought an evil sign, was the inundation of the Tiber; for though it happened at a time when rivers are usually at their fullest, yet such height of water and so tremendous a flood had never been known before, nor such a destruction of property, great part of the city being under water, and especially the corn market, so that it occasioned a great dearth for several days.

But when news was now brought that Cæcina and Valens, commanding for Vitellius, had possessed themselves of the Alps, Otho sent Dolabella (a patrician, who was suspected by the soldiery of some evil purpose), for whatever reason, whether it were fear of him or of any one else, to the town of Aquinum, to give encouragement there; and proceeding then to choose which of the magistrates should go with him to the war, he named amongst the rest Lucius, Vitellius's brother, without distinguishing him by any new marks either of his favour or displeasure. He also took the greatest precautions for Vitellius's wife and mother, that they might be safe, and free from all apprehension for themselves. He made Flavius Sabinus, Vespasian's brother, governor of Rome, either in honour to the memory of Nero, who had advanced him formerly to that command, which Galba had taken away, or else to show his confidence in Vespasian by his favour to his brother.

After he came to Brixillum, a town of Italy near the Po, he stayed behind himself, and ordered the army to march under the conduct of Marius Celsus, Suetonius Paulinus, Gallus, and Spurina, all men of experience and reputation, but unable to carry their own plans and purposes into effect, by reason of the ungovernable temper of the army, which would take orders from none but the emperor whom they themselves had made their master. Nor was the enemy under much better discipline, the soldiers there also being haughty and disobedient upon the same account, but they were more experienced and used to hard work; whereas Otho's men were soft from their long easy living and lack of service, having spent most of their time in the theatres and at state shows and on the stage; while moreover they tried to cover their deficiencies by arrogance and vain display, pretending to decline their duty, not because they were unable to do the thing commanded, but because they thought themselves above it. So that Spurina had like to have been cut in pieces for attempting to force them to their work; they assailed him with insolent language, accusing him of a design to betray and ruin Cæsar's interest; nay, some of them that were in drink forced his tent in the night, and demanded money for the expenses of their journey, which they must at once take, they said, to the emperor, to complain of him.

However, the contemptuous treatment they met with at Placentia did for the present good service to Spurina, and to the cause of Otho. For Vitellius's men marched up to the walls, and upbraided Otho's upon the ramparts, calling them players, dancers, idle spectators of Pythian and Olympic games, but novices in the art of war, who never so much as looked on at a battle; mean souls, that triumphed in the beheading of Galba, an old man unarmed, but had no desire to look real enemies in the face. Which reproaches so inflamed them that they kneeled at Spurina's feet, entreated him to give his orders, and assured him no danger or toil should be too great or too difficult for them. Whereupon when Vitellius's forces made a vigorous attack on the town, and brought up numerous engines against the walls, the besieged bravely repulsed them, and, repelling the enemy with great slaughter, secured the safety of a noble city, one of the most flourishing places in Italy.

Besides, it was observed that Otho's officers were much more inoffensive, both towards the public and to private men, than those of Vitellius; among whom was Cæcina, who used neither the language nor the apparel of a citizen, an overbearing, foreign-seeming man, of gigantic stature, and always dressed in trews and sleeves, after the manner of the Gauls, whilst he conversed with Roman officials and magistrates. His wife, too, travelled along with him, riding in splendid attire on horseback, with a chosen body of cavalry to escort her. And Fabius Valens, the other general, was so rapacious that neither what he plundered from enemies, nor what he stole or got as gifts and bribes from his friends and allies, could satisfy his wishes. And it was said that it was in order to have time to raise money that he had marched so slowly that he was not present at the former attack. But some lay the blame on Cæcina, saying, that out of a desire to gain the victory by himself before Fabius joined him, he committed sundry other errors of lesser consequence, and by engaging unseasonably and when he could not do so thoroughly, he very nearly brought all to ruin.

When he found himself beat off at Placentia, he set off to attack Cremona, another large and rich city. In the meantime, Annius Gallus marched to join Spurina at Placentia; but having intelligence that the siege was raised, and that Cremona was in danger, he turned to its relief, and encamped just by the enemy, where he was daily reinforced by other officers. Cæcina placed a strong ambush of heavy infantry in some rough and woody country, and gave orders to his horse to advance, and if the enemy should charge them, then to make a slow retreat, and draw them into the snare. But his stratagem was discovered by some deserters to Celsus, who attacked with a good body of horse, but followed the pursuit cautiously, and succeeded in surrounding and routing the troops in the ambuscade; and if the infantry which he ordered up from the camp had come soon enough to sustain the horse, Cæcina's whole army, in all appearance, had been totally routed. But Paulinus, moving too slowly, was accused of acting with a degree of needless caution not to have been expected from one of his reputation. So that the soldiers incensed Otho against him, accused him of treachery, and boasted loudly that the victory had been in their power, and that if it was not complete, it was owing to the mismanagement of their generals; all which Otho did not so much believe as he was willing to appear not to disbelieve. He therefore sent his brother Titianus, with Proculus, the prefect of the guards, to the army, where the latter was general in reality, and the former in appearance. Celsus and Paulinus had the title of friends and counsellors, but not the least authority or power. At the same time, there was nothing but quarrel and disturbance amongst the enemy, especially where Valens commanded; for the soldiers here, being informed of what had happened at the ambuscade, were enraged because they had not been permitted to be present to strike a blow in defence of the lives of so many men that had died in that action; Valens, with much difficulty, quieted their fury, after they had now begun to throw missiles at him, and quitting his camp, joined Cæcina.

About this time, Otho came to Bedriacum, a little town near Cremona, to the camp, and called a council of war; where Proculus and Titianus declared for giving battle, while the soldiers were flushed with their late success, saying they ought not to lose their time and opportunity and present height of strength, and wait for Vitellius to arrive out of Gaul. But Paulinus told them that the enemy's whole force was present, and that there was no body of reserve behind; but that Otho, if he would not be too precipitate, and chose the enemy's time, instead of his own, for the battle, might expect reinforcements out of Mœsia and Pannonia, not inferior in numbers to the troops that were already present. He thought it probable, too, that the soldiers, who were then in heart before they were joined, would not be less so when the forces were all come up. Besides, the deferring battle could not be inconvenient to them that were sufficiently provided with all necessaries; but the others, being in an enemy's country, must needs be exceedingly straitened in a little time. Marius Celsus was of Paulinus's opinion; Annius Gallus, being absent and under the surgeon's hands through a fall from his horse, was consulted by letter, and advised Otho to stay for those legions that were marching from Mœsia. But after all he did not follow the advice; and the opinion of those that declared for a battle prevailed.

There are several reasons given for this determination, but the most apparent is this; that the prætorian soldiers, as they are called, who serve as guards, not relishing the military discipline which they now had begun a little more to experience, and longing for their amusements and unwarlike life among the shows of Rome, would not be commanded, but were eager for a battle, imagining that upon the first onset they should carry all before them. Otho also himself seems not to have shown the proper fortitude in bearing up against the uncertainty, and, out of effeminacy and want of use, had not patience for the calculations of danger, and was so uneasy at the apprehension of it that he shut his eyes, and like one going to leap from a precipice, left everything to fortune. This is the account Secundus the rhetorician, who was his secretary, gave of the matter. But others would tell you that there were many movements in both armies for acting in concert; and if it were possible for them to agree, then they should proceed to choose one of their most experienced officers that were present; if not, they should convene the senate, and invest it with the power of election. And it is not improbable that, neither of the emperors then bearing the title having really any reputation, such purposes were really entertained among the genuine, serviceable, and sober-minded part of the soldiers. For what could be more odious and unreasonable than that the evils which the Roman citizens had formerly thought it so lamentable to inflict upon each other for the sake of a Sylla or a Marius, a Cæsar or a Pompey, should now be undergone anew, for the object of letting the empire pay the expenses of the gluttony and intemperance of Vitellius, or the looseness and effeminacy of Otho? It is thought that Celsus, upon such reflections, protracted the time in order to a possible accommodation; and that Otho pushed on things to an extremity to prevent it.

He himself returned to Brixillum, which was another false step, both because he withdrew from the combatants all the motives of respect and desire to gain his favour which his presence would have supplied, and because he weakened the army by detaching some of his best and most faithful troops for his horse and foot guards.

About the same time also happened a skirmish on the Po. As Cæcina was laying a bridge over it, Otho's men attacked him, and tried to prevent it. And when they did not succeed, on their putting into their boats torchwood, with a quantity of sulphur and pitch, the wind on the river suddenly caught their material that they had prepared against the enemy, and blew it into a light. First came smoke, and then a clear flame, and the men, getting into great confusion and jumping overboard, upset the boats, and put themselves ludicrously at the mercy of their enemies. Also the Germans attacked Otho's gladiators upon a small island in the river, routed them, and killed a good many.

All which made the soldiers at Bedriacum full of anger, and eagerness to be led to battle. So Proculus led them out of Bedriacum to a place fifty furlongs off, where he pitched his camp so ignorantly and with such a ridiculous want of foresight that the soldiers suffered extremely for want of water, though it was the spring time, and the plains all around were full of running streams and rivers that never dried up. The next day he proposed to attack the enemy, first making a march of not less than a hundred furlongs; but to this Paulinus objected, saying they ought to wait, and not immediately after a journey engage men who would have been standing in their arms and arranging themselves for battle at their leisure, whilst they were making a long march, with all their beasts of burden and their camp followers to encumber them. As the generals were arguing about this matter, a Numidian courier came from Otho with orders to lose no time, but give battle. Accordingly they consented, and moved. As soon as Cæcina had notice, he was much surprised, and quitted his post on the river to hasten to the camp. In the meantime, the men had armed themselves mostly, and were receiving the word from Valens; so while the legions took up their position, they sent out the best of their horse in advance.

Otho's foremost troops, upon some groundless rumour, took up the notion that the commanders on the other side would come over; and accordingly, upon their first approach, they saluted them with the friendly title of fellow-soldiers. But the others returned the compliment with anger and disdainful words; which not only disheartened those that had given the salutation, but excited suspicions of their fidelity amongst the others on their side, who had not. This caused a confusion at the very first onset. And nothing else that followed was done upon any plan; the baggage-carriers, mingling up with the fighting men, created great disorder and division; as well as the nature of the ground, the ditches and pits in which were so many that they were forced to break their ranks to avoid and go round them, and so to fight without order, and in small parties. There were but two legions, one of Vitellius's called The Ravenous, and another of Otho's, called The Assistant, that got out into the open outspread level and engaged in proper form, fighting, one main body against the other, for some length of time. Otho's men were strong and bold, but had never been in battle before; Vitellius's had seen many wars, but were old and past their strength. So Otho's legion charged boldly, drove back their opponents, and took the eagle, killing pretty nearly every man in the first rank, till the others, full of rage and shame, returned the charge, slew Orfidius, the commander of the legion, and took several standards. Varus Alfenus, with his Batavians, who are the natives of an island of the Rhine, and are esteemed the best of the German horse, fell upon the gladiators, who had a reputation both for valour and skill in fighting. Some few of these did their duty, but the greatest part of them made towards the river, and, falling in with some cohorts stationed there, were cut off. But none behaved so ill as the prætorians, who, without ever so much as meeting the enemy, ran away, broke through their own body that stood, and put them into disorder. Notwithstanding this, many of Otho's men routed those that were opposed to them, broke right into them, and forced their way to the camp through the very middle of their conquerors.

As for their commanders, neither Proculus nor Paulinus ventured to reenter with the troops; they turned aside, and avoided the soldiers, who had already charged the miscarriage upon their officers. Annius Gallus received into the town and rallied the scattered parties, and encouraged them with an assurance that the battle was a drawn one and the victory had in many parts been theirs. Marius Celsus, collecting the officers, urged the public interest; Otho himself, if he were a brave man, would not, after such an expense of Roman blood, attempt anything further; especially since even Cato and Scipio, though the liberty of Rome was then at stake; had been accused of being too prodigal of so many brave men's lives as were lost in Africa, rather than submit to Cæsar after the battle of Pharsalia had gone against them. For though all persons are equally subject to the caprice of fortune, yet all good men have one advantage she cannot deny, which is this, to act reasonably under misfortunes.

This language was well accepted amongst the officers, who sounded the private soldiers, and found them desirous of peace; and Titianus also gave directions that envoys should be sent in order to a treaty. And accordingly it was agreed that the conference should be between Celsus and Gallus on one part, and Valens with Cæcina on the other. As the two first were upon their journey, they met some centurions, who told them the troops were already in motion, marching for Bedriacum, but that they themselves were deputed by their generals to carry proposals for an accommodation. Celsus and Gallus expressed their approval, and requested them to turn back and carry them to Cæcina. However, Celsus, upon his approach, was in danger from the vanguard, who happened to be some of the horse that had suffered at the ambush. For as soon as they saw him, they hallooed, and were coming down upon him; but the centurions came forward to protect him, and the other officers crying out and bidding them desist, Cæcina came up to inform himself of the tumult, which he quieted, and giving a friendly greeting to Celsus, took him in his company and proceeded towards Bedriacum. Titianus, meantime, had repented of having sent the messengers; and placed those of the soldiers who were more confident upon the walls once again, bidding the others also go and support them. But when Cæcina rode up on his horse and held out his hand, no one did or said to the contrary; those on the walls greeted his men with salutations, others opened the gates and went out, and mingled freely with those they met; and instead of acts of hostility, there was nothing but mutual shaking of hands and congratulations, every one taking the oaths and submitting to Vitellius.

This is the account which the most of those that were present at the battle give of it, yet own that the disorder they were in, and the absence of any unity of action, would not give them leave to be certain as to particulars. And when I myself travelled afterwards over the field of battle, Mestrius Florus, a man of consular degree, one of those who had been, not willingly, but by command, in attendance on Otho at the time, pointed out to me an ancient temple, and told me, that as he went that way after the battle, he observed a heap of bodies piled up there to such a height that those on the top of it reached the pinnacles of the roof. How it came to be so, he could neither discover himself nor learn from any other person; as indeed, he said, in civil wars it generally happens that greater numbers are killed when an army is routed, quarter not being given, because captives are of no advantage to the conquerors; but why the carcasses should be heaped up after that manner is not easy to determine.

Otho, at first, as it frequently happens, received some uncertain rumours of the issue of the battle. But when some of the wounded that returned from the field informed him rightly of it, it is not, indeed, so much to be wondered at that his friends should bid him not give all up as lost or let his courage sink; but the feeling shown by the soldiers is something that exceeds all belief. There was not one of them would either go over to the conqueror or show any disposition to make terms for himself, as if their leader's cause was desperate; on the contrary, they crowded his gates, called out to him the title of emperor, and as soon as he appeared, cried out and entreated him, catching hold of his hand, and throwing themselves upon the ground, and with all the moving language of tears and persuasion, besought him to stand by them, not abandon them to their enemies, but employ in his service their lives and persons, which would not cease to be his so long as they had breath; so urgent was their zealous and universal importunity. And one obscure and private soldier, after he had drawn his sword, addressed himself to Otho: "By this, Cæsar, judge our fidelity; there is not a man amongst us but would strike thus to serve you;" and so stabbed himself. Notwithstanding this, Otho stood serene and unshaken, and, with a face full of constancy and composure, turned himself about and looked at them, replying thus: "This day, my fellow-soldiers, which gives me such proofs of your affection, is preferable even to that on which you saluted me emperor; deny me not, therefore, the yet higher satisfaction of laying down my life for the preservation of so many brave men; in this, at least, let me be worthy of the empire, that is, to die for it. I am of opinion the enemy has neither gained an entire nor a decisive victory; I have advice that the Mœsian army is not many days' journey distant, on its march to the Adriatic; Asia, Syria, and Egypt, and the legions that are serving against the Jews, declare for us; the senate is also with us, and the wives and children of our opponents are in our power; but alas, it is not in defence of Italy against Hannibal or Pyrrhus or the Cimbri that we fight; Romans combining against Romans, and, whether we conquer or are defeated, the country suffers and we commit a crime: victory, to whichever it fall, is gained at her expense. Believe it many times over, I can die with more honour than I can reign. For I cannot see at all how I should do any such great good to my country by gaining the victory, as I shall by dying to establish peace and unanimity and to save Italy from such another unhappy day."

As soon as he had done, he was resolute against all manner of argument or persuasion, and taking leave of his friends and the senators that were present, he bade them depart, and wrote to those that were absent, and sent letters to the towns, that they might have every honour and facility in their journey. Then he sent for Cocceius, his brother's son, who was yet a boy, and bade him be in no apprehension of Vitellius, whose mother and wife and family he had treated with the same tenderness as his own; and also told him that this had been his reason for delaying to adopt him, which he had meant to do as his son; he had desired that he might share his power, if he conquered, but not be involved in his ruin if he failed. "Take notice," he added, "my boy, of these my last words, that you neither too negligently forget, nor too zealously remember, that Cæsar was your uncle." By and by he heard a tumult amongst the soldiers at the door, who were treating the senators with menaces for preparing to withdraw; upon which, out of regard to their safety, he showed himself once more in public, but not with a gentle aspect and in a persuading manner as before; on the contrary, with a countenance that discovered indignation and authority, he commanded such as were disorderly to leave the place, and was not disobeyed.

It was now evening, and feeling thirsty, he drank some water, and then took two daggers that belonged to him, and when he had carefully examined their edges, he laid one of them down, and put the other in his robe, under his arm, then called his servants, and distributed some money amongst them, but not inconsiderately, nor like one too lavish of what was not his own; for to some he gave more, to others less, all strictly in moderation, and distinguishing every one's particular merit. When this was done, he dismissed them, and passed the rest of the night in so sound a sleep that the officers of his bed-chamber heard him snore. In the morning, he called for one of his freedmen, who had assisted him in arranging about the senators, and bade him bring him an account if they were safe. Being informed they were all well and wanted nothing, "Go then," he said "and show yourself to the soldiers, lest they should cut you to pieces for being accessory to my death." As soon as he was gone, he held his sword upright under him with both his hands, and falling upon it expired with no more than one single groan to express his sense of the pang, or to inform those that waited without. When his servants, therefore, raised their exclamations of grief, the whole camp and city were at once filled with lamentation; the soldiers immediately broke in at the doors with a loud cry, in passionate distress, and accusing themselves that they had been so negligent in looking after that life which was laid down to preserve theirs. Nor would a man of them quit the body to secure his own safety with the approaching enemy; but having raised a funeral pile, and attired the body, they bore it thither, arrayed in their arms, those among them greatly exulting who succeeded in getting first under the bier and becoming its bearers. Of the others, some threw themselves down before the body and kissed his wound, others grasped his hand, and others that were at a distance knelt down to do him obeisance. There were some who, after putting their torches to the pile, slew themselves, though they had not, so far as appeared, either any particular obligations to the dead, or reason to apprehend ill-usage from the victor. Simply, it would seem, no king, legal or illegal, had ever been possessed with so extreme and vehement a passion to command others, as was that of these men to obey Otho. Nor did their love of him cease with his death; it survived and changed ere long into a mortal hatred to his successor, as will be shown in its proper place.

They placed the remains of Otho in the earth, and raised over them a monument which neither by its size nor the pomp of its inscription might excite hostility. I myself have seen it, at Brixillum; a plain structure, and the epitaph only this: To the memory of Marcus Otho. He died in his thirty-eighth year, after a short reign of about three months, his death being as much applauded as his life was censured, for if he lived no better than Nero, he died more nobly. The soldiers were displeased with Pollio, one of their two prefects, who bade them immediately swear allegiance to Vitellius; and when they understood that some of the senators were still upon the spot, they made no opposition to the departure of the rest, but only disturbed the tranquillity of Virginius Rufus with an offer of the government, and moving in one body to his house in town they first entreated him, and then demanded of him to be head of the empire, or at least to be their mediator. But he, that refused to command them when conquerors, thought it ridiculous to pretend to it now they were beat, and was unwilling to go as their envoy to the Germans, whom in past time he had compelled to do various things that they had not liked; and for these reasons he slipped away through a private door. As soon as the soldiers perceived this, they owned Vitellius, and so got their pardon, and served under Cæcina.

INDEX

DISCUSSION GUIDE

1. As Plutarch says in the beginning of his Life of Pericles, "Such objects we find in the acts of virtue, which also produce in the minds of mere readers about them an emulation and eagerness that may lead them on to imitation." Can these lines be said to encapsulate Plutarch's project in writing the *Lives*? How is Plutarch more a moralist than a historian? How are morals and virtue central to the lives you have read?

2. Although Plutarch's *Lives* are, without a doubt, one of the greatest historical works of antiquity, Plutarch has often been criticized as an inaccurate historian, for including apocryphal anecdotes, citing facts from questionable sources, and especially for ignoring historical events that would contradict his depiction of the figure. Do these lapses in historical accuracy weaken the credibility of the *Lives*? Do they strengthen them by reinforcing his purpose in writing? Are such modern concerns about historical methods even applicable to a writer of antiquity?

3. Attempt to characterize Plutarch's moral beliefs as they are revealed in the *Lives*. What traits does he most esteem, and what traits does he most condemn? How does he depict these traits in the men he describes, and what is the lesson to be drawn from each depiction? Does he have moral consistency from one life to the next? To what extent do you believe these morals to be held by his contemporaries as opposed to a modern readership?

4. In the case of the "Parallel Lives," what purpose is served by the structure of Plutarch's biographies? Why dedicate a passage to their

comparison? What were the criteria upon which he based his comparisons? Why did he choose to compare these particular figures to one another? Finally, why would Plutarch always choose one Roman and one Greek figure to compare? Was it to show the similarity of the two cultures to his Greek or Roman audiences, or was it for an entirely different reason?

5. While the bulk of Plutarch's *Lives* is concerned with historical figures, Plutarch also includes biographies of several mythological characters who held an important place in the history of Greece and Rome. What function is served by the lives of these mythological figures? How are these lives fundamentally different from the other lives he recounts? Does their inclusion weaken the historical believability of the *Lives*? Would it have done so for an audience of Plutarch's contemporaries?

6. Plutarch's *Lives* is a compilation of the biographies of the greatest men of antiquity. Consider the nature of greatness as it is depicted by Plutarch in several of the lives you have read. What characteristics are common to these great men? How does Plutarch connect their success and the character traits he admires? Can the depiction of such great men serve as a blueprint for greatness today?

A Note on the Type

The principal text of this Modern Library edition was set in a digitized version of Janson, a typeface that dates from about 1690 and was cut by Nicholas Kis, a Hungarian working in Amsterdam. The original matrices have survived and are held by the Stempel foundry in Germany. Hermann Zapf redesigned some of the weights and sizes for Stempel, basing his revisions on the original design.